P9-DYD-361
3 1502 00816 8047

THE DOVE'S NECKLACE

RAJA
ALEM

THE DOVE'S NECKLACE

Translated from the Arabic by
Katharine Halls and Adam Talib

OVERLOOK DUCKWORTH
NEW YORK • LONDON

This edition first published in hardcover in the United States and the United Kingdom
in 2016 by Overlook Duckworth, Peter Mayer Publishers, Inc.

NEW YORK
141 Wooster Street
New York, NY 10012
www.overlookpress.com
For bulk and special sales, please contact sales@overlookny.com,
or write us at the above address

LONDON
30 Calvin Street
London E1 6NW
info@duckworth-publishers.co.uk
www.ducknet.co.uk

Cataloging-in-Publication Data is available from the Library of Congress

Book design and typeformatting by Bernard Schleifer
Manufactured in the United States of America
ISBN US: 978-1-59020-898-4
ISBN UK: 978-0-7156-4586-4

FIRST EDITION
2 4 6 8 10 9 7 5 3 1

THE DOVE'S NECKLACE

Preface

Dedicated to my grandfather Abd al-Lateef's house

THE BIG RED *X* ON THE SIDE OF THE HOUSE MEANS IT'S GOING TO BE DEMOLISHED soon. Demolished to make room for a parking garage to house those strange four-wheeled creatures that look as if they're about to take over Mecca, just like in the stories of the apocalypse. When we were kids, the words "And gold will be strewn along the byways" seemed like the most far-fetched nonsense we'd ever heard, but with the astronomical prices people pay for the cars that are fast outnumbering the population of Mecca, gold's being strewn right and left before our eyes. And hills are being leveled, too, disappearing just like the old buildings, one of which was my grandfather's house. The house stood at the summit of what used to be called Sanctuary Portico, in the Istanbul neighborhood. That guileless past is gone now and it'll never exist anywhere again, except in the pages of this book.

I'm telling this story to my great-great-grandfather Yusuf Alem of Mecca, who could make bread appear from beneath his prayer rug when he was praying in the Sanctuary, and if that seems like no big deal to us now, it's only because sending a message from Mecca to China with the click of a button is no big deal to us now either. Yes, my ancestor was one of those people who could cross great distances in the blink of an eye.

He was a scholar who believed that traditional learning was just material passed down from one dead person to another. Death was something you could achieve easily enough, he felt, but spiritual life—well, that was something that bubbled up out of the sea of the living. That was why he shunned any kind of learning that could be passed down, and devoted himself to that knowledge which sprang forth from the sea of life and sent bread pouring out from beneath his prayer rug, whisked nations beneath his feet, and shone a light through the faces of his descendants—including my father Muhammad—which illuminated all that was unseen.

PART ONE

The Lane of Many Heads

THE ONLY THING YOU CAN KNOW FOR CERTAIN IN THIS ENTIRE BOOK IS where the body was found: the Lane of Many Heads, a narrow alley with many heads.

The first thing you should know, though, is that it's not me who's foolish enough to try to write about a place like the Lane of Many Heads; this is the Lane itself speaking, me and my many heads. I am that narrow alley in Mecca, off the highway where pilgrims make their ablutions and don their white robes to begin the Umrah rituals: the cleansing of the soul, washing away the past year's sins in preparation for another year of debauchery.

I'm the Lane of Many Heads, a champion at holding my breath; it's a title I've earned through my enviable skill at confronting the impossible. Since no one ever bothered to dignify me with streetlights, I've learned to sit in the darkness, getting high on deep drags of the stink of trash and sewage, the clamor of discordant voices, like any old forgotten backstreet. I like to hold my breath for a few minutes before I slowly let it out through my mouth in rumors and legends and whispers of forbidden things. It's how I torment the people who live here, how I'm able to send them trawling through their history for some antidote to the unholy gloom they live with, something to protect them from the atomic age that's about to crush them.

My story may not go as far back as the tribe of Jurhum and the Amalekites — it's true—but I can at least say I've witnessed the collapse of one great kingdom and the rise of another, as well as many wars and much blood. I know enough to be able to tell the story of one of the Hijaz's greatest valleys, al-Numan, whose name, as any dictionary will tell you, is one of many words for blood, one of the many disguises it likes to hide behind.

My name's all right, I guess, but I probably envy Elbow Alley most of all. That's where the Prophet's companion Abu Bakr had his silk shop and house, or so they say. In the wall opposite the house, there's a stone that passersby touch because they think that every time they do it, the Prophet receives a blessing. This may, in fact, be the very stone the Prophet was referring to when he said "There is a stone in Mecca that used to bless me on the nights when I received revelation." Across from this stone, on the left as you're approaching, there's a slab in the wall with an elbow-shaped depression at its center, and this, too, is visited by the masses, who believe it's where the Prophet used to rest while chatting to the adjacent stone, his sublime elbow eventually wearing a groove into the wall. People also say that any Meccan who suffers from impotence or infertility need only walk from Khadija's house to this stone, to be blessed with all the children they could ever want.

Of course, I'd love to be the kind of street that's the star of its own magical fable, an alley with walls that chat to passersby and respond to the touch of their fingertips. I know I can't compete with those kinds of streets and their legends, but I've still got more going for me than scores of others. I like to think I'm better than Embrace-Me Way, which is so narrow that the only way two people can get down it is if they entwine their bodies like lovers; there's not a step you could take in that alley that wouldn't get you stoned to death. Or what about Funeral Lane, the tragic path that people only go down once? Or Mortar Alley, which likes to grind down the cheerful souls whom I actually welcome into my nooks and corners? I'm far superior, likewise, to Wretches' Lane, with its bonfires surrounded by beggars and dervishes and other unsavory types; and to Coal (or Red) Alley, too, for that matter—the only thing it has to brag about is a single carob tree that produces bloody fruit. I'm the Lane of Many Heads; I'm better than that.

Sometimes I sit down to pray—that's right, don't be shocked: everything prays—and when I shut my eyes, I get carried away on a mental wave under the influence of my Tryptizol, which is prescribed for both depression (large doses) and incontinence (small doses). I take a 50 mg capsule between my fingers and open it to reveal tiny beads, which I divide into five piles. Some nights I increase the dosage, and other nights when my insides feel like they're coming apart, I abstain completely even if it means I end up wetting the bed . . .

I'm the Lane of Many Heads. My name stands for an alley that's unknown to anyone who's known, to anyone who has the power to change my destiny, to put me on the map of Mecca, which is where I belong.

The Dress

LANE OF MANY HEADS. WHY THE HELL HAVE I PUT UP WITH THIS OVERPOPULATED, headbutt-evoking name for so long? A long time ago, well before I came to life, the heads of four men were found buried here, beside one of the stations of pilgrimage. Please notice that I make no mention of the woman's corpse that's at the heart of this book, the only reason I broke my silence. No, instead I'm telling you about four heads, which were lopped off during the reign of one of Mecca's Sharifs—maybe Sharif Awn's—or under one of the Ottoman viceroys. These four men, you see, had taken advantage of the opportunity presented by the arrival of the new kiswa. A drape of green and red silk, the kiswa that covered the Kaaba was brought every year from Tinnis in Egypt in a great celebratory procession, and every year the Sharif and his soldiers, as well as the rest of Meccan high society, went out to meet the procession, while the attendants laid the old covering in a pile near Victory Gate, which faces Mount Marwa. They would leave it there for the Shayba clan to come collect it and take it to the jewelers' market, where the gold and silver thread that had been used to embroider the glorious names of God onto it would be melted down. This was the Shayba clan's annual stipend. The four men waited until the Sharif and his soldiers were out of the way, then dashed in and made off with the old covering on camelback down the pilgrimage route. When the Sharif's soldiers finally tracked them down, they discovered that the men had pitched the covering like a tent and were receiving the poor, the sick, lepers, and madmen, who, after lying beneath the cloth, emerged as if born anew, cured of their diseases, disfigurements, and woes, and occasionally of their earthly bodies themselves!

News of the theft and the miracles the thieves had wrought was hushed up, lest other greedy souls attempt to imitate their blasphemy. Instead stories were spread about how the four men had snuck into Mecca dressed as pilgrims, as so many Western travelers and other outsiders had done before, be they Jews, Christians, false prophets—all manner of the damned. The Chief Judge of Mecca was forced to issue a snap ruling, saying that the men were heretics and must be executed, and so one night they were simply beheaded. Their bodies were thrown into the Yakhour well, the final resting place of all Mecca's garbage, and their heads were stuck on spikes in the spot where they'd been apprehended. At this point, the plot requires me to mention the woman who used to walk here barefoot from Mecca every day to sit beneath the heads and mourn them with poems and songs, occasionally reciting verses from the Quran, which were believed to protect the dead from the torments of the grave. People said she must have been in love with all four of them to turn up each morning, her feet burnt by the scorching Meccan sand, and sit there making conversation with the severed heads, goading them to compete with one another for her affections. She even used to wait until nightfall to retrace her steps toward home so as not to arouse gossip. This alley sprang up out of that woman's tender whisperings of grief, and so I must confess that I'm nothing more than the water of desire pooling in a woman's lap or in the lacerations of her heart and hands, even though she never shed a tear for those four severed heads; not even as crows circled overhead, pecking at them incessantly, hoping to snatch a chunk of eyeball or flesh. The woman did nothing but lament and sigh, until the alley was rent in two, and I can tell you now that the culprit behind this split was none other than feeling itself. At the top of the alley beside the Radwa Mosque, in the midst of the hordes of seeking pilgrims, there was longing, and at the end of the alley by the shops that dealt in the instruments of passionate music, there was ecstasy, and in the middle, a history that buried its head in the sand, humming the call of demons and fading away into nothingness. And yet along the edges of the alley, the doors to sadness were still open a crack, and the windows stayed up late looking for love, while the grandest gates of all were the ones that made room for secrets. The gate of passion and yearning stands in this tranquil garden, which was founded by the first of the Sharifs or the last of them (either Sharif Awn or Sharif Hussein, what difference does it make?) and has become rather more like a mirage, a glimpse of water to the thirsty, drawing in the miracle-seekers and with them soldiers to guard against brigands who are hooked on gum arabic and the kind of booze that's made in backyards and cellars.

Before the Body

I TOLD YOU THIS STORY WOULD BEGIN WITH A BODY, BUT BECAUSE IT'S MY STORY I've decided we're going to hold off on the body for the moment. Let's not worry about the dead for now, not while we can still chase the living. I'd gone to great lengths to hide all traces of love and revenge, but the body gave us away. So when I mention Azza or say everything there is to know about Aisha, I'm not being lazy and simply picking the first girl who comes to mind; the body could've been any of the girls from the Lane of Many Heads, really. I should be more precise: I mustn't mix up the names of the parties involved or hurry to point the finger at whoever did it. Not before we've been through the story, and heard and compared the different versions of events told by the four heads, each of whom was a suspect at one point or another. Those heads of coal shall tell their stories, from beyond the veil that separates me from them.

There was Yusuf the history nerd. He had a bachelor's degree in history from Umm al-Qura University, signed by the dean in green and sealed with an unfakeable blue. He got it for his research paper on historical minarets in the mountains around Mecca. Yusuf was the Lane of Many Heads' Minaret of Love, calling to his two beloveds, Azza and Mecca, and he didn't climb down off his family's roof—or his delirium—until he managed to combine them into one.

Then there was Mu'az, who was being trained to take over from his aged father as prayer leader at the mosque. In the meanwhile he decided to kill time by helping out at the photography studio. There was also Khalil, who had a suspended pilot's license and rejection letters from every single private airline. And, last of all, there was the adopted son of al-Ashi the cook, the Eunuchs' Goat, who gathered human limbs to practice his perversion. They all deserved to have their heads paraded on spikes.

That much was vouched for by Sheikh Muzahim, who arrived in the wake of Ibn Saud's campaign in 1926, after King Ali ibn Hussein gave up Jeddah following a long siege and Mecca surrendered without hostilities. Muzahim was fifteen when he was orphaned by the Battle of Taraba—it was news of that massacre, in fact, that caused the Hijaz to surrender without putting up a fight. He stayed in Taraba for a long time, the only survivor, and witnessed the piles of fingernails, which according to legend were all that remained of Taraba's slain inhabitants, blowing slowly away in the wind, silvering the contours of the sand dunes. People have attempted to tarnish his reputation, as a man and as a religious scholar, because of the silver he pilfered from the tribe's legacy before finally fleeing to Mecca where he used the silver to start a business. His family name was left in tatters; he buried it along with the last of the silver in the ground beneath his new store. He began trading in "sustenance," which is what the people who lived there called the bags of flour, rice, wheat, sugar, and tea he sold. Sheikh Muzahim made his money off of human sustenance. He suffered from chronic, debilitating constipation, too, and the only thing that eased his suffering was an almond-oil coated finger. That was why he found Ramadan such a torment. Inevitably, by the time the month was over, his anus would be besieged by hemorrhoids and his intestines would have turned to stone. He finally went to the trouble of seeking a religious ruling to affirm that almond oil in the rectum didn't break one's fast.

The Body

MU'AZ, THE PHOTOGRAPHER'S APPRENTICE, WAS LEAPING BETWEEN TWO ROOFS when he froze in mid-air, transfixed by what he saw below. Deep in the cleft between the two houses was the body. In her death the woman was a breathtaking nude portrait, one leg bent and the other stretched languidly out, rebellious breasts pointing in opposite directions, reveling in the attention of the sudden crowd, who were captivated by the bloom of darkness between her legs.

"Such perfect death! What a shot!" cried Mu'az as he snapped a photo.

At one end of the alley, an oud fell silent, though a drum still rattled under an amateur's clumsy hand. From the other end came a squat penguin of a woman in a flapping black abaya and white mourning dress—Kawthar, the wife of Yabis the sewage cleaner, mother to Ahmad the emigré. "For the love of God, cover the poor woman up!" she cried as she waddled back and forth around the body. The crowd jostled against her great hunched back, which shielded the dead woman from sight.

An older man with an orange beard broke through the commotion with his cane. His liquid blue eyes settled on the woman's nipples, each looking pertly out to the side, and he was struck by one terror only: "May my daughter Azza never have a body like this, shameless even in death!"

To prevent the murdered woman from possessing his daughter's body, Sheikh Muzahim muttered to himself, "Azza's like a falcon. When I slapped her yesterday, her eyes pecked me to pieces. Azza doesn't live like this, and she's not going to die like this either. Lord, let it be a simple death, dignified, and let me awaken among the houris in the pools of Paradise!"

"Hmm Hmm Hmm . . ." Inside houses women murmured, and outside mothers blew on the corpse to keep disgrace from spreading to the other girls in the Lane of Many Heads.

An officer, two police cars, and an ambulance rushed through my narrow entrance into the confused melee around the body. Everyone fell silent when it came time to record the victim's name on the official forms.

"Unknown."

For the first time, the woman lay unveiled in the alley for all eyes to see. They covered her in white and lifted her onto a stretcher; her slender right leg escaped and dangled over the side, trailing in my dust all the way to the ambulance, where the nurse gathered her up and thrust her inside the van alongside festoons of resuscitating equipment.

The dead woman left no mark except for the line that her neatly trimmed, rose-scented toenails traced across my back and the bloodstain between the houses of Sheikh Muzahim and Aisha the schoolteacher.

At the Bottom of the Vat

HALIMA LOOKED OUT FROM HER ROOF, HER GAZE FLITTING OVER THE SURROUNDing walls of my houses, running over my crumbling, impoverished rooftops where the remains of old furniture languished. Her roof was bare except for some potted herbs. She marveled at those who lived in my alley, those who never turned their noses up at a rotten chair or a soggy couch but were content to share their spot with the rain, the heat, the passage of time till they themselves were as damp as the old sofas, as dreary as the threadbare carpets. She played memories of Azza over in her head, allowing herself to feel the pain of some of those scenes. Around her, every family in the neighborhood counted their daughters and washed their hands of the scandal of the body.

She had no idea how long she'd been sitting there in silence when she was roused by the sound of a crow that had gotten stuck somehow in a forgotten water vat at the edge of the roof and was struggling to escape through the half-open lid. It burst out in a streak of black, followed by a sparrow.

As soon as Halima lifted the decaying wooden lid, she could make out the papers that filled the vat. They were wrapped in trash bags. Her hand trembled, and the yellow of the papers nipped at her heart. "These aren't drafts of my son Yusuf's articles." His rational, carefully indexed articles were piled up in the corner of their room. Halima scooped the papers out excitedly and pressed them to her cheeks and nose. The sweat of Yusuf's hands, his unspoken passion, his madness wound its way through the words, from the first clipping at the top of the pile to the thick paper of a cement sack that bore a drawing of a pregnant woman. The charcoal line-drawing stopped her in her tracks: it showed a woman's body from her waist to her knees, emphasizing her thighs and her round, pear-shaped stomach.

Halima was illiterate so she couldn't read any of the papers, all of which were dated, but still she memorized them: pages that spilled over with words fading away in the distance like a caravan of camels loaded with firewood, and others on which the camels had left marks where they'd kneeled. The words agitated her, bounding over the page like cats in heat, sniffing each other's tails, scattering ink and meows left, right, and center, words, which were no more than a pit in the center of the page, a boulder poised to tumble off the bottom right-hand corner, a fishing net of tangles and runs.

Halima realized that the papers she was clutching were her son's insides. Her son, whom the body had driven away.

She didn't know what to think. There were dozens of pages fashioned out of cement sacks covered in tire tracks, blackened with charcoal drawings of creatures, a cross between humans and motorbikes, accompanied by signs—some bearing neon lights, others rusted and old—reminiscent of the shop fronts that lined the Lane of Many Heads. Halima knew they were Yusuf's letters to Azza; once hidden in the broken radio, they must have been retrieved by Yusuf before he disappeared.

Halima held the corner of her scarf over her nose as a cloud of dust rose from the charcoal; it was still moist. Her heart was beating hard. She put the lid firmly back on the vat and turned away.

"If only I could read . . ."

Angel Girls

I SHUT MY EYES AS SOON AS THE STORM BROKE OVER MY ALLEYWAYS AND HOUSES. Everyone had to take his or her turn being questioned at the police precinct, and the raids, searches, and seizures went on endlessly. They confiscated all the most popular videotapes from the café. There were more crows circling over Mushabbab's orchard than usual; he had taken off after the bank foreclosed on both house and orchard following a disastrous stock market venture that took place just a few days before the body appeared. Yusuf had disappeared along with Mushabbab, so no one was surprised when his mother Halima, the tea lady, was called in for questioning. A masterful mind-reader, I closely observed the features of those going into the precinct, and the ashen looks of those coming out, their index fingers stained with ink from marking witness statements. Halima, on the other hand, looked like she was on the way to one of her tea-pouring ceremonies. She'd even touched up the half-moon of henna on her palm, ready for the fingerprinting. When she stepped into Detective Nasser's office, they were both surprised; she'd been expecting to see Ali, the officer who'd dealt with the body that morning. This Nasser lacked the air of indifference and flaccidity that Ali had affected as he strolled around the body, laughing flirtatiously at the feminine voice emanating from the cellphone that never left his ear, waving orders to his assistant before finally gesturing to him to move the body and clear the scene.

"Aren't you going to take fingerprints from the body first?!" Khalil the taxi driver's voice boomed absurdly, as if straight out of a movie script. Everyone turned to look. The official smile on Ali's face congealed suddenly in the heat. Without putting his phone down, he answered the challenge: "Is anyone here related to the deceased?" he demanded, staring defiantly into the eyes of the crowd around him. "If so, perhaps they'd care to come with us for a preliminary interrogation, so we can file charges and open a case. Then we can apply to the relevant authorities to take fingerprints. It'll take some time, and, as you know, the victim's relative will have to meet with us frequently over the course of our investigations. They'll need to make sure they're free for, let's say, a month, maybe a year—who knows? Investigations take time. This isn't a TV show, folks." The crowd shrank back. Ali gestured to his assistant to clean up.

Halima looked at Nasser; he didn't have that naive, vacant look of authority that Ali had. Nasser looked like his pride had dried him out. The Sony air conditioner stiffened him; the ceiling fan whipped at his face and flaked the paint off the corners of the room; spiders had paved webs over the electrical wires and were working their way over the detective's face as he examined the same grim, murderous mugs filing past, asking the same questions, dealing the same blows till his rough skin started to look like an extension of the brown camel-hair carpet on the floor. Detective Nasser al-Qahtani had interrogated thousands of people during his quarter century as head of the criminal investigation bureau, and they all left him feeling the same. Even though Nasser was not himself the human embodiment of Israfil, the archangel who will sound the trumpet on Judgment Day, he did derive his strength from him. The archangel worked as Nasser's assistant, hiding in the beat-up Sony air conditioner and blowing at the faces of the accused.

"This Nasser guy's possessed," Halima thought to herself, pity showing on her face. Nasser turned his swivel chair a half-turn to the right, stretching his shoulder across the width of the gray office, blocking her pleading look with the insignia on his uniform. She reminded him of his aunt Etra, queen of Wadi Mehrim in the Surat Mountains. Aunt Etra had married half a dozen men, each of them years younger than she was. She was famous for her snake-like ability to paralyze a man with a single look and make him crazy with desire. They said that she could peer right through a man down to his semen, that her eyes could pierce through to his spine, that she knew how to touch all the most vital points on a man's body. They said that before she passed away, she'd leave the secrets of her wisdom to the wildest girls in Wadi Mehrim, but only if they could read and write, so that they could record her teachings about these special spots and one day publish them. The old men of Wadi Mehrim, though practically on their deathbeds, still fought over her, desperate to have her trace a map of vital points across their bodies, to breathe life back into them.

Aunt Etra haunted his dreams. He always saw her in that final scene: she'd dared to stand up to his father at his sister Fatima's funeral. The thought made color drain from Nasser's face, and a smell of blood wafted into his office from the past, the same smell that his sister Fatima's body gave off when it was wrapped in the white burial shroud. Denuded by that white shroud, all that could be seen of her body was the protrusion of her breasts, which bore into Nasser's consciousness. He was five at the time and the events of that day had faded. He could remember little other than the smell of heat mixed with peril. Those breasts were engraved upon his memory. They were crowned with inch-wide dark circles that seemed to float on their surface in that dusty street in the Martyrs' Quarter in Ta'if. Nasser had watched the astonished male eyes appearing, multiplying, orbiting those two dark circles. His father scrambled past them, pulling off his white robe as he ran, and threw it over Fatima's naked body. As if possessed, he wrapped her up and dragged her into the house. He shoved her through the door, and with the same movement tore his robe off of her and flung it aside in disgust. Fatima was getting to her feet when his father seized the first thing he could find, a coffeepot: whack. Nasser had never been able to shake the sight of the coffeepot spout piercing Fatima's forehead, the channel of blood that suddenly spurted out over her face and neck, his father's threatening finger: "Your sister died of an asthma attack . . ." His father burned that robe, the one he used to wear for holidays and Friday prayers.

A doctor relative of theirs filled out the death certificate, his eyes lowered, embarrassed and sympathetic to the father's plight. He'd had the story before coming: "The father who'd refused the neighbors' son who was smitten with his daughter; the cousin who, as soon as he'd heard she had a love-interest, washed his hands of his betrothed; and the young woman herself and her giving, playful, thrumming heart that sent her, naked and crazy, out into the middle of the street." The neighbors played their parts perfectly in burying the scandalous affair: they came to the house to mourn with the mother and father, telling countless stories of deaths caused by asthma, or insect bites and the like. You'd be forgiven for thinking the girl had simply forgotten to keep breathing. Their deeply sorrowful expressions and their commiseration ate at Nasser's young sisters, for whom Fatima's death might as well have been the death of their own reputations and any chance they might have had for a decent marriage or life. Only Nasser's aunt Etra swore she'd never set foot in that house again. She marched down to the police station and reported what had happened with the coffeepot, but was met with nothing but pitying looks. She realized she'd have an easier time getting into the *Guinness Book of World Records* than penetrating those thick, almost armor-plated heads and their ideas about honor.

That was four decades ago now. The climax of the plot was his own father's death: it wasn't grief for his daughter that killed him, rather the tragedy of his lost reputation. Nasser grew up an orphan, hostage to that crippled reputation, and he seized the first chance he got to flee to Mecca, to escape the sour blood that stained the threshold of their house. Years later, when the Lane of Many Heads case came across his desk, he felt compelled to discover the identity of the body and the person who'd flung it out into the street. He wasted no time in getting down to the task.

Halima's affectionate gaze pierced through his insignia straight to his heart, to the cowering child still grieving the death of his sister. Sweat began to trickle between his shoulder-blades and down his temples.

"Your son Yusuf is a suspect," said Nasser hoarsely, trying to regain the menacing aura he'd always relied on for strength and protection. It didn't stop her from pitying him. He needed one of her potent coffee blends, she thought sympathetically. She picked one out, and seeing that the samovar had boiled, she polished her tiny coffee cups, stirred up the soul of her copper coffeepot, and poured out her encyclopedia of the neighborhood:

"Yusuf gets scared easily, that's all. He caught a glimpse of death on his doorstep and ran away. My son eats, sleeps, and breathes history; he graduated from Umm al-Qura University with honors. Then they gave him an important writing job on the *Umm al-Qura* newspaper." Nasser let her continue. He listened to the ceiling fan whirring softly above; the aroma of Halima's coffee evoked the love he felt toward Mecca. "This is the sacred womb whose honor I swore I'd protect," he thought to himself. A pinch of ginger, thought Halima.

"Mushabbab's one of his friends. That boy's all about Mecca and its secrets. Ever since we've known him, he vanishes every so often and comes back with some discovery." The coffee boiled over, and she moved the pot to where hot embers lay beneath a layer of ash.

"As for the girls of the Lane of Many Heads, 'O fire, be cool and gentle!' The angels still smile on them. They each live in their own little world.

"Aisha and Azza, goodness me. Whenever I visit Aisha, I see her sitting clammed up with her computer in that tiny room of hers—as if it's her entire world! And Azza, if it weren't for me distracting her with my fabrics from time to time, she'd have long since drowned in her paper and charcoal! None of the girls in the Lane of Many Heads has done anything to deserve murder or punishment.

If you give me a Quran, I'll swear to you that Yusuf wouldn't hurt a fly. His entire life is paper and ink. The only legacy he's going to leave is the stack of papers that's rotting in the old vat on the roof, getting pecked at by crows . . ."

Confiscated Documents

April 6, 2000
A Window for Azza

Azza was the first of my miracles. I wrote to her, and she made me fall in love with her.

Why do I love Azza?

I watch her; she hides her secrets in an old radio at the bottom of the staircase that leads up to the roof. She takes out the very first scrap I ever sent her when I was nine years old. It was a drawing of a triangle-shaped girl with hair like seven violin strings, freshly cropped. That was the day Azza first picked up a charcoal stick and tried to talk to the girl. With three strokes, she turned out another girl just like the first, and I followed her with another, this time with shorter strokes for hair. The sheet of paper flew back and forth between us, but then she surprised me with a boy, breaking my stride. When she said his name was Yusuf, I felt her touch for the first time, felt there was nothing more to say. There was nothing that could express transgression and passion like the appearance of that boy.

If it weren't for Azza, I'd have never learned how to make love. I experienced my first orgasm at that precocious age. Azza was every woman, every girl I met.

I realized then that the boy had liberated the girl—as if she were a dove—so he could massage her neck and break into the world of women that lay behind closed doors. The dove never looked back, not even on the day I took it out from its nest inside the busted radio and wrote "Azza has the eyes of an angel" between its eyes with my finger.

At these words of romance, the sheet crumpled and the girl's heart shrank back, and I could hear her laughing as she said, "If I could undo the collar and cut the girl's hair that's tied to my tail, I'd have swallowed the boy and flown away."

Yusuf's enigmatic diary was laid out in a pile in front of Detective Nasser, who was slowly making his way through it. Part of it dated from 1987 onward, but another part covered the period from 355–1120 AH (966–1708 AD). They'd recovered it from inside the water vat on Halima's roof. It was prefaced with a report by the expert who'd examined all the episodes and their arrangement. The report ended, "The defendant Yusuf refers to his memoirs as 'windows,' and he divides them into two sections: 'windows for Azza,' in which he describes the alley to his beloved, and 'windows for Umm al-Qura,' in which he dredges up incidents from history."

It was almost midnight, but detective Nasser al-Qahtani was still at his desk, going over stacks of interrogation transcripts and back down the dead-end where his investigation had stalled. Each day brought dozens of cases like this one—sealed by murder, or torn open by rape—that would eventually go cold, pinned on SUSPECT UNIDENTIFIED. But the Lane of Many Heads case was different: this many-headed alley knew exactly who the murder victim was. It was just daring him to figure it out, thumbing its nose at his storied career as a detective. He could've ignored the Lane of Many Heads case. He could've let the archives swallow it up along with hundreds of pages of Yusuf's diary and all of Aisha the schoolteacher's emails, but something in those stacks of paper—something hidden—was taunting him. He couldn't even tell the difference any more between what was real and what was a delusion brought on by the high blood sugar and cholesterol he'd developed after all those sleepless nights and fast-food meals eaten hurriedly at his desk.

Nasser put off looking into the folder labeled "Emails from Aisha," which his men had downloaded and printed out from a folder named "The One" on the missing teacher's computer. The report stated that they "were sent from one party to an unidentified second party over the Internet." What dormant cell lurked in those emails? Who was going to rouse it? And to what explosive end?

August 30, 2001
A Shroud for Azza

If the earth were a bolt of fabric, how many meters would you need to wrap yourself up warm? What if there were a child or two, and Azza, to wrap up with you? I already know what size the shroud has to be: it's a cotton weave, white, eight to ten meters long, with strips to cover our genitalia, and drapes over our faces like a head-cloth in case our mouths fall open. "Mouths do nothing but bring shame. They're never sated, not even in death." To me, a shroud represents the ultimate act of shedding whatever the world might try to do to us. Do I have your permission to dream of making a home for you inside it, somewhere where we can have a child?

I look around the cardboard room on your father Sheikh Muzahim's roof, where my mother and I live. He lets us have it out of the kindness of his heart. I am twenty-eight years old. I've got a fiftieth of a square meter for each year of my life: fifty-six hundred square centimeters for me, and about twice that for my mother the tea lady. That includes everything: the bedroom, the roof, and the bathroom in the far corner. And yet we don't pity ourselves either. We live on the gone-off leftovers from Sheikh Muzahim's storeroom and whatever the tea money brings in, touching the sky like angels.

I sit at my mother's tea stall in the midst of her samovars and glistening teacups, which distort my face, reflecting it back at me mixed with the faces of angels. It's a little game I play to make myself feel better. I'm obsessed with it.

I'm going to write about veils as I watch your apparition reflected in my mother's samovar. Do you mind if I write about death? You see, I got my start by corresponding with my father, who was veiled by death at the very moment I announced my existence in my mother's belly. I corresponded with him so that I could reach you, Azza, so that I could pierce the even greater veil that separates us and falls over me like the night.

I try to write with the simplicity of the dress I remember you wearing as a young teenager: black, with slits at the chest and the wrists.

Don't make fun of the way I write.

When a man sits down to write, to jostle the dead so they can't enjoy their eternal rest, he's choosing to write as a substitute for living the life he dreamed he would: a world in which his sons could live contentedly, assured of the knowledge that their father had fought and been broken, but that he'd done it all for them. That he was a hero and that his children were the only medals he had to show for it. The most painful, most deceitful words a man will ever write are the words he writes to a woman so that she will give him something she's never given to any man before him and will never give to any man after him. Imagine the hopelessness of a man who writes for a living and who, after writing books upon books, discovers in his writerly solitude that he's gone down a dead-end of illiteracy; that he writes but isn't read, that the volumes of his life are nothing more than moth fodder.

We write to give life and to take it away (that's how you should see me).

I realize I'm not writing to you, but to whomever inevitably reads my journal after you're gone. They will, of course, try to read between the lines; so, to those who will wear themselves out trying to deduce who I am, let me save you the trouble: I am the writer and historian Yusuf, half-man, half-

robot, twenty-eight years old. For some sin or transgression, I was born deformed in the 1980s and have lived on into the twenty-first century.

But I will record my secret here: I swear to you, reader, that I was born, healthier and more handsome, in the fifties and grew up in the sixties. Azza met me back then. She fell in love with me, and we sailed through time together.

Don't ask whether the things you're reading are true.

Just tell yourself you're reading about a freak who wakes up in the twenty-first century to unfurl and stretch like the monsters looming before us, all these limited and unlimited liability corporations.

My nom de plume is Yusuf ibn Anaq, the giant who plucks fish out of the bottom of the ocean and grills them on the eye of the sun. It takes days for the caravans I send from my head to reach my feet where they discover that the nipping flies they set out to rid me of are actually wolves. I'm the one who survived Noah's flood, which didn't even come up to my waist. I'm the one who traveled through time and met the Israelites in the desert, who picked up a boulder the size of a mountain, which would have crushed them all had Moses not begged God to protect them. The boulder was instantly hollowed out and fell like a collar around my neck. The column I write in Umm al-Qura newspaper is a salute to my namesake, Awaj ibn Anaq.

Detective Nasser had the feeling that Yusuf was writing all this to make sure he'd be involved. He was writing to be read. He wasn't writing like someone trying to hide a secret; he wanted to defy the veil. He wanted to look the reader straight in the eye and say the things that people usually tried to hide. Nasser was annoyed. For a second he thought about stopping—so as to deny this gloating exhibitionist an audience—but the detective in him told him he could do it: he was capable of combing through even the most innocent-sounding testimonies to track down the criminal hidden within. He carried on; the challenge he'd accepted weighed on him greatly.

September 20, 2004
A Window for Azza

Dear Azza,
When I get close to home, coming down the narrow lane, the window of your bathroom becomes the direction of my prayers. I look for the signal we've agreed on: a scrap of red cloth tied around the iron bars of the window informs me of your father Sheikh Muzahim's movements.

I see it from far off. A red rag, shouting: "Danger! Do not approach."

I slip my "window" under your door and go on up to my room, which is directly above yours. I step heavily on the floor, wanting to impress myself upon your head and your body, to inhabit you and the loneliness that surrounds you.

I should have stopped writing these windows to you. We're not kids like we were back when we started playing this game of life. Back then my secrets were silly. I still remember what I wrote to you when I was in fourth grade: marriage?

My ears flushed red when I watched you read that word; I thought it meant something like "making out," or "sex" even! Do you know how far a word will go to disguise its meaning, just so it can hold on to the connotations of its first rhythms?

That's the beat the word played on my heart, the chill it sent up my spine, and no matter how many times the religion teacher explained and elaborated, the word still winks at me and whispers: "Take her in your arms, crush bones and distances in one go."

I still look for a word like that, a word that says something so it can say something else, and for faces that present certain features so they can disguise others. I look out for those dreams, as well, that make us dream so they can hide us inside the dreams of another being, even though that being doesn't want us to be part of their dreams either. Their dreams, too, are the dreams of another being that doesn't want to release them from the library of dreams dreamed by all the people who came before.

I rave and claim that I'm going to tear off all the masks. The first mask is yours.

Azza, have you really become a woman like you threatened when you said, "There's a veil between my face and yours now, Yusuf!"

Okay, fine, then that must mean I'm a man now, and like all the other men in the Lane of Many Heads I need a veil to cover my impotence so you don't see my shame.

How can you expect a man to be nothing more than a white scrap addressed to you? I've lost sight of the man I once promised you I'd be; his head's been unplugged.

I've got to keep breathing so I can fill your chest with oxygen. I, too, can hear the contradictions in my voice. That's always how it is when I'm with you. It's what gets to you.

I'm sitting on the bus writing this scrap of paper to you. Did you know that I'm an Aquarius and that Aquarius empties his bucket for all of eternity? Suddenly fate—that eternal emptying—dragged me to my feet in the middle of the bus, my papers scattering everywhere. The dusty eyes of the immigrant workers all turned to stare. These men didn't let a fear of emigrating hobble them, they chased their dreams—me on the other hand . . .

How old am I now?

My head sways every time the bus stops, every time a body beside me stands up, sits down, or slumps in its seat. I've got to collect all these shreds of my identity; me and everyone else in my petroleum generation.

Did you know that bodies can tell a story in sweat? Like the sweat of this worker who just sat down with his plastic bag, stained with oily chicken and rice; he's between a rock and a hard place. He's in a rush to get to the building site where only yesterday one of his friends fell off the top of the scaffolding. They waited for hours for a vehicle—any vehicle—before they could take him, finally, to the nearest clinic in the back of a truck, racing against death. They were charged four hundred riyals just to have him admitted, and he ended up dying on one of their stretchers.

The sweat of these men tries to wash over me, tries to seep out of me; it says we're all running from a construction site to a destruction site.

My gaze takes refuge in the scrap of paper that longs for your eyes, and in the view of the road ahead. Every time I raise my eyes, people, shops, and colors flash past, jolting me. I'd bet you there's nowhere else on earth where you can find two square meters with such a mix of complexions. Mecca is a dove whose neck is streaked with colors that surpass the spectrum of humanity.

Do you also see how the rails of goods in the storefronts cry out? Newly arrived migrants are hatching a new generation, and in doing so they're splitting the physical and human geography of Mecca into two classes: the improvisers—whose one care in the world is selling as much as they can of whatever they can—and the consumers. During the pilgrimage season, alongside the religious ritual, they buy and sell to the tune of five billion dollars a month. They drink tea with milk, mint with pine nuts, strong coffee, Seven-Up, Pepsi, herbal teas, Boom Boom, and Bison ("Makes you move!"); they gobble up basmati rice and buy prayer rugs ("One hundred percent guaranteed to answer all your prayers!"). My mother used to warn me: "Make sure you fold up your prayer rug when you're done praying, or else Satan will use it!" and as the bus speeds along I watch devils praying on rugs laid out on display in shop windows. If you ask me, marketing really is the answer to the devil's prayers. O rugs of

Mecca, if only you'd give me one that was guaranteed to answer my prayers!

"Meccans are slippery and sly, hot pepper that brings tears to the eye. They're born businessmen who'd sell you the shade and the breeze. Never mind wool, they'll pull your own mother's placenta over your eyes!" My mother, Halima, loves repeating this little pearl; it's like scrawling a naughty smirk onto the face of the mountains around Mecca.

I just got out of an interview with the recruiting team at Elaf Holdings, the company that handles most of the urban development and investment projects in Mecca, trading in soil that's worth more than enriched uranium.

It was for the position of "historical researcher." I'd be tasked with investigating potential sites for real estate development, with regard, of course, to preserving the unique nature of the Holy City.

The other interviewees had a real mixed bag of qualifications (priority was given to graduates of foreign universities!). When the man who was chairing the hiring committee, who also happened to be the managing director and the lead developer, asked me if I was Yusuf al-Hujubi, I wanted to punch him in the face. He said it like he was suspicious and he didn't even wait for an answer. "If we decide that your qualifications are satisfactory, we may need to hire you on a probationary basis. If we were to take you on as an assistant, would you be able to put together a list of properties in Mecca whose charitable endowments are now defunct? And to find out whether the endowments are defunct because of a dispute among heirs, or just because they've been forgotten about?" The superior look that accompanied his question got on my nerves, and I was tempted to say, "I specialize in history, not family dramas." The look was amplified when he said, "Leave us your number. We'll be in touch."

He dropped the sentence like a wall between our faces, yours and mine, severing every link: our noses and your full, peachy lips.

I stopped off to see Mushabbab on my way back. He was suspicious when I told him they were on the lookout for abandoned properties. We sat down in front of his computer together and searched for "Elaf Holdings." You wouldn't believe what we found: it's like an octopus, with tentacles in companies, factories, hotels, hospitals, private universities, etc. It's an empire on which the sun never sets. Mushabbab said it was vital that we keep track of the consortium's activities on the ground—you never know what you might find out. To be honest, as I wrote down my suspicions it was like my eyes opened for the first time: the map was being redrawn right under our feet.

I'm not going to continue with Mushabbab's line of thinking. I'm as deflated as a balloon today.

I dreamed of white thread last night. I dreamed that I tied the end of a string around your hand and flew you like a kite. You were leaning on your hand, as if seated in a chair, and I was flying you up over the mountains attached by only the thinnest string. We were watching Mecca wake up, though Mecca doesn't have to wake up because she never sleeps: she only dreams, of the prayers and the footsteps of circumambulating pilgrims. And the dove: we undo the collar around its neck and the dove shakes it off like a splash of water. The thread that connects me to you makes a rainbow out of these colorful feathers, fanning them out over the Meccan horizon.

God, I'm so thirsty! And for some reason your dad chose not to take a nap today even though it's sweltering.

I'm desperate to see that black rag at your window telling me: My father's gone out, for . . . ever.

On days like this, allow me talk to myself rather than to you.

Who would hire a guy who can only think about the first Abbasid dynasty, or at a push stretch to Islamic Spain in time to fall alongside Granada in the space of a single night and hand over the keys? We always come back to the key, the epitome of my nightmares. I'm searching for the keyless lock to everything that's shut off from you and me.

Detective Nasser reached for another scrap of paper impatiently, his mouth feeling dry as he read stealthily, like an intruder creeping into a house that was off-limits, slipping into bedrooms, finding their inhabitants stark naked, framing them for crimes, seeing right into their minds without the slightest difficulty. A "window" for the city of Mecca, the Mother of Cities, found its way into his hands:

Roofs

Our ancestors were obsessed with roofs. Meccan men were fulfilled—they were ready for death—once they'd made certain that they'd built a shelter for their heirs. Some Meccans endowed their property, entrusting their houses and their land to God—thereby returning it to Him who created it—while also giving themselves and their progeny the right to build on it, live in it, or rent it out, though they could never sell or leverage it. Their heirs were forbidden from selling or dividing up the inheritance of stones and soil within the confines of the sanctuary. The wisdom of our forefathers could be summed up thus: dust turns to liquid only for the purchase of other dust (that is to say, liquidating or selling land must lead to the purchase of substitute land that will be endowed to God).

A wise principle that is today being eroded, as can be seen in all the empty spots on the map of Meccan endowments.

Reading a Footprint

HALIMA SLIPPED INTO THE MASS OF BODIES CIRCLING THE KAABA IN THE CENTER of the Sanctuary Mosque, and as she moved she became aware of the reflection of the full moon on the marble courtyard of the mosque, casting a silver glow over the faces around her. She was borne around the first two circumambulations by the melodic Persian wail of a young Iranian man leading four women in full white cloaks who smelled of damp and dough. From the upper galleries of the mosque she could hear the wheelchairs that were provided for old men too weak to perform the circumambulation or even walk at all. She knew Yusuf was pushing one of them—a temporary means of making a living. One full Umrah ritual only cost about two hundred riyals, if the customer was willing to bargain a little.

Halima continued her circumambulation, invoking His greatest name—O Almighty!—over and over in the hope that He might restore to her what she'd lost. Her body trembled as she noticed a thin figure that had pulled away from the crowd begin swaying beside her, but without raising her eyes from her supplicating palms, she continued her rotation, finishing on the seventh circumambulation with the words "In the name of God, God is great." When she raised her face to the corner of the Kaaba that held the black stone, she saw the names "The Living, The Everlasting" embroidered in gold, shimmering against the black silk of the covering. Without turning to look at her companion, she grasped his hand firmly and held it against her chest as she'd done so often since he was born to rein in his crazed episodes, to give him some of her tranquility:

"Are you sleeping well?" Yusuf was used to this eternal question of hers and the red blaze of insanity in his eyes diminished some.

"I gave them your papers. Forgive me." He didn't reply. She felt his pace quicken suddenly, and like a bird he tugged at her hand, pulling her away from the circumambulation toward the rock on which the Prophet Abraham had stood to build the Kaaba, leaving behind two footprints that were now covered over with a crystal dome set on a marble base, all enclosed in gold-plated latticework. Around the footprints was a band of silver engraved with the Verse of the Throne, and beside them, on a cushion of green velvet, lay the key to the Kaaba. Halima avoided the look of burning coals in her son's eyes and stared instead at the key that was at the center of so many of his writings: millions of people have examined these footprints and this key, and they'll go on doing so until the end of time. What's the hidden message here? She wanted desperately to follow the key and the footprints, if only for a step or two, through the door to the impossible world that had possessed her son and all the other sons who were lost like him. "My whole life revolves around a key and all these doors that either open or shut in our faces."

Halima felt even guiltier when she saw how pale and scrawny Yusuf was, and she hastily pulled her hand out of his. "They're looking for someone to pin this body on," she said. She hesitated before going on to tell him: "Sheikh Muzahim might ask me to vacate the room on the roof." She could sense the anger in Yusuf's footsteps, and it flustered her. "Some disagreement over the legality of his ownership . . . Sheikh Muzahim says they have doubts about his deed for the house. You know that house used to belong to my father, who sold it to Muzahim, but now someone else is claiming they have an even older deed."

"Muzahim never stops complaining. He's trying to make everyone in the neighborhood think he's fighting for some noble goal, but the truth is he wouldn't let anyone cheat him out of a grain of sand. And when it comes to you, he'll just go on playing the gallant knight forever . . ."

"That's true, but it's still up in the air. If worst comes to worst I can always go live at the home with Yousriya, Khalil the pilot's sister, and the other women."

"You? Live there?! Mom, you earn your living from making music and livening up weddings with your tea ceremonies. You'd die in that depressing place! Maybe Mecca's getting back at us because we're both such hypocrites!" Halima could feel the crackle of electricity in Yusuf's voice, and it reminded her of that morning a few months earlier when Imam Dawoud was leading the prayers in the mosque in the Lane of Many Heads and he recited Verse 32 from the Banquet Chapter: "If someone kills one person, other than to avenge a murder or prevent wickedness on earth, it is as if he has killed all mankind; and if someone saves a life, it is as if he has saved all mankind." Something went off in Yusuf's head when he heard that verse. One moment he was on the roof and the next, he'd leapt down to the alley in a single bound, his eyes shooting sparks like a wounded animal, and he broke through the door of the mosque with a thunderous clatter. The worshippers tried to ignore him, but he pushed them aside as he elbowed his way through their ranks in the direction of the air-conditioning unit. He snapped it off, and then he turned out the lights as well, ricocheting from one switch to the other like a bullet, and then he went up and snatched the microphone from under Imam Dawoud's nose.

"You, people of the alley, whom I cherish and whose lost causes I've defended tirelessly in my column . . ." His eyes bored into the alarmed faces arrayed before him. "You've stolen my life. You've suffocated every youthful spirit in the neighborhood. You're nothing but a bunch of hypocrites and liars who've banded together to fight life itself. You poison the minds of young people in the Lane of Many Heads. You've turned this place into a den of spies who pry into our most profound desires, our most intimate dreams. You've managed to turn the most private moments in our lives into a living hell. And you still have the nerve to stand in a house of God, blasting your prayers over the loudspeaker five times a day! You pray to ingratiate your way into heaven after you've gone and made our lives unbearable." Yusuf avoided the sympathetic look in the cook Abd al-Hamid al-Ashi's eyes and directed his rage at Sheikh Muzahim. "You. You build prisons with your left hand and mosques with your right. You're always preaching about faith, but what faith? The faith of burying your daughter alive every day? The Lord knows you'll be held to account on Judgment Day for all these prayers and prostrations. And you—" Yusuf turned to Yabis the sewage cleaner. "You dream of making it to heaven by cleaning up our shit! You're killing yourself day in and day out, but you think that our excrement's going to win you God's favor. What kind of role model are you for us and your own children? What if we all followed your lead and became cockroaches living off the neighborhood's waste? Of course, I'm a hypocrite, too. None of us knows what it means to live next door to God's holiest sanctuary, what it requires of us. Are we supposed to celebrate life? Or to fight against it?"

The loudspeakers carried an explosion of anger from inside the mosque. "That's the voice of Satan himself speaking!"

"The kid's crazy, look at his eyes . . ."

The speakers had drawn an audience. A cloud of dust rose in the alley as people poured in from the fringes of the Lane of Many Heads, rushing to see the spectacle. Even those who didn't usually get up early enough for dawn prayers couldn't miss the appearance of the devil himself in their neighborhood mosque.

Some of the young men came forward warily, hoping to wrest the microphone from Yusuf's trembling hands. At the other end of the Lane of Many Heads, Azza burst out of nowhere and ran down the length of the alley in her abaya to the door of the mosque, where she hesitated. She wanted—no, yearned—to push past the men and get to Yusuf, to calm him down, but some fear, like the fluttering of a dove's wings, stopped her.

"What kind of believers are you? What are you doing here, bowing and kneeling like robots, when true religion is out there, in the streets and in people's homes, in the good deeds you do, whether great or small!" A cloud of heat settled over the mosque and the neat lines of prayer rugs began to sway and overlap; sweat trickled between men's shoulders, daubing wet patches onto their shirts, sliding into the scene. A group of young men had Yusuf surrounded. Yusuf sent his first assailant flying through the rest of the circle with a forceful shove.

"God give you strength! Don't be frightened by the devil. Don't let him weaken your faith!" shouted a voice somewhere in the back, cheering the attackers on. Raising his voice, Yusuf answered him, "Have faith in life, in the breath of life His spirit gave us! Don't fight the breath which brought us into this world. Know its many blessings. Heaven begins in the street and ends at the threshold of the mosque!"

"Muslim brothers, block your ears to Satan's blasphemy! Repeat God's name and attack him. This is the devil himself speaking to you through Yusuf, an angel of hell!"

That morning Halima woke from a deep sleep to the sound of her son's rage booming out through the mosque's loudspeakers. She leapt up, grabbed her abaya, and raced out into the alley. The air exploded as Yusuf, now cornered by the men, screamed at the top of his lungs, "Look at the deal you've made!" Amplified by the loudspeaker, his shriek tore through every breast in the Lane of Many Heads. "A prison in life and a paradise in death!" he yelled, as fists pounded him and feet smashed into his face and his ribs, not even sparing his broken knee. They were beating Satan himself. They beat Yusuf until he collapsed, crushed under the weight of their rage, until even his breath fell silent.

Halima broke through the ring of bodies to find her son had been tied up with cables and his head wrapped in a red scarf so as to hide the face of the devil.

"Move, woman. Stand back or Satan will get you!" Halima paid no attention to the warning and pushed her way through the crowd of men to her son's unconscious body. Her abaya slipped as she knelt down to cradle Yusuf's crumpled frame in her lap and the men retreated at the sight of her bare chest. As soon as the ambulance appeared at the end of the alley, they surged around her again and shoved her aside. She found herself stumbling feebly into Azza's arms outside the mosque. Meanwhile, Sheikh Muzahim and his bright orange beard stepped forward to fan the men's rage:

"Fear for your religion! The devil has taken over the body of this cursed boy. Cast him into hell! Show him no mercy!" His hand trembled as he grasped his black prayer beads, urging the paramedics and policemen to expunge the satanic presence.

"He is an angel of hell," echoed Imam Dawoud. "Who is more wicked than he who seeks to destroy God's mosques and prevent worshippers mentioning His name therein? Only disgrace awaits such people . . ." His son Mu'az went to turn on the air conditioner to end the disgrace Yusuf had caused.

Yusuf was taken to Ta'if and booked into Shihar psychiatric hospital. He was strapped to the bed in a crowded ward where six patients lay immersed in their own feces, spraying everything around them with putrid froth every time they shrieked at the orderlies or at Yusuf when he tried to escape. He was unimaginably furious: to end up in Shihar hospital was a fate worse than death. Shihar . . . The name alone was considered an insult back in the Lane of Many Heads in Mecca; it was where disturbed girls, who were virgins, suddenly gave birth, where the healthy dropped dead by morning, where sanity trickled away down drainpipes and heads were emptied slowly of their identities, where a person's human qualities would be washed away by the surging onset of idiocy and stupefaction.

"My mind's never been in such a shockingly pure state before! Please, you must listen to me. You can't just run away from me! We're all hypocrites and liars!" It was Yusuf's eyes, not his words, that gripped the nurses and doctors. Two popping eyes that shot sparks and never clouded over, not even when he was pumped full of enough tranquilizers to floor a camel. His body would go limp and his tongue would become tied, but his eyes still pierced the faces around him with burning rays, all day and all night.

The technician fixed wires to Yusuf's head, while avoiding that gaze, which streaked through the heads gathered around him like a shooting star. The first charge tore through the whorls of Yusuf's brain and lifted his convulsed body several centimeters into the air, but it didn't succeed in forcing those eyelids shut. The technician doubled the voltage. He could almost smell the unblinking eyes burning.

The sessions continued for a week, but they couldn't put Yusuf to sleep. His memory exploded into fragments that caused wounds, which looked like dove's footprints, to appear across different parts of his body. They placed him in isolation, in a cell resembling a metal box, to monitor these symptoms. The shocks increased, but they did nothing to crack open the store of rage that was pumping poison straight into his bloodstream, turning his skin a dark purple.

Just when Yusuf had finally managed to subdue the poison and pull a mask of calm over his features, it was time for him to be examined by the chief consultant supervising his case. Yusuf mustered every mask he had and pleaded to be allowed to make one phone call.

On Yusuf's seventh day in Shihar, al-Ashi appeared, accompanying Yusuf's mother on her visit. "I'm no less crazy than any of you," said Yusuf. Al-Ashi contemplated Yusuf, who was sitting strapped to a bare white chair—patches of untrimmed beard, features contorted from inhuman pain, pleading with an incandescent glow—in the starkness of the visiting room and the chill of the air-conditioning, which iced their faces. Despite the cold, sweat ran in little rivulets from Halima's temples down to her chin and dripped onto her great chest. Something about that sweat made Yusuf's gaze even glassier; his blackened body seemed dried-out and wide-awake, burning with some internal fire. The voice hissing out of his chest sprayed them with coarse splinters:

"You're my only hope of escaping this wretchedness. I'm strapped to the bed, I lie in my own shit like an animal, in a paddock with other animals pissing and shitting in their sleep." Al-Ashi turned to look at Halima questioningly.

"Crazy or not, this place isn't fit for human beings," Halima answered, and for the first time in her life there was a bitter edge to her words.

"Just take me to the Sanctuary and leave me there," Yusuf begged.

"The electrical activity in his brain has reached ninety-five microvolts. Five more and this young man loses any chance of getting his mind back," the doctor said, attempting to convey the gravity of Yusuf's condition to Halima and al-Ashi. "Usually, when the mind is active,the frequency of beta waves should be between fifteen and forty waves per second. But your relative's mind"—the doctor scrutinized al-Ashi carefully for any indication that he understood this bombardment of medical information—"is registering a constant rate of thirty-two hertz, sometimes even more than forty. The mind needs deep, dreamless sleep in order to produce the delta waves that help the body recuperate and regain its natural internal balance, but not even the strongest tranquillizers we've got have managed to put your son to sleep. He's hanging on to his sanity by a single thread, and I can assure you if he leaves the hospital now, it will be severed." The only thing al-Ashi and Halima got out of all the jargon was that Yusuf needed to be taken to the house of God to be rid of his beta, delta, and satanic waves. His attempt to intimidate them having failed, the doctor could do nothing but sign the discharge papers and order that Yusuf be tightly bound and strapped into Khalil's waiting car.

The moment they were off the hospital grounds, al-Ashi undid the restraints and Yusuf immediately—and for the first time in a week—closed his eyes and fell asleep in the back seat. Khalil's usual acerbic comments deserted him when he laid eyes on the pitiful sight in the rearview mirror. The car went through Ta'if and headed in the direction of al-Hada and the Kara mountains, and down to the Plain of Arafat. Halima, al-Ashi, and Khalil listened the whole time to the remote sound of Yusuf's breathing. It sounded like he was trying to breathe life itself into his lungs, to breathe in the sanity that had been taken from him at Shihar. But no sooner had they reached the Sanctuary in Mecca—the car hadn't even stopped—than Yusuf shoved the car door open, leapt out, and disappeared into the crowd. Halima grabbed al-Ashi's arm to stop him from chasing after him.

"He's in God's hands now." Indeed, she didn't attempt to look for him at all but merely sent Mu'az to check on him later and make sure that he was still remembering to sleep. For three days straight he didn't leave the Sanctuary, not even to use the bathroom. He was like an empty shell, living off handfuls of holy Zamzam water, feeling ever more weightless and transparent. He would stand purposefully in the great courtyard of the mosque, in the middle of one of the marble passageways that led to the Kaaba, and block the path of the people entering. People walked straight through him as though they were walking through a sunbeam. His body no longer had any solid, substantial presence, and people could penetrate through it now. Instead, his body functioned as an X-ray, revealing their innermost essences.

Each day Mu'az would stand watching Yusuf from a distance as he took up his position at one of the mosque's doors. When the call to prayer sounded, Yusuf would greet those entering, grabbing the hands of strangers and clasping them with childlike joy in a gesture of welcome: "You're a good man! I salute you!"

Sometimes he would chase someone maniacally through the colonnades, as he did to one toothpick-seller. "You're evil!" he screeched. "I see the devil in you!"

People would run to get away from him, and they took care to avoid crossing his path, terrified by this man who might equally welcome them or condemn them. It pained Mu'az to see Yusuf slipping like a phantom in and out of the colonnades in pursuit of visions that eluded him. Perhaps the only place they existed was inside his head. He gathered his strength and approached Yusuf, who seized his hand eagerly.

"It makes me so happy to see you through these new, insightful eyes of mine. I see you're an extension of my body, Mu'az, like a third knee that nothing can break. I know you're not shocked by what I'm doing to the worshippers, because I can see right through you just like I can see through them."

"I don't know if what you're doing is right, Yusuf. Why are you just repeating the stuff Sheikh Muzahim always says, dividing people into angels or devils?!"

"No no, Mu'az, it's not me who's dividing people up. I'm no longer a body. I'm weightless like a beam of light. Try to catch me!" Mu'az retreated; he thought he was going to walk straight through him.

When Yusuf returned to the Lane of Many Heads several days later, he was as silent as the grave. The neighbors watched as he spent his nights wide-awake, his eyelids never even drooping for a moment. He was in a state of such terrible animation that he couldn't lie or sit down. He would pace back and forth, tearing up his papers: he started with his identity papers, went on to his signed diploma from Umm al-Qura University, then drafts of unpublished articles from *Umm-al-Qura* newspaper, his memoirs of Mecca, personal photos taken by his university classmates.

"I'm not going to leave a single word behind. I've got to free myself from this deceitful sham of a life that's taken everything from me," he repeated agitatedly to his mother Halima, who watched him wordlessly as he tossed scraps of his innocent past out into the alley. The people of the Lane of Many Heads awoke each morning to find themselves treading on fresh piles of Yusuf's shredded-up life.

All that came after Azza's first betrayal.

A dove alighted by their feet in the Mosque of the Sanctuary, bringing Halima back to the present. The dove hopped about in little circles, cooing and fixing its red gaze on Yusuf. In front of them, a blind Quran reciter chanted invocations in a low tone, his white eyes rolling. The Quran on his lap was open to the Verse of the Light: "God is the light of heaven and earth. His light is like a niche and within it a lamp . . ." His eyes grew whiter as he recited.

"It won't last for long. Just until they find out what really happened with the body, and then, gracious Lord, let this adversity pass."

They were suddenly interrupted by a great crash that tore through the tranquility of the courtyard. The worshippers around the Kaaba scattered and the crowds retreated. Glass smashed somewhere in front of them, and Yusuf instantly understood what had happened: a man, his face covered, had pulled the dome off the case covering the Prophet Abraham's footprints and was now circling around it, threatening the guards with a chainsaw. People were shrieking in panic: "He's stolen the key to the Kaaba! Stop that infidel!"

The terrified guards hesitated, keeping out of reach of the chainsaw, and the man darted toward the Mas'a gallery, a passage spanning the two holy mountains. In a split second, Yusuf took off after him, taking a shortcut around the Well of Zamzam, where he'd left his wheelchair by a row of taps. The thief was making for the outside gate of the Mas'a when the wheelchair hurtled into him, sending the chainsaw flying through the air. It crashed to the ground right in front of Halima, who had come running after Yusuf: "The thief! Watch out, Yus—" The hoarse cry had barely left her chest when the two bodies connected and went rolling across the floor. As the crowd watched the struggle between the two mismatched forms—skinny Yusuf battling a giant with mad, supernatural strength—the key shot out and went skimming across the marble floor. Yusuf dived after it. The crowd gasped as the key spun toward the drain beneath the rows of taps and was swallowed up. Yusuf plunged his hand into the drain vainly while behind him, the thief vanished into thin air. By the time the police arrived and the cleaning company had been called to open up the drain, there was little trace of what had happened except for Yusuf and the lost key. Even those who'd witnessed it happen doubted they'd really seen the key fall into the drain.

A heavy silence lay over the mosque, and flocks of doves settled motionless on the tops of the colonnades. The smashed dome gaped open over the plinth where Abraham's footprints, after their calamity, lay bare in the Meccan night. The two prophetic feet seemed desperate to continue their eternal journey.

Aisha: Potential Identification of the Deceased (preliminary)

I, THE LANE OF MANY HEADS, PLAYED DEAD AS DETECTIVE NASSER AL-QAHTANI, a cold cup of coffee on the table before him, sat fiddling with a few date pits in the protective shade of a cafe at the entrance to my alley. He waited patiently, sheltering from the blaze of the sun, which his heavy uniform seemed to suck right up, leaving him dripping with sweat. He watched Sheikh Muzahim in his shop until the sun was halfway across the sky and Imam Dawoud sounded the call to prayer. When Sheikh Muzahim picked up his cane and headed over to the mosque to pray, Nasser leapt up, crossed the alley, and slipped easily through the shop to the small door at the back. He went through to the storage area beyond, where he was swallowed up by a maze of tiny rooms, each stuffed to the ceiling with sacks of produce, leaving scarcely enough room to set a single foot inside. Nasser crept forward, urged on by the obvious emptiness of the place and the smell of foodstuffs long past their sell-by date. He spotted the huge old-fashioned radio set that had been hollowed out and concealed under the staircase leading to the roof where Halima and her son Yusuf lived. This was the radio set in which Azza hid Yusuf's letters. Nasser headed past the furthest aisles of the storage area to the back, where Azza's kitchen was. Before him was a small stove placed on a low table, and next to it were copper pots and non-breakable melamine plates drying in the sun under a wide skylight in the roof. A rusty hosepipe, still dripping, poked out of the bathroom, with its squat toilet and peeling walls. Nasser looked up at the narrow window close to the ceiling and saw, on the bars of the window, the offcuts of fabric that Azza used to signal to Yusuf to inform him of her father's whereabouts.

Most of the scraps were black; in the middle there was a single piece of red fabric. Nasser couldn't translate the message. His attention was drawn to some pieces of fabric used as sanitary towels. They'd been washed and hung out to dry, they'd stiffened but they still bore the faint scent and outline of impossible-to-remove bloodstains. Was it safe to sneak into Azza's room? Standing in that narrow space, looking at those scraps of fabric, Nasser felt like he was the one being watched.

A room eyed him from the middle of the storage area. It had to be Azza's. When he pushed open the door, the room surprised him with its starkness, mocking his uniform and eavesdropping on his cement-muffled footsteps. There was no trace of life in the room: no personal belongings, no clothes, no forgotten handprints on the walls. A plastic wardrobe stood there, thin and split; a broken drawer poked out of it as if Azza's entire life had been rent open. A hard cotton-stuffed mattress lay on a slightly elevated section of floor beneath the window. Nasser couldn't catch his breath all of a sudden. The room was totally bare. It didn't give off any feminine scent whatsoever. Nasser, who could sniff out a drop of sweat on a corpse, couldn't detect the slightest whiff of perspiration, not even a stray hair fallen in a corner or stuck to the mattress. It was a stock scene wiped clean of any feminine traces. But even so, it aroused him: he dropped onto the bed, imagining Azza tied to its hard surface, and was immediately blinded by his erection. He closed his eyes, cursing himself. He forced his legs to heave his trembling body up off the bed and his mind to focus on the facts around him. The second call had sounded and the early afternoon prayers had begun; after just four cycles of standing, bowing, prostrating, and kneeling, Sheikh Muzahim would return to his shop. Nasser examined the window again. Someone had ripped out the wooden crossbeams in the window, leaving only the rusty nails behind. Yusuf had written in his diary that the window was nailed shut and was never opened. Had Azza been killed and thrown out of this broken window?

Nasser knelt down and lifted the edge of the thick cotton mattress to find a hollow storage area underneath. From inside the hollow, Batman stared back at him from the cover of an old comic, yellowed from having to hear the desolation in that room and the alley outside for such a long time.

Nasser heaved the mattress onto his shoulder and bent down to see what else the drawer contained. Suddenly, a body landed on top of the mattress, burying him beneath it. Nasser's face was slammed up against Batman's, and he felt a pair of sticky knees ram into his back before the attacker fled, yanking the door open with a bang and making off like a flash into the storehouse outside. The taste of blood filled Nasser's throat and nose. For a moment he felt like his neck had been wrung like a chicken's, that his face was covered in blood like Batman's mask. Terror rooted him to the spot. Looking around him, he could see no trace of anyone, only the unsettled air in the room and the open door. Too late, he bolted after his attacker, and had to stop, confused, surrounded by the different storage rooms, all of whose doors were open and whose dusty thresholds bore no footprints. Small prints like those of goats' hooves led Nasser to the last room, which looked like an old bathroom. The door was ajar, strengthening Nasser's suspicions. He attempted to squeeze through the opening, into the fetid darkness of the room, but the door was blocked by a pile of sacks behind it, and the opening was too narrow for a human to pass through.

A hubbub from the mosque speakers suggested that prayers had ended, and that Nasser ought to leave right away, but a sudden movement in the deepest dark of one corner of the room caught his attention. It came from behind some sacks of coal. He thrust his head through the narrow opening in the door, half-expecting a blow to knock it right off his shoulders, but the eye peering fierily out at him was only that of an enormous rat, a Lane of Many Heads rat, which began nibbling hysterically at something. Nasser's eyes widened in disgust as a mocking laugh filtered into the shop from the alley outside. It was only Imam Dawoud's salutation announcing the end of prayers that finally forced Nasser to extricate himself from Sheikh Muzahim's storeroom. The Sudanese cashier at the cafe gave the detective a derisive look as he burst out into the afternoon sun, his face bloodied and his eyes chasing a specter.

Hurrying down the alley, Nasser was no longer certain what had happened inside Muzahim's shop. Had Azza stashed Batman under her mattress so as to distract the police dog inside of him with a hunk of poisoned meat?

Over the two decades that Nasser had toiled away to earn and keep his reputation as a first-class criminal detective, he had developed his own theories about how to analyze negative phenomena encountered in investigating crime scenes and how to put seemingly illogical clues to use.

Like a police dog, Nasser had trained his intuition to seek out the characters who left no trace. For him, a blank spot where there should have been fingerprints merely confirmed the existence of a killer. He felt that a criminal's sweat and breath were like weathering agents that always left a faint trace, and that he could read those traces. This led to rumors among his colleagues that he sought the assistance of genies to help him solve tricky cases, as some intelligence agencies were known to do. Their proof was the circle that presided over his noticeboard. He began every investigation by drawing a circle: a dot in the center represented the victim, and concentric circles spiraled out around it. He would usually begin with the characters who had fled to the furthest points on the periphery, and his excitement would grow as he searched for the hidden threads that linked them back to the center and thus to the victim. It was just a plain old circle, but it amazed his staff: they were convinced it was magic.

Nasser could have sat in the cafe forever, going back and forth over that magic circle. What perplexed him in this case was that the center was missing; it goaded all his police instincts. He couldn't leave it empty so in the center he wrote "Lane of Many Heads"—me, the victim! And on the periphery, the spot furthest from any suspicion, he was again at a loss so he put "Lane of Many Heads" there too! Nasser leaned back and surveyed his ingenuity: the criminal and the dead woman were both me, the Lane of Many Heads. Though the symmetry of it invited ridicule, I must admit I was flattered nonetheless. I felt it meant something that I'd succeeded in adding a little spice to the stifling lethargy around this Nasser fellow.

Nasser distributed dots around the concentric circles, which represented the people and houses he would rely on to reconstruct the Lane of Many Heads case. He built his case around the eternal axis of Eve's role in the fall from Paradise: he paid special attention, therefore, to women and their involvement in the issue at hand. Azza and Aisha, for example, he left floating between the center of the circle and the area of suspicion, owing to the secrecy and denial that surrounded their simultaneous disappearance from the neighborhood—not to mention the abundance of documents written about both these women. Detective Nasser began a mental list of the various small signs that pointed to them, and he added these to the copious amount of information linking them to the other concentric circles and to the center of the crime. A passing reference in Yusuf's diaries brought him up short: Yusuf had described Aisha as being "cold."

What made her cold? Being "cold," to Nasser, meant something sexual: a woman who couldn't even charm her own reflection in a mirror. Nasser's canine instincts warned him not to get distracted, but for the man inside him it was too late. He began searching Yusuf's diaries for evidence of the coldness he'd mentioned:

October 12, 2004

I'm dropping Aisha. I'm kicking her out of my diary. I'm not going to write about her, because she's <u>cold</u>. For me, she is dead, was dead, long before the rest of her family. Sometimes I imagine that she's reached the age that tightens around people like a snare. I doubt she reads, despite all the books she *beat me to, or that she even writes, although she used to be a teacher. Aisha's like a box of words. Aisha is obsessed with cleanliness these days, but she's still engraved upon the mind of the neighborhood as the fish-girl: we would wait, barefoot, for her to get off the schoolgirls' bus and follow the odor of dried fish emanating from her. We would watch the heel of her left foot carefully, looking for the fine thread of blood we'd noticed one day staining her socks red. We all knew she'd got her period before the other girls in the Lane of Many Heads, who eventually turned the school bus into a can of dried fish.*

"Let Aisha write herself into thin air! I'm not going anywhere near her."

The expressions "cold" and "already dead" stuck in Nasser's head. He hurried to the file containing all of Aisha's emails addressed to an unknown German man, which they'd found on her computer in a drafts folder entitled "The One." Nasser took out the first page and began to read:

From: Aisha
Subject: Message 2

You said that you were twenty-four when you got a job at the hospital carrying corpses from the morgue out to their relatives. You had nightmares, you said, until one day the old-timer who worked there said to you, "Is a human body really so different from a plank of wood? Just imagine that's what it is."

When you touch me, do I feel like a plank?

During those three months of accompanying the dead, were you ever able to turn one of those planks into trembling softness at the mere touch of your hands? When did you acquire that skill?

Can you believe that we're writing messages back and forth between a hospital in Germany and a backstreet in the Arabian Peninsula?

Is this simply another symptom of the disease that's had me in its grips for the past year—am I just raving deliriously?

Why do we feel so small and lost when we lie alone like this in bed? Is this what the solitude of coffins is like?

If I close my eyes, I can hear the fat as it bubbles inside the folds of my stomach.

Six of us used to sleep in a space three meters squared.

They say there are microscopic creatures that can't be seen by the naked eye, and can't be wiped out by cleaning or sterilization; they hide in our blankets and beds waiting to eat our flesh. They can eat us alive. Can you bear that thought?

Away from you, I lie alone in my bed carrying the torsos of dead bodies back and forth through the operating theater in my head.

Have I told you? In Arabic, *Aisha* means "alive," not "living."

The tea tasted strange to Nasser, and all the sugar he'd added—four teaspoons—coagulated on his tongue at this woman's talk about the body and flesh-eating mites. All his police instincts, indeed his entire body, reacted to this message: what sort of coldness was this that was being eaten by mites? Mites are attracted to decomposition, heat. Suddenly the air conditioner and the fan were no longer enough to cool the room. He continued reading:

The universe is swarming with messages sent back and forth. In the virtual world, borders have been shattered and people in every corner of the globe are engaged in an exhausting quest for love, desperate to exchange a laugh or share a little company . . .

My words mingle with throngs of other desperate voices searching for a way out.

I'm on the Internet because I want to learn how to talk to a man. Does that make me sound naive? A divorced girlfriend of mine once said to me, "How was I supposed to know what to do with men's clothes? How was I supposed to know that you have to starch a man's headscarf in a specific way to keep it sitting at just the right angle on his forehead like a nest? I grew up an orphan surrounded by a bunch of women. I'd never even looked at a man face-to-face. What was the big deal about this nest thing anyway? How was I supposed to know what temperature to wash a robe at to keep it soft? Men's robes, like their bodies and minds, are toys I don't know how to care for or keep looking shiny. I didn't know that men were obsessed with cars and football and sexy dancers in music videos. I'm on the outside of that world."

That day, I felt a sense of superiority toward the divorcée, because I knew no headdress was plotting my divorce. Ironing men's robes was right up my alley—I had six brothers, whose robes were as smooth as paper and whose headdresses hung down as rigid as drainpipes, not even buckling when they knelt to pray.

But the other masculine languages, the language of actually living with a man, had passed me by. When the time comes that I have to interact with a man's body, I freeze up. There's a story from somewhere back in the mists of time about the little girl who's born to a man obsessed with chastity. From the moment she was born, the man imprisoned his daughter in a world he'd built himself in the basement of his house, with not even a skylight to the outside, and he erased from that world every last trace of masculinity. He didn't even let words that were grammatically masculine enter the space, so instead of sending her food on a masculine "plate" he sent it to her on a feminine "saucer." He never fed his daughter lamb, but the meat of female cows. The girl didn't sleep on a bed—which was masculine—but on a feminine chaise longue. He didn't adorn her with masculine necklaces or earrings, but with feminine bracelets, and so on. He entrusted her to a wicked old lady to bring her up in that feminine environment. The world in which the young girl grew up wasn't merely devoid of masculine elements; they'd never existed in the first place. It was an indestructible, impenetrable world of unadulterated femininity. Then one day, a pair of scissors somehow found their way into the basement and fell in the hands of the young girl. The masculinity of the object shocked her and she immediately hid them, aware of the danger they posed. Of course, she then used the scissors to dig a tunnel through the wall of the basement so she could look out upon the outside world. One day when she was contemplating the outside, she heard someone talking about the handsome prince Harj ibn Marj, who'd never been defeated in battle and whose hair was so long that it had to be pleated seventy times and piled up on the back of his saddle when he rode his horse. Needless to say, that single masculine instrument was all the girl needed to escape, and then to fight and vanquish Harj ibn Marj. An escape that we, the women of the Lane of Many Heads in the twentieth century, had failed to achieve. We were raised in similar subterranean worlds, and when the time came for us to be allowed out, our faces had to be effaced with black—an invisibility cloak that makes us a non-existence—so the masculine world would not notice us. We've been trained so that we're blinded to masculinity, this castrated masculinity that's lost its ability to extend any kind of salvation to us as it did in the story of Harj ibn Marj. The weird thing was that this regime of effacement was a sign of modernity in the Lane of Many Heads, for throughout the neighborhood's history, right up until the early twentieth century, women's faces had remained uncovered for all the world to see, for the sun to shine on.

On mornings when nothing can get me to open my eyes, I just have to imagine the taste of dates and then I can get out of bed. Throughout the history of the Hijaz, dates were idols; they were worshipped but they were also eaten without any feelings of guilt. With the utmost piety, in fact.

I'm in thrall to the date paste they make in Medina; it's dark and it looks desiccated, but it melts in your mouth. Medinan dates transmit all the desires of a city that calls upon one to travel in pursuit of one's faith—follow your faith no matter where it takes you—and that's why they taste twice as sweet.

The date paste on your tongue is me: you have to chew it for the flavor to come out. The **paintings** you send me, with their vivid colors, soak my face in splashes of spring morning. My God, how is it that a few simple paragraphs can bring so much intimacy and joy?

Tell me, why do you insist we find our own private language? Does my Arabic not get through to you? Do I not understand your German? That leaves us with broken English. Thank God you can chalk up my incoherence to the language and not a limited intellect.

But let's turn our backs on this talk and chatter. Let's talk like people lost in a forest: don't pretend that you can understand the forest that's taken hold of you, but carry on walking; your feet plunge into rain-soaked earth, branches laden with last night's dew graze your forehead, you bask in the scents of untouched blossom and greenery and submit to the forest's entreaties, its gentle breezes.

This is the language I want us to use to get to know each other. Talk to me like you talk to a trail; walk over me, walk over me and through me, in silence or chaos; run or tiptoe or crawl so that every muscle of your torso brushes over me; allow me to extend my tongue and devour you as you pass over me.

If you were here in front me—like you were the whole time I was being treated at your hospital—**your hand** could grasp mine, could be my confusion and my guide. You would name the trees growing in my head and the darkness that spreads over me whenever I want to give free rein to my dreams, and this dew that spreads out from my core whenever I see your face reflecting mine, seducing me. Have you become my mirror so I can check to see how I look? To see how your passion shows around my eyes? How your desire has become a scattering of pimples across my forehead?

Tell me, am I still "beautiful and refreshing like a desert moon?" That's what you said the day it snowed in Bonn. Has my attachment to you made me ugly?

It was you who, with a pat on the shoulder, spoke my today, my yesterday, and my tomorrow. Dream-Words. Words of languor that put me to sleep under your hands, words like tiny thrones I sit on and hop between like a pampered child.

Aisha

Detective Nasser flung the message away, then moved Aisha's name closer to the center of the circle. The hound in him said, "She ought to be put to death." He resisted an urge to stick a finger down his throat and vomit up the bile brought on by Aisha's email, the way she'd smuggled this stranger into the Lane of Many Heads. From her few words it was clear that Aisha had a ticking desire inside of her—accompanied by treacherous urges that, as he knew from his experience of criminal practices, were embedded inside every woman. Nevertheless, he couldn't yank out the wire or predict when the timer was going to go off.

Much as his inner hound was tensed, ready to pounce, it was actually the beating arousal of his inner man that spurred him on. He wanted to see this dissolute woman stripped naked before him. Detective Nasser found himself trailing after a short phrase in a message that wasn't numbered like the others.

From: Aisha

You answered all my doubts about whether you still had feelings for me when you said "I see you!"

This is my face. Are we the ones who carve these maps onto our own skin? Eastern faces like mine are heavy with sadness, while your faces are like plastic, without even a single wrinkle of suffering. I believe our souls are old. These are secondhand souls, encumbered with the weight of having known life and death.

In my early adolescence, I read that pain was what scorched away our faults to reveal the gold beneath,

I would often sit and experiment with pain, from a starting point of no pain,

I had something deeper than pain, this need for something, for a hand, here,

I had this photo of a tree trunk that had been gouged by ibexes, sharpening their horns for the mating season in spring,

every time I looked at those marks on the trunk I felt that deeper-than-pain . . .

It had never occurred to me that I'd ever say what I'm saying to you now, because I knew you couldn't read my Arabic . . . But now . . . It's caught up with me. I won't say "pain," it's something deeper, what lies beneath all pain . . .

Has my face turned into a tragic Kabuki mask?

Aisha

He couldn't stop. Nasser flicked through page after page, racing against the German guy toward this brazen, naked woman. From the mental archive of crimes he'd seen, he knew that Meccan women were experts in unspoken love: in his interrogations he often had to rely on slips of the tongue, or otherwise use all kinds of "pressure" and even threats to extract their deepest secrets and use them to unravel the knots . . . This one, on the other hand, had written her love down; her own words had indicted her, even if they'd never left her drafts folder. Words weren't supposed to be a striptease like this—certainly not those of a woman from the Holy City. If Aisha was the victim, this was the first time Nasser had ever come across a victim who insisted upon documenting her own improprieties from beyond the veil of death.

Detective Nasser started when a cadet appeared in the doorway to tell him his shift was over, and wondered guiltily whether the cadet had been able to read the sinful thoughts on his face.

"God spare us this nasty business," the cadet began abruptly. "Did you hear? Officer Ali's taken over the investigation into the theft of the key of the Kaaba. They found the thief dead and half-eaten by dogs in Umm al-Doud, outside Mecca."

"Seriously?!" Nasser was irritated by the junior officer's lack of ceremony.

"They should've assigned the case to you, sir. Everyone in the crime unit said that there was no choice but to give it to Nasser . . ."

"That's kind of you to say, but my hands are full at the moment."

"What a curse it'll be if they can't find the key! If I were handling the investigation, I wouldn't be so sure that the young guy who attacked the thief isn't an accomplice. What if he's got the key? The maintenance company went through the drain and the pipes, but they couldn't find anything."

"With a lively imagination like that, you could be a first-rate detective." The cadet blushed. The police hound in Nasser perked up at the mention of the theft of the key to the Kaaba, but he ignored it. He was itching to get back to the naked emails in private.

"What will happen to the Muslims of the world if we don't find the key? Does that mean that God has shut the door to His house in our faces? Are we cursed?"

"They'll just have to cast a new key until they can solve the puzzle of the stolen one," replied Nasser in an attempt to end the conversation.

"They've tried several times, sir, but all of the keys have broken in the lock. They might have to take the whole door off . . ."

"They just need to find a specialist locksmith; that's all there is to it." Nasser moved toward the door so the cadet was obliged to leave. As he was leaving, Nasser paused and returned to his desk. He picked up the box of papers where he'd put the file of Aisha's emails and then left without hesitation, as if he were simply leaving work at the end of the day with his things. When he got into his car, the hound growled: "You've really got yourself mixed up in it now."

Fragments

HE CARRIED THE PAPERS TO HIS SMALL APARTMENT IN THE ZAHIR NEIGHBORhood. It wasn't much more than a large bedroom with a table and hotplate in one corner and a small bathroom off to the left. Two whole decades of his prime had been chewed over by this place.

Words from the letters and diaries he'd been reading had clung to his body, and they began to tickle him, arouse him. He reined in the eager police hound inside of him, letting the man take over. He dumped the papers on the bed and threw his work jacket over the back of a chair. Then he stripped off his pants and faced his own short, stocky body in the mirror. He ran a hand over his muscles, and as it sank lower, he asked himself: "How do you think a girl like Azza or Aisha would react to a body like this?" It took him some time to satisfy the eyes and hands gasping and spasming over his virility, to ride out their agonizing, ecstatic wave. He was sweating by the time he was finished.

He looked around sheepishly as if apologizing to an imaginary audience. He felt as if the hound inside had been watching him through indifferent eyes. He walked to the bathroom, averting his gaze from the small mirror that reflected his body from the shoulders up, turned on the faucet and submitted to the gush of water, soaping and scrubbing away every trace of what he'd just done. Wrapped in a towel, he went back out into the room and quickly made himself a cup of tea and a cheese sandwich with cucumber and greens. His body was still alert and in no mood for clothes, so he lay back down on the bed naked, enjoying the sensuous touch of skin on soft sheets. He could feel the cotton of the pillowcase and covers all the way down his back to his legs as he lay half-watching the forty-five-inch television, which he'd paid for in installments over three years so as to give his cramped room a view of oceans and mountains and to allow him to play host to seductive women whose nubile company he could now enjoy every evening.

He opened a file of letters that lay on his bedside table, ignoring the damp box on the floor below him—complete with his own personal signature across the cover of one of the diaries—and began to eat his sandwich. With one ear on the sports channel, he trained his eyes on Aisha's emails and continued reading where he'd left off, letting every page and word trace its imprint on his naked body.

From: Aisha
Subject: Message 3

Do you remember how many times you had to wake me up after a massage? You used to run the back of your finger up my cheek to my temple . . .

Did you know that you were the first person to ever pat me on the back? At our house, love used to pause at the front door to stick out its spines like a hedgehog before crossing the threshold. Love could only be found in my father's pockets and my mother's pots and pans: if you wanted to know how much you were loved, you had to count how much money Dad spent and how many meals Mom cooked.

My father couldn't afford to be extravagant on a schoolteacher's salary, but he did indulge us with little treats from time to time. On Friday evenings he used to take us out and buy us each a shawarma sandwich and a plain baguette, and we'd divide the meat between the two to fill us up. My grandmother used to like to say that we had snakes in our bellies eating our food, which is why we were always hungry. My father never stopped trying to trick those snakes into feeling full.

That was one of our sacred rituals; fruit was another. My father did everything he could to make sure we each had an orange a day and one peach a week, and a bunch of grapes in summertime. My youngest brother, who was the apple of my father's eye, used to get a peach every day during the summer, and we'd all watch him eat it, hovering about like crows for him to throw away the stone because he never figured out how to strip it right down to the pit and we were more than happy to see to the task.

You said you grew up feeling like you'd been pushed away, isolated, after your parents sent you to that boarding school when you were six years old. That you graduated at eighteen without ever having felt the touch of another heart. You told me you'd been born tough, but not tough enough to swallow your mother's cold heart at breakfast. I think you're alienated and untamed, that you've come to me now looking for the jungle. You're chasing after crumbled bridges that lead into the void with no route back, not even a glimpse of what you've left behind, should you look over your shoulder . . .

In your hands I began again, starting from nothingness, nothing but pain, like someone weighed down by a twin around their neck.

While your hands massage and dig into the hidden pain, I suddenly wake to find my heart halfway round the racetrack, doing eighty miles a minute. It slipped away from me somehow while I was distracted, leaving my mouth dry and my lips cracked and salty.

Your hands must have felt its first kick, its acceleration and the willfulness of its first shot, before my head even noticed you or it.

My heart took me by surprise that day and slipped away to alert my body, as your hand massaged this shattered pelvis of mine. I no longer know which bits of me are metal and which are living bone. I imagine that now, in the heat, it's becoming acutely sensitive, that it burns at the touch of your large hand, those fingers. "My hands are beyond all standards of human beauty," you said sheepishly.

I imagine that they're long and slender and stretch from Bonn to Mecca, that they were created in a single, smooth movement out of clay that's still fresh and dripping. After all these months, I can feel your fingers, clay-like and soft, against my spine, kneading into it a suppleness I hardly recognize in my own body.

That hand of yours kneaded my back. You cared. Your palm was gentle, as though you were touching a child. When I received your email I understood that you believed—though I most certainly do not—that our paths may cross again somewhere down the line.

I need to stop writing. As you know, before the light forces my eyes open and my body surges with an uncanny energy, just at that moment, I feel I could fall in love every dawn, or drop dead.

For years, before I met you, I used to stand at the door waiting for Khalil to arrive in his taxi to take me to school, and when the light burst through, the inexplicable eruption always made me nervous. The accident had put me on the shelf, useless and neglected, but I couldn't shake off the wakefulness and the early-morning bursts of energy. To be honest with you, I was relieved to be done with the gloom of being a teacher. Did I say "teacher"? What a joke! I was just one of the neighborhood's many tentacles; one of a countless many who wage war against fate, stifling young girls.

I was essentially a timekeeper. My only duty was to ring the bell to signal the end of one class and the beginning of the next. The poor spinster headmistress and I fought a minor war over that bell.

But I also mastered the art of catharsis. I used to stand as still as an idol in the schoolyard in the mornings in front of the lines of students—two-hundred lungs burning with life, arrayed before me like mummies—for a whole hour as the morning radio program was broadcast. They feigned interest in the antiquated parables and didactic poems in classical Arabic, and the stories that had failed to make anyone laugh since the beginning of the last century. Two hundred granite faces. Any hint of a smile, any meaningful glance, any simple string of beads, any colored hair ribbon or trace of nail polish, any attempt at self-expression at all was enough to get a girl dragged up to the stage where I stood. There I would slowly, carefully—and in front of two hundred pairs of horrified eyes—rip out and crush this self-expression before it could blossom.

I was the executioner in the doll factory. Their bodies were our private property and my job was to color them, head to toe, in a drab gray moderated only by black shoes and white hair ribbons.

It was for this instinctive sternness that I earned the headmistress's confidence and the right to ring the bell now and then without having to wait for a nod from her or a jerk of her finger.

Does the Lane of Many Heads have a problem with girls? Maybe it's this: life is a **scorpion's egg that emerges from its mother's back**

and then, as soon as it hatches, fatally stings its mother.

Every move we make taunts the Lane, its many heads and its octopoid tentacles. Do you know how many heads have sprung up in the spot where we dared to sever just one? With one of its heads, the Lane of Many Heads imagines us as untouched virgins, and with another, as lascivious sex dolls.

The challenge we face is how to be superwomen, a cross between our Bedouin grandmothers who never raised their face-veils, not even when eating with their husbands, and the pop stars and dancers who writhe and moan in music videos.

I feel like there's a woman made of stone inside of me.

My salvation lies in writing to her.

Your bird,
Aisha.

P.S. This reminds me of my father's cane. My father died, but the cane remained, beyond the reach of death.

We, the children of the Lane of Many Heads, grew up, every last one of us, in the shadow of a cane, stored inside a water tank to keep it supple, ready to spill and drink our blood.

When I first got back from Bonn, alone with the weight of the empty house and the death of my family pressing down on me, I was stopped short by the sight of the cane resting in the water tank in the hallway that was connected by a pipe to the drinking fountain, which stood in the alley for the benefit of passersby. My father hoped that the chilled water of that public drinking fountain in which his cane lay would clear his path to heaven; my mother used to clean the tap diligently so as to make sure she would slip in along with him.

Maybe the cane gave me a frightful look (or maybe it recited the Fatiha for my father's soul) as I walked over, picked it up out of the water, and set it on the shelf to the right of the entrance, leaving it panting with thirst.

P.P.S. The first time I felt you, and I closed my hand around your stem, you surprised me by saying "This is what I wanted to give my mother!" Something about what you said made me ache deep inside, but I was absent. Do you know how old I am now? I'm in my thirties, and I was even married once, but still I'd never uprooted a man before. Taking a man's very being in your grasp. Now I know that our hands were made for this, to hold this root of life, to feel this erection from head to toe. You had no idea how new it all was to me, the shock of discovery. You were absent, lost in your past and your mother:

"Recently my mother confessed that she loved me more than any of my brothers. But I was born stubborn, a heavenly creature, while my mother is a peasant, the salt of the earth. Already when I was three, I used to go exploring in the woods near our farm, and they would come looking for me at sundown. I'd spend the whole day as far away from human contact as I could; the plants of the forest fed me. My mother, on the other hand, lost her heart growing up an orphan. There was a big bundle of fear where her heart should have been: a fear of life and the thought of giving in to its joys."

You kept talking while I, Aisha, usually so sober, was absent, crazy, trying to shake you out of your depression.

"Aisha, let me explain it to you. The sun was in Gemini when I was born, you see. We Geminis have a problem with either-ors. We see all the choices that life offers us as possible. Nothing's forbidden to us. As far as we're concerned, we can accept every proposal without having to discriminate. But sunlight brings some clarity to this problem of either-ors, allowing us to see past multiplicity to the singularity beyond."

Am I allowed to say that all of you Westerners are Geminis, while here we're all handcuffed Libras?

You once said to me, "You're a bird, Aisha. I'll be your stretch of sky so long as you promise to never stop soaring joyfully."

Reading these words, Nasser suddenly felt like his body had been buried alive in an endless pit for the past thirty years. Buried beneath stacks of investigations, murders, betrayals, clues. Now Aisha's words taunted him; they dared him to jump up and discover that he was still alive.

She wasn't the only one who submitted to the hand of a healer against her back. No, Nasser al-Qahtani was also lying down and baring his back for her to massage his eternally tense muscles and finally loosen up their toughness.

Nasser peeled himself from his victim's repose and stood up, angry with himself. When he went to take off the dog's collar, he found it sound asleep. He turned out the lights and lay back down. He was still tossing and turning when the sun came up. He didn't bother with breakfast, just put on his uniform, drawing the sturdy khaki fabric around him tightly, and left the house.

In the Land Rover marked with its official badge, he briefly ruffled the fur of the dog inside him and reassured himself that last night's weakness was simply part of the magic formula he'd been dreaming about since childhood: to show off like Superman in a comic book, performing heroic feats that would impress even the criminals. He'd always thought of criminals as being outside the spectrum of humanity. Rather than become one himself, he'd chosen to become the person to whom murder victims would first disclose their murderers' brilliance. To train his ears to listen, even though his heart was full of the kind of stress that no heart—or ear for that matter—could ever bear. To be a friend to the truth in this exhausted, decrepit body. That was why he'd specialized in homicides, so that his heart would be as tough as the heart of al-Malah Cemetery. So that it would be a sanctuary for all those tableaux of violation, all those disowned corpses. He'd decided that he, too, would have to leave the spectrum of humanity behind.

The Prince

THE PAKISTANI ELECTRICIAN HAD BEEN STANDING AT THE SIDE OF THE UMRAH route for about an hour. The midday sun, directly above him, was fierce, and as soon as the bright yellow taxi pulled up he jogged toward it, pulled the door open, and threw himself into the front seat beside the driver in a halo of curry spice. When he took a look at the driver, his blood froze. Hoping there was still time to escape, his hand reached for the door handle, but the car sped away at a demented pace.

"Excuse me, sir, this is a taxi?" The question rang out stupidly, which only tickled Khalil more.

"Of course it's a taxi. Where do you want to go?"

The Pakistani stuttered before managing to reply, "Gaza Market, please, sir . . ." His hand fumbled comically with the door as he attempted to open the window.

"It's broken." Khalil grinned spitefully.

The Pakistani floundered, groping for the words that might save him. "Are you making joke? Excuse me, sir, you are . . . Same same Saudi prince?" Khalil's delight doubled at the man's agitation.

"Don't worry, you're not on candid camera, I really am a prince and I'm driving you around. The world is finally smiling on you!"

The Pakistani smiled back at him uncertainly. "Sir, you serious? This is why you wear fashion clothes?" He took in Khalil's embroidered silk robe, the gray wool cloak trimmed with gold thread, the bright white Lomar branded headdress and the fancy black band that held it in place, coming to rest on the gleaming black Zimas dress shoes, one of which was pressed hard on the accelerator, keeping the car hurtling along at a diabolic speed.

"Please, sir, slowly—"

"Why? Don't you like how princes drive?"

"Please, sir . . . In Pakistan I am have six children, and my mother is sick, will die soon—"

Khalil stamped on the brake. "Get out. May God shun you! And your six kids and your mother, too!"

The Pakistani shoved open the door and leapt out, reeling. Khalil took a bottle of mineral water from under his seat, emptied it in one gulp, and sped off, thirsty for the next humiliation.

His second victim was a woman with her teenage son. She looked like a tent of black in the abaya, which hung from her head right down to her feet, and the black knee-length socks and elbow-length gloves, which picked up where the abaya left off. She stuffed herself into the back seat with her son. At the decisive clunk of the doors being locked centrally and a foot slamming on the gas, the car—darting forward hysterically—was suddenly filled with panic.

The boy attempted uselessly to open the door, then at his mother's urging squeaked as loudly as he could, "Stop! Let us out here please!"

"Brother—" Terror had induced even the mother to speak, "Let us out, for the love of God!"

"Not until you take your socks and gloves off. Pretend like you're making the pilgrimage!" Khalil laughed, abruptly and jarringly.

"What?! Fear God!"

"I'm a disturbed man," replied Khalil baldly. "The color black upsets me. I could drive this car into a wall at any moment." The car accelerated. "But as soon as you take your gloves off . . ." The boy frantically tugged his mother's gloves from her hands.

"See, we're slowing down. As soon as you take your socks off we'll stop and the doors will be unlocked." The boy leaned down to take his mother's socks off, and the moment he dropped them onto the front seat with the gloves, the brakes squealed.

Driving off, Khalil watched in the rearview mirror as the woman flapped about, her hands and feet suddenly exposed to the sun, struggling to cocoon herself and protect her skin from the light and people's eyes. "A real-life Dracula!" Khalil cackled with glee.

The third victim was a solidly-built man in his sixties wearing a robe, waistcoat, and snow-white skullcap, and a yellowed silk stole draped over his left shoulder.

He climbed into the back seat and sat in silence. Khalil tried to provoke him: he drove fast and he made several sudden, violent stops that sent the car's contents, including the passenger, crashing into the back of the front seat. He changed direction from west to east to south again, and stopped at every traffic light to rearrange his headdress in the rearview mirror, looking defiantly at the impassive face in the back seat as the cars trapped behind them released a torrent of indignant honks. Finally, in the isolated valley of Mina, he came to a stop. "Get out. I'm not going any further," he ordered. The man gazed out at the bare mountains and the empty land sliced into asphalted plots in preparation for the construction of yet more accommodation for pilgrims.

"What on earth am I supposed to do here? I told you to take me to al-Rusayfa."

"Yeah, and I say get out here."

"Take me back to where you picked me up, or else I'll have to sit here till Judgment Day."

"Be my guest!" Khalil turned off the engine, and they settled into a silent standoff.

"You're out of your mind," said the man. "If I knew how to drive, I'd kick you out and drive off myself."

"You have no choice but to get out."

"You want me to go out there with all the demons? They're your tribe. You sure drive like one . . ."

"How perceptive of you!" laughed Khalil. "You know, I almost like you!"

"I bet you don't even like yourself," said the man, examining him. "Look at how you're dressed! You're making an ass out of yourself."

"Is that so? Just a few minutes ago, I managed to scare someone into taking off their clothes. Some passengers wet themselves all over that seat you're sitting on. That's why it's got that plastic cover on it."

"You're just a silly little boy in a man's body."

"Yeah, and sometimes the little boy dresses up in a traditional Hijazi outfit like you're wearing. I have all kinds of disguises in the trunk. I even dress up like cartoon characters to entertain the more mature customers like yourself."

"You're pathetic, a lost soul, that's my diagnosis."

"I wouldn't worry about it if I were you. I don't have a soul."

"Is that the only thing you have to be proud of? Listen"—the man straightened up in his seat and spat the words at the back of Khalil's neck—"I have all the time in the world, even for blue demons like you. I buried my three sons in their prime. Azrael plucked them like fruit when they each turned twenty. I lost them all to car accidents, the plague of our age. Nothing fazes me any more. If you want to sit here until the crows peck out our eyeballs that's fine by me. But if you try and drag me out of this car—I swear to you—all hell will break loose."

"You mean my inane little performance hasn't shocked you?"

"You know, if you need a shrink, I'm all ears. My wife and relatives actually tried to make me go see one when they felt they couldn't get through to me any more."

"I'm looking for men like you," said Khalil accusingly. "Men from the bowels of Mecca, like my father. You're all alike: you're like fish out of water as soon as you leave the tiny circle around the Sanctuary. You're all flapping around on the ground, getting further and further away, and crushing your children's throats in the process. What were you going to do in a modern, plastic neighborhood like al-Rusayfa anyway?"

"I was thinking of getting married again and having some more children for Azrael to feed on. My wife's not interested in helping."

"Just like my father," Khalil laughed bitterly.

The man studied Khalil's profile. "Who are you? What do you want?"

"Sometimes I'm a respectable taxi driver and stick to the highways. But most of the time I drive into the guts of the city, entertaining myself by toying with all these nobodies."

"Nobodies? Listen, boy, one day you're going to come face-to-face with death, and you'll realize you can't go around talking about human beings like that."

"You've almost convinced me"—Khalil turned round to look the man in the eye—"that you're not as bad as you look."

"Meeting people like you is a lot like looking in the mirror."

"Now you're boring me."

"Get rid of me then, take me to the nearest place where I can find another taxi. There's no way I'm going to let you abandon me here in the wilderness."

Khalil turned the engine on. "Maybe I'll take you where you wanted to go."

"No, thanks," the man said quickly. "I've decided I don't want to bring any more children into the world now that Azrael has turned taxis into race cars. Sooner or later this life of yours is going to fall to pieces in your hands. You'll see."

A Window for a Window

WITH THE EXPERT MALICE OF EACH OF MY—THE LANE'S—MANY HEADS, I MADE Nasser spend his morning between two windows: Azza's, which was nailed shut, and Aisha's, which was blocked by an air-conditioning unit. In the end he retreated to his seat in the cafe to see which of my secrets he could unearth by comparing my geography to the information contained in Aisha's messages. He read:

FROM: Aisha
SUBJECT: Message 4

Dear ^

Like a sip of coffee on a cold morning, your name revives me.

Do you remember the day you took out your encyclopedia because you wanted to learn more about Mecca, my city?

"Wow . . ." You were amazed that it was the center of the universe.

The Mecca of books is beyond the internal geography of our neighborhood.

The Lane of Many Heads is a scandal just waiting to be exposed.

I once dreamed that the Lane of Many Heads was a woman's body dumped by the side of the road.

The sky over her was clear but for the clouds over the only neutral space: a jewel-like garden that was nestled in the navel of Wadi Ibrahim. It belonged to **Mushabbab**, a descendant of the freed slaves of the Sharifs and a lover of music and water. To the right was Radwa Mosque, and to the left the house of Sheikh Muzahim the wholesaler, where Auntie Halima lived on the roof. In the shadow of these lay our house. Aside from all that, from head to toe it was a down-home but cosmopolitan body that prayed and would stop dancing at prayer times, and during the pilgrimage season would cater to the pilgrims with improvised clothing stalls, hide away its musical instruments, empty its rooms to rent them out, and give over its kitchens (even though "the devil pisses in their food," according to the old ladies in the neighborhood, who'd long since surrendered to the cooking of strangers).

If you investigate the history of our neighborhood, the Lane of Many Heads ("Abu r-Ru'us" or, the way we say it, flouting the rules of correct pronunciation, "Aboorroos"), you'll find that it emerged as people began settling here. The municipality made it official when they gave the neighborhood a major makeover and excised its name and history. They changed the name of the street to Radiant Passage, but the Lane of Many Heads remained fuzzily in our memories, intimating some warmth whose origin we couldn't put a finger on. Then Sheikh Muzahim came along to blast it away and shove his own memory into that spot instead:

"We never hear a single voice in the Lane of Many Heads praising God. Even the angels have washed their hands of you!"

There was no one as obsessed with perdition as the wholesaler Sheikh Muzahim. He shoved it under our noses so we could smell nothing else when we went to bed and when we rose with the birds' hymns. Sheikh Muzahim gathered up all the original melodies, while the discordant notes gathered like a murder of crows over the Lane of Many Heads, warning us of hell.

Nasser stopped reading for a moment to hate Aisha, then continued:

"You're driving the angels out of our neighborhood with this nudity!" he exclaimed, cursing their screens. But then the neighborhood dared to fight back:

"Land in Mecca is worth its weight in gold, but Sheikh Muzahim got his piece of paradise just by laying claim to it. He claimed this piece of land as his reward for building a mosque, a house in heaven at a discount price. Then he installed Dawoud al-Habashi as imam of the mosque, but left his salary to be paid for out of the neighborhood's charity."

The minaret sprouts more and more loudspeakers by the day, and neighborhood gatherings overflow with improvised sermons, trapping in their corners genetically modified rats of heresy and other unidentifiable rodents.

Why am I being so hard on the Lane of Many Heads? Have I begun to see it through your eyes?

Aisha

Azza: Potential Identification of the Deceased

IT WAS THAT SILENT TIME OF NIGHT THAT ONLY COMES HOURS AFTER MIDNIGHT. Nasser's imagination sprang up from the silence and crept out alone to survey the Lane of Many Heads, listening carefully to how the heaps of filth on the ground sucked up his footfalls, investigating forbidding doorways barely wide enough for a human to pass through and backyards where stray horses, donkeys, and demons lived; he wanted to catch the Lane of Many Heads red-handed. He walked for hours, unaware that the Lane of Many Heads was baiting him, leading him to an old man slumbering on a low platform by the door of a beat-up old house. The neighborhood sensed Nasser's footsteps as his bleary eyes drew him drew closer. Nasser spun round, looking for a way out, but the neighborhood had him surrounded. Like a hedgehog, it puffed out the spines of satellite dishes, which bristled from every tumbledown house, ruined backyard, and cheap prefab home of people who hawked ice or home-made food.

"Nothing's new to an old neighborhood like me."

Nasser's shoulders slumped suddenly, and a feeling of immense fatigue overcame him. He collapsed onto the bench beside the ageless body, who spoke as if the voice of the alley itself were rising from beneath the bench.

"Today's loaf comes from yesterday's leaven: learn this lesson from my history. At first, I was inhabited by devils who helped Eve tempt Adam to leave the Sanctuary. That was back when Mecca was one of the pearls of Paradise nestled in the heart of remote Wadi Ibrahim, which I think was nothing more than the lap of a woman—first Eve, then Hagar—who spread her legs from Mount Safa all the way to the end of Mount Marwa: from the peak of splendor to the depths of beauty. Hearts were broken, and thus began the ritual of walking between the two peaks."

The Lane snorted at Nasser's sudden tiredness and went on with his history lesson. "You see, when God created Adam and put him in paradise, the only thing missing from this distillation of perfection was death. That's why He cleft Adam's breast and tore out a bone and then rolled it up into a ball, stretched it out, and made it writhe in front of Him. Adam was anxious to get his bone back, but when he grabbed it and pushed it back into place between his other bones, it was death he'd picked up. A bone outside of Adam's breast is death itself . . ." The voice of the Lane of Many Heads hissed from inside

Nasser's chest. "We must bury all Eve's daughters alive and put an end to the rift they tore open in our breasts. We must restore our bones." Women, women: Nasser felt uneasy. The alley had hypnotized him. He was surrounded by the specters of old sheikhs, who echoed in chorus the Lane's voice as it rose up from underfoot.

"How can you cook up the present moment without a measure of the past or a hint of the future? Allow me to reveal the key to this riddle you're trying to solve: death is a ram that will be made manifest on Judgment Day, and life will be embodied in a towering mare with a million transparent wings that rustle sweetly as they beat. When the terrors of Judgment Day are over, after the hell-bound have betaken themselves to their hell and the heaven-bound to their heaven, the ram will be brought out and slaughtered, and the mare will be released to go forth in boundless freedom. You, Nasser—" The old man directed the accusation straight at Nasser, who couldn't be sure whether the voice was coming from in front of him or behind him, or raining down like a curse from above. "You could collect all these stories and discover that the ram and the mare were merely a fantasy that came out of Adam's breast. That is, that Adam overcame his imagination so he could commit suicide. It's exactly like this case you're investigating. It'll never go further than the slaughter of the ram and the release of the mare, which is also Adam's mount, incidentally, and his bone. All you have to do is ask yourself: who in the neighborhood is most likely to kill themselves, like our ancestor Adam? Believe me, there's only Yusuf—but who's the mare?"

The seven minarets of the Sanctuary sounded briefly, then paused to take a deep breath. As the minarets rested between calling worshippers to the dawn prayer and announcing that the prayer was about to begin, Mecca's backstreets purified themselves in the waters of their ritual ablutions, and in that moment of stillness, the Lane of Many Heads grabbed Nasser by the throat.

"Can you hear the blood pumping through the veins of all these men I've lured here from the four corners of the earth with dreams of black gold? Men who left their families and children behind and swarmed here like lice to take up residence on my heads. Men who suck my blood while I devour their lives and their dreams in my shacks and squalid huts. I'm a spiteful old man: I take their youth in return for my putrid decay. There's nothing like the dawn to awaken in men the anguish of what they've sacrificed in their lust for the illusion of fast food and easy riches." Nasser tried to get up. "Why are you trying to catch one killer who killed one victim? Are you stupid enough to think that you'll ever be able to keep an alley like me on the up and up in this ballistic age? I'm like the circle of toilets they erected, like a public fountain, at the entrances to Mina, Arafat, and Muzdalifa—innumerable toilets in adjacent square cement cubicles whose sole purpose is to receive the excrement of the faithful. I'm warning you, Nasser—don't go digging around in my memory for a murderer. You'll find yourself drowning in sewage and you'll never make it out."

In the ephemeral instant before prayers began, the universe fell silent in anticipation of the exaltation of God's name, and in the furthest corner of his memory the Lane of Many Heads recalled with wicked pleasure the light footsteps that used to make their way across his every dawn before the body appeared—footsteps which stopped when the dove in Yusuf's diary went wild at the sight of that body.

The neighborhood deceitfully hid the night that had replenished the charge of Yusuf's mind from Nasser. That night, Yusuf's sleep had been interrupted by those fleeting footsteps crossing the alley like a dove flying low to the ground. From his spot on the roof, he saw a young woman in an abaya running toward him. Although Yusuf wasn't in the habit of looking in any detail at female bodies that suddenly appeared before him—out of loyalty to Sheikh Muzahim's daughter, Azza—something about this girl's abaya caught his eye. He thought he knew her, but she didn't give him the chance to work out who she was: by the time Imam Dawoud al-Habashi had called the dawn prayers in a hoarse, deeply pious voice, turning the alley into a lining of embroidered cotton, she'd disappeared. Yusuf tossed the papers upon which he was milking the dawn into a poem for Azza aside. In the blink of an eye, he'd crossed the flight of steps leading down past Azza's bedroom door and followed in the girl's footprints, moving in the opposite direction to the people heading to their prayers, led by those flying steps whose tiptoes skimmed the ground toward Mushabbab's venerable old garden. What a devil that Mushabbab was, he thought to himself, tempting the girls of the neighborhood with his curiosities so early in the morning.

The Lane of Many Heads remembers that the gate to the garden was always open, as an invitation to passersby; just then, though, it had been closed. Yusuf pushed it open and went in, to find himself staring Mushabbab in the face. Mushabbab's eyes glimmered in the darkness as he rinsed his mouth out with mastic-scented water from the Well of Zamzam. He then carried on what he was doing, averting his eyes from Yusuf's searching, accusing gaze. Something in the air made Yusuf long for Azza, though he hid his love for her even from himself. He was seized by an urge to shock Mushabbab by telling him about her. But which words would he stun him with? Would he say that he was born to adore Azza, that she had bewitched him in a previous life? That she had propagated inside him like a vaccine? When Azza's mother had died, and Sheikh Muzahim buried her in the darkness from which she'd never emerged after giving birth to Azza, Halima took her under her wing, and twinned her with Yusuf. Yusuf didn't bottle-feed Azza out of joy so much as he did it out of a fine, insistent sadness, like the dull hum of a toothache. None of the epidemics that featured during the pilgrimage season—influenza, cholera, meningitis—had succeeded in raising Yusuf's temperature for so long and without interruption, even though he'd caught them all and had barely made it through alive. Mecca's epidemics were nature's own beneficial vaccines: they killed thousands, but those who survived gained total immunity. Not even Mecca's fabled bad knee, which crippled every woman and man it struck, could impair Yusuf's joints, which, far from becoming eroded, were like iron. In Mecca, what doesn't kill you makes you stronger, which is why the people of the city have always sent their children out into the pilgrim-thronged backstreets to crawl around, stumble over, and generally fraternize with all kinds of diseases and nationalities, or to peddle goods or work in the Sanctuary pushing aged pilgrims around for their obligatory circumambulations. That's why death was forced to find more modern means of infiltrating the Lane of Many Heads—like the one that smashed Yusuf's knee, for example, or the new habit Meccan youths had of going after their livelihoods on the backs of *shaytan arawat*—"Satan's devices"—which is what the aged Bukharan woman in the neighborhood called motorbikes.

"As children of the Sanctuary, Azza and Yusuf are twins, born from an egg that split in two," Halima would say, laughing. "And if the day ever comes that eggs cease to split apart, Mecca will fall into the hands of demons . . ."

The One

DETECTIVE NASSER AL-QAHTANI FLICKED THROUGH THE PHOTOS OF DEATH piled up around his bed. He could almost feel the tingling sensation as it waited for him to doze off, ready to take over his hands from Yusuf's memoirs and those emails of Aisha's that overflowed with an urge for dissipation. He was confused, perturbed, desperate to smell her depravity. He picked up one of the emails.

FROM: Aisha
SUBJECT: Message 5

I turn on the webcam for Skype and throw myself onto the bed.

On the screen, movements envelop me like a wave, taking me to places I'd never dreamed of going.

I reach climaxes I never even got close to with Ahmad, the husband I paralyzed.

David, I'll use this symbol to address you: ˆ. You need to be concealed in case someone discovers my messages.

And someone will. So please delete this message. It's the only one that contains the key to your identity.

Your messages are beams of light, and soon there won't even be a single word of them left in my veins.

I store your messages in a folder in my email called "The One."

ˆ is like the smell of cigarettes on my breath that I cover up with lemon scent as the tar rattles in my lungs. You can hear me coughing all the time when I'm alone at night.

My auntie Halima asks me, "Is it a dry cough or is it wet?" and makes me swallow a spoonful of sesame oil.

How dare we leave our hearts at the end of the world and just return home, instead of dropping dead on the spot?

ˆ, I watch the firefly circle the lamp in my hand, I close my eyes and it grasps my hand and dances and spins me around, as you and I did in the physiotherapy room that morning.

I'll pick out certain words that point to the things I love and write them in bold so that you trip over them like rocks in your path. Sometimes they'll cause you to bleed. (I swear to you, I'll leave rocks here and there and a scrape of what delights me). Am I talking too much? I used to always be so silent. I'd never let anyone get into my head. But then where's my heart? Inside my chest, where it should be, there's just a void.

Me and the sun—which I can't actually see—have a lot to talk about. Can you imagine, ^, I'm a radiant woman in a country that they mark on maps with a sticker of a laughing sun.

Meanwhile, I know nothing about the sun except for that sentence that's in all the grammar books, the sentence that's supposed to explain the concept of subject and predicate adjective: "The sun is resplendent; the moon is radiant." Inside my room, bits of it come at me from behind the veil: in dots and dashes so I can punctuate the sentences of the world outside. In my country, where the sun is ever-present, I treat my frailty with Vitamin D and Osteocare—manufactured in Britain and the U.S. from calcium extracted from seashells from the shores of the Far East.

So don't tell me things like "Your sun brightens my room," because active sentences are beyond my experience.

The droplets of sweat on my upper lip are spreading, and even your face is damp, exactly as it was on the morning you said goodbye to me at the hospital door before the embassy car took me to the airport so I could return to my country.

"Her health has recovered," said my hospital discharge papers, but to tell the truth it wasn't just pain that I was smuggling back with me but a man, too: you were in my head and under my skin as I swept, without flinching, through the scanners at customs in the Jeddah airport.

The scent of your shaving soap still arouses my senses, tickling me awake each morning.

I turn to look at my back in the mirror and examine the long scar. It's made red by the many stitches that look like a dove's footprints. You continue to massage it with Vaseline, and I wonder to myself: how on earth are you able to touch a wound so gently? You apply yourself with nothing but tenderness to something so hideous, so disgusting, that even I'm revolted. You told me the tissue and muscles needed time to rebuild, fuse together and fill the cavity—but it took you no time at all to fuse together with me.

You should number your messages too—so that we keep an eye on time as it seeps away.

Isn't it Time that keeps the dead company?

Aisha

The Lane sniggered at Nasser that night as he paced beneath its windows as he did every other night. Every evening as the smell of toasted bread poured out of their houses, the people of the neighborhood made jokes at the expense of this "Siren Man," a reference to the police siren in which they all heard a finger of accusation pointed at each and every one of them.

The Lane of Many Heads was apprehensive all of a sudden and watched closely as Nasser pushed open the door of Aisha's abandoned house and slipped into the dark hallway, where he halted in front of the dried-up faucet. The neighborhood didn't attempt to stop him as he sought out her father the teacher's cane, whose history had been recorded on their bodies. They decided to let it spill Aisha's tragedies out into his narrow eyes, which reminded them of a bat's. All those years of trying to pierce through into the hearts of the guilty and the suspicious had made them into drills.

Nasser went up to the roof, but no sooner had he set foot there than he forgot what he was doing. The sudden shock of open space had blinded him. He couldn't remember why he was there, and he felt that the slightest movement, a breath even, would summon Aisha: sitting there, with the face of his sister Fatima, whom they'd nicknamed Dawn because she was so radiant. He could almost hear Aisha writing, asking him "Do the dead take Time with them for company?" Nasser pushed these delusions from his mind and walked to the edge of the roof to see how far it was from there to the place where the body had been discovered. "Could she have fallen off this roof?" There was no straight line between the two points, so unless the body's trajectory changed as it was falling, it couldn't possibly have landed in that spot, which was quite a way off and nearer the end of the alley.

Suddenly, he felt a crunch of glass underfoot, and when he stepped aside he saw fragments of crystal; he spotted other beads scattered about, glinting in disparate corners, and he trailed them to the pile of boxes to his left, where he found more crystals: twelve-millimeter gems. He picked through the pile of boxes and came across a sleeve torn off of a dress, the whiteness of its lace grimy with dust and the underarm thickly stained where deodorant had stewed in sweat. For a moment, Nasser lost himself in the feminine, yellowed scent, but the hound in him had already identified the smell: Aisha. He had no desire to complicate the matter by wondering who could've torn the sleeve from her arm, and when . . .

What's the sweat of death like? If he knew anything about the chemistry of sweat, he could've reconstructed the moments that preceded that tearing: were they moments of passion or terror? He inhaled the scent deeply and staggered: life flared up inside of him. He stuffed the sleeve into his pocket and left. The hound inside him curled up inside the sleeve. It had discovered itself; it swooned.

Yusuf's Rib

YUSUF LOWERED HIS EYES, SHIELDING HIMSELF FROM THE OUTSIDE WORLD WITH his eyelids in an attempt to disappear among the Sanctuary's many columns. His intervention in the theft of the Kaaba key meant that he was now not only being pursued by the killer but also by the police. The money he'd made from pushing elderly pilgrims around the Kaaba had dried up after the police confiscated his wheelchair, and he could no longer feign the weightlessness of the insanity that had sustained him during his refuge in the Sanctuary. He felt like his skeleton couldn't bear the weight of his body any more. He moved around alone, crawling with his torso flat against the cool marble floor of the courtyard, listening to the ravenous emptiness inside of him. The body pursued him. For the first time, he began to miss the wretchedness of the Lane of Many Heads, a wretchedness he'd rebelled against ever since the day he'd opened his eyes to life. He raised his eyes to the Kaaba and prayed: "Dear God, free me of this corpse I bear and transform me into a man." In the presence of God, he summoned Azza in the hope of working his way back to the point at which the rift between them had first begun. It would have been better if she'd been the one killed, for he would much rather have mourned her than have her despise him, and cause him to despise himself. But however hard he tried to identify it, the moment at which Azza first wished to exist outside of him eluded his memory. She was in his blood, an extension of his rib. She had the same big wide eyes, her legs had the same strong kick. It wasn't his mother Halima's face that had been the young Yusuf's entire world but Azza's tiny, soft-skinned body as she crawled, and later when she learned to walk even before he did. And then she began to grow up.

Her black abaya swallowed her up, and she was told that she would have to amputate that extension of her body. Azza had suddenly become something shameful, ripe for being buried alive.

Now, at twenty-eight, Yusuf finally knew what it meant to be down and out. Azza's absence had driven him to the streets, not because he was afraid that he'd be accused of murder, but because he was afraid of being implicated in the scandal that the woman's murder had brought to light. They say that twins can sense when their other twin is near death; so far, Yusuf's senses assured him that Azza was alive.

And yet, ever since the theft of the key Yusuf had felt a watchful presence pursuing him, lying in wait, holding off before it pounced so it could use him as bait. Mushabbab had warned him: "The body's just one element in a big conspiracy against us. Lay low until things blow over. Go take refuge in the House of God and don't come out until you hear from me."

Yusuf mocked him at the time: "The whole of the third world suffers from conspiracy theory paranoia. Anybody who can't get their wife pregnant says it's a global conspiracy!"

"I have a theory," Mushabbab said, ignoring his mockery. "I think they need you to lead them to something. That's the only possible explanation for what's about to happen in the neighborhood. That corpse signifies far more than we think we know. As soon as it appeared in the Lane of Many Heads, everything went topsy-turvy."

Mushabbab was full of nonsense, no doubt, but the message imprinted upon the body smoldered in Yusuf's mind. Could taking refuge in the Sanctuary save him? What other choice did he have?

There Yusuf was, constantly moving, never stopping in one place . . . If he stopped, his pursuer would catch up with him. But whenever he looked around him, all he could see were the pillars in the Sanctuary's many colonnades beginning at Victory Gate and stretching, dizzyingly, all the way to Farewell Gate and Cemetery Gate. How on earth could someone hope to disguise themselves within the House of God?

Yusuf would wrap his yellowed headscarf around his head and then adjust it in case his veiled face looked too conspicuous and gave him away. He blended in during the prayers. Whenever he listened to the worshippers praying around him he heard them muttering litanies of requests and supplications; some even dared to offer up a list of curses. Yusuf trained his senses to conjure up the angels he used to see when he came to the Sanctuary—the playground of angels—as a child. Every Friday, his mother Halima would perfume herself and accompany him and Azza to the Sanctuary Mosque, leading them in through the Ajyad Gate, which stood in a spot that faced the oldest mountains on earth, from which the very first horses had sprung to life at the beginning of time. From there the three would enter the Sanctuary courtyard surrounding the Kaaba. It was like a cake cut into slices: marble walkways crisscrossed the courtyard between the areas where pilgrims prayed, which were covered in fine pebbles washed in musk, agarwood, and ambergris. The pebbles had long since been replaced by slabs of white marble, yet when Yusuf walked barefoot his feet still tingled with delight at the rough touch of those ancient stones.

Yusuf pressed his head to the marble floor, listening for the conspiratorial female voices in the courtyard of those childhood Fridays.

Directly after Friday afternoon prayers, Halima would go over to the same stone slab to the right of the Well of Zamzam, spread out a rug, and take her seat at center stage. The black abayas multiplied around them as women with their little ones spread out brightly colored rugs. Mopping the perspiration from their temples, they sipped tea from tiny gold-rimmed cups and devoured roasted almonds and watermelon seeds. They played their roles masterfully. Each circle of abayas was its own stage in which the husband played the starring role in a boisterous drama seasoned with ennui.

"Don't worry, Wadoud. Count out four thousand prayers on your prayer beads over water and then give it to him to drink. That'll have a troublesome lover wrapped around your little finger in no time . . ." This tried and true advice was punctuated by the disconsolate sobs of a woman who'd been abandoned, bursting into tears at stage right; to the left a mother prostrated twice before God, pleading to join her young son, to whose green funeral procession, headed for al-Malah Cemetery, she had just bid farewell.

All around them women sent cries of supplication to God, begging Him to send down angels who would alight upon their amulets and the clouds of incense that clung to the Sanctuary's colonnades.

Hungrily, Yusuf submitted his body to the pull of the black stone and pressed his face into the worn-down surface set in a silver surround, seeking the taste of Azza's lips among the millions that had imprinted their kisses there over the ages. His mother Halima had inscribed onto their memories what she'd been told by her grandfather: the stone was "one of the great sapphires of Paradise, over three cubits long, which if tossed into water would float—despite its awesome size! When God most exalted took the covenant from Adam's descendants, He wrote out their destinies and fed them to the black stone. On Judgment Day, the stone will be resurrected with two eyes, a tongue, and lips, to testify to the loyalty of believers and denounce the heresies of infidels." Azza would always take her time kissing the stone, by way of some secret agreement with the soldier who stood guard beside it. Azza's tongue never tired of licking the stone, and after its blackness began to drip from her fingers, she started to draw. "We used to think she drew with charcoal," Yusuf thought to himself, "but in reality she uses the black stone, which she sipped up in those lingering kisses."

"Recite the Surah of the Earthquake from the Quran and blow in their direction. They'll get off your back then . . ."

"The Fussilat Surah. If you recite it after evening prayer with the intention of resolving the problems between you, and making the truth known, even your bitterest enemies will be made to come to you, willingly or otherwise, and do right by you." With hopes of splitting asunder or bringing together, illiterate women and those with enough learning to make out letters exchanged wisdom—both occult and commonsense—while their children listened, awestruck. Yusuf realized that the mystical tokens they shared with one another with the utmost discretion were capable of summoning the angels down from heaven and into a woman's pocket. He began to understand that a wronged woman could tear open the doors of heaven and cause angels to rain down. These heads wrapped in black, these women prostrating fervently around him, they confirmed his suspicion that a woman's tears were a dangerous thing, and that to women faith was a dough they baked into bread for food, warmth, and control over their husbands. By feeding her man, she gets her claws into him. He couldn't stop thinking about the girl who was reciting verses from the Surah of the Jinn to make the future appear before her.

He would pull Azza away and make her chase him through the colonnades where children played in the shade of the columns' intertwining capitals under the watchful eyes of the affable sanctuary wardens. Sometimes Yusuf's gaze would stray upward, and he would see the angels coming to life in the tulip-like adornments atop the columns and inside the gilded circlets that embroidered the ceiling with Quranic verses and the Names of God, angels for whom time stands still in the moment of their revelation. In those venerable colonnades, Yusuf came to understand that art and recitation were synonymous with the sacred. The angels would beckon to him, and he'd fly on his long legs, not stopping until he reached what little remained of Mount Marwa, where Azza would finally catch up with him, narrowly avoiding a collision with the girl who rented out scissors to the pilgrims wanting to cut their hair. Yusuf would stand rooted to the ground, absorbed in thought, in front of the great barrel where the hair piled up in layers, hair of all colors and textures, amassed into the form of a vast bird-like creature. It smelled like the very essence of human desire. A cipher that was shorn during the ritual circumambulation and the running between mountains, cut and brushed off of pilgrims' napes; the Umrah washed away an entire year's worth of sins. He'd stand there, enraptured, before the barrel of sins and desires.

Now, with the awareness of his exile intensifying around him, Yusuf was seized by a sudden need to unburden himself, not only of his sin-drenched hair, but of the life that weighed so heavily upon his shoulders. Next to the doorway leading to the concourse between the mountains, he knelt and offered his head up to the razor of an Ethiopian adolescent, who denuded it in five strokes, leaving its surface smooth and gleaming with a greenish shine. He stood up feeling light, almost transparent, and allowed his toes to sink deep into the talismans and charms that accumulated in the courtyard of the house of God. Surely one of these contained his salvation from the bruising weight of this shadowy persecution.

Evening prayer was over and night had long since fallen, turning Mecca into a great marble platter overflowing with a neon glow. It was rush hour in the Haram Mosque, with the weary workers coming to find refuge from the tribulations of their day. Wrapped in his ritual ihram, Yusuf walked out of the Sanctuary, stepping over the vast piles of worshippers' shoes at the King Fahd Gate and crossing the exterior plaza, all beneath the glare of the Vegas-style spotlights trained permanently on the House of God. Yusuf turned around, his back to the shopping mall opposite, and looked at the whiteness of the Mosque, arranging the edge of his ihram so that it covered the side of his face to ward off the glances of curious passersby.

He was waiting for Mu'az, Dawoud the Imam's son, who was bouncing like a tennis ball when he arrived. He was a bundle of contradictions—a mixture of pious and modern stuffed into a white Chinese-made tracksuit and sneakers, crowned by an unkempt chest-length beard that looked more like a costume accessory than the real thing. He stood there looking around him for a moment; he obviously hadn't recognized Yusuf.

"Mu'az!" Yusuf hissed, causing him to jump.

"I didn't recognize you with all the pilgrims here! With your hair completely shaved like that, and that ihram on . . ."

"I'm so tired, Mu'az. I'm living like a hobo, and the marble floor's crushing my bones . . ." After so much time spent by himself, Yusuf's voice sounded like it was coming from far away. "I'd give my life for a soft bed and a pillow."

Mu'az gazed at Yusuf's ghost-like form. "I know somewhere you can stay. Meet me Friday afternoon by the bike shop at the beginning of Mount Hindi . . ." A clueless look crossed Yusuf's face for a moment. "You know, the guy we used to call 'Son of a Hag?' When he wasn't watching you used to steal a bike for a ride around the block . . ." Yusuf nodded, remembering.

"Take this for now," Mu'az went on, thrusting two hundred-riyal notes—a generous share of what remained of this month's wages—into Yusuf's hesitant hands. To dispel the sudden awkwardness, Mu'az hurriedly began his update from the neighborhood.

"The Lane of Many Heads is undergoing cosmetic surgery. The sound of strangers' footsteps in the neighborhood never dies down. They're digging up Mushabbab's orchard in search of the amulet. They've begun a cleansing campaign to drive the squatters out of their shanties and huts. We went into hovels we never even knew existed. They've evicted women and children and beggars who have no one to go to, people living in cellars and beneath roofs made of a few rags strung between two crumbling walls, hordes of people without papers . . . The Mercedes 4x4s park at the entrance to the alley and out come the surveyors . . . It's all so strange. Mutairi the oud seller sold his shop, loaded his instruments onto the back of a truck, and left the Lane of Many Heads . . . What do you think's happening? Is this all because of one body?!" Yusuf looked around them. A dozen or so Afghan children were sniffing about, looking for pockets full of booty and soliciting pilgrims' charity with heaps of prayer beads, prayer rugs, and cheap hats. They carefully skirted around Yusuf, remembering all too well his history of madness.

"It's hard for me to imagine what you're saying . . ." He fell silent for a moment, then continued. "If we were the kind of people who thought like Mushabbab, I'd say the body was simply a full stop at the end of the last chapter, and that this is the beginning of a new one. . . Maybe this is how progress is meant to happen . . ."

After Mu'az had faded away, Yusuf stayed facing the Sanctuary, absent-mindedly watching the doves ascend the clouds of incense, tracing circles in the sky above the house of God as if to guard it through the night.

It was midnight by the time Yusuf returned to the Sanctuary. He stopped to take a last look out at Mecca and his gaze settled on Mount Abu Qubays, the home of many legends. Its peaks were swathed in darkness, with not even a window from which light might trickle out to passersby or a lantern carelessly left on a doorstep. The mountaintop had been completely shorn of its houses and left to sink into ravenous emptiness. All of a sudden, there was a light. That oughtn't to have been unusual, but a jolt of electricity tore through Yusuf's mind, sparking the dry tinder of his insanity. To him the hesitant flicker of light was like a shriek of death or a desperate cry for help. Yusuf ran back to the pillar in the colonnade next to al-Salam Gate where he stashed his bundle of clothes, and quickly changed out of his ritual ihram into an ordinary robe whose aged cotton had yellowed slightly, wrapping his headscarf around his face. Then he left his hideout and ran—on a mission to save something, whatever it was—in the heights of Abu Qubays.

For a moment, Yusuf was a child again on a regular Saturday morning outing. When they were little, his mother Halima would walk them both from the Lane of Many Heads out to Mount Abu Qubays, passing through the Small Market just outside the Sanctuary's Farewell Gate on the way; it was the gateway through which anyone leaving Mecca had to pass. As they walked through the market, they were awash in the laughs and cries of vendors. Their eyes gorged themselves on the vivid greens that vied for the attention of their senses. Pyramids of dew-dappled tomatoes were ringed by rows of parsley bunches, fragrant mint and radishes, and the pumpkins, stacked on the ground in a pyramid, toppled over and rolled about at shoppers' feet. Every morning, camels who'd started their journey at dawn would deliver the succulent bounty of the orchards and gardens of Ta'if: al-Shafa, al-Hada, Wadi Mihrim, and Wadi Fatma, to market.

Yusuf's hunger—a hunger for Azza and Azza alone—would surge as he watched her surrender her senses to the scents of the Small Market. She would dash to the stalls that sold miro kebab, where she'd score one of the deep-fried balls of meat mixed with millet. The doughnut vendor was generous too, drenching his fried creations in sugar or seasoning them liberally with pepper. They'd stop to look at the great pots of fava beans cooking in homemade ghee and listen to the tune of the wooden pestles grinding up bread in big vats and mixing it with honey or banana to make ma'soub, until finally Halima would take them to the King of Heads. The King of Heads sold the finest sheep's head meat in Mecca. Like a sculptor he would hew out the choicest morsels for Halima, wrap the lot up in brown paper and hand it to Yusuf, saying: "Here you go, my man. Carry this for your dear ladies."

With the paper package tucked under Yusuf's arm, Halima would lead the two children up the steep slope of Mount Abu Qubays. Their ascent was easy and spontaneous, without any formalities, at the start. They followed along dusty tracks lined with old houses bearing roofs decorated with perforated gypsum. Collapsed skylights had left many houses open to the elements; they'd been replaced with a layer of bare wood, like a cry of "Lord help us!" Halima encouraged the children to be tough as they continued on their journey upward. Planted on the rooftops around them, elderly men betrayed by their crippled knees sat watching, stinking of Vicks and chicken fat—the prescription of choice for arthritis—their legs stretched out in front of them like flayed rabbits. In their stiff white cloth caps and faded colored waistcoats, they sat there like a collective memory going stale, watching passersby walking up and down the hill, watching what took place and what didn't on the benches out in front of the houses—nothing ever did happen, in fact, except for the wait until the next prayer, when they would join their families and pray, looking out over the rows of devotees in the Sanctuary below.

The young Yusuf's body memorized the benches outside each of the houses on the mountains around the Sanctuary—which lay like a navel below, as if Mecca were a big crater, its four sides plunging down toward the House of God and the Kaaba at its center—and the lines of innate wisdom etched onto the foreheads of the old men. They, too, were crumbling, dilapidated. Halima would urge the two on, and they'd continue upward toward the open summit, nearer and nearer to God. As he climbed, the blood would pump more violently in Yusuf's temples and he'd lose the ability to see out of his left eye, seeing only with the right, which was trained on the sky, while Mecca and its Sanctuary, the corners where the four Sunni schools of law were taught, and the domed roof over the Well of Zamzam, lay down to his left.

As they ascended, little Azza's eyes would pop out like an insect's so she could see in all directions, and her skin would lose color as her blood drained out into the well below them until they eventually made it to the Cave of Treasures. The opening received them like an iwan set into the rocks. Goat droppings and traces of previous visitors gave the place some life. From the clearing in front of the cave, it looked like it was just a crevice in the mountain, its mouth blocked by stones stacked up like a puzzle without any mortar. According to Yusuf's many historical reference works, it was built by Noah, peace be upon him, to cover the final resting-place of Adam and Eve and their son Seth, who had been given ninety tablets of divine secrets and knowledge of humanity's destiny from on high and had hidden them in that spot where they lay in wait for the person who would discover them. Yusuf and Azza's imaginations were piqued by the cracks in that stone curtain, which must have been there to allow a little light to filter into where the three lay, but they never dared to steal a glance into the cavern. In Yusuf's history books, it said that the rocks had been softened by the flood and that Noah's feet had sunk into them as he strode across the eastern cliffs, leaving footprints a meter long. Visitors would gather around them every Saturday morning, tracing the steps of the Prophet Noah as he came to return Adam's coffin, which he'd carried on the Ark, after the great flood receded. Only today did Yusuf realize that the stone on which they'd always had their picnic was a pool of water left over from the flood, the depression left by Noah's foot as he went to bid his final farewell to Adam. There, Halima would lay out their picnic and divide up the sheep's head, picking out the tapered end of the tongue meat for her son to spear and butcher, and the three of them would devour their snack by the graveside of Seth, son of Adam. Yusuf would be overcome by a manic urge to write, his pen quivering at the thought of those ninety tablets Seth had left to him, which held the secret to his nine hundred years, and to humanity's longevity—a secret that Seth buried before he was buried himself beside his father in the cave on Abu Qubays.

Halima would explain to Azza's father, Sheikh Muzahim, that the aim of these trips to Abu Qubays was to seek healing—to cure Azza of her terror of falling asleep and Yusuf of his headaches. Meccans believed that eating sheep's head there strengthened the heart and cured congenital headaches. Yusuf thought back to Azza's heart when she was a little girl, squeezing an eyeball between her molars, biting into it, causing the white of the eye to spurt out onto her tongue. The thought of what she was doing would seize her suddenly and she'd spit the white fat out.

"Don't spit out God's blessing. He'll strike you blind!"

So then she'd bite into the head of a spring onion and her eyes would water. He would watch her and wait for the sunset, which signaled it was time to head home, hoping that the moon would rise and break upon her face in the same place that people claim it broke upon the Prophet's face—peace be upon him—and Yusuf's pounding headache would make the scene at the top of the mountain wobble and blur. It occurred to him that when he stood at Azza's side, holding her tiny melting cotton-candy hand as they gazed down on the dizzying sight of the pilgrims circumambulating the Kaaba, they must have appeared taller than Noah's ark and the graves of Adam, Eve, and their son Seth with their long-destroyed tombstones. In Yusuf's history, it wasn't just the Kaaba that was sacred. Mecca's mountains were existential secrets and healing.

A great rumbling noise tore Yusuf back from his past to the hungry, empty present. The night was pitch-black with no moon to relieve its agony. When he opened his eyes, he found himself facing an imposingly high wooden barrier, which protected a construction site on that same mountain peak. He could feel the rock beneath his feet tremble: under cover of night, colossal machines were grinding away. Yusuf leapt over the fence, landing on his bad knee inside the construction site. Just a few meters away from where he'd landed, a bulldozer sank its teeth into the stone wall around Adam, Eve and Seth's final resting-place. Rock after rock fell from the painstakingly stacked wall. The puzzle was disintegrating into chaos. Letters, black and white, piled up and rolled away, tracing out scattered lines of poetry and proverbs. Yusuf was too worried to take too close a look at the destiny that he imagined was written upon the ninety tablets Seth had received from the Lord at the dawn of creation.

Behind the bulldozer, the hoist of an enormous crane rose up, its fangs closed around a shrouded bundle shaped like a pointed obelisk. Each side of the obelisk was a body. Yusuf shook with terror: those were the bodies of Adam, Eve, and Seth, huddled together defensively as the crane wrenched them out of Abu Qubays and hauled them into the air for eviction. In the blink of an eye, Yusuf too sprung into the air, propelled by his good knee, stupefying the Ethiopian crane-driver who was suddenly shoved out of his seat as Yusuf took the controls. Sirens ripped through the night at Abu Qubays and glaring headlights surged at the crane. Yusuf struggled to control the machine, which lurched forward, swinging the pyramid-shaped bier through the air and smashing into the oncoming attackers. He had no choice but to save this ancient treasure from the construction—or rather, destruction—site. As the crane crashed through the site's main gate, Yusuf was startled by a streak of yellow and a squeal of brakes off to his right. The taxi driver who'd nearly hurtled into him stuck his head out of the window to curse at him. For all the pandemonium and the fizzing, popping madness in his brain, Yusuf was fully lucid and recognized the driver. He could see it was Khalil, who'd once been a pilot and also his rival for Azza, though he was several years older. The contrast suddenly appeared absurd to Yusuf: to fight for Azza in the Lane of Many Heads was surely more worthwhile than fighting over stones in the House of God!

All of a sudden, the pulsating energy in Yusuf's head sputtered out, the crane ground to a standstill and he slumped back in the seat. His will to react had dried up, as had any desire to keep going. He sat pallidly in the cabin waiting for the guards to surround him and escort him away. But his pursuers had also frozen in position, their cars forming a wide circle around him. None of them dared to go nearer in case the madman who had stolen the crane caught them by surprise. Khalil took advantage of the suspense and drove closer to the cabin, opening the passenger door for Yusuf.

"Jump," he urged, with the warmth of an older brother. "Let's get you out of here." Yusuf studied Khalil's face. A current of electricity zipped around in his head. He was at a loss. Was Khalil laying a trap or genuinely offering a helping hand? The Khalil he knew excelled in bullying both Yusuf and Azza, especially on Saturdays when they'd get back from their sheep's head picnic at the top of Mount Abu Qubays. Envious and spiteful, Khalil would greet them: "So? Feel better now? Now you've eaten our ancestor Adam's head and drunk the aspirin of Abu Qubays?" Azza would stick her long tongue out at him before the refreshing cool of the alleyway swallowed her up. Yusuf thought Khalil, with that malicious look of his, was capable of swallowing Azza's head whole. From the crane cabin, Yusuf scrutinized the face that his mother Halima had always likened to that of a broken-winged eagle.

From the corner of his eye, Yusuf could see that his pursuers had gotten out of their vehicles and were creeping toward the crane. His neighbor from the Lane was Yusuf's only hope of escape, so without another glance over his shoulder he leapt out of the cabin and threw himself into the seat beside Khalil.

"Fool!" Khalil cackled as he sent the car shooting forward at cinematic speed. The brakes shrieked and the wheels spit dust into the faces of their pursuers. Yusuf just gazed pop-eyed at the bodies of Adam, Eve, and Seth, which hung fused together like an obelisk in the sky over Mecca.

Memories on a Shelf

WHY DO PEOPLE PUT MORE FAITH IN WHAT THEY READ ON PAPER THAN WHAT'S scrawled onto clay or talismans? Look at the filthy plastic bags muddying my unpaved surface and you'll see what my many heads consume and reuse.

Nasser plowed on with Yusuf's diaries, ignoring all the intersections and stop signs that I, the Lane of Many Heads, placed in his way, going through page after page of Yusuf's memoirs, all of which pointed to the fact that Yusuf was Salih the foundling's closest friend. Salih was also known as the Eunuchs' Goat—but then, I don't want to implicate any of my heads in that headache. To tell the truth, these young people and the schizophrenic crazes they go in for are driving a stake into my historical behind. This guy Nasser . . . How could he ever understand that the seemingly trivial apparitions in my fishing net of misery were rooted in history? Like that nickname "the Eunuchs' Goat." At some stage in history, the castrated chamberlains who'd consecrated their lives to serving the Sanctuary became famous for a virile billy goat they kept. Livestock owners used to get the billy goat, known to everyone as "the eunuchs' goat," to inseminate their flock, borrowing him for several days at a time and letting him loose among their goats so he could spread his exemplary genes. The only condition was that the borrower was responsible for feeding him for the duration of the loan, and the borrowers were indeed very generous, if only so as to ensure the quality and fecundity of his seed. Most of the city's blessed stock were descended from the eunuchs' goat.

Salih got the nickname on account of his rosy vigor when he when found, as a newborn, by al-Ashi the cook in the yard outside his kitchen. Al-Ashi and his wife Umm al-Sa'd adopted the baby. There's more to the story than that, but Nasser likes to sit in the cafe, like he's doing now sipping his coffee coolly, and flicking through the diaries, so I'll have to pay attention, to find out what stories Yusuf has been inventing about the heads on my shoulders:

February 6, 2000

Just like every morning, I bumped into al-Ashi at the entrance to the grocer's. He turned his head as if he were following the scent of something delicious cooking.

"Your 'window' was longer than usual today," he commented. The shop boys and a customer stopped to hear what he had to say about my article. His verdict would determine the way they felt about me.

A cat squeals, its tail caught in the closing shop door, and shatters Nasser's concentration. I, the Lane of Many Heads, will have to intervene and continue the story from my point of view, to demonstrate just how peculiar al-Ashi is.

At exactly six in the morning, as precise as an hourglass, not a second before or after, al-Ashi went over, as he always did, to the newspaper stand that one of the shop boys had just wheeled into place outside the store, and stood at the side of the road, rifling through Umm al-Qura *newspaper. Having enjoyed many gifts from his kitchen, the shop boys turned a blind eye, though they knew he was looking for Yusuf's daily column, entitled "A Window," that surveyed this, the Mother of Cities. He read the column slowly and with pleasure, and measured it with his handspan before closing the newspaper, returning it to the stand, and reaching automatically for the official newspaper, al-Riyadh. He handed over the money and turned his back on Yusuf's window, secure in the knowledge that it was there behind him.*

Tucking the newspaper under his arm, al-Ashi disappeared into the courtyard of his kitchen.

He pulled out his immortal chair, its tired iron legs screeching on the cement floor. The bare chair was cool in a way that made it seem as if it looked forward to his morning perusals. He extracted his glasses from the cloth tied around his middle like a sarong, then sat down, stretched his arms and legs out to the full length of the newspaper and lost himself in the front page of Al-Riyadh.

"Al-Ashi has connected the transmission wires," the kitchen boys whispered. The courtyard door was open so no passerby or neighbor could fail to notice that the reading ritual had begun, and that the outside world had begun to flood into the neighborhood through that newspaper.

Umm al-Sa'd sent her stepson the Eunuchs' Goat down with tea, in one of those tall collectible Kraft cheese glasses, which he placed on the floor to the right of al-Ashi, who let the tea vapors, infused with Umm al-Sa'd's breaths, waft up to him as he began his second round of reading. "Umm al-Sa'd reads and writes." I, the Lane of Many Heads, always made sure I kept my heads well out of reach of the deluge of that woman, who could sweep walls away and always cleaned up in the stock market. Nevertheless, I observed with interest the stupid morning assemblies she held for her acolytes in her apartment on the first floor of the apartment block that belonged to her father the milkman and was known as the Arab League building.

That morning, Umm al-Sa'd was tense as she greeted Kawthar, the wife of Yabis the sewage cleaner, whose oldest son Ahmad was married to Aisha the cripple and worked as a PA to some big shots. He had promised—

Nasser paused the action. He was taken aback by the word *cripple*.

Ahmad had promised he'd look for somebody who could take care of some papers for the Eunuchs' Goat, who, having been left to grow up with the cats in al-Ashi's backyard, had never been granted citizenship, and was now finding it nigh on impossible to get it. In my minds, Ahmad stood out for being a well-connected node: he built relationships with influential people, the kind of people who could turn the sea into tahini, as the saying went, who could fix all the intractable problems I faced when I tried to keep up with progress. He sold permits for music shops, for example, and allowed video games to be played in cafes in exchange for bribes that were peeled from my flesh. He guided me step by step through a series of cosmetic procedures—a total makeover, in fact—the complications of which transformed me into a monster like that woman who got plastic surgery to make herself look like a cat. Ahmad claimed he was doing it all as a favor to me, but the truth was he was sucking my blood on behalf of those people who were biting the flesh off my shoulders.

Umm al-Sa'd slumped regally on her throne in front of her computer. Her Internet browser was open at the website of the national stock exchange and the women from the neighborhood were arrayed around her, munching their way through roasted sunflower seeds and the latest news and rumors. They all watched her when she sat up straight and—with a heart like steel—clicked to confirm the purchase of a thousand shares in Shams Ltd., which had been losing value over the past few days. She reclined on her throne once more. The rim of her coffee cup was branded by her garish red lipstick. The numbers on the screen jumped about incessantly, never settling not even for a moment, and each tiny quiver brought new gains for market parasites like Umm al-Sa'd, who would jerk upright with a tremble whenever the value of her shares rose unexpectedly, and with a click, issue the order to sell.

"We've pulled it off! Out of the lion's jaws, and we made a thousand!" The women gave a collective sigh of relief, filling the room with the smell of roasted watermelon seeds. They rallied under the banner of her stock market piracy. They entrusted her with what little wealth they had, giving her power of attorney so she could sell and buy on their behalf in the hope she would bring them unimaginable wealth. This fills me, the Lane of Many Heads, with an overpowering desire to crush that lone female head sprouting up like a parasitic weed among my male heads.

"Women like Umm al-Sa'd must have enormous vaginas that are capable of swallowing up the entire stock exchange, the Lane of Many Heads, and even death itself all in one go!" The idiotic thought took root in the women's minds as they watched Umm al-Sa'd penetrate the market, leaning toward her computer without bothering to sit up. They called her "Steelballs" behind her back. I'm certain that if the women of the Lane of Many Heads were ever allowed to nominate their own candidate to chair the local council, there wasn't a single man who'd dare challenge Steelballs. She could win all the women's hearts with a mere flick of her index finger, which lay poised on the keyboard, and she'd have posed a very real threat if she hadn't been so preoccupied with the problem of how to secure citizenship for her adopted son, the Eunuchs' Goat.

"God knows Ahmad's tried his very best," Yabis' wife Kawthar said, relaying her son Ahmad's message, "but his contacts weren't shy about put-

ting a figure on it. They want eighty thousand up front and the same again once it's taken care of."

Umm al-Sa'd gasped. "Selling favors is like selling shade, or water from the Well of Zamzam. It was the downfall of earlier nations, you know. When the Amalekites lived in Mecca, they were as wealthy as could be but they got greedy. They started renting out the shade and selling water, so God expelled them from Mecca. He hit them with a plague of ants that chased them out of the Sanctuary, and then He drove them away with drought. He sent bountiful rain ahead of them and they followed it, and that's how He was able to drive them back to Yemen, the birthplace of their forefathers. There they were dispersed and perished. God replaced them with the tribe of Jurhum, but they, too, eventually became greedy and so He exterminated them."

The history lesson didn't ruffle the satisfied look on Kawthar's face. Umm al-Sa'd shifted in her seat, making her displeasure clear, and picked the bowl of red apples up off the side table. The women looked on anxiously as she peeled them methodically one by one, heaping the peels on a plate and chopping out the core and seeds. She then began feeding the slices to her guests, who chewed mechanically, as if carrying out a military order. Umm al-Sa'd herself pounced on the plate of peel. The women watched in disbelief as she wolfed down the entire heap, with inexplicable lust and a dripping red mouth. It only confirmed the legends about her past that the women had tried to put out of their minds. They couldn't stop watching Umm al-Sa'd, who'd never eaten an apple in her entire life, just apple peels; to them the peels looked like a victory banner that she raised every time she'd fought and triumphed against the injustice of men, a banner bloodied by years of unconscionable imprisonment.

"Newspapers are al-Ashi's drug. He reads but he doesn't write. He's half illiterate."

The Eunuchs' Goat liked to spread these kinds of rumors about his adoptive father, and no one knew for sure, or cared very much at all, whether or not al-Ashi really could write. He read closely, engrossed in the pages as if discovering great secrets, obsessively studying the photos of the Custodian of the Two Holy Mosques, King Abd Allah, and Crown Prince Sultan, with whom he was infatuated. He was always cutting their pictures out of the color photograph supplement, and then he'd hang them compulsively on the walls of his lean-to, like a barrier between himself and the greasy-smelling, bloodstained yard; between himself and the eye-shriv-

eling ovens. The photos made him feel a sense of connection between his yard and the aspects of existence that remained out of reach, even for his imagination.

He studied the photos of the soccer players with a sport-obsessed child's delight, and when he reached the sports supplement he'd always have to pause his reading to adjust his glasses, which had remained unchanged for a quarter-century. In fact, every surprising news item caused him to grab the corner of his sarong, exhale warm air from the depths of his soul, and polish the lenses.

Only then, confident that he could make out even the tiniest news items that lurked in corners almost beyond the reach of his lenses, would al-Ashi cry, "All is well in the world!" Then he'd lean over to take the first sip of the tea his wife, Umm al-Sa'd—the mother of his happiness—had prepared.

The moment the sun touched his feet, he folded up his arms, legs, and the newspaper in one decisive movement, and stood up, adding the paper to the stack on the shelf opposite the door.

As he did every morning, al-Ashi paused and stood with his back to the yard, sipping his tea and contemplating the trove of newspapers arranged according to date and compelling subject matter: he knew, for example, exactly which stack contained the beginning of the terror campaigns and the crackdowns and police raids that followed, and he kept pictures of the dead security forces officers and the list of the country's thirty-six most wanted.

Al-Ashi cast an extra glance toward the stack of double-sized special editions announcing the deaths of kings—Faisal, Khalid, Fahd, al-Hasan, and Hussein—and news of who would succeed them. This pile contained the telegrams sent to congratulate them on the occasion of their investiture and to commiserate after their funerals.

Here, too, laid out horizontally, he kept the issues that contained special stories: the Lane of Many Heads made a rare appearance in the story about the miracle that was Aisha, the sole survivor of a bus accident that had killed three families from the neighborhood while on their way to Medina. This was followed by Prince Abd al-Aziz's promise to cover the costs of her treatment in Germany at His Majesty's personal expense.

Al-Ashi also held on to reports about the performance of the stock exchange and significant donations, and reports about the vast "economic cities" projects inaugurated by King Abd Allah. He stacked these horizontally so he could keep track of their claims.

Half a century's worth of dust was lined up there neatly; Hamid al-

Ashi knew that he was laying his memory out on that shelf: he could forget everything, become as senile as he liked, as long as the box of recollections stayed up there out of dementia's reach; a standalone repository that he could link up to the void inside his head whenever he felt like it, to become a young man or a child once again—any age from six onward, in fact, because that was the age at which, in this very courtyard, his fascination with newspapers had begun. And just how old was he now? Whenever he was accosted by that question he would steal a furtive glance at the shelf and know that he was as old as that heap of the kingdom's history, years of growth and plenty that had transformed the yard from the site of slave auctions into al-Ashi's kitchen. And yet in reality they still hadn't passed through my, the Lane's, net of despair except for on that shelf, with its photos of monuments and galas and foundation stones being laid and ribbon-cutting ceremonies with little girls wearing coronets of flowers and clutching golden scissors. He carefully organized and arranged even during the years after the boom had petered out, years that saw the music shops in the vicinity of his kitchen multiply, closely followed by the kingdom's accession to the World Trade Organization and the first municipal elections in forty years. Al-Ashi scrutinized the short row near the end and picked out the first photo of a Saudi woman ever published in a local newspaper: it was a photo of the broadcaster Samar alongside Maha. Then he carefully picked out the first angry response to the photos of Saudi women appearing in the pages of newspapers, addressed to all the dailies and weeklies, and even the supplements which carried short news items. The photos became so commonplace after a while that it was almost impossible to continue collecting them one by one so he decided to make do with his archive of the earliest examples. Whenever al-Ashi looked at the row of papers, he had the sensation of a vast female army advancing. It had only just been detected, in the years from 2004 to 2006, but it was decisive and it was sweeping the country. Particularly notable was the news that a number of women had been elected to the Jeddah Chamber of Commerce. The most important photo of them all was the one of Hanadi, the first young woman to obtain a civilian pilot's license, standing in front of a massive airplane with Prince al-Waleed bin Talal and her parents. This was to mark her joining his aviation firm, and it was accompanied by a two-page-long message of congratulation from the Prince. Al-Ashi took the flood of newspaper-ink faces in warily; perhaps one day Umm al-Sa'd would turn up in the middle of this forward march. There was no point trying to pin down exactly how he felt about that possibility, which would turn the Lane of Many Heads, me, upside down if it came to pass. What if she also decided to publish her memoirs? She would definitely make the front page of all the papers. She'd make a hell of a splash, and anybody who could afford the two riyals for a newspaper would get the chance to see her do it. Goodness knows how many people would read the newspaper that day. Would the readers sense the power of her strong thighs and the vortex that lay between them, a perfect copy of her bright red lacquered lips, which would become a craze every woman would imitate?

"I'm in deep shit tonight with al-Souq Telecoms. I'll be eating hay when the market shuts." Al-Ashi had trained himself not to notice his wife's comments about the stock market. He didn't understand anything about that empire of numbers whose swells and ebbs his wife monitored constantly. The only thing it meant to him was that she'd embrace him with all the frustration and power of her broad shoulders, flat chest, and masculine frame. He'd trained his senses to switch off and allowed himself to be swallowed up by her womb in a nightly implantation from which he was revived every morning. On nights like tonight, however, when he could sense she was agitated, he'd look deep into her womb to see all the defenses she hid there. He understood very well what it meant to enter a body that had already been inhabited by that coldest of metals, gold.

I, the Lane of Many Heads, left him to his terror, thank God. I've managed to keep her tragedies hidden on that shelf for the last quarter century, partly because they no longer entertain me. But al-Ashi couldn't forget that stretch of time in which he did nothing but submit to her fearsome appetite. He, the talented cook, had a secret side to him that nobody knew about other than Umm al-Sa'd: he loved playing the role of the woman, giving in to her domineering masculinity and the cave of treasures that lay within.

Serpent of Serenity

IT WAS TEN IN THE MORNING WHEN THE SUN'S LIGHT WOKE YUSUF, WHO'D BEEN lying against a pillar by Farewell Gate. He looked around him in panic, but there was nothing there except the huge air-conditioning unit humming away and flocks of doves around the Kaaba. He was careful not to look in the direction of Abu Qubays, frightened at the thought of seeing the bier as he'd seen it yesterday, swinging in mid-air. For a moment he stayed there crouched like an animal on all fours, pinned down by an orphanhood so disturbing it was like there was a void where his heart and belly should be. He didn't want to think how long Adam, Eve, and Seth would remain swinging in the air or in the emptiness inside him.

He sensed a pilgrim eyeing him up in his crouching position, so he struggled to his feet and staggered to the taps of Zamzam to the side of the Mas'a, the very spot where he and the key thief had come to blows. After having been cordoned off for several days, the area had been re-opened and the taps once again distributed the flowing water that was free to all, as they had throughout Mecca's entire history.

Yusuf splashed water from the Well of Zamzam on the back of his neck and dampened his aching heart before purifying himself for prayers. He headed toward the Hijr of Ishmael, the part of the Kaaba that's not covered over, where people could get a taste of what it was like to be inside the House of God. Stealthily, he pressed his body against the black cloth embroidered with verses from the Quran and closed his eyes, sinking his face into the stone between two of God's names: "The Greatest" (a disguised name) and "The Everlasting" (a revealed name), so that his pursuers would lose sight of him. He knew that if he ever left the Kaaba they would be able to see his nakedness. He hid his face where Hagar lay beneath the rain-sluice and where breezes of agarwood and ambergris emanated from the cloth covering the Kaaba. His pulse and his nervous system slowed, taking his body to within reach of death. He waited for the serpent, over whose body the foundations of the Kaaba had been laid, to encircle him, waited to see it just as it appeared to Ibn Saj: it had the head of a cat, and wings; it could talk, and it moved like a delicate breeze. It had come from Armenia with Abraham, Friend of God, who'd been led by an angel to the site where he would rebuild the House of God. When they eventually arrived in Mecca, they found Ishmael, who was just twenty at the time and who'd long since buried his mother in the spot now known as the Hijr of Ishmael. The angel showed Abraham the location of the House, and he and his son Ishmael began to dig, looking for the foundations. They hit huge foundation stones, emeralds the size of a camel that not even thirty men together could move: the first foundation stones ever laid by the descendants of Adam. As they built over the foundation, the Angel Sakina—Serenity—came forward and coiled itself over the foundation and cried, "Build the House over me, Abraham!" So he did. That's why whoever circumambulates the House of God, be they timid Bedouin or fearsome giant, is filled with the same engulfing sense of serenity.

Yusuf could have stayed there all day and night were it not for the guard's hand upon his shoulder: "Make some space for your brother Muslim." Yusuf remained still for a moment; suddenly, he felt a sweaty hand slip into his pocket. He was torn from the grasp of the snake of serenity. He opened his eyes and looked around him; there was no one there other than an elderly man rocking back and forth as he made his rotation, repeating, "God Everlasting!" Yusuf didn't dare touch his pocket. He flew on the wings of that snake back to the colonnade, where—heart pounding, fingers trembling—he slid his hand in his pocket and drew out a small piece of paper folded around a tiny key. The paper was damp and the ink had run, but he could just about make out the words "Locker 27." Yusuf was shaking. His loitering was no longer something he'd chosen for himself; he'd become part of the plot that Mushabbab had dreamed up. He knew instantly that the key would lead him to a point from which there was no hope of return.

Locker 27. He racked his brains, trying to work out where the locker might be. By the entrances to the mosque, there were shelves where worshippers stored their shoes, but they didn't have doors or locks. They were open for anyone to use . . . Without thinking, he hurried through Ajyad Gate toward King Fahd Gate, which had recently been added as part of the expansion of the Sanctuary complex. With the Tawhid Intercontinental Hotel to his left, he made for the modern building that served as a cloakroom, a tall aluminum-encased construction with a glass edifice set in the middle of the marble plaza. He wanted to test his hunch.

The dark-skinned doorman stopped him at the entrance: "Locker number, please." Yusuf fished the slip of paper marked with the number 27 out of his pocket. The attendant took it from him and led him to a locker at the very end of the row. Blood thumped against his temples, and the attendant could see he was shaking. Yusuf stiffened: in front of him inside the open locker was the silver amulet, a locket shaped like a half-moon. The sight of it, lying there, threw the switch on Mushabbab's conspiracy theory. The day the body had turned up, he'd confided to Yusuf that he had documents he was going to hand over to them, not on a tray, but in a silver amulet. At the time Yusuf hadn't paid any attention to what he assumed was a metaphor, but now he'd come face to face with the amulet. There was no time to lose. He had to get the evidence out of Mecca.

Mushabbab had warned him: "When the amulet comes into your possession, call me on this number and I'll guide you to where I am. Any delay could cost you your life." Mushabbab had been sure to get ready for the challenge. The whole time Yusuf thought that the supposed appearance of the amulet was just a storyline out of a cartoon, but the amulet in front of him turned the game into a nightmare.

The faint rustling caused the cloakroom attendant to crane his neck to sneak a glimpse into the locker; he was taken aback by the silver amulet inside.

Yusuf hurriedly stuffed it into a paper bag and scurried away. The attendant's gaze was following Yusuf's thin form as he hurried toward Misyal Street in Misfala when two men—their faces hidden by their red-checked headscarves—swooped past him on a motorcycle. The man riding behind ripped the package out of Yusuf's hands and shoved him into the path of an oncoming bus as the motorcycle sped away and was lost from sight. The bus, brakes squealing, screeched to a halt, and Yusuf, who was almost between its front wheels, leapt to his feet. The scene, which had lasted only a few seconds, was over. When the cloakroom attendant's shock wore off and he took a look around him, it seemed none of the passersby had noticed anything; even Yusuf had disappeared.

In a narrow side-street, Yusuf stood panting. He found a phone kiosk and dialed the number.

"They stole it off me." Silence. Yusuf's plans for escape crumbled before his eyes.

"Maybe we rushed. We missed things . . . We need to take a few steps back." His instruction to Yusuf to lie low seemed insufficient. They both knew that it was only a matter of time until he was run over—though by which set of tires and from which direction they'd be coming was anybody's guess.

The Pilot

If they'd interrogated me under oath, I'd have said that Khalil was the killer. The tricks he played on his passengers were beyond even Nasser's twisted imagination. If only he'd consulted with me before summoning Khalil for interrogation . . . But then Nasser wasn't capable of forcing a spiteful old alleyway like me to snitch on a head that was like a novelty decoration among my other miserable faces. Khalil was fun to watch, to observe, to challenge and hate, and if it weren't for him, life would've been depressing. To me, Khalil belonged to some cyborg race, and nothing entertained me more than his blind tenacity. He'd simply been programmed. I'd watch him slipping along like a thin, glistening water snake, taking care not to go near any of my filthy corners. This snake didn't want to have anything to do with me, holding his breath and sticking out his chin as he moved along. He'd stop under Azza's window, take a deep breath, and repeat his oath—"Either I'll have you, or the Angel of Death will"—then he'd continue on his way to her father's store. Sheikh Muzahim never invited him to sit down, never reached out to turn over a cup and pour him some coffee, so Khalil always repeated his request for Azza's hand standing up, and he continued to do so even after he'd married Ramziya, Yabis' daughter. At times like that the signs of madness would show on Khalil's face: a deeply buried disfigurement rose to the surface along with an anger vicious enough to tear your insides apart. Have I mentioned that I was rather proud of this Khalil? No doubt every sensible head resting on my shoulders will despise me for that slip of the tongue. Let's just say he was the best at Action and Horror. His thirst for sadism certainly did make me uncomfortable, as did his noble descent and family history, and the way he identified with machines like the taxi he earned his living from part-time. In truth, it was a vehicle of deportation, and I felt as if he were draining me, the Lane of Many Heads. His withering looks left scars on my pride. Nevertheless in my mean old age I spend my nights feigning interest in his nostalgia, listening to him resurrect in obsessive-compulsive detail the legend of his father Nuri bin al-Hadrami, known to one and all as The Pilot because he was so very well-traveled. I'm supposed to listen enraptured while he goes on and on, staring at a photo of charming, sunny Nuri, gray adorning his jet-black locks. He went down in history as the first gentleman to bare his head in a public gathering. Every day, from afternoon prayer till midnight, he would hold court—as if a king—from the first-floor balcony of his large house, which was jam-packed with aunts, uncles, and grandparents, and look out over the Sanctuary complex amidst the spellbinding melodies of the famous Taher Catalog's endless oud playing. Mecca's men of note would pass by to greet him, or simply linger to listen to the jokes and hearty laughter that rained down from the balcony onto the Sanctuary. Nobles and common people alike would stay up half the night listening to his many stories about the magic of the Nile and its naiads, who dissolve pearls in flutes of champagne for their lovers to sip and light cigarettes rolled from green banknotes. His wild stories were shocking and they multiplied; passersby below would catch refreshing breaths of them, and they would drift through Qarara Hill and Shamiya Hill. The whole city fell under charming Nuri's spell. They followed his every move. Like how in the pilgrimage season, he'd uproot his entire family tree—branches, leaves, and all—and plant them on the roof while he rented out his castle to visiting pilgrims. That brought in enough to last him the whole year. That was until eventually charming Nuri was lost to the nymphs of the Nile for good. His only son failed to fulfill his dream of becoming a pilot, and poverty dragged Khalil and his sister unceremoniously from their balconies on affluent Qarara Hill all the way to where the Lane of Many Heads gave them refuge. My arms are always spread wide to accommodate the dregs of reputable families who have fallen on hard times.

Even Nasser was captivated by this complicated personality. There he was, up all night, out in my coffee shops, rummaging through his files on Khalil.

Not even a few loose stones in a crumbling wall in one of my corners escaped his attention. My throat constricted, I darkened my winding alleys in the hope of spitting him out. The cafe had closed, leaving Nasser seated with a cup of tea—three sugars—going cold in front of him. We were long past midnight. He finally got up and headed toward his car.

As he passed in front of Imam Dawoud's house, something happened that was beyond my control. A body burst out of the darkness and crashed into Nasser, who sensed fleetingly a mocking hiss before he fell to the ground. In the second it took him to get back to his feet he made out the body of a monster torn out of black with a large square mud-colored head. He heard it roar and watched as it shoved the Imam's door open and disappeared inside. Nasser rushed to follow when a cry for help rang out: "Someone broke into the Imam's house and kissed Sa'diya on the mouth while she was asleep in bed next to her brothers and sisters!" Nasser couldn't believe his ears and started knocking angrily, but the hubbub died down straight away. He could sense Imam Dawoud was irritated when he opened the door. He yawned and eyed Nasser sleepily.

"Are you all okay? Did someone break in?" The words died in Nasser's throat.

"Faith is our fortress," replied Dawoud. From where he was standing in the doorway, Nasser could sense Sa'diya lying stunned in her bed inside, licking her bloody lips. He was dying to push the door open and inspect the room, but the Imam's beatific face obliged him to withdraw. It made him wonder to himself if perhaps he'd imagined the whole thing.

The next thing that caught his attention was Aisha's front door, which was ajar. It creaked as he pushed it open and slipped into the corridor. The dark was like lumps of coal. He took out his lighter and proceeded carefully, his shadow, tall against the damp, cracked walls, following closely behind him. A faint snapping sound led him to a spot at the bottom of the stairs, and suddenly his foot sank into something soft, terrifying him even more. He bent down with his lighter, and there before him in the meager spotlight lay the coal-black body with the brown square head, the twisted grimace, and the popping eyes. Nasser's hand trembled and the lighter fell to the ground, ricocheting off into the darkness. He cursed himself for being such a coward and knelt down to feel about for it on the floor. The feeling of silky fabric in his hands filled him with revulsion, but he finally managed to find his lighter and light it. He leaned down closer to examine the body. It was just an old, stretched-out abaya topped with a hideous mask. The thick lips were still wet with Sa'diya's blood. A forged ghoul, and right at Nasser's feet. He was certain it was a message meant for him. But who was it who was trying to scare him off with these threatening messages?

He couldn't bring himself to touch the ghoul on the floor; he was still trembling. Something inside him told him he was face to face with Aisha's ghost.

"That's Aisha's ghost!"

Nasser jumped in terror. The voice cutting through the darkness had broadcast his fear out loud. It was Mu'az, standing in the shadows, watching and sniggering. Nasser wanted to break his neck, but he was frozen, like an idiot, to the spot where he knelt on the ground. "Don't let it frighten you," teased Mu'az, "it's just a ghost from our childhood. Every kid in the Lane knows the Veil Monster." Nasser felt like a fool for falling for the trick.

"But it crashed into me . . . Are you sure it wasn't you playing a trick on me with this Veil Monster?"

"I wouldn't dare," Mu'az replied. "And anyway, it's a game that mothers and grandmothers play. To be honest, it still scares me. It's just a silly, childish game, but somehow it manages to arouse the devil in us."

"But it was really there; I saw it running down the alley to your house. It must have been you."

"I swear on the Quran it wasn't me." He lost his smirk. "It must've been that thing," he added, gesturing to the heap on the floor in the corridor. "Someone must've been here, waking up the Veil Monster." His voice trembled. He came into view standing by the staircase, carrying a candle that threw their shadows leaping toward the great heavy door as if rushing to escape. The smell of burned meat took hold of their senses and the walls of the corridor.

"You don't think—" Nasser was silent. "If Aisha has indeed run away, why would she draw attention to herself with a game like this?" He was more interested in quelling his own doubts than those of Mu'az. "Who could it be?"

"Well, that's hard to say, but the only person around here who's known for playing dress-up games like that is Khalil—" The absurdity of his own idea took him by surprise. "But he's never shown any interest in Aisha. Not in a woman with that kind of intellect . . ."

"Well what is this Veil Monster then?!"

"It's a ghoul made of masks, or face-veils. Our mothers play the Veil Monster trick on us whenever we act up." He stood examining the features of the mask, which were scrawled in coarse coal, as if it were a face that had burnt to a crisp, black and gauzy with fresh blood on torn lips.

So there they were, all of these heads bursting with apprehensions and suspicions—those of Mu'az and Nasser, for example—and they were completely out of my control.

Nasser summoned Khalil for interrogation. On the day, however, Nasser clean forgot and left Khalil the pilot waiting outside his office while he rifled, utterly engrossed, through Aisha's letters, looking for any mention of the Veil Monster.

From: Aisha
Subject: Message 10

I asked you to grant me some faraway corner of yourself.

The corner shouldn't be a cellar, or a storeroom on the roof even. It should be more like a treehouse in a forgotten backyard, where you hid out as a child and pretended to be a pirate or an angel of revelation, where you hid your possessions, your little anxieties, your adventure comics.

I hole up in there with you, and we spy through the bathroom windows of the surrounding buildings at the girls bathing directly across from the green almond tree with its round birds' nests that fall to the ground every morning to wipe away the Lane of Many Heads' fatigue . . . When a girl is washing herself, she will often pause for a moment, rooted to the spot, and stare into a golden mote, imagining a book, a man's faraway hand, or that of an angel, or God even . . . Then she plunges herself beneath the fast-flowing stream. Or she scribbles a few words on paper in ink whose sighs bleed under the water pressure, their intimacy washing away. . . As unsuitable as ink might be for writing in water, it's perfect for writing about the deepest secrets and sins and caresses . . .

A nest of straw, no more . . . With you.
Aisha

P.S. I had a dream. This isn't me speaking, it's the voice of **the Veil Monster**, the Lane of Many Heads that's forced its way into my mind. It was a silvery night, and I was crawling toward the darkened hallway, feeling my way along, led by the sound of muffled laughter from a spot at the bottom of the stairs. My mother and grandmother were there, squatting on the ground, flattening out a brown paper grocery bag between them, cackling wickedly as they slashed the shape of the Veil Monster's hideous features onto it with a fat charcoal crayon. From my hiding place I could hear its flesh tearing, and the black abaya being eaten away by its own gluttony to the point that it was worn and frayed; the mouth was bared in shrieking anger. Topped off with that growling voice, it was the picture of torment. Suddenly, the Veil Monster was looking directly into my eyes, and then crawling toward me, its voice squeaking. I fled, but its strangled voice was licking my body, and it was only then that I realized I was naked.

With its rasping voice, it caught me at the door to my cubbyhole, where any resistance I possessed left me, and I froze like a bare tree stump. The Veil Monster was bearing down on me; it wanted to **drink** my blood. Then my auntie Halima appeared, pretending she'd come to protect me, but she let it grab my leg, here, then my hand. Something hot and wet made my leg slippery, and the Veil Monster couldn't manage to drag me away; I'd peed myself.

I was woken by your index finger on my spine.

The leg that the Veil Monster had taken hold of stayed numb for a whole week. The parts in that play had been masterfully shared out between my mother, grandmother, and Aunt Halima. In the course of it, they left behind fragments of our hearts broken off by the Veil Monster so they could be certain we'd be tamed. Having watched the Veil Monster being created didn't lessen the terror he provoked in us in any way: he had only to make the slightest movement for a satanic spirit to rear its head within me, more frightening than my mother and grandmother could have calculated.

I think it's the Lane of Many Heads transforming himself into a fearsome creature to keep us under control, and I don't think we'll ever be strong enough to tear off his masks.

The Veil Monster is the embodiment of a repressive urge hidden inside the women of the Lane of Many Heads, a chain of docility passed on from mother to daughter.

Do you think that's what sharpens and guides Azza's charcoal when she draws? Or is it her passion?

Azza has never taken fear seriously. Even love is just a flickering flame for her. "Why would you expect love to last forever? It's just a feeling like any other feeling. Do you expect fear or upset or anger or sadness to last? They're all temporary. They only come so they can go away again."

For Azza, love has always been more like flu than cancer, so she flutters from heart to heart, reveling in the fever of constantly falling in love and always emerging from it lighter in heart and soul, ready to take on another, more highly evolved virus. She doesn't face life or men with grim seriousness.

If only you knew how much fun it was to be around Azza! It's like being in a patch of **sunshine that never dries up,** like being in an endless painting.

Still, I pity those consumed by cancerous love for her, like Yusuf!

Nasser was choked up with anger at Aisha. He couldn't quite put his finger on the reason, but he felt a malicious satisfaction that she'd nicknamed the Lane of Many Heads "the Veil Monster."

When Nasser finally permitted Khalil to enter, the fortysomething threw himself nonchalantly onto a chair and relaxed into it, leaving Nasser to read his body language. His shiny black leather shoes clashed loudly with his bright white leper's socks. His features were elongated; his eyes and mouth were rectangular and uniform, and his cropped-looking ears stuck out like airplane wings. Khalil didn't let Nasser finish looking him over, but began abruptly:

"My father continued to cover our expenses for years, even after I graduated from the Aviation Academy in Miami. He only cut us off after that Egyptian wife of his had a baby." Suddenly Nasser's suspicions about Khalil being the Veil Monster who'd escaped down Aisha's corridor fell apart.

"And the fire that burnt down your house in the Lane of Many Heads—was it really caused by faulty wiring?"

"Oh yeah, thanks again for your efforts," he drawled. "You and the firemen whose truck got stuck at the entrance to the alley and didn't get anywhere near the fire at all." The same devil goaded him to go further still: "You're in the middle of an ocean of drug dealers and illegal migrants, fires that happen over and over, sewage floods, overcrowded, crumbling buildings that collapse here and there. The police and the fire department are a joke. Your emergency vehicles can't even get down the Lane of Many Heads because there's no suitable road, and now all you want to know about is a body? This neighborhood desperately needs an enema to be followed by several microsurgeries."

Nasser met his insolence with a question. "Do you realize that you've made a lot of people in the neighborhood feel very uneasy recently?"

"That's to be expected. This place is in one time zone and I'm in another," he said, gesturing upward.

"So then what's keeping you here in an alleyway in the underbelly of the world?"

"It's temporary . . ." A drop of sweat formed on Khalil's temple. If the detective had asked him "How long is temporary?" he wouldn't have known what to say.

Nasser didn't think Khalil was giving away his real age. There wasn't a single gray hair spoiling his youthful appearance. "I hear Saudi Airlines decided they could do get by without your services. Something to do with you hitting a female flight attendant?" The sweat on Khalil's temples trembled, and he could feel the heroin, which had destroyed his dreams and ambitions and driven his life to the brink, flowing through his veins. He'd put too much faith in the brakes and in the autopilot inside himself. That day was the first time he'd flown without waiting for two days to let his system clear itself after a fix; he was still strung out six hours before takeoff. Everybody who looked at his eyes and dilated pupils during that flight could see that he'd crossed the red line.

"You can't mess around with the chain of command onboard a plane. A plane is like a kingdom in the air. The pilot is the king, and everyone else is a subject who must obey him blindly from the moment the plane doors are shut until they're reopened after landing. If anyone has any kind of objection, they have to present it in writing to the authorities after the flight because arguing with a pilot while airborne is a capital offense . . ." He didn't want to mention what it was that had made him lose his better judgment on that flight just yet. Was it that the Turkish flight attendant had rebuffed him or that she'd upgraded that passenger to first-class without first checking with her supervisor? How was he supposed to know that that cursed Turkish woman with the faded eyes was one of Satan's demons herself? With a single swipe of her paw, she knocked twenty years of service off his personnel file.

Nasser seized the opportunity presented by the glimmer of arrogant lunacy in Khalil's eyes to catch him off guard: "And Yusuf, what's your connection to him?"

Khalil exhaled derisively. "Yusuf comes from the time before Abbas ibn Firnas and the Wright Brothers. In the century he's from they haven't even discovered flight yet . . ." A note of malicious satisfaction in his voice left question marks in the air.

"Do you think he has anything to do with the body?"

"Don't implicate me in other people's accusations; I fear God . . ."

Nasser wanted to be reckless, to give in to the rumors and search the trunk of Khalil's taxi for the disguises the whole neighborhood was gossiping about.

"What about Mushabbab?"

"Myth."

"A myth?"

"This whole web of tiny alleyways is built on myths."

Nasser was still waiting for an answer. He was well aware that Khalil was trying to distract him with that generalization.

"So you're married to Yabis the sewage cleaner's daughter, and yet they say you proposed to Azza recently but were refused?"

"Have you got a problem with that?"

At that moment, Nasser caught sight of the madness that the neighborhood folks whispered about. Khalil retreated in the face of the detective's attack, guarding himself with sarcasm. "The old man's lost it. He believes in myths too. He told me not to ask for Azza's hand during times of bad omen: I'm not allowed to propose to her in the month of Muharram, when bloodshed is forbidden, or in Safar, when it's said that provisions are scarce, or in First or Second Jumada, during which our fortunes are fixed and unchanging, or in Ramadan because, as you know . . ." He winked at the detective. "Threads of piety and threads of desire woven together to make a web. I'm also supposed to refrain from asking for her hand in the months of Shawwal and Rajab, and abstain in Dhu'l-Qada, and then the old man goes on Hajj in Dhu'l-Hijja . . . What about you, Mr. Detective? You married? Or are you just planning to fast for eternity? Your breakfast's on me: dates, halva, Turkish delight, Egyptian bonbons . . ."

Veil Monster versus Siren Man

NASSER LAY IN BED, SOMEWHERE BETWEEN SLEEP AND WAKEFULNESS. THE LANE of Many Heads' unending, day-and-night torrent of odors and chaos assaulted his every sense, getting back at him for taking Aisha's side and accusing The Lane of Many Heads of being The Veil Monster.

Whenever Detective Nasser appeared, they shouted: "The siren man is here!"

Naked, barefoot, and with dusty snotty faces, the children flocked around his official Land Rover. The rotating, flashing light on the roof was still on. Nasser left it on deliberately so that it would point its accusatory red finger all across the entrance to the alley. The ice-seller came running after him, begging him to move the vehicle just a little so that the indictment wouldn't completely hide his fridge from the cars passing by in the fast lane. The children, meanwhile, ignored him and clambered up to the roof to turn their faces blood-red in the light, or sat on the hood tickling their cheeks with the windscreen wipers, leaving scratches across the Land Rover's brilliant shine.

Half asleep, Nasser could hear the voice mocking him: "Officer, you're up to your eyeballs in pages and pages of the Lane's faked memories. They're luring you into that memory, and then they shut their eyes and stop up their ears to trap you inside the nightmare nesting in their heads. They aren't even memories; they're a counterattack against a disappointing reality . . ."

Some of Yusuf's phrases that he'd read that morning floated around in his mind:

March 3, 1995

Do you think we've sinned against the revelation that made its home in Mecca, the revelation whose battlefields and great men we're reducing to mere legend by erasing every physical trace leading back to them?

Hulagu Khan drowned the works of generations of scholars and thinkers in the Tigris so as to destroy the legacy of the Abbasid Dynasty and before them the Umayyads.

And here, nothing remains of the Well of Zamzam now but a row of pipes and taps—who knows where the water actually comes from. A mere quarter-century ago, the froth of longevity and blessings used to drip directly from the bucket of the well into the hands of the nation of Muhammad. These days God's gift, the water of Zamzam, is being sold. There's no froth left any more. We're up against risk factors like high cholesterol and premature death and we take anti-depressants to treat our delusions.

Delusion 1: We used to think of the nation of Muhammad in a vague sort of way as something like a tall, alluring servant girl who lived in the desert and suckled all of humanity's children from her vast breasts. She could never die because everyone we knew prayed to God every day for her longevity.

Nasser buried his head fast under his pillow, rubbing it against the sleeve of the robe he'd found and promptly hidden as if it were the limb of some woman he'd murdered. He didn't want to return to her, but her scent filled the air. The robe with the missing sleeve appeared before him, called out to him to come. Detective Nasser al-Qahtani was trembling as he followed the scent, which pushed him toward the sleeve between the lines of Aisha's writings. Lately his sleep had become fitful and troubled. He'd wake up and immediately begin recording every suspicious item in Aisha's letters, marking a red *X* at every explosive spot and copying out some of the phrases that particularly took his fancy so he could carry them around with him and reread her secrets wherever he was. He felt like every word concealed some transgression or temptation, the silhouette of a man. By her own account, "getting caught with a book was like getting caught hiding a man inside your school notebook." Nasser searched for that man's face, wondering if it resembled his own and wondering: how many men had she hidden so they could enjoy that scent in solitude?

As soon as he'd woken from a night of troubled sleep, he picked up another of Aisha's letters, and once he'd drunk its scent he added it to the pile of letters he'd read through next to his bed. He leapt out of bed—the damp morning air free to view his naked body, the air conditioner free to attack it. He was aware, for the first time, of his own body as he strutted about before the world in lazy arrogance. He liked the way it felt when his legs rubbed against the stove as he made himself a cup of instant coffee. Then he got back into bed, his mind preoccupied, and reread the same letter for the tenth time. He picked up a red pen, and after a moment's hesitation, scribbled a title across the top of Aisha's letter:

Women in Love

From: Aisha
Subject: Message 6

There are things that guide me to discover them.

That book I'd forgotten about . . . When? Since my first year at the Teachers' College. Stuffed in a nook under the stairs for years.

My friend Leila had curves like creamy condensed milk. She stuck out her lips like a bird's beak when she spoke; her voice was hoarse, but tinged with laughter, and she loved stealing glances. She'd smuggled the book out. She said she'd found it waiting for her in the corridor where it had fallen out of one of her uncle's moving boxes. He was the director of Mecca's famous Falah schools, and ordinarily his office was out of bounds to all. He was planning to bequeath it to his male offspring once his long life was over.

"Do you want it or should we bury it?" she said. That was how the book's destiny became tied to my own.

Leila and I both risked expulsion: getting caught with a book was like getting caught hiding a man inside your school notebook. I tucked it beneath my buxom chest, where the gray expanse of my school pinafore concealed it easily, and I yanked my abaya down slightly. That was a signal agreed on between the girls that meant your clothes were stained with period blood.

Leila and I were like two bats. We spent the day in the bathroom reading the first lines. I came across the words "Lawrence ran away to Germany with his female tutor." The words pricked me somewhere deep in my insides, and we both averted our eyes. A single word more would've stopped our hearts and given us away.

Of all the books she'd smuggled out, this one seemed most like a sinful time bomb.

Returning home with the book would have been suicide. I crept in, and without even looking at it I stuffed it into that hole under the stairs to the right of the door. It's been there all these years. It was only tonight that the rain brought it out, wet around the edges, pages yellowed, binding falling apart. It still had the same sting of fear and awe, though . . .

Leila and I didn't even read the title. I just imprinted the cover image onto my memory: those long red stockings and the woman wearing them, a bundle of sketchbooks tucked under her arm.

That's how you saw me, ^: leaving the hospital wearing your long red socks and thereby fulfilling my legs' oldest dream . . .

Women in Love . . . Can you believe they were lying stuffed under the stairs—right under the nose of my mother, father, and Ahmad—and in love, too? Of all the books I managed to get my hands on and dared to read, this book (which I'd have preferred to call *Women in Love* in the Arabic translation rather than *Lady Lovers*) terrified me: from the moment I set eyes on those red stockings I knew that I was risking a lot—perhaps even my life. Do you understand why? One woman becomes two becomes three. Like rain. Drops of women in a downpour of love, like the battery acid that jealous men hurl at the women they love in the short items in the newspaper.

Today, I'm grateful for the innate prudence that made me understand, even at that young age, that I needed to bury *Women in Love* in that nook under the stairs.

Now it's popping back up.

Good Lord, did you notice? That English writer's name reveals your name, ^. Can these little voices, which lead us suddenly and unexpectedly to detours and forgotten secrets, really give us away like that?

My body has suddenly started to tremble. Does it seem logical that the mere sight of a book should be able to slough off our scales? This book is scrubbing the prints off of the tips of my fingers so that they're ready to be replaced with others. The book is chopping time up into cycles that spin me round like a cement mixer.

I'm lost to the mystery—do you see what little sense any of this makes?

Are you bored yet?

One time I caught the Eunuchs' Goat sneaking a **mannequin** into the backyard of his father's kitchen. I was shocked. Not because of whatever he might be about to do with the mannequin, but because the plastic doll reminded me of me in my **wedding dress**. It reminded me of how Ahmad had carried me as if he were shouldering a bundle of firewood. If you ask me, these mannequins are invading the neighborhood, possessing our bodies, sowing tumors in men's imaginations.

I know that you can't decipher Arabic letters yet, ^. It all looks like a painting to you. You still write to me in a mixture of pictures and English words. I sit on my over-the-top bed and allow the Aisha beneath my skin to pop her head out and flirt with you in a way that surprises even me—but she doesn't pay any attention to me. She just flows on automatically, ready for you to receive her on your screen. And when I make you lose your cool, and the German words sigh out of you, I receive them with my body. I let them crush my ribs in their embrace, bite my chin and the edge of my cheeks, bore into my skull to reach the pressing need inside . . .

I don't know where all these violent temptations are coming from. I don't want D. H. Lawrence's loving women to steal your heart. I could become even blacker and more violent, because wherever I look in Lawrence's analysis of love, I find the words *blackness* and *black truth*.

What's with all this **blackness**? Is this me? On top of all these red lines which surround the black smear of my abaya?

I don't know when they started coming to me in the alley with all these life-maps, demanding to bury them in my head as if I were a memory dumping-ground. Even I forget that they've come . . . And who were they anyway? Was it the anesthesia from the series of operations I had that left these sunspots in my memory? Who was just here? All I can hear is Mu'az singing in the corridor, and even that sounds like the echo of a memory someone left behind.

"They want to undo the collars of death around my neck with their tragedies."

Release the weight against my neck and disappear. I can feel the cartilage in my neck weakening and snapping and pressing down on my spinal cord. Maybe I shouldn't listen! I want to have fun with you, be entertaining. I want to tell light-hearted, trivial stories. You, on the other hand, want me to write long letters like my rigid old self used to do. My body's my dictionary now, a dictionary of much more than language and phonetics: a dictionary of this delicious laziness, of all my new discoveries . . . With every movement I discover another **forgotten** part of my body, with every action I shed another husk of fear and another layer of material . . .

The game of masks is over now.

P.S. Me too . . . I'm also as light as a ghost.

Piece by piece, we die after those we love.

P.P.S. I dreamt of a newborn baby, its umbilical cord still intact, with the following dedication written on its forehead:

To the tiny child who entered the world and left it in a violent **termination** . . .

It came and went quietly, no one heard the womb tearing or the umbilical cord being cut.

We neither repudiated it nor did we give it a name . . .

P.P.P.S:

'Do I look ugly?' she said.

And she blew her nose again.

A small smile came round his eyes.

'No,' he said, 'fortunately.'

And he went across to her, and gathered her like a belonging in his arms. She was so tenderly beautiful, he could not bear to see her [. . .] Now; washed all clean by her tears, she was new [. . .] made perfect by inner light [. . .]

But the passion of gratitude with which he received her into his soul, the extreme, unthinkable gladness of knowing himself living and fit to unite with her, he, who was so nearly dead, who was so near to being gone with the rest of his race down the slope of mechanical death, could never be understood by her. He worshipped her as age worships youth, he gloried in her, because, in his one grain of faith, he was young as she, he was her proper mate. [. . .]

Even when he said, whispering with truth, 'I love you, I love you,' it was not the real truth. It was something beyond love, such a gladness of having surpassed oneself, of having **transcended the old existence**. *How could he say "I" when he was something new* *and unknown, not himself at all? This I, this old formula of the age, was a dead letter. [. . .]*

[T]here was no I and you, there was only the [. . .] consummation of my being and of her being in a new one, a new, paradisal unit regained from the duality.

(D. H. Lawrence, *Women in Love*)

I sit down to pray and my heart dives . . . into deepest sleep to re-emerge, reciting. I can hear you reading Lawrence's words to me.

I return to bed, where I speak to God so that I don't forget how to speak. Yesterday's dream hovers around the edges of every word.

Between consciousness and dreaming, I'm rocked gently by your call, ^. If I lean a little too far, I'll fall back into yesterday.

With the same sense of surprise.

As long as I don't turn the lights on, the room will hold its breath and remain in yesterday's labor pains. Only the clock tells me when it's daybreak.

I leave my cubbyhole sunk in the delusion of night and savor *Women in Love* like the taste of coffee mixing with my saliva. Strong nicotine making my hands tremble.

I shine the intimate yellow light of my wobbly lamp on the page and drink the words along with their pallid background. It increases my thirst.

Do we cease to see when love calls on us to come out of ourselves? On the route between the I and the Other, is there some moment of blindness that you can occasionally pass through, but that occasionally stays with you, obliterating the whole universe around us?

One sees and the other is **blind**; is that how love is put together?

I speak out loud now to reassure the picture I took of myself with my cellphone: "I never said that Ahmad didn't love me!"

The picture refuses to respond, however.

Maybe running away is love; even hate can be love . . . But I didn't flee, I didn't hate, did I?

I guess that means that my send and receive function is faulty when it comes to love.

When we renounce words, we shouldn't complain that our interiors shatter into perplexing, repellent stutters.

Maybe we need to train our words to be tender, to flow like water and sink like perfume into the body of an idol; maybe we ought to be born equipped with a dictionary for the words of worship . . . I don't know . . .

Attachment: A photo of the cubbyhole where I sleep.

My bedroom. We call it the cubbyhole because it's between two floors, carved out like a tomb cut into the space of the dark room below. It weighs down on my chest. The house is just two rooms stacked one on top of the other, with my room in between. The upstairs room was where we slept as a family; downstairs was where my father sat and gave his private lessons.

As you can see, there's no room in the cubbyhole for a lover. Nevertheless I keep you crammed in here, in the empty space in my head. I stuff you under my fingernails, so I can slip you past them and smell you from time to time, like the body's first, strongest scent.

Aisha

When Nasser reached Aisha's signature, he picked up a pen and paper and wrote down the name Ahmad. He repeated it in a long line and underlined it twice. "Another man in Aisha's life. Let's see where he fits into the puzzle of the Lane of Many Heads." He ignored Birkin's belief that there was "a gladness of having surpassed oneself, of having transcended the old existence" in taking the love of a woman to its furthest end. The sentiment irritated him. It set off warning signals in his head. It condemned his existence, which was beyond just "old." It was the threadbare existence of someone who'd never experienced the kind of stormy exchange with another person that Aisha searched for in books and in real life, across an ocean, from Germany to a forgotten alley like the Lane of Many Heads. He put off facing up to that thought for some other time.

X-Rays

THE SHOPS THE LENGTH OF GATE LANE WERE OPENING UP, AND THE MUNICIPALITY workers were sweeping the gutters, making the most of the relative quiet to gather up the plastic bags and empty soda bottles littering the road. Nasser stood watching. Their fortitude seemed like a provocation. Faced with those mountains of trash, he would have lost his mind a long time ago, but they just carried on, earning only the meagerest salaries, shielding their heads from the Meccan sun that turned their uniforms to dust. They were there at their positions every morning, their patience solidifying with each movement until it became a layer that protected them from anything that might happen.

Nasser laughed at the sight of the one worker who was using gloves and a gigantic claw grabber to pick up the trash while his colleagues worked with their bare hands. He turned and stepped into the tiny Studio Modern, surprising Mu'az, who had just opened the place and was polishing the front window. Mu'az tucked the cloth away and drew down the wooden counter, placing a barrier between himself and the detective.

"You and I need to sit and talk a few things over," said Nasser. Being a photographer had landed the young man firmly within the circle of suspicion. The detective had stumbled across a crumpled photo of the dead woman: a high-angle shot, taken from a rooftop through the lens of the imam's son, whose photographic talents aroused whispers in the Lane of Many Heads (they were careful, however, never to let these whispers get back to his father the imam, so as not to endanger the boy's chances in that profession in the future).

"I didn't want to call you in to the precinct this time. I just want to have a friendly chat." Alarm flashed in Mu'az's eyes. He led Nasser into the studio, where a backcloth painted as a forest scene covered an entire wall, and showed him to a seat directly beneath a waterfall. He left the door open so he could keep an eye on the shop entrance.

"You're a bright young guy—" At that opening, Mu'az folded his arms in front of him and hugged his body. Nasser clocked the defensive reaction but pressed on. "The people in the neighborhood say that you take sneaky pictures of the alley from a window halfway up the stairs of the minaret. Am I right in thinking that you're the only one who has access to a view of the alley from above?"

Mu'az hurried to correct the detective. "I don't take pictures from above, I take pictures from within. The Lane of Many Heads has never taken me seriously enough to hide its secrets from me. Do you know what memorizing the Quran did to me? It's like I swallowed a powerful flash that never goes off. It lights up everything I look at. I had this internal camera long before I knew anything about photography. And by the way, if my father knew what we were talking about, he'd throw me off the top of the minaret and you'd have another crime on your hands."

Nasser replied with a short, forced laugh, giving Mu'az a little room to relax so he could study his features more closely. His body was bunched up like a ball. He wore threadbare trousers and his hair was tucked into his scarf. He was a photomontage of modernity and ancient misery. Nasser glanced down at Mu'az's feet and his huge Chinese-made imitation Nike sneakers, then raised his eyes once again to Mu'az's dark face pierced only by the glimmer of his eyes. Mu'az was visibly uncomfortable under Nasser's gaze. Nasser aimed his next question.

"What do you know about Azza?" Nasser could see he'd hit his target: he was well acquainted with that involuntary twitch of the eyelashes that meant the person being questioned was hiding something. Mu'az stared at Nasser's face: it was predatory, like the face of one of those falcons trained to hunt bustards. The unexpected response exploded in Nasser's face:

"Azza was like a time bomb in the Lane of Many Heads." The exchange of fire eased the tensions between them. Mu'az spread his palms on his knees, and silence fell. The sounds of that morning were still streaming through Mu'az's head. He had dozed off, sitting by the window on the stairs inside the minaret, and was awoken by a loud thud, which he was now certain was the sound of the body hitting the ground. He didn't open his eyes for a little while, however, not until he heard the sound of hurrying, frightened footsteps, almost inaudible, because the alley was sucking them up like a sponge. He thought they were part of a dream at first—yet his keen hearing, even from that height, could sense their fear. By the time he opened his eyes, it was too late: he only just glimpsed the black Cadillac at the head of the alley, a small foot poking out from a hem before it disappeared into the back seat, the head of the black driver covered with a spotted scarf, as he leaned down, closing the door behind her, before the car sped away and the noise of the engine receded into the distance. Whose foot was it? He didn't know.

The hound sensed these images whirling around in Mu'az's head and broke in, "You think she's the victim?" No sooner had he asked the question than Nasser sensed the pungent smell of denial radiating from Mu'az's body.

"I don't know," he said. "Her face was totally smashed up. My lens had never captured anything so hideous. Beneath her veil, Azza had a golden face that dazzled anyone who saw it; you know the sweet scent of paradise that they say the true believers can smell? Azza went places they didn't want her to go to."

Detective Nasser was really no different from the street cleaners outside; he had to rake through all these layers of rotten deceit, tossing bones to his hound to chew on, until he arrived at the truth.

"So you're sure you didn't see anything suspicious? A strange person hanging around? A thief that could have snuck into one of the two houses?" A chill emanated from the studio walls.

"All I heard was a loud noise," said Mu'az. "But I didn't look. It never occurred to me that someone could strip a person naked and throw them down into the street like that."

"You said you've memorized the Quran . . ."

Mu'az nodded. The threat implicit in the detective's question hadn't escaped him.

"You're not doing anyone any good by hiding information, you know. You might be helping a murderer walk free when that girl's lying dead in the morgue," Nasser warned. "I'm told you also work for Aisha the schoolteacher? Is there anything you want to tell me about that?"

Mu'az was terrified that the finger of suspicion might suddenly turn to point at him. "No, no, don't accuse me of covering something up. I'm a hard worker, Detective. My father sent me to help the schoolteacher out after she came back from Germany. I used to run errands for her once a week and sweep the hallway. A week before the body, she told me to stop coming because she was leaving the Lane of Many Heads to move in with one of her relatives."

"Did you see her leave?" asked the detective.

"Aisha?" Mu'az snorted. "She might be the only person who could never leave. Detective, Aisha lives behind her computer screen in a world of images like me. When I worked for her I got used to hearing that same sound from my spot in the corridor. I'd stop sweeping when I heard her tapping the keys on that old computer of hers. Actually, to be honest, I got addicted to that sound. It sounded like it was coming from some incomprehensible faraway world. Often, the clicking would come thick and fast with no intervals whatsoever, so I'd hold my breath and try to move gingerly and quietly so I wouldn't disturb her reverie. Her fingers would chase one another to a world where she'd withdraw into nothingness, so much so that I'd risk creeping up the stairs and even sneaking a look at that unearthly creature with her back turned to the door of her cubbyhole. Her hair shone with an ethereal blue light. It was twisted into a bun, always messy and listing to the right, toward the door, with a pencil stuck through it to stop it coming undone. I never felt uncomfortable nor did I restrain myself; I just stared at God's exquisite creation, draped atop that neck. I'd follow the nape of her neck, which was craned forward, looking for some weakness in the curvature the crash had left her with. But there's nothing weak about it, in fact it's more like a miracle. I envy her; I wish I could run my finger over my lens shutter at that speed. I wish I could photograph worlds like the one I could hear in her fingers tapping on the keyboard."

The hound began to salivate, but Nasser's mouth went dry at the cipher. "There you go," Mu'az continued. "I've laid out everything I know for you, like a film that burns up when exposed to light."

Nasser felt vindicated in his decision to lure Mu'az out of the Lane of Many

Heads; he felt like that trickster of an alleyway was urging them all to mislead him. Mu'az continued, revealing yet more: "You should charge me, or understand how weak I was in the face of that *being*—I don't want to call her a woman. She's a feminine miracle just in herself . . . I could never do harm to such a symbol . . . Can you imagine? She—out of all the women in the Lane of Many Heads—saved herself and made it out. I try to figure out what's stored in her memory. The worlds she must have seen to set her fingers loose on the keyboard with such—" He paused, searching for the right description: "lust." His mind offered nothing but the image of one of the springs in Paradise. "Aisha's fingers are the spring of Salsabil, flowing over the keys, setting her apart from the rest of the lane's lifeless living. Do you know the Verse of Light? That verse, from the Chapter of the Cow, lives in my heart. Aisha was lucky enough to be cast from the energy of pure light. I line my little sisters up, one after the other, with their skinny bodies and their wrapped hair, like links in a chain. Try to understand me . . . Understand what my life's been like. I'm a self-made man. I taught myself photography. I memorized the Quran. I earn the money I need to support the children of the imam, who doesn't believe in birth control."

The detective stood up suddenly, and as though he'd been sleepwalking, he saw the world Mu'az inhabited, took note, and left. He wouldn't be returning to him as a potential suspect.

Nasser went back to some of Yusuf's articles, which spanned two years. He read an article by Yusuf on the unprecedented and simultaneous rises in expenditure in three sectors (real estate, psychiatry and cosmetic surgery, and livestock, specifically camels and goats) in which he tried to uncover the links between them. He noted how Yusuf compared—in red ink—the disparity between the value of his friend the Eunuchs' Goat and the market price for goats, which averaged as much as 160,000 riyals for a billy goat.

The detective rifled through, looking for mention of the kid Salih, known to all as the Eunuchs' Goat. At Imam Daoud's Quran memorization classes, the children had sat in a circle bisected by a blue curtain, the girls on one side and the boys on the other. The sweet little boy had fallen in love with the round protrusion in the curtain where the girl Sa'diya's elbow poked through. He'd spent many evenings breathing in the smoke of his father's cooking and the smoke of their ridicule for being head over heels for a girl's elbow. Salih was tied to an invisible rope that ran between al-Ashi's kitchen and the mosque to keep him from going out to the main road and falling into the hands of the immigration police.

A Window for Azza

August 16, 2005

It's summer, you see, when everything around us dies. The Lane of Many Heads flops limply like a salted fish laid out in the sun to dry, and our burning hearts, desperate to escape the putrid stagnation, eat away at us.

Every summer I spend with you, Azza, brings such a conflict. The days stretch and my patience shrinks; I can't stand you being hidden away from me, I can't stand all these Meccan windows shutting in my face. When night comes, I happily tear off my clothes, knowing that I'm peeling away the barriers between us. That is, if you too shed your layers.

Our constant complaints had driven Mushabbab crazy so he decided to test us: "What are your greatest fears?" he asked. "Lay them out on the rug in front of me and I'll squash them for you like bugs."

"The immigration police," said the Eunuchs' Goat, retching with sour fear at the thought. "The deportation truck with the bars over the windows . . . It paralyzes me. I'm trapped in the alley, and if I do leave, I'm blinded by visions of plainclothes immigration police. At every bend in the road I expect them to pounce and drag me away. Where would they send me? Me, the one whose umbilical cord they cut in the dirt in the yard outside the kitchen, nameless, voiceless; I only learned to speak as an adolescent. Will I live and die without ever leaving the Lane of Many Heads?"

When it was my turn, the trump card I'd hoped for didn't materialize. When I posed that prying question to myself, I realized that I, Yusuf, am the source of my own fear. My thin body is possessed by Awaj ibn Anaq, the giant of legend from the time of Noah. I am chained to the distant past, but I move around on a spaceship. Everything around me is automated, but my mind belongs to legends and the time before.

Maybe my fossilized body needs a quick renovation.

It occurred to me to surprise him by turning the question back on him: "So, Mushabbab, what's your greatest fear?" But I chickened out. I knew Mushabbab was our axis: if he weakened or slipped, our entire circle would collapse.

It made perfect sense to us: no fear was so great that a woman's abaya couldn't fix it.

Mushabbab wrapped the Eunuchs' Goat up in it carefully and we all bundled into Khalil the Pilot's taxi. When we approached the checkpoint, Mushabbab instructed him to slump limply in the abaya. The indifference in the soldier's gesture as he waved us through sent tingles down the Goat's spine.

It was as if he'd turned feverish when he realized we'd crossed the sanctuary boundaries and were headed toward Jeddah, on the Red Sea coast. Tales of the mermaids there had burned holes in the imaginations of the young men in the Lane of Many Heads.

"The chicks in Jeddah, sweet lord. . ." We weren't going there to check out God's gifts, though. Mushabbab directed us along the ring road toward the old Jeddah airport.

The sun had risen by the time we got there. Stretching before us was an expanse half a kilometer wide, carpeted with men and women of all colors and races. The image of people assembled for the Day of Judgment came to mind.

"This is where everyone who wants to abandon the petroleum paradise flees to. Here in the open air is where workers take refuge when they're waiting to be picked up by the immigration police. It's the rapid delivery service back to the homeland," said Mushabbab.

"Some people wait a week or even a month before someone comes along and picks them up," added Khalil the Pilot. "Some even end up having to bribe soldiers to hurry the process along."

"One man's hell is another man's heaven."

Mushabbab's proverb was directed at the Eunuchs' Goat, who quickly asked, "You mean they don't round up the people without papers here in Jeddah?"

"Nah, they round up bribes: one to get you a residence permit and another to deport you. Right, out." Mushabbab gestured to the Goat to get out of the taxi. He left him there with those waiting people, while we stopped at a distance to observe.

The section editor at the *Umm al-Qura* newspaper had deliberately drawn a veil over that window onto the hell of deportation. "These 'windows' of yours are supposed to shine a light on Mecca. Not on the sea." Before tossing the draft article into the wastebasket, he took a thick black marker and crossed out the following section:

In the first few hours, the Eunuchs' Goat lost his ability to hear and speak. A flood of vehicles swept past in a flash; the humidity that clung to his nostrils prepped him for the question "What country?" With no homeland to be sent back to, he was sure he'd rot in detention.

A voice in the crowd kept repeating: "People who are forced to wait a long time get so hungry they eat their blankets!"

They were all telling their stories in broken Arabic that reeked of sour spices.

A Sri Lankan maid chattered non-stop about the lazy husband she'd been sending her wages home to for the last ten years, only to discover that he'd remarried and had children on her earnings. She was flying back home on the wings of a buraq to teach him a lesson.

He could barely fathom the Egyptian giant who'd left his waste disposal business and his shanty at the dump between al-Samir and al-Ajwad in East Jeddah in the hands of a relative, and come to turn himself in so that he'd be sent home for free to spend his holiday with his family. He claimed his first stop was going to be the sulfur baths in Helwan, where he'd scrub the layer of scabies off his body before going home and impregnating his wife with a son. This he'd follow with a new escape, courtesy of a pilgrim's visa, and return to reclaim his trash heap. Or rather his gold mine, which yielded him 500 riyals a day! The Egyptian was full of stories of his adventures against attempts to regulate international money transfers, the sums he'd smuggled across international borders through the black market using devilish tricks, the tower block he'd had built in the smart Cairo district of Heliopolis, his position as economic consultant to shady African trash-heap moguls.

He was being watched with great interest by a tear-streaming African face that told the story of a dying mother and his race back home against the Angel of Death.

An Indonesian offered strong competition with a photo display of the women who vied for his heart: dozens of faces plastered with lime, followed by eye shadow, and lips painted a garish red. They struggled fiercely to make it into the top four whom he'd marry as soon as he touched down in Jakarta, returning as a newly crowned emperor bearing the wealth of a year and a half in exile. Obviously, to him, ten thousand riyals was the wealth of Croesus.

The Eunuchs' Goat lost count of how many stories he swam through there.

As evening fell, the touch of a salty breeze reminded him he was alone. The crowds had all disappeared, though to where he had no idea, and their place had been taken by the smells of human urine and desperation, a pungent odor rising from behind the trunks of ornamental Washington palms, in the blueness of the Saudi Airlines office across the way and the continuously replenished ATM with a camera's eye to guard it.

The Eunuchs' Goat felt like the ATM screen was following him as it repeated cheerfully, "Welcome to this automated teller service."

Automated deportation service . . .

By midnight, his eyelids were drooping over a vast nothingness. He still didn't know what he would say his country of origin was if he were to be detained.

At dawn the calls to prayer flocked on the horizon. He needed to empty his bowels, but his feet wouldn't obey him. His entire being was tensed, erect, ready for the moment when the police vehicle and officers turned up. The moment of fear hung like a noose around his entire life. When it came, he might run, he might drop dead; the important thing was confronting that moment.

He didn't know whether Mushabbab was serious about leaving him there or whether he himself was serious about persevering.

At first light, he awoke to find the eyes and stories thronging around him anew. Yesterday's crowd had reappeared from nowhere and they seemed to be joined by a new body with every passing moment. The city dribbled fatigue and anticipation on them, drop after drop.

And that woman who kept nursing yellow water from a jerrycan, dozing and staring at him. At some point when the heat was at its fiercest, he imagined three women—blonde, raven-haired, and brunette—winking at him.

As the call to prayer rang out at noon, a bus with bars over its windows appeared, and the heaps of bodies suddenly pulsed with life. Conversations, jokes, complaints fell silent, and the mass surged toward the bus. The Goat's eyes were glued to the bars over the windows. He noticed that as the bodies jostled to get onto the bus, hands attached to khaki uniforms pushed them back, and then grasped banknotes held out by other sweaty hands, which they then allowed to board the bus. It was soon full, the tires compressing under their weight, and then it heaved away, covering the remaining faces with dust.

The fit that seized the Eunuchs' Goat left him bewildered; his body suddenly felt prepared and on edge—against what, he didn't know. Around him, crestfallen faces lamented their missed chance at freedom.

His heart opened up like a cave that had been blocked up for centuries; the deep shadows of fear dyeing its walls dissolved and oxygen flooded in. He felt he could breathe again. No sooner had the fire entered him than his longing for Sa'diya al-Habashiya the Imam's daughter became acute: hers was the only freedom he wished for any more.

He looked around him and still he couldn't see Mushabbab, so he walked boldly to the road, in a strange city without knowing where he was headed, and continued down it over the bridge, which led to Road 60, amid the car horns' shrieking. There, at the intersection, Khalil's taxi caught up with him. Mushabbab opened the door for him wordlessly.

"If my mother knew what you did to me, she'd turn the whole neighborhood on your heads! She'd boil you in kerosene, no joke." His mother Umm al-Sa'd's stocky build and features were an exact copy of those of her father the milkman whose photo hung in her room beneath the caved-in red ceiling—like a sword above the neck of anyone who entered. She even had a mustache just like his, which she plucked every morning with her decorated red tweezers.

"They say angina's the cool new birth control for 2005–2006." That snide comment was characteristic of Khalil.

Mushabbab interjected, "In her capacity as mother to a goat, your loving mother has proclaimed a period of mourning for a herd of camels that were poisoned in Wadi l-Dawasir, and what with the snare of the stock market and the hundreds of thousands of the best she-camels being poisoned by fodder from the silos in the south, her liquid assets have been wiped out. As you can see, your mother's busy with important things." We were saying the first inanities that popped into our heads to celebrate the occasion of the Goat's victory over his fear.

Disquiet

I, THE LANE OF MANY HEADS, APPEAR TO BE THE ONLY ONE PAYING ANY ATTENTION to Nasser's addiction. He's become a very regular customer at the cafe, where he sits for hours reading Aisha's emails. I personally never paid any attention to the schoolteacher's emails, which she always crammed full of revolting emotion. In fact I've never once bothered myself with a female opponent, since I know women were created simply to submit to the status quo, my vile status quo. But there were her words, spreading cancer-like from Nasser's head to my own.

FROM: Aisha
SUBJECT: Message 7

Did you notice I called you "sir" at the end of our conversation today?

I never knew my own father's name; my mother always called him "sir." The say she said it with such tenderness that he became the servant and she the queen.

Sir

If only my voice were as husky as my mother's was, I could summon you here with that word.

I took *Women in Love* to bed with me this evening . . . My mouth was dry and I began to tremble—I'm still trembling.

How dare I bring that interloper into my bed?

The literal translation of the title brings me up short once more. Women *in Love*. In Love.

A fly dips its bitter wing and leaves its sweet wing breathing on the surface. The fly pauses on the surface of my cup of tea, with milk, perhaps **drowning** on its own, never to emerge again. I wonder: who will drink me?

I can feel my dead father's eyes boring through the back of my head. I always leave the house to his darkness, and take refuge, with a flashlight, beneath the thick blankets to sneak a few words:

> After the First World War, Lawrence began a **savage pilgrimage** in search of a **lifestyle** that was more fulfilling than what industrialized European society could offer him . . .

I still don't feel safe so I read *Women in Love* again from beginning to end.

I steal a few words, a few passages,

Risking sleeplessness, I point the flashlight at certain words in the introduction to the Penguin Classics edition that I feel speak to me personally:

> Lawrence's lover Frieda wrote upon his death in 1933 that 'Lawrence's writing conveyed to his fellow human everything he had seen, felt and known: the splendor of life and the hope for more and yet more life . . . that inestimably heroic gift.'

The flashlight goes out and I throw off my blanket and everything else.

Where can we get more of this more from life? What kind of more?

I review every detail of my life, searching for a droplet of that "more."

Attachment: This is my Auntie Halima's palm. It's scary how small it is, lines running parallel and intersecting.

A "wounded palm" is a piece of gold jewelry that runs from around the ring finger down to the wrist forming a triangle. Auntie

Halima couldn't afford one so she traced the shape of one on the back of her hand.
Aisha

P.S. "Why don't you buy **red** towels?" asked the fetus I miscarried in my dream last night (every night, in fact).

For two whole years I kept praying: Ahmad—please, God, let him sleep with me just once and release the collar of that dirty word *divorce* from around my neck. Just one thrust toward life, dear God: a **child**!

And now here's Ahmad, reopening the hotline between us, pleading for us to pick up where we left off.

What would make a hunter return to the prey he's left to rot for two whole years?!

Words like these were a challenge to Nasser. Whenever he stood at the entrance to the alley beneath Aisha's window, which was taken up almost entirely by an air-conditioning unit, he felt a weight descend on his heart. It was the burden of her obsession with the things she called the "splendor of living" and "more and more life." What could it be?

He was torn between Aisha and Azza: which one of them could he tie to the body? The wretched, crumbling houses around him defied him; Nasser felt he was being watched in that moment in which he was seeing through to my body and my many distracted heads.

At nightfall, he watched them as they slumped in front of their television screens. It was like looking through department store windows. They tore away the image so they could dive straight into the story. He disappointed them so much when they compared him to the detectives from *CSI*, whose science fiction plotlines were firmly stuck in all my heads. Nasser felt small and ignorant stacked up against those fictional detectives.

For all his horror at how uninhibited Aisha had been toward that German, he could still close his eyes and in an instant replace that annoying "^" with his own name, Nasser, pretending to himself that he was the one she was writing to. Why shouldn't he be the object of that surge? He wanted to bash his head into hers so their thoughts would start to mingle.

"May God smash your heads together!"

My mother Halima's expression fascinated him. It summed up the need to be open to the other, even to the point of butting heads.

The Hell List

NASSER PARKED HIS CAR AT THE ENTRANCE TO MY WINDING NETWORK OF ALLEY-ways and stood for a moment watching approvingly as my parasites woke up and began their day, before heading to the cafe where the Pakistani waiters greeted him with a stack of molasses-flavored shisha tobacco. He sat down and contemplated the freshly washed colors of the dawn sky over Mecca, quite different to the glaring sunsets, when it seemed to him as if Abel's blood were dyeing the evening sky over the Sanctuary. He could still just about make out the old page, which had been torn away, leaving behind a fresh one; every morning the inhabitants rewrote the city's fate upon it in Cain's breaths. Is that what Yusuf's diaries were trying to do?

The cashier, a Sudanese bachelor, had spent the night on one of the cafe chairs wrapped in a blanket and was just stirring to the scents rising off a teapot that one of the Pakistanis had set down on a tray beside him, along with a cup sitting in a pool of water left over from a hurried rinse.

Nasser didn't know what kind of message the neighborhood was trying to send him by following him even through his dreams . . . Nasser's thoughts were interrupted by a sudden kerfuffle from just outside where the African woman who'd been sitting at the side of the road with her goods had leapt to her feet and shot away down the street.

"Good morning to you, too!" snorted the detective as he watched her disappear from sight, leaving behind her mat and the cheap wares piled up on it. She didn't run so much as the alleyway simply opened up and swallowed her. At precisely that moment, a truck emblazoned with the logo of the Market Inspection Service—"Safeguarding the Holy Capital"—appeared, and before it had even stopped the doors burst open and two officers leapt out to pounce on the miniature stall. They kicked over trays of roasted almonds and watermelon seeds and ground them into the dust. Then they began picking up the bags of snacks and foodstuffs that had been packed and tied carefully by hand and tossing them into the back of the truck. Ready-to-use sachets of hibiscus tea processed by a company called Vitaminat Group, Bakura bars—short, curved, tamarind-flavored sugar sticks—colored imitation lollipops produced in improvised kitchens by illegal workers, cheap toys and games made in Taiwan.

Once they were done and their truck continued onward, deeper, into me, I was seized by a fever of activity. The makeshift stalls that were laid out down the length of the alley all disappeared, their owners having managed to hide inside the entryways to people's houses, as cats clustered around the bits and pieces that had been spilt and scattered around, licking and sniffing disdainfully in an effort to determine what was good to eat.

Nasser watched as the waiters huddled in the bathroom of a dilapidated house, shutting the door behind them, while the kitchens hid their poor day-laborers in tiny coal rooms. Nasser didn't watch so much as feel himself one with the endless, obstinate movement in the neighborhood. He thought, "If the angel Israfel's trumpet rang out, heralding the coming of Judgment Day, the Lane of Many Heads would simply lay out its sinful red carpets and its staff of heretics and carry on being unruly after the trumpet was blown. Chickens would still be roasted on spits over flames, flatbread would still bake in the tandoor, biryani would simmer on in its pot, the grease would bubble up, unceasingly, lying in wait for stomachs that were ready to renounce their deeper hunger and all that they'd accomplished in the day." I won't pretend that the notion didn't flatter me or that I wasn't filled with pride.

I wasn't quite sure how to understand Nasser's yearning to possess everything, even a neighborhood like me. He'd spent so much time here that he'd begun to see my miserable winding alleyways as an extension of his own body. That's right, I'd tricked him into thinking that he himself was just another one of my many heads. I entertained him with little crumbs of my inner thoughts, all the while keeping him far away from the place where I stored all my secrets and sins. He even began thinking that he was incognito; that he knew exactly how many undocumented wastrels were hanging around, that he knew who was splitting the rent on the shacks where they took turns enjoying what pleasures they could on my lumpy, bumpy beds; that he knew all the petty offenses—merely human nature—and the crimes that violated both religion and the regulations on public safety in the Holy Capital; that he could count every single sigh sighed by the women as they watched episode after episode of reality TV behind boarded-up windows, before the next round of confiscation and destruction put an end to it.

Once the municipality truck had left, Nasser headed to see Imam Dawoud, who led him into the mosque. As he stepped in front of Nasser to open the door, Nasser had the chance to take a good look at him: he was a stocky, rotund Ethiopian. His robes hung from his round belly halfway down his rough calves, casting a shadow over his callused feet in their blue flip-flops. His white head-cover hung on his head, as if pinned to an invisible hook, down to his scarf as it cascaded down between his shoulders and spread like a fan over his backside. His beard struggled bravely; a few of the hairs had made it to over two inches. He had no mustache. His eyes were protruding and bulbous, piercing and slashing from behind thick lenses.

Nasser didn't know how to begin. "The people of the lane hold you in special regard, sir. Your children were all born here. Is it hard for them never to have visited Ethiopia even though they carry Ethiopian citizenship?"

"We have served this mosque for a quarter century and so I pray that the Lord will give us the reward of those who live in the vicinity of His holy house. Praise be to God, we now have regular residency papers because of my work with the Committee for the Promotion of Virtue. They have also begun citizenship proceedings on my behalf. And yet with one foot in the grave, what need do I have of citizenship? If I have any desire of it at all, I want it only for my children."

"Tell me . . . What's all this about your lists? Lists of the people going to hell and those going to heaven?" The imam's gaze froze on a point on the wall in front of him and bore deep.

"You should ask about the box for bribing the VIPs. A certain woman claimed it was for collecting donations when she set it up, but all it is is a way to collect protection money from the people in the neighborhood," Dawoud replied, carefully avoiding the sin of mentioning either Umm al-Sa'd or her stepson, the Eunuchs' Goat, by name. "God forgive her. She's collecting money to bribe some officials to issue an ID card for her son and get him citizenship." The ancient air conditioner, which was doing its best—with the assistance of the ceiling fan—to drive the burning clouds out of the mosque, reminded Nasser of his office. "That woman is hell's kindling. Satan gave her his devilish skill so she could bewitch people and force them to donate to her fund. But then, what do you expect from a woman who fell from Azrael's jaws? She's capable of any sin."

"Even Sheikh Muzahim talks about 'the woman who fell from Azrael's jaws.' What do you mean by that?"

"Be sure you don't tear off Satan's mask before you've fortified yourself against his fiendish horror," he replied. He continued after a pause, "With those marketing skills of hers, she's gone and hung a donation box for bribing those officials on the door of her father's building so she can watch who donates, and then she divides the Lord's Muslim believers into those who give and those who abstain, splitting them into two factions: the kind-hearted and the empty-hearted." He suddenly fell silent once more. There was no way he could expect a man like this, in his Western uniform, to understand the defense plan he'd put in place. It was based around the certainty that both briber and bribed were condemned to hell; they, and everyone who donated to the fund, were on the list of those bound for hell. Those who abstained were on the heaven list.

"It has come to our attention that the donors are mostly men blinded by lust. They're donating hard currency as well as gold trinkets on occasion." Nasser had no clue what the imam was talking about. "It is not for me to describe to you the satanic urges they stuff into that box along with their hard contributions." Nasser didn't know what to think of the imam's deliberate use of the adjective "hard," but in any case the imam had regained his deep silence, leaving the ceiling fan to put a finer point on his insinuations and scatter them around the darkness of the mosque.

Those Who Meet Azrael

IT WAS ANOTHER PITCH-BLACK NIGHT IN THE LANE OF MANY HEADS, AND NASSER was hovering around the Arab League building trying somehow to solve the riddle of how Umm al-Sa'd had "fallen from Azrael's jaws." He paced back and forth between the building and al-Ashi's yard across the street. Everyone's eyes were fixed on the smear of soot on the wall of the yard: it was never cleaned or scraped off, it remained there as if it were a testimony to al-Ashi's good luck. The shocking affair, which had taken place in that exact spot a quarter-century ago, had left its stain upon my memory. I had been temporarily blinded that night by the misery that swept down my alleyways and clouded the moon above, setting the scene for the drama about to be played out. Even the shadows were pinned against the walls and the neon lights merged overhead to form a curtain for an operating theater that was preparing for an imminent disfigurement. Cats skulked on crumbling sidewalks and rooftops, while doves buried their heads deep beneath their wings and feet, sneezing at the putrid smell that had turned the howling dogs rabid. They scrapped like starved wolves, nipping one another's tails to win a bite of the plastic-wrapped mass that had been tossed in a heap at the bottom of the wall in the yard. Al-Ashi was a young trainee at the time, fighting to move up the ladder in the kitchen. It wasn't the smell of cooking oozing from his clothes that woke him up but the manic barks that shook the room overlooking the yard where he lived. He hurriedly wrapped his green towel around himself and staggered, still half-asleep, down the stairs to see what was going on outside. He was assaulted by the same putrescent smell that had besieged the entire alley: the smell of a body. Grabbing rocks, bones, whatever he could find, he chased the dogs as far away as he could from the plastic bag that had been tossed in the gutter. When his shaking fingers finally managed to tear the bag open down the middle he found himself face-to-face with a skeleton. I admit that even I, the Lane of Many Heads, usually so phlegmatic—even when faced with the most hideous abominations—was overcome with nausea at the sight. I was speechless; even after a long time had passed, I could never bring myself to utter a word to anyone about that disgraceful secret. I couldn't bear to look at the clotted black mass between the wide shoulders; there was hardly more than a ribcage topped by an elongated skull, which grinned at al-Ashi with a set of mouse-like teeth. The smell of bodily decay surged out so violently that it was impossible to tell whether the body was alive or dead, female or male. The acrid burning odor blinded al-Ashi and brought tears to his eyes. The dogs were snapping at his anklebones, angling for their share of the ribs, but he bent down and gathered up the body, then set off at a run. Deaf and blind to the world he ran and ran, a foul trail dripping behind him, followed by a pack of barking dogs and curious eyes peeping out in terror. He ran on—his animal pursuers having long since given up—until he reached Zahir General Hospital. They say that he ran for miles and miles, in search of refuge or salvation, because he knew he was carrying his own doomed fate in his arms. He finally laid his heavy burden to rest on a yellowed stretcher in the emergency room; a strong smell of chloroform suggested that another body had departed quite recently on these sheets. The doctors and nurses were revolted at the thought of touching the body, but al-Ashi begged them.

"Please! Have mercy! This is a human being," he entreated, tearing apart the plastic to reveal the hideous skeleton patched with decaying flesh. The ER team spent a goodly amount of time just working out whether or not the body was still alive and deserving of medical attention. Frustrated, al-Ashi grabbed an oxygen mask and fitted it over the gaping skull, covering the murine teeth—but it wasn't the surge of oxygen through the arteries so much as al-Ashi's faith that sent a shudder of breath through the large ribcage, which was followed by a hacking cough that sprayed the disgusted faces surrounding the body with mucus. The spray of slime left the medics with no choice but to examine the body. From the plastic bag, they pulled a woman with a crushed chest and abdomen swollen with fever, most noticeably around her pubic region, and they hesitantly began cleaning her body, though they expected it to collapse in on itself at any moment. The stench of bodily decay grew with every stroke of the alcohol-soaked sponge. It took the team more than an hour of routine examination to establish that they should indeed treat the body as a living being. Yet at the very moment that the doctor touched her stomach, the body reared up angrily and tore away the hand that had dared come near the swelling in her pubic region.

It took five Filipino nurses to hold the thrashing body down so they could inject her with anesthetic. The hard swelling in her pubic region puzzled the medics; they were astounded all the more when their probing hands met solid metal. The radiologists and medics stood, amazed, looking at the images of the woman's vagina and uterus. "Is that an earring?!" asked one. "I've been on my feet in the emergency room for twenty-four hours receiving one casualty after another. I'm beginning to wonder whether my eyes are playing tricks on me and all this chaos is just my imagination!"

"Wait, is that a necklace?"

None of the people who'd been lured by the hubbub to come gawk at the strange X-ray could believe their eyes. When the doctors decided that surgical intervention was necessary, al-Ashi assumed the role of the woman's next-of-kin and signed the consent form.

"She's got a vagina like a bank vault! We dug out all kinds of twenty-four-karat gold jewelry from there: necklaces, bracelets, earrings, solid gold coins all lining the woman's vagina and womb!"

The riddle demanded police intervention, and of course the fingers all pointed at al-Ashi at first, but further investigation soon revealed the woman's true identity. "It's Umm al-Sa'd, the milkman's granddaughter and the only girl among four brothers. Just look at that flat chest, like a man's, those wide shoulders, the gaping mouth with mouse teeth—those features can only have come from her grandfather al-Labban. Her brothers announced her death a while back. And they kept their father locked up, saying he'd gone mad, until Azrael the angel of death came to save him from their ingratitude."

"We suspected they might be keeping someone prisoner in the back room—you could see that mop of hair through the bars on the window. It was their sister they'd locked up in there. The only thing they gave her to eat was pieces of stale bread and apple peels, and in the meanwhile they took her share in the Arab League building—the same inheritance that had led them to get their father declared insane so that they could stop him from giving it away to any young man from the Lane of Many Heads who was allowed to build another floor on top."

"Finally, after she'd been locked up for years, they thought she'd died and tossed her out in the alley for the dogs to eat her. That's when al-Ashi found her."

"She inherited all that jewelry from her mother. She was determined not to let them get their hands on it, no matter how badly they starved her for all those years. She never cracked. Never revealed where it was."

"Noah's treasure buried in a vagina! No one could ever dream that up, not even a Hollywood director. And to think, it was all the work of an innocent teenage girl."

"Even if her brothers had had suspicions, who would dare dig for treasure in a hiding place like that? Who would dare profane his sister's virtue, her womb? That girl was something else!"

The drama swept through the lane like a tornado. People began saying that Umm al-Sa'd had fallen from Azrael's jaws, loaded with unimaginable riches, and they crowned her with the title: the neighborhood's roomiest vagina. In order to get her to drop the charges against them, her brothers agreed to let her marry her savior al-Ashi, and they gave up their claim on the first-floor apartment in the Arab League building. Nevertheless they never truly gave up their attempts to rob her of her fair share, even as they watched each year—in horror—as she littered the alley with crates of apples and showered the neighbors with roasted seeds whose husks would be sucked on and spat out in celebration of her heroic survival, which had left her ever more robust and ravenous. For a quarter-century, whenever Umm al-Sa'd relapsed into silence, al-Ashi followed her inside her head and alongside her he traversed those many years of imprisonment in that back room where she'd lost her innocence. He kept the starving teenage girl company as she exposed her womanhood in the darkness and carefully dug down into her own vagina, hiding hard metal away within her soft flesh, her stomach swelling and hardening, in preparation for the day when she'd be freed from her imprisonment and begin a life built on those riches.

Al-Ashi's eyes would fill with tears when he looked at her. "This woman is the treasure life has granted me. She and the massive hoard she used to buy me this kitchen and invest in the stock market." He embraced her every untiring effort to transform her inconsequential treasures into a small fortune. She'd paid a heavy price: her womb had become too hardened ever to be able to accommodate a soft human body.

"Any fetus of her own flesh and blood would just stay in her womb, hoarding gold. The infernal girl brought the curse upon herself!"

I pressed the wisdom of all my heads into service to mock Umm al-Sa'd, without the slightest compassion. I was afraid that if her womb were to be taken seriously it might swallow me right up. I watched al-Ashi on the nights when his anger was too much for him, when he'd take the burning logs from his ovens and march out into the alley, threatening to burn my heads in an attempt to stamp out my snickering. Umm al-Sa'd didn't need fire's help to defeat me, though. She'd been rearing a tech-obsessed genie inside of her, and it finally appeared in the form of a laptop and an AwalNet modem that connected her phone line to the Internet. She defeated all of my macho heads by getting to the stock market first.

In record time she announced her victory with a vivid red sheen upon her lips, giving away her bloody methods. The other women imitated her style; it was open rebellion.

"The women see her as a symbol of perseverance in the struggle against men. The men, on the other hand, can't stop fantasizing about her savage vagina. They are drawn there compulsively, only to drown. That's why they're so keen, so passionate, about donating their hard gold to her famous box. Following, in a waking dream, as the donations take shelter in her vagina and never come back out."

"Don't be deceived by her flat boylike chest. Look further down, at her pelvis. That will always be the source of devilish pleasure . . ."

"Some might envy her husband, al-Ashi, but mostly he's pitied. Just think about that teenage girl excavating her womb with her own fingers. That means she wasn't a virgin when they got married. What kind of a fool agrees to that? They've both been cursed for it. Now al-Ashi's paying the price for having been a jackass: the orphan they adopted, the Eunuchs' Goat, is a jackass in human form."

Yabis the Sewage Cleaner

IT WAS MU'AZ WHO SENT NASSER LISTS OF THE PEOPLE WHO WERE GOING TO heaven and those who were going to hell. In studying these lists, the detective found that the sewage cleaner Yabis was the only person to be excluded, to be left off of both the contradictory rosters.

The children of the lane ran on ahead, leading Nasser to the sewage cleaner who was clearing out the Arab League building's septic tank. His burly body came into view; he was naked from the waist up and his bottom half was covered by a garbage-colored apron that stretched to mid-calf. The sewage cleaner was busy pulling the hose up out of the tank, disconnecting it, and wrapping it up the length of the tanker truck. Before Nasser could catch up with him, he'd flipped the tank over, ninety percent of which had been cleaned out by the pump, and in the space of a moment, he was swallowed up by clouds of methane. Nasser hesitated for a brief second, but he could see through the gas to the kids pointing to the center of the tank: "It's Pokemon!"

Nasser was blinded by the methane fumes, his eyes watering so hard he could hardly follow what the man was doing down at the bottom, up to his knees in solid human waste and reptiles, barefoot and without any gloves or a mask for protection. It was as though he'd been made out of this primordial soup as he dug through layers of waste, preparing it for his colleague who scooped it up into a bucket, which was hauled up by the assistant at the surface. He in turn piled it up at the edge of the lane, unleashing a cloud of terrified, terrifying cockroaches in every direction. That's the truth; it happened before our very eyes. But Nasser's focus waned. I wondered if he'd begun to doubt whether the entire investigation was worth it, whether it was worth trying to save a neighborhood that kneaded and fermented its excrement so that they could get drunk on methane.

Nasser couldn't linger at the cafe: he was running away from the eye-stinging, hallucination-causing methane cloud that had washed over my every corner. He felt he'd fallen into some space outside of known time.

When Nasser came back, he was determined to catch Yabis when he wasn't at work. He headed to the two rooms with planks for a ceiling at the end of one of my narrow alleys. He was surprised to find the front door a half-meter off the ground and open to the alley but for a curtain drawn across it. The green flowers on the curtain reminded him of the violet hem of Azza's mother's dress, which was stuffed in the bars of Azza's window. He could sense Kawthar, Yabis' wife, moving behind the curtain, which was swaying in the wind. He knocked and waited. Nasser ignored the blank space where Yabis' mother Matuqa used to sleep. Yabis had kept her bedroll folded up on a shelf beside the bathroom, which was the source of the most horrible odor ever to have blocked Nasser's nostrils, the smell of human excrement. The curtain was pulled back first to reveal the edges of the sewage cleaner's new purple sarong, and then the man himself. Nasser tried to ignore the hole in the shoulder of the man's threadbare tank top—just how much use and sweat that must have seen. There was a smell of camphor in the air, as if a body had recently been washed on the other side of that curtain in preparation for burial. Resignedly, Yabis led him away from the room back toward his tanker truck at the top of the alley. Nasser looked at the end of the hose, which was covered in something disgusting. They sat on a crumbled doorstep, looking out toward the Lane of Many Heads, and without any preliminaries Nasser said: "Aisha was your daughter-in-law? Tell me about her."

"Aisha was soaked up to here," he said pointing to the top of his forehead. "A bunch of the kids here learn to read and write, but for Aisha it was like her mom and dad were books. She spent her whole life chasing books. I mean, for a lady. A lady isn't a lady unless she's like good soil, willing to receive her man. Aisha wasn't soil. Lord knows she wasn't. She was just dust. That's what made my son's guts get scattered here and there." There was no bitterness or blame in Yabis' response. "And of course she was the only member of her family to survive the accident." Nasser was filled with a sudden delight that Aisha had been spared. "Would you believe she used to sleep on top of her books? She had an ocean of books hidden under her bed." The man was sitting directly beside Nasser, unaware of the halo of putridity that surrounded him. Something in Nasser's insides reacted to the latent smell.

"Did your wife Umm Ahmad happen to see the body?" The sewage cleaner looked at him. It was like he could detect something rotten in his question, the sour smell of an imminent accusation, but he answered anyway.

"My better half Umm Ahmad, the teacher's mother-in-law, washes the dead. She attends to all the bodies. May God grant you that blessing." Nasser was stumped. He could only stare at Yabis, holding back his laughter at the thought of a sewage cleaner marrying a corpse washer. It was a case of what you might call self-sufficiency, or self-cleaning, or self-recycling even. The hysterical synonyms swirled in Nasser's head. A city could try to get by without tradespeople of all stripes except for these two—it would drown in its own disease and dissolution otherwise.

"Men are weak . . ." The sewage cleaner scanned the two sides of the alley, the people and the shops loaded up with food and toys and products. "All this is going to end up on the bench for washing corpses or down the sewer." He stretched his hand out to secure the hose against the clip on the end of the truck, and then he wiped his hand on his new towel as a reflex. He left a smear on the purple fabric covering his thigh. "This is all just the earth's manure," he said, indicating his entire body. Nasser sensed there was some invisible blemish deforming Yabis' body despite his good looks. The jet-black hair that fell over his forehead looked like a hump he'd put on, like the torturers who appear to the dead to swallow them up! Nasser drove the thought from his mind and wondered instead what would induce a man to take up a job like that in a time of technology and sewer systems, and in the holy capital, too. Nasser was drenched in sweat, but the sewage cleaner, who said he'd answered the official call for people to perform the job, wasn't affected by the heat and carried on talking. They discussed the government buildings he serviced without going into great detail, and then he gave Nasser detailed information about how often he serviced the major residences in the Lane of Many Heads. Al-Labban's house, better known as the Arab League building: "We clean it out every other day. That means, at a hundred riyals for the tanker, it comes to fifteen hundred riyals per month. I knock off two hundred riyals for them so their monthly excrement ends up costing them thirteen hundred riyals a month. You know, it costs a man money whether it's going in or coming out." Nasser was embarrassed that the sewage cleaner expected him to record these filthy details in his case notes.

"I told them they should get a separate tank for the cellar. God commands us to hide our shame. You know, nothing's going to hide the shame of their tenant, the Turkish seamstress, and her guests, except a proper sewer."

He had no idea what Yabis was getting at with his repeated "You knows." From where they were seated on the doorstep, he examined the Labban building. The fight over who owned it started up at exactly the same time that the body was found. The windows of the cellar were open like the eyes of a genie traveling down a road. There was a toddler lying on the ground in front of the building, sneaking over to the cellar, spying on the ghosts who still played the role of girls sitting beneath those windows, their coconut-oiled locks falling down over the style patterns, taking lessons in the art of preening from the Turkish seamstress. The sewage cleaner felt that his body didn't suit clothes, or a burial shroud even. That he was at his best when he was alone, half-naked, in the darkness cleaning out a septic tank. The true scents of the body and its excrement reaching his senses. Now that his mother, Matuqa, was dead, his loneliness had become complete.

"I may not have anything useful to give you for your investigation. Look at my sons. Yusuf was right when he attacked me in a fit of craziness. So far every son I've had has run away. Musfir most recently, and before him Ahmad, the oldest. They were adopted by a relative of mine who wanted to give them a clean life, far away from septic tanks." He thought he'd strayed away from the case at hand, but the detective's eyes sparkled at the mention of another lead: Ahmad. There were plenty of witnesses who'd seen him scurrying down the alley the night the body was found. It would be easy to accuse him of murder. He wanted to ask Yabis whether his wife Kawthar had seen her daughter-in-law in the corpse, but he was afraid of the answer.

Instead, he said, "Ahmad lives abroad. He left Aisha two years ago, two months after they'd got married. People in the neighborhood say he used to hit her. That makes him a suspect in the murder and it makes Aisha the victim, potentially."

"Aisha and Ahmad went away together. She had to go with him. He came to see us before they found the body. I let him have it. I was so angry he'd abandoned Aisha. He told me he'd put an end to their separation. When my son says he's going to do something, he does it."

What really complicated things was that there was a disappearance larger than death. The crux of the issue wasn't the murder victim, it was mistaken identity. Whether Azza, Aisha, or the body. There was a mass of crushed woman in front of him, and he had no hope of making out the murdered from the insane from the one who'd slammed the door in the face of the Many Heads and run off. Nasser was faced with the challenge of teasing out that spiritual DNA from the mass, so that he could absolve Azza of the stain of suicide, passing it on to some other girl in the Lane of Many Heads, and so that he could exclude Aisha, as well, and thereby not draw attention to the woman sitting in his own heart, speaking to him with an intimacy he'd never experienced from a woman—or another person—before.

"And Azza, Sheikh Muzahim's daughter, where did she go? Any ideas?" The detective traced Yabis' glance as he looked up at Azza's empty bedroom and her father's shop, as a male pigeon danced, courting two females, among the clay soldiers on the roof. He was flying out from his wooden coop to the ruined building and back.

A laughing Yabis interrupted his train of thought. "They only ask me to come clean for them once or maybe twice a year."

"Is that because Sheikh Muzahim's a tightwad?"

"It's 'cause their output is so meager. The only people in that house are a girl who's buried in her papers and charcoal drawings, and Yusuf's mother, who's in her fifties and spends half her life at weddings, serving and drinking tea. That woman's whole life is wrapped up in tea leaves and mint leaves and the leaves of her son Yusuf's notebook. In the case of Sheikh Muzahim, what comes out isn't even a tenth of what goes in. He lives off of dates and unsweetened coffee. In short: those people are vegetarians . . . That's beyond the scope of the kind of work I do." Nasser looked at the sewage cleaner as if he were something beyond the scope of life. A parasite subsisting on life's rituals, like aging and decay, like an illness that removes the weakest elements from the human mass; he was like the kind of death that scrapes the surface of the earth clean so it can celebrate new births and deaths.

"You're not curious about who the victim is?"

"I didn't even lay eyes on her." Suddenly Nasser was filled with shame. "We're talking about our women. We look down at our feet when we sense a woman walking past." A sandstorm wind blew toward them; Yabis waved his hand in the air as if to drive it away. "What with this stifling air and sandstorms, what's so weird about a boil swelling up and exploding one night in the Lane of Many Heads?" A moment later, he said, "People are strange." Nasser kept quiet so as to let him carry on. "During the holidays, people defecate twice as much. And I make twice as much money. I don't mind going out to empty tanks during the holidays. That's celebratory excrement even if it's a bit gluttonous."

The detective couldn't bring himself to continue down this path any longer so he brought the conversation back around to Ahmad. "People say your son Ahmad has close ties to a lot of important people."

"For example, I would never want to empty the septic tank of a building where Ahmad lives. Ahmad's crazy about wheeling and dealing. Everything he expels reeks of the same odor: rotting food the likes of which has never been seen in the Lane of Many Heads. That might not matter much to you, but I'm picky about my customers."

"What if we need you to come empty the tank at the criminal investigation unit?"

The sewage cleaner laughed. "Your unit doesn't really suit me, no offense. The walls of your septic tank are probably covered in all kinds of nuclear, chemical, and conventional weapons." Nasser laughed, and then they both fell silent. The detective's silence puzzled the sewage cleaner somehow. He continued, "You should've seen the fast food invasion. You can clean a septic tank a thousand times, but you'll never get rid of that smell of fast food, especially hamburgers—"

The detective cut him off. "Who would have a motive to kill someone in the neighborhood? Who could the murderer be?"

"Have you heard about depression? I just heard about it recently in the Labban building. Umm al-Sa'd, al-Ashi's wife, took her adopted son the Eunuchs' Goat to a shrink. 'He's depressed,' she said. And she said we shouldn't be ashamed of psychological problems. A month later when we went to empty the septic tank, it smelled like colocynth incense. Painkillers turn the bowels sour. It knocks the bugs out without any insecticide. Even we sewage cleaners, as soon as we breathe that stuff in, our tongues get tied up and our faces and limbs begin to twitch."

Nasser asked Yabis about the state of his own mental excretions. Yabis looked into Nasser's eyes. Apropos of nothing, he said, "You seem like an enlightened man, detective. Ever since Yusuf left I don't have anybody to talk to. Yusuf was the most educated person in the Lane of Many Heads. He understood how we spoke, and he spoke for all of us, every last one. He was our reflection. When we lost our minds, he was the one who went to the Shihar Hospital and received electric shocks. Shocks straight to the brain." The sewage cleaner was desperate to talk, so Nasser just let him, pulling on the thread that led to Yusuf.

"Yusuf's like me. He's digging his way through the Lane of Many Heads, you know? Some people's heads are filled with the same stuff you find in people's stomachs. Then he'd publish the remains in the newspaper and call it the history of man. He told us, and he was talking to me the whole time, about the revolt of the army and the common people during the rule of the Sherif Muhammad bin Abd Allah, when they forced the mufti and the wazir to expel the Shiites from Mecca in 1732, because they accused them of sullying the Kaaba, because according to their rites the pilgrimage doesn't count unless the pilgrim dirties the Kaaba. What they thought was filth was actually lentils mixed with oil, which had gone runny in the Meccan sun. Detective, what's all this waste if it's not the thing that gets us drooling, makes us pay any price—high or low—to fill our bellies with it so that it comes out of our orifices, the superior and the inferior."

Yabis' youngest son, the one-year-old, ran up to them and clung to his father's knee. He pressed his wet mouth against the dirty patch of his father's purple loincloth. The child peered at Nasser and then suddenly raced down the alley, toddling in his worn-out tank top and orange tracksuit bottoms. He dodged the Mitsubishi motorcycle carrying sugar cane as it zoomed toward the space between the two shops where the sugarcane-juice seller had set up his extractor and lined up his yellow plastic cups on a shelf beneath the counter. Behind the counter, he hid the bucket he used to wash the cups after every customer. The motorcycle sped past him, trailed by a bunch of children who, if it had slowed down, would've have nabbed a sugarcane and run off. The little boy hesitated for a moment—he didn't know whether to follow the sugarcane or the scent of the roasted chicken one of the cafe patrons was eating. By the time he'd made up his mind, one of the cafe staff was clearing the table, and when the boy appeared beneath the table, he threw him a wing. Like a cat he scurried off as he chewed. Yabis watched him lovingly. He swallowed. He was silent for a while and then he said, "Sometimes I wonder—what's the use of a job like mine at a time like this?"

"You mean because of the sewer system?" The sewage cleaner looked up at him and then he nodded. Face to face with those severe features, Nasser chose not to speak the conclusion that had suddenly occurred to him: there's no need for sewage cleaners in heaven. Waste ceases to mean anything in that paradisiacal realm where nothing can be consumed, or digested, or go rotten and decay. Is that because the only thing left behind is light?

Corruption

"NOTHING ROTS IN HEAVEN." THOSE WERE NASSER'S PARTING WORDS. THE detective chose not to return to his office. He felt an overwhelming need to go back to his tiny apartment, where he shut the door behind him, took a deep breath, and headed to the bathroom. He stripped off all his clothes and laid them in the laundry basket. Then he sat down to relieve himself. He laughed. After the day he'd had, he felt he could now appreciate what was coming out of him. "One man's trash is another man's treasure." He was sure to wash his hands with Dettol before he took up his lover's letters. Therein lay his humanity, his paradise.

FROM: Aisha
SUBJECT: Message 8

Time is a pit here.

I stand on my bed so I can reach the window that's blocked up with an air-conditioning unit.

I look out at the neighborhood through a long aperture. It's like a hedgehog covering its back with satellite dishes. It's the communal longing to get away from here. We lose so much when we live and die in the same spot, the same alley, the same smell of the same breath, when we don't get mixed up in the saliva of others. One oxygen atom and two hydrogen atoms (forgive me if I get the proportions mixed up), that's what water is made of. I haven't made my own water yet.

Attachment 1: photo.

Is this **Jameela**? It's hanging up beside the door of Sheikh Muzahim's shop.

Her clothes don't change. They just get grimier at the chest and turn a pale yellow. If you chewed on Jameela, you'd smell turmeric. Saliva dribbles from the corner of her mouth. The girl's mouth watered and her saliva washed away the ground beneath Sheikh Muzahim's feet.

Aisha

P.S. Do you hear the singing coming from the hallway? That's Mu'az, Imam Dawoud's son. Every morning at dawn he comes to clean the hall. I stand at the top of the staircase with burning incense while he splashes songs of water and Danat against the stairs. For days I've been burning the same charred chunk even though you're not supposed to re-use incense because it'll smell of burning. The last thing he does is spray water in front of the house to "put the shadows to bed" like my father used to do.

P.P.S. When Azza was a child, there were always ants swarming over her diaper, and my mother Halima would say **"She's got sweet pee"** in a singsong voice. I wanted to ask her what she made of my urine.

As soon as I reached puberty, I started spending long stretches in the bathroom. I looked warily at my body, this thing that was erupting out of control, the scandalous contours of my chest, the sloping of my torso toward what came next. Now when I confess these things to Azza, she laughs hysterically. "It's weird but I was never embarrassed by my body."

Then I get defensive. "I had to monitor my body so that I could hide it. I was embarrassed to see it transforming into an adult woman. I didn't want my teachers, who were all women, or my mother to see my shame." Azza looked at me like there was something wrong with me. I can understand how she wasn't embarrassed by the danger of her body: she was an innately alluring creature. Made of seduction but in its raw form, before it's become self-aware. She used to augment the danger, too. She'd wear a **rocket** bra that pushed her breasts out for all to see. She'd add a belt to any skimpy thing she wore to cut her in half at the waist and accentuate her curves. Even without a belt, the way she stood was seductive: hands on her hips, as if she were re-sculpting the latent thrill of her body. Am I allowed to say that even her sweat was dew?

P.P.P.S. Do you still smell of firewood and rosemary? Which parts of you should I lick to know what kind of mood you're in today? Tell me which of your black parts is off-limits so that I can start there. There's a lot for us to enjoy as we wait for the grill to heat up and we feed the moons and cats. Do you still walk barefoot in the garden? One day, when I'm rubbing your feet, you'll see rose-water and damp spots in the places where your foot rests against my lap and in my hands. You look so much like me.

Nowadays when I pray it's like a door that opens for you to slip through, like a chatty conversation or one in which we tell each other our dreams. I wait impatiently for that moment when I'm **standing before** God and I make you stand next to me so we can replay our most intimate conversations. Just imagine!

Apple Smoke

DETECTIVE NASSER STEPPED OUT OF HIS APARTMENT BUILDING AND TOOK A LOOK at the empty space around him. For the first time, he actually wanted to see the place where he'd lived for two decades. This was one of the neighborhoods that had sprung up after the oil boom twenty years ago and although it was new, it had begun to decay. Buildings still under construction were sprinkled here and there, and between them lay wild and empty spaces. The neighborhood didn't deserve a second look: all the buildings were copies of one another, the products of minds lacking any imagination. They had tiny windows, and all the columns were concrete pillars that ran up the entire length of the building. Three or four columns, sheathed in golden aluminum, covered each building's main entrance. The street looked like a steaming corpse. There was no foot-traffic to give it life, just a row of cars on either side of the street, carrying ghost-like riders, unseen. One car disappears as another comes around the corner, both covered in dust so you can't even see the windshield.

Nasser gave The Lane of Many Heads his undivided attention in an attempt to become part of that neighborhood: the old ghosts, the buzz and din, the vivaciousness that threatened a quarter-century-long routine of robotic discipline, robotic lifelessness.

Nasser sat at the cafe in the Lane of Many Heads, engrossed in the soap opera, a favorite among housewives who were perpetually depressed because of it: *The Happy One*. He took a deep drag on his water-pipe, relishing the burnt apple taste. He'd become addicted to that type of flavored tobacco, and he'd smoke constantly as he interviewed people. He took a look at Mu'az, who'd always stop by when he saw Nasser sitting there. He'd come up and take a seat beside him, silently joining the television viewing. I, the Lane of Many Heads, was never comfortable with the way Nasser toyed with my younger heads. Ever since Mu'az's latest confession, the two of them had built upon their flimsy trust. Nasser had the feeling that Mu'az wanted to tell him something but was unsure, and so he resorted to telling Nasser about himself. He wasn't embarrassed about telling him the details of his home life:

"It took us fifteen minutes to get through the Dawn Prayers this morning. My father the Imam got confused when he was reciting the verses. I was standing behind him in a row with the other worshippers. The voices of the men who knew the Quran by heart rose to correct him, and he struggled to pull himself together. He sat down and read from the text. My mind drifted during the pause. I thought of my sisters. They, like me, were frightened that the Quran would begin to slip away from him. I heard his own frightened voice in my head: 'They're not going to let me lead the prayers any more if I start forgetting the Quran.'

"'Years of raising children and looking after the mosque have turned my hair gray.' I watched him run his fingers through my mother's gray hair.

"He reassured her: 'This grayness won't last forever, God willing. Consider it the price you pay to be thirty-three in heaven.'

"'Thirty-three?'

"'Yes, it's the best age for a human being. It's the age Jesus was, peace be upon him, when he was raised up to the sky. It's the age at which we're reborn when we enter heaven.'

"My sister Maymuna went to answer the early-morning knock before the rest of us could, so that, as my father would say, blessings would be revealed to her. Before decline beset The Lane of Many Heads we were used to the Eunuchs' Goat coming to our door in the early morning: 'From my father al-Ashi of the cooking courtyard. Empty the pot out and give it back.' The Eunuchs' Goat was always disappointed to find Maymuna's hand snake past the door to take the pot he'd brought over so early, hoping to hand it to Sa'diya. The Eunuchs' Goat was quite the devil. He'd try to nudge the door open slightly with the side of his foot to get a look at Sa'diya, who was rubbing her sleep-puffed eyes with one hand and with the other emptying the pot into a bowl, adroitly avoiding the layer of burnt rice at the bottom of the pot. She could no longer distinguish between her dark hands and the blackened pot, scraping here and there. These morning handouts irritated her no end. When she's asleep, she dreams of throwing rice-missiles at the do-gooders who never think of them until their food's about to go rotten. Gaining blessings for a new day with yesterday's inedible leftovers. She sleeps with one eye closed and one eye on the worms clustered around the streaks of filth on the floor of their concrete bathroom. Bunched up in a line between her feet, she had no idea where they were headed.

"'Those are the worms that are going to feed on you in the grave if you don't shield yourself with faith.' My mother almost tore the worms open with her finger.

"Sa'diya handed the still-wet pot back to the Eunuchs' Goat, but it did nothing to extinguish his passion. 'God bless you and may He count this among your good deeds on Judgment Day,' she said softly. Her smile is special, it plays on the corners of her lips when she pictures the scales of their good deeds crawling with worms depending on how stale their charitable offering is."

"And what about your father?" Nasser asked.

"My father has his daily routine down to a T. Every morning after dawn prayers, he exhorts the angels of good fortune with his chanting, and after night prayers he chants that the followers of Muhammad will grow and multiply. Every year brought my father another child. With each of them, he increased the number of the poor and the blind. The people in the Lane of Many Heads used to make fun of him with stealthy glances, but they also envied him the number of sons of his who'd become Quran reciters. The burden he bore wasn't because of all these mouths that needed feeding, but because of the forehead-splitting sadness that came from knowing what punishments awaited man.

Sa'diya was convinced that our father had memorized all the Quranic verses about perdition and the various punishments that awaited unbelievers. 'Diabetes has put out the light in my eyes,' he complained. 'Diabetes is like disbelief. One takes away your ability to see with your eyes—may God have mercy on us—and the other takes away your ability to see with you heart.'

"Whenever he slipped deeper into infirmity and thus nearer to death, he'd brace himself by filling his heart with the fear of the torments that awaited him after death and filling his mind with visions of the angels of paradise. Then he would recite the Quran in that sweet voice of his as though to line his grave, making it more comfortable, in preparation to receive his body."

From where they were sitting, Nasser saw the imam going into the mosque. Mu'az turned his back to hide from his father because he didn't want to be spotted loitering with the rest of the cafe crowd. Once his father was out of sight, Mu'az carried on:

"My father is constantly frowning. The only time his features relax is when he's standing in front of the shelf of Qurans that people have donated to the mosque. Then he gives in. At sunset, he stands there patiently going through the donated Qurans, smelling their ink and leather binding. He bides his time till he can pick out a rare one and add it to his shelf, which is brimming with Qurans of all different dimensions. My oldest brother Yaqub, who wears glasses as thick as the bottom of a tea glass and is the Quran reciter at the Umm al-Joud Mosque, will come over and take a Quran off the shelf to the right of the door and sit down across from my father. Then the rest of us, boys and girls, are expected to fill out the arcs of the study-circle, to connect their two poles.

"*When a man dies, his good deeds end with him except for three things: an upright child who prays for him* . . . Whenever we sat down to memorize the Quran, our father's blind eye would be there, pleading with us: 'When you feel the flocks of the Quran slipping away from you, gather them up against your chest and bring them to me in my grave.' My siblings would shut their eyes and begin swaying as they recited. The recitation would begin at the bottom of their spines and work its way up, causing their bodies to sway until it reached their tongues. My father's cane was hot on their heels, though:

"'Don't read with your eyes closed! You were blessed with sight so you might as well keep your eyes on the verse as you're reciting.' We trained our eyes on our Qurans in a pathetic attempt to follow the verses, but it didn't take long for our eyes to shut once more, causing us to sway again; miniature copies of my father."

"The Eunuchs' Goat used to attend the memorization classes at your house. He said he was in love with Sa'diya."

Mu'az laughed. "In love with her elbow, more like it. I was the first person to notice. I sat there paying attention to all of them. I took the largest share of my father's caning: whenever I'd sit on the outside breaking the circle, whenever I'd look in the direction of the door, whenever I'd play with the mat or the pools of light in the middle of the circle, or when I'd lay my voice out over the circle, soaking up the rhythm, training my voice, or when my father would sense that I wasn't reciting the verses, rather floating and bobbing on the surface of the music, dipping my vocal cords in its sweetness. His cane and his shouting both stung: 'Recite properly, boy!'"

Nasser cut him off, laughing: "Do you sing, Mu'az?"

"No, I cry . . . I pin a recitation on the scales of a melody. I uncover new horizons for my voice in the rules of Quranic recitation." A light flickered in Mu'az's eyes and he carried on:

"Whenever my eldest sister, Maymuna, begins to recite, her tears begin to stream but only out of her right eye. We never know what to think. Her tears don't just stream down over her cheek, they spill out of her eye into the air and fall on her chest and onto my younger sister Sa'diya's shoulder. Sa'diya says that there's an angel with a watering can who sits in Maymuna's eye and sprays us with her sweet tears. As soon as the first tear falls onto my father's hand, he swells up with joy and says, 'Praise be! An eye that cries for the sweetness of the Quran won't be touched by hellfire. The fire won't come near your eyes, Maymuna. God willing.' Sa'diya would leave the tears where they landed across her neck as shield against the fire.

The detective was surprised by how nonchalantly Mu'az mentioned his sisters' names in conversation; that wasn't how things were done. Mu'az watched the television in front of him in silence for a while and then went on with his story. "Sometimes I ask myself, what's life like for my sisters? Even television is a novelty to them. Look . . ." Nasser looked over at the black triangles huddled in the doorway of the Imam's house: Mu'az's sisters dressed in abayas that covered them from tip to toe, cones of black crowding one another to peek through the narrow crack in the door at the television in the cafe.

"When they're sleeping sometimes I wish I could see beneath their eyelids. I want to see how they make dreams without the help of a satellite dish. I hear them whispering: 'Which of the boys in the neighborhood are we going to marry? Who should we recite the chapter of Ya Sin forty times for?'

"'The Eunuchs' Goat?'

"'His name's Salih, don't call him the Eunuchs' Goat.'

"'Yusuf?'

"'Yusuf's disappeared.'

"'Mushabbab?'

"'Our father says he's no good.'

"To get Yusuf to come back to the neighborhood, Maymuna recited the Ya Sin Chapter of the Quran forty-one times, as though it were a raft that would carry her to him."

"You're talking about when a girl recites Ya Sin forty times?" Nasser asked.

Mu'az looked at him, shocked that police officers knew anything about occult rituals. "You've heard of it?"

"Ever since I was a kid, that ritual scared me. I was worried that a ghoul-girl would cast a spell on me so she could marry me." He could tell that Mu'az had suddenly stopped listening to him. He'd turned his head to look at the thin old man dressed in blue wool robes and a red-checked head-covering who'd appeared at the end of the alley. Nasser followed Mu'az's line of sight. "Who's that?" he asked.

"That's sheikh Muflah al-Ghatafani, Mushabbab's friend."

Nasser threw a fifty riyal note on the table and ran after the sheikh, leaving a bemused Mu'az in his wake. He followed close behind him until he reached Mushabbab's orchard. He slowed for a moment before charging in after him. When he entered the orchard, he found the old man rummaging through the shelves and beneath the cushions.

"What did you come here to look for when you know full well the owner's gone missing?"

The old man was clearly embarrassed. "I'm looking for something that belongs to me."

"My name is Detective Nasser al-Qahtani and I'm investigating a murder. The owner of this orchard is wanted for questioning as a potential suspect in the crime. The fact that you've turned up here is enough to make you a person of interest in the case."

"Listen, detective sir, I don't have anything to do with this neighborhood or the people in it. I left an amulet with Mushabbab and I've come to take it back."

"An amulet?"

"Yes, it's an antique silver amulet that's hollow on the inside and can be worn on a belt. I inherited it from my grandfather but I had to sell it to be able to buy a gold ring for the mother of my children."

"So how did it end up here?"

There was a flash in the old man's eyes and there was scorn in his voice. "Mushabbab collects antiques and he wanted the amulet, so he asked me to leave it with him so he could examine it closely. Didn't you say he was gone?"

There was something cunning and ill-tempered about the way the old man looked at him and Nasser just knew that he was only giving him part of the truth. Nasser looked the man up and down; he wasn't carrying anything other than that menacing smile.

"And did you find what you were looking for?"

"You didn't give me a chance. Are you going to let me go?"

"Give me your address in case I need to call you in. Then get out of here. This place is off-limits."

Mu'az: An Occult Future

At mid-morning, Yusuf met Mu'az at the foot of Mount Hindi. The son of a hag's store had closed, and in its place was a new building with a cheaply-finished glass frontage, and a vast sign proclaiming APARTMENTS TO LET. Yusuf snorted at the thought of how long the flimsy building would last.

They set off up the hill in silence, Mu'az leading and Yusuf following. Yusuf didn't want to look around at the houses he used to see as a teenager when he passed by on one of the son of a hag's bikes. He kept his eyes to the ground and his brows firmly knotted together, but sounds still filtered through: children cackling like mountain goats, clambering about and shrieking at one another. Like the call to prayer, the smell of cooking rose from each of the tiny houses at exactly the same time. Female voices spoke a jumble of foreign tongues and Meccan slang. Windows opened and closed quickly to catch the attention of passersby, their distant clatter mingling with radio quiz shows, the clink of spoons on plates, coughs, and songs. Rocks tumbled; the steps up the hill were clearly defined in some places, but in most crumbling away.

Mu'az's voice brought them to a halt. "We're here." Yusuf looked up to see an old wooden door. A mihrab was engraved on each leaf, and the knocker, positioned where the inner niche would be, was shaped like a dove in flight, its beak striking a flat plate of copper. The graceful old house towered above Yusuf, reaching up the slopes of the mountain so that its roof was level with the foundations of the square Mount Hindi citadel. It was perhaps seven stories high—attempting to count them just got him lost amidst the solid volcanic stones, mined from Mount Abu Lahab, from which it was built. A bunch of keys in Mu'az's hand suddenly caught his eye. They had appeared out of nowhere. Mu'az took the largest one, the handle of which was shaped like a mihrab, inserted it into the cavernous lock with a trembling hand, and opened the door.

It creaked loudly and released a breath of cold air. Their skin crawled at the musty odor of dereliction and the motes of dust that billowed out.

"This is where my treasure's buried, Yusuf," said Mu'az. Yusuf's mouth felt dry. He didn't dare to look up at the endless ceiling as he stepped into the hall. On both sides of the hall, windows looked out from spacious sitting rooms, and toward the back, stairs descended to both left and right, no doubt leading to cellars below. In the center, a wide staircase led upward.

Mu'az led Yusuf to a room at the back of the hall on the right, as he himself had once been led by Marie, the owner of the house, when Mushabbab had taken him to see her. He thought he had seen a visitation of the Lord come to answer all his prayers when the woman had said she wanted him to work for her in place of the Pakistani who was leaving her service. "A servant in the Lababidi house on Mount Hindi," recalled Mu'az. "It was just what I needed to convince my father the imam. The salary they offered was persuasive, and he let me leave high school. What I found here was something I would spend the rest of my life looking for." He went first into the small room, Yusuf following. It was bare except for a bed on the floor.

"This was mine," Mu'az gestured. "No one will look for you here." He hesitated to give the whole bunch of keys to Yusuf—he was tempted to keep the key to the front door and the upper stories—but he couldn't bring himself to separate the bundle of linked mihrabs. He reluctantly placed the bunch in Yusuf's hand. Sighing, he looked around the austere room where he'd lived throughout the time he had worked in the service of Marie, the wife of al-Lababidi the photographer.

"God is great . . ." The first words of the noon call to prayer pierced the room. They cleared Mu'az's indecision, and he took the keys back from Yusuf. "Come on, I'll show you the house." Yusuf followed him to the wide central stairs. The incline was so shallow—each step was no more than ten centimeters—it was more like a slope. They raced the call to prayer up to the top floor, so Mu'az could begin Yusuf's tour there, just like his own first tour of the house had begun.

Mu'az's recollections mingled with Yusuf's observations. When they got to the roof, as Mu'az had done the first time, the stairs opened out into a room. Engraved wooden windows in all three walls looked out onto the expanse of the sky, and on the fourth side, splendid teak arches gave fully onto the roof. Neither of them looked toward the room, its door ajar, at the end of the roof; instead they looked at the damask floor cushions—now covered in dust and dove droppings and feathers—where he had first seen the Lebanese woman. She was so unlike the black-cloaked women of the neighborhood and his skinny cinnamon-stick sisters; no houri, certainly, but enchanting nonetheless with her thick cigars and smoke rings. That was how he'd seen her first.

Mu'az stopped Yusuf there, under the canopy where the stairs led up to the roof, as the second call to noon prayer exploded like a fountain from dozens of minarets below them. It was as if the roof was being lifted aloft by the voices. Mu'az wished Yusuf could see Marie as he'd seen her that day, when he and Mushabbab had followed the young Pakistani to the rooftop. Standing there at the top of the staircase, he was bewitched by the woman reclining with her legs crossed. She was perhaps in her sixties, though she could easily have been in her forties, and the adolescent Mu'az didn't notice the flabbiness around her knees—only the shimmer of the silk stockings hugging her bare calves, which stood like two of heaven's white-sugar columns. He had been startled for a moment, astonished to see a woman like her within the circle of the Haram Mosque. At the end of the roof the half-open door caught his eye; a washing line hung inside the darkroom beyond. He made out freshly developed photographs pegged up to dry on the line, but he couldn't tell when or where they were taken.

He stood with Yusuf in front of a portrait of the lady of the house and introduced him to her, as Mushabbab had done with him. "Marie," he said, with the same mix of deference and embarrassment that a real, living woman would occasion. "Mr. Lababidi's wife. Al-Lababidi was the first Meccan photographer. He was taking photos from the beginning of the twentieth century right up until God took him away when he was nearly a hundred. That was in 1979, the year Juhayman al-Otaybi seized the Haram Mosque. Al-Lababidi left his photographic archive of Mecca to his wife." Yusuf had no idea why Mushabbab should have been visiting this lady—Mu'az hadn't understood either—an interloper among the women of Mecca with her Christian name and religion, which she gave up in exchange for the right to accompany her husband into the Muslim-only Haram compound. In fact, the only way she had actually entered was through the telescopic lens of the tripod-mounted camera that stood on their lofty rooftop next to the citadel, shaded by the minaret of the Turkish baths.

Al-Lababidi had met the fifteen-year-old Marie in Beirut when he was in his sixties. The girl born to a soundtrack of Hiroshima's echoes had fallen inevitably, definitively in love with this Meccan born at the dawn of the twentieth century who had spent years moving back and forth with his merchant-fighter father between Syria and the Hijaz, his plans put on hold by two world wars that ended up turning him into a pro at photography, life, and faith in a soon-to-appear Hidden Imam who would end all wars and turn the deserts into Eden.

Mu'az was lost a while in the memories of his infatuation with the Marie he had seen the very first time he stood in this spot. He was fresh from the neighborhood back then, and his adolescent gaze just couldn't put together all the contradictions, all the strokes of passion, struggle, and transformation that had gone into sculpting this female idol. He trembled involuntarily when she stood up in a single fluid movement, thinking to himself that if he'd taken her photo just then she would have appeared as a droplet of water falling from her bijou ruched muslin hat.

Marie walked ahead of them to lead the way downstairs into her vast old house, taking them into sitting room after splendid sitting room, hidden store rooms and cozy parlors. Every time she led them down to the next floor, the servant scurried ahead, unlocking high-ceilinged reception rooms where sculpted doves crowned each arch and flanked tall mirrors that shunned reflection of the present and instead revealed a hundred years of the Holy City. Having stood empty since the beginning of this century, the three-hundred-year-old house was now inhabited not by people but by black-and-white photographs of all shapes and sizes that covered every wall, from the floor right up to the gilded cornicing of calligraphied poetry.

Mu'az wished he could draw Marie for Yusuf, not merely as she was but how she looked in motion; wished he could create a film so that she could walk before Yusuf, leading him as she'd once led Mu'az. On the upper floors he and Mushabbab had walked, as Yusuf was doing now, past photo after photo of the courtyard of the Holy Mosque where the pilgrims walked circles around the Kaaba: scenes of the whirlpool of human movement circumambulating the courtyard taken throughout the decades, showing infinite numbers of tiny dots sinking to kiss the black stone or prostrating en masse against the Hateem Wall or swaying, supplicating in front of the multazam or washing in foaming buckets of water from the Well of Zamzam or reciting their night prayers. The pattern was repeated and varied endlessly across the years. The thrill of seeing the old courtyard like this, when he'd thought it had been lost forever, had shaken him violently, just as it shook Yusuf now.

On the next floor down, Mu'az waited at the door of a parlor, as he remembered Mushabbab had done, to allow Yusuf a few moments alone with some rare photographs of the architecture of the Haram Mosque taken at the beginning of the twentieth century, long before all the expansion and demolition projects. They showed the green-domed Well of Zamzam, the Gate of the Shayba Tribe, the spot where Abraham had stood, where Imam al-Shafi'i delivered his classes, the Hateem Wall around the Hijr of Ishmael, the outposts of the Hanafi, Maliki, and Hanbali schools of law, and the surrounding buildings that jostled for a view across the mosque's central courtyard: the Ottoman governmental palace known as the Hamidiya, the triple-terraced Ajyad Fortress with its rear towers, and the Vali's office with its twin minarets and three domes.

On the next floor down, Yusuf found photographs of Mecca and stepped forward to mingle with the people walking through its ancient neighborhoods: Mount Turk, Mount Hindi, the Sulaymaniya quarter where the Afghans lived, the Moroccans' Alley, the Bukharans' Alley, and the settlements of the Africans, the Jawanese, the Kurds, the Sindhis, the Syrians, the Yemenis and the Hadramawtis. A whole maze of alleys like the Lane of Many Heads, overflowing with faces with which Yusuf and Mu'az no longer crossed paths as they went about their daily business: black, white, and narrow-eyed children playing barefoot in the street, slave musicians beating drums and dancing with rattles, hoof castanets, and wood blocks, Indian merchants in black cloaks over white robes haggling with Turkish officers whose belts held inlaid swords and whose pedigree camels were adorned with silver brocade sashes, and madly grinning Sharif children—those descended from the Prophet, peace be upon him—in short gold- and silver-belted jubbahs that showed their booted feet and wrapped cloth turbans, similar to Ottoman fezzes, studded with starry pearls. The sons of the Vali and other dignitaries were more serious, wearing cloaks cinched with cartridge belts bearing jeweled daggers. Then there were the children of the Shayba Tribe, the custodians of the Kaaba, who exuded nobility and splendor in their brocade-trimmed robes, leaf-embroidered jubbahs, and gold egals. There were muezzins who traced their ancestry back to Ibn Zubayr, merchants with their Circassian slaves, women reclining in their gardens smoking hookahs or hurrying down dusty streets, wearing brocade-striped belts and airy, white embroidered burkas that framed their eyes with gleaming gold coins. There were Meccan brides drowning in layer after layer of pearls, and pilgrims from India, Baghdad, Kabul, Bahrain, Melaka, the Bacan Islands, Sambas, Jawa, Sumatra, and Zanzibar. Bukharan dervishes, in their wide-belted short coats and the fur-trimmed conical hats they wore even in the sweltering Meccan summer, held staffs and jangled bunches of keys that—so they claimed—unlocked paths and destinies before them wherever they went. Knowledge seekers busked their way from Yemen to the Great Mosque, drumming and dancing to earn their keep while they stayed in Mecca and were educated in religion.

Tentatively, imitating the Pakistani who had preceded him as guardian of this treasure, Mu'az locked every floor as they descended to the next, giving Yusuf no chance to go back and contemplate again the decades of Mecca's history they had passed through. Each floor was a different face of the city's existence. The lower they went, the more alienated Yusuf felt: as they moved into more recent years, Mecca's immense spirituality receded into the distance. Floor by floor, the old alleys became wider, and their cobblestones, over which water once ran in rivulets to cool and refresh the city, were picked off, until they reached the ground floor where the houses had lost their teak-wood windows altogether. Poor squatters had taken over the old abandoned houses with their roof terraces, and the hillsides had been eaten away to make room for asphalt that bit through them. Yusuf got to the point where he couldn't tell if he was still wandering among the photos of al-Lababidi and his wife Marie or if he had been booted back to the modern Mecca he knew.

With dilated pupils, Mu'az turned to Yusuf, wanting to convey in his look that he had seen—and wanting Yusuf too to see—the transformation of the world around him into an ugly rectangular box, the blade that had sliced through old stone houses leaving staircases and footsteps dangling in mid-air and reminiscences of wooden windows teetering, about to crumble into nothingness or fall into a deep dream; that had unceremoniously chopped up sitting rooms mid-soirée so that half a divan still stood in its place here, perhaps the leg of an evening guest still resting on it, and eager oud strings or laughter still echoed there, only to be chewed up by bulldozers and paved over with asphalt, cement and aluminum punched through with narrow windows where air-conditioning units crowded out most of the light.

Mu'az and Yusuf stood in front of a room on the ground floor that was stuffed with al-Lababidi's photos of the Mecca he'd continued photographing until his last breath, taken during the period when Mu'az had worked at the house; to these, Marie had permitted Mu'az to add his own black and white photos. Standing there, Yusuf could see how Mu'az had raced to take those pictures, panting to keep up with the pace of the changes sweeping the city. As the photos progressed, they seemed to drag Mu'az and Yusuf into a hole. Around them, the heart of Mecca was transformed into a courtyard paved with marble slabs that erased the Small Market, the Mas'a Market, the Mudda'i Market, the Night Market, and al-Salam Gate Square to the southeast where pilgrims entered the Haram Mosque. Nothing whatsoever remained of the two public squares at al-Salam Gate, only the great courtyard like a crater left by a meteor, overshadowed by glass towers that ate into what flesh remained of the bare mountains. In that pit, gone were the faces of the Meccans who had sought wisdom and proximity to the Great Mosque, and in their place were the faces of mercenary salesmen, infiltrating from every side, and their stores, uninterrupted like prayer beads, which confronted the approaching visitor to Mecca upon his arrival at the gate that opened onto the graves of the martyrs and Umm al-Doud and covered the city's peaks and depressions. Holes had been drilled in the façades of old houses where parlor windows had once been, and protruding glass vitrines now displayed clothes made in Taiwan, China, and Korea. The makeshift stalls selling caps and robes dyed with saffron and embroidered by Meccan fingers had disappeared, while new restaurants, stores, and stands, more of which were opening all the time, sold every kind of fast food under the sun amidst stacked-up white plastic jerrycans of Zamzam water for wholesale purchase.

Standing in that cold hall, Yusuf realized—as Mu'az had also realized—that he was moving in a condemned space, in a holy sanctuary where Old Mecca had come with its history, its people, and its stone houses to take refuge. Here, in al-Lababidi's house. A beggar, he had come to take refuge with them.

Yusuf knew that Mu'az had arrived before him to the world that he'd spent his life trying chaotically to sum up in a word. He was seeing it now summed up in a picture.

Abraj al-Bait Towers

SINCE THE PREVIOUS NIGHT, NASSER HAD BEEN UNEASY. HE FELT NOT ONLY LIKE he was being watched, but like someone was directing his movements, as if by remote control. Thinking for him, impelling him to go poking around after events and faces that even the Lane of Many Heads itself had forgotten. It wasn't just Yusuf's diaries or Aisha's letters—there was something else. Nasser was trapped inside a puzzle, and the puzzle-master was moving him—the central piece—back and forth, either to build or to destroy the case.

That morning, the player had him follow the thread that wove Thursdays together through Yusuf's "Window" in *Umm al-Qura* newspaper. Yusuf had become a ghost who surprised them by peering out of his newspaper column, corresponding with his editors from the many Internet cafes scattered about Mecca. His last piece had been banned, but Nasser had managed to find it on *al-Sahat*, a dissident website, using a personal proxy server. It gave him a great sense of superiority; he could reach everything blocked by the National Anti-SPAM Firewall—Electronic Crimes Division—with their bland message: "This website is unavailable. If you think this website should be available, please click here. For more information on Internet services in the Kingdom of Saudi Arabia, please visit www.internet.gov.sa."

Nasser read:

> *Yesterday when I entered the courtyard of the Haram Mosque, I couldn't see the Kaaba. I looked around, wondering for a moment if David Copperfield—famous for making the Eiffel Tower and the Statue of Liberty disappear—had come to play his tricks on the circumambulating worshippers, but by feeling my way ahead, my fingers finally made contact with it,*

having penetrated the thick vapor of pilgrims' breaths, which there was no mountain breeze left to dissipate.

And when I slipped into the masses circumambulating the Kaaba and raised my eyes to the sky, I realized there was no space left there for the moon; it struggled to squeeze past the Abraj al-Bait towers that dazzled the eye and flooded the mosque courtyard with their silver glare. There was no empty firmament, just the skyscrapers clawing at the bare flesh of the volcanic mountains. I don't know how Mecca breathes any more. Throughout history it had always breathed through those mountains.

I realized then that the day when the Kaaba truly disappears isn't far off. Either it will be suffocated, and suffocate every pilgrim who dares to approach it too, or Wadi Ibrahim's legendary flood rains, which once swept a camel all the way to the mosque's pulpit, will burst forth from the tips of the skyscrapers surrounding it and wash the entire courtyard to a pit at the bottom of the universe. Our eyes, which used to reach the silk-swathed Kaaba long before our bodies, will strain to make out its distant form but fail, and only with infrared night-vision goggles will we dare to venture toward it.

The detective glanced at some of the comments below the article.

"Chill out, grandpa . . . You'll be beefing with our ancestors Adnan and Qahtan at this rate!"

Nasser smiled wryly and wondered how he could track down this ghostly character who left his fingerprints all over the Internet. He was struggling, too, to work out what the puzzle-master was cooking up by bringing this magician Copperfield into the whole business.

Dulcimer

Dear ^^^,

Azza makes me feel guilty. She talks about everything, whereas I don't breathe a single word about you. What she said about him today was both titillating and frightening. Let me tell you what she said:

"I'm a child.

Yeah, a child. And I want to play. What do you expect of someone who was born into a little container? Someone who was nursed on her mother's post-partum depression?

Mushabbab isn't depraved or evil. He's a child like me. Yusuf wrote about Mushabbab. He wrote about him until the slave of the sharifs appeared in the flesh like a genie when I was lonely and heavy-hearted. I sleepwalked that night all the way to his garden.

Don't laugh. Girls were always getting abducted in the stories they told us when we were children. Why do you think that is?

Because the girls of the Lane of Many Heads are born into little containers. The only way they can get out, the only way they can stand in the doorway of their houses and get some fresh air, is magic.

There were times when the secret of my sleepwalking was close to being exposed. At that moment, I'd see fear in the form of agitated camels. Real-life black camels coming toward me, blocking the alley. But I wouldn't shut my eyes, wouldn't shield myself. I run straight toward the center of the herd and at the moment of impact everything disappears. My brow sweats and my throat bleeds. The herd grows larger every time and the houses join in, collapsing as I walk past, and I know that one day they will **crush** me without mercy.

I ignored the rush of blood and sweat until I made it to the orchard gate and pushed it open with both hands.

As soon as I took off my shoes and buried my feet in the sand, I opened up on the inside like a rose. Even my scent changed. There was a burning down the length of my back and between my breasts. I don't know how to describe it to you. Mushabbab calls it "the smell of water breaking." Like all men, Mushabbab is naive. How would he know what it smells like? I, on the other hand, can sense the chemical effects it has. It's still there when I wake up and for days after. It's like a combination of genie hair and the scent of Arabian jasmine.

Do you know how thin and cottony pollen can be? If one were to take hold of me, I'd turn into dust.

I walk around in circles in the orchard while Mushabbab laughs. Aisha, you don't know the Azza I discovered in the orchard. My limbs are longer and more flexible. My smile is wider, my eyes are bigger. The Azza whose eye broke her out of the little container knows how to flirt and talk in ways that you won't even find in those books of yours that scare me so.

The orchard was always full of small things. It's as if they've known you since you were born, as if you can travel backward through time with them. Whenever I went there in the evenings, I found little treasures worth stopping for. One time there was an instrument from Basra, a hammered dulcimer inlaid with mother of pearl. It had precision tuning pins that gave the notes a deeper tone and a longer resonance, one string for each note. When I tried playing it with the two hammers, the smooth, ringing sound that rose up came from those passions that I don't dare to face.

One time, I went in and found the sitting area covered in piles of books that Mushabbab was in the middle of organizing, dividing them up between the shelves on the wall and the shelves beneath the seats. He hid the copies that were nicer and older, and replaced them with copies that were more run of the mill. Mushabbab's passion for hiding things drove me insane. I always made fun of him for it, but he didn't care. For nights on end, the amulet that I'd spied lay there stuck between books in the shelf beneath his stand. I examined it stealthily: it was in the shape of a half moon and it was made of pure silver. It was engraved with intersecting pleas for help shaped like little amulets, which reminded me of my mother Halima's one and only bracelet. She never wore it, of course, rather she hung it proudly on her bed; it was the only gift her husband had given her. The Jews of Yemen had them made to mimic the moon-shaped birthmark on the palms of Solomon's daughters, which symbolized the moon under which they'd been born.

The amulet didn't hold our attention for long. Spring brought the inescapable pandemonium of clogs: some decorated with shells, others with pearls, still others with brocaded Indian fabric, and there were even some made out of fragrant sandalwood. The women of Mecca wore their clogs in their bathrooms and on the roofs of their houses, clicking and clacking wherever they went. The night they arrived, we moved the Persian carpet in the sitting area out of the way so Mushabbab and I could dance on the bare floor. We experimented with every type of tap-dancing imaginable. Dawn snuck up on us that night, as we tap-danced lightly on our feet, until I finally realized just how long I'd been gone and knew that I was in deep trouble. Whoever goes to Mushabbab's orchard is transported into a dream-state; it's as though it's one of the dreaming stations par excellence.

Things were always appearing and disappearing there, but I never asked any questions. He didn't used to rescue me with any answers either. Where does he get all this detritus? Where does he go when he leaves? Sometimes I would come across patches in the dirt in the orchard where bodies had lain recently, and I could never imagine the orchard in deepest night, full of people who'd taken shelter there, waiting for sunrise so they could earn their living. At dawn, one time, I'll hide on one of their collars and see where it is they go.

Those faces crop up and disappear as if by magic; Mushabbab and I are the only ones who hang out there. Aisha, if only you could see the place. From the outside, the orchard looks constrained by the fence and time, but on the inside, there's no fence, no time. You get lost whether you're going forward or backward. It looks to me like a piece of silver that's fallen from the sky. I knew that my game had to end where the trees began; one step farther and the game would no longer be a game. I didn't dare cross over alone. Mushabbab had to wait for me at the entrance to one of the paths or he had to escort me somewhere and bring me back as well. He would always come fetch me in time so I could get back home before dawn. And there was always that same smell. Smelling like the blood of a slaughtered animal, sacrificed there by an old man on the old ground that was still there in the orchard. A scream I still can't perceive.

Tonight I went to the orchard unexpectedly, where I encountered the **guest**, who looked dangerous, what with the bodyguards he had waiting for him at the end of the alley. I darted past, but they spotted me and were about to follow after me before I reached Mushabbab. He was in a state. He hid me off to the side of the orchard as he said goodbye to his visitor.

I waited before I headed back to him. Gathering my courage, I headed for an alleyway that led northeast; at the end of it there was a thicket, dried up, growing wild. At one point, I was stopped by a hand that stretched to cover my entire face. I could feel the hand even if I couldn't see it. But I didn't resist. I peeked through the branches to see three white bodies, naked, talking in a huddle. I felt my vitality goad me as I stood there. I was worried that if I moved backward or forward, they would be on to me. I let out a sudden gasp when I felt Mushabbab's lips rub against my braids.

You think I'm overdoing it? I could feel hot lips against the end of my braids; I smelled fire. Mushabbab led me back. When we got to the sitting room, he sat me down in a Louis XIV armchair he'd chosen for me at an antiques auction, which he always kept in the same exact place in the courtyard facing the sitting area. Only then did he settle my curiosity. "What a wild imagination you've got! What you saw was nothing more than three column capitals. The same columns that were left forgotten in the colonnades of the Great Mosque after they were removed from the Hanafi corner and the Well of Zamzam. They disappeared completely, and we had no idea where to look for them even. Then one day a friend of mine who's got some pull brought them here." To assuage my doubts even further, he said, "The most complete one is the **column** that loomed over the Well of Zamzam, its oil lamp lighting the pilgrimage rituals for centuries. Memories of the faces of believers and a faith unlike any humans can conceive of are alive inside that column's memory."

The thought of running my hand over those column capitals makes me shiver with a pleasure I dare not explain. Aisha, you're free to roam through books and the minds of those who wrote them. But my world is here between these four walls, which reflect nothing but my own face. In my room, I miss the feeling of coming across these small things, I miss the whims and the laughter. And they don't remind me of the windows. For my own is nailed shut and the only way I can get out is through Yusuf's writing. And that's not real.

You know what I need? To throw a stone. A stone that will force the bird out of my chest into the open air.

Every time I visit the orchard, my desire to go even farther grows.

You'll probably laugh, but I'm dying to get my lips on a teat. To drink directly from a nanny goat's teat. That was what Yusuf did when they couldn't get him to wean. None of the substances they rubbed on Halima's breasts—aloe vera, pepper, chili—succeeded in keeping him off, so his mother let him run loose in Mushabbab's orchard and suckle on the young nanny goats.

What do you think? What must the mixture of dung and wool and hot, pulsing milk taste like?

Mushabbab lays a mat over the sandy ground where we're standing. He sits down and starts playing a Danat, a Yemeni song. A shawl of silence floats, translucent, above us. It's nearly touching the ground, but every time it gets close, a night breeze raises it up.

"Ha! You're going to take her, Mushabbab? Your beloved? To reality TV, to Fashion Academy?" I used to pick fights with him whenever that desire to touch bubbled up inside me.

"Where do you belong if not among beauty queens? When they finally get around to starting Miss Saudi Arabia, you and I are going to have to put our heads together. You'll show us a flirtatious side that's been buried like treasure."

"Everything is buried treasure and keys with you, Mushabbab. Really!"

That's when he stands up. He pushes away all his wooden instruments and starts playing on the live string in my feet. When he reaches my ankle, bodies spring from my body and Mushabbab crumbles. He has one of those episodes that he calls "a moment of dislocation." A moment of submission in which he is stripped of his skin, and his nerves are all exposed to the refreshing breeze.

"Your foot is the buried treasure and the key." I can feel his heart breaking over my foot. I feel awkward and I have to suppress a giggle. How come we don't laugh when a man's worshipping us? I can barely make out his whispering. "Men may dream of kissing your lips, but I don't dream of anything except for this foot. Your foot running over my lips, washing over my face." I shudder, terrified God might punish me for enjoying the man's desperation. This same man who doesn't dare lust after anything above my foot. He stands up suddenly, looking at me as if lost beyond hope. I'm so scared of what I might do to him I begin to tremble."

IT WASN'T NASSER WHO DECIDED WHICH OF AISHA'S LETTERS TO READ; IT WAS THE puzzle-master. Nasser read them out loud so that he, too, would suffer from their many disappointments. He put this Mushabbab character's name down as a suspect, as an adversary, and he went looking for him in Aisha's letters to see if she too had fallen under his spell.

The way the women conspired to break a man's spirit frightened him. He went digging for more of the erotic suspense that outraged him, that whorish glimmer. The puzzle-master had dropped him into a stifling scene, the only cure for which was to throw Azza and Aisha, crushed and naked, onto the side of the road.

P. S. You found the masculine river, Yang, and the feminine river, Yin, in my body. The river water is like magnetic tape: every scar of our desperation and happiness is written onto it beginning from when we are children, and the moments of our sadness pile up, blocking its course, getting it caught.

My whole body caught fire when your fingers touched my nude back. You knew which keys on my spine would unlock the energy: rubbing the small of my back, then up my spine to the back of my neck and the base of my skull. I chased after the void that rose up from my spine through your touch. Suddenly the river split into two streams and oxygen flowed, pulsing, from the end of my spine to the base of my skull. That's when you sighed softly and said, "That's right. Take a deep breath and let it out. Let the dolphin that's trapped in your spine out."

You set my senses free so that they could trap the first thing they encountered, which was you.

And then suddenly I could **smell**. For the first time in years, scents reached me. Your scent.

Now the scent of pine on the inside of your wrist enthralls me.

Oh, how you played the Yin of my body off the Yang. First you raised the level of Yang, and my body burned, then you raised the Yin, and I began to soak. What kind of balance am I supposed to reach through your hands?

I now understand what it means that I was born in the autumn. You said that's when "femininity is at its peak."

Aisha

Al-Busiri's Mantle Ode

NASSER WOKE SUDDENLY TO A POEM INSIDE OF HIM THAT WAS MIXED WITH mastic-scented water from the Well of Zamzam. He'd learned it in secondary school, and it had never held his attention, but still its scent was carried by Yusuf's diaries, and it made him trail after it through his window for Azza:

I'll go with you, Azza, to the ceremony Mushabbab has every year on the twelfth of Muharram to conjure the blessed Prophet.

Location: Mushabbab's orchard. Time: yesterday.

I entered as the call to prayer rang out from the nine minarets of the Haram Mosque. The ground was immediately covered with rugs for prayer. The floor of the sitting room and the ground in the orchard became rows and rows of worshippers facing in one direction, and foreheads began sinking toward their Creator's house.

The wings of angels are not made of feathers but of the sound of warm muttering.

On the Prophet's birthday, once prayers were over, the worshippers formed a circle, the novices spreading themselves out. Mushabbab walked around, his arm covered up to the shoulder with prayer beads, some of them with a thousand beads, which are stored in ivory inlaid boxes that smell of amber and perspiration.

Mushabbab held onto his own prayer beads, which he never relinquished during the celebrations of the Prophet's Birthday. They are made of serpent's bones and whenever he flicked the beads, the life in the bones would whisper secrets of the afterlife to him.

I took my prayer beads of amber cat's eye. The Eunuchs' Goat ran his agarwood beads through his fingers, conjuring his fealty to the fire. I knew that you'd have picked the ebony beads like Mu'az does if you'd come.

Mushabbab sat in his spot to the right, at the tip of the crescent moon formed by the participants, while Mu'az, the Eunuchs' Goat, and I stood by the doorway to the parlor, against the branches of the carob tree and the shadows of the volunteers who were circling with pans of Zamzam water, which was nearly foaming with the breath of the Mantle Ode and the remembrance ritual.

You, Azza, would've stood beside me, exposed to the parlor and the space that lay behind where the volunteers lit fire pits to warm the giant frame drums. The circle was formed in the utter whiteness of robes and headdresses, as our breathing rose, and the gold-trimmed pillows, carved wooden ceiling, and the remnants of the column capitals slipped from our awareness.

"O Prophet of God, O brilliant star,

"You lead all men, from behind the stars.

"Pray for the soul of the one who is present in his absence.

"Muhammad, God bless you and keep you and reward you!" Voices resonated around the room, followed by fingers in the air; millions of prayers for the Prophet Muhammad.

Beads whispered, breaths muttered, as they floated between index finger and thumb, encircling the prayer niche of the assemblage.

You could see the hands raising the prayers they've harvested into the air: "a thousand, ten thousand, a hundred thousand . . ." The leader of the birthday celebrations gathered five hundred thousand prayers and blessings before he bent time: bodies stood straight; hands locked together in a circle of energy, interlinking to form a large field.

Welcome, light of my eye,
Welcome, grandfather of Hussein,
Bless you, O Messenger of God
Bless you, O Prophet of God.

The circle enveloped those present. They all breathed in time as the drums beat their praise, welcoming the Purest One who had been summoned and had arrived.

As though fire were as wet as water
in its grief, as though water itself were aflame.
The demons wail, the lights flash, and truth
in both word and meaning is made plain.

Then the entire group, in the painful throes of passion, prayed in one explosive voice: "Give us strength!"

"Give us strength!" I walked, I slapped the air, I was engulfed in al-Busiri's Mantle Ode. "Give us strength!" I rose from the ground. My face breached the surface of a cool inundation, but Mushabbab's voice brought me back:

"Yusuf. Yusuf, give blessings to the Prophet," he whispered in my ear before splashing me with the poetry-foamed water of Zamzam from a pan, and I snapped out of it.

"The boy's got a tender heart." I smelled butter and milk mixed with the scent of agarwood and mastic. When I opened my eyes, I saw three thousand pairs of hands eating from massive trays of rice cooked with butter and milk. Some of the hands were spotted with warts, others are smooth and blemish-free.

I watched one grease-glimmering hand with a variety of the grimes of toil beneath its fingernails, as it scooped and squeezed rice alongside and in time with another hand with painted fingernails, wet and shining from the juice.

Hands, which in the light of day keep to separate spheres, came together, all of us, in passion and yearning and delight.

When I left Mushabbab, who was dressed in embroidered robes for the birthday celebration that hung loosely and smelled of fragrant oil, which meant it had been blessed to rub against part of the Kaaba's covering, a sense of ecstasy had softened the corners of his mouth. I shut the orchard gate behind me. Behind it was Mushabbab; I don't know what he got back. His private life is a well-kept secret, which he only occasionally gives me a peek of.

Azza, I carry you like the froth of that Mantle Ode. I once heard Mushabbab, raving that "We become orphans if the poem dies; we become naked if we allow it to disintegrate in our neglect."

People say that al-Busiri was paralyzed, and that he saw the Purest Prophet in a dream and recited this poem for him. The Prophet, they say, gave him his mantle and when al-Busiri woke from his dream, he was cured of his ailment. I give you this mantle, Azza, so that you'll be wrapped in the sweet black smell of it, so you'll be bundled up so I can carry you around the Kaaba. I wash you and purify you and absolve you as if you were a sip of briny Zamzam water. Even if we both dissolve, its verses will drip honey on your tongue. Even in your shadowless room, you can hide inside of it.

Nasser was exhausted by all Yusuf's effort. He'd nearly reached the conclusion that Yusuf didn't care about Azza as a person, but simply considered her one of the spirits of the letters that he made submit to his will. He litters them here and there in his histories of Mecca, but in poems, he sets them out deliberately. He enlists them for his paranoia, but when they disobey him he goes on a rampage with his pen, crossing them out of the neighborhood. Why not?

From: Aisha
Subject: Message 11

"This novel, which Lawrence considered his best, tells the story of the lives and complicated relationships of two sisters, Gudrun and Ursula. Ursula falls in love with Birkin, a stand-in for Lawrence the author, while Gudrun pursues a tragic and macabre affair with Gerald. These conflicts: intellectual, emotional, and doctrinal epitomize the course of love in modern society."

Good lord, how much more shameless could I be?

I was reading *Women in Love* on the steps by the front door, as if just waiting for my father to come home.

Gudrun brought out the spitfire in me. I know now that I always wanted to be *normal*, to be Ursula, not Gudrun the rebel.

The passion of those two women was more than I could handle. More than I could take. Even now that I've been married and divorced. Perhaps your presence inside of me would allow me to reach those roiled heights. I was surprised tonight to read Gudrun saying on page ten: "If one **jumps** over the edge, one is bound to land somewhere."

What if what we have to do now is to jump? Jump to make things change? Jump to detach the Lane's many heads? To put them back in place? As a first step toward changing the fate of the land we live in.

If I were to throw myself from here to Bonn, I would still end up here. My passport is temporary, for one trip only: I need a close male relative or guardian to renew it for me. Not having any male relatives left, I won't bother looking for a miracle if I'm going to be stopped by a piece of paper in the airport. Guardian's consent: "I allow this woman to travel and vouch that she will return." That form gets men's blood pumping with visions of rulership and regalia. Try asking your father or husband or brother to sign that form and you'll understand what's meant by the phrase, "The sky shut in on itself." Without it, I can't even choose to jump.

Can words be thrown out after they've been used? Where does a word end up after it's been read? There are two kinds of words: poisonous and not. Certain words make my mouth taste differently after I read them.

My skin changes colors. At the moment, I'm bluish. Poisoned by anger and these desires, which only grow the more I chew on toxic words.

I occasionally burst in on the passage at the end of the book when Halliday is reading Birkin's letter about the union of darkness and multitudes of corruption: "There is a phase in every race [. . .] when the desire for destruction overcomes every other desire. In the individual, this desire is ultimately a desire for destruction in the self [. . .] **a reducing back to the original**, a return along the Flux of Corruption."

What if the souls of the dead were to merge with our own souls and expose our thoughts? Will my desire for destruction poison my father?

P. S. I shut down my computer. I turned off all the lights in my cubby-hole. Darkness everywhere. I closed my eyes and when I re-opened them, I noticed that even in darkness the light streams and crowds.

It occurred to me that this is what the grave will be like. After they've shut you in and you know with full certainty that no artificial light can penetrate, light will come up out of the depths of darkness. It will illuminate for your eyes what lies beyond.

There is life in the darkness.

Aisha

Nasser didn't pay any attention to what Aisha had written about "jumping" and "self-destruction." He spent the entire evening thinking back on Aisha and what she'd said about "merging with the souls of the dead." He knew deep down that the puzzle-master was using the pieces to move him, using Aisha's emails to read him. He was laying bare Nasser's inner thoughts, laying bare the end of his conversation that morning with Yabis the sewage cleaner. He still couldn't get over the fact that he'd voiced those delusions of his after he'd sprung the question on Yabis.

"Your wife, Umm Ahmad"—he didn't dare say Kawthar, her name—"Yusuf wrote somewhere that she can detect the souls of the dead." That was his question, and when all he got from Yabis was a blank look, he continued, "I've spent two decades around crime scenes and corpses. I know what it means when a woman can make out the souls of the departed in the air." Yabis still wore that blank look; he was simply waiting for the detective to spill everything out. Nasser had never spoken these ludicrous imaginings out loud before. "Most of the time, when we get to the scene, the body's already decaying, but on the occasions when we make it there while things are still happening and a victim dies in your arms, I swear you can make out the outline of their soul in the air right in front of you. Sometimes the person tries to whisper their last words into your ear, but their soul slips in instead. Do you know what that's like? It's like a blast of heat straight through to your brain. For a second you feel like another being has come over you and that you're living two lives, with two souls, just for a fleeting second before the being slips out of you and its soul rises to the sky."

The Donkey Empress

The Turkish woman charged into his office in a burst of color: vivid red and yellow, white skin, a streak of blue eyeshadow and a ruby the size of a pigeon egg sitting between her enormous breasts, framed by the low neckline of her robe. She adjusted her loose headscarf, which had slipped to reveal a shimmer-dusted forehead and a peroxide mane sculpted to show off her fine ears and shoulder-length chandelier earrings—amidst all this glitz Nasser scarcely noticed the jubbah she was wearing instead of the usual abaya, and the green sequins and red studs that adorned it. He and the puzzle-master sensed a heat radiating from her that defied Israfel's icy blasts from across the small office, and her glowing locks coiled into his throat and around the words they exchanged. Nasser spluttered and began abruptly, "You're the Empress?"

She gave an unintelligible laugh. "The Donkey Empress!" she corrected. Nasser flinched. "'The Donkey Empress is a butcher,' that's what was written on the wall of my atelier after the corpse appeared. It wasn't hard to figure out that the accusation was meant to smear my professional reputation. The Turkish Empress of Fashion. I vowed to make up for everything my Ottoman ancestors inflicted on the women of this country, to get rid of the seclusion and the black masks, the head-to-toe black tents covering their bodies and the white veils over their faces. And beneath all that lie the forgotten spots: the sad kurtas and sirwals and Jawan sarongs. I came to the Lane of Many Heads bringing joy, modernity—and a good few conflicts too, what with all the men complaining "That Turkish woman's turning them all into vamps!" She looked at him with her world-weary gaze. "I won't deny," she continued, "that Aisha's dress was my breakthrough in the Lane of Many Heads. Before that, I'd had my big break in the city: I was the one who got the first bride ever to ditch the Hijazi get-up. If it weren't for me, the Lane of Many Heads would still be stuck in the eleventh century and brides would still be suffocating from all that padding they stick under the traditional dresses, weighed down with necklaces made from fruit and silver-dipped cardamom pods. A stuffy dress with a million clasps can't compete with the carefree present!" She paused to let her words fill the room, then carried on with a wink: "And Azza? Those rags I strung together for her to pull her out of her father's spider web? Who knows where they took her! The Lane of Many Heads is so ungrateful. So ungrateful! There's no pleasing it no matter how hard you try."

Daughters' Dowers

NASSER CORNERED HER WITH A DIRECT QUESTION: "TELL ME ABOUT THE DRESS."

The Turkish woman looked up. An instinct for seduction lifted one corner of her smile, and she arched one tattooed eyebrow so high it almost reached her hairline. "The dress?" she cackled. "Let me tell you: hems keep climbing up and necklines keep falling down." She shook with laughter. Nasser was so surprised that his question had missed the mark that he didn't notice the innuendo.

"Aisha the schoolteacher. Her wedding dress, everyone says you designed and made it."

She raised her head proudly and snorted. "She and I picked that style out together. It was the embodiment of everything she'd read about the French and

Russian courts! A flower on each shoulder, elbow-length taffeta, and lace gloves, and pearls all over the bodice. We kept the details a secret so the girl could make a grand entrance. I staked my reputation and talent on making her a masterpiece of a dress. She arrived at my atelier for the first fitting in a procession. Her parents came with her, and the whole neighborhood was watching them. I had to close the shop to customers so as to keep the party out, and I managed to prize her away from her parents and get her in the fitting room with me alone. I locked the door and had her stand on the little stage I use for fittings—it's not much bigger than a cake stand really, just a few feet across and one foot off the floor—anyway, I plunked her up there like a fruit on a plate, and the first thing I did was take off the drab gray robe she was wearing. I made sure she knew that I was unraveling a cocoon of her ugliness, picking her locks, peeling her, turning her into a beautiful sliced peach." She said it with lust, and a steamy patch of humidity began to spread on the ceiling above her in the otherwise bone-dry room. "I was getting her ready to be presented to a husband; I knew what I had to stoke and what I had better leave, cooking gently among the coals, waiting to be consumed with care. The poor girl didn't know what to think about all the ruffles and fish scales and layers I poured all over her, rustling and cruel, like a dead-end tunnel, and yet still as light as a cloud against her trembling, newborn body. I artfully arranged the lace to rub and excite her budding breasts, let the taffeta lick her legs, layered stiff net and starched cotton into a petticoat that pecked at her ass and nibbled her silky thighs. By covering her here and uncovering her there, with only air and ruffled fabric, I was able to replenish desire where it waned and reshape her so that she'd catch her husband's eye, make him pant and salivate—" Suddenly, mischievously, the Turkish woman stopped speaking and just stared at Nasser. She enjoyed handing him this forbidden fruit naked on a tray, and then she burst out laughing, knocking him out of his trance. He realized she was choosing and polishing her words aggressively before she poured them into his ears, molten, the steam sizzling, to clothe the demons inside his mind. Nasser looked back toward her to find her staring impudently back. He could see that she'd opened up a route ahead of him and was urging him to take it; she left him with that realization and continued to stitch together her story:

"Then the door flew open, tearing Aisha's flower-strewn tulle and pearl veil and baring her shoulders to her father the teacher's face. He was brought up short by the snow-white starburst that clasped his daughter and revealed that divine body like a blossoming lily. Next to her he looked comically short, hopping about energetically like one of the seven dwarves, thunderstruck by her femininity, honed and rearing. I laughed, because that's my game! He began to complain, 'Where are the jewels? It needs more—more . . .' More flesh or more fabric? I couldn't tell. But his words summed up everything I'd known about the Lane of Many Heads. You know, I'm where excitement gets its start. I'm the one who sparks the desire to get through to the flesh, to the sheath; to the wound beneath, and to the surface, raven-black.

"The poor guy kept yelling, 'What about the sequins? What about the glitter?'

"So I asked him, 'Would you like me to add a few crystals?'

"'A few?!' he spluttered. 'Listen, sister, do you know who the groom is? Ahmad the sewage cleaner's son! He works for some seriously important people,' he bragged by way of explanation, 'and he gave us the best dower the neighborhood's ever seen. So we need to be up to standard!'

"He gave some instructions and left. Aisha was deserted, robbed of her lovely gloves, and we had to add shoulders, a chestpiece, and sleeves sturdy enough to hold all the crystals her father had demanded. They nearly broke her neck with their weight, and brashly outshone her lucky stars, which dropped out of the sky one by one.

"The day of her wedding, of course, the women were awestruck, craning their necks enviously to get a better look at that glittering vision. Poor thing. He left her two months later. The whole neighborhood blamed me for ruining the marriage from afar, and for the death of her family in that crash . . . They said it was all because of that unlucky dress! Any time anything bad happens to you guys in the Middle East, you always blame me, me and the Ottomans. When we brought those black robes and face veils you shouted, 'You've brought the Black Death!' and now when I design revealing dresses you scream, 'You've unloosed the Evil Eye!' At least our veils had slits for women to see and breathe out of; when the hurricane blew out of your desert it sealed them all up!

"Anyway," she finished with a wink, "I'm beyond all of that." Nasser hoped that wink wouldn't drag him into another snare.

That night, he went through Aisha's emails looking for the dress.

Dear ^,

I freed the dress. I spent a whole night snipping **crystals** off the fine lace, and ripped off the sleeves, and when I stood in front of the mirror with bare shoulders I felt such ecstasy. I went up to the roof and stood on a barrel to recreate that first fitting, and let the Meccan night and the lace take turns licking my breasts. I wore it directly on my skin and raised my weightless arms to the sky, ready to fly like I do in my sleep.

Aisha

Rubber Membrane

David,

The sentence I'd read in Yusuf's Window in *Umm al-Qura* floated around in my head: "The Kaaba refused the first covering that was placed on it by the king of the Himyarites: he had it covered in skins and hessian but the House rose up and shook them off, and then it did the same when he had it covered in woven palm fronds. But when he clothed it in water and patchwork Yemeni silk, the Kaaba assented."

Believe me, there are clothes that torture.

I recall the coat my father was wearing when he turned up unexpectedly in my bedroom the day after my wedding. The heat was stifling and there was no reason to be wearing such a heavy coat over the crumpled robe he'd been wearing since the celebration the night before. I was still lying where Ahmad had left me, barely able even to bend my legs. I'd heard the door slam when he'd left in fury at midnight, and then again when he returned at dawn, about an hour before my father appeared. These details are chiseled into my memory. I try to find an explanation for the scene that's stuck in my mind, but I don't dare face the **knife** he hid there. I remember my father came in without knocking and leaned against the doorjamb; he looked as if he were wavering between two possible decisions. It was as though he'd cornered Ahmad in my bedroom cubbyhole, in the bed that filled the entire space. Without uttering a single word, he handed over a piece of paper, and I knew, I knew exactly what it was. I remember how my father's face was flush with blood. This was his second heart attack, and it cast a bloody shadow over the bedroom. The first was when he saw the pan of still-warm blood that had come from between my legs and his face turned the color of raw liver. I was twelve at the time.

My adolescence began in distress. For three whole days, a feverish grape of menstrual blood, my first, grew between my legs. The doctor came to our house with a nurse in tow and rendered a diagnosis as unmitigated as his scalpel. You see, David, I have a history with scalpels. They laid me down in that same bedroom and shut the door. I could sense tiny, shining, curious eyes that turned dull when a needle was stuck in my vein. The world began to recede as a voice ordered me to "clench." I was clenching and my mother was spreading my legs farther apart when the cold scalpel hit, and the world was blown open in that red bubble between my legs.

I was twelve years old, and when I came to nothing was left except for the pan, which our neighbor Halima could attest to. The blood that had stored up in my womb for three days burned as it poured out of me.

And thus my father handed Ahmad, who felt duped, that piece of paper. He looked at it blankly.

"A **medical certificate** signed and sealed." The conversation was one-sided. It was only then that I noticed the knife in the inside breast pocket of my father's coat. A knife?! What's a knife doing on the morning after my wedding?! The room was suddenly calm now that Ahmad had surrendered completely to silence. Even now when I think back on that knife—in the pocket of that small man of many slogans, my father—and the sealed certificate, it still seems like a border between life and death. Ahmad had no idea that even just a glance, whether mocking or incredulous, in the face of that piece of paper would have been enough to make one of us cross that border.

The certificate wasn't on my father's mind that morning. It was my mother who'd got it out and slipped it into his pocket. He'd picked up the knife! Was it Ahmad, the doctor, the nurse, or was it me? Who had my father been planning to stab before chickening out at the last minute?

"**Rubber** hymens." I was the first person to introduce that novelty to the Lane of Many Heads. And Ahmad nearly bought it.

My father took his rage out on what he understood a honeymoon to mean. "He's going to take her somewhere and mull it over? No fucking way." It was the nightmare he'd feared.

Even now my menstrual blood burns, between my legs and his.

Aisha

P. S. The scalpel, the cleaving between my legs, propelled the blood all the way up to my nose. I can still taste it in the back of my throat. All that to be rid of a rubber barrier. But that wasn't all. There were more barriers, devious barriers that no scalpel, no doctor, could tear down. Ahmad failed as well. And yet two years later, you came and you conquered.

The Bundle Girl and the Dinosaur Age

VAGUE RUMORS HAD BEGUN TO SPREAD ABOUT THE MASQUERADE GAME KHALIL liked to stage in his taxi, but Nasser did his best to ignore them—in part because his only meeting with Khalil had caused him so much consternation—but the puzzle-master was prodding his suspicions about that skittish, agitated character. Likewise the police hound inside Nasser wouldn't let him pretend not to know that Khalil was capable of suicide. He'd already committed career suicide, so what was he capable of now that he was about to turn fifty? It's a turning point in a man's life that causes him to start making calculations and the thought of how to regain what he's lost consumes him. How could he pursue a man who was in his prime and yet so full of anger, defiant?

In any case, tracking Khalil down in the neighborhood wasn't going to be easy any more. This was perhaps partly because his backstory had taken place outside the Lane of Many Heads, but more than anything it was due to the dispute over al-Labban's building, the Arab League, and the forced evictions. Khalil had simply left his wife Ramziya on her father the sewage cleaner's doorstep and disappeared. Nasser worried he'd never be able to find him again, but Halima had some advice for him: "Your best bet now is his sister Yousriya. Ask her and she'll lead you to him. She lives in Hajj Silahdar's home for the destitute. The Pilot's well known there. No matter where he's hidden himself or how long he stays away, he's bound to go back to Yousriya. He adores her and she adores him." It never occurred to Khalil that I, the Lane of Many Heads, could be the reason he had to burrow down into the network of banishment places that eroded my perimeter.

Nasser brought some tinned food and a couple of bags of rice with him. He parked his car at my entrance, by the cafe, and followed behind some children who'd promised to show him the way. They bounded ahead, racing and sparring with one another—with the shadows they cast on the crumbling walls even—each trying to kick up the biggest cloud of dust, while Nasser followed passively, surrendering himself to a map that was beyond his control. They took him down alleys within alleys, beneath decaying buildings, which Nasser feared might collapse on their heads at any moment, until they came face-to-face with a hundred-year-old house. Nasser read the inscription over the door: ENDOWED BY HAJJ MUHAMMAD AL-SILAHDAR. The excited children tossed pebbles at the Yemeni guard lying on a bench to the right of the door, and he in turn gleefully opened his mouth as wide as it would go, revealing a tongueless cavity, blackened by licorice and rotting gums. Nasser tried talking to him, but quickly realized he was simple. Delighted by the children's shrieks of laughter, the guard repeated his grimace with a throaty gurgle, but when he noticed that Nasser was holding a bag of donations he went ahead to the door and knocked. There was scuffling and murmuring on the other side. Three loud claps came by way of reply and then a woman's voice barked: "Media or charity?"

"I've brought some provisions for Yousriya on behalf of her brother Khalil the Pilot," Nasser replied without looking inside.

The door clove open and a damp smell gushed out as the women scurried to hide behind the doors to their rooms. As lonely and forlorn as the Seven Sleepers, they eavesdropped on the newcomer and peeped at what he was carrying from behind the doors. A tall, broad-shouldered woman in a blue and white floral prayer shawl came toward him, yanking one corner of it across her lower face so that only her eyes, which studied him carefully with every step she took, could be seen. Slipping back off her forehead, the shawl revealed a few white locks poking out of the tight green kerchief she'd tied around her hair. She surprised him with an elegant gesture of greeting—a remote handshake formed by a thumb pressed to the palm, three fingers swept through the air and the littlest extended gracefully outward—and then she led him to Yousriya's room, the first of several doors along either side of a dark corridor on the first-floor.

"Has Khalil visited you recently?" Nasser asked her immediately.

"You from the press?" she asked anxiously.

"No, no," he reassured her. But she didn't appear to be listening.

She didn't stop for his answer, just plowed on: "because we're not allowed to talk to the media." Then she added, "Khalil said there was something he had to sort out in Ta'if."

"Ta'if?" echoed Nasser in surprise. They were separated by the doorway, but she pushed a chair out into the hall so that he could sit down as she sat facing him on an ornate chair just inside her bedroom. Yousriya began speaking, her lips writhing like a chrysalis behind her shawl. Every time Nasser asked a question, seasoned memories poured out of her, unrestrained. For a moment it seemed to him that it wasn't even Yousriya speaking but the puzzle-master, unlocking women's heads so he could peer inside and leading him into storerooms full of their memories, which were crumbling like the walls of the home they inhabited, atrophying like their forgotten bodies. Nasser was amazed by her closely and vividly sketched memories, which seemed trivial now and sluggish compared to how much had changed so quickly. Details, details, details; he listened intently.

She began, "Khalil is possessed by a black and white dinosaur. He will tell you in great detail about how our father used to take him to the ravine in the South Martyrs' neighborhood in Ta'if, to the cinema where our father himself went to watch films with his grandfather and his friends in the sixties. Such a shame they always repeated the same movie—the one about the dinosaur that tramples cities with his enormous feet. Would you believe that, in the sixties, our father was able to buy a ticket to the cinema and go and watch a movie with other people? That would be an impossible luxury nowadays, even in a modern city like Jeddah, or in Dhahran or al-Khubar in the land of oil. Our father was a furnace of money, or rather like a pumpjack that spewed money like crude and pumped Khalil into the finest aviation school in the USA. He used to always say that we could fly, and that we pissed all over those barefoot naked shepherds with our constitution that dated from the time of the Sharifs. A load of good those words did him—he ended up a broken man in Egypt and he had to cut us off. The money he used to give us stopped at the banks of the Nile, and the old man retired and flew away. I left the world to them, and Khalil started to say, 'Embrace evil . . .' Khalil's been shaken by two earthquakes in his life: coming back from America, and losing his job at the airline. Returning to Mecca from the other side of the Atlantic was like being placed on a road between heaven and hell. Khalil was like a lion in a cage, traveling from Mecca to Jeddah to attend movie screenings organized by the British Council on the invitation of the son of the last sultan of Hadramawt, who'd taken refuge in Jeddah with his family. Khalil had met the man at Heathrow on one of his stopovers on the way to Florida, and they became good friends, until the guy moved to live permanently in London. With the sultan's son gone, the cinema was closed in Khalil's face, just like all the concerts and art exhibitions were closed in everyone's faces by various embassies when terrorists began threatening the expat communities."

The scarf fell from her face, exposing her dark lips. Yousriya coughed and fanned the air around her mouth with an elegant, practiced wave followed by three light raps on her ample chest. She continued with her face uncovered, chewing every word with pleasure:

"Khalil considers himself part of the generation who were taken to the sea and came home thirsty—the generation who fled to American movies to escape the image of the belly dancer—it was either Taheya Carioca or Samia Gamal, I can't remember—pouring champagne into her shiny stiletto for some Pasha who's crawling around her on all fours like a dog. Khalil felt like he'd been transformed, as they say—into a monster. A cross between a Pasha, a dog, and the Incredible Hulk. Just to make it absolutely clear to us that he was made of different stuff than ordinary people, that he was a modern-day combination of movie hero and space explorer who belonged to a world of science fiction, they took away his pilot's license—what a shame—and let him loose in the streets of Mecca, to make the rounds with his taxi . . . He would say that inside an airplane he always became a silent drop of night, gliding transparently, searching inside himself for the young woman who made him fall in love after thirty years of liberty.

"I used to tell him, 'Khalil, you've only ever seen the shadow of her abaya!' But he'd say, 'Yes, but still my mind is licked!' He'd captivated and conquered nightclubs in Florida and Los Angeles, he had adventures to his name like those of Abu Nuwas and dervishes and hashish smokers. He was excessive in everything he did, even in his daydreams, apparently, which all revolved around that cunning temptress, Azza the idiot, who was half his age. Khalil's philosophy was absolute: he was looking for an odorless woman, and he thought he'd found her in Azza. He thought she was a different species from the kind he'd tried on his airplanes. The thing that terrified him most about those women was how promiscuous they were. His stomach would be whisked away and turned upside down in disgust; he'd lose control and become violent, and say he was the dinosaur and that he'd awoken to go on a pitiless rampage. I remember the night after the first screening of the dinosaur film: Khalil's body was taken over by the dinosaur, which was something he'd inherited from our father when he was only nine years old. He stepped out of the house at noon to find a Thai man had spread his watermelon stall out on our doorstep. Suddenly Khalil was throwing watermelons left and right, hurling them down Qarara hill where they exploded like bombs. The Thai man's shrieks brought our mother to the window. Her loud, forceful clap was enough to rein us in, and she tied us up with the firm rope of a threat: 'Wait till your father wakes up and sees what you've done!'"

Yousriya laughed, quickly covering her mouth to stifle it. "The dinosaur was suddenly a mouse cowering, paralyzed in a corner, waiting for the stick. When our father got up from his seat to descend upon us he really warmed us up with those lashes. Fresh welts across our shoulders, feet, and behinds, ready to have salt rubbed in. The marks that that stick left on our bodies were the only words we exchanged with our father. 'Miserable bastard' was how Khalil eloquently put it when the subject of our father Nuri's severity arose. The language had been handed down from the time of Ottoman rule in Mecca, to our grandfather Ateeq, then Sulayman, and from him to our father Nuri, and now it had reached Khalil. Prophets of torment, all of them. People would say they 'stood on the doorstep weathering necks,' which meant the mere sight of one of them was enough to crack a person's neck with fright.

"After weeks of not talking, and tormenting each other, their moods would relax and our father would take Khalil out on trips to look for Uncle Ismail—whom we didn't know and never had known and never would know.

"Khalil's a good boy. He never once fell out with me. Even now he comes every Thursday to pour his heart out into my hands. The two of us got on like a house on fire, but sometimes during the punishments the fire would go out. The cracks of the cane brought our bodies closer together.

"Khalil was ground down hard. He's severe in his affection, too, though. Even at that age, he wanted to imprison me hot cold, but after the fire I forswore this new world—I just couldn't endure it. I decided I'd kneel and pray and serve my sisters instead. I look after the aged and sick, and when their time comes, I shut their eyes and pray over them . . . I know my path: it's here with my isolated sisters, here with these twenty-seven women who are trapped between two darknesses, the darkness of glaucoma and the darkness of these rooms they haven't left for thirty or maybe even fifty years."

Yousriya's eyes settled on Nasser's form as if awaiting sentence, but quickly relaxed into a knowing smile. "And you, what's your story?"

"I haven't got a story!" he answered quickly, embarrassed, but he found himself adding, "I'm also being pursued by nightmarish dreams about a woman." He had to repeat his words for Yousriya like an echo, but she was completely deaf and still couldn't hear him. She must have been able to read his features, though. "The same one?!" she asked.

"No, a friend of hers." She gave him a look of surprise, which soon turned into pity.

"Same thing," she said, before retreating to her memories. "Khalil and I found refuge from our father's harshness with our grandfather, our mother's father. His house looked over al-Malah Cemetery so we got to watch all the funeral processions in Mecca. We played a game where we'd try to tell the different kinds of dead people apart: the elderly were covered in gray, which was very different from the green draped over those who'd died when they were still young; the biers of children could be distinguished by the bright, embellished drapes, and then there were the cages laid over women's bodies which our grandfather explained to us.

"These cages were first widely used in the time of Fatima, the Prophet's daughter, peace be upon him. She was the first Muslim woman whose bier was covered in this way, having been told about the tradition by Asma bint Amees, who had said to her, 'Shall I tell you about something I saw in Ethiopia?' She asked for some pliant palm-frond stalks, bent them and covered them with cloth, making a canopy like a bridal howdah. We used to imagine how Fatima, the Prophet's daughter, had ordered that nobody be allowed to see her dead body and how it emerged in that bridal litter. Khalil used to terrorize me by saying, 'I can picture you as a silent bride in one of those cages for dead women!' And here I am, a spinster. I never married and never even went out into the world, and I'm waiting here in my cage for my funeral procession to set off. Death and I know each other pretty well after all this time.

"From a window in my grandfather's house, Khalil and I used to watch the Yemeni gravedigger. We'd watch him eating his flatbread and leek with one hand, while the whole time using his other to collect bones from fresh graves, which were only a month or so old, and transferring them to a mass grave at the far end of the cemetery. We knew all about that pit of bones and it hardened our hearts. That was where all the skulls of Mecca got to know one another, teeth chattering in the cold. In summer, we'd see him come out in his red sarong and light white headscarf, barefoot on the death-molded, sun-fired earth, walking across the plots in the blazing sun, sprinkling water to cool the dead, stopping at the freshly-dug graves to take a hit of the strong rot.

"We spent our childhood between death and my severe father, coming and going through the carnival of Mecca's old markets in the vicinity of the Holy Mosque. We knew all the traders at the Night Market and the Mudda'i Market because we were the grandchildren of the Sheikh of al-Malah—the biggest Wihda fan in Mecca.

"Khalil used to always wear the red and white Wihda uniform at Grandad's. We were eternal rivals for our grandfather's pride and affection, but Grandfather called me 'top of the bundle,' meaning the choice bit that's placed on the very top of a bundle of surprises, and he always took me out to show me off. He'd take me by the hand and we'd head out to the Mas'a and all the neighboring markets; starting from the house of Abu Sufyan at the Turkish Qubbaniya Hospital, we'd enter 'Egg Alley' where there were stalls displaying handicrafts and caged pets—we always stopped to look at the red-eyed rabbits—and then move on to the auction at the Night Market and the goldsmiths' alley, then turning east toward the Gaza Market where we'd stroll past the masterpieces of joiners and wood-turners, met on both sides by greetings:

"'God preserve you, sir!'

"That was Bafaqih, the silk merchant, who was echoed by al-Fadl, the perfumer.

"'Us and you both, my man!' Grandfather would reply. He had a booming voice that made me wide-eyed with pride.

"Next we'd head north to al-Mudda'a Market where Sheikh al-Wazzan would always greet me with a 'God bless you!' The market was full of huge food and perfume storehouses, nut-and-sweet shops, and fabric stalls. 'Oh generous Lord, a pot of gold and a righteous girl . . .' the dervishes would cry as we walked past.

"Those were the days," sighed Yousriya. "We used to dip our bread in salt and that was enough to fill us up. I live off these memories here, and share what I have with my sisters. They take our minds off things. We don't need a glowing TV to fall asleep in front of, just a little yellow lamp that won't go out in the evening when there's a power cut . . ."

Her eyes shone at the memory of a distant yellow glow. "On the twelfth day of Rabi' al-Awwal, our grandfather would take us on an outing that began at the Prophet's birthplace, the house of Ibn Yusuf in an alley called Ali's Path that lies at the foot of Abu Qubays, at the end of the Night Market. We'd imagine all the torches, candles, and lanterns gathering there after the early evening prayer, and he'd stop to tell us gravely: 'Under the Kurdish bookshop here, in the earth right beneath this spot, is where our beloved Prophet was born. Remember this!' He'd pinch my earlobe, pinching Khalil's with the other hand, and repeat his words once more before shepherding us on toward the wonders of al-Jawdariah, the market of the cobblers and cotton merchants and quilt-makers. We'd stand for hours watching them card the cotton and watching the cobblers as they made shoes and other leather goods. We'd go next to al-Malah market where there were seed-sellers and piles of vegetables, clover, charcoal, and firewood. Finally, we'd end up at the Friday afternoon auction where they sold antique furniture. One Friday he bought me this Syrian-made inlaid chair. I rescued it from the fire, but I forgot my own mother! I was determined to bring it here with me. I used to sit on it just waiting for it to accompany me on this trip."

Nasser watched her. He was no longer a detective; she'd made him a witness. "Don't you miss all that?" he murmured, but she didn't hear him and she didn't reply. All she did was ask him to wait a moment and then got up and disappeared inside the room. She returned with a bundle and unfolded it in her lap in silence, spreading her palms over the old satin fabric like a dove spreads its wings. Without looking up from the bundle, she said, "This contains everything that's dear to me. Feast your eyes!"

When she lifted her hands off of the bundle, there appeared four embroidered rose bushes, their pots at each corner of the fabric and their branches and flowers leaning toward the center, where a woman in a full skirt with rings on her fingers and bright red lips stood against the white background, clutching a bouquet, a foot in a black high-heeled shoe stepping gaily forward to present the green bouquet . . . To whom? Who was she stepping toward? Nasser felt prickles like fireflies glowing in his skin, the prickle of a single name and of letters emerging one on top of the other from the weave of the satin to announce its owner—

Yousriya flipped open the bundle and took out a golden wing spread around a circle. "This is the lapel pin that Saudi Airlines pilots wear. And this is his hat, with the same logo—Khalil left it with me. He hasn't needed it since that damned day when he was fired."

She was interrupted by someone knocking on the wall. "Sister," called a voice, "are you talking to someone from one of the charities? Ask them why they haven't delivered the bedpans yet. My sisters' backs are broken from carrying me to and from the bathroom all night!" Yousriya tapped back to acknowledge she'd heard, but Aminah wailed again, "We were born in a box and we'll die in a scrap of cloth! Give us some light! Help us pay the electricity bill, good Muslims!"

"Yes, yes, I'm sure it'll be sorted out, don't worry," said Nasser, getting up. He wasn't quite sure what he was promising. The curtain that divided the room into two twitched and a dumpy face peered out. "Come back and visit us," it implored. "I haven't left this room for thirty years! Don't forget us, son. No, don't take photos! Not even of the curtain . . ."

You ought to come back, Nasser, he thought to himself as he left. It won't cost you anything. He thought about what he'd read on some website—the ideal charity menu: "a quarter-chicken, a handful of rice, one samosa, four dates, a bottle of water and a small pot of yogurt. 300 riyals can feed all twenty-seven residents." Some local do-gooder had arranged for the set-menu meals to cost donors just six riyals by making up the rest himself.

You really ought to come back to visit once a month, Nasser, and bring them a donation once a year. It wouldn't cost you anything.

From: Aisha
Subject: Message 10

I'm amazed by the battle you went through with your wife to try to give her what no other man had ever been able to. That constant, exhausting effort on the long road of insatiability . . . You two tried everything you could—specialist books, couples therapy, pornography —for four years, but by the end of it your morale as a virile man was totally destroyed.

Looking back, though, I wonder if maybe that process wasn't the hellfire that forged you into the person you are now. I don't know what magic it is you do, but you make me soar. With your hand at the center. That's real flying. A woman's body is the storm's slumbering eye. Do you know where to find the thing that gets it going? **Spreading** all over the world, and the wider you spread open, the higher you soar.

Higher and higher, sharpening that lightning tongue, spreading in from the tips of the wings to touch the core, so close to the agony of death, a beating of wings between the ribs, the belly, and the legs.

The eye of the storm opens up to swallow the whole world and still asks for more,

The male body is nothing more than an ejaculator. The female body vacuums up the whole universe!

An hour later, a muscle was still twitching involuntarily in my thigh—do I come off as an amateur to you? I could go on explaining forever—and I could still feel that branch of lightning cracking all around me.

Yours,
Aisha

P.S. Do you remember that morning when we bumped into each other in the library? You were so surprised to see me. You stopped for a while to have a look at the research I was doing on the computer. It was about an extinguished star, which had a black hole at the center and a green halo around it, and had been discovered accidentally by some amateur. Your eyes kept flicking nervously to the door, however. You must have had a date with some girl. I felt sorry for you so I tried to distract you by saying, "There are black holes in space threatening the young stars that are trying to come fully to life, like this one."

"And was this one also discovered by an amateur like me?" you said, teasing me in turn and laughing.

P. P. S. I just remembered that song my mom and Auntie Halima used to sing about how babies are made: "Water mixed with water . . ." They'd giggle and say, "Can you believe we used to sing that out loud when we were young?"

An Eye and an Eye

Mu'az waited eagerly for his free moments so he could go and visit Yusuf. He knew he might attract people's attention, but he couldn't stay away from the treasure whose keys he'd given up willingly. He felt deprived; it pained him for that world to be taken from him.

The moment he stepped into the hall, he sensed the profound change that had come over the house all of a sudden. It was as if the house was conspiring with Yusuf. It was giving him access to places Mu'az had never been to, showing him photos Mu'az had never seen.

His first thought was to kick Yusuf out, then he calmed himself down and considered locking Yusuf into the central hallway and taking back the keys to the upper floors, but the kind soul within him, the one who'd memorized the Quran, intervened on Yusuf's behalf. Nevertheless he was still possessed by a burning jealousy. What was it about Yusuf that exerted such power over the house in a way he never could?

Yusuf avoided Mu'az's accusing gaze, hiding a deep sense of guilt. Over the days he'd spent alone in the house, he'd fallen into an arid solitude, which had driven him to sneak into the parlor where all those faces were, impelled by a sudden urge to be among those Meccan features. There must be faces he knew or faces that knew him and could make him feel at home. Just one face might be enough to give him a sense of place and bring a sense of center to all the broken vignettes around him and the wholesale destruction of ancient landmarks. He stared at every photo; he didn't pass a single patch of wall without interrogating every picture, looking for threads to tie him to Mecca or to the Lane of Many Heads, examining events that he hadn't noticed at the time, which had brought him to this destitution. He'd known full well that Mu'az wouldn't be happy, but the house was reeling him in like it wanted to prod and revive his memory.

Mu'az bored into Yusuf's face. The eyes, which evaded his own, worried him. Was Yusuf seeing the Mecca hidden in that place through the eyes of history? Whereas he, Mu'az, had only ever seen through the eyes of art and technique, like al-Lababidi? Art's eye was restorative and healing, but history's eye liked to pick at scabs. Why had he let that coarse eye in here to pick through Marie and al-Lababidi's treasure? Without realizing what he was doing, Mu'az hurried to beat Yusuf to the biggest scab in the place.

"It was off this very roof that I threw away my book of sins," he said, pausing to see whether the words had any effect on Yusuf. Unlike Mu'az's father, though, Yusuf wasn't frantically obsessed with catalogues of sins, so Mu'az carried on. "Because I was so proud that Marie appointed me to be guardian of the house—even though she warned me never to go through any of the floors without her express permission." He gazed down at the feather duster he was holding. Yusuf kept silent, having taken note of Mu'az's tone of accusation, which was no doubt due to the temerity he'd shown by going into the parlor.

"I used to dust Mecca's every epoch with this peacock feather duster, making sure the pictures on the wall were straight, and I'd clean the developing baths and change the red lightbulb." He pushed the switch a few times but the lamp didn't come on. Yusuf felt sorry for him. "They must have cut the electricity off ages ago . . ."

Mu'az stared at the floor in front of him in silence, unable to describe the part of himself he'd discovered in that house. "Do you know Verse 260 from the Surah of The Cow? When Abraham asks God to show him how he resurrects the dead. Do you remember how God responds? 'Take four birds and tame them. Then put a part of them on each hill and call them and they will come flying to you.' How he called them through his faith, and the parts came flying back to him whole? I'm those birds. I was scattered across Mecca's mountains and scattered among you boys in the Lane of Many Heads, then along came this house and this camera, and it brought me together so I could fly whole . . ." He strove to impress all this upon Yusuf and to undermine his apparent affinity with the house.

"It's like a treasure hunt. We are—I mean, each one of us is—scattered about in caves and on mountaintops and in deserts, in places and in people all over the world. And we find—or at least the lucky ones find—a little piece of that treasure as we go along. I found a huge piece of my treasure in this house. Marie allowed me to discover it through a camera lens. I found another part by memorizing the Quran . . . No, the Quran is the power or the faith with which I called those parts together. They came 'flying to me' and made me whole."

After a pause, he went on, "You never saw me, Yusuf. I was just a shadow of you golden boys in the Lane of Many Heads. I was your negative. I was just a blank sheet for you to scrawl your heroism on. But here . . . I discovered the image of a black and white Mu'az, who wasn't just programmed to record you. I develop this world. I am its continuity. All that time it had been waiting for my lens and my flash and my patience as an artist. Marie saw all that in me with her trained eye. She gave me this professional camera and told me, 'It's yours.' It was like recovering a lost piece of myself—like some amputated part suddenly returned to my body to make it whole. When I wandered up and down all the floors, al-Lababidi took over my body. Took me out of the world. And Marie made time to teach me how to use the camera. The sound of the shutter made my entire body tremble! You know? When I was growing up my body could always sense the lost camera. It could sense its twin somewhere in that void—until the twin was embodied in this little light-sensitive contraption. Marie taught me what to see and how to see. The Quran taught me how to find light in the darkness, and Marie showed me how to capture and manifest it. I flew with my camera above the citadel, my heart racing, and I said to myself, 'I'll begin where al-Lababidi began. I'll capture a beauty equal to, even rivaling, my own worth. But I could feel the difference in the camera from the very first shot; the truth hit me and it hurt. Al-Lababidi's lens had captured growth and construction, mine captured destruction and decay. It could recognize the magnitude of the changes that were happening to the city, not only to its body but also to its spirit. A spirit that had once called out to the Hidden Imam was now preparing for the monster that would smack the ground with its tail and bury the city alive. My eye would flicker thousands of times a minute, following the rapid movements of the shutter leaves, before a wall of collapsing skylights, or a mirror retrieved from the splinters of a house, or the still-standing vaulted ceiling of a caved-in sitting room, or a beautiful doorway closing for the last time with panels bearing the fingerprints of old world craftsmen—wood and plaster panels that vied to out-exquisite the other. They shyly cast their verses of Quran and poetry onto forgotten courtyards, to wait under a layer of dust for resurrection, but they were threatened from both sides: on one side the grasping fist, and on the other the decay eating away at their sweat and blood.

"I can feel Marie watching me now in silent pain. She wanted me to see this, to suffer as I realized how fast the encroaching sands of ignorance and fear were advancing, cementing over and obliterating everything in their path, and getting closer and closer to her heart too. She didn't want to come too close to the worlds of my camera, but she taught me how to develop them and she used it to record her purification and her innocence for posterity. Straight away, my lost-cause creatures began appearing in al-Lababidi's photo-worlds—forgotten, snatched, improvised—and Marie began to wilt slowly at the same time. The thought of beginning with death terrified me so I never picked up the camera on days when Marie had nothing to say. She eventually lapsed into total silence . . ."

Mu'az told Yusuf how one day he'd woken up and found himself up in the little kitchen on the roof, lying on the ground, his head resting on the millstone. A revolution broke out inside of him: he would either bring the outside into the house so that it could become a new pulse for the city or he'd take that pulse out into the pulse of the modern street and let them blend together. He decided to begin with the latter.

When he'd stood there, trying to choose between those worlds embodied in black and white, he'd found he didn't dare. He just about managed to wrap up a few faces of pilgrims from the thirties in a folded sheet of ihram fabric he found, and leave.

He hadn't walked so much as been carried along by those old bodies, who were still tramping on their pilgrimage from the ends of the earth. He was overcome by the heroic urge to release those beings to resume their lives of spirituality in Mecca, but he didn't know where he should take them to set them free. His feet had led him to the teacher at his old primary school, where all the kids in the Lane of Many Heads had been taught. He had a notion that the pupils should see those photos, that they should form part of the curriculum of handwriting and reading that they all went through, so that the photos and the children could grow up together.

The teacher flicked through the stack of photos, then looked up at him and said, "All these people and stones and trees . . . You'll be asked about them. Will you be able to breathe life into them on Judgment Day?" The teacher had recently been reading an eyewitness account of the end of days. The big red *X*s that were slashed across the heads of animals in the drawings in science and reading textbooks crisscrossed in Mu'az's mind. He pictured them advancing on the necks of his nobles and pilgrims, who'd run out of there.

Realizing he wasn't going to wait for Judgment Day, he grabbed the photos and dashed out. No second life for these faces.

After that lengthy confession, Mu'az couldn't stay away from the house. He hurried to the Lababidi house to see Yusuf whenever he could to continue telling the story, fearing that if he stopped, the house would surrender to Yusuf completely. It didn't take long for Nasser to notice his routine.

Making use of the lunch hour when the shop was closed, Mu'az hurried to catch the public minibus, and Nasser followed him on his trip to Mount Hindi. Beneath the building with the APARTMENTS TO LET sign, Nasser saw him with a tall young man, a skinny specter of a guy who reminded Nasser of the ghost in Yusuf's diaries. His heart started beating faster as if he were about to come face to face with his adversary, and he jumped out of his car, slammed the door, and sprinted toward them. His rapid footsteps caught their attention right away, and the tall young man hurried away while Mu'az turned back toward Nasser and blocked his way.

"Who was that you were just with?" Nasser asked, panting.

"Who are you talking about?" Mu'az asked, answering the accusation with total calm.

"The guy you were just talking to." The man had disappeared, swallowed up by the mountain, and there was no sign of which path he'd taken.

"Oh, he just stopped me to ask how to get to al-Salam Hotel."

Nasser was at a loss. "What are you doing here, anyway?" he asked.

"Buying sweet dates for my dad," replied Mu'az, nodding at the shopping bag he was holding.

His silencing stare bored into Nasser long after he'd left. Nasser's police nose could smell the prey he'd been searching for all this time, and the heat in his temples agreed. He spent the searing midday hours walking back and forth on the mountainside, peering into people's houses and faces, sneaking into corridors wherever he found a door ajar and investigating ruined buildings, looking for that tall specter. He knew his target was somewhere in this labyrinth.

That evening, Mu'az tried to find a way to go back. He had to make it absolutely clear to both Yusuf and the house that they couldn't get rid of him, even if they started making deals with external forces like this Nasser, whom he'd only just managed to stop from uncovering his treasure.

The mountains ceased to tremble when they were both shut up in the Lababidi house together. Mu'az sat sulking on the roof in the shadow of the minaret of the Turkish bath, where he could keep an eye on Yusuf and the house. He wanted to be enveloped by the restful sunset over the rooftops like usual. The old pain attacked him during his long silence. But suddenly, he didn't need to be jealous any more—didn't need to possess or to tire himself out. After they had both performed the evening prayer on the roof, he told Yusuf the most important of his secrets. Still facing the Kaaba, he began:

"The day we discovered the corpse in the Lane of Many Heads, I came here to escape everything. Marie was sitting like she usually was, one leg over the other, leaning on those damask cushions and resting her head to the left-hand side, where she had a diamond flower-shaped brooch pinned on her chest—a moon hovering over a flower—and her muslin hat was sitting on her chignon of black and gray hair. My lens was still shaken from seeing the body in the lane so I sat on the floor in front of her, still trembling a bit. We sat there for hours, maybe days, and she said nothing the entire time, so finally I looked up at her. I realized that I'd seen yet another loss. I'd witnessed the death of a whole century. I didn't dare touch her!

"I still don't know whether it was me who killed her or not. Did I bring the germ of death with me when I came, destroying her world?

"That evening, the Meccan sky looked like an empty, colorless mirror that didn't reflect the person looking into it. It was splintered by paths leading into and out of the Holy Mosque like ant trails around a nest, and you could no longer see the inside from the outside. I felt like I'd entered into her moment and I realized that she wanted to be left where she was, looking out over the Haram Mosque, which she'd spent half a century photographing. I was worried it would be disrespectful to the body, though, so I pulled her seat, just as it was, to the darkroom over there, read the Surah of Sovereignty over her, and closed the door. I gathered up my sinful, intimate photos, went down the stairs, locked al-Lababidi's front door safely on all those heads that had been threatened with decapitation, and left. I buried the set of keys with the interlocking prayer-niches under the top step of the staircase in the minaret in the Lane of Many Heads. And covered them up with my father's calls to prayers and recitations of the Quran, and I left them undisturbed until you, Yusuf, needed somewhere to escape to. I locked myself out of there; that was as far as I was going to get: shop assistant to the owner of Studio Modern in Gate Lane. Two simultaneous deaths made for a great ending, don't you think?"

The air around them trembled. The desire for his approval, the desire to please him, held Yusuf in its hot thrall. Could Mu'az have possibly had a hand in—he quashed that train of thought, ignored it. "I know how difficult it is for you to get here."

"It's not as bad as going there."

"Have they found the Kaaba key yet?" Yusuf asked, as a way of distracting him from his sadness.

"No," sighed Mu'az, "but they're casting a new one in Turkey and they say it'll be ready for the next pilgrimage season, in time for the ritual cleaning of the Kaaba . . . "

Mannequin

DETECTIVE NASSER TOOK NOTE OF WHAT YUSUF HAD WRITTEN IN HIS WINDOW about the Eunuchs' Goat, the character who slaughtered sheep every day. He wanted to ascertain whether what Yusuf had written in his window could be a possible alibi for why he wasn't in the neighborhood when the crime took place.

I doubt you'll know me when I call to you with this voice: "Azza."

I've lost my most important face in the mirror; I've lost the Eunuchs' Goat.

No one can see me the way the Eunuchs' Goat sees me. Every time he looks at me it's like he's saying, You exist, you're a citizen, you belong, you're a historian.

They caught him selling black-market carcasses to the restaurants in the Lane of Many Heads! You should've seen it, Azza. It was a parade of photos and titles in the pages of Umm al-Qura newspaper: the brave men of the municipal government and the Holy Capital's licensing bureaus who'd performed the early morning raid against unregulated slaughterhouses.

I read out loud by your window while the finger of charcoal rattles between your fingers. Are the torsos you draw still fleeing a massacre? Did you make sure to get them marked them with veterinary certification stamps? I can't stop reading and re-reading it.

"140 tons of spoiled meat intended for distribution and human consumption were seized today, along with the culprits who slaughtered camel mares, sheep, and goats. Authorities stressed that camel mares must be slaughtered systematically under the supervision of veterinarians . . . Several experts warned in their testimonies of the danger posed by careless treatment of sick animals, pointing to more than 200 diseases common to both animals and humans. Some of these include Malta fever, valley fever, anthrax, tuberculosis, rabies, tapeworm, which can be transferred to humans through contact with a slaughtered camel mare, and there may even be other diseases that are more dangerous."

Most of them are here this very moment, living side by side with the people of the lane in perfect harmony, sharing their viruses generously. As you can see from the experts' testimonies, Azza, the Eunuchs' Goat is a vector for no less than two hundred epidemics. What's worse, though, is the lie they're spreading that the Eunuchs' Goat stole the donation box, "The Bribe Box," and embezzled all the donations that were meant to help him get his papers.

"Do you agree with me that this is all just a rotten plot, timed suspiciously to coincide with the recent news about changes in the stock market and the reports of Iran's nuclear reactors?"

In the Lane of Many Heads, people joke that the Eunuchs' Goat has fallen victim to the vagina of the woman who took him in, Umm al-Sa'd. Surely you noticed the fire. When al-Ashi heard the news, he burned all his records, and Umm al-Sa'd left without her loud red lipstick. She had a nervous breakdown and bailed. She hailed a taxi on the main road and abandoned the neighborhood.

The sun overhead was exactly perpendicular, not unlike his doubts, when Nasser left the police deportation center in Umm al-Joud. He'd actually taken note of these sleights of naming that were considered a form of municipal beautification: The Lane of Many Heads became Alley of Light; Umm al-Doud,

Mother of Worms, they changed to Umm al-Joud, Mother of Munificence. He knew that if he spent any more time there—in that den of forgery, deportation, passports, and nationalities—the worms of the massacre that was taking place there would begin penetrating his bones.

He drove off with uncharacteristic calm as images of sweaty-faced men in khaki uniforms holding endless lists of deportees—none of which contained the name Salih, the Eunuchs' Goat—floated through his mind. Unless he'd used a pseudonym, this meant that the Eunuchs' Goat had escaped after his arrest. Either he paid a bribe, or seduced a soldier with his good humor and good looks, or maybe fate just gave him a lucky break. He was stuck with that nickname, the Eunuchs' Goat. Could you really tell an officer or government official that that was your name?

What were the official documents that were being processed by the Interior Ministry? The ones that al-Ashi and his wife had drawn up and gotten notarized. The ones they'd paid bribes for so that their middleman, Ahmad, the sewage cleaner's oldest son and Aisha's husband, would make sure they got through? No matter how many favors he called in at Civil Affairs, or the Passport Authority, or the Interior Ministry itself, Nasser could find no trace of anyone who'd been naturalized with the name "the Eunuchs' Goat" or "Turk" or "Salih" or "Defiler" or "Marbleskin." Those were all nicknames by which the handsome Turkish boy was known in the Lane of Many Heads. He was the one, people said, who'd be getting all the girls in the lane pregnant on account of his good looks and fair complexion!

Nasser made a note: *Questions remain re: Eunuchs' Goat. Still a potential suspect.*

Nasser drove to the Lane of Many Heads. He snuck through the window at the back of al-Ashi's courtyard kitchen into the firewood store and then into the chilly courtyard. The walls were covered in foul-smelling grease, cooking pots lay silently on their stoves, cats inhabited the pits in which the lamb was roasted for mandi. It was as though the kitchen had been in disuse for ages, not just since Umm al-Sa'd's recent trouble. Her nervous breakdown, which everyone in the neighborhood made allowances for. "Who could cope with three shocks like that? The arrest of the Eunuchs' Goat, the stock market crash, and losing the share in the Arab League Building she'd inherited?"

"Umm al-Sa'd had survived the clutches of death but the boy she raised was her downfall."

There was nothing of interest in the yard except for the buried remains of newspaper in the pits, which served as a pen for the cats and whatever overflowed from the sewers. He picked up a pile of ashes that bore the headline

"Mile Tower"; it looked like a spear or a pen stuck into the sands on the Red Sea coast. It towered in the sky over Jeddah at a height of sixteen-hundred meters and had been built at a cost of fifty billion riyals in cooperation with Bechtel Corp. The wind blew pieces of other headlines around him in the yard:

Rattles Saber
Market Crash
World Silent Despite Rising Death
Women Driving: External Pressure, Interior Funda—
Food Inflation 30–50%, Affects Milk, Sugar, Rice
Barrel of Crude Breaks $100 Mark
3 Billion to Expand the Haram Mosque Complex Toward

These were just meaningless scraps, which the wind would use to supplement its own historical archive. Nasser suddenly noticed something at the bottom of the cooking pits. He reached down into the nearest pit to examine the base. It felt strange. It didn't feel like soil, it felt like something thick. Nasser touched something prickly; it was like plastic covered with real hair, as if the bottom of the pit had been coated with a half-plastic, half-animal skin layer. He had no idea what could have made for a substance like that.

Nasser hadn't come to rifle through al-Ashi's memory. He'd wanted to make sure that no one, especially the Eunuchs' Goat, would be able to come hide out here in the yard. He could have spent hours there, and still not made head or tail of those sooty memories.

Detective Nasser carried on upstairs to where, according to Yusuf's diary, the Eunuchs' Goat's room should have been. The door was locked. He rammed it with his shoulder, knocking it out of place and tumbling into the room, where he landed on a heap of women's bodies. They were all in pieces and rigor mortis had long since set in, but they were still wrapped in evening dresses of lace and tulle and satin, embroidered with beads and crystals, girded in velvet and silk. What kind of a sicko had dreamt up this cocktail party massacre? Nasser was still half-blinded by the searing pain in his head, but when he regained his composure, he realized that he was surrounded by a phalanx of life-sized cork dummies, mannequins. Nasser sat there, staring at those amazing imitations of women. It had simply never occurred to him. What could these mannequins add to the case? What could the Lane of Many Heads know about the fetishes of a man with no identity who'd disappeared without a trace as if he'd never existed.

That evening, Nasser found something Yusuf had written about the mannequins in his diary.

March 2, 2004
After Mushabbab had liberated him from the terror of being deported, the Eunuchs' Goat underwent a complete transformation. He started following his whims through Mecca. He stopped making furtive escapes, stopped always keeping an eye out for the deportation vans. His body tasted freedom for the first time: it was like biting into a peppercorn, or a cinnamon stick, or a clove; the sweet aroma stung.

I receded. It was like I was just recording the life of the Eunuchs' Goat, who now had a feel for Mecca that I never had. The thing that most made him want to take his body outside the neighborhood and into the world of the markets outside was his love for the traffic and the way it pulsed. He discovered that he wanted nothing more than to surrender his body to the crush, to bump into and be carried along by the masses, never raising his eyes to look anyone in the face. He understood that parts of his body became parts of other bodies. Don't laugh, Azza. He works in a kitchen. He enjoys slaughtering animals and butchering them, preparing them for the oven, slicing them up into pots. All his senses have been trained to slice, and to relish the act of taking bodies apart and cutting them up. When he sees someone's leg or their rear or even their back, he feels like his leg is being summoned, that his own rear end wants to join all the others, that his back is unconsciously falling in line with all the backs of man. To him, these are just separate parts ready to join whatever body calls on them.

As night fell, Nasser's body surrendered to the putrid smell giving form to the mannequins around him and I, the Lane of Many Heads, found it a perfect opportunity to perch on the threshold and whisper to him in Yusuf's voice, "I am the Eunuchs' Goat, one of the many heads opening up for you so that you may walk across the stage . . ."

Nasser carried on reading.

March 11, 2004
That Friday evening, he was meandering through the Gaza Market when he was blinded by a cacophony of lights in a store window he'd walked past dozens of time before. He'd never seen it like this before: it was like a planet with human life! Then came his epiphany: for twenty-eight whole years, his life had been nothing but a massive encyclopedia of black, from cover to cover, entitled Women: An Illustrated Encyclopedia. Every time he opened it looking for page X, he found a smear of black, or a photo of Y: also black, or—God forbid!—Z: black, again. His entire adolescence, his every waking

dream about a woman's arm or leg or shoulder: black. He used to try to conjure up some tender image, but the encyclopedia would always blot it out with blackness before he could.

Then as Soviet expansion brought on more and more Jihadist groups, the blackness veritably poured out from the pages of the encyclopedia, layers of black were pasted over other layers of black, shrouds sewn onto other shrouds, till the whole world was covered over. The only female reference the Eunuchs' Goat knew was the woman who raised him, Umm al-Sa'd—broad-shouldered, flat-chested, with narrow hips—and if he tried really hard, he could add to that Sa'diya's delicate wrist from behind the curtain.

Then suddenly, and without any prior notice, those women fell out of the sky to land before him: garish travelers preserved behind glass. He stood there for hours, in a daze. His encyclopedia absorbed the woman in the apple-colored muslin top with the lace décolletage and the embroidered leaves, which wound their way up from her left breast to her shoulder, leaving the top of her right breast and shoulder bare. Her flat belly was wrapped in pomegranate-colored silk, and chiffon hung from her waist—like a waterfall—down between her thighs and over her rear. The pain of desire pressed on his kidneys as he stood there like a taut string planted in the sin of that nearly transparent layer that ran from her navel to the top of her breasts. And those drops of bead falling over to touch her delicate toes and forming a long train followed him all the way into his dreams. A cart full of bolts of cloth swung past, knocking him unceremoniously to the ground and out of his own body. He didn't bother to get up. He just stared up at the soft chest, twisting every last drop out of his body as it was rocked by wave after wave. He understood then that the female body is the secret we never dare expose. It is the intention that precedes movement. He knew that if he stayed there looking at it his body would pass through any solid barrier and that his desire would carry him over any distance, no matter how far. This was the secret behind the black covers of his encyclopedia.

An Afghan boy selling bundles of jasmine walked by, trailing the flowers across the Eunuchs' Goat's nose and giving him a knowing look as he followed the Eunuchs' Goat's gaze toward the shop window. The Afghan boy's smile spread across his red cheeks before he walked off down one of the brightly lit market's many aisles, followed only by a faint trace of jasmine. The sadness of the flowers revived the Goat's desperate need to be touched.

The next day, when the Eunuchs' Goat had mustered up the courage to go into the clothing store, he started having seizures. He could've sworn that he'd died and been resurrected in heaven, surrounded by all those beauties. Their bodies with the tiny exposed gaps and the mere suggestion of slight curves. He put up with the kicking from the Pakistani security guard in the blue uniform who threw him out onto the street. He disappeared from his father's kitchen and scrubbed himself clean of the layer of rot that had settled on his skin. He didn't eat for days as he wandered from clothing store to clothing store: paradises like al-Ceyloni, al-Bajiri, and Bin Siddiq. He knew that he would grow senile but that these women of his harem would never suffer the touch of old age or headscarves. Clothing stores became his entire focus. He derived more pleasure from going into a clothes store than from all the victories over all the devils that haunted his dreams. There among those silks was the greenery that would cover the entire peninsula, the rivers, the freely grazing ostriches alongside the night, and the beauties, whom he'd fight to liberate from their hell. You see when we, children of the lane, dream, we don't dream about fairy godmothers, we dream about the war of the Hidden Imam who will come to earth and transform the Arabian Peninsula into heaven. We dream of death so that we can give life to the beauties in the peninsula's rivers.

The only thing the Eunuchs' Goat wanted was for the entire world to forget about him and leave him there with that woman. He fought off all Yusuf's attempts to get him to go back to the yard. And his usual academic attempts to give them a date and time. He tried to tie it to modern history for him, calling it a flavor that had abandoned the city during the long, lonely years of religious sermons, which mirrored the jihadi campaigns in Bosnia and Afghanistan. Yusuf drew him a diagram in words of how the spiritual and financial capital reserves of the Arab World were depleted in the eighties and nineties, just before the incursion of satellite hegemony, which arrived in the period between the First and Second Gulf Wars, when the illustrated and sensory encyclopedias of real life were being rooted out and banished. During that time, the guardians of the encyclopedias turned their attention to denuding. At the portals to land, sea, and brains, they planted censors who pored over all printed materials, blotting out any form that resembled a woman, whether in advertisements or even in dress patterns drawn in Chinese ink. Mannequins suddenly disappeared from all the shops—except for in the lawless cities of Khobar and Jeddah—and were burned in secret. Yusuf summed up his theory in a single sentence:

"After centuries, women want their revenge. This is what the harem of today looks like." He pursued the economic liberalization plan that had been sketched out in bold. "At the dawn of the third millennium of democracy, promoted violently by the West, we found ourselves cresting a wave that would lay the encyclopedia of women bare: women in chamber of

commerce elections, women in the arts, women in advertisements, in the journalists' syndicate and in official delegations, women in politics and ministries, women educators and humanitarians, a woman leading the organization for human rights. The mannequins were attacking and they were about to overrun all our biggest cities."

As he went from clothing store to clothing store, the Eunuchs' Goat was flabbergasted by the attention paid to a certain inconsequential Lebanese man who looked like a designer of cheap knock-off fashions. All the biggest clothing boutiques in the Gaza Market, in Street 60, in al-Awali would hire the man at a rate of three hundred dollars an hour to come and give life to their limbs of cork. All he had to do was play around with the fabrics to arouse the devils of temptation.

For days, the Eunuchs' Goat kept watch. He learned that the Lebanese man only ever turned up at closing time, and was astonished by the warm welcome all the boutique owners gave him. They would hand over the keys to their supply rooms, pile all the beauties around him, shut the door to their shops and walk off! Standing on the other side of those locked doors was true hell for the Eunuchs' Goat, and he spent nights on end standing there, prey to his own wild imagination, wondering what that Lebanese jerk and those beauties were up to on the other side. Jealousy blinded him and left a bitter taste in his throat. He began stalking the Lebanese window designer, following his every move, recording, to the second, how long he spent on his own in the biggest boutiques, the ones with the most exquisite, most captivating, beauties. A desire for vengeance burned inside him. He spent night after night calling the office for the enforcement of public morals, begging them to come and break up these rendezvous.

One night, he took advantage of the break for evening prayers to sneak into the stock room of the al-Ceyloni clothing store. He hid in there, waiting patiently for the store to shut after evening prayers. He bore the claustrophobia, the stifling feeling of all those bolts of cloth and cardboard boxes on top of him. He expected to be discovered at any moment by the stock boys, who kept coming in and out of the room to fetch more fabric. Finally, at exactly midnight, closing time, he heard that warm welcome ring out and a grimace settled on his face: his Lebanese lover had arrived.

"Please, my dear, be sure to keep all the doors shut, just to be safe. We don't want any problems with the authorities. They're already not very pleased about our half-nude mannequins and the fact that you spend so much time alone with them!" With that, the manager, shut out the lights in the back of the store and left.

From his hiding place beneath all that cloth, the Eunuchs' Goat felt he'd been stripped bare, now that he was finally going to confront his adversary. But for some reason he couldn't bring himself to announce his presence or raise his head to check out what was happening, let alone to pounce on the guy as he'd planned. Minutes passed like epochs and the Eunuchs' Goat was convinced that he'd die right there in his hiding place, that they'd find his bloated body in the morning under piles of imported cloth. But then as the temperature rose in the store, he knew that what he'd been expecting to happen was actually happening. He flew into a blind rage. He got up and headed toward the front of the store, guided by the faint purple light, to where the Lebanese designer was standing face to face with a blonde female figure. Crouching to watch, he could feel her breathing grow faster as the man bent over her, his shiny, dyed-blond hair grazing her breasts. He was fumbling with her silk trousers, undoing the belt then the two pearl buttons. There was a flash of panties and a glimpse of her slender waist topped by a perfectly round navel. The Eunuchs' Goat's heart leapt into his throat, and he experienced a thirst unlike any he'd ever known before. The Lebanese stopped to contemplate that creamy torso for a moment and then, slipping one hand between her legs and another between her shoulder blades, he lifted her up off the ground. The way he grabbed her made the Eunuchs' Goat's blood run cold. His entire body, including his face, was transformed into shards of dark-red glowing glass. He lost all feeling in his limbs and fought to stay upright, gripping at bolts of cloth that fell with him to the floor, causing a racket. The Lebanese was in thrall, however, and didn't even bother to look to see what was happening. He carried the beauty over to one of the low display tables, which was padded with layers of bright fabric. The body was laid out plainly, trembling at the thought of the touch to come. With unexpected force, the Lebanese decorator stripped off her trousers, exposing her bare legs, and flapped them about like a hot silk cloud to air them out. He placed his left knee between her legs, spreading them apart roughly and with a second thrust, separated her left leg from her body, which crashed onto the ground, hitting the Eunuchs' Goat. When the beauty's toes pushed against his belly, the devil overtook him. For an instant, the Eunuchs' Goat surrendered to the tempting pleasure, but then he simply stood up and walked, breathlessly, forward into the pool of purple light where neither adversary really existed any longer.

As he was busy struggling with the body, the Lebanese window designer didn't seem the least bit taken aback. He looked at the Eunuchs' Goat like he was just another red mannequin, and allowed him to reach out and help. In silence and harmony, they worked together, stripping her, piece by piece, greet-

ing her nudity warmly. The Eunuchs' Goat didn't dare bring his body closer, touching her only with his fingertips, which turned red hot anytime he felt her shoulder or her arm, as his body grew as stiff as an actual mannequin. Only then did he notice the wound around the woman's left eye, it was like a torture scar, which wrapped around her eye and down to her neck beneath her left ear. His tongue yearned to lick the laceration, to cleanse it. Another scar appeared across her waist as he wrapped it in satin, another torture scar slicing her body in two. The Eunuchs' Goat thought back on the Indonesian woman who was married to his father's kitchen helper. The woman entertained every hidden desire in the Lane of Many Heads, and her motto was famous. "This," she said, pointing from her waist to her head, "is for my Lord, and this," she said, pointing from her waist to her feet, "is for my lover." The Eunuchs' Goat fought the designer's attempts to reattach her leg; all he wanted to do was to grab the leg and run. But then, when the designer turned to him and placed one of his hands between his legs and the other between his shoulder-blades and picked him up and carried him out of the shop, throwing him into the street, the Eunuchs' Goat said nothing. He fell onto the sidewalk where he lay for hours on the floor of the market, completely drained, having lost the first woman he'd ever laid his hands on to his adversary, who wrapped her neck and waist with coarse crimson fabric to exaggerate the contrast between her modern jeans and the striped silk across her torso.

From that night on, that Lebanese joker became his one and only obsession. He'd stand outside the doors they shut behind him and bark, imagining him on the other side of those doors stripping them and redressing them in even more seductive outfits. He knew which bits to touch, what to cover and what to lay bare so as to drive the Eunuchs' Goat's senses wild. Love was challenging all his primal urges. He was suddenly, bitterly desperate to exterminate this infatuation that was polished with lotions and make-up. His hair grew longer every time he saw the Lebanese decorator's pony-tail bouncing between his shoulders. The pretty boy went to the barber every Friday afternoon for an hour to have his hair combed, conditioned, and straightened, but when he went into a working-class neighborhood he'd stuff his ponytail into a cap bearing the insignia NY. A deeply despairing Eunuchs' Goat planned his attack for Saturday. It took him a whole week to coordinate the movements of his enemy with those of the General Motors SUV belonging to the public morals enforcers. When the mirage appeared on al-Rusayfa Street at two o'clock in the afternoon, the boys from the Lane of Many Heads–led by the Eunuchs' Goat—pounced on the Lebanese designer and the poor guy took off running. The stones they threw at him forced him to run in the direction of al-Rusayfa Street's main intersection where, just as he got there, a Public Morals Authority SUV drove past, patrolling for high school students on their way home. The man had no time to grasp what was happening, or to understand why these demons were chasing him and pelting him with stones, because he instantly came face to face with the gray SUV, which appeared out of nowhere, as if from the folds of the earth. A policeman and three bearded sheikhs jumped out of the SUV, surrounded him, and ordered him to remove his baseball cap.

The Eunuchs' Goat was pleased to see that the man's ponytail caused a flash of anger in the eyes of his captors, who immediately forced him to his knees roughly right there on Street 50 in the midst of crowds of white-collar employees and schoolchildren on their way home at two o'clock in the afternoon. They shaved off his hair (and dignity) in broad daylight, making an example out of him. People say that the Pashtun barber the authorities brought with them on their raids was actually an expert sheep-shearer who used wool shears, but when the Lebanese designer stood up and walked off, he held his head as high as Yul Brynner.

Last month, the Eunuchs' Goat lost the last of his patience and good sense, and it didn't take much courage or forethought for him to carry out his next reckless move. He suddenly found himself with his arms wrapped, shivering, around the torso and legs of his beloved—passion and fear have driven you mad, Eunuchs' Goat, look at you, your fingers are colder than a dead fish in a supermarket freezer! He calmly covered her with her wine-colored muslin and smuggled her out through the narrow alleyways of the Gaza Market till he reached the Mas'a, where he boarded a bus that was just pulling away from the stop. He couldn't believe how easy it had been for him to steal the body. By the time he got it back to his bedroom above the kitchen, evening prayers were over. He lay down at her magical feet and let out a deep sigh. "This is the fragrance of feet that have never once touched the soil. Virginal feet. Nothing has ever spread these toes apart before."

He was in seventh heaven, and for days the Eunuchs' Goat had to fight the desire to dip into that wine-colored cloth, to strip away its many layers and reveal its amazing truth. For days he kept to his room, constantly parched, ignoring his foster father al-Ashi's calls and foregoing lunches with his foster mother Umm al-Sa'd. When his resistance finally crumbled and he knelt down between her feet, all his limbs were numb. He shivered as he lifted up the hem of her dress, and he was shocked to find a hard wooden pedestal instead of her feet and cold metal columns where there should have been calves and thighs. His blood sugar dropped suddenly and his ears began to ring. With his teeth he tore the straps off her shoulders and ripped the wine-colored muslin to shreds, exposing the woman's torso. It was perfect and sealed; nothing had split it open, neither scalpel nor desire. The feeling of encountering this woman before her body had even been formed was frightening. She was the mold of a woman, the body of woman before the Fall, before opening up, before extending her limbs.

The Eunuchs' Goat was frantic but he carefully avoided the al-Ceyloni store and headed instead for its large competitor, the massive Bin Siddiq Outlets. While the security guard was watching, he bent down at the feet of the woman nearest the door. He wanted to make sure they were delicate and when he revealed her calves and saw how perfectly they were executed, his mouth went dry. Without any hesitation, he picked the woman up, wrapping her left arm around his shoulders and walked out. The security guard sitting at the other end of the shop simply finished his tea and said nothing. No one would try to pull something like that unless they were the rightful owner.

The Eunuchs' Goat took off running, blindly, the fiery satin stinging his tongue. His entire body was propelled toward the Lane of Many Heads with his treasure in tow, deaf to the horns and screeching brakes around him, and it wasn't until a flash of yellow crossed his path that he was awoken from his trance. A massive blow knocked him sideways and the muslin-covered beauty was mangled under the taxi's wheel. The mocking laughter was like a slap in the face, but he ignored it and bent down, yanking and pulling, trying in vain to free the woman's torso from beneath the tire. He lost it. He started beating the door of the taxi with both his hands. Khalil got out and grabbed the Eunuchs' Goat by the collar. He shoved him against the bent metal of the car's body and penned him in with his superior size. "Want me to show you the woman trapped inside that doll's body of yours?" he said, mocking him for being a pretty Turk. The Eunuchs' Goat kicked and punched him hysterically, but Khalil was enjoying the violence. He then suddenly shoved him to the side, got back in the cab, and reversed a few feet.

"When I was a king in heaven, I knew exactly what this country needed. I used to use my connections with the airlines to smuggle in dolls like you for seamstresses and tailoring workshops." Khalil was getting off on insulting the object of his infatuation, this boy. "I'd bring in one or two dolls each time, disassembled and laid out in my suitcase, and I'd put them back together as soon as I made it past customs. The cheapest mannequins you can get abroad are priceless in this country. Maybe you should try Afghanistan, you'd probably be worth millions there." The Eunuchs' Goat took off his robe, which had been torn to shreds during the altercation, and

knelt down to gather the pieces of his beauty up in it. Then he walked off, not once looking back, and Khalil, who was back behind the steering wheel, watched him sneeringly, appreciating the cute young man's curves under his long white trousers. There was a smell of poison, mixed in with a hint of yellow satin, in the air.

Alone in his bedroom, the Eunuchs' Goat confronted the frightening perfection of thighs and knees. His eyes weren't aware that the torso was shattered; he'd never once imagined that his heart could be so enthralled by two knees and the silence that separated them.

It was then that he realized that he'd fallen under the control of women with closed fists, closed mouths, closed—impenetrable women! No matter how hard he tried, his saliva didn't soften the cork, his touch couldn't knead it. The first time he looked into her eyes to beg with his own, he saw there was no eye there, no head.

"God curse American democracy! It can't even give the beauties in shop-windows their heads or severed limbs back. A democracy of cork arms and legs that can't wrap around men's necks and waists and make the blood flow back through them."

He became addicted to those bodies. He no longer had any qualms about stealing them from wherever he could find them. He was consumed by his conflicted feelings about those beautiful women; their skin that never sweated and thus left him craving. Every morning he woke up disgusted with himself. The only thing that he could hope for was that Sa'diya, Imam Dawoud's daughter, would save him. Sa'diya who was wrapped from her head to her toes in black, who had never been programmed by a fashion designer or by love scenes seen on TV. Sa'diya was his "Surah of the Cow." Her heart contained the "Throne Verse," where he would stretch out and be loved like no man had ever been loved before. The Eunuchs' Goat swore to himself that he would be the recipient of that tiny flame's love. That he would surrender himself to her completely. That she would make up for all the rejections he was getting from the beauties that were cluttering his bedroom.

From where he was standing in the doorway, Nasser could see the delicate arm, its palm stretched flat and index finger pointed in his direction. In the light coming through the tiny window, the mannequin's subtle gesture brought him nearer to her. He shut his eyes and the taste of blood overcame all his senses . . . This was the Eunuchs' Goat's blood; there was no doubting that. Nasser fought his attraction to the Eunuchs' Goat, whom he called to mind through the mannequin's body, though hers was more feminine.

Discovery

From: Aisha
Subject: Message 11

The bird scrapes at the air-conditioning unit, with its stock of feathers and chicks, to build a nest. "Is it spring?" I ask out loud. He doesn't answer. He disappears and then comes back again. Like you . . .

Every Sunday since my back was introduced to scalpels and crow's-foot stitches, my heart feels as if it's been left here in this chair by the window to wait, and is reluctant to speak to me.

You look out.

You cover me with that heavy raincoat that smells of **pine nuts**!

Your slender body kneels in front of me, you set my feet on the footrests of my wheelchair.

Your lips graze my knee for the briefest moment.

You jump up and come around behind me to push the wheelchair.

All the stores on the sidewalk of that narrow lane are closed.

Then we arrive at the **river**.

In the small village, I let the wheelchair spin in whatever direction it pleased. I discovered that **wheels** are bolder, more curious than feet.

The old woman who knits socks in the tiny shop and the **red** pair you gave me.

No one ever spoiled me before you.

Why is it that we never get the opportunity to **spoil** the ones we love and to **be spoiled** by them?

Aisha

Attachment: A photo of Aunt Halima's samovar. Half the Haram Mosque have drunk from it.

Also a photo of her drum.

Aunt Halima always repeats her motto to me: "I'm my own woman. God have mercy on anyone who tries to tie me down!"

Discovery signed this drum for me.

Discovery is the Beyoncé of the Lane of Many Heads, ^. She and her whole band with all their instruments sit atop Aunt Halima's heart. "She's so beautiful, so sexy, so young. She's one of a kind, she's a star!"

She was always waxing lyrical about Discovery and she'd go to all the weddings just to see her, Halima and all the other women who couldn't get enough of joyous celebration.

P. S. The first meal I ever ate with a strange man, alone, in the **open** air. It makes my body writhe with passion even now.

P. P. S. Azza loved the bracelet that you and I picked out for her. That day you were surprised, ^, by my naive suggestion that we get our two initials, A & A, Azza and Aisha, engraved on it. I didn't feel I had to justify anything, but then I said one "A" would be enough. Whenever I dream of life outside the Lane of Many Heads, I become Azza, **who becomes me**.

Aisha

Manumission

One day, Yusuf discovered a small storeroom behind the sitting room on the third floor, which al-Lababidi had devoted to pictures of Mecca's largest cluster of papermakers and booksellers, the area between the Great al-Salam Gate and the Little al-Salam Gate on the left side of the incline leading from the Haram Mosque to the Mas'a. Booksellers' and bookbinders' stores were mixed with perfumers and kohl-sellers dating from the third and fourth centuries AH; it was a river of ink and perfume welling up from the Haram, flowing alongside the Mas'a.

On the right-hand side of the storeroom were engraved the words: *The Perfumers' Market. Soul of books and soul of oils. Book lovers believe the words of books are what give the perfumes their wonderful scent, but the old fragrance connoisseurs believe that perfumes are what give the books their magic. The truth is, it's the human spirit diffused in the air that does it.*

Yusuf spent the nights gazing at the pictures. He strolled in a waking dream from the Sidra dorms, which had been endowed as lodgings for seekers of knowledge, to the ranks of innumerable small bookstores like Fida, al-Baz, and Mirza, with their tiny dark interiors and traditional arched doorways at which Mecca's great men—Fida, al-Baz, and Mirza themselves—sat surrounded by piles and piles of manuscripts. Yusuf gazed at a black and white photo of the founding bookseller, Fida bin Adam al-Kashmiri, a hundred years old with feet still dusty from traveling to Istanbul, Egypt, and India in search of books. He had scarcely to utter the first missing title that he noticed—*Fath al-Qarib Ala Abi Shuja*, say—when his grandson Abd al-Samad would throw him a small cotton cushion to put on the paved ground of the square while he went around to the neighboring stores to bring him the title *Fath al-Qarib al-Mujib Ala l-Taqrib* by Sheikh Abu Abd Allah al-Shafi'i. He'd come back, having fetched the book, repeating what he always said: "Price is final. Price is final." Time was suspended and merged, allowing Yusuf to walk slowly and arrive in time for the audience at the bookshop after sunset prayers, where he was enveloped in the most beautiful Quran recitations, by sheikhs Qarut, Bahidra, Qari, Jambi, Ashi, Mirdad and al-Arba'in. Whenever one ended, another would start up somewhere in the twilight. Then, as soon as the evening prayers were over, the chanters would come—Jawa, Abu Khashaba, Bukhari—to salute the night with their hymns and folk songs. Yusuf wandered from bookshop to bookshop, stopping to see the calligraphers, disciples of Muhammad al-Farisi and his student al-Kutbi, who flung out lines of calligraphy to the cadences of the recitations. He stopped to read every one of the signs that were hung on the walls and over the arched doorways—QURANS AND THEOLOGY BOOKS, ARABIC LITERATURE—and witnessed an argument which broke out between some market traders in Sheikh Muhammad Salih Jamal's bookstore. He stopped at the narrow frontage of the store owned by Abd al-Karim bin al-Baz, heir to the great dean of booksellers, which had become a center of intellectual activity under the auspices of Sheikh Abd Allah al-Urabi, and went in, joining the crowd of youths who were watching, entranced, the poetic duel taking place between al-Zamakhshari, al-Siba'i and Abd al-Jabbar.

Next, leaving the books in the background, Yusuf went out to the square where entertainers and storytellers were narrating the adventures of Abu Zayd al-Hilali to circles of listeners. On his left, sermons still echoed from inside al-Sawlatiya School every Thursday, along with sighs rising up from all the other schools and the homes of the great scholars of Mecca who either taught, led prayers, or delivered sermons at the Haram Mosque. Yusuf examined old title deeds and leases, some of which granted just one side of a store to a bookseller, while another bookseller took the other side; such was the booksellers' rush for victory in the honorable occupation of bringing books to life.

As night wore on and the stores closed, Yusuf lingered alone, taking deep drafts of the night breeze, which was laden with the scent of ink, old paper, and perfumes, and echoes of the readings and recitations that were still going on. He stood amidst the network of stores, facing the awesome idol Hubal, who had been thrown out of the mosque, one of many idols that had stood in the area around the Kaaba in the pre-Islamic age and were removed after being smashed. Al-Lababidi's shots were taken from angles that conveyed the vast might of the idol, which lay keeled over with its head, eyes, and nose squashed into the ground under one of the bookstores and its vast stone body stretched out. It was one-armed, because its arm, fashioned entirely out of gold, had been long since hacked off and melted down to make jewelry and gold bullion coins; the rest of the body had remained at the entrance of the Haram Mosque for worshippers to tread on or disdainfully leave their shoes on, until one night during the redevelopment, when it disappeared without warning.

In the dim light of the storeroom, Yusuf examined all the bookstore signs, in particular the attractive sign advertising the services of ABBAS KARARA, MAS'A, MECCA: ANY TOOTH REMOVED COMPLETELY PAIN-FREE, ALL KINDS OF FALSE TEETH FITTED, HALLMARK-GRADE GOLD CROWNING, ALL AT REMARKABLE PRICES.

Reliving his past in al-Lababidi's photographs, Yusuf realized the danger he'd exposed Azza to. He had been fifteen when he'd dragged Azza to Sheikh Abd al-Razzaq Balila's bookstore, which was a space of no more than four square meters where the air was laced with the aroma of books. The solemn old man in a white robe and matching muslin turban who greeted them didn't lift his eyes from the parchment he was reading, part of a volume on mythical creatures that was bound in camel leather and stamped with gold leaf. The old man seemed to come from some immortal ancient time. Behind him were shelves loaded with old manuscripts—Ibn Sirin's *Interpretation of Dreams*, Jahiz's *Book of Animals*, *The Soul* by Ibn Qayyim al-Jawziya, *The Necklace of the Dove* by Ibn Hazm—side by side with stacks of parchments written in the hand of such great Sufis as al-Suhrawardi, al-Niffari's *Stations*, and Ibn Arabi's *Meccan Openings*. Abd al-Razzaq Balila's bookstore represented stages through which the knowledge-seeker had to progress: when the student arrived from the Haram Mosque, laden with protestations of God's oneness, he would travel through the old Arabic manuscripts, the exoteric sciences dispersing into irrelevance as he learned the esoteric ones.

When Yusuf had become engrossed in the Sufi section, Azza had gotten restless and tried to slip away, so he'd shaken off his abstraction and gone to hang out with her in the cartoon section.

They'd lurked there until the old man headed out to perform his afternoon prayer in the Haram Mosque, then Yusuf grabbed Azza's hand and pulled her down the steps into a storeroom tucked between the houses in the Hajla neighborhood, where the modern-day mind could journey across the continents and see inside the minds of men, from *The Courts of Great Men* to Hugo's *Les Misérables* as translated by the poet Hafiz Ibrahim. He pulled Azza in between the shelves. To their right, were Marx's *Capital*, Kant's *Critiques of Pure Reason, Practical Reason*, and *Judgment*, Hegel's *Encyclopedia of the Philosophical Sciences* and *The Union of Soul and Matter* and his idealism based on the capacity of thesis and antithesis to create synthesis, Cervantes' *Don Quixote* and his ill-fated war on windmills—books that had inspired many of the great upheavals that changed the path of humanity. To their left were the world wars—Hemingway's *For Whom the Bell Tolls*, Tolstoy's *War and Peace*, Dickens' *A Tale of Two Cities*, Maxim Gorky's *The Mother*—and the intellectual trials that had shaped humankind, from Asia to Europe to America—the Bustani translation of *The Iliad* and *The Odyssey* by Homer, prophet of the Greeks, Frazer's *The Golden Bough*, Sartre's *The Flies* and de Beauvoir's *The Second Sex*, Goethe's repurposing of Sophocles' model of tragedy, Orwell's *Animal Farm*—along with a smattering of the works of Rimbaud, Mallarmé, Maupassant, Foucault, Chekhov, Turgenev, Alexandre Dumas, Shakespeare, William Faulkner, Edgar Allan Poe, Aldous Huxley, Jacques Prévert, Balzac, Camus, and finally Colin Wilson's *The Outsider*.

The yellowing pages of those old minds had made Azza cough, so Yusuf had distracted her with stories of wide-eyed young girls who ventured beyond the limited world of reality: Thumbelina, scarcely as tall as a thumb, who was nearly married to a mole, Rapunzel who let down her long hair from her prison at the top of a tower so her lover could visit her, Alice in Wonderland whose one teardrop flooded the underworld, and Cinderella with the fairy godmother who turned insects into horses and rags into jewels and silk so she could escape from the soot of her kitchen . . .

In the silence of al-Lababidi's house, Yusuf's soul peeled away and floated alone through time and space, wandering through a black and white world where Mecca's past and present bled into one another on the walls. There was nothing to separate the photographs from the things that could be seen out of the windows. There was no longer any link to reality other than the diaries, which Nasser was as addicted to reading as Yusuf was to those photographs; the pair blended together in their shared addiction.

Nasser read on:

June 6, 1995

Azza, your addiction to comics—particularly Batman issue 135, where Batman meets Batwoman—shocked me. The jealousy killed me. I was jealous of your obsession with that superhuman being. I realize now that Batman's surprise attacks were your model for all those fleeing bodies in your sketches . . .

Aisha was my unbeatable competitor. That secret conflict with Aisha robbed me of two decades of my life, though maybe she was never aware of it. She had her brothers working as emissaries who'd race me to the bookstores at the Salam Gate and buy books for her, hunting out titles I'd never even heard of, then sneaking them in plastic bags past their father the schoolteacher who'd forbidden the termites that books put into people's heads.

Aisha, whose weak sight got ever weaker, always read in bed after her family had all gone to sleep. I always imagined her like that, curled up in their reinforced concrete pressure-cooker house, while I sat on our mud roof and we competed to get as much light as we could from the municipal street lamps. I'd finish off a whole book in one night. But where she hid her habit from her parents, I, the fatherless, would read, and love what I read, in the open, because my mother Halima believed that my demon was made of paper—and anyway my book obsession kept me away from smoking, sniffing glue, and sneaking around harassing women, which was what all the other boys my age did.

My greatest loss to Aisha was Marcel Proust's In Search of Lost Time, the only available copy of which she'd managed, by some inexplicable miracle, to get hold of. She beat me to that lost time, which remained a hole in my heart like a keyhole through which my time trickled out, and sometimes it seemed to me that if I'd managed to get my own copy of that Lost Time then I might have lived a totally different life, might not have been betrayed like I have been.

On the roof of al-Lababidi's house, Yusuf realized just what a damaging effect Aisha had had on his life, and realized that it was she, not Azza, who'd betrayed him. The one he'd excised from his diaries, the one he hated, even—he saw now what she'd stolen from him.

Yusuf was tempted to break into Aisha's room right then to look for Proust's Lost Time. He trembled a little at the thought. But he was pretty sure that she was sneaky and daring enough to have taken that Time with her.

He thought about Batman, wondering if Batman could have stolen Azza.

Did Batman remind Azza of him, Yusuf? Or of some nocturnal creature that penetrated the darkness and avoided obstacles using sonar?

Yusuf was turning into the remnants of a bat, crashing into the remnants of her. He understood for the first time the meaning of all those red lines he drew as a teenager under Kant's words: space and time are both finite and infinite; matter in itself is both finitely divisible and infinitely divisible; will was both constrained and free. He called out from the roof, "Azza! You're all of those contradictions. Finiteness and divisibility of the infinite go beyond the surface. I mustn't give up hope that you're still there. I'll search for you wherever you are, even in death, because your death means my death too . . ."

Yusuf missed bringing Aisha to life in his diaries, but he knew that fate had consigned those days to the past. There was no place for them in the present.

Ring Road

CHECKING THE PASSENGER LISTS OF ALL OUTBOUND SAUDI AIRLINES FLIGHTS for that Thursday and Friday, Nasser discovered Aisha's husband Ahmad's name on a dawn flight to Casablanca on the day the body had been found. His sudden appearance and disappearance made it look pretty likely that it was Aisha who was dead, but Nasser shuddered at the thought of going down that line of investigation.

That day, he was trapped for hours at the Gate Lane exit, which led to the Haram Mosque. The engines of all four lanes of cars groaned, pumping fumes into the Meccan heat in competition with public buses, refrigerated vans transporting foodstuffs, trucks piled high with live sheep, and tourist buses whose drivers stood on the gas and zoomed through the traffic, terrorizing the little cars that shoehorned themselves into the tiniest gaps in attempts to escape the creeping paralysis of the traffic. In seasons like this, and especially in the Umrah season during Ramadan, those buses played a leading role on the roads. They looked like mythical monsters, with the dense rows of pilgrims' heads peering out of their darkened windows, and they mercilessly sliced paths through the masses of humanity before them, which is why Meccans simply vacated the center of their city and left it to the pilgrims, crossing the ring road around the Haram and heading for anywhere outside the first or second belts that encircled the heart of the city and from which all the main trade arteries branched off.

Nasser left the car running to go and buy some laddu balls, a specialty sweet made from yellow gram flour, raisins, and a hint of cardamom, which he stuffed—all six of them, each the size of a golf ball—into a sandwich under the amused eyes of the sweetseller. He'd eat that sweet for breakfast and lunch if he could, without a thought for the risk of diabetes that loomed over him like it did all the children of the Gulf's oil boom. He enjoyed the greasy snack at the wheel, the car idling in the same spot thanks to a bus that had stopped in the middle of the road to offload pilgrims—Saudis from other cities whose cars were kept in designated spots at the outskirts of the city while they were loaded onto public buses to be dropped right in front of the Haram Mosque, then loaded back on and returned once they had performed their Umrah obligations.

Nasser looked at the bare shoulders of the male pilgrims and the unveiled faces of the women. If so much as a corner of cloth brushed one of those faces, a sheep had to be slaughtered in recompense. He thought it was weird that a woman's face had to be uncovered for religious rituals, but sealed up again for life—he was an active participant in that contradictory habit, of course—and he realized that his heart wasn't racing, his mouth hadn't gone dry, the sight of those female pilgrims didn't cause his body to stiffen—he looked at them as if they were some kind of non-masculine, non-feminine third sex—whereas the mere glimpse of a local woman was enough to nail him to the spot! The thought of meeting an unveiled Azza or Aisha in the courtyard of the Haram and stepping on the marble that their feet had touched caused his body to seize. Suddenly he had no appetite and he wrapped the uneaten half of his sandwich up and placed it on the seat next to him.

Ahead of him, the river of cars was dammed between banks of shops: Nour Grocery, Nour Valley, Nour Bakery, Nour Shawarma, Nour Juices . . . Harra Supplies and Salam Beverages were the only two names that interrupted the broken record repetition of the word *Nour*, light, over every sign. The repetition resumed a little way down the road, where the offices of the pilgrims' guides were loudly decorated with lights trained on pictures of the two Holy Mosques and their custodian, the King, which hovered over the heads of the men sitting on long couches, waiting to receive visitors. By one of the offices, Nasser spotted a copy of *Umm al-Qura* sitting on a rack in front of a small bookstore stuffed with Qurans and biographies of the Prophet, so for the second time he left the car running and went over, paid the three-riyal cover price and grabbed his copy. Back in the driver's seat, the traffic was still motionless, so he opened up the paper and flicked through in search of Yusuf's Window, which caught him unawares with the headline "A View Over al-Malah." He read:

Al-Malah is being extended upward to form a multi-story cemetery.

As fans of conceptual art we're keen to see the cemetery remodeled as a tower. Our deaths will be truly modern—if not post-modern! A more creative contractor might even fashion the upper stories out of glass so our corpses can lie watching the more freshly dead decompose artistically above them.

I'm afraid to go on my morning stroll around al-Malah these days.

Here in Mecca we've become specialists in religious tourism and our mission is to deport our dead. The bodies who were disinterred from al-Shubbayka know all about that. Developers razed the cemetery and moved all its dead to make way for skyscrapers, parking lots, and five-star hotels.

Long corpses were stacked on giant trucks, their legs sticking off the end. Those of us who saw that sight as kids, still see them now, floating in midair down al-Misyal, following the drainage sewers to Majin Pool. Who knows where they took them from there.

The traffic suddenly started moving and a motorcycle roared past Nasser into a narrow gap ahead, belching fumes straight into Nasser's face. He quickly closed the window and turned on the air-conditioning, laughing at himself for needing living, rather than mummified, air. He regarded the pate of the bike's back passenger, which was shaved so closely it shone, and the ihram robes that fluttered as the motorbike sped along, contrasting with the driver's tracksuit and helmet. He found the frivolity of motorbikes so irritating. They'd started to replace taxis as the main form of transport in the past few years since they were so much faster in traffic. A ride cost as little as fifty riyals, but the accidents were innumerable.

Nasser had lost his place when he'd stopped reading, and when he went back to it the word *revolution* caught his eye.

You could say the dead were the first to form an opposition movement because in Mecca death is the frontline. Meccan graves have a history of rebelling against extortionate taxes. The most famous instance was the Gravediggers' Revolution in 1326 AH. When Sultan Mehmed V acceded to the throne and the Committee of Union and Progress got their way, the Ottoman constitution was reinstated throughout the empire, including in Mecca and the Hijaz. The Ottoman constitutionalists established a specific tax of five riyals for burial of the dead, which was allegedly to cover the cost of maintaining the graves. They summoned the leader of the gravediggers' guild and instructed him to exact full payment from the relatives of every dead person, but he refused categorically and stormed out of the government palace with the famous words

People of al-Malah, rise up!
Death may well be free today
but tomorrow to die they'll make you pay!

His cry roused the anger of the people of the Hijaz. No longer impressed by the constitutionalists' principles, they lost what faith they'd had in the Young Turks' revolution against the Sultan. Their crier called for a holy war, and young men from every neighborhood responded, coming out with their weapons and clamoring for a revolution against the Turks. They clashed with soldiers in markets around the city, and small numbers were killed and injured on both sides until the Turks managed, with the help of several Sharifs, to suppress the mutiny a few hours later. The Sharif of Mecca, Ali bin Abd Allah Pasha, was accused of fomenting and aiding the revolt and promptly deposed. Sharif Hussein bin Ali was installed in his place. A hardline conservative, he paid no attention whatsoever to the principles of the constitution that granted ordinary people a bare minimum of political rights because it went against the tradition of total separation between the ruler and the ruled, which was something he cherished.

The traffic finally eased when the troop of pilgrims crossed the road toward the Haram behind a young guide, chased by a little Afghan boy selling miniature prayer mats, decorated with glittery pictures of the Kaaba, out of a plastic bag. Nasser bore right, toward Hafayir, though he wasn't planning to go anywhere in particular. Since he'd taken on the case, Mecca—the city he'd left his birthplace, Ta'if, for—had stirred in his heart; more than once, now, he'd driven around aimlessly at night, for no other reason than to check that his Mecca was still there and that the angels hadn't carried it away to punish its unworthy residents.

As soon as he turned into al-Mansur Street he was surrounded by shining black faces. He felt safe in that narrow alley, which was named after the dervish who lived there, al-Sayyid al-Shanqiti, who was famous for materializing out of nowhere. He would wander the alley or sit down on the sidewalk in front of the mosque, perform some miracle, then suddenly disappear again. Nasser parked opposite al-Shanqiti Mosque and continued on foot, looking around him without knowing what he was looking for. People always hoped that some crisis would persuade al-Shanqiti to return from his occultation; Nasser could feel anticipation in the air, the hope that he would appear like he had once when a father had accidentally slammed a car door on his son's hand. Al-Shanqiti materialized, read some verses from the Quran over the crushed hand, and then breathed on it. The boy's hand had healed immediately. Or once when a motorcyclist had an accident with a car and his leg was smashed up; al-Shanqiti appeared, recited, and breathed, at which the wounds sealed themselves up and the bones set themselves. The young man got to his feet as good as new and set about collecting the broken bits of his motorbike and hauling them over to the nearest mechanic's. The stories,

Nasser thought, would be perfect for those shows on satellite where they read the stars, cure people's problems with magic, and turn ugly ducklings into graceful swans through epic cosmetic surgery operations.

Nasser glanced around him, following the eye of the puzzle-master who supervised him and guided his investigations. He saw no trace of the glory that Yusuf had found in the history of al-Mansur Street, which used to be known as "the Chamomile." In the early twentieth century it was easily the most fashionable area in the city, equivalent to Hyde Park, or Central Park, or the Champs-Élysées, where everyone who was anyone would promenade each afternoon to show off how elegant and radiant they were, their bejeweled rainbow-like costumes easily eclipsing the finery of their Turkish overlords.

On the other side of the alley, a black man stood up, drawing Nasser's attention to a threadbare red couch, a water urn next to it, and a peeling Formica bookshelf whose three shelves bore a few leftover rounds of dry bread and a couple of open cans of food. A living room out in the street, on the bare earth. The man came over, arms outstretched to greet Nasser, and Nasser yielded to the hand, discovering too late its leechlike softness; it was as though his hand was encased completely in squelching clay. The man's palm was firmly glued to his and he stared into Nasser's eyes as he said, "Women! They come with knives. Some of us can read their sharp edges. You will. But take it slowly. Don't read with your heart. We have nothing to do with it. Women are their own biggest problem." The man let go of Nasser's hand and vanished down the street.

Nasser's feeling of annoyance mounted. He was sure he'd seen that face somewhere before, but he couldn't recall where, and although he wanted to follow the man to find out, his inscrutable words stood like a barrier in Nasser's way.

Nasser went back to the car and drove off in irritation. When he got to al-Rusayfa Street, the word "knives" resurfaced to prod him, and he remembered one of Yusuf's old columns that had been published online was about knives.

June 20, 2000

The eighties began with a phone call from a woman to the office of the City of Mecca. She informed them of a peculiar phenomenon: "Firstly, I'm Meccan born and bred," she said. "Now, my husband and I noticed a while ago that all the knives were disappearing from the markets. We asked around, and discovered that the cleavers and other sharp instruments were beginning to disappear too. We've found out that African workers are buying them in record numbers!"

The municipal employees naturally scoffed at the woman's laughable conspiracy theory, but it brought to light a story that had been taking place silently under the surface of the city: the Emir's deputy subsequently discovered that his undersecretary, Ba Ali, was in the process of embezzling a tract of land in al-Rusayfa belonging to the al-Qabuji family, who had been unable to evict the squatters who lived there and who had discreetly agreed with Ba Ali that the Public Security forces should be called in to remove them. They surrounded and attacked the rebel neighborhoods in total secrecy, so the news didn't reach any other neighborhoods in the city. The residents resisted, fighting with blades and rocks in the hope of routing the soldiers, until the municipal authorities received the woman's phone call and were alerted to the crisis. The Emir ordered an immediate end to the cleansing operation, and it was the end of the undersecretary Ba Ali's career, but the luxury developments crept in anyway.

"Women!" snorted Nasser, remembering the letter preserved for twenty years in his boss's archives. It was just one of a whole wave of letters that had flooded their office at the time, along with Public Security offices, research centers, universities, the municipal authority, and the Royal Court, all offering the exact same suggestion, the brainchild of a certain "Dr. Farida, Concerned Citizen":

To confront the problem of the armies of illegal foreign workers who come to the kingdom to perform the pilgrimage and then go underground, we propose that the authorities consider taking the following steps:

Two camps should be constructed in the desert, the first for females in the Nafoud Desert, and the second for males in the desert of the Empty Quarter. Any foreign national who is unable to produce proper residence papers should be transferred to the appropriate camp immediately. If any criticism arises on the part of the so-called civilized world, as is to be expected, our official reply will be that the government that objects should open its own borders to the masses of immigrants currently hosted by the Kingdom of Saudi Arabia. Otherwise, a portion of the state budget should be allocated to provide for the immigrants until their time is over (and it is highly unlikely their number would grow). There should also be a dedicated effort to disseminating news of these camps in order to counter the idyllic image that attracts immigrants from all over the world to come here and scrounge from our overburdened budget.

Nasser sniggered at the cruelty of the female imagination. He pictured scenes from a film he thought of making, entitled *Transistor States*. The plot would revolve around a world ruled by women. One character would head the inspectorate for the knife industry and she'd demand to see buyers' entry visas before authorizing any sales, and the other would draw up plans to populate the world's deserts with a new unisex subspecies of human.

As he was waiting for the light to turn green, Nasser suddenly—and apropos of nothing—remembered a black and white photo of Mushabbab that hung on the wall to the right of Mushabbab's couch. The face in the photo was identical to the dervish al-Shanqiti. The light went green and Nasser accelerated then made an abrupt U-turn, brakes screeching, to head back toward the orchard in the Lane of Many Heads.

He ran the last stretch to the orchard, rousing all the neighborhood cats and dogs, threw the gate open, and rushed into the yard. On the wall to the right of the couch there was a patch of yellow brighter than the paint surrounding it; someone had taken the picture. Nasser felt like he'd been tricked. He drove back to al-Mansur Street, only to find that the little living room in the street had also disappeared. All the alarms in his head were going off at once: someone was messing with him. The dervish he'd shaken hands with was Mushabbab. How could he have been so stupid as to fail to confiscate the only photo of his antagonist?

Nasser hurried to his office to look for a case from a while back involving the dervish al-Shanqiti. The file he found recounted that a black man had escaped arrest after being caught smuggling cannabis to the daughter of a prominent personality, Sheikh Khalid al-Sibaykhan. The man had apparently disappeared without a trace, and the report went so far as to claim that he possessed magical powers, which allowed him to hide from his pursuers!

Nasser pieced the information together with something he'd read in one of Aisha's emails.

From: Aisha
Subject: Message 18

Dear ^,
You want to know: am I consumed by guilt? Does what's going on between us make me feel schizophrenic? By which you mean, do I ever compare this to how I grew up? You asked me if the Lane of Many Heads was a threat to me somehow, or to you, and I assured you that the only threat to you was me! This construction called "me" . . .

It WILL be amusing to take part in German Bohemian life . . . I don't delude myself that I shall find an elixir of life in Dresden. I know I shan't. But I shall get away from people who have their own homes and their own children and their own acquaintances and their own this and their own that. I shall be among people who DON'T own things and who HAVEN'T got a home and a domestic servant in the background, who haven't got a standing and a status and a degree and a circle of friends of the same. Oh God, the wheels within wheels of people, it makes one's head tick like a clock, with a very madness of dead mechanical monotony and meaninglessness. How I HATE life, how I hate it. How I hate the Geralds, that they can offer one nothing else."

The thought of the mechanical succession of day following day, day following day, AD INFINITUM, was one of the things that made her heart palpitate with a real approach of madness.

Gerald could not save her from it. He, his body, his motion, his life—it was the same ticking, the same twitching across the dial, a horrible mechanical twitching forward over the face of the hours. What were his kisses, his embraces. She could hear their tick-tack, tick-tack.

Then, with a fleeting self-conscious motion, she wondered if she would be very much surprised, on rising in the morning, to realise that her hair had turned white. She had FELT it turning white so often, under the intolerable burden of her thoughts, and her sensations. Yet there it remained, brown as ever, and there she was herself, looking a picture of health.

Perhaps it was only her unabateable health that left her so exposed to the truth. If she were sickly she would have her illusions, imaginations. As it was, there was no escape. She must always see and know and never escape.

(*Women in Love*)

Gudrun puts me in this disturbed mood. I can't stand this emptiness that Gudrun opens up for her men, opens up inside her men.

How I laughed at your naïveté in secret! If only you knew what girls' bodies were made of in the Lane of Many Heads. The dough of little liars, digging with lies, daily digging to get through the layers upon layers of warnings, restrictions on movement and restrictions on existence, to penetrate into life lightly . . .

Aisha

P.S. "I'm hanging on one," meaning her husband has said the divorce formula once.

"I'm hanging on two."

"I'm on three." The third time means the irrevocable end of the marriage.

"I'm on four, but looking for a fatwa to erase two."

"I'm on five, and we've exhausted our options with sheikhs and fatwas. Now we're looking for a third party who'll marry and divorce me without touching me so my counter will be reset to zero."

"How about you, Aisha, what are you on?"

"I'm an outcast, I don't fit in anywhere in this musical **scale** of divorce. . ."

Correction: Azza's in a state. There's a rumor that Mushabbab was arrested for dealing hashish to the daughter of someone important.

P.P.S. Here's the story as Mushabbab told it to Azza:

Mushabbab went up to the gate of a palatial house, looking with awe at the sky-high walls, more than eight meters high. From a window in his post adjoining the gate the guard watched him, knowing that the young miss had been expecting the man and had left orders at the gate for them to receive the parcel. Seeing the name on the parcel, the guard took it without questioning, and immediately, from the evasive look on the poor man's face, Mushabbab realized it was a trap, even before the gate slid open and the police car appeared, and a circle of policemen closed in on him. They shoved him up against the car, and from there he watched, as if in slow motion, the parcel being transferred from hand to hand. No one even bothered to look inside. They kicked him unconscious on the spot, and by the time he regained consciousness he found himself lying by the side of the Mecca-Jeddah highway. He struggled back home and hid out in his orchard for more than a month, but his attackers saw no need to pursue him afterward. Apparently the broken ribs had simply been a warning to Mushabbab to forget whatever he'd seen in that palace.

"But how?" asked Azza, touching the makeshift bandage wrapped around his broken ribs. "How could you be so reckless?"

"If only you could've seen the poor girl . . . She can't be older than twenty-four, and she has no life. She lives in harsher conditions than the prisoners in Guantanamo. Her father's an international business tycoon, but she's not even allowed access to a cellphone—even the maids are allowed that much. She's under round-the-clock supervision and all she can do is sit there and watch while her life slips between her fingers."

Azza couldn't bring herself to ask whether a cellphone was the only thing he'd smuggled in that parcel. Instead she ventured, "May I ask how you got mixed up with this girl and this action movie plotline?"

"Her father's one of my clients. I supply him with a traditional dance troupe whenever he wants to organize a showcase evening for his foreign guests."

Azza regarded him sardonically. "Did you provide his daughter with the same service?"

Mushabbab was pleased to hear the jealousy in Azza's voice.

"The whole thing started last month. The father asked me to go over there and he told me that his daughter was suffering from acute depression and that she'd tried to kill herself several times over the last ten years. She'd been taken to see the best psychiatrists but nothing worked, and since they'd heard that I practice healing through the Quran they wanted me to give it a shot. I'm always careful not to get involved with powerful people, but they wouldn't accept any of my excuses; they just made an appointment for me to go see the girl."

There was no sign of life at all anywhere around the sky-high walls, only the opening to the right of the gate from which the guard peered out. When Mushabbab presented the permission slip he'd been given, the red-checked headscarf vanished for a few minutes and then a door beside the gate opened and swallowed Mushabbab up. Amazed, he submitted himself to the secretary who'd come to receive him. He was shown to a car and driven through gateway after gateway until they reached a cluster of modern villas set amidst scattered palm trees. The place was an artificial tableau of lurid green. Nothing moved other than him and the palace secretary, two crows disturbing the plastic lushness of the scene as they headed toward what the secretary referred to as "the girls' villa."

He left Mushabbab alone in the reception room, some three hundred meters squared—another perfect tableau of luxuriant nothingness. A Filipina maid in a blue- and white-striped uniform appeared and asked him, "Anything to drink, sir?"

"Just water, please." His voice came out muffled in the void. A tray bearing fresh orchids and a crystal tumbler of water was set before him and sat untouched as minutes stretched into an eternity. For nearly an hour he was left there, sitting by a coffee table weighed down with a variety of the finest dates, glazed nuts, and rich sweets. He was expecting somebody to pop up at any moment to inform him that the girl didn't want to see him, and to show him the door. The furniture was exquisite—everything upholstered in pure silk—even the walls were covered in golden brocade. The entire space was freeze-dried by the powerful central air conditioning into a mummified tableau of grandeur.

Finally, a golden door at the end of the room opened with a faint sound, and a young woman appeared and padded barefoot toward him across the silk flowers of the Persian carpet. For the sake of her modesty, Mushabbab didn't look up but the girl came so close that her feet came into view, and he could see the patterns of the carpet reflected on her pale crystalline skin, a sheen of blue and crimson.

"So you're one of them? A charlatan who hasn't got a shred of professionalism left?"

Mu'az didn't say a word. She stamped on his foot, hard. "Apparently you're a magician. You think I'm a child who likes magic tricks? Life's just a broken toy."

"There's no magic involved, just your inner strength enhanced by my recitation. You could even try reading the Quran on your own to find inner peace." Some sixth sense felt a tremor in the air. The call to prayer rang out in the silent emptiness around them, but it wasn't that; Mushabbab felt like he was being watched. He ignored his apprehension.

"Next you'll tell me to try the Surah of the Cow! My sisters already treat me like a mad cow that isn't even good enough to make leather out of. I haven't seen a street in ten years, apart from in video games and on TV. My mother left for the land of cuckoo clocks, chocolate, and secret bank accounts. Have you seen how they use remote-controlled robots to race camels now? Well I'm the camel. My sisters are the robots and my mother's holding the **remote control**." Having to listen to oppressive paranoia like that got under Mushabbab's skin. "And when I don't respond to the remote, they try to break me in with anesthetics—I had a suitcase full of every drug you can think of. First they got me addicted and then they took the suitcase away to keep me docile with pain. Now they've brought you along to annoy me."

Mushabbab had just arrived back at the orchard when a messenger arrived. "Don't come to the palace again. Your services are no longer required."

I'd been videoed and they'd already screened me; apparently I'd been deemed unfit.

"Can't you do anything?" asked Azza.

"Her father said he'd have me burned for practicing witchcraft! They said I should be grateful they let me go safely after I defied his orders and tried to smuggle that stupid package to her."

Juhayman

TUESDAYS WERE MU'AZ'S DAY OFF FROM THE STUDIO, SO THAT MORNING HE headed for the Lababidi house, taking a roundabout route to be sure no one was following him. When Yusuf opened the door, he was preceded by the warm scent of shurayk bread, a local specialty made of mixed gram and wheat flour and fragranced with fennel, which he'd bought from Shaldoum's bakery. Shaldoum always got that old-fashioned taste just right.

This time, when Mu'az led Yusuf upstairs, he kept going past the first rooftop and up to the tirama, the balustraded terrace elevated above the rest of the roof. "You could sleep up here on really hot nights," he suggested. Yusuf sensed arrogance and superiority in the offer, as if Mu'az saw himself as the unchallenged sovereign of the domain and was deigning to toss Yusuf a few crumbs. He was letting Yusuf walk around in his kingdom and inviting him to enjoy a few fruits from the orchard of photos.

Suddenly, Mu'az noticed the metal gleam around Yusuf's neck. "You devil!" he yelped, and without thinking leapt on Yusuf, who was caught unawares and crashed to the ground under Mu'az's weight. He had no choice but to fight back, and the two bodies rolled and grappled on the bare summit of the roof. The only sounds that could be heard were their grunts and Yusuf's attempts to block Mu'az's blows. He finally managed to get on top of Mu'az and pinned him between his legs. "Are you nuts?" he panted. "What are you doing?"

Too furious to speak, Mu'az replied by spitting at Yusuf, spraying saliva uselessly into the air between them. He saw Cain in Yusuf's face. "How dare you take it? Those keys are mine! You have no right!"

Yusuf realized he was talking about the key hanging round his neck. "This? It doesn't even fit any of the doors! It's bigger than all the locks!"

"You tried all of them?" hissed Mu'az in outrage.

"Of course not! It was obvious—this one's all rusty. The three mihrabs on the bow reminded me of a key I saw once in a manuscript Mushabbab has about the Kaaba, so I thought I'd check if it had anything to do with that. I just took it off the bunch so I can compare it with the picture next time I get a chance to sneak back to Mushabbab's orchard."

"You had no right to polish it! It was a beauty, and you've gone and wiped years off it. You've erased the time! I never even dared photograph it. Now you've stolen it."

"Don't be dramatic. I just want to put it back into its context. I didn't mean to take liberties—I thought I'd been allowed into this house for a reason. You know Mushabbab and I collect keys that've been retrieved from old houses and the Zamzam Well. When the time comes, the keys might unlock some of the mysteries we're after."

Yusuf didn't mention what had really made him take the key: a feeling that it was meant for him. The first time he touched it, his hand recognized it—it was his key, he could feel it . . .

Mu'az pushed Yusuf's weight off his body and crawled to the other side of the bare roof, where he sat in a sulk looking out over the city. He avoided looking toward Yusuf. Neither of them made any attempt to give or take the key back. It was a fait accompli.

To dispel the awkwardness, Mu'az went downstairs to the kitchen at the back of the roof and took out a jar of Nescafe. This had been his celebratory drink on the morning he'd first entered that world. He spooned out the coffee and added a share of milk powder to each cup as Marie used to do for him every morning. He took the two steaming cups back up to the tirama, and they sat down on the edge of the teak wall, beautifully engraved to look as if it were braided, where they sipped their Nescafe and dunked pieces of shurayk, tasting of ghee, fennel, cumin, and nigella; they cracked the coffee-soaked seeds between their teeth. They shared the intimacy of their truce meal in total silence.

Mu'az watched Yusuf like he used to watch Marie at her post in the shadow of the minaret of the Turkish baths, hunched over her camera lens spying on the Haram Mosque, and repeated what she'd said when she first invited him to look through the lens himself: "You're not being invited into a house, you're being invited into a dying world. The end of days . . ."

He could feel Marie staring at him intently; she could see in him what he couldn't see, as if looking into a crystal ball. "Well, since you know the Quran by heart, do you know what this is?" She reached out and took his hand, opening it up like a piece of paper on which she was about to write her last will and testament. She pressed the big pile of keys, with their interlinked domed bows in the shape of interlinked mihrabs, firmly into the palm of his right hand, then took his left and placed it over the treasure. "You're the closest person to these pictures," she said. She released him with that entrusting gesture, and he knew then what he had to do; he still knew. He opened his senses as wide as he could and breathed in the motes of the past, which still hung in the air here. He was amazed by the fading faces he dusted, as he himself faded into a trance.

"The last thing al-Lababidi photographed was the courtyard of the Haram Mosque on the first day of Muharram, 1400 AH, or 1979 AD, the day that Juhayman al-Otaybi barricaded the doors after dawn prayer, he and his fighters on the inside, preventing the masses outside from coming in to pray. We have rare photos of the funeral processions that al-Otaybi used to smuggle weapons into the mosque . . ." Mu'az wasn't sure where her words began and ended. "They smuggled a whole arsenal of weapons into the mosque's recesses under the cages of women's funeral biers, along with sacks of dates as provisions for the rebels' long occupation of the House of God." Yusuf and Mu'az went downstairs, guided by Marie's ghost, and followed her to a staircase that led from behind the rooftop kitchen down to a hidden room. It was from there that Marie had witnessed al-Otaybi's attack. The walls were covered in photos of weapons, dates, and decaying bodies strewn around the Kaaba. Mu'az channeled Marie's deep, grief-stricken voice as he repeated her words for Yusuf. Yusuf didn't know if it was Marie speaking or his own apprehension as he listened to her explaining to Mu'az that day:

"We were photographing what we thought was the beginning of a new hijri century, during which the Mahdi would appear, when suddenly we heard gunshots and a flock of pigeons taking off in terror and fluttering around the mosque's minarets. Al-Lababidi was killed by the first shot fired from the courtyard. Thank goodness he didn't live to witness what happened after that. Al-Lababidi wasn't a photographer, he was a hermit, and he gathered Mecca's spirit into his photos as though he were reciting the ninety-nine names of God on a string of prayer beads. His lens faithfully followed his subjects—scholars, people who came to the city just to be near the House of God, its custodians, the Shayba Tribe—and in their faces he reverently awaited the coming of the Mahdi. I was al-Lababidi's constant companion, this man whose heart was connected to Mecca, who took photos like he was pumping his own blood into the city. It was like his veins ran through the House of God, so when those shots were fired in the heart of the city, he had to die. On the same day the Haram Mosque was broken into. We weren't able to parade his bier through the city as is the Meccan tradition. His funeral procession couldn't pass through the Haram Mosque's Funeral Gate, or cross the Mas'a to the covered market of al-Mudda'a and the Night Market so that the locals could ask God to have mercy on the deceased. He died with his spirit intact. He hadn't been broken: neither by his rivals nor by the frequent spells in prison he had to endure whenever he was caught sneaking forbidden shots of the Mount of Mercy in Arafat or the courtyard of the Haram Mosque because, they claimed, photography stole the spirit and desecrated the sacred. When he was deprived of a proper funeral they said the Haram had shunned him on account of his temerity, and that his burial was cursed because the people hadn't prayed over him and he hadn't been admitted into al-Malah. What with the curfew and the heavy sniper presence on all the city's minarets, we had to bury him here, behind the house, at the top of Mount Hindi. It was Doomsday on the Arabian Peninsula then . . ." Her voice was still there with them, and in the half-light the photos watched them. Before them was the Haram courtyard stained with blood and corpses, trucks piled carelessly with bodies streaming in from Ajyad Gate, Abraham Gate, Farewell Gate, Funeral Gate, and King Abd al-Aziz Gate; the last of these had been added during the expansion.

"Those bodies are the rebels. Marie took these shots of the destruction—or perhaps it really was the end times—which descended upon us at the turn of the century instead of the Mahdi we'd been hoping for."

The eyes around them had begun to move, and came out of the photos in a huge procession, streaming from every corner of the house and from the fear-misted camera lens—*Say: There is no god but God!*—to pay their last respects at the funeral processions of those who departed during those final days of the old times.

Umm Kulthoum's Sighs

SITTING AT THE ENTRANCE OF SHEIKH MUZAHIM'S STORE, NASSER RESEMBLED A wormlike appendage. The neighborhood stared at him with open dislike, and he was totally ignored by Sheikh Muzahim, who looked drained and hadn't bothered to reach over to his tray and upturn a cup to welcome Nasser with coffee, or even refill his own cup, which was encrusted with desiccated grounds. He'd been getting the man at the cafe to prepare his routine morning coffee for him since Azza's disappearance, but the man boiled it to death, spoiling the aroma of the blend with his slapdash approach and leaving a bitter taste in the Sheikh's mouth. He'd left a plate of dry, half-eaten dates unfinished, and a fly was hovering loudly around a pile of pits that had been tossed into one corner of the shop. A fly was hovering around his whole life. Day after day since the body had been found, Sheikh Muzahim sat in his store staring into the void Azza had left behind in his heart. It wasn't the pain of love or of missing Azza—sitting there, he couldn't remember ever missing Azza or ever allowing her to forge any bond between them at all; he'd never had a thought to spare for her and so she'd closed in on herself and pushed him over the edge of her heart and down into the abyss of his store, where he could rot alone for all she cared. Just like her mother: he'd hated every morsel of food she'd ever cooked for him and would try to escape through the storeroom to go sit in the store, but she'd still reach through the door with an arm like a slippery snake to leave a tray of food a meter in front of the chair where he always sat, as though she were feeding some kind of feral cat. But the food dripped with cold resentment and would sink silently down his throat to choke his intestines like heavy stones. Azza was exactly like her mother, who'd died of childbed fever just to provoke him. "That's what a woman does to you when you let her into your heart, she sticks her muzzle in and drinks your blood." Thus he was careful to keep a safe distance between Azza and himself.

"Since we came under Ibn Saud's leadership, after Mecca surrendered to his army and was then followed by all of the Hijaz—since he founded the Kingdom of Najd and Hijaz—no one's been able to escape his dominion except for that devil the radio and now these satellite dishes too . . ." He only said it to fill the silence brought by Nasser's arrival.

"Where's your daughter? Is Azza dead? Who do you think killed her? Did Azza kill herself to escape your cruelty?" Those were the questions the detective had prepared, but Sheikh Muzahim grabbed the reins and beat him to it.

"Have you found the devil yet? Satan's been throwing the rotting flesh of his followers in our neighborhood. They chose the alley right in front of my storeroom so as to trash my business, to get revenge on me; they want to hurt me and my daughter, because I'm the only one fighting back against their depravity! They're walking all over us and herding us like livestock with their fiendish media and God knows what else!"

Sheikh Muzahim was foaming with rage. Nasser struggled to keep up with him as he went back in time—to long before this most recent crime—reciting a litany of Satan's offenses he himself had witnessed.

"Satan has many faces, God help us. The main one is the accursed radio, an evil that wormed its way here in the sixties via Gamal Abd al-Nasser's speeches. It snuck into his followers' houses in secret, through balconies all over the city, and into the palm groves between al-Abtah and al-Hujoun, to Wadi l-Zahir and the gardens of al-Misfala and the foot of the mountains overlooking the Majin

Pool. Then, when the Lane of Many Heads came to life, it was accompanied by that demon singing out of a box in the Sharif's garden, which was given to Mushabbab's halfwit grandfather, Ali Bao. Sharif Awn singled him out for preferential treatment to humiliate the people of the Hijaz. Don't ask me about his story, ask one of Mushabbab's acolytes, like Yusuf—God help him—that guardian of history. I wonder what he has to tell you about that despicable family? Mushabbab's father, who was the Sharifs' protégé, was a dissolute wretch. He used to hold monthly parties in his orchard for that witch who'd enslaved Mecca's men, Umm Kulthoum. They'd listen to her concerts live on Radio Cairo—Heaven help us—and they were all head over heels; her sighs drove them wild. I only witnessed it once, when I was a teenager. It was just after the pilgrimage season and that wicked old man's pockets were stuffed with what he'd made off the pilgrims, so without even a thought to the sanctity of the holy months, he held a party to celebrate the coming of the month of Muharram and invited everyone who was anyone in Mecca—but he left the gate open to passersby too, to all the dervishes, lowlifes, and travelers staying in the adobe houses around the orchard. That night after evening prayers, zealots like me flocked there along with Mecca's rich and famous, but we kept to one side and watched, expecting the sky to fall on their heads at any moment. It wasn't long before we began to see arrogance, dissolution, and poison stuffed inside the baklava, fried doughballs, and Turkish delight along with ground pistachio, rose petals, and honey. Our blood boiled at the sight of the hordes of men in their Hijazi waistcoats and cloth caps, but that was nothing compared with those degenerate women, who we could see shaking their rumps behind the curtain which separated them from the men while they waited for the music to begin. Suddenly, the huge wireless began to shake with singing and sighing, and all ears and hearts were glued to it, drinking in that satanic voice. I remember how we begged God's forgiveness, sensing the disturbance to the column of light rising from the roof of the Kaaba to its counterpart in the Heavens. Suddenly the Sharif's green parrot squawked its favorite warning—"Bala bakash, bala bakash! Don't joke with me!"—and the lanterns hanging on the orchard gate flickered in a sudden breeze, and at that moment our sheikhs burst in with their hennaed beards, night air trembling in the rustle of their black cloaks, short white robes and red checkered headscarves. They made straight for the radio at the edge of the open sitting room; the men reclining on Persian carpets and the youths sitting around on the orchard's earthy ground had no time to react. The sigh emanating from Umm Kulthoum's bosom seemed strained and lengthened under the weight of that first rock as the beards surged forward and attacked the men dancing to the pipe music with coarse wooden sticks—thin, strong ones that left marks all over the shoulders and split the foreheads of more than a few children, including those of Mushabbab and his friends, who were too frightened to burst into tears even. They concluded their raid by finally silencing the radio with a boulder, but then, equally suddenly, they began to lose ground. Al-Labban, Umm al-Sa'd's grandfather, spearheaded the resistance."

Sheikh Muzahim paused for a moment and watched the effect his words were having on the detective. "Are you following?" he asked. "Do you see how these people strayed into sin? Do you care?" Nasser nodded, and the old man went on.

"Al-Labban—the milkman—was nothing but bad news. He was one of the devil's two horns. He was always making trouble. They used to call him "Full Cream" because he was so fat. His twin brother was as skinny and sparky as he was podgy and slow, so they used to call him "Son of the Night." He never sat down and never got tired; he was the backbone of that dairy. He used to milk the cows before it got light, skim off the cream and fill the yogurt vats, ready to wish the neighborhood a good morning before anyone had even woken up. No one knew the truth until the religious folks raided the cellar of the milking yard at midnight one Monday and found him smoking with his friends. Having caught them unarmed, the attackers brought the cellar down on top of their heads, then dragged them in chains to Farewell Gate where they flogged them and beat them with sticks, leaving them for dead. Worshippers who'd come for morning prayers hurried to dress their bloody wounds and carried the dead to al-Shifa hall in the center of Mecca, on the side of the Haram Mosque facing Shamiya Hill, where all the perfumers and herbalists had their shops, while the injured were taken to Qubbaniya hospital, which stood on the site of the house that Abu Sufyan had bought from Khadija bint Khuwaylid. That was where Full Cream found the corpse of his twin, Son of the Night. His heart was consumed with rage. May God pardon them both." Sheikh Muzahim fell silent so as to savor his own words in the silence of the shop, and such a long time went by he almost forgot his voice.

"It was Full Cream who led the counterattack," he picked up, "on the night of the Umm Kulthoum party in the orchard. He awoke from Umm Kulthoum's sighing, which had stoked his pain at the loss of Son of the Night, and cursed the zealots—the same curses that had accompanied his twin's bier during the funeral procession. Demons clamored in his breast, and suddenly with a leap he was possessed by Night, his dead twin. All his usual lethargy seemed to melt away and he snatched up his club and began thrashing every one of the attackers he could get his hands on. When the other men, both gentlemen and slaves, had gathered their energy they formed ranks behind him, and soon the beards and checked headscarves began to retreat. By the time they reached the gate of the orchard, they found themselves encircled and were forced to surrender. They were tied up and blindfolded and dragged to the desert near the road to the Umrah station, where they were beaten again and had their beards ripped out. Then they were thrown down a hole and left in the darkness . . ."

"And what's the link between Full Cream and the place they call al-Labban's house here in the alley?"

"He was their grandfather. He left his only son the milking yard and a wine press, and the son—Umm al-Sa'd's father—sold the milking yard and used the proceeds to build the building they call the Arab League. The devil's money, that was . . ."

"How much did he get for it?"

"I told you, there was a wine press in the milking yard, and al-Labban the milkman used to come out every dawn carrying three cans of milk on his right-hand side and three cans of wine on the left, distributing each to whoever requested it. There's a very over-the-top story about how he died, now I come to think of it," he added, spraying spit in excitement. "Are you interested in the hallucinations of devil worshippers?"

"Of course," replied Nasser. He felt like he was being pushed into the past; he wasn't seeking out these memories but rather they were being inserted into his head whether he liked it or not, like external memory drives.

"Some people say his children declared him mad and locked him up, so he ran away and was soon arrested by the Committee for the Promotion of Virtue for selling "vice." They escorted him to their leader, our sheikh. He was standing before the Kaaba and turned to the milkman to rebuke him. "Aren't you ashamed?" he asked. "How will you face your Lord with these sins?" "Shall I show you?" replied al-Labban. He asked for some water so he could wash for prayer, and then began to pray. After two genuflections he remained prostrated on the ground for some time, and when they touched him they found he was dead. Death while praying, Detective, is the fastest route to Paradise. As you can see, these types grant themselves license to do whatever they want, claiming that they're spiritual people, and even have the temerity to say they're going to go to Heaven!"

"So Umm al-Sa'd is this dervish al-Labban's granddaughter?"

"Her father kept the wine press in the hallway of the Arab League as a memento, God help us." He whistled sarcastically. "The milkman's depravity jinxed the whole family. See how viciously the grandsons fought over their inheritance and how they ended up turning on their father, and their sister too? She gave them away in the end, though, when she escaped from Azrael's jaws and came back to wage her shameless war on men. Well, like father, like son!"

"And what about Aisha? I heard she was friends with your daughter."

Sheikh Muzahim glared at Nasser as best he could through clouds of glaucoma.

"Lord help us! She's a weevil in the flour barrel, that one. She's a curse: she corrupts the children first and then the adults. I was always careful not to let her near my daughter. Her marriage brought her and the whole lot of us bad luck. It was that crystal wedding dress that did it . . ." The mention of the dress surprised Nasser, and he sat up, hoping to hear more. "Ask that Turkish woman," said the old man, but at that moment the sun must have set, because the call to sunset prayer sounded and he stood up to go and wash. "Are you coming to the mosque?"

"Sure," said Nasser. "Go ahead and I'll catch up with you."

He'd finally got to the dress. Soon, he'd get to the body underneath, too, and the moment he touched it, life would shoot through his veins.

It was getting late, so Nasser went straight to the Arab League to deliver the Turkish seamstress's eunuch assistant a summons for her to come in the following morning. On the wall of her cellar studio was daubed sloppily in red paint: THE DONKEY EMPRESS IS A BUTCHER.

That night, the stories he'd been listening to brawled in Nasser's head, leaving him with half a headache. Automatically, he opened his wardrobe and took out the shameful ripped sleeve, spread it out on his bed like he did every night, then lay down with his face buried in it and fell asleep. Yusuf's surreal article about Ali Bao the lunatic ancestor was waiting for him in his dreams.

> *Sharif Abd Allah ibn Muhammad ibn Awn (1299–1323 AH) picked out one of Mecca's madmen known as Ali Bao, who used to roam the streets naked, and brought him into his circle of intimates—once, of course, he'd ordered for the man to be washed and shined and dressed in finery befitting someone who was to sit in the parlors of noblemen. They became close companions, and the Sharif ordered Mecca's gentry to kiss the man's hand, and treated him as the most important gentleman of all. He wanted to build the madman a grand palace, so he bought several houses close to the mosque in al-Qushashiya—the most important street in Mecca, where the fanciest, snobbiest of its people lived, such that even a Turkish pasha would take care to pick out his best clothes if he were passing in that direction—and forced the owners to move out before demolishing them and building the palace in their place. Next, he selected a large area in front of the palace that was also full of houses, ordered their inhabitants to move out too, and demolished them to make way for a lush garden that would delight the*

madman's eyes whenever he looked out from his palace. Then, he decided to demolish the whole adjacent area, up to the edge of the Gaza neighborhood, so as to give an unobstructed line of vision between the Emir's palace and the madman's palace. In the end, whether it was cleared so that the Sharif could plant an enormous garden, or to build lodgings for pilgrims in accordance with the wishes of the Caliph, Sultan Abd al-Hamid II, the land remained empty for some time, but Sharif Awn died before anything was built, and it was eventually overrun by small houses and stores. Some like to believe that Sharif Awn associated with lunatics because he was wary of Sultan Abd al-Hamid—it was well-known that he was highly suspicious of the more precocious of his employees and servants—while others claim that Sharif Awn himself was a loony, as was patently clear from his approach to governance. They tell stories about the elephant he was given by a dignitary from India, which he used to let wander wherever it liked through the streets of Mecca, accompanied by a minder, and which he would take to summer in Ta'if with him. All this is to say that over the years, Mecca has become perfectly accustomed to madmen and elephants wandering around in the vicinity of the Haram Mosque . . .

From: Aisha
Subject: Message 19

Ignorance is not in the head but in the hand and its nerve endings, and in the heart. The worst death is death of the hand.

Under my clothes I was an electric toy that had lost its battery; all the wires that led to my senses and my heart had been cut.

I envy Azza, Sheikh Muzahim's daughter, as I see her clearly now: Azza, when she glimpses a swarm of bees, doesn't run away but walks right into the attack with a laugh, and comes out immune to their stings. Sometimes rashly, sometimes innocently. I always feel sad for her, but only so that sadness for myself doesn't overwhelm me . . .

If I had just a jot of her recklessness I'd probably be settling down in Casablanca with Ahmad now. As it is, he turned his back on me the second month after we got married, and threw those two words over his shoulder as he went: "You're divorced."

I hid the blow, knowing my little father's heart wouldn't be able to take a third shock. I built a cocoon around the words, and everyone in the neighborhood just took it for granted that he'd left me;

the Lane of Many Heads never imagined that the legendary crystal bride would end up divorced.

So why's Ahmad suddenly so keen to get me back? Is it your scent on me?

He never actually filed for divorce—maybe he just totally forgot about me. When he was forced to accompany me to Bonn, his face floated in front of me for the brief duration of the flight then he fled, leaving me to an endless string of operations, no doubt scared he'd be trapped by my crushed pelvis.

But now my cellphone rings at all hours, as if to say: what do you have left but me?

Does our love have a smell? What was it that created it?

Do you remember our last goodbye in the hospital room in Bonn? I skimmed you with my eyelashes, my chin, and the tip of my nose. I traced the pale whiteness of your belly with my features. Do you know what living flesh smells like? I can still smell it now.

In bed now, the tip of my nose can still feel the contact, and my eyelashes. It brings you to life so vividly.

Ahmad isn't attracted to my scent; it's your scent he's sniffing for. Both the battery's electrodes are connected, the energy is surging and the light has flicked on, luring the insects in . . .

Attached: you asked for more old photos, ^ . . .

This one's from the first month, or rather the only month, of my marriage. Can you follow the plot of this psychological thriller, where all the characters are **chopped** to bits under the skin, but without guns, murders or ghastly diseases?

Aisha

Data Bank

"THE WESTERN FOOD CORPORATION—A SUBSIDIARY OF ELAF HOLDINGS—HAS finalized a deal to purchase a plot of 50,000 square meters in the far south of Mecca. Vice President for Development Salim al-Muriti has said that the land purchase forms part of the company's strategic plan for new factory development. Steps are being taken to build the most modern food-processing plant in the region, which will comprise six standalone factories as well as centralized storage facilities. It is understood that purchase agreements for the necessary equipment have already been signed. A spokesperson for the corporation said the new factory will help fulfill the growing demand for food, especially in the critical seasons of both greater and lesser pilgrimages, which have seen steady year-on-year growth in the numbers of pilgrims."

Yusuf was glued to the computer screen, even though there was a smell of stagnant sewers to the row of computers around him. Like every morning, Yusuf had snuck out of the Lababidi house and headed toward the nearest Internet cafe he could find. After handing over his five riyals for two hours' use, he'd sat down in front of the last computer in the cramped room. Any hall of a house or corner of a shop that could fit two or three computers was enough to set up an Internet cafe that would bring in a steady stream of income for the owner.

Another day had come and gone and there was still no news from Mushabbab. Yusuf typed Elaf Holdings into the search box and hit enter. He looked through the corporation's website, local newspapers, and discussion boards, searching for information about their extensive, almost octopoid portfolio projects: factories that made cement, plastic, bottled water, and prayer rugs; meatpacking plants where they processed the animals slaughtered in the pilgrimage ritual; real-estate developments for both low-income and high-income housing.

The Pakistani employee noticed the thick force field around Yusuf's body and smiled as he set a cup of tea beside him by way of welcome, since he was a new customer. In an attempt to settle his nerves, Yusuf began writing an article. That morning he'd woken up to distorted images in his mind; he didn't know whether they were the tail end of a nightmare or a reality about to befall the Lane of Many Heads. He paused to consider just how absurd what he'd written in his first article seemed compared to the destruction he could see from the roof of al-Lababidi's house.

> *God sent his angels down to Adam on earth with emeralds, plucked from the gems of paradise. These angels were the first to master the art of building in Mecca, so they built, and Adam learned the art from helping them. Then he circumambulated what they had built.*

Loud banging drums in his mind repeated the words that he chewed over constantly in all his articles:

> *At the time, the earth was home to demons and beasts. The angels took up their positions before the Haram Mosque, their backs to God's House, looking out over the wasteland beyond and preventing the demons and beasts from entering the Sanctuary. Eve had also been forbidden from entering the Sanctuary. When Adam wanted to beget a son, he would go out to see her and lie

with her and then return to the hollowed-out gem the size of a tent that God had sent down to earth for him to live in, as a consolation for having been excluded from Paradise, and which was raised back up after he died.

He searched for words that would neutralize last night's nightmare and the sight of that adversary that was punishing them: faceless businessmen dressed in long, fine, gold-embroidered wool cloaks greeting men dressed in elegant black suit jackets and loud ties, individuals and groups, but all nameless. Faces and stars from the fifty states to the fifty-first and the fifty-second . . . Plus a woman with high heels and a facelift, standing for ruler of the world.

Yusuf only got gloomier. Staying in the Lababidi house had added heft to his gait; he dragged the whole house behind him. "One day Mushabbab and I were crossing the alley beside our house and he said to me, 'I never noticed those stones before.' I looked and saw faces as if they were out of a picture inside the house. Distress had turned human faces to stone." He scratched those lines out.

He gave up on trying to finish the article, knowing that it would be censored—yet maybe it would provoke some reader or other, or throw up a key to Azza's disappearance. As he was flipping through his old articles, he came across this:

January 22, 2003

Last night when I opened my eyes and found myself inside the Haram Mosque, circumambulating the Kaaba—and I don't think it was a dream—I increased my pace and slipped in among the construction workers behind the wooden screens that had recently been erected around the Kaaba. We spent the whole night digging for the green gems at the foundation of the Kaaba, and when an emerald as big as a house was finally revealed, I fainted. I knew the workers were digging it up so as to remove it and dump it into the ocean. Every time they chipped at it, it would spark and Mecca would tremble. From where I lay on the ground, I tried to hold back one of the workers: "Why are you trying to get rid of the last remaining piece of heaven on earth?"

In the beginning, God sent down his house for Adam to live in, then Ishmael came to live in the Kaaba and took to using the unroofed part as a pen for his sheep and goats. Our journey away from divinity began when we led Ishmael's animals out of the ruins and shut the Kaaba in our own faces.

Yusuf was annoyed by the emptiness in these words, knowing they were no match for the threat he felt in the air around him, but he couldn't put a name to it.

At noon, Yusuf set out for the Lane of Many Heads, stealthily making his way to Mushabbab's orchard. The sun had filled the sky and the temperature was over 49 degrees Celsius. Mirages formed over the surface of the lane as Yusuf walked along, joining the workers on their way to lunch, a wave that began after noon prayers and receded at half past two, leaving the neighborhood spotted with reeking plastic bags of rice and chicken, the eternal meal.

Yusuf moved warily, conscious of the eye that was following him carefully, but he was pretty sure Nasser wouldn't be expecting him to show his face in the Lane of Many Heads in the middle of the day like this.

He sneaked in through a gap in the fence at the back of the orchard and made it to the stairs leading to the open sitting room. There on the mud stairs he collapsed. He couldn't move. He surrendered totally to despair, not giving a damn what might happen to him. He felt that the last thread he could cling to had been cut. A stray cat appeared out of nowhere. It was missing its right eye and there was pus suppurating from where the eye should have been. It stared with its left eye, which was still intact, straight through to his heart. As he sat there, Yusuf lost all track of time. He was thinking back to the last time he'd sat there, when he'd watched as Mushabbab woke up.

Mushabbab doesn't get up from the pile of dust he's been lying on naked like a corpse, like a charcoal sculpture laid out on the ground of the orchard. Instead, still lying on the ground, he buries his head in green silk scraps from the covering of the grave of the Purest Prophet, peace be upon him, and breathes in the scents of three-quarters of a century's worth of the Prophet's tranquil sleep. He's drunk on the sun so he begins to pick at the strings of his rebec with his left thumb, and sighs rise from his body. It's a melody a woman sang to him on some occasion he can't quite remember; nevertheless, he still passes it on in that singing, and it carries with it the weight of many souls. Some of the rebec's strings do nothing but carry sighs:

"O Lord, you formed me out of the separation suffering soot of your creation.
I am your slave.
I long for nothing but to hear your voice.
I yearn for nothing but for you to reverberate through my body.
O Lord, I've left behind everything I used to carry except your echo."

Mushabbab continues his secret conversation with that hidden melody until the sun lights up his still-high mop of hair. Then he knows it's nine in the morning and time to cover up his nakedness.

He puts on his silver and white striped African robe to walk around the garden. He prepares for his daily ritual: reviewing the curvature of the arches created long ago by masterful hands, and examining the mosaic trees and their birds, and the decaying wooden carvings on what remains of the roof. He can sense the hands of the artisans and the adobe of the builders who mixed volcanic rock with mud and spread its warmth over the walls with the ancient crenellations they called "stone soldiers." Like a snake that slithers along and feels the soil of the orchard against its belly, he can feel the vaults beneath his feet, full of fragrant oils and history. In the air in front of him, he thinks back on the travelers who passed through his orchard the day before, including the Bangladeshi man who left him a stone tablet the size of a man and told him it was one of the tablets of Seth, son of Adam, which contained the destinies and wisdom of man from the beginning of time to the end of days.

"Rock candy, narcissus and wild thyme, ginger . . ." He squats by his stove and mixes up his secret preparation. "Sweetens the breath in the chest, helps the breath flow . . . When air finds a capacious emptiness inside of you, it speaks and comes out clearly, and takes inspiration from the rhythm of your diaphragm." He drinks the mixture and it makes him feel full. He sets the cup down on the base of the mosaic and a hovering bird lands and drinks the last few drops. He heads for the only closed door in the orchard, to the left of the sitting area. As he turns the ancient key, the sun crowds against him on the threshold before he enters the bathroom. Only once has Mushabbab let Yusuf into that mysterious vaulted bath, which is the object of the curiosity of every young man and boy in the Lane of Many Heads. Yusuf was blown away when he saw it; it was a masterpiece. The floor was made of ceramic tile that looked like it had just come out of the oven; it was the color of fire. The walls were covered in blue mosaic up to Yusuf's head, but above that they were bare adobe and the ceiling was cement, its dinginess contrasting with the turquoise hint in the blue. Mushabbab had brought this bathroom to life out of rubble. He himself had mixed the cement and laid out the tiles, arranging them according to how much fire they'd absorbed. He himself had laid the pipes that fed the wide pool.

Mushabbab closes the door in the sun's face and drops his robe on the doorstep. He continues his daily ritual, ignoring anything higher than his head. He pulls up a tile to the right of the door and extracts his cigarettes, hand-rolled from darkened reddish weed, picking up his lighter, too, and walks to the brimming pool in the middle of the room, where he plunges his entire body into the water, hissing and bubbling like a burning piece of coal. The water soaks every bit of him, sending up bubbles of thyme and ginger and the sweetness of the rock candy. He lies back, lights his joint, and the drug spreads through his limbs.

The earthenware jars lined up along the sides of the pool are filled with mud from the Well of Zamzam and plants from the sacred circle of Mecca's deserts. He reaches toward the jars and picks a few leaves, dunking and swirling them into the water next to him.

Time stops while Mushabbab is lying there, hidden behind clouds of smoke and listening so he can tell his disciples how he was reborn out of the bottom of the Well of Zamzam.

"I had the chance to touch like a truly living, waking person touches, and stagger like a dreaming person staggers more than a quarter-century ago, in 1979 or '80, when I dove to the bottom of the Well of Zamzam in diving gear, in shifts with several other divers. They were hired to deepen the well, while I dove down to deepen its springs in my chest.

"I dove down—just as Yaqut al-Hamawi says in his *Encyclopedia of the Lands*—from the top of the well to the bottom, sixty cubits, half of it through solid rock.

"I was in a rush to get to the bottom of the well and the three springs there: one coming from the corner of the Kaaba, one from Mount Abu Qubays and Mount Safa, and one from Mount Marwa.

"Good God, when the vapors hit me: the smell of the beginning of death, the beginning of hell, the beginning of paradise, the beginning—Amen . . . Suddenly its gasp, or my gasp, dissolved my wetsuit, and those springs flowing from the Black Stone compressed my body into a crevice even more violent, baring me to their powerful flow.

When the two divers dredged the well, it was actually my breast they were dredging,

when they picked up pieces of pottery, and keys, and metal, and mud, and brought them up to the surface,

when my remains were the last thing that Muhammad the Egyptian or the Pakistanis Bin Latif, Hamid, Yunus and Shawqi pulled up from the well,

when I came to on the floor of the Haram,

I was as sad as Adam, who moved the angels to tears. To this day, the grooves worn by the water still run across my chest.

From: Aisha
Subject: Message 20

Dear ^^^^,
A cat was run over on the asphalt. That's me. Crushed under my own loneliness this morning.

If you don't reach out to me through the screen, through the air, I'll . . .

I'm erasing everything I've just said.

From the Lane of Many Heads to Bonn in one fell swoop. From the sublime to the ridiculous, as my Aunt Halima would say.

I found a young Aisha laid out on a stretcher, heavily drugged, suddenly among all those white, ruddy European faces. Their language, not just their speech but their body language too, locked me out.

You know, ^, I went into a succession of operations "the way the Lord created me," in only that shirt that came down to my knees and had the hospital insignia over my heart and was open all the way down the back. I had no sister or mother there to cover up my rear when I turned around. And that female nurse who weighed me at the last minute to determine the dosage of anesthetic.

Arab and non-Arab alike, our bodies share different kinds of surgical stitches, ingenious ways of splitting us open, whether longways or crossways or laparoscopically, and with radiation: sedative, inductive, tumor-destroying. There were more than a few Gulf, African, and Asian faces in casts or bandages. The waiting rooms were crammed full of relatives. They read books to pass the pains of their ill loved ones, or listened to their iPods through earbuds, blocking out the sounds of the world, or passed cookies and cups of instant, vending-machine coffee back and forth. A universe of faces flashed past as my gurney was carted into the operating theater, with no face to follow after it with a concerned look, or muttered prayers, or even a trembling lip.

I passed by like a ghost: Patient Nobody. I was received by the elevators which waited silently in corners or suddenly appeared in empty sections of hallway. A single warning was repeated over and over: it might as well have read "Elevator to Outer Space: Return Not Guaranteed." The elevator was as big as our bedroom in the Lane of Many Heads, but made of a metal to which no emotions could stick, metal burnished with pains unknown to humans. No matter how much I hurt, it outdid me. With a single, definitive "ping!," it spit me out into the next unknown. I got the feeling that the elevator wasn't expecting me to return from the operating room or the post-operative care unit, but it didn't stop to shed a tear.

How much time went by while I was in your hospital? If you asked me, I'd tell you the first day lasted forever. In the three months that followed, I regained my sense of time. The six months after that went by like the blink of an eye—the blink of an eye is a lifetime—with you.

I'm just getting it back now.

Calendars are a deceptive invention.

They exist so we won't measure time with the units of our hearts (the units of existence).

Dividing time into years and months and weeks and days and hours extends the void. Or it limits eternity.

Ahmad was always working for some big shot or other. Before his most recent job, he was PA to a Gulf millionaire in Cairo for years, and having to keep the man's many secrets turned him gray.

Who was crying on the phone last night?

The fog of Rovinac clouded most of Ahmad's call. His fear pressed into my cubbyhole bedroom: "My friend the military attaché died alone in his kitchen. It was days before someone by chance found his body. Promise me you'll be at my sickbed, my deathbed! Aisha, do you understand? Life here . . . The women aren't like in our neighborhood; they just want you to be virile and strong with a functioning credit card . . ."

Under the shower this morning, my mother's soap gave off the smell of aloe vera, and I heard his voice again. "You're the shroud I'll be buried in!" I didn't catch the single tear that burned my left breast.

In its faint saltiness, I made a **promise** to myself that I'd never get ill or old and infirm. Not in the Lane of Many Heads and not elsewhere.

Aisha

P. S. You scared me when you said, "We used to have a poultry farm, and when one of the chickens died, we wouldn't notice it in the middle of that vast sea of chickens. We would only realize one had died when the putrid odor spread through the farm. You have no idea how rank a dead chicken smells! It was my job to clear up that rotten mess, including the worms crawling all over it, with my bare hands—I'd act like it was no big deal to impress my mother. At times like that, the distance from the farm to the woods, where I had to dispose of it, seemed so endless. My only hope was to block my sense of smell, and my sense of touch." You added, "I pretty much can't **smell** anything any more." How can I leave my scent behind me when you can't smell?!

Wedding Night

KHALIL DROVE ON WITHOUT STOPPING. ANYONE WHO GOT INTO HIS CAB GOT in with a stomach churning, knowing that this guy was trying to escape from his own shadow. Wherever he stopped, Ramziya's shadow would catch up with him and be all over him like a rash. A car with tinted windows raced ahead of him in a pack of other honking cars, decorated with scraps of tulle and white flowers. Out of the corner of a back window the bride's white veil flapped in the wind. He hadn't even given Ramziya a wedding procession, Khalil thought to himself. He didn't give her a wedding at all except for the primitive ceremony called the khamsha, which was when, without any preliminaries at all, her female relatives chased after her like a frightened animal, threw a sheet over her, wrapped her up like a corpse, and bundled her behind a screen they'd erected to keep her secluded. For a week, she was excused from doing any housework and fed constantly, so that she'd plump up and her complexion would be rosy. In the end, Khalil didn't notice the brightness to her features. They married on a moonless night, a night without any light at all, nothing except for the blood of the sheep they'd sacrificed and invited the neighbors to partake of. She was handed to him in a basket without any effort on his part. The feelings of guilt gnawed at him. He replayed the night over in his mind: the first night he spent with Ramziya, the pilot woke up drenched in his own sweat. In the dark he looked at the body wrapped in a cheap wedding dress and white veil, which was still clipped to her hair, one end undone and dangling down, the pin that held it in place lying neglected on her cheek like a wound. He stared into the smell surrounding them. Her body smelled like fertilized soil when it's moistened by nighttime dew. He withdrew into his dreams of Azza, slipped into sleep, and began to snore.

In his wedding night dream, he followed Azza until he pinned her against a wall. She didn't mind when her abaya slipped but she clung on tight to her face veil. He was having sex with a faceless entity. He couldn't visualize its features at all—only the features of Azza as an eight-year-old, which was when he'd last seen her face. He worried that the child's features would kill his desire and impatiently undid her braids, which cascaded black water into which he dove down, only to surface terrified and agitated, his body soaked. He hurried to get rid of that wetness by throwing his underwear into the heap of ruins behind their house, but the heap of manure lying beside him was still stinking of methane, an odor like blinding snuff, making his eyes and nose run. He remembered suddenly that he'd married her to spite himself, as if to cauterize his heart, which had been paralyzed by Azza. When he loomed over Ramziya, her eyes burst open in terror, arousing him so much he lost all control. His body even forgot how it had refused her the night before when the door to their bedroom had been shut behind them. Suddenly he was no longer Khalil with the invalid pilot's license. He was a slave like the slaves out of the *Thousand and One Nights*, where the evil queen parades their virility in front of her husband, whom she'd turned to stone from the waist down with a wicked spell. He had an absence inside him that devoured both the tender and the desiccated, and it was met by her hunger, digging away in the simple room on that narrow wooden bed decorated with cheap, now tattered lace, and those rock-hard cotton-stuffed pillows that gave the neck a permanent crick. When they rolled onto the floor, the rough Afghan wool carpet, from the area near the border with Turkmenistan, lacerated her elbows. Two patches of blood spread out and the rug became greedier, taking bites out of her shoulders and the edge of her pelvis as blood poured from her knees and Khalil's groans filled the room.

In a sudden moment of disgust, Khalil wrenched himself out of Ramziya and crashed backward into the door, panting. The oily touch of its glossy blue paint stung his nakedness. His disgust was directed inward: how could his body have submitted to this woman when his mind was preoccupied with another? He forced his clammy body into his old clothes, ignoring his wedding outfit with the starched and embroidered collar. The Turkish seamstress in the basement had made it for him, designing it specially to resemble some of the embroidered robes her grandfather had inherited from Ottoman governors, which she had on display in her workshop. She'd presented him with the replica as a wedding present. The Turkish woman was laying her hands on the Lane of Many Heads; with her little gifts and her recipes for beauty, doors in the neighborhood were opening, and daughters were being entrusted to her basement, where she taught them embroidery.

Without even turning to look at the red-splotched body on the woolen rug, Khalil rushed out of the apartment and down the stairs of the Arab League, which was awaiting a final settlement in the matter of its inheritance. "This marriage of yours is an insult," he said to himself, "from the bride herself down to the cheap furniture that's going to be thrown out into the street when the male heirs rob you and all the other tenants of the deeds that dead al-Labban made out for you." He bit his tongue to refrain from adding "May he rest in peace" about a man who'd hatched and raised four greedy vultures who felt no compunction about undoing their dead father's final good deed.

As he went past the first floor, he was careful not to make any noise that might wake up Umm al-Sa'd, al-Labban's daughter, and her husband, al-Ashi. He slipped warily across the foyer to the basement vault where the Turkish seamstress was running her scissors over women's bodies, making dolls, hiding defects. "No eunuch or Turkish seamstress is good enough at cutting or measuring or stuffing or lining to hide how ugly Ramziya is in that sticky mess I've just left her in," thought Khalil gloomily.

As if he'd uttered the name of a genie, the Turkish woman suddenly appeared out of the darkness and blocked his path, her bright dyed-orange locks licking at him.

"How many times are you going to turn down my invitation and break my little heart?" she purred. "It's the morning after your wedding! Let me read your coffee grounds for you." Her demonic face tied his tongue. She carried on reading his mind. "There are demons frolicking over your face. It's no wonder the prophecies were sent down to Mecca, to a cave. Let me tell you: the young men of the Valley of Abraham are like the very red fire of hell itself."

Foolishly he tried to get around her, but she breathed her poison into his face. His movements were drowsy, drugged. She led him backward, toward her studio, and the doors parted, swallowing them both. Her eunuch servant disappeared on the other side of the partition, keeping watch.

"Your muscles are all so tense. Just a breath and they'll snap!" Her voice was a cool salve, like the raw steak his boxing friends in the States used to put over their swollen eyes after a match. He'd almost become a pro, just because he loved pain so much. That was what always attracted him: pain. Maybe he got off on the torture of Azza being so impossibly out of reach. With dizzying torment, the salve spread over his skin, still swollen from Ramziya, and sucked up all his bruises and blood clots. For a moment, the world ceased to exist and he imagined all his internal wounds had risen to the surface because of the salve and its sucking. He imagined that the salve could spread to cover his breathing and take his soul away without his body noticing the theft. Rather than beginning to decompose, his body would go on for ages after his soul had left, and he would be embalmed in that salve like the most elegant of pharaohs. When she began to sway him, he didn't even bother to open his eyes to see where his feet were landing, he just let her whirl him around, and it wasn't until bliss began scaling his spinal cord that he realized he was dancing. He was dancing with the same hunger that had conquered the nightclubs of Miami.

But then when she lay him on the floor, he suddenly felt the need to be covered up, and he reached up to the hangers above his head, carelessly pulling the newly tailored clothes onto his body. He grabbed the finest and softest pieces, the silky, the ruffled, the fluttering. When he stood up, he slipped on the silk and fell. But there was no reason to ever move again; his body submitted to the will of the silk. All that time he'd spent chasing his father and the impossible beloved, and flying planes, and carrying strangers through the streets of Mecca aimlessly—the whole time, he now felt, he'd been chasing after this softness, this effortless body, which didn't go after anything but had things come to it. There was a mirror in front of him; he peered into it. The figure looking back at him shocked him out of his reverie: the almost-naked woman draped in silk had his face. Behind her, a peal of Turkish laughter smelled of Turkish delight, halva, palaces, consolation. She was all over him like a young scorpion riding on its mother's back. In panic he tore her clothes off his body and scrambled out. He found his own clothes, strewn like evidence of sin, across her doorstep. When he made it out onto the street, his clothes were on inside out and the pen in his breast pocket was digging into his chest, reminding him of his loyalty to pain. In the middle of the Lane of Many Heads, he stripped off and put his clothes back on the right way round without the slightest embarrassment.

From the alley, he shot a look back toward the Arab League behind him, his annoyance climbing from the Turkish seamstress in the basement vaults to the third floor, where he'd built his dreams for Azza but had installed Ramziya instead. He tried to summon up some affection for Ramziya, something like acceptance.

"There's something invisible in Ramziya's body that wants to expose itself. Something that won't keep quiet, can't be sated, refuses to behave itself. A base demon that fights any attempt at being dragged to a higher level. Her body is a storehouse of desires, driven not by passion but by disgusting appetite and excess."

A monstrous morass; that perfect description was what he'd been desperately looking for. "Ramziya's like the Well of Yakhour, enough to make my body erupt with warts and ulcers and pus if she gets her hands on it again. What else do you expect from a sewage cleaner's daughter?"

That night, Khalil came face to face with the humiliation of his kinship with pain. He admitted he'd enjoyed that Turkish battleship that could take gunfire and incendiaries without sinking. She took the same pleasure in giving and receiving pain as he did. There was a rhythm that linked Khalil's limbs to the Turkish woman's flesh. In the blink of an eye, a bruise would appear here and then another there, lighting up like green bulbs with each of his blows. They drove him wild, adding to the pleasure he took in the silk clothing from her basement studio. When he'd put them on, his movements became pure femininity, which then soon became a ghoul that assaulted the Turkish woman's shimmering rolls of fat.

Khalil flew down the Lane of Many Heads like a bat. He spat to his left and avoided the taxi parked outside the alley, which he slaved in day and night. He went ahead on foot, gathering up the desiccated neighborhood and pressing it to his own moisture; he knew that every step he took that night was a step away from himself. His good looks faded away, falling to the ground, their lines drooping and slackening, his face sagging like the houses around him. His heart twitched like the garbage heaps dotted here and there. All this trash filled his heart with misery.

"What is it, Khalil?" said the trash, addressing him directly. "Are you getting all high and mighty? No one's bigger than the Lane of Many Heads. You might be strong and capable now, but what about in a decade? We all have a lifespan: you have yours and we have ours. Read the expiration date stamped on the back of your neck. You human beings are trash. You manage to stay on your feet for sixty or seventy years, or ninety or a hundred even, but in the end your legs give out and leave you here. You pile up beside us, and everyone who passes by curses how you stink. There won't be any garbage trucks to cart you away; the municipality trucks can't get down streets as narrow as this. Who cares if you have a pilot's license or a driver's license, how long did you think your eyesight was going to last? Look how your bald spot's growing and your black hair's graying. The veins on your hands are starting to bulge. The fire that used to run through your insides is flickering feebly over the surface now and in a little while it's going to leave you for good. Today it's anger and passion that make your hands tremble, but soon it will be decrepitude and diabetes. And just wait till you smell of piss and turn the stomach of anyone who tries to hand you a bite of food. No, don't be scared. Don't let the thought of that kind of ending stop you; just be gentle now while you're stomping all over people and their joy. Be a little a bit kinder. You never know, maybe that little bit of compassion will come back around when you're thrown on the heap."

By the time Khalil got to the end of the lane, all the lights in the cafe had been turned off, except for one hanging from the roof of the shed where the Pakistani and Sri Lankan waiters slept. They rented out the corners to undocumented workers and exchanged smuggled pornographic photos, which they kept for company and used to sate their devils until they were interrupted by the dawn call to prayer. The Sudanese cashier, who was still awake and sitting behind his desk, scratching at his ledger, greeted Khalil, and absentmindedly Khalil raised a hand in return. He sat down on a chair that had been forgotten at the edge of the cafe, in limbo, one of his feet inside the cafe, the other in the street. He sat there like the embodiment of ruin: his arms lay slackly in his lap, his palms stacked one atop the other, his head drooping forward slightly, his eyes trained gravely on a spot of ground before him, the point of prostration in prayer. The mosque was in front of him. He knew, without even looking at his watch, that dawn was at the edges of the city, about to dissolve as the calls to prayer began and intermingled—"Prayer is better than sleep"—and then the single lightbulb hanging from a wire in the doorway of the mosque would flick on, Imam Dawoud's silhouette would appear behind the barred window as he stood in front of the prayer niche, which was marked by an arrow drawn onto the wall, and he'd announce the dawn prayer.

Khalil looked to the sky: "Don't cut me . . . " he said, trembling, his sister Yousriya speaking through him with the voice of a helpless, desperate woman. He sighed. "Kill me in an accident, God, crush me with metal so there's not even a scrap left to rot, but don't take away my strength, don't take away my eyes. Those who are disemboweled or slandered die martyrs. Disembowel me and let me die a martyr! But before you kill me, kill her first, that—"

"God is the Greatest." The call to prayer rang out from a distance like an "Amen" of assent to his own prayer. It was received by the first angels of the dawn. His soul trembled. He remembered that he hadn't washed off what he'd done in the night so he avoided going into the mosque lest the angels turn his prayer into a black rag and slap him in the face with it, striking him dead in front of the men lining up to do their ablutions in front of the mosque.

From: Aisha
Subject: Message 21

"'Look,' said the Contessa, in Italian. 'He is not a man, he is a **chameleon**, a creature of change.'" (*Women in Love*).

The chameleon Birkin in my clothes.

Do you know what a miracle it is for the one you've prayed for to appear at the end of your prayers?

You popped up on my screen this morning—completely unexpectedly—just behind my left shoulder when I turned my head, exactly when I whispered my greeting to the angel Raqib, who perches there, noting down my sins. That angel is the embodiment of creativity, always ready to erase pages and pages and give us another chance to start writing afresh.

This is what you bring out in me: I woke up with a blast of energy, massaged my poor injured body then poured the energy into this message to you.

In the past few days, I've had trouble figuring out whether I'm praying or writing. Everything has melded together into a corner which I escape to.

Aisha

P. S. You said, "I don't want you to miss waking up with the Lane of Many Heads, or with God for that matter. How many of us are there waking up in the same bed now? **Four**? Or forty?"

Do you realize how beautiful the melodrama was that played itself out on your stage?

In that scene, you, the Western man, appeared on stage as an individual, as the possessor of your own body. You took an entirely personal step, playful and carefree. For you it was just a treasure hunt. I, on the other hand, whenever I looked up, I locked eyes with my father and mother and my siblings and the Lane of Many Heads. They were all watching my every move, every flirtation; your every touch was felt by the body of that audience.

Do you see? Where can I find the words to explain it to you? I never came to you as an individual. I was a sheet of white paper covered in ciphers, the eyes of the Lane of Many Heads. You were an elephant stomping on the sheet.

I gave you what wasn't mine to give. I couldn't believe how much I smuggled into your arms with every single moment. No matter how hard you squeezed me in your arms to extricate only me, three bodies emerged: one starved and made thirsty, a second that had been encoded with years of "this is forbidden, that's forbidden, that's allowed," and a third, a tiny, tiny body, which grew smaller and darker in the presence of God, despite my long-ago divorce and the verbal agreement you and I made that morning in the park beside the train station.

Try to imagine me like I was in that room. As you were being lashed by the waves, I was being buffeted, too, as I tried to excise a single body that could be yours and yours alone while they jostled and brawled with one another on my bare shoulders.

Aren't you blown away by how spontaneously I performed in front of that unsympathetic audience?

Cyber Life

MU'AZ WENT INTO THE MOSQUE AND PRAYED. THEN HE LINGERED THERE UNTIL all the other worshippers had gone and only he and his father were left. His father watched him with pride as Mu'az prayed for forgiveness, tracing the chains of sin that were weighing him down. He asked for forgiveness a hundred times—a thousand times—for every photo he'd taken, every face he'd abused. He summoned all the angels that had abandoned him for his private abominations, and he apologized for the keys he'd burdened Yusuf with and the trouble he'd gotten him in. He begged for mercy and renounced everything except for the book he'd stolen from Mushabbab's library. It was a sin that couldn't be erased. He couldn't bring himself to put it back or even part with it. He insisted on taking it with him everywhere, even into his dreams, constantly flipping through it in the studio or in the Lababidi house on Mount Hindi, which the angels had long since abandoned owing to the mass of photos stored there. Mu'az discovered that his dreams were the only place where he could enjoy privacy, the only place he could be alone with his intimate belongings, whether or not they were sinful. Like the desires he had, which were brought to life in the snapshots he took of girls' bangs and legs, or this book, which was packed full of the work of the earliest photographers. They took him along with them, from the early 1860s all the way to the end of the 1950s, and he stood beside them as they snapped rare shots of Mecca and the Hijaz. He met the traveler Muhammad Sadiq Mirza and his sons in the photos of the supplication of pilgrims on Mount Arafat; Snouck Hurgronje, disguised as Abd al-Ghaffar, showed him what the pilgrimage looked like in 1889. He spent time alone with Ibrahim Rifaat, who'd taken some of the rarest photos of Mecca and Medina; Clemow and Hallajian at the turn of the twentieth century; Lawrence in 1916. In John Philby's photos from the first quarter of the twentieth century, he saw the pilgrims alighting from their ships in the port of Jeddah, and then he moved with de Gaury, Rendel, and Thesiger into the 1930s and '40s. In his dreams, they all became one: his genes climbed up the scaffolding of their genes, ascending through their genius, in-mixing. He woke to find that he was like Dolly the sheep: just a clone. No more, no less.

"Mu'az," called his father, interrupting his pleas for forgiveness. "God bless you, my son. The Turkish seamstress—God reward her—sent us a sheep for the poor. We shall slaughter it and divide the meat among the people we know."

Mu'az folded up his prayer rug, his father's voice following after him: "Mu'az, don't forget to keep the head and the tripe for us . . . And the skin as well." Mu'az nodded reluctantly.

"I'll be late for work now." Mu'az left the mosque, his father's blessings following him out the door, and he left his own voice to hang in the air: "I hate slaughtering."

Whenever Imam Dawoud sensed any weakness in Mu'az, he gave him an assignment like this to strengthen his constitution. "I'm going to become a vegetarian," Mu'az thought to himself. "I hate meat."

Mu'az had only ever seen meat that was covered in fat and veins and pericardium, and looked like the froth of death itself, from the charity they'd been raised on and celebrated with on feast days. "Are you too good for the meat that built your bones now, Mu'az?" Mu'az didn't want to anger God by refusing His blessings. "In the Quran, heaven is said to be full of fruits," he thought to himself. "Whenever meat is mentioned, it's usually birds or fish. Okay, fine, it does mention livestock, but . . ." He pushed aside the thought.

He untied the Turkish woman's sheep from their front door. This was what was going to do away with his weakness and sin. The sheep the Turkish woman had donated for slaughter was large and embodied all the mystery and desire rising up out of her basement; it even embodied his own desires and sins too. He couldn't bring himself to look into its tearful eyes; he couldn't stand the sight of its tongue—still licking—or its teeth—still chewing. He didn't know who it was who remarked, "They should've stopped giving it water last night so its veins would be ready to open."

An idea occurred to Mu'az. He led the sheep to the spot between the two houses where the body had fallen. The ground there was dry. There was no trace of what had been. Facing the direction of prayer, he pushed the sheep onto its side and knelt down on its chest. He picked up the large knife and was instantly transported to that last attempt at toughening up his constitution. One Friday after night prayers, he and his father were sitting with al-Ibsi, the executioner. Al-Ibsi was a regular at the mosque and the other worshippers all regarded him with respect. He introduced himself to Mu'az with consummate modesty.

"I carry out executions in the western region—Mecca, Jeddah, and Ta'if," he said. Then he introduced the delicate young man he'd brought with him. "This is my son, Mishari, my pride and joy. With God's help, he's going to inherit my trade. I've trained him well, now he just needs to be approved and examined." Mu'az nerves were jangling. His father and al-Ibsi went off to speak in private, leaving Mu'az and Mishari to get to know each other.

"You chop people's heads off? You're an executioner?" Mu'az asked incredulously.

"My father's heart is filled with nothing but care and concern when he's removing people's heads. That's what he's been teaching me during my apprenticeship. I can't even count how many beheadings I've seen. I look right at the point where the sword should fall so the head comes off with one strike. The challenge is testing your fortitude—seeing whether you can keep your cool."

"Are you married?"

"Yes, God has blessed me. I'm a newlywed."

"And what does your bride think?"

"She married me when I was still a soldier, but when I told her about my ambitions, she didn't object. She just asked me to think it over for a while. When I told her I was certain, she supported me."

"Isn't she scared of you?"

"No. She knows I'm carrying out God's law. At home, I'm like my father: gentle. We were never scared of him, not before he'd carried out a punishment and not after. He does his ritual ablutions first and goes to a beheading in a state of purity as if he's going to the mosque. In clean robes, with a headscarf and igal. Last time, he took off seven heads in seven seconds. Each head popped right off and he didn't once need to strike a second blow."

"Doesn't he have nightmares?"

"No, because he's a very pious man."

"What heads do you train on?"

"The training is abstract, but the actual procedure is carried out in the square. Tomorrow's going to be my first actual beheading assignment. You can come watch if you want." If it weren't for his father, Mu'az would've run screaming from the invitation.

"You're going to use a real sword tomorrow?"

"God willing, the government will provide me with one. They're very expensive. They're usually around twenty thousand riyals. My brothers and I always sanitize my father's after he gets back from a beheading."

Mu'az remembered that early the next morning he and his father, the prayer leader, had taken up their spots in the square outside the Haram Mosque by the King Abd al-Aziz Gate. They saw the police shut the streets leading to the square before the execution, but Mu'az didn't even notice the crowds that encircled them. All he could see was a man surrounded by military guards. He had no idea where he'd come from. The brute was dressed in white and his head had been shaved bald. From where he was standing, it looked to Mu'az like the man had no eyebrows or eyelashes or eyelids, or mustache, even. Mu'az knew he was one of the thirty-six terrorists who'd been sentenced. Photos of their arrest had filled every newspaper. The danger he'd once posed had been completely stripped off him now, though. He was nothing more than the vibrant quintessence of his audience's voyeuristic impulse.

Al-Ibsi appeared beside the condemned, and Mishari quickly tied the man's hands behind his back and blindfolded him. The scene was so horrific that Mu'az didn't catch a word of the sentence as it was being read out by the official in the square. There was a collective shiver around Mu'az as Mishari recited the profession of the faith three times, the convict repeating after him. Mishari's father al-Ibsi was standing nearby, watching nervously, in case his son botched his first assignment. He was ready to step in if Mishari's nerves failed him and he was unable to carry out the procedure. For a split second, Mu'az sensed that Mishari was on edge because of the huge crowd, and remembered what he'd heard him say the day before: "My father's determination is so immense it dwarfs even the crowd in the square." At the exact same moment, the same words ran through Mishari's own mind, and when the official signaled to him to proceed, he lowered the convict to his knees facing the direction of prayer, though he wasn't in a posture of prayer but halfway between prostration and standing. The flash of the sword cut through the scene, eliciting a sigh from everyone watching, and then the slightest nick on the back of the convict's neck. The head reared back, a blade of sunshine fell across the bend of his neck, and the man's head was separated. The blow was so light his blood didn't even spill out. The body remained kneeling, solid and strong, while Mishari turned away, wiping his sword with a cloth he produced from his pocket. Mu'az's eyes were trained on something in the background, though. He watched al-Ibsi's enchanted eyes as he traced the head falling in an arc and landing nearby; he could hear the head fall at his feet.

MU'AZ FLINCHED WHEN THE SHEEP TURNED ITS HEAD TO LOOK BACK AT HIM; IT WAS as if he'd heard the exact same sound. "In the name of God, the most merciful, the most compassionate." He ran the knife across and the same old blood came spurting out, but not from the severed neck. It came bubbling up from the ground beneath his feet. Mu'az dropped the slaughtered sheep and ran. *No doubt about it: he didn't have Mishari's mettle.*

"Mu'az chickened out! Mu'az is a chicken, Mu'az is a chicken!" The taunts of the neighborhood children pursued him until he disappeared into the maze of the Lane of Many Heads. At midday, his brother Yaqub went to finish the task of butchering and picking out the parts their father had asked for.

From: Aisha
Subject: Message 22

'No,' said Ursula, 'it isn't. Love is too human and little. I believe in something inhuman, of which love is only a little part. I believe what we must fulfil comes out of the unknown to us, and it is something infinitely more than love. It isn't so merely HUMAN.'

Gudrun looked at Ursula with steady, balancing eyes. She admired and despised her sister so much, both! . . . 'Well, I've got no further than love, yet.'

Over Ursula's mind flashed the thought: 'Because you never HAVE loved, you can't get beyond it.'

(Women in Love)

I wonder whether I'm Gudrun, but at the same time, there's some Ursula in me, I find.

Your cruelty comes so unexpectedly; sometimes you cut me off for one night, sometimes more.

I know you're always pursuing new victims for your massage table, but what I can't stand is how much I depend on you. And how I burden you with my feelings, which change from one second to the next. I can't help but feel my feelings have wiped you out. I pity you sometimes.

But you put up with me, unless there's a new body on your massage table. You were up-front about everything from the beginning, you sounded a little martyr-like when you said "My passion in life is healing the injured. I want to help by giving them a little pleasure in the midst of all that pain." But when you help one body by giving it pleasure, you put all the leeches, which are stuck to your flesh, on hiatus.

I've been a leech for the past two days in a row. I drink serenely from the cruelty of your cold shoulder. I know you won't leave me waiting for long. You'll come back to me. And you'll say, "You're a sex bomb." It wouldn't be wise of you to detonate me from afar.

A sex bomb?! Is that what you've been blowing up in my face every time you turn up or disappear without warning like this?

I remember when Azza was only five she used to sleepwalk—or, at least, she used to pretend she was sleepwalking when anyone caught her—across the alley into our house, through the door that we always left ajar, up the stairs, across the six laid-out sleeping rolls where my brothers slept, and into my bed. I could feel her tiny body squatting there beside my sleeping head. "Aisha," she whispered. "I hate sleeping." Without opening my eyes, I'd lift up the edge of the blanket for her to crawl in. When she settled in the bed, she wouldn't press her body up against mine, rather she brushed against me lightly where it mattered. Making her body into a crescent, she left space between us: her forehead against my lips, her left hand tucked in my armpit, her toes between my thighs. Our bodies connected at three points, we'd both fall into a deep sleep. I felt my heart go out to this child who'd abandoned sleep to come find me.

There was a time when I thought I could bring you into my bedcovers like a child, but you shattered the parts of that child inside of me.

Aisha

The Mahmal

An ancient silence lay over the Lababidi house. Yusuf could sense it in all the rooms, the narrow passages and the open spaces of the parlors, and inside the mirrors that lay on either side of the arched doorways. Yusuf sat in the silence on his own, eyes watching him out of the photos. In the silence, his life came to him out of corners he'd never noticed before. Everything he'd missed came to visit him in al-Lababidi's house.

One night, he was dozing on the floor of one of the sitting rooms, surrounded by photos of the people of Mecca, and when he woke up with a start at midnight, he'd realized he'd been thrown back into the same dream he'd had on the night the body was found, when he was nodding off on their rooftop in the Lane of Many Heads.

He'd been watching the neighborhood that night from the rooftop. The book *Saudi Arabia by the First Photographers* by William Facey and Gillian Grant lay in his lap. Mu'az had brought it to show him, opening it to the page with a picture by an anonymous photographer found in a file on the First World War. "You need to see this for yourself," Mu'az said, raking up a circle of fear around Yusuf. "I fear God's wrath! I won't be the one to expose people's secrets." Then he disappeared.

Yusuf spent the entire night examining that photo, but he couldn't figure out the secret Mu'az had tried to get him to see. It was a photo of the mahmal, the procession of the kiswa, moving through the Meccan streets having arrived from Egypt. The mahmal was always occasion for celebration; those gifts were like a yearly revival for the poor Hijaz. Between glances at the photo and down at the alley, Yusuf was nodding off, and at one point the photo and the alley infiltrated his dreams. He dreamed of them both as one and the same. All of a sudden the mahmal was passing through the Lane of Many Heads, guarded by soldiers at the front holding their swords pointed toward the ground. In front of them were the down-and-outs of the Lane of Many Heads, mingling with the great men of Mecca who walked behind the Sharif in decorated headdresses, the religious scholars in white turbans and the Bedouin in headscarves and igals. The women were dressed in black abayas and white yashmaks, diaphanous veils that covered their mouths but left their eyes and foreheads bare for all to behold. A single tree recurred in the image; military drummers girded the procession. Women peeked enviously at the procession from behind screened windows and cracks in the wall. Yusuf's heart stopped when he spotted the men on the roof at the left of the picture. Half-hidden behind the minaret on the roof, a man dressed in white traditional clothes seemed almost to be waving at him; another man had turned toward the wall so Yusuf couldn't see him; Mu'az was watching the scene surreptitiously from behind the minaret with the two other men. The houses in the Lane of Many Heads looked like they'd been patched up. Some parts bespoke great past wealth and others had been fixed with new pockmarked bricks or cement or wood, or even mud. It was a mix of planks and patches, through which the mahmal passed on its way to Mushabbab's orchard, where the camels would rest.

Yusuf came right up close to the decorated canopy on the back of a camel in which the covering of the Holy Kaaba lay. It looked like the kind of cage they put over a woman's coffin to conceal her post-mortem allure. "Who's under that cage?" wondered Yusuf.

"Azza," said a voice inside him.

"Aisha," said another.

Yet another said, "Yousriya. Salma. Maymuna. Sa'diya . . ." It couldn't decide on a name. Some presentiment was telling him to decipher the designs and words embroidered in gold on the kiswa and the canopy of the litter . . . When they got to the orchard, the men began lowering down the magical-looking mass of the kiswa. Yusuf was expecting the girl wrapped up in there to appear. But the men weren't taking down the cloth, but rather the writing itself. Word by word they decorated the orchard, the pride and joy of the Lane of Many Heads. When the silver- and gold-couched words had all been hung up on the walls of the orchard, a young woman in trailing black appeared all at once out of the writing-denuded camel howdah into the orchard. Yusuf's heart was pounding;

it told him he knew her. In that instant, the trumpets and drums, the ruler and notables, all the celebrants, disappeared as if they'd never been there, and in their place was a huge fire. The neighborhood people were adding firewood. They said it was to melt down the gold and silver in the orchard's decorations so it could be donated to the people of the neighborhood. The fire raged and smoked, and the walls began to melt from the heat; the girl was melting too. When she had melted down completely into a puddle, a giant reared up out of the puddle and with a single flick of its tail knocked the alley upside down.

When Yusuf woke up, a certain tranquility had settled over the lane, but it was almost instantly shattered by a scream: the body had been found.

Alone in the Lababidi house, Yusuf pored over the photo of the camel litter. He spread it out in front of him; for days and nights he examined its every last detail. He looked at all the men's faces, searching for the man responsible for withdrawal. Among the people celebrating, he noticed a face he recognized. It was one of the notables; he was dressed in modern-looking robes and surrounded by lackeys. He'd seen him before. With his driver and PA. All those faces had actually been through the Lane of Many Heads a month before the body was found. He tried to find a way to blow the photo up, so he could see the features better, to find that man and find out who he was. He knew that if he could just put a name to the guy, he'd have discovered who the killer was. Or who the kidnapper was, or who the woman was. He replayed the image in his dream in slow motion to get a better look at the young woman as the curtains of the litter parted and she made her way toward the orchard, or leaving the alley in the magma of the giant . . .

Subconsciously, Yusuf knew the woman who had snuck out of the Lane of Many Heads. Who was she? Azza or Aisha? Or just another daughter? A sister? A woman who couldn't bear the neighborhood any more? He looked back and forth from the photo of the camel howdah to the image of the event in his mind. The events of that night were impressed on his subconscious. Although he'd been sleeping, he'd still been aware of that quick rustling movement: the body that fell and the other that ran from it.

From: Aisha
Subject: Message 23

I sank into the deepest of deep sleeps last night. I missed the dawn prayers, and waking up this morning was like having my soul torn out.

If death turns out to be a deep revival like that, I long for it. After all, the Quran does tell us that sleep is a **minor death**.

Do you ever ask yourself, "When is she going to give up and stop writing to me?"

A single word from you is enough to wipe out my darkest thoughts.

"Best strive with oneself only, not with the universe." Lawrence says toward the end of *Women in Love*.

Imagine if you only had one local channel, then the signal was cut, and then suddenly you were reconnected and plugged into all the cutting-edge channels we have today. My father's death was like that. Whenever I look at the channels Azza is plugged into, I can't help but pity myself.

There was a sour taste to the yeast in our bread this morning. Do you think that Azza is coming up with all those channels herself? She says there's nothing to the world but portals, and there are too many for her to cross. "Just close your eyes and spin around and start bouncing from doorway to doorway. The important thing is not to let any doors close on you." That's her mantra.

The photo of you standing in your **kitchen** is making me hungry. Remember how I tore at the bag of shopping you brought home that Sunday? I had no idea what I was going to make with leeks in that modern kitchen of yours. One day I'll make a meat and leek pie for you. It's not an easy dish to make and it must have eaten up so many of my mother's days.

Don't be surprised by the amount of leeks it uses. Leeks warm the blood. Did you know that? They're related to green onions. Our grandmothers used to mellow them out by adding ground meat, tahini, and pastry.

I look back and I see the leeks of my childhood. Strange, exciting images whose focal point is the Yemeni porters. They were literally the backbone of the Lane of Many Heads. Their backs had witnessed all our homes coming into being. Their backs, half bent under the crushing weight, had seen our furniture move up and down the floors of our building, sometimes during pilgrimage, and for the last time when I settled in my cubbyhole for good. They left their heavy vests on even when they slept and they would sit in the corner of the lane, out of the sun, each with a bunch of **leeks**, which they ate with rounds of white bread.

My father was irritated that the strong, well-built Yemeni who'd appeared in our narrow neighborhood had chosen to sit leaning against the nude brick wall of our house, the smell of his white, leek-steeped undershirts reaching up to me as plainly as anything. I would peek out at his green loincloth, which changed color like a sunflower, rising and loosening as a reptile crawled inside it. Every time a woman walked past, she'd screech like a crow and crash into walls as she tried to flee.

"A **Yemeni** got up, his compass pointing north, he needs a **nest** to stick it in but he hasn't got a dime!"

I wait for the children's rhyme. They sing it as loud as they can and smiles break through the frowns of windows quivering to open.

I could never bring myself to say those raw, naked words. Words like that stick in my throat and send blood rushing to my face, because they don't come out level and neatly cut, but take me by surprise, their bodies appearing out of nowhere on my tongue.

The Lane of Many Heads doesn't sing those songs in the middle of the day any more. Perhaps their giant has left.

If the Yemeni man were still alive, I'd have sent you his picture. The rumor was that he'd been magicked into a bunch of leeks and devoured by the female crows in the impenetrable hideaways of the Lane of Many Heads.

We the girls of the Lane of Many Heads grew up with all these dreams and all these things we'd read. We were raised to think the world revolved around love and that love would save a girl from suffocation. I know now that the world revolves around sex and food.

I finished last in that race—it took me thirty years to have my first orgasm. The whole world is built around two bodily orifices.

Everything else is just padding that disappears at first contact.

Aisha

P. S. Dear ^,

'Do you love me?' she asked.

'Too much,' he answered quietly.

She clung a little closer.

'Not too much,' she pleaded.

'Far too much,' he said, almost sadly.

'And does it make you sad, that I am everything to you?' she asked, wistful. He held her close to him, kissing her, and saying, scarcely audible:

'No, but I feel like a beggar—I feel poor.'

She was silent, looking at the stars now. Then she kissed him.

'Don't be a beggar,' she pleaded, wistfully. 'It isn't ignominious that you love me.'

'It is ignominious to feel poor, isn't it?' he replied.

'Why? Why should it be?' she asked. He only stood still, in the terribly cold air that moved invisibly over the mountain tops, folding her round with his arms.

'I couldn't bear this cold, eternal place without you,' he said. 'I couldn't bear it, it would kill the quick of my life.'

(*Women in Love*)

Every time I read this conversation, I find something new.

Is this what I've been missing all along? Begging?

And what comes before begging: **poverty**. A hunger you would steal to sate?

It takes **another person** to make a beggar out of you. Because if your indigence becomes paranoia it will chase him away and you'll be left hungry.

P. P. S. My computer crashed all of a sudden.

Don't ask what made me download this cutting-edge program. This program excels at testing our curiosities and whims. Sometimes it opens us up onto a world in which a single click makes magic happen and other times it wipes your entire hard drive. Just like a human relationship.

I was in a coma for hours. Without our computers, we cease to live, I thought. And why? Because we are removed from the digital truth.

I'm out of order now, but still this list of commands is penetrating deep into my memory. It took me a couple of tries to get this service to work. These are the steps:

All Programs —> Supplementary —> System Controls —> Reset or Restore

Renew System Time or **Revert** to an Earlier Point in Time

All of a sudden you find yourself in front of this calendar and you can choose to go back one day, or a whole month, and with a single click you can delete the whole intervening epoch from your system. You can go back in time to when things were still working perfectly.

Should I look into my head to find the virus that disabled this service?

Should I think about which time it makes sense to restore to? Which periods to delete so I can go back in time?

Maybe I should start by erasing my name

Aisha

Maybe I should change it to

Hayah.

Aisha

P. P. S. 1. You said you like the digital photos I send you. It amazes me that though they come from this muddy darkness, they're light when they reach you (and museum-worthy!).

2. A photo of Umm al-Sa'd? None exists.

Attachment 2: Hamid al-Ashi: this is his yard and his shelves of paper.

Attachment 3: This is a sheep tied up in a fire-pit. The Madbi cooking yard is never without a **feast being prepared** for the fortunate people who can afford it—people from outside the Lane of Many Heads, of course. The aroma makes its way to us.

You can't smell.

Nasser turned up at my, the Lane of Many Heads', entrance tonight. And he uttered these words, as if they were an oath: "I wasn't made for this poverty and I won't let the Lane of Many Heads ruin my career. Not now, and not even when I'm old and feeble." And yet I still draw him in deeper and deeper. The dark circles under his eyes and his hollow cheeks tell me he hasn't slept in ages. I notice everything. I watched him sneak over to Aisha's house for the second time. I knew he was looking for *Women in Love* this time. It was vital for him to find that red sock, anything that represented Aisha, any snippet of her dreams. The smell hit him as soon as he walked into the hall. The whole building smelled like the inside of his undershirt. Nasser felt like he was walking through his own personal paranoia. He felt his way up the stairs, which were enveloped in darkness. Every door in the building was wide open. None of them had been shut except for the door to the cubbyhole. He knew it was the room squeezed in between two floors. He did try the lock, but in the end he had to break it. As soon as he took his first step into the room, his eyes ceased to see the world around him. In front of him, he saw only her bed, looking like a battleship. He fought the desperate urge to throw himself onto that space that had been inhabited by her body, her suffering, by the German demon who accumulated in her loneliness.

"Aisha is the very devil. But what, Nasser—you think you're a holy sheikh? And you've come to exorcize the demon from inside her? You want to extract it from her eye and blind her? Or from her toe and doom her to a wheelchair? Which body part are you going to have to sever to get him out and punish her?"

He didn't dare go forward. There was a satin sheet covering the bed—it was the color of lavender, light purple—and it was ruffled and twisted like a body in love. He scanned the entire room, looking for *Women in Love*. Wherever he looked, the scent of lavender lured him on. He moved forward. He dug through the drawers in the dressing table. He looked in all four corners, but he didn't dare touch the bed or the balled up sheet. There was no trace of the book. Everything in that house was stretched out; it was as though the people who lived there had left the place very, very slowly, with plans to return. Everything except for the cubbyhole, which looked tapped out. As if it had had enough of waiting for the women who loved to return. They'd been gone a long while.

He shut the door quietly behind him and left.

He would definitely have chosen to go from her lips downward. The opposite direction to the German. The thought turned his stomach.

Jameela

BETWEEN YUSUF AND AISHA'S PAPERS, NASSER FELT LIKE HE WAS MOVING AROUND in a fantasy Mecca. It wasn't the Mecca he knew from his usual beat. That night, he stopped over some pages of Yusuf's entitled "Sheikh Muzahim's Biggest Secret: A Farce":

January 1, 2005

Jameela was like butter stuffed into her black abaya. It was open all the way down the front, concealing nothing. The beautiful Yemeni girl's headscarf lay nonchalantly on her shoulders, leaving her black braids uncovered. Sheikh Muzahim's heart leapt into his throat at the sight of her. She was a luscious round pumpkin dripping with butter. Sheikh Muzahim's right eye, less afflicted by glaucoma than the other, dived into her lap and buried itself there.

"Welcome, priceless ornament, exquisite face, may the Hijazi earth welcome the beauty of al-Mukalla!"

"I'd like a Galaxy." Her voice echoed in the empty depths inside Sheikh Muzahim. He nodded.

"Your Sheikh Muzahim, his store, and all his sweets are at your feet. I have every kind of candy: lollipops, lemon bonbons, Mars with caramel, Kit-Kat, coconut Bounty . . . But your choice is the sultan of chocolate, Galaxy!"

Sheikh Muzahim believed that Yemeni workers were the best at all trades and it was good luck, too, that their lust for life made them reproduce more.

Jameela had spotted the Galaxy bars in a dark blue tin and was instantly hypnotized by the rancid cacao. He held out a bar for her, making sure to brush the edges of her fingers; his eyes practically popped out and the blue clouds of glaucoma roiled at the touch. No snuff, qat, or mahaleb cherry could compare with the electricity that crackled between him and the soft-skinned beauty.

At the first simmering of femininity, the scent would shoot through him to the very tip of the big toe on his right foot. In that smell glimmered the Bedouin charcoal-seller who had hidden him under her dress when his tribe came under attack, as happened constantly in the desert. He was seven at the time. The girls in his tribe started embroidering their dresses when they were still children, then got married in the dress, and never took it off for the rest of their lives. It secreted away every memory of every moment of passion and sadness until it passed on with them. All that wrapped itself around him inside the dress of the Bedouin charcoal-seller; he got an instant erection the size of Mount Tuwayq and ejaculated a flood bountiful enough to irrigate an orchard.

The same mountain reared up now whenever he saw fifteen-year-old Jameela. She brought back the moan that echoed in the the well inside him that he'd turned his back on long ago, along with the dream of a male heir. Jameela's gaze had the placidity of a cow's; what was it that was absent from her face? Disgust and defiance. There was none of that in Jameela's sweet, animal gaze; she gave him back what Azza's mother had taken from him.

A Hair

"NASSER, SON!" HIS MOTHER'S VOICE ON HIS CELLPHONE CUT SHORT THE NAGging of that phrase from *Women in Love* in his head, "best strive with oneself only, not with the universe." It was the middle of the night. "I've found you a bride! She's rich, pretty, and respectable." The Lane of Many Heads roared with derision inside Nasser's skull.

"Oh God, Mom, not this again . . ."

"You bury yourself in work! You'll be the end of the family line and you'll never have the chance to have a kid who has your name."

Nasser fidgeted with some paper. His bed was covered with Yusuf's diaries, and Azza's sweat was leaking out of the pages onto the bedclothes. He couldn't even close his eyes against it; the smell seeped out anyhow. Going back to his mother's ways was inconceivable. He struggled to focus on what she was saying. "She's an orphan. Her uncles are very modern and would be happy for you to meet her, with a chaperone and so on, of course. Please, Nasser, make me happy before I die!"

"God keep you here for us, Mom . . . Can we chat about this tomorrow? It's pretty late."

"Son, don't go to your grave a dried-out stick!" Her words darkened the already-dim room. He hung up. He closed his eyes and tried to slow himself down, fleeing to that remote spot in the corner of his heart, where no murder or misery could sneak in. There, he'd hidden the image of a girl: a girl whose veil he'd never dared to even tug on, so that throughout his adolescence and maturity she'd remained wrapped head to toe in her abaya, though she was still as light and joyful as a shadow.

Tonight, though, he reached out a feverish hand to that cloud of black he'd concealed throughout his adolescence, and began pulling off layer after layer of the endless blackness. But when he at last got to the center of the cloud he didn't find the women he'd been collecting—glimpsed through the windows of cars speeding past him in the traffic, or the windows of his neighbors in Ta'if. Back then, whenever he looked up at a girl's bedroom window, he'd find a sandal dangled out the window, sole facing him, in a rude rejection of his presumptuous advance. In the mirrors of those dirty soles, Nasser saw his own lonely face waiting for a female face to inhabit it.

He took his memory tin out of the bottom of his wardrobe. All there was inside was a single long hair and a hairclip decorated with a tiny red diamanté apple. He remembered how he'd found it on a side table in his friend's house, how the blood had rushed to his temples when he'd picked it up and stuffed it quickly into his breast pocket. His hand hadn't stopped trembling for days; the apple next to his heart was a fully formed girl and she had captivated him for years. He never said she was imaginary, the Apple Girl. He'd spent his prime obsessed by that apple and the single long hair that he'd wrapped in velvet and laid in a long thin box like a precious, jewel-studded sword in its sheath, as if waiting for great men with jet-black beards and glittering eyes to uncover it and forge its blackness into the path of their destiny.

Vague scenes haunted him; he thought they were from that film starring the famous Bedouin singer Samira Tawfiq. What was it called . . .? *Amira, Daughter of the Arabs*? Maybe . . . The one where the handsome prince falls madly in love with a black hair that he finds in the middle of the vast desert, and abandons his tribe and kingdom to travel the land searching for the woman it belongs to.

Nasser felt like all the men of his generation could have been that Arab prince, capable of falling in love with a nameless hair. A name *is* a woman—it's a woman's self, her honor—and could be enough to kill a man out of passion. He remembered his mom's trips to find a bride for his older brother. The whole family used to join in the offensives she led on houses where she'd heard there were available daughters. There was an African woman, Hajja Hawwa, who used to go round the houses helping families out with their laundry and ironing and would bring back descriptions of the girls wherever she'd been: "Al-Mukharrij's daughter, her braids are as thick as a palm trunk and reach down to her ankles . . . The al-Asiri girl is as curvy as a moringa branch and has breasts like home-grown pomegranates . . . Al-Zahraniya's eyes are fatally seductive . . . Al-Ghamidi's girl is quicksilver, whoever gets her'll be a lucky man . . ."

Her usual trade was smuggling forbidden features, but one time, she came with just a name. She breathed the name like she was breathing a spirit into his brother's body: Salma. It was love.

The name started a hurricane inside Nasser's brother. Like our ancestor Adam when God breathed the names of all creatures into his back so we could be created, his brother built an idol on the foundation of that name, Salma, molding her out of the breasts of the most gorgeous movie actresses, Umm Kulthoum's deepest sighs, and the loveliest kidnapped brides out of Fairuz's plays . . . He prepared a dower of twenty thousand riyals, a neckpiece of pure gold rashrash-work like a shimmering cascade, bottles of rose, musk, and ambergris, and a set of make-up with bright turquoise eye-shadow, pink rouge, and blood-red lipsticks, and he furnished the splendid open sitting room in the Qarawa Gardens in Ta'if, where he worked as a supervisor at the Bugariya orchards. But when he finally met Salma on the night of the wedding, she turned out to be a demon, and he fell into a terrible depression.

Nasser recalled the pall that marriage had cast over his brother's life. He'd drawn his lot from a bundle of names three times, and every time, she turned out to be either a demon, or just a "woman with no salt," as they say, meaning unremarkable and insignificant. He finally settled on the fourth: his Filipina maid. Every time, Nasser used to live off the crumbs that fell from the names and descriptions of his brother's dreams, just like he was feeding now off David's leftovers from Aisha's letters, which had shattered all his teenage fantasies and replaced them with women like herself, women capable of penetrating his mind with their words, of desire and fruition. "Nasser, you've stolen a sleeve from that cheap flesh and now you're worshiping it!"

Dogs barked in the distance, and Nasser thought to himself that the municipality should go back to culling them using meat mixed with broken glass. It would mean dog corpses filling the horizon with their rotting smells, though. He put his hand under his shirt and felt for his heart, which he'd never faced up to before. Bringing it out into the air, he could tell from the cracks all over it that there was a gaping hole inside of him like a cage, for a lover like Aisha or a wild bird like Azza, and that it was still beating and capable of loving Azza's bare feet padding up the stairs to the roof as she crept out in her sleep to visit Mushabbab, or sinking into the sandy ground of Mushabbab's orchard, or even when Mushabbab knelt down humbly to cover the tips of her toes. Nasser knew that all the men who'd had those two women had left cracks in his heart where oxygen was seeping in, feeding his infatuation, and teaching him how to outdo all of them in courtship. If either Azza or Aisha fell into his cage, he'd show no mercy: he'd starve her to make her eat his live flesh, he'd interrogate her and wring out her femininity, he'd tear away all the pages that Yusuf or the German had imprisoned her with, he'd wash her long hair with his hands and wipe everything she'd said from behind her ears with fragrant kewra water, and rest his own ear on her lips to break her fast . . . She, the one Yusuf's diaries described as fasting from words.

"But Nasser, she's half your age, and besides—you've been fasting all these years and now you're falling for a dead woman!"

A Window for Azza

December 2, 2005

From California, USA, a motorbike has been imported to the Lane of Many Heads . . . You must have heard the roar of its engine.

Note all the details on the delivery slip, Azza:
Make: Yamaha, imported 2004
Color: red gloss
License: Florida 946248, 01/06143234
Owner name: Mushabbab Ateeq Al Nayib

Order name: al-Sheikh Khalid al-Sibaykhan

Notes: With thanks for your assistance in organizing private events.

Mushabbab was as happy as a child, saying that at last he could cross the whole city now and get out of the Lane of Many Heads.

Nasser couldn't believe his eyes when he saw al-Sibaykhan's name. He circled it in red several times before carrying on reading.

That Mushabbab is a rocket launcher. He's thrust me out of the manual age and into the petroleum age with this motorbike of his.

"Life's like gas, you burn it or you get burnt!" My hands respond to Mushabbab's motto, pumping another shot of gas into the motorcycle, and I shoot like a screeching arrow along the Mecca ring road on my way back from Ajyad to Sittin, heading for the masses of people in the crowded neighborhoods where I drive around displaying the Starbucks logo on my T-shirt. Don't laugh, Azza. I can't be deformed, not even by a dubious logo on the back of my green shirt. I was hired by the advertising company on the condition I provided my own motorbike, so I'm using Mushabbab's.

I fling off the logo behind my back. We won't waste gas by stopping to look behind us; you're here with me, the speedometer is showing "Azza," you're the point I was naively aiming for in my history studies.

Yes, this motorbike is the real me.

Speeding through tunnel after tunnel that cuts through Mecca,

I start with the glass and steel towers that surround me. They're solid but I find my way in; all it takes is a firm foot on the gas and they start unraveling and peeling off the city's skin to reveal the hidden kernel underneath.

Azza, burn all your patience and come race me in this speed,

Can't you feel that I'm light, for the first time in my life? All I need now is to touch you in the rushing air and be blown away with you.

From: Aisha
Subject: Message 24

Dear ^,

Did you really paint me from memory???

Even my mirror doesn't greet me with a face like this! And the lips, my God . . . What a scandal! And that nose, sticking itself up in the air to scorn me.

You shouldn't make my face so open; otherwise my features won't have anywhere to hide from you.

I can read even your faintest trembles in the photos you send me. I can even read the scent of your mood now.

You smell like me now.

You're like Birkin, who doesn't need to admit his excessive sensuality, his darkness. For him, that deep, piercing gaze is enough to terrify Ursula, for me to know, with a new sense in my body, what he'll say and how he'll wreck the scene.

I think your challenge is the same as Birkin's—not to fall in love with an Ursula but to test your ability to **be subsumed** in another person, someone who will understand you not through words but through touch, to move slowly, to keep sex from burning her—sex devours handfuls of one's innermost core, it ignores those places that long most to be heard, it fails to give them expression or to allow them to express themselves, but soft touches are like butterflies fluttering at the edges of edges where it wouldn't even occur to you that there were any nerves.

Birkin might submit to desire, Birkin himself might even act out that desire and sweep away, but that non-desire, that hunger to reach oneness that went beyond sensuality, remains like a delicate butterfly fluttering at the edge of his soul, unconsciously, without a backward glance to spoil it, swiftly rubbing its wings and leaving behind a colored stain of wing-dust on the soul.

Attachment 1: Jameela covered head to toe in a **red wrap**, with a man on either side: her father to the left, the registrar to the right.

Mu'az took this shot for me. I didn't show it to Azza. I was too scared.

Attachment 2: After some hesitation I'm sending this picture of Matuqa, Yabis the sewage cleaner's mother.

As you can see, her bed is like Noah's Ark, carrying Matuqa's whole existence: there are rags and scraps laid out lengthwise which take up half the bed—so many that she's lying twisted to make space for them—and scraps of dry bread hidden in readiness for the famines that are to come, you can see bits of them here and there, and there's a plastic bag holding her eyebrow pencil and her silver engraved kohl container and applicator, incubating bacteria from Noah's times; at her feet are the leftover clothes of a dead husband, reeking of lamb fat, and under her stiff, neck-breaking pillow there's a copper plate that was one of her wedding gifts, a camel-leather shoe with broken straps, and a string of sandalwood prayer beads that Yabis brought back from Medina; at her left is a packet of stiff, moldy strawberry bubble gum to bribe passing children, and underneath that a half-eaten tube of cheese'n'chili flavor Pringles. Goodness knows what else is in there, but the main thing is she's ready to set sail as soon as Israfel blows his horn.

Mu'az, Imam Dawoud's son, managed to snap this picture of her spontaneously. He wanted to capture the flowers on her Shalky label dress, with the enormous fuchsia-colored flower across her chest and an orange and red one splashed across her pelvis.

I wonder: what does this ninety-something woman dream about? What are dreams like when we're about to step over the threshold at the end of life? Do they care about us? Do they show us any bonus footage? Does life change position so that it always moves forward, not backward or toward the present? Do we think our beauty will still be there, waiting for us, on the other side of that threshold? At what age do our bodies retreat and stop dreaming, and our eyes begin to look ahead to what's beyond the threshold?

Matuqa's part gets wider and wider but not a single white hair invades it. A woman's will to live resides in her hair, and a woman who shines her hair with coconut oil every morning and braids it around her head like a crown will surely never die.

Aisha

P.S. When I woke up after the accident, my whole life seemed like just a moment, like it had passed me by, because my limbs weren't responding and no mirror would face me.

For days I avoided looking them in the eye, certain I was somewhere else and that another life, which wouldn't die, was waiting for me.

When the nurse exposed whatever part of me to wash it with a warm flannel and antiseptic soap, I didn't care enough to cover it up, because the body that feels ashamed was somewhere up there, hovering in some spot above everyone's heads, and focusing on some other point that was even further away. No matter how much I craned my neck I couldn't quite see that point which comes after death. Who said I didn't die? Even now, whenever I close my eyes, they look toward that point beyond pain, beyond humanity.

Who said they all died?

They made me undergo psychiatric treatment with the doctor with the Egyptian accent who was going to help me come to terms with my orphanhood.

He assured me that the anti-depressants were enough to bring my soul out of that emptiness and make it swallow their death, one in the morning and one at bedtime, like a glass of sugarcane juice.

My eyes bothered him. In between us were the lenses of his glasses and their heavy green frames, which framed and contained his every look.

I gave up nothing from the inside of my head but the bubble of fake everything's-okay. He soaked it and starched it and ironed it and folded it to see if it was still crumpled, to repolish it with his tranquilizers.

All the while, my head's central safe was still hovering in the air, where not even dynamite could get it, staying out of reach of all the questions aimed at figuring out the secret combination to its lock.

"Do you feel a sense of loss? Do you want to express your pain?" Are your dead relatives contributing to the problem of global warming?

His questions were like the endless pages of Chinese horoscopes or personal ads in women's magazines.

I made it through all those questions without giving up a single digit of the secret combination.

When I got back from Bonn, I stuffed the safe under my bed. I avoided the room on the top floor where they still sleep . . .

In the middle of the night I can hear their dreams,

Once one of them woke me from a nightmare,

And once my dad came to the door and stared at me while I was sleeping, and said "Don't forget to wear your **nightguard**!" The plastic mold that I have to put over my top teeth to stop me grinding and squeaking them all night.

P.P.S. Azza sleeps with her legs wide open . . .

I find that so disturbing.

Do you dream of having a woman like that in your bed?

P.P.P.S. I remember the first nights after Ahmad left me:

One night, while I was fast asleep, I sensed my father standing at the door of my cubbyhole watching me sleep—he came once at midnight, and then again around dawn,

He found me in exactly the same position: lying on my back with my hands one on top of the other in prayer position and my two long braids lying undisturbed on my chest,

He shook me violently, thinking in panic that I might be **dead**.

Do you think Azza sucked all my energy so that she could be extra open, extra free?

Can you hear the sound of the Muhammad Abdu song coming from the cafe? "Push me to my limit . . ." I tremble at the **limitlessness** you've opened up within me . . .

An Apology for Azza

April 6, 2006

How long has it been since the Yamaha slept?

Tonight the Yamaha veered expertly to avoid the bus that had suddenly left its lane. It was the motorcycle's sudden responsiveness that foiled the bus's attack; it only managed to nick the back bumper of the bike, but that was still enough to send it skidding down Shamiya Hill. All the lights shining on me kept me from feeling the asphalt tearing up my legs. All I was aware of was the crushed metal and spilled gasoline. When the many lights became a single light shining into my face, I woke up to find myself in an operating room and then suddenly in an operating theater as long as a bus.

"As a trainee on his probation period, he is not party to the medical insurance benefits we make available to our permanent employees." With that the advertising agency washed their hands of me, and I was forced to rely on the free medical services at the Nour Hospital.

Azza, don't cry.

My mother brought me the cloth on which you'd drawn in chalk and charcoal. You'd written out an order on its tatters: "Stay alive!"

She also brought me your words: "No hope."

And, "Get well soon."

Are you actually angry?

Do you remember that day we were trying to save those black puppies on the roof of that abandoned building? When the walls collapsed on us, I broke my leg but you landed on your feet like a cat, if a bit dinged up. You started hitting me wildly when they brought me back later that day with my leg in a cast.

You didn't speak to me for days.

I understood that you were a glance; as soon as you fall you fly off again. You amputate the damaged limb.

You strip off anything that slows you down.

They swapped my crushed knee for a metal knee. Mushabbab had to pay twenty thousand for them to perform a surgery that was meant to be free. I have no idea why he was so keen on investing in my misfortune or why he uttered prayers over my knee that it would be repaired.

It looks like I'm going to be laid up here for a while. At least until your anger runs out.

I promise you I won't be a burden and that I'll resume my plan for making inroads as soon as I get out of the hospital. As you can see I'm slowly turning into metal, starting with my knees.

Here I am, jettisoning all my limbs like the bodies you draw, so that I can escape this picture-frame.

Sitting cross-legged Gandhi-style on the floor so much means that the knee joints of most women in Mecca wear out eventually. And they all have to replace them with metal ones; the female sex is racing to be transformed into steel. Do I look like I'm changing sex, too? Let me talk nonsense . . . Don't be mad.

Nasser made a note: Yusuf limps.

From: Aisha
Subject: Message 25

'Death is all right—nothing better.'

'Yet you don't want to die,' she challenged him.

He was silent for a time. Then he said, in a voice that was frightening to her in its change:

'I should like to be ***through with it****—I should like to be through with the death process.'*

'And aren't you?' asked Ursula nervously. They walked on for some way in silence, under the trees. Then he said, slowly, as if afraid:

'There is life which belongs to death, and there is life which isn't death. One is tired of the life that belongs to death—our kind of life. But whether it is finished, God knows. I want love that is like sleep, like being born again, vulnerable as a baby that just comes into the world.'

'Why should love be like ***sleep****?' she asked sadly.*

'I don't know. So that it is like death—I DO want to die from this life—and ***yet it is more*** *than life itself.'*

(*Women in Love*)

Dear ^,

In the mood for dying, I read *Women in Love*—a scandal—in the open air of the rooftop. The Lane of Many Heads took in the scent of a woman in love. And the down on the back of Ursula's neck. It stood there, yearning, waiting for the musician who'd just then opened his mouth and begun to sing.

By reading it out in the open like that I knew I wasn't just goading my father, I was challenging every one of the Lane of Many Heads' many heads. Including my own.

We were raised to fear the outside world. You probably can't believe that the woman you treated, and then invited out, had never been alone in a room with a strange man ever before. Had never walked in the street by herself before. Had never been alone before. Had never exited the bubble of fear to see what she was capable of.

The thing I feared most was waking up without an address. That I wouldn't get off at the Lane of Many Heads one day. You're the first *address* on the outside I've ever longed for.

That's why I simply couldn't die in Bonn. It was impossible. Not even when I was brought to the very precipice, more than once, as my lungs failed.

In my mind, moving will always be associated with a black-stuffed yellow cube. Can you guess what the cube is? *The setting: Women's Teacher Training Academy.* Time: 1985.

I set the cube before you, and I warn: what is it?

The security guard shuts the door of the academy, locking it with a chain and padlock. On the other side of the door:

We girls, she-goats, sweating in the heat, stinking of adolescence.

We get ready in a hurry. Our heavy black: abayas.

Our translucent black: headscarves. We put on our abayas and lay our headscarves over our faces. One layer, a second, a third, a fourth . . . It makes us proud to break the record for how many layers of fabric can be worn without tripping up.

We crowd together and are crushed. There wasn't space for a single hair to pass between one abaya and the other. There was even less room in our lungs for breath.

The door parts and spills us out. We take no notice of anything.

You didn't know where your abaya ended and your friend's headscarf began. You were carried between the two doors: the academy and the bus. Whatever part of you popped out in the bus would be your claim to infamy in the line-up the next morning.

When we reach the bus, you need to be a gymnast and up at the front of the crowd, if you want to score a seat.

Breathing was forbidden. Speaking was forbidden. There was no laughing. Girls' Schools Transport. Most of us stood.

When you sat down, there was the chance that bodies would be pressed up in front of you where your feet should go. The chassis groaned and the bus was transformed into an utter blackness but for a single whiteness: the driver's robes.

And a redness: the chaperone's pen, writing down a list of any girl whose body parts were exposed or were made to be exposed.

I don't remember ever being exposed. In the morning line-up my name was only ever mentioned under the section: **"jostling"** and **"talking"**.

I have no idea how the chaperone was able to tell whether we'd sneaked a peek at the opposite sex or not. And apparently with no difficulty at all.

The free transportation wiped Mecca's streets, and the female students, clean.

Then when we reached the Lane of Many Heads the black mass dissipated.

You don't know what the neighborhood boys are like. They never got bored. Every afternoon they waited at the top of the lane for our bus to arrive.

Look: this scar on my nose is from a stone hurled indiscriminately at a group of us by a young boy.

He wasn't hoping to land himself a beautiful angel or anything, but perhaps only to touch one of those faces out of the mass of all those girls' faces. Even if only with a rock.

Aisha

P. S. Just imagine how far I've come: from four layers and a headscarf to a Bonn hospital gown.

P. P. S. Have you noted that I'm most like Ursula? Well in that case what the hell are Gudrun's socks doing on my legs?

Confidential Attachment: A photo of the black triangles, i.e. Imam Dawoud's daughters, crowding behind the door, trying to steal a glance at the television in the cafe.

Attachment 2: The song of a turtledove (singing alone because the other birds were suddenly alarmed by the sudden light).

The joy of that turtledove spread all the way through to my pillow and I cried.

After dawn prayers, I leave the birds to make supplications on my body.

It is the sound of healing and penetrates deeply into one's mind.

The idea of death as a rebirth, which came up in that section of *Women in Love*, caught Nasser's attention. Nasser was paying special attention to the death extracts that Aisha selected for her letters, and to the severed stumps that piled up in Yusuf's diary, wondering to himself just what kind of deviancy he was dealing with. Nasser thought back to a particular expression from Yusuf's diary entries that occurred over and over again like a cry for help:

December 12, 2005

I know women from books. And women know me in dreams. There they bring me to climaxes my waking body has never known. Because I'm a coward. And because I'm desperate to stay white, never to stray, never to mix with the darkness.

Every morning I wake up terrified by those female visions. I'm a deviant. I can't enjoy a woman unless I write her. I can't enjoy myself unless I write myself. Not even Mecca pleases me unless it comes in a window written for a newspaper that is destroyed day after day.

That day it felt to Nasser that Yusuf was using the darkness that ran through the heads of women like Azza and Aisha to get the better of him. The heads of these women, wrapped in abayas even darker, were primed, one way or another, for tragedy.

A Henna Half-Moon

I WOULD NEVER PRETEND—ME, THE LANE OF MANY HEADS, DESERT LEECH THAT I am—that I wasn't used to the 45-degree Celsius heat. The scorching middle-of-the-day heat is my favorite kind of high. Who would believe that my legendary senses have begun playing tricks on me lately? I lapped up the stink and the sweat and closed my eyes tightly to try to sleep, but the buzzing of Nasser's curiosity kept me awake. He was standing by the side of the road chatting, and Halima was looking down on all my hustle and bustle from the rooftop. She made me feel self-conscious. Through the doorway she handed him the Arabic coffeepot and a tulip-shaped demitasse, and pressed a handful of dates into his palm.

"Lord, I haven't tasted coffee like this since my aunt Etra left us . . ." Her smiling eyes brightened. All that precise measuring and tireless preparation was so she could hear a stranger sigh like that when they tasted her coffee. Halima's face stuck out from her headscarf, which was wrapped around her face, accentuating her smiling eyes, and leaving the part in her hair uncovered, the ends resting against her chest. Hers was a youthful face that had made peace with the world, and her preoccupying worry of late—that Sheikh Muzahim would turn up to evict her any day now—hadn't caused any wrinkles. The half-moon colored in henna on her palm appeared and disappeared with her every gesticulation as she spoke. Nasser began to suspect that she might have been meeting Yusuf secretly. Absorbed in the motherliness of her face, Nasser stood there by the side of the road listening to her and trying to follow any thread that would lead to Yusuf.

"My father came from Jawa in the Qasim Oases originally, but he became a city-dweller. He used to sit out in the alley, dressed in a striped sarong like the people of Jawa who come to live in Mecca. He even started to speak with a Meccan accent." She bit off half a date with her tiny teeth and squeezed the other half into her palm. The stone she threw at a crow perching on the lip of a water vat; it flew off and landed on the shoulder of the one of the stone soldiers, its eyes trained on her. She polished her samovar with clay dust, which made all my coverings shine as well. Stories trickled out from her giggles:

"This house used to belong to my father. He sold it to Muzahim when the drought wiped out our orchards in the Fatima Valley. He sold the soil for mere cents and used it to prop up the men who came to see him who'd been wiped out. He took in a Yemeni man who came on pilgrimage from Aden and gave him a job selling the dates he used to harvest from the orchards in Fatima Valley. He rewarded him by giving me to him as a wife just like Jacob did with Moses. My father wasn't impressed by his trustworthy character so much as the story he told: he claimed to be related to a Meccan family." She pointed toward the sky. "They kept the name a secret, though, until they could prove it."

From his eternal spot in his shop, Sheikh Muzahim listened in on their conversation. He would interject, but then pull back, not wanting to expose his opposition to the story. "He wasn't a Meccan, her husband," he cut in. "Not on your life, God help us. He was a descendant of King Solomon and the Queen of Sheba. He was raised in the happy land of Yemen by their genie servants. He was cursed because he dared to alight in Mecca and pretend he was related to its servants."

Halima didn't pay any attention to his sarcasm. She was in the thrall of her own tale:

"I fell madly in love with the handsome Yemeni. I didn't care who he was related to! Every time I looked at him it was electric, my heart trembled. But we weren't allowed to enjoy it. The old men in the Lane of Many Heads used to make fun of him for the claims he made. They said that throughout Mecca's history there were always Jews and Christians and infidels pretending to be Muslims so they could spy on the House of the Lord. But God cursed them and wiped them out for their insolence."

"Hmph," Sheikh Muzahim snorted. "How these birdbrained women dream!"

"My father, though, he adopted the Yemeni and took him to the venerable memorizers of Meccan lineages, al-Qurashi and one of the sons of Na'ib al-Haram. They saw that he carried the ancient blood and features, and they were ready to testify to his lineage, especially after they heard my husband talk about the moon-shaped birthmark on his mother's palm." She looked wistfully at the henna moon on her own palm, which defied all the neighborhood's customs and traditions. "He told me that this moon here used to remind him of the one on his mother's hand." She showed Nasser her palm, ignoring Sheikh Muzahim's snarling derision. "What I gathered was that my husband was descended from Mecca's devoted servants who'd gone to Yemen in search of the key."

"What key?"

"He showed me a drawing of the oldest key to God's house. They said that an Iranian pilgrim once had stolen the key and fled to Yemen with it. Mecca's most loyal servants, among them the Shayba clan, went looking for it, but the happy land of Yemen stole their hearts and they married Yemeni women, had children there, and never returned."

"But what was it about that key in particular?"

"I don't really know the true story, but they believed it was the greatest key. God knows best. The one that the books of the Shayba clan say unlocks all doors. Don't ask me how. Over the centuries, the doors of the Kaaba have been changed, but that key is blessed. It unlocks them all. The historians spotted that key in the drawing that my husband had inherited from his grandfather. It had been passed down from father to son for generations in the Shayba clan."

"But what exactly did your husband the Yemeni have to do with that key?"

"It was a message he'd inherited from the servants of Mecca. They raised their children to search for the missing key and bring it back to Mecca. My husband told me that his father was one of the servants and that he'd told him to return to Mecca so that he could prove his lineage and go searching for the key. They believed that the key had been taken to al-Andalus. An ancient Andalusian traveler had either taken it back there with him or made a forgery. The traveler had gone halfway across the world, from southern Spain to the village of Solomon in Yemen, where there'd been an earthquake that destroyed everything in the village. The only thing left was the doors, so he took them all back to al-Andalus. People say that by tracing the seals of Solomon that were etched into all the locks he was able to make a key that unlocked them all and that it was an exact copy of the greatest key."

Sheikh Muzahim cleared his throat. "The woman's head is stuffed full of her husband's delusions. Those Yemenis all bring Solomon's hour with them: at sundown they chew qat and start having hallucinations of the key that unlocks all doors, including the door between genies and humans."

I confess it does amuse me to hear them go around in the same circles like that, and their imagination always heats up the neglected corners of my mind.

"My husband didn't come to Mecca to plant roots and settle down. He came chasing the dream of the key. His father had driven it into him and he'd made sure that all his descendants would go looking for it after his time was up. My husband was killed, though, before he'd even appeared before the judge to verify his lineage. And on that same day, Yusuf kicked in my belly to announce his presence. I named him Yusuf after his father. I wanted to pull him back into life through his son."

"Who do you suspect of killing your husband? The Many Heads?"

"They claim to have seen his body being eaten by rabid dogs, but we could never prove that he'd actually died. He left us no body to mourn or bury." Sorrow spread through her voice.

"But you still believe he's alive?"

She hesitated for a moment, but then she came clean. "Somewhere in God's great land. I've never felt like he's dead. Men who are possessed don't die. The thing that possesses them swallows them up." The look of skepticism Nasser gave her forced her to elaborate. "On the night he disappeared we were sleeping in the same bed. I woke up in the darkest darkness. There had already been rumors of Portuguese pirate ships roaming the Red Sea and my husband had decided that that was a sign that he need to go searching for the key. He'd heard about the pirates abducting men and forcing them to work on their ship."

Sheikh Muzahim coughed, spraying them with a hail of cardamom and sour coffee. "Detective, you know Meccans," he said. "Their imaginations are as impenetrable as their mountains. They still weave horror stories out of the Portuguese fleet's invasion of Mecca and Jeddah in 1541! You know, the Portuguese came with eighty-five warships and landed at the port of Abu l-Dawa'ir near Jeddah. They were met by the Sharif Muhammad Abu Nama, the pride of the Barakat tribe, at the head of legions of Meccans and tribesmen from the surrounding area, and the fleet was repelled. Ever since then whenever a young man goes missing in Mecca, they say he was abducted by the Portuguese and taken back to Andalusia. They have a hard time believing that some of their own flesh and blood are little devils who would leave the proximity of the Holy Mosque."

A long suppressed ache in Halima's heart was awoken and the scene from twenty-eight years ago replayed itself:

A sudden movement in the darkness interrupted her sleep. She could feel the heat coming off her slumbering husband's body, which pressed against her own. She wanted to warn him but she was paralyzed by fear. She lay there for a while, looking into the darkness, watching the black figures fill the room. They approached the bed, and in a flash they pounced on her husband. Innumerable hands covered his mouth and stuffed him into a bag and then they simply carried him out. Halima fell deeper and deeper into her nightmare until dawn broke her screams open and the whole neighborhood came running. Innumerable hands reached out to soothe her, and hands held her back when she ran out into the street, trying to chase after the bag. In daylight, she was surrounded by pitying faces and the spiteful rumor started to spread that the angels had torn the Yemeni to shreds and fed him to the dogs because he'd had the temerity to ask for the key to the Kaaba. That night even the drawing of the key had disappeared, leaving no trace.

Halima had fallen silent and was watching the television in the cafe downstairs. A music video of song by Abd al-Majid Abd Allah was showing. For a second, her silence tempted me. I, the Lane of Many Heads, nearly started to tell the truth of what had happened that night, but I restrained myself. I wasn't going to make it any easier for Nasser to tie together all the loose ends in his case.

"What exactly was the lineage your husband was claiming anyway?" It was sarcasm more than curiosity that impelled Nasser's question.

"I'll be honest with you, I don't know what kind of fire my husband was playing with. I didn't want my son Yusuf to fall victim to the same curse so I let the lineage my husband claimed stay buried. I remember my father used to like to call my husband "al-Hujubi," in reference to his ancestors the custodians, so that's what I nicknamed Yusuf. But when he needed a pen name to sign his Windows in *Umm al-Qura*, he chose Yusuf ibn Anaq, as if he were descended from the historical giant Awaj ibn Anaq."

Women prattling always make me lose my mind. It feels like my heads are exploding into a million chaotic shards. Night fell on my desolate corners and to shut Halima up I covered the houses in the neighborhood in an even thicker gloom. Halima watched Nasser leave the depressive darkness after he'd gone for his customary walk around Mushabbab's orchard. She pulled herself away from her permanent overlook and got ready to go out for her Thursday evening bridal tea-pouring ceremony.

As usual, she hung her mirror on the back of the door, her face lit by the streetlamps, and began to make herself up. The eyelashes of her left eye fluttered as she ran the kohl over them and suddenly she felt something watching her in the darkness. She dared not turn around. For a second, she thought her time had come—that after the murdered woman her turn was next, that the hidden killer had come looking for her. The kohl hardened in the corners of her eyes. The death ritual replayed itself in her mind like a video: She'd washed that afternoon, and her hair, which she'd tied into a bun behind her head, still smelled of Abu Ajala soap. She'd performed her ritual ablutions before squeezing into the outfit the wedding planner had sent over. It covered her from tip to toe and had a white apron that tied at the waist and draped to her knees like folded wings; it matched what the rest of the servers would be wearing. She didn't have to worry about being unclean, she thought; she was as ready for death as you could be. If only this person who'd snuck up on her in the dark had given her the chance to pray the evening prayer: four obligatory sets of prostrations plus two extra for supererogatory blessings. If only he'd done it while she was prostrate in prayer. But it occurred to her that dying on her prayer rug on all fours, like an animal, would leave all her curves exposed to the eyes of the policemen who'd come to find her body. Even if dying in prayer was the quickest way to enter heaven. For the first time, she understood the wisdom of her grandmothers' prayers: "God grant us a good ending!" She thought she should repent, but in that gossamer limbo between life and death she couldn't think of anything she had to repent for. In her mind's eye, she could see the image of that specter, the visitor who used to appear at night in the Lane of Many Heads back before they'd found the body.

Halima drove that madness from her mind and focused on her tongue. The tongue is a secret portal that can open up under a Muslim's feet at any time, plunging them down into the lowest circles of hell. Her grandmother had driven that image into her memory. There was no way she could repent for every rude thing she'd ever said. Instead she thought back on that bag of high heels she'd come home with one night. They were given to her by a woman in a car that was worth as much as the whole Lane of Many Heads neighborhood itself.

"Pray for Khalid Bin Nura, Auntie dear," the woman had bent down and whispered to Halima, who was sitting on the floor in front of the Abu Dawoud Mall selling pots of waxing sugar. She motioned to her driver to give the bag to Halima.

Halima's tiny feet were swimming in those size thirty-nines but she didn't let that stop her. She stuffed each shoe with cotton so she could strut around like a peacock at weddings, and she generously let the neighborhood girls borrow them, too.

She had no idea who was weighing her soul down with all these heavy thoughts at precisely the moment when she needed to concentrate on one simple thing, one simple sentence. Out of the darkness emerged the figure of a man. "I testify that there is no god but God and that Muhammad is his prophet!" The profession of the faith had scarcely burst out of the lump in Halima's throat when she recognized Mu'az. "You scared me, God damn you!" She noticed how thick his eyelashes looked, and he cut her off:

"Yusuf is in a safe place, Auntie Halima. He asked me to check on you."

"Thank God, thank God a million times. Does he have enough to eat? Does he have enough to drink? Is he feeling well? Is that electric in his brain keeping him up at night? Is he sleeping?" The whole neighborhood was used to Halima worrying about her son's sleep and the electrical activity in his brain. "How about his metal knee? Is he keeping it warm? Take him some Zamzam water that prayers have been read over. And give him this." She reached three fingers into her cleavage to pull out some rolled-up banknotes and pressed them into Mu'az's palm.

He looked her up and down. "My, my Halima, bird wings and high heels?" he teased.

"If the job demands it."

"Give me one of your outfits. I can put a veil on and come help you."

"No boys allowed."

"I'll come as your little assistant boy and help carry your stuff. I can just peek through the door."

"You call the prayers and you've memorized three-quarters of the Quran and you're sharp enough to steal the kohl off an eyelid—and now you want to come peep at girls?"

"Just from the doorway. I want to see what an eight-star hotel looks like on the inside. I want to see what Mecca looks like from a skyscraper. I promise you I'll look down at my feet the whole time. I'll only look up to see the sky."

"Everything in the neighborhood's topsy-turvy now. I don't know what to think. Even you all, sons of the imam! You're not like you used to be."

His pure eyes stared straight into her own and pleaded. For a moment she looked to him like the very embodiment of tragedy. Her deep-set eyes were like graves for her husband and son, the whole neighborhood even. He could have lain down to die in one of her all-enveloping eyes. Tragedy stopped at her neckline, however. Maybe if he'd been able to picture one of those great big breasts, he'd have enjoyed a glimpse of paradise, the promised land of milk and honey.

She draped her veil over her face. She didn't permit him, nor did she forbid him, so he followed her in silence. They walked down the alley amidst barking dogs and jangling music videos.

It was night. He was all in black and she wore heels with flashy diamante buckles on the side. They got into Khalil's cab. The scent of olive-oil soap preceded her into the back seat. Khalil turned the car over robotically and set off into the Meccan night, smirking with menace, searching for what to say to annoy Mu'az.

"So," began Halima, "How do you like being married?" It was the question all of the Lane of Many Heads had been wanting to ask ever since they attended his wedding to Ramziya the sewage cleaner's daughter. The question came as a shock.

This woman was the definition of a trooper, he thought to himself. Nothing—not a body, not the disappearance of her son or beloved—nothing could put an end to the rituals of her life. Here she was, made up and tottering on high heels off to a wedding, and asking him about his bride.

"Well, to tell you the truth, Auntie—"

"Now don't you start complaining!" she warned him with her usual giggle.

He couldn't help but laugh.

"I haven't laid eyes on Ramziya since we got kicked out of the Arab League. I sent her back to her father's house and I started living in this cab." His voice conveyed a mixture of relief and sadness as they drove through the al-Zahir district.

"Khalil, don't just abandon her like a house that's been left to someone in a will. God will curse you for wronging her!"

"My body's been sucked into a void and my mind's in a different space altogether. Please, Auntie, stop giving us headaches with this curse business. I'm a man and I won't be beat. I defeated cancer. Doctors in the U.S. said I was a miracle case. It had spread through my stomach despite the intense chemotherapy, and they'd given up hope." Khalil looked at himself in the rearview mirror and ran his hand over his hair, which had grown back sparsely after his treatment. "I was determined to make the angel of death choke on my dust. I fought back with yogurt and garlic, clinging to life like a flea on the back of a bull. I drank buckets of that stuff. One morning I woke up and discovered the cancer vanished. It was a miracle. The will to live can make miracles out of Moses' staff, or yogurt, even. But it's not working at the moment, now that I've got Azza eating away at me. She keeps metastasizing. And Ramziya's like a bucket of garlic, burning up all my cells, benign and malignant together." Khalil's expression was all bitterness now. Everyone knew that the chemotherapy had left him infertile. The day he went to ask Yabis for Ramziya's hand he surprised everyone with an award-winning performance.

"It's your daughter's decision. If she wants to have children, then it would be unjust to tie her down to a man like me. The doctors robbed me of that option. They could've frozen some of my sperm before they put me through the chemotherapy, to give me the chance to have kids in the future, but they gave me the treatment without letting me know what the side effects were." The light shining through his thinning, almost glowing, hair gave him a boyish air, a vulnerability that played on the heartstrings. It was a miracle when his hair started to grow back after the chemotherapy and he started treating his hair as if it were a child. He would oil it and comb Minoxidil through it every night. He was as careful as he possibly could be and he never suffocated it under a headscarf. He spent more on that desiccated chaff than he did on his entire body—the body that had already betrayed him once and given life to that dinosaur, cancer. That day, standing in the alley in front of the sewage cleaner's house, he could be heard as he explained, in detail, how the doctors had failed to freeze a portion of his sperm. As he delivered his scientific exposition to Yabis, the look on the man's face reminded him of a cow drinking happily from a muddy puddle. His response was entirely unexpected:

"I know my daughter. Who are we to question God's wisdom? Who knows? Did you hear about the Indian lady who got pregnant in her seventies? When the Lord wills it, milk will pour from stone udders." Their blind faith was almost defiant and Khalil decided to punish them for it by going through with the marriage.

On their wedding night, that same inner demon goaded him. As she walked toward him resignedly, he stretched his arm out, blocking the doorway to of their bedroom. "You're going to walk out of here just like you walked in, childless, all the way to your grave. Nothing but burnt firewood. There's no point to anything you do in there. It's pointless. You're just a toy for me to play with." His idiotic talk pained even his own ears.

"Leave it to God," Ramziya had said, sighing, emitting a faint whiff of something rotten. She defied him by replaying the same pious tune her father had. "Don't reject God's blessings. When you get to the bottom, say, 'Praise be,' before you say, 'It's tar.'"

Halima's probing questions made him uncomfortable and in an effort to distract her he nodded toward the mass of white buildings that had come up on their right.

"Those are the Sayf buildings. There are forty-four of them in total. They're kitted out like spaceships and all lit up. They were built over where the mountain and citadel of the Dabba used to be."

"Yusuf's obsessed with that mountain," Mu'az chimed in. "Those are the rocks from which horses first emerged in the beginning of time and it's where the Dabba will appear at the end of time. It will wipe the earth out with its tail and then comes the resurrection. He still writes about how they destroyed the citadel, which was more than a century old, despite Turkey's objections and their pleas for UNESCO and the heritage protection bodies to get involved."

Khalil shot to life as if he'd been stung by a scorpion. "You still see Yusuf, you son of—an imam?"

Mu'az brushed off the insult. "Don't you follow his column in the paper? He said that they'd promised to rebuild it on a different mountain farther away, complete with all its original underground vaults and secret passages. Including the Ottoman chests that are still shut up with great big padlocks on chains and the old guns and cannons that are breeding-grounds for rats now and haven't been fired in more than three-quarters of a century."

Khalil stared at Mu'az for a long while, irritated by his idle chattering. He was looking for his point of attack and then he said, "Is Azza with him?"

The accusation riled Halima. "God protect us from your devilry, Khalil. Don't go making trouble. And keep us out of your twisted obsessions." Halima turned to look at Mu'az. She wanted to get into his head to know the truth. Why hadn't it occurred to her?

Mu'az broke through the apprehension that had settled over the three of them. "Apparently the princess is still lying there in a sandalwood coffin at the top of the citadel. People say she still winks and braids her hair with camphor and rose perfume."

"Camphor makes you infertile," Halima interjected.

"No, camphor comes from one of the springs in paradise. And the princess is still waiting for the Turkish pasha who locked her up in there until he could defeat her father the Sharif of Mecca."

"Mankind has had free will ever since it was a speck of cells on our ancestor Adam's back. You can go look for what you want in the citadels of the Turks, developers' high-rises, dovecotes, wherever," said Halima, making Khalil wonder whether she was hinting at what he'd gotten up to in the Turkish seamstress's basement. "But it's pointless vanity," she continued. "All Eve's daughters are the same in the end. Deep by night and sweet by day. As for the ones in coffins, God knows best."

Khalil looked back and shot Mu'az a disdainful look. "You still digging up graves? Huh? Has your camera flash got any bones to fess up to yet?" He was trying his hardest to irritate him.

Mu'az was defiant. "They told me that human waste has been piling up and that it attracts crows. They said we've become the biggest crow colony on earth."

Halima cut through the tension between the two men. "That detective's getting more and more suspicious. He's chasing down every single thing in the neighborhood, his own shadow even. You two know he's been asking about you both." As soon as she said that, she regretted it. She felt sorry for Khalil and she didn't want to give him something else to worry about. He was gloomy enough as it was! She couldn't imagine either one of them being involved with the body in any way. She was quick to add, as if to apologize, "Never mind the Seven Wonders of the World, these days there are two thousand and seven! There's a murder on every TV screen—and all for entertainment. Men stay up all night in cafes, smoking shisha, to watch that stuff."

The look of worry in Khalil's eyes only intensified. Everywhere he turned, the phrase "He's been asking about you both" followed. The cab was filled with a glum silence as they each followed the course of their own private apprehensions. The night outside the window was less heavy. Mu'az thought about the meanings pregnant with meanings that lay behind words. They felt like thick honey on his lips.

Khalil took them up Hafayir Hill in silence. He felt as empty on the inside as the top of Mount Omar to his right, which had been shorn of all its houses and leveled. Thoughts ate at his black insides, which were exposed to the elements. He saw the neon yellow bulldozers that were parked, waiting for morning, waiting for flying saucers to land atop the spacescrapers.

"God help me. Not a day passes without another mountain in Mecca disappearing. Where are the houses at the top of Mount Omar that we've always known?"

"Their misery was wiped out in the name of progress! The land they used to occupy is called Ground Billion now. They're planning to build the tallest buildings in the world on Mecca's mountaintops."

"Taller than the minarets of the Holy Mosque?"

Mu'az saw Mecca through Halima's eyes. "The development here is out of this world, Auntie. They're pouring billions into it every day. The massive corporations are like their own world order. They don't answer to the laws of any one country. The last deal they signed was with Elaf Holdings for three billion dollars to develop one mountain here and another one in a different area. Not even Manhattan's like this! The Valley of Abraham is lit up like a Christmas tree. I swear if the Many Heads went out for a stroll in Mecca, they'd think they'd been resurrected in New York City."

"God help us. Why are they trying to make the holiest city into George W. Bush Land? Turn here."

Khalil veered right toward al-Misfala and Abraham the Friend of God Avenue, in the direction of the royal palace. "That's globalization for you," he said sarcastically. "I've got a pilot's license from America, Auntie. But I married into a sewage cleaner's family, I'm tied down to a convent full of old women and I drive around all day in a taxi. My only hope is in the private airlines, Sama, Ama, and Nas. But they're not hiring. May God let us die believers!" Khalil sped up as he veered left toward the tunnel that led to Ajyad.

Mu'az thought that if he took a shot of Khalil the pilot's head it would come out all blown up. Khalil still felt he was too *big* for the neighborhood. He'd decided that the skill required to switch on a commercial airplane's computer system was greater than all the locals' brainpower put together. Khalil was weighed down by his frighteningly heavy technical know-how in a neighborhood of illiterates who had no interest in books and no idea about the power of neutrons and atoms. And they all called Khalil "The Cabbie." *You can pound the earth and pierce the sky, but you're still a cabbie.*

"So who's singing at the wedding tonight? Discovery? Or Qamari al-Hafayir?"

His question took Halima by surprise. He was trying to drive the phantoms from his mind.

"Tonight's the crème de la crème! It's at the Scepter Hotel, at the top of the towers. It's the wedding of Sheikh al-Sibaykhan's secretary."

"That Sheikh al-Sibaykhan is chairman of the board of Elaf Holdings, which owns three-quarters of Mecca. It has investments everywhere, like an octopus, and the right to requisition private property within belts one and two in the perimeter of the Holy Mosque in the name of development." When Mu'az heard the name Sheikh al-Sibaykhan, he knew his decision to come was the right one.

"They've brought the singer Ahlam and her band all the way from Bahrain for the occasion!"

"And why do you think they requested an old-fashioned tea-lady like you, Auntie?"

"Nothing looks prettier than when you mix the local and the exotic! Your Auntie Halima ties it all together, boys. Among all those chefs and waiters from the eight-star hotel, I'll be the local color."

Khalil pulled up in front of the entrance to the hotel at the Baraka Tower. Halima stepped out of the cab and walked toward the entrance, her abaya open over the peacock-like outfit they'd had made for her. Mu'az followed her. She breathed in before stepping into the elevator, to allow the attendant in his red and white uniform who pressed the button to share the confined space as they ascended. Mu'az noticed how little attention the attendant actually paid them. The golden walls inside the elevator stripped Khalil's bitterness off his face, and the golden glow of life returned to his dark cheeks. He was keenly aware that they were on their way to a place that people like him never got to see, not even in the afterlife. Suite after suite overlooking the masses praying in the courtyard of the Haram Mosque. The prices ranged from fifteen million to fifty to a hundred.

They reached the ballroom near the top of the building.

Halima crossed to the other side of the partition that separated the hall, shooting Mu'az a look that warned him not to follow. On the other side lay a forbidden world. It occurred to him that he could get his hands on one of his sister's abayas and cross over to the other side—like those gatecrashers who came to weddings firmly wrapped up in abayas and veils so no one could see who they were—if only he wasn't afraid of Halima's wrath. He stood there as if standing outside heaven's gates. Dancing and music and makeup and beauties.

His heart wouldn't obey his commands to leave. The female guests were walking through to the other side and Mu'az was dawdling by the entrance, ignoring the abaya-clad female bouncer standing nearby. He retreated slightly to a spot where he could still watch the women as they entered. You could see their hair was piled elegantly on the top of their heads underneath their headscarves, and they shone like crystal dolls.

He checked them all out. He wasn't looking for a face so much as he was looking for a body whose language he knew. The language that permits a man to read a woman's body beneath her abaya. He could've picked Sa'diya out of a crowd of a thousand abayas, and he knew Azza's fleeting black form, though he'd never told anyone about her little nighttime outings. He simply memorized how her pinky stuck out while she was drawing, guarding the surrounding area like a scorpion's tail. He often crossed her flitting nighttime path, and followed her form, which emerged more often than not out of his imagination rather than Sheikh Muzahim's house. Her disappearance would forever be a rupture in the ties that bound the neighborhood together. From within that rupture, he tried to guess where she might have gone. There were a billion stopping points between the morgue and the wide world. He thought back on the dawn the body was found. The black Cadillac that belonged to the social insurance employee. How much blackness on wheels had stopped at the entrance to the alley that day?

Mu'az was mesmerized by the drums and the colored glass and the jewels all around him. Where did luxury like this even come from? Even Mushabbab's orchard, the neighborhood's pride and joy, would feel embarrassed by these riches. Where did Mecca hide all these nude-clothed women? They were unreal. They were woven from cyber-fantasies and science fiction and grandmothers' fairytales: "Beauty sculpted by hand or by God Himself?" Even the old legends were dumbstruck by the beauty of these women.

Mu'az had no idea where this particular woman had appeared from. She came from behind the partition, rushing against the tide of the other women, lifting the hem of her headscarf to cover her mouth as she went. She turned around and in that sudden movement her hair came loose and cascaded over her cheek. She reminded him of a dove laying its neck against its mate's. The woman was gone again suddenly. She hid herself away in the image she kindled in his mind so she could disappear. Another bouncer, who was standing beside the elevator, nudged him, so he turned toward the elevator to make his escape—and that was when he spotted a slender foot disappearing behind a narrow door at the end of the hallway. He headed straight for the door without thinking. Every part of him was being pulled toward that crystal-studded shoe. When he opened the door, there was nothing to greet him but silence. He walked down the short corridor to another door, opened it, and walked through. This time he was met by the hush of an empty ballroom. He walked toward the faint light in the direction of the red-satin padded elevator; there was that alluring scent he couldn't name. When he stepped forward, his footsteps sunk into the shiny redness and it enveloped him entirely. When the elevator launched him upward, his breath caught in his throat. He could feel his heartbeat in his temples. His blood was rushing as if it were about to burst out. When the elevator doors opened, he was hit by the scent of an orchid in the center of the hall. An icy draft leeched the energy from his body and the sluggish pulse of everything around him made him feel as if he were walking not through a room, but through the inside of that woman, who'd lured him here into this suite. Pale and trembling, he proceeded down the corridor, which led to a floor-to-ceiling window overlooking the rows upon rows of worshippers making their rounds in the courtyard of the Haram. The door he'd thought was a side exit opened up onto a large study. He instantly zeroed in on the table where a silver amulet lay beside several ornate antique perfume bottles—as if it had been waiting for him all along. It was hollow, in the shape of a half-moon, engraved with tiny diamond shapes. He recognized that amulet instantly. Mushabbab had once asked him to store it in locker number twenty-seven in the cloakroom next to the Holy Mosque.

Mu'az was dumbfounded that the amulet had found its way to this tower; perhaps—as Mushabbab had suspected all along—the centerpiece of a great conspiracy. Perhaps it was just a copy of the original, and yet Mu'az was completely mesmerized by it just as he'd been the first time he saw it. It was a suicidal idea, but he grabbed the amulet and ran. He crashed through doors and hallways until he made it into the elevator and began slowly descending the many floors. When the doors opened, he walked out into the lobby, which was silent and frozen by the central air conditioning, squeezing the half-moon in his hand.

Loss of Sadness

THAT NIGHT—IN THE HUSHED AL-LABABIDI HOUSE—YUSUF STOOD FOR A LONG while in front of a picture of Bull Cave. He could see his life in that photo: the day he turned eighteen, the time he took a visit to that cave where the Prophet had hidden from the polytheists of Mecca on his escape to Medina. Yusuf went to Bull Cave to subject his lineage to the oldest test in Mecca: to go up to the cave and try to squeeze himself past its narrow opening, for if it was too narrow, you were a bastard, and if you made it through to the cave, your lineage was legitimate. It wasn't Khalil's repeated taunts and aspersions about his lineage that made him go; he was motivated by something inside himself—he needed Mecca to accept him. He needed to be able to present his true self to this city, as if he were presenting his credentials, to put himself on the table without any character witnesses, save the Eunuchs' Goat, who went with him everywhere, like his shadow.

The moon came out as they were climbing up Bull Mountain. When they got to Bull Cave, the Eunuchs' Goat held back and let Yusuf go ahead on his own to submit to the test. Yusuf felt like he was facing death head-on. The crevice looked too narrow for a human body to pass through. Yusuf held his breath; leading with his skull, he plunged himself into the heart of the mountain. His animality, his femininity emerged in the pains of that labor. The moon surrounded his body thickly, kneading it into the whorls of the crevice, and as he shut his eyes and mustered all his animal strength to push himself deeper, his body was sucked in, as if by a whirlpool that he was powerless to resist, and came out into that animal womb. When the Eunuchs' Goat came in through the cave's wide main entrance, he saw Yusuf naked before him, his clothes having been torn off in the ordeal. He looked like a leech born backward and returned to the womb. Yusuf had not only been proven to be his father's son but also son of this mountain, and this sanctuary, and the prophecy it had hosted, and of God, who was incarnate in the weakest of his creatures so there was no room left for weakness, aggression, or sadness. The Eunuchs' Goat turned around and walked out silently.

After a while, Yusuf began to sense the movement of the plants behind him. Sensing earthy fragrance, he got up to leave; he came to stand beside the Eunuchs' Goat, shoulder to shoulder with the mountain rock; its body was wet and dripped on them. A strange-tasting bliss settled heavily over Yusuf's limbs, a weighty feeling of belonging. He realized that proving his lineage meant he'd proved his responsibilities as well. Below them, Mecca spread out from the foot of their mountain, and in the center, a single ray comprising all human existence streamed up toward the heavens from the Kaaba.

As Yusuf retraced his steps back toward Mecca's giant glass monsters, he felt restless. He remembered when his mother had told him that anyone who entered Bull Cave would be relieved of all sadness forever. A tremor passed through the mountain's stones and the moon blinked coolly, revealing Mecca naked before Yusuf's eyes. She had discarded her eternal sadness, surrounded by grand mountains, preparing to cast off, without a shred of sadness, the old features that stood in the way of the new architects of her present.

Bodily Reality

From: Aisha
Subject: Message 26

With perfect fine finger-tips of reality she would touch the reality in him, the suave, pure, untranslatable reality of his loins of darkness. To touch, mindlessly in darkness to come in pure touching upon the living reality of him, his suave perfect loins and thighs of darkness, this was her sustaining anticipation.

And he too waited in the magical steadfastness of suspense, for her to take this knowledge of him as he had taken it of her. He knew her darkly, with the fullness of dark knowledge. Now she would know him, and he too would be liberated. He would be night-free, like an Egyptian, steadfast in perfectly suspended equilibrium, pure mystic nodality of physical being. They would give each other this star-equilibrium which alone is freedom.

. . .

He gathered her to him, and found her, found the pure lambent reality of her forever invisible flesh. Quenched, inhuman, his fingers upon her unrevealed nudity were the fingers of silence upon si-

lence, the body of mysterious night upon the body of mysterious night, the night masculine and feminine, never to be seen with the eye, or known with the mind, only known as a palpable revelation of living otherness.

(*Women in Love*)

Dear ^,

Would you translate this load for me?

This sinful rendezvous with physical ambiguity.

This unbearable morning knowledge.

I won't come back to re-read this passage unless, by some miracle, you and I should meet again.

Unless the unknown should answer my pleas and put you back in my path once more, for another moment, if only for . . .

Do you remember that night in Bonn? The night I left you and walked back on my own in the dark? I'll admit I was frightened for the first few paces. Do you know what it means for a woman like me to walk somewhere by herself for the first time, on an unfamiliar street—or on any street? With every step forward I was expecting to drop dead, or to be attacked and have my head split open and my brains spilled everywhere. The Lane of Many Heads was walking with me in my head, watching and ready to poke around in there and tell all the locals what it had found.

At one point, I was taken aback by the shadow limping beside me as I walked along the river. Then, instead of one shadow, there were five shadows pouring out of my body as I limped along. For a moment, I thought it was something inside of me coming out to attack me. To punish me for the strange scent that still clung to me, and for the desire that was renewed with every step I took away from you. But then suddenly, I could see those five shadows for what they actually were: happy ecstatics dancing around me. Those shadows knew something I could never even dream of knowing, sated to the point of yet more hunger. Some fear had snapped and released this multiple me. But still there's more to this me that hasn't been discovered yet. Every one of your looks releases another me that I had no idea about. I walked on—no, the five **I's** walked on, with a sinful delight, back to the hospital. Somehow, though, I—and my other I's too—hated you for leaving me to face this fear by myself, leaving me to bear this sin alone. Because sin's not in your make-up, whereas for me, every charge of pleasure I experience releases an equal charge of guilt. Guilt about what sometimes gives pleasure so intense I can't bear it. With every breath of love I took, I hated you, while you just kept asking me, "Are you okay? Is your conscience okay with this? Feeling any regrets?" And I just kept repeating, "I'm giving myself to this moment, no further. I'm floating along with the present, with life, with the deal we made."

I was too scared to say I was giving myself to God. I didn't dare utter God's name after what . . .

Do you think I'm cursed now? No, you don't think that. You believed what I said about giving myself up to life. But I was really just giving myself up to your taste. The taste that now poisons me even in my humblest prayers. I feel like I've lost something. Not my dedication, but rather the emptiness from life. Now, I've got indigestion from life. Indigestion from you. Can you call that a distraction?

I owe you. I owe you for the joyful lightheartedness you brought to our brief connection. How long did it last? Three, four months?

Every time my feelings ground me down, you made me fly. You massaged my sluggish conscience so that it could fly unencumbered.

Did you say that my demon is the story of the fall from grace? Why do you deny the fact that there was one thing that caused us to fall from grace? When the body discovered its taste, and its secrets, it became too **heavy** for the heavens to support and its plunge to earth was inevitable. So that we could spend our lives looking for the self-respect we lost back in paradise. Now, ^^^, you made me wonder: can life be boiled down to regret? Regret over what? The apple? The fall? The loss of face?

But you just laughed smugly and said, "Life's all about avoiding abstraction!" Do you think this life of mine is an abstraction?

Do you actually agree with me when I say that our fates are predetermined? We determined them. When God lifted us up in his palm like specks from Adam's back, he made an oath. That was the day each of us had our fate determined and it was granted that we could plunge forward into it to reach the truth. We're here on earth as an experiment to see if we can reach that truth.

God, what a weird writer of fate I must be for choosing this storyline as my experiment: Being torn between Mecca's Lane of Many Heads and Bonn, Germany.

I'm starting to think this plot's more than I can handle.

I spent the entire day today going about dumbfounded by the absurdity of our intercontinental relationship. The laughter and the bursts of affection. What is this cyber-relationship compared with real life on a city morning where you wake up to a woman of real flesh and blood? I am a woman made of thin air, amusing herself—unwisely—with a man made of solid stuff, surrounded by solid bodies and a concrete life. How long can ether and a solid hold together? Does eternity have a chance when it's only made of thin air?

Attachment: A photo of the cubbyhole with the bed in the middle. I put the **lavender** coverlet on the bed, spread it out and try to reincarnate the dolphin you encouraged me to visualize in my spine.

Nasser's body tensed with those "fingers of silence upon silence" upon it. He stopped reading abruptly and got up, and like a sleepwalker drove magnetically to the morgue at the Zahir Hospital, where he was met by a chill silence lying over the refrigerators in the purplish light. His vision was filled with that purple and his fingers trembled—not out of fear, no, but out of the longing as huge as the fog that had accompanied him along the roads and down the hospital corridors to this place, to this drawer that the morgue supervisor opened for him, to this silent, swaddled body. He didn't dare uncover her face but he was desperate to touch her fingertips, he was certain that those fingertips held a message for him. He sighed deep inside—*I'm exhausted*—he wanted her to reach into the depths of his exhaustion and erase it, to stamp her fingerprints onto his lips. As soon as he'd pulled the cover down off the shoulder an indescribable scent rose up. A torrent of sadness spread through the morgue, blinding him. A pearly cloud enveloped him and he could feel his hair crackling and turning gray. The cloud dissipated, slipping through the doors to the corridor outside the morgue, leaving Nasser empty, hollowed out. Finally, and with effort, Nasser was able to get a hold of himself, his eyes having gone as rigid as the sculpture laid out before him. He entered into the perfection of death: "Death is the body of a woman." He knew it for certain now. His clouded eyes floated over her chest, over the two dark peaks and back down to the triangle of darkness, and to . . . His eyes froze, his throat went dry, it felt like he was grinding glass between his teeth; he stood for a long while in that silence, searching for an equal silence inside himself (in all the silences that had swallowed his feelings, all the female bodies he'd silenced since his adolescence, wrapped in blackness of abayas), and for a moment he was one with her absolute silence, he penetrated as deep as the wound that killed her, to the floor of her abyss.

It wasn't he who moved to leave; his body simply slipped out the door in a frozen sadness born of silence.

He didn't know where he could go to escape this Meccan heat that swirled around him as if to melt her silence, which still enveloped him. The heat taunted him:

"You poor bastard. It's like you take pride in deceiving yourself. All you had to do was turn her over to look for scars from the surgery, or order an autopsy to find the metal in her pelvis. But no—it's just another example of what a coward you are."

He stopped in his tracks. Am I really a coward or just greedy? You want to dissolve the truth of her into every woman so that nothing can break the bond of love you've clung to for the past quarter century, during which you've played the part of a man in the void that surrounds you.

He returned to find the chill of death had beaten him back to his own bedroom. Was it death or some legendary sadness that was released when he uncovered that body? What was certain was that it had a woman's voice, which took form in the night to whisper into his ear:

Aisha

P.S. Are you serious when you say you want to love a woman like me?

Do you know how many men you've got to be? As many as the number of times a girl like me has fallen in love since puberty, as many as the number of teenagers who didn't chase after me, whose eyes didn't lust after me, as many as the number of men who weren't kept awake at night by the thought of me, those who weren't widowed by me or whom I didn't cause to take their own lives, as many as . . . Can you love like that? As many as the nights my heart spent in agony, desperate to know why, and the nights I was supposed to spend sleepless in love that I spent sleeping beside my brothers instead. As many as the heartbeats my heart was supposed to beat if only I'd met the someone who could make it. As many as all those love scenes in books and movies and songs that I knew with all my heart were about me. Do you know how to love me with that kind of love? A love like a book of coupons I'm spending all at once to make up for the love I missed out on in the years I spent trundling back and forth between school and this cubbyhole in that yellow box of a school bus, blindfolded like a falcon so it doesn't panic when it sees too much.

Maybe it would be easier for you to love a woman who'd already cashed in all her coupons one by one by the time you came along, so she didn't expect you to settle the debts of those who'd come before and those who hadn't . . .

Don't laugh at me. I know I'm **old-fashioned**. I missed out on the era when people used to kill themselves for love.

An era of hearts whence love would not sprout.

P.P.S. Jameela the Yemeni girl's mother left a gift for me. I found it on my bed: a set of lingerie woven out of fresh white jasmine flowers.

The people of Jazan weave their underwear out of jasmine . . .

I slipped out of all my clothes to try it on. I pranced around my room caressed by the jasmine petals as they were crushed against my petals. The perfume seeped down into my veins.

One day, I'm going to leave a pair of trousers made out of jasmine for you. Just so you can experience the pleasurable suffering of that sweet-smelling freshness for yourself. The dew of the deepest, gentlest touch. I imagined that I was clinging to your back, that the petals were smashed against your solid frame.

I spent the whole night tossing and turning. I couldn't sleep properly for the disintegrating jasmine and the perfume it released every time I rolled over.

In the morning when I put on my jeans, the jasmine was crushed even further. Imagine what it's like to face the world in a skin of jasmine.

Attachment: Photo of an **amulet** the shape of a half-moon, which Mu'az pilfered from somewhere, having taken a shine to the special trinket, and which then made its way into Mushabbab's possession. Look at the silver half-moon, one of those old hollow charms which Bedouin women stuff with handwritten scrolls, talismans that can attract, or repel, or make fertile.

For the first time ever, Nasser didn't shave. He didn't stare worriedly at the damp patch that was forming on the ceiling above the shower, and the dirty drips from the ceiling didn't break his train of thought. The gray-haired figure in the bathroom mirror surprised him. That unexpected whiteness was the only evidence of what he'd nearly done the day before: he'd wanted to have sex with a dead woman. Nasser stood there for a long time contemplating that face in the mirror, lost in the truth about himself that had been revealed the day before. Nasser felt a bleak whiteness plundering the Meccan air around him. Was this some disfigurement in the city or was it part of his own body?

Suddenly, out of nowhere, a face appeared in his memory. That old man Mu'az had pointed out, whom Nasser had then followed into Mushabbab's garden where the man was searching for a silver amulet!

Nasser wiped the steam off the mirror then quickly went over to his noticeboard. He found the name and phone number, but then another business card bearing the same name caught his eye. How could he not have noticed that they shared the same last name and phone number? Muflih al-Ghatafani and Son, Research and Investigation, Pilgrimage Research Center. He ran over to his phone to dial the number, not noticing how late it was. It rang and rang, and Nasser thought the number must be out of service, when suddenly a woman's voice, sluggish and drowsy, picked up: "He's not in."

Nothing could daunt the detective. "Where can I find him?" he asked.

He'd woken her up now. "Lying in the National Guard Hospital."

It was only after Nasser had got dressed and was about to leave the house that he noticed the time.

A Layer of Tar

"The nearest National Guard hospital is in Umm al-Salam, on the Jeddah road." This time he didn't wait for the elevator that was always dawdling somewhere between floors so that even the attendant could never locate it no matter how much he banged against the door on the ground floor. To Nasser it felt like everything around him was slipping on a thin layer of tar, skidding, still not keeping out a leak of damp. Without hesitating, he scurried down the dark staircase, which was covered in the yellow of the last sandstorm that had blown through Mecca a week before. Nasser headed for the Jeddah road, passing through the Barbie-like facade at the entrance to Mecca in the direction of al-Rusayfa and Road 60. He drove past the cafes and amusement parks and brightly-lit new fish restaurants, finally coming onto the bleak asceticism of the highway that wended between the sand dunes, getting narrower from time to time around volcanic mountains, the expanse only broken by billboards advertising the Sawa and Mobiley cellphone networks or tourism in Malaysia. Nasser felt like he was a long way away from the Lane of Many Heads now, but he wondered whether some stranger was leading him back to the lane and its secrets, which had come to matter more to him than finding out the identity of the murdered woman or her killer.

"Do you have a patient by the name of Muflih al-Ghatafani?" The receptionist's eyes flicked impassively between Nasser's face and his police ID a few times, and then consulted the computer:

"Urology ward, room 7." A moment later, he added, "His doctor signed his discharge papers today."

Nasser followed the signs until he reached the door of the crowded room with its seven beds. He sighed when he saw the man's frail body and aged, sunken face. "Mr. al-Ghatafani. We've met before. Do you remember me?" The whole row of patients turned to look at him except for the old man, whose eyes were as piercing as a hawk's.

"Are you from the police? I hope nothing's the matter," said a voice behind Nasser, taking him by surprise. He turned around, to discover it was the man's son.

"We're still investigating the murder that took place in the Lane of Many Heads, sir. I'll cut to the chase so I don't waste your time and mine." Everyone's ears perked up. "I know this isn't a good time, but I wanted to ask you about the silver talisman, uncle."

"Can't you see this isn't the right time for this sort of thing," the son chided.

"I'm very sorry, but your father's name has cropped up in Yusuf al-Hujubi's writings. He mentions that your father owns a lot of old maps and deeds. Can I see them?"

The father cleared his throat and finally spoke. "Really, please don't drag us into all this crime and terrorism stuff . . ." He was cut off by the nurse who came in with his discharge papers and a prescription. "Give this to the pharmacist before you leave," she said.

Nasser could see the man was slipping out of his grasp. The son frowned but said nothing as he helped his father into his wheelchair. He wanted to get away from the suspicious looks around them. He picked up their bag and set it in the old man's lap, as if claiming innocence of the aspersions cast, knowing well that that booby-trapped word, terrorism, could blow up in their faces.

"I'm begging you, sir. You're not well enough for me to have you come to the precinct for questioning or to give a statement." The only response he got was silence, so when they got out in the corridor, the detective caught up with them, unfolded a map showing a line graph and placed it over the bag on al-Ghatafani's lap. "Have you seen this before?" he asked. Muflih's wheelchair stopped suddenly and he answered.

"We gave it to Yusuf al-Hujubi. He was doing research on forts in the rural Hijaz at the end of the pre-Islamic period. We gave all our evidence to the son of the slaves, that one with the orchard. This is my cellphone number. You can call and make an appointment any time."

Nasser followed them down the hospital's long corridors, to the pharmacy and then out to the parking lot. He helped them into the car and before they shut the door, he leaned down next to Muflih al-Ghatafani and said, "Don't worry. I'm just trying to gather information. I'm not accusing anyone of anything."

Muflih al-Ghatafani looked back at him, looked through him, and asked a question that caught him off guard. "Are you working for the police or for Bin al-—" Nasser didn't catch the name; it had been drowned out by the noise of the engine that had been turned on at exactly the same time. The car moved away. Nasser stood stock still, desperately trying to work out what the sounds al-Ghatafani had uttered were: Bin al- . . .? The car was nearly out of sight by then. Nasser ran to his own car.

Nasser started the engine distractedly. He was passing the guards at the hospital gate when a police car overtook him, siren blaring into the silence. When he reached the highway overpass where one exit led to Mecca and the other to Jeddah, a whole cluster of police cars and their sirens brought him back to reality. From the overpass, he could see a traffic jam below, cars queueing up to rubberneck, as well as the huge truck and beneath it, flattened like a pancake, a blue car. His heart began to pound before his mind had time to process the information.

"Al-Ghatafani's car!" He drove back down the bridge, into the oncoming traffic, toward the Jeddah exit. He parked his car and got out, zigzagging through the lines of cars. There was no sign of life in the crushed blue metal; the bag of possessions and medicine lay at the man's feet. The truck driver wasn't injured but was sitting stunned at the edge of the highway.

Whiteness spread over Nasser's skull. This was the death or the gloom that had driven him out of the morgue the day before, piling up everywhere around this case, streaming out icily from Aisha's fingertips.

Roundabout

NASSER WAS LOOKING THROUGH YUSUF'S DIARY FOR ANYTHING LEADING BACK to Muflih al-Ghatafani when he came across overwrought, preposterous words:

June 5, 2006

I died today.

Without any warning, lighting flashed over the neighborhood and a sandstorm covered the sky when Sheikh Muzahim took Azza over to

Mushabbab's orchard. They married her to him then and there. The registrar and Sheikh Muzahim took their leave as the angels pelted us all with dust.

Damn this diary. Damn this place.

Yusuf

From: Aisha.
Subject: Urgent

O God, what's awaiting Azza in Mushabbab's beautiful garden? Her father handed her straight over to the son of the Sharifs' slaves when he saw the colossal amount of money he'd made in the stock market.

Azza followed Sheikh Muzahim without blinking. Or maybe her eyes just got wider. Remember that day you told me, "Don't pluck your eyebrows. It'll make your eyes bigger and then they'll swallow me."

Without any plucking, and despite the darkness of her eyebrows, Azza's eyes were wider than **all our eyes**.

Yusuf limps like a madman up and down the Lane of Many Heads.

Aisha

It was like a bomb had exploded inside Nasser's head. He couldn't believe it: Azza had been handed over to marry Mushabbab. Why hadn't anyone from the neighborhood told him? Something as big as this, why would the neighborhood try to cover it up? Halima, Muzahim, Mu'az, Khalil—none of them had spelled it out for him: Muzahim had agreed to marry Azza to the son of the slaves of the Sharifs. It was a secret. They'd hidden this major event from him, here in these papers, left him to crawl around looking for it all this time, and only told him when they felt like it?

Nasser was gripped by panic. Something had changed, there was no doubt about it. All he had to do was take another look at the case for all the masks to fall, right before his eyes. But right now they were clouded by a comfortable white noise; he wasn't prepared for this game of pulling off masks.

There was a bitter taste in the back of Nasser's throat. He took Azza's marriage as a personal betrayal. He rummaged through letters and diary entries to find out anything else he could about the story.

June 8, 2006

You say, "He covers me.
Not with words, but with my abaya."
I don't hear you.
Starting from the bottom of your feet,
the silk of your abaya flutters, brushes against your belly
shivers against the tips of your breasts, the gap between your lips,
finally the silk relaxes over the hair that's come loose
from your braids.

A naked demon, that's who Mushabbab is when he lays the silk of the abaya over your nakedness to cover you. The moment your face is covered up, every last drop of my strength and the voice that tortures me with that scene, both dry up.

You're cursed, Azza. I'm not writing you any more. Go die, and good riddance, from your face to your feet. God has no mercy for you.

Yusuf

Yusuf's words tumbled over one another in rage:

June 9, 2006

That trivial speck of nothingness of a woman lies and says things like this:

("At dawn, lying in his arms, I woke up suddenly, burning for you, Yusuf.

If, while sleepwalking, I'd rushed to the doorway of my bedroom, to our old radio, a note waiting for me would have woken me up.

In your old handwriting. But didn't you say, 'the handwriting of Zayd ibn Thabit?'

You'd be crazy to stop writing.

Yusuf, if you were to write to me about lying here with him,

'I read it and then re-read. To bring it to life . . .' That's from the lines you wrote, among whose capers I grew up; they lived for me more than I've lived myself.

Who was it who said, 'Nothing has any taste unless it's written with your saliva'? Can't you see my engine runs on your confused, impassioned words? My lips mutter with the pleasure of reading what you've written.

At dawn, in his arms, I saw that you, Yusuf, were writing me more than you were writing the world or yourself. I was the page on which you would scrawl out your being. Drafting and revising your attempts, failures, and retries.

I'm your ink, your scribblings.

No matter how hard I tried, Yusuf, Mushabbab wouldn't be written. This night is bigger than me. You'd have been better off writing it. If it had been you writing me, I'd at least feel pleasure.")

I've put the lies between parentheses.

Yusuf or Azza

Next were some huge scrawls that had been erased:

June 12, 2006

The fourth night.
Should I write her or not?
I can't decide.
I'll stop writing so she can die in her sleep.

Yusuf.

This outpouring of naive sentimentality annoyed Nasser. He wanted to know what crime had been cooked up in that disastrous marriage. Nasser could find no other option but to race breathlessly between Aisha and Yusuf, who'd both fallen into a funk. Nasser sensed that Azza's fall had happened at the same time as the loss of morale that came across in Aisha's letters; Azza had taken a leap toward Mushabbab while Aisha was planning a cold end.

The alliance between Azza and Mushabbab was the breaking point in this case and any detective worth their salt would have been skeptical about Nasser's capabilities after seeing how late in the game he'd discovered it. Nasser began to read the diary entries and the letter as one, unbroken text. He came across this page in the diary in a strange hand:

June 15, 2006

Like a falling stone,
It wasn't in her, but in the well
Lying between the three springs that feed it

And he drinks, not just like a dove a cat or a beast, but also like a plant. Like a stone, with all its pores, with its skin and its heart all at the same time.

It drinks saltiness and the taste of metal, from the ankles upward. Who's that who can't be in two places at once?

Crowned with saltiness all the way down to his ankles,

When he was inside her mud, all the jars in his bathroom fell, spilling their mud all over this cosmic flesh.

In this volcanic landscape.

The earth became salty, metallic, centered on his lap whenever he wanted to penetrate to her core.

His body could only respond by collapsing. O God, how they've colluded against him: desire and its collapses!

There was no one left in the Lane of Many Heads that didn't celebrate the news: the devil in the orchard was impotent!

I die and he's reborn in the same lap. Where whatever's watered dies.

The Lane of Many Heads had no entertainment so it amused itself with Sheikh Muzahim's beard, which was led to a Mercedes that took him out of the neighborhood on shady errands, dropping him at offices where men showed him statements from his bank accounts and those of his son-in-law, the descendant of the Sharifs' slaves, alluding to possible solutions and get-outs; but these meetings soon ended definitively with the nullification of the invalid, impotent contract he'd concluded in the shack in the orchard between his daughter and Mushabbab. They produced a notarized document for him laying it all out.

Even contracts can be nullified: marriage contracts, ownership contracts, sale contracts, rental contracts, The Unique Necklace (or Contract), your contract.

Yusuf.

From: Aisha
Subject: Message 27

It was very consoling to Birkin, to think this. If humanity ran into a cul de sac and expended itself, the timeless creative mystery would bring forth some other being, finer, more wonderful, some new, more lovely race, to carry on the embodiment of creation. The game was never up. The mystery of creation was fathomless, infallible, inexhaustible, forever. Races came and went, species passed away, but ever new species arose, more lovely, or equally lovely, always surpassing wonder. The fountain-head was incorruptible and unsearchable. It had no limits. It could bring forth miracles, create utter new races and new species, in its own hour, new forms of consciousness, new forms of body, new units of being. To be man was as nothing compared to the possibilities of the creative mystery. To have one's pulse beating direct from the mystery, this was perfection, unutterable satisfaction. Human or inhuman mattered nothing. The perfect pulse throbbed with indescribable being, miraculous unborn species.

(*Women in Love*)

Isn't it a strange thought that I could fail to develop and be replaced by my siblings!

The Chinese write the character for crisis by combining two characters: danger and opportunity. It's as if crisis equals danger with the possibility of resisting it, like a vaccine to induce the antibodies of change inside a body. This current is you.

^, I write to you with two words, with a hug that crushes my left rib as happened on that rainy day when my ribs were crushed by your embrace—you, the healer—and I don't show the slightest sign of pain.

An energy that prepares me for everything, anything, even death itself.

Now even my voice has changed because of the painkillers, my face is swollen, even the breaths I take don't taste like my breaths.

Aisha

P.S. Just now the loudspeakers of the mosque across the street announced the beginning of the **eclipse** prayer. They pray until the moon reappears. "It was He who created the heavens and the earth . . . so that He might determine who among you does most good," Imam Dawoud recited. They believe that our sins blacken the surface of the moon and that prayers for repentance clear it.

Which prayer can clear my face?

P.P.S. You've helped fix my computer more than once through remote desktop access. Yesterday you simply said: "Click OK to give me access to your files, your heart, your soul. Let me see who you are, where you've come from, your wallpaper, the people who make you who you are."

I was trembling. Clicking OK seemed like tearing the veil off the Lane of Many Heads . . .

Yusuf has lost his mind because of Azza, and attacked the people praying in the Lane of Many Heads Mosque. They beat him savagely and he was taken to Shihar hospital in Ta'if. For two weeks the Lane of Many Heads was as silent as a tomb, incredulous that they'd sent the only voice that wrote their dreams—Yusuf—to a psychiatric hospital.

In the end it was al-Ashi who took the initiative to go to Shihar to get him released. We rarely see Yusuf now, though. Can you hear him limping about on the roof?

He tore up all his papers; the alley outside my window is covered in his shredded words, his anger, his identity. Every dawn, the Lane of Many Heads awakes to find a new pile of his possessions on the ground: articles, diaries, personal pictures taken by Mu'az, his ID card, his emblazoned bachelor's degree from Umm al-Qura University.

Finally there was nothing left for him to tear up,

And then he came out into the Lane of Many Heads, and flitted about collecting blackened bread from houses, trash dumps, the heaps outside bakeries, and cooking yards, taking them back to the roof to build a horrifying sculpture that smelled like fire. Even the pigeons stayed away from it. The people in the alley joked: that's the Many Heads, being consumed in the fire of our sins, with the overflowing fountains of minds. And they named him "he who is not eaten, **nor burned**."

The name made me curious. I spied from the roof. Seeing it there in the sun gave me gooseflesh, like a glimpse at death leaking the yellow essence of a life that had once been.

Mu'az was convinced that this was actually the unholy devil himself and that Yusuf had erected him on the roof so he could watch everyone coming and going.

There was an emptiness inside Yusuf. I felt like it was himself he'd erected up there. He'd reassembled whichever pieces of his brain had survived the shock therapy they'd put him through, and then one day he'd ground them up like dust and left the result out for the hot sandstorm winds to blow in our faces.

What's he going to tear up next?

> He's tearing Azza to shreds, he's cut her off completely. He didn't write a single word to her even after she was returned, defeated, to Sheikh Muzahim's house. No one had any idea how they'd forced Mushabbab to divorce her. Yusuf kept to the Eunuchs' Goat's empty room above al-Ashi's kitchen; God only knows what he's doing in there. The Lane of Many Heads has gone topsy-turvy. Without Yusuf's words, Azza can't find her way.

The handwriting in Yusuf's journal began to alternate, and Nasser struggled to work out if someone else was planting entries in Yusuf's journal. There was something that had him worried: some of the pages were written in splendid *naskh* script, of the kind often used in old manuscripts, and decorated with gold pointing and marbling. For a moment, he thought it was excerpts from the Quran, written in Mu'az's handwriting, but Mu'az swore it wasn't him: "Yusuf plays the part of the storyteller. He adopts our personalities so as to expose us to ourselves."

Could Nasser believe, alternatively, that an alleyway like me could have its own handwriting? The thing is, although I took Yusuf's madness with good humor, it's not like he managed to pull the wool over my eyes. His madness hit me like a stroke, a gray patch that spread instantly over each of my different heads, and if it hadn't been for al-Ashi, savior of freaks, I'd have left him to rot in the loony bin at Shihar. That's why, ever since he got back, I've spent my time following his every move. Look at that deep trench between his eyebrows; he spoils my nonchalance and sense of humor. Maybe I'm slowly losing my lust for life, but my foolproof cunning still has the power to outwit. I'm not going to let him trick me.

The moonlight penetrated through the ripped-out window in the Eunuchs' Goat's bedroom, which overlooked the cooking yard. A patch of milky moonlight deepened even further the shadow over the faces of the heavenly maidens who gazed longingly at the dark body on the bed that occupied the narrow space along the wall behind the door. Yusuf hadn't slept a wink for several nights on end. Like a worshipper he strained his eyes to read something in their pensive looks. He was fasting, surviving only on water from Zamzam and five dates per day, which Mu'az got him by sneaking a little money out of the mosque's charity box. The whole time he spent lying there, Yusuf could feel Mu'az's idolizing gaze keeping vigil over him through the slightly-open door, though he was careful not to open the door and go in. They spent several nights sitting on the narrow doorstep, leaning on the door. They looked like a photo and its negative, a young man on the inside and his dark shadow on the outside, leaning against the same door, each feeling the heat of the other's body through the crumbling wood, one watching as the other performed a postmodern play for his audience of girls. Yusuf and Mu'az shared their hunger; they were both thin. They told themselves that the early believers had fought great battles and won, with only dates to keep them going.

Even Yusuf's heart quieted in the presence of those women. The light of the moon kindled the scent of the bed Yusuf was lying on—a mixture of blood and rancid cheap food. Yusuf had abandoned his books and begun working as an errand boy for the nearby kitchens, before submitting to depression, withdrawn and alone in that room. He himself smelled of food; he was too drowning in the intoxication of having discovered that world to bother feeling any guilt for having taken on the personality of his friend the Eunuchs' Goat and invaded his plastic and cork harem. He was switching roles in my web of despair. That Mu'az always turns the pupils of my eyes back at me, to make me look inside my many heads, exposing faults that I wouldn't allow one of my heads even a glimpse of. Mu'az was the first to notice that the Eunuchs' Goat had possessed Yusuf when he interrupted prayers in the mosque and Imam Dawoud confronted him with the Verse of the Throne, which drives away the devil. That dawn, the Imam ordered the devil that had taken over Yusuf's body to make himself known:

"Which devil are you? What is your name?"

A Satanic voice deep in Yusuf's chest replied, "I am Salih." The name literally meant "good."

"Salih son of whom?"

"Salih till the end . . ." The answer frustrated them; the imam and the other sheikhs didn't have a list of devils without expiration dates. Nor did they know what immortal devils like this one were capable of, nor how they could be resisted.

It was past midnight by the time Nasser gave up in despair at the Lane of Many Heads' red herrings, the diary's hallucinations, and Aisha's schizophrenic emails. Their predestined fates—no, the life decisions they'd made themselves—were an affront to a conservative man like him. He'd never even heard of this job of "DJ" that the boys of the Lane of Many Heads dreamed of becoming; when he Googled it he discovered it was a man who manipulated women's bodies through music. It was basically like being a pimp. Nasser sensed the mocking eye that had been toying with him and directing his movements since the very beginning of the case. He pushed Aisha's sleeve deeper underneath his pillow. His anger dissipated and he got up to look in his dresser, not for anything specific, but for any sign that he belonged. What did he know about this world around him? He went through all the trinkets he'd carried with him since he was a child, such as the bullet-adorned leather belt with a dagger sheath on one side. The leather smelled of his grandmother, the scent of banquets on nights gone by. When he looked through his dresser, there was no sign of Nasser, who like his father used to be smart enough to snatch kohl off an eyelid, but just a bunch of his uniforms: six, seven, eight, ten, forty uniforms, two for each year he'd served. He spread them out on the floor of his room. The uniforms started out as thin as the ghosts of a famine and got progressively wider. There was no mistaking the pot-belly that had filled out over the years. The jacket shoulders had begun to slacken around his shoulders like they belonged to someone else. He'd spent more on dry-cleaning these uniforms than he'd spent on his own body. These uniforms were lord of this room, and he was their servant. The bedroom floor looked like a graveyard of soldiers, for forty men in one.

That night the room looked bigger with its wide-open window which paid no attention to the graveyard inside, its corpses each paler than the next. Nasser slept soundly amidst the clamor of the traffic below. He had no idea how many nights he spent in that cemetery of his; he'd lost all sensation. He was conscious only of Aisha's eyelids stamping their silence over his entire body, and though time passed, he wasn't aware how many times the sun had risen or set.

He was rescued from between her eyelids by the smell of grilling meat from next door. He realized he was famished; he couldn't remember when he'd eaten his last meal.

"The wolves of this hunger are howling inside your mind, and it's making you delirious." He got up, dragging his feet over to the refrigerator and stood there, completely at a loss. Ever since he'd gone to the morgue, he'd been unable to stand the sight of the refrigerator or the thought of a morsel of food going down his throat. With a shudder, he reached for the tub of date biscuits beside the stove and started robotically stuffing them one after the other into his empty belly. The sugar rushed to his brain, waking him up. Through the haze over his eyes and the windows, he couldn't tell what time it was, whether night or gloomy dawn. He took out his five bottles of Dunhill cologne, the last five remaining of a dozen he'd bought heavily discounted a year ago from a friend of his who smuggled goods into the country in a suitcase. He poured them down the toilet and flushed, and left the door closed until the sweaty, rank-smelling cloud had faded away.

FROM: Aisha
Message not numbered

Don't search, ^, for message number 1; we mustn't write it yet. We'll leave it for when we've stopped speaking and fallen silent so that our words can go on imagining us and waiting for us, impatiently, at the edge of every sigh, so that they can say what we're not able to express in any language.

I also skipped all the tens when numbering my messages. We've left them for the unknown, because we won't consume everything—we'll leave something secret. The important thing in our correspondence isn't the search for freedom or love, but the **puzzle**. We lean toward it unaware, not translating, not even thinking. We don't allow our consciousness to break it open, so we can stay clinging to the rope of its amazement, which could be severed at any time by anything, which relinquishes the reins so we can enter. There I find the dream that keeps me awake with thoughts of you, that keeps your dream company, and shares with it this sadness charged by us.

The most beautiful sadness is this moon.

You're the most beautiful moon.

When the nurse was distracted, you seized the opportunity to whisper to me, "This is our secret . . ." Of course, you and I have to have a **secret**. Some kind of feverish sadness, so that we can cling to it.

"Do you give yourself to me in marriage?"

"I give myself to you in marriage."

I made sure my words could be heard by the two witnesses, who for their part broke out in grins, rather taken aback and desperate not to miss a detail, when I surprised them by adding, "On the condition that I have the right to initiate divorce proceedings." They applauded in delight, thinking themselves extras in a rehearsal for some comedy on that bright morning.

"Bear witness to this contract before God . . ." They shook our hands enthusiastically as the sunny garden paths fell silent, and signed our verbal marriage contract with an impromptu violin duet, making the morning seem even more gilded.

"This is my second wife. I'm still married to my other wife as well and she lives in the same city. I'm Harun al-Rashid, the

Caliph," you said, laughing, to shock them and make their performance even friskier.

All along, you were performing that ceremony as a joke. You never did believe me when I told you "all it takes to get married is an offer and an answer in front of two witnesses. A divorced woman like me doesn't even need a male guardian to be present."

"God, life is so wonderful **without papers**! May God strike me dead if I violate this ethereal contract."

All the people enjoying themselves in the park turned to look when you started shouting, and then you grabbed me and held me so tightly you might have broken a rib, or three, and they grinned encouragingly. I soared on those smiles; even though you didn't sense any change, I felt like a mountain of sin had been lifted off my neck.
Aisha

P. S. I was like a **stone** thrown through the air that day. I shook at the thought of that inevitable moment when it would crash to earth.

Yusuf had successfully managed to change Nasser's perception of Mecca. He'd begun to see the city as a woman. Nasser was robbed of the Mecca he'd known and had sacrificed his life protecting. He had fallen into a spider's web of contracts sealed and broken in the Lane of Many Heads. Yusuf's words were making him dizzy: "every time Mecca was on the brink of dying of thirst, a woman brought it something to drink: Hagar, Zubayda, Fatima." Aisha took the complete opposite position:

From: Aisha
Subject: Message zero

Can you hear?

I'm possessed by the doves' cooing.

I don't know why I'm haunted by the events of the day I came back from Germany.

It was during the last ten days of Ramadan, and the clock showed eleven at night when I came out of King Abd al-Aziz Airport in Jeddah with my small suitcase. On the highway, the driver missed the exit for the Mecca road, so we had to take the Medina road that runs through Jeddah, north–south, and found ourselves stuck in celebrating crowds and traffic: it was the 23rd of September, National Day. It took us five hours to get across the city—a journey that normally took a quarter of an hour. I was somewhere between ecstatic and fearful as our car was swallowed up by a sea of cars of all different types—you couldn't even imagine—fancy cars, beaters, wrecks, all draped with the green flag with its sword and the profession of faith—there is no god but God—faces painted green, green clothes of every kind, green scarves, green hats, fluttering from car windows and boys' and girls' bodies as they hung out of windows or popped up through sunroofs, dancing, exchanging victory cries, blocking all the city's main arteries, or congregating around the main roundabouts and monuments to join dance circles where crazy hip-hop mixed with dignified traditional Gulf dances.

In Mecca, we'd often heard the rumors about Jeddah's fanatic nationalism, but we never took it seriously. In a country leery of any kind of celebratory motorcades, this was the one day in the year when the streets were given over to public celebration. There was no official sanction, but laws were bent and young people took advantage of the blind eye that the religious police turned to that holiday in particular. Headscarves slipped off girls' heads and every street was a party.

I rolled down the car window with trepidation, a strange mixture of intimidation and utter abandon as the driver weaved in and out of traffic James Bond–style, taking every unannounced shortcut he could to rescue us from the storm we'd found ourselves in the middle of.

A strange dreamworld in which car radio speakers blasting Gulf dance music vied with mosque loudspeakers broadcasting verses from the Quran during vigil prayers in the Ramadan night.

You should've been here, ^^^, to taste the Saudi hodgepodge for yourself. Sow-Dee Champagne cocktail!

Aisha

P. S. We grew up hearing mother Halima's words: "All the demons are chained up in Ramadan, so any sin we commit during that month stems from our own impulses. It's ours and ours alone and we'll be held accountable for it. No help from the devil." Azza always laughed at that, muddying up the gravity of those words.

When I look through the emails I've sent you, I wonder: Do you think I'm making up for Satan's absence? Adding enough of his flavor? Or are they boring, the lines I write you?

It isn't Ramadan at the moment but my stomach's completely empty. Not a bite of food or a drop of water in twenty-four hours. I weigh almost nothing right now. It was so windy at sunset today, the air-conditioning unit almost flew out the window.

With people starving like we are now, it's no trouble at all for the wind to pick us up and blow us through the air like it does all those plastic bags.

P. P. S. What will it take to break the bond between us?

I tried to do it a few times, but I was too fragile to send us both on our way.

And yet the whole time it would've been so simple:

Just a **step** in the air.

P. P. P. S. There's something I haven't been able to bring myself to say to you. If **Azza** jumps, there won't be anything left for me to hold on to.

"Jumps?" Nasser leafed frantically through the emails, in hot pursuit.

Bad Is Good

You once enchanted me by saying "Love is sharing our normality . . . Taking pleasure in our normality, without magic or charms."

Why do I complain? Isn't that the essence of living?

To deepen the pain, I listen again to the tape you gave me of music by de Falla. I told you one day how I adored Don Quixote, so you got me this tape of his ballet about Don Quixote but told me that you liked the other piece, about the nighttime secrets of the gardens of Andalusia . . . You told me more about Don Quixote and explained that Sancho Panza had spent years creating **Don Quixote**, honing him with every forbidden dream he didn't dare to carry out himself, and every adventure he'd always wanted to embark on, till he finally got Don Quixote to bring them to life . . .

Azza and I wonder now: which one of us is Don Quixote and which Sancho Panza?

I have to be honest with you—I can't keep living in my computer screen like this . . .

Aisha

P.S. I was reading about Prize for Oddest Title of the Year at the Frankfurt Book Fair, and apparently the book that won this year was called *If You Want* ***Closure*** *in Your Relationship, Start with Your Legs.*

I think that I probably need to start by letting go of Azza . . .

And you, I know you're bringing me down from the sky bit by bit, and you feel guilty—don't . . .

After seeing your last photo, with veins bulging at your temples and fatigue dripping from your nose, which looks so long now, I felt like a creature of a totally different caliber, from a whole other world, maybe of light . . .

You, on the other hand, are a hole, whose emptiness no passion or pain can fill, and you'll carry on swallowing us all one after the other . . .

Just now, at this moment, I was appalled to realize that I don't love you any more. In fact, I never loved you! You were nothing but a placebo whose narcotic effect I willed my body to imagine . . . To end up, now, faced with your pitiable baldness and the way your hips start to hurt when you try to get into certain positions. The first time you pushed me onto a bed, you slumped heavily like a bear, your face distorted by panting, oblivious to my fear and my body, from which you proceeded to strip every illusion of passion. I put up with it just to get to the end of the tunnel, whenever and wherever it would come. I have this ability to close my eyes to things, even when my body's all eyes . . .

There's something dead about you, can't you smell the stench? There's something missing in the look of a man who has lost his virility. You confided in me once that your idol was Federico Fellini, because despite his own impotence, he attempted to feed off his friends' sexual glories and turn them into artistic masterpieces.

I understand, you can't believe this is happening to you; you go after every new face in the hope they can give you back that electric shock—don't you get it? Your wires have been cut.

That's it.

The current flowed again once with me, but it was just a fluke. It isn't going to happen every day. That day, you called me a "sex **bomb**"!

I wonder if it's you I'm talking to or Ahmad. Whichever one shook the kaleidoscope of my head, tangling my wires and electrodes so I can't tell who's who or what's what any more . . .

Now, how far can I limp without an idol to worship that'll distract my body from this pain?

I wonder: can an impotent man fall in love? Can his heart thrash with passion or skip a beat? What is love? Just a physical reaction? In that case, according to your theory of existence, you're finished!

Intelligent young men rush headlong, blinded by love, and then as they age, their virility betrays them and they take refuge in clinging to that slim alternative, the thing they call sensuality, going totally overboard in their obsession with the senses and their desperation to satisfy them. Who was it who said that?

June 30, 2006

Aisha, that thieving script-writer—why did I let her write the last act?

She called out to me. I was going past her house when I noticed her hand signaling to me from the doorway. My mouth went dry . . . But no, it's not true that her hand reminded me of Azza's.

Despite my resentment, I went closer, scarcely believing I'd find that it really was Aisha. She addressed me from behind the door in a whisper: "Come in, take them to . . . There are minds who could live off these books; maybe you're one of them." I could hardly make out where it was she wanted me to take them.

I confess I was shaken to hear her hoarse voice for the first time in my life. It was as if she were really saying "these books should be saved from the Lane of Many Heads." Rats are the first to leave a sinking ship, I felt like retorting nastily, but I didn't dare, and instead went into the dim hall to find a row of cardboard boxes, overflowing with books, waiting for me. The dizzying smell of damp paper and ancient minds poured out of the boxes . . . I wanted to lie down and inhale to death.

When I looked up to catch a glimpse of Aisha, she'd already gone, leaving a patch of darkness on the wall of the stairs after disappearing upward.

She didn't wait to see if I'd carry out her instructions—she knew my weakness. A faceless woman; I'll never know what she looks like.

I ran outside and stopped the first Mitsubishi pick-up, then went back in to get the boxes. I wasn't sure about giving them to the library at Umm al-Qura; I knew they'd set up a whole load of committees to examine the books before accepting them, and then end up destroying most of them, so I took the liberty of taking most of them to the library of the Literature Club.

One last confession: right in the fast lane, in the middle of all the cars, I made the Mitsubishi stop, and started going through the boxes like a crazy person. I checked them page by page, title by title, but I couldn't find a trace of Marcel Proust's In Search of Lost Time. I slumped against the books in dismay as the truck drove on. She's mocking me, mocking all of us, by keeping that Time locked up in her room . . .

Yusuf

Closure

"I COULD CLOSE THIS CASE WITH THE SNAP OF A FINGER."

Nasser was stunned to find that the Lane of Many Heads case had been taken out of his hands and transferred, without any notice whatsoever, to the counter-terrorism unit, and that he'd been summoned to explain himself. Facing that staring eye, Nasser felt unreal.

"The Lane of Many Heads is leagues ahead of you," the cold, sardonic voice lashed at him.

"I arrested Khalil, but he was released . . . Some force behind the scenes is working against me. But you have the means to correct that, sir. Believe me, we're letting a real criminal loose in Mecca with that Khal—"

"Khalil is pathetic, that dinosaur of his makes him an easy target . . . Concentrate on the armies of vermin who make up the very soil in the Lane of Many Heads . . . You can't expect to succeed in a plague-ridden environment like that unless you examine it microscopically."

The air in the luxurious office chilled tangibly.

"I picked you specially for this case based on your life choices. For a quarter century you've had the option of living or being promoted, and you've always chosen to leave life behind, without hesitation or regret. That's why I gave you free rein in this case, but you've disappointed me. Your twenty-five-year career looks like a joke. You're broken, letting yourself be taken in by words. I carefully chose you, to polish and powder like a fine billiard cue, but you've turned out to be just another ball rolling around on the table with the others. And you're taking the case like it's like a personal tragedy—look at your hair, it's gone white in less than a week!!

"Give me another chance . . . Please . . . Just one last chance!" beseeched Nasser, dying to be that favorite billiard cue again.

"History moves like a wave, all ebbs and flows, and you can never ride the same wave twice." Both men listened appreciatively to the hollow echo of those words. "That said, I'll be even more generous than I usually am and give you a head start in the second round with the Lane of Many Heads. So you can be in control of the game, I'll let you see from above what happened before the corpse was discovered, and show you the four moves that you missed when you were drawing that circle of suspicion.

"Come here, take a look . . . Focus on those four steps in the air . . ."

First Move: Cadillac

AROUND SUNSET, THE PURRING BLACK CADILLAC PARKED AT THE MOUTH OF THE Lane of Many Heads, blocking the alley. It was carrying a female social worker, come to conduct a study of the socioeconomic conditions of the neighborhood, whose rickety old houses heaved and jostled, flaunting their poverty to catch her attention. The driver stepped out followed by a woman fully armored in black from her head to her socks and her elbow-length black gloves, and the pair walked the length of the alley, followed by eyes peering surreptitiously out of windows, until they reached Sheikh Muzahim's place.

"Good evening, sir. This lady's come to visit you from Social Security. She'd like to have a chat with your family and find out how things are for you."

The Sheikh's face lit up and he gestured toward the door in welcome. "God bless her," he murmured.

The woman knocked lightly at the door. No sooner had Azza opened than the abaya pushed her back into her room and clamped a hand firmly over her mouth, the veil slipping away to reveal the face of a man. Azza recognized him; he'd gotten in her way several times before, but she froze in shock and he yanked her toward him easily. She scattered like a broken string of prayer beads; she was deep in his abaya, which reeked of agarwood oil; she couldn't hear or see, wasn't conscious of how she tore him away or how he left.

She leaned against the wall, her stunned eyes fixed on her father Muzahim.

She wasn't sure at what point she stuffed the envelope full of money into his hands and rushed to her bathroom. As she stood under the shower, the man's smell surged back with the warm water, along with the words he'd bored into her head.

"K.S. is security itself. His miracles make the miracles of Moses and Joseph in the court of the Pharaohs look pitiful. You don't need to read about him, just look at what he has planned and his dazzling smile . . . Soon he'll write a book: *K.S.: Making Billions* . . . He's got his eye on a satellite network. His commercials and his conquests will be everywhere—East and West, from the North Pole to the South in bold face—taking the financial supplements by storm, disproving every theory, engineering new global relationships. K.S. is an economic empire, above states and political borders, above passports, above obstacles, above fingerprinting and retina scans. Just watch him. He can tear down mountains and rebuild them. We're immortal, we run the universe with our satellites, we're a race above humans, prepared to mate with demons if that's what it takes to inherit the earth and everything on it."

Outside, an earthquake had struck the neighborhood, and the Lane of Many Heads was a commotion of competing voices. Someone could be heard yelling: "The Lane of Many Heads is on Al Jazeera!"

"Halima, Matuqa, Aisha and Jameela, Mushabbab and Dawoud, Yabis the sewage cleaner, and the Yemeni and Ahmad, and Amina and Bakhta and Noon. . . All of us, we're all on there!"

"The Lane of Many Heads and all its dirty laundry is on screen! We're all on TV!"

"The Lane of Many Heads is on the news! We'll be making money soon!"

A viral video that was posted to YouTube has caused controversy recently. The video, which is less than ten minutes long, shows photos of one of Mecca's poorest neighborhoods, the Lane of Many Heads, against a cartoon backdrop. Presenting a satirical portrayal of the life of women in that neighborhood, the short film attempts to show some comic aspects of poverty as well as shed light on the criminal networks that operate in the neighborhood. The video has provoked a huge range of responses and the number of comments on one site had already reached an estimated 60 million. The video has prompted renewed debate on the ethical implications of the totally free exchange of information as well as the negative impact on the individuals who appear in the video who were photographed without their consent . . .

"They've disgraced us!"

"Who was it?"

"Has to be someone from here, one of us."

"Who?"

"That spiderweb Internet, God curse it," marveled Halima with a wry smile. "We've all become international celebrities now!" The way she pronounced it, the word *international* sounded less harsh.

In the Lane of Many Heads, feelings toward the scandal were mixed.

Second Move: Desperation

AN HOUR BEFORE THE DAWN OF THE BODY:

He turned the key in the lock. The door slid aside like a curtain to ease him into the silence inside. His suitcase sloughed away from him in the hallway. He took a single step and was paralyzed by a clear peal of laughter, deep and satisfied like velvet. A shiver attacked him at the joy in that laugh, the abandon, the vigor, the recklessness—he didn't recognize them, though it was definitely her voice. That joy, so full of life and death. Who was making her laugh like that?

Blending into the dim light, he held his breath at the half-open door to the room where he and Aisha had slept. His bones were groaning from the six-hour flight. The air was trapped in his chest at the sight of the cubbyhole, which was getting smaller as time went by. Like in a Pharaonic temple where farmers engraved their annals and their gods, he'd succeeded in engraving his history onto the oily paint of the walls, though it didn't give him any sense of pride. He'd left scars on the room's memory. The deepest of his engravings had been the word *divorce*, which, in his carelessness, had formed a layer of armor over her body, giving her voice that poisonous tone when they spoke on the phone.

He watched Aisha lying peacefully by herself, illuminated by the light of her computer screen, stretched out across her entire bed, nude but for her red knee socks that drew his eyes toward her dark triangle like a flame. With him she'd never been definable or had any substance; she had no surface and no relief; she always reduced herself to an ink spot washed a thousand times; she contracted and withdrew in his hands and let him drill into her so he could create his own fantasies. Now, her neck was arched on the pillow for a kiss or a droplet of saliva, that neck which had never arched for him to kiss. He didn't even know what it tasted or smelled like. He always identified women with their smells; for him a smell could embody a woman. One onion was enough to reincarnate the aunt who'd brought him up, while the smell of bleach and Dettol always brought back his mother. At the beginning of his marriage, whenever he beat Aisha, he'd soak her in Dettol out of regret and say, "Lie and rest on my mother's chest, and lie me down too!" He'd ladle it out and feel safe. Even the women who consoled him in Casablanca strutted about with bodies made of rotten smells—sweat, or a garlic mixed with perfume. The garlic bodies were huge, inducing tyranny and control, inducing murder; when a garlic breast descended upon him, he'd be convinced that he'd come out ripped limb from limb and carted off as booty. Those bodies shrieked and scandalized with every touch. Aisha was the only bodiless woman; he'd still never manage to grasp her scent.

"Maybe now, stretching on the silky bedclothes and the fluff of her dreams, she'll give off an animal smell or the warmth of new satin." That lavender-colored satin coverlet—whenever he was there she'd be careful to fold it and keep it out of his reach in her closet, and in the two years since their marriage and divorce he'd never touched it, as if his touch on its uncovered body would leave a stain or a burn! This lavender coverlet, which she'd taken out in his absence, was the one thing Aisha brought to the marriage from her teenage closet of dreams, and was probably also the only piece he'd let her add to the furnishings he'd chosen, and then only grudgingly. He felt drawn to it, wanted to touch the forbidden item and leave his mark on it, if only for the last time.

"Aisha gets out her hidden scents and lies in them, dreaming and flirting with her dreams . . ."

He was struck by a sigh at that reserve of passion that he'd never experienced, and swift as a reptile he was on that altar-bed; he didn't know how his body managed to execute that entry: it was as if a second flowed like a drop of water and let him flow into her, he spread the length of Aisha's body, violating that satin, and suddenly his body was satin and Aisha's fluff. The moan that heaved through her body came up through his lips. The moment kneaded the room into a single dough: somewhere in a dream, he grasped it or it grasped him. Suddenly his body was being crushed, returning to what it was, the sob that came out tore through the dough, and Aisha was torn too, in a flash she awoke, saw who he was, and he was outside her. This woman's eyes were popping in wrath and a coldness harder than death; he the ever-absent repudiated usurper had returned, and he was unbearable. A monstrous anger and need to possess erupted out of his chest and he reached for her, to destroy that coldness and those red socks, and again she was in his hands, under him. He didn't know when her hand began hitting, not wanting to know him let alone love him, he was a rejected nobody on that blank sheet of a non-body, he was despicable, he was outside of everything, alone.

Suddenly the house felt empty, apart from the text-filled computer screen and the book, which had tumbled to the floor, open and face down, beneath his feet. On the front cover was a woman, and on the back a man. The woman, standing there with her red kerchief and bold red knee-length socks, and the blackness of her woolly hat, and a sketchbook under her arm, didn't pay any attention to him. The man facing her, to her left, had sleek hair parted over his forehead like a curtain and sleepy, half-open turquoise eyes. He felt them closing on him. He felt menaced by the man's beard; it reminded him of the sheikhs from the Haram Mosque, though this beard was nothing like theirs.

In a final, resigned gesture he picked up the book, and on the open page read the lines highlighted red:

> *Birkin watched the cold, mute, material face. It had a bluish cast. It sent a shaft like ice through the heart of the living man . . . Birkin remembered how once Gerald had clutched his hand, with a warm, momentaneous grip of final love. For one second—then let go again, let go for ever. If he had kept true to that clasp, death would not have mattered. Those who die, and dying still can love, still believe, do not die. They live still in the beloved*
>
> (*Women in Love*)

When Ahmad left the cubbyhole and the house and her deadly silence, the Lane of Many Heads didn't know where to hide him with his suitcase. Her features floated at his heel on every wall and bend in the alley, she was screaming at him to notice the red sock crumpled in a ball and hung on the cafe's satellite dish. How come it was there, watching him? He avoided his father the sewage cleaner's house and the cafe, where the doors were still shut and the workers still asleep in the shacks round the back. He ended up, dragging his suitcase behind him, at the old-style Mahawi Cafe at the entrance to the city, which was open 24/7 to receive the eternal flow of pilgrims. He stared blankly at the Pakistani waiter for an age, he didn't know how long, and then suddenly realized he was supposed to order a drink—to add taste and smell to her silence . . .

"Apple shisha . . . No, wait—just plain Persian tobacco." The waiter smiled, understanding his need for the strong tobacco. "Some bread? Stewed beans? Masoub? Tea? Liver and kidney? Dough balls with honey or cheese?"

"No." A single breath expressed the void in his wide, staring eyes. An hour went by while he watched the glowing embers turn gray in the bowl of the shisha pipe, which he hadn't even taken one puff of. The forgotten mouthpiece sat like a corpse in his hand, like his own body, which groaned as if it had been crushed under the wheels of a car.

"That cursed woman is my scourge. She's like a cat—she has seven souls . . ."

Third Move: Jaws

DAYS AFTER THE BODY APPEARED AND AZZA DISAPPEARED, THE CLOUDS OF senility settled over Sheikh Muzahim's shop. He'd woken up in the middle of the night to the sound of gnawing canines. He listened intently, unable to believe what he was hearing. He followed the sound to the room at the very back of the storage space and opened the door. The sight of Jameela, lying there gnawing a corn cob between her hands, hit him like a ton of bricks. She simply stared back at him, and for a moment he didn't recognize her. Who stuck her in here, he wondered. Then he suddenly remembered how they'd married her to him that very night.

"Did you really marry Jameela, you gray-beard?" he asked himself.

He recalled how it had all taken place mere hours before the body was found nearby. Her father, Hasan the Yemeni, had brought a registrar from the Hafayir neighborhood.

"Don't worry about it, Sheikh, it's all in accordance with the customs of God and His prophet. People told me about this guy. He may work outside the law, but it's to serve people who live outside the law, illegals."

When the father returned, Jameela was trailing behind him dutifully, dressed in a faded abaya. He pushed her forward at the entrance to Sheikh Muzahim's shop, her back to the street, and stuffed the five thousand, a whole stack of bills, into his pocket. He disappeared without a word. Sheikh Muzahim didn't even look at him, he was so entranced by Jameela. The words stuck in his throat, gagging his lust. He was so enamored, he couldn't bring himself to utter even a breath. He had no idea how much time passed as he just sat there staring at her. He heard the door at the back of the shop swing open and he saw a look of terror on Jameela's face as she stared at the doorway. He was too scared to stand up lest his passion flood the room. He wanted to gather up everything he had for her, to enjoy her pumpkin plumpness, to store her up and consume her in small portions or maybe squander her entirely in one go. He didn't know what greed it would take to possess her. He got up, limping, and she followed him, submitting to a flick of his wrist. They walked through the door at the back of the shop into the storeroom.

He laid his desire out, crushed like a scorpion beneath a stone, and covered it with the dome of Jameela's body. It wasn't enough. He was in a frenzy. He wanted to spend eternity watching her from below and he would have if it hadn't been for the commotion outside in the lane. He left her there and went to see what this storm was that was brewing in the neighborhood. On her wedding day, he shut her up in a storeroom.

In the days that followed, she broke through doors into the depths of his storeroom. She lived off her fear, her loneliness. She made her way to the sacks of dates, starting with the ones nearest to her, leaving gouges wherever her fingers had dug.

Sheikh Muzahim was terrified that his lust had betrayed him with Jameela, and then he woke up and found her gnawing. In the doorway of the storeroom, he watched her; saw what days of neglect had done to her. She'd fattened up, and left a sticky trail on the floor, which led him to her. Just below her chin, her neck had grown fatter, like a cushion for her little head. Her waist had filled out, and fat bulged from her chest and hips, weighing down her short frame. His eyes, which had been wild and hungry for her, were suddenly repulsed. His eyes cut her down to the bone, laying bare the hungry child standing before him. Where had this monster come from?

Suddenly he recognized the black and white, most of which had been erased: those were Azza's charcoal drawings, which a terrified Jameela had destroyed. The edges, which had been spared erasure, were enough to remind him of the body. He stood by the door, paralyzed. The need to live slapped him across the face. To strip off his clothes and walk out into the middle of the Lane of Many Heads, raving about a sin that no outburst of repentance could wipe out.

Sheikh Muzahim slammed the door on that threatening creature, gnawing, monstrously fat, scratching about in Azza's charcoal, and lay down in his shop, despairing and alone. Tears began to stream down his face, grooving his puffy cheeks. He hadn't cried since he was a child in diapers, but he'd stopped caring now. He began searching for Azza under every single sack in his shop. They ended up piled outside in the street, most of them bearing long-past expiration dates, and he slumped disheveled between them, his head uncovered and his beard long undyed.

As night fell over the Lane of Many Heads, Sheikh Muzahim was left on his own. Insomnia ate away at his eyelids and he couldn't sleep. "Did she spot Jameela in the shop when we were signing the marriage contract? God, please tell me Azza didn't run away because she saw her." The thought of Jameela, that rat, skittering around in Azza's place burned him up inside. "Who can bear this pain, Lord?"

In deepest night, he sharpened his senses, waiting for Azza's footsteps, but all his finely tuned senses could hear was Jameela's gnawing, which was constant, night and day. She paced and munched and grew. Her canines had started on his bedding and his dreams of drought. He didn't dare stir from his bed in case he should startle her, worried that she'd tear open his belly and consume him alive. All that time he spent listening, he never once heard her go into the bathroom to expel what she'd devoured. It all just rotted inside her, surfacing as pallor on her skin.

"Did Azza see her? Did this rat make you run away, Azza? My darling. She chased you away so she could have this old man, your father, all to herself!"

Pepsi Can

Sheikh Muzahim woke up that morning at dawn with the realization that he'd had enough. He got out of bed, and for the first time in ages he wasn't limping. He was determined to put an end to his agony. He performed his ritual ablutions quickly and announced the dawn prayer from the mosque, as Imam Dawoud had overslept.

"Every stone that's ever heard me call for prayer will testify on my behalf on judgment day," he thought to himself. He was hoping that the stones and the soil itself would help him with the day's mission. They watched him march toward his house, his beard faded, and with huge effort unlock the storeroom, and venture toward the ratty animal within. When she saw him, her jaw dropped, spraying chewed-up wheat, and she went goggle-eyed. He led her into the shop and emptied the whole shelf of sweets into a burlap sack for her. He handed her the bag and said, "Okay, you get going now. Back to your parents."

She fumbled with the buttons of her abaya, one flying here, the other there, stubbornly determined to cover herself up modestly; she was a married woman now and her husband was the biggest merchant in the Lane of Many Heads! But he stuffed a coffin-like stack of five hundred riyal notes into her cleavage and pushed her into the street. With one eye on her buttons and another on the fading henna dye in his beard, she grabbed her bag and walked out. It was her job to soak some Aden henna and re-dye his beard for him, she thought. She'd steal some of that henna from her mother's bag—after all it was her own grandmother who went up into the mountains above Sanaa and picked the leaves, drying them and sending her family bags of the stuff.

He watched her roll away from him, her abaya jutting out over her ballooned-up belly and breasts. He had no idea when he'd chase her down with the word *divorce*. He should've wrapped the word *divorce* up in that bag for her so she could chow down on it greedily along with the candy.

For a second, he thought about throwing the word at her from behind, but he hesitated, worried that she'd trip on her own weight, that she'd explode in the street, her fat spraying everywhere like Azza's blood, sullying the road in front of his home for the rest of his life.

He watched her until she disappeared, and then, as silent as before, he leaned on his cane and walked to the entrance of the Lane of Many Heads. There he got into the municipality sewage tanker that was waiting for him.

"Are you sure about this, Sheikh Muzahim?" Yabis asked him.

"May God help us, and may He forgive me."

Neither of them spoke of what lay before them as the truck got moving, leaving the Lane of Many Heads behind. A pack of children caught his eye; they were running after a bright yellow bulldozer that was carving its way from the top of the Lane of Many Heads, wiping out the empty sheds and shacks in its way as it rolled along, plowing into Sheikh Muzahim's chest, which was hollowed out like a grave. The tanker slowed for the two men to watch the bulldozers in the rearview mirror. They sank their teeth into Mushabbab's orchard and bit hard, tearing up the vaults concealed beneath. With a single stroke, clouds of dust and smoke and leaves and old stones flew out in every direction, causing sparks where they landed on the Lane of Many Heads. Sheikh Muzahim didn't turn to look when the bulldozers smashed old mosaics and crushed antique books beneath them, ink mixing with dirt. The neighborhood kids skipped about, grabbing any chunks of engraved wood, old artefacts, and musical instruments they could get their hands on. The vaults beneath the orchard, which were filled to the brim with treasures, caved in. Furniture, jewelry, house signs, salvaged pieces of inlaid wood, everything Mushabbab had spent a lifetime collecting, heard a single crash and was churned up in the dirt. The jewel of the Lane of Many Heads was torn to pieces and left strewn over the crumbled ground.

When Sheikh Muzahim arrived at the police station, a bunch of officers and sergeants were sitting in a semi-circle watching a single computer screen, which was showing stock market trades. The police officer sitting closest was selling stocks one minute and buying others the next. He seemed to be an expert in timing his deals; with every successful tap of the keyboard, he sighed a sigh of relief.

"Pardon me. The profits are nothing major, I know, but I'm going carefully. Little by little here and there to rescue what I can."

An officer patted him gratefully on the shoulder. "We'd be in serious trouble without your help."

"These small stocks are like stocks in magical companies. A total blessing. If it weren't for these, we'd all be bankrupt. The big corporations are in free-fall. The market is swinging like mad and we're liable to fall off into hell. What's up with you, Qahtani? Have you stopped breathing?"

"I got offered half a million for my she-camel, but I didn't want to sell. Then I watched her die because of that rotten feed from the south."

"Only a deranged person would invest in stocks or camels, I'm telling you."

Sheikh Muzahim was leaning against the door frame, propped on his cane, adrift in a sea of hesitation and shame. He tapped his cane against the ground.

"Are you alright?" asked one of the officers, his words tinged with impatience. Cigarette smoke hung in the air over the trades being executed. Their lips were faintly stained around the edges; Sheikh Muzahim felt like they'd all been dipped in some kind of ink. Their smiles were strained and the smell of tea coming off their crimson-tinged lips soured to the air. The moment Sheikh Muzahim opened his mouth to speak again, he had a coughing fit.

"The girl in the morgue is my daughter," he hissed, his eyes watering.

He'd armored his heart and his head with that fear, without which he'd never have allowed an unidentified corpse in a morgue to drag him out of his comfort and respectability. The terror of that single phrase had shocked the Lane of Many Heads and turned all its heads gray. He didn't know who it was who by chance had thrust that terror into his heart: "They send all the unidentified bodies to the medical school. The students lean on their breasts and drink Pepsi."

Fourth Move: Direction of the Qibla

THE DARKNESS MELTED AWAY AT MIDNIGHT. SHE MOVED AMONG BEINGS OF both sexes, and words and actions and reactions dissolved.

This young girl was flying for the first time, and she could define the course of her journey in colors:

Red: the inside of the black car that picked her up, starting from an unopened point in time, which she left behind like a sealed tin can tucked on a shelf.

Veined marble: the transitory tower overlooking the courtyard of the Sanctuary, a last glimpse as she was leaving Mecca.

Gold: everything in the villa where she stayed temporarily in Jeddah: a transition point.

Silver: the color of adrenaline, pumping in huge doses, blinding her along with the water pressure of the jacuzzi on her body—no matter how vigorously she was scrubbed and churned, that skin didn't dissolve or peel off.

Three points of black: the eyes of the Filipina servant who took her ripped black abaya from the bathroom floor and pushed it into the trash can, and then immediately removed the bag so as not to dirty even the gold rim of the trash can.

Mustard: the seats of the private airplane, which smelled of new leather and were whisking her through the air right now.

Navy: the silhouette of the VIP air hostess to whom she'd been entrusted, who fastened her seatbelt, checked the pillow behind her neck, poking at her new identity and picking curiously over the tidied-away clutter of yesterday—of the time before the adjustment.

"Welcome on board today's direct flight to Marbella. We will be flying above giant cities, maxi-cities, super-cities, hyper-cities, at a cruising altitude of 1,000,000 feet. In the seat pocket in front of you, you will find a list of the in-flight entertainment available today and a menu of our snacks and hot meals. You will also find paper bags should you feel unwell during any periods of turbulence. The journey might take a long time . . . But it often flies by. . . No need to fasten your seatbelts!"

Large chignon: the hair she'd embarked with now cascaded down her back and all over the seat, as thick as a horse's tail.

Translucent white: the outline of her arms hugging her chest tightly in that silky white shirt. She didn't look up in response to the inquisitive glances around her, or even raise her eyes once: an entity practicing total self-erasure, total absentia.

Cold mercury: the mirror in the villa on the Red Sea that played games with the face she knew. Slippery metal whose eye she evaded, though she knew it, knew its secrets.

Brown: the wide, frightened eye that took her by surprise through the crack in the storeroom door that dawn. A look of fear that stripped her body of its previous obedience and launched her away with an illiteracy beyond illiteracy: no suitcase, no name, not even an outline of what might be ahead.

Red: the knee-length socks that her memory had managed to save and were floating in a ball over her complimentary plate of fruit.

Transparent: Zamzam and all those ills of hers for which it had been prescribed: bitterness, sickness, hair between the eyebrows . . . Her right eye was the prey and the left was the hunter, wall-eyed; everything they looked at dissolved.

Her scent no longer had any hope of drawing her back to what she was before that dawn.

Envious eyes: somewhere in her memory.

Hot flashes: for the heart she left behind under a stone in the alley, a heart crushed beneath a stone, erasing a criminal record in that smashed-up face. She locked it up and left, capable of—anything? Everything.

The pans of a weighing scales: a woman's eye on one side and another woman's eye on the other. Which one fell and which one gave up?

The musk of conclusion: darkness, with which she wiped her forehead, erasing her dumb, uncovered face—which didn't know and didn't want to know—entirely. She wiped behind her ears, she didn't want to hear the clink of metal inside herself, she wiped under her chin with the palm of her hand like she was following the water of her prayer ablutions; she bent her head forward and placed her index finger on her lips and silently, silenced, realized what was happening, became aware of the separation in the kernel within the lips closed tight on a secret. Her finger slid upward and touched the point between her nostrils. She threw her head backward and sighed: "Everything becomes flexible when we leave territorial airspace . . ."

In her head the clock was still showing twelve, the time of takeoff. She felt like the airplane was propelling time before it, pushing that first split second of twelve o'clock forward, leaving open-ended time behind it. On the screen in front of her a diagram showed the direction of the qibla: a miniature airplane linked by a black thread to a miniature black cube representing the Kaaba. She watched the airplane in front of her plow westward, pulling the thread to the black cube tighter and tighter. The airplane tugged and the cube tugged back, until she felt the thread snap and the cube tumbled backward into the void while the airplane shot forward toward its destination.

Vibration

He opened his eyes. It was morning. Someone had painted the autumn morning bright yellow, and the hot sandstorm wind was blowing, howling across Mecca's mountains and its high-rise buildings, the migrant laborers' bitterness seeping out of the fissures in those haphazard, cheaply finished tower blocks.

Nasser knew it was the season of palm tree pollination, and the sandy wind made him wonder: are there any palm trees left in Mecca to be pollinated? This was the land that Abraham had made sacred, forbidding that any trees be cut down here or any animals be hunted. All these transformations that were taking place now, did they not deserve God's curses, and those of the angels and mankind, too?

He started his car and headed over to Mu'az's studio. He didn't bother to look to his right or his left. He'd stopped double-guessing and double-checking all the details now.

"Do you have a photo of Azza?" he asked without any preliminaries. It surprised them both.

"Of course not!"

Nasser drove to the Lane of Many Heads for a final visit. When he got there, he hardly recognized the place. Nearly everyone had left and the cafe was the only building still standing. The Sudanese cashier explained to him what had happened:

"The neighborhood didn't fall silent all at once. The houses were knocked down gradually, one at a time, like teeth falling out. Last week, the last of the residents received notices that they had to move out within a month."

"What about you?" Nasser fought to keep his guilty feelings at bay. Had that fatal melancholy he'd let out of the morgue begun to slowly spread through Mecca?

"So long as the cafe's still standing, I'll be here. It might take a while. The whole neighborhood got rich overnight. They took their compensation money and got out of Mecca."

"Even Imam Dawoud?"

"He's lodging with the Imam of al-Malah mosque until they find him another mosque to serve." Nasser felt like someone had pulled the entire scene out from under his feet, leaving him suspended in a void. The neighborhood had emptied out right under his nose. Maybe the next time he came looking for it, he'd find a big hole instead.

"What about Yusuf's mother? Where did she go?"

"She came by and told me she was going to stay with Haniya, right after Sheikh Muzahim went to live with his relatives in Ta'if. She left a note for Yusuf in case he came looking for her."

"Did Yusuf come by to get it? Can I see it?"

No, I can't give it to you, but she did leave another copy. She said she tied it to her window on the roof."

Nasser ran over to Sheikh Muzahim's abandoned house and up the crumbling stairs to where Halima had her room on the rooftop. It was the first time he'd seen the place devoid of Halima's sunny presence. The window of her bedroom, which looked out over the roof, was directly in front of him. Her prayer shawl was tied to the bars of the window and at one end of it there was a knot in which she'd tucked her note. He undid it and began to read:

> *Yusuf, I didn't go to the home. You were right. May God give me the blessing of faith as death draws near, and surround me with people. Tala helped me write this note for you. God bless her. She gave me her time even though she's really got to study hard to get good grades so she can get a scholarship to study abroad. Life here isn't the same as in the Lane of Many Heads. Tala writes stories like you. She's only seventeen and I tell her to dream. I tell her that every girl should write her dreams. Otherwise they'll just pass her by, or get ground into the dust and chaff . . .*
>
> *Tala was the one who suggested I could come live here with her grandmother Haniya. Haniya's a joy to be around. She loves life and she can get drunk on a single grape. She welcomed me with open arms. When I lived with them, it was the first time I'd ever seen a house without a man, except for their Indonesian driver. She has two unmarried daughters who have no children. They have jobs like you: all papers and trips abroad. I thought that maybe if you traveled, you'd find the world you were looking for. And don't worry about me, Yusuf. I've been to Jeddah and seen the world! Haniya takes me to the seaside every Friday. We eat chili chickpeas and ice cream from snack vans. People put up windbreakers and spend their whole vacations by the sea. They fly plastic kites and pay a little money for pony rides. They swim until sunset and then they pray right on the salty sand. We go to the Pyramid department store, too. The whole world's there buying their clothes, and everything's five riyals. No one goes without. Life here is easy. We only knew it was pilgrimage season because she took me for meningitis and flu jabs yesterday. So, your mother is doing just fine. When you settle down, give your address to the Sudanese cashier. Haniya's going to send her driver once a month to check. You can call me on 0559722147.*
>
> *I leave you in God's hands for He never neglects His charges. Please, don't undo the small knot at the end of the prayer shawl. I made a vow that if you made it back safe, I'd give away coffee and almond sweets.*

Nasser could feel time catching up with him. He'd lost the nickname Siren Man since he'd stopped coming to the neighborhood in his official Land Rover and now came in plainclothes in his own Infiniti instead. As he walked back through the neighborhood that night, examining the crumbling houses, searching for what had passed him by in that plotline he'd now exited, a dog came running up to him. It was a Saluki, but bred in some poor neighborhood so it had lost its distinguishing features. It still looked beautiful to Nasser, though, with its long neck and cropped tail. When it got close to Nasser, it halted and began to sniff the air. He'd never usually stop to pet a stray, but this dog charmed him somehow, so he followed after it as the dog led him past various abandoned houses in the Lane of Many Heads. He saw houses that had fallen off the human map. They'd been abandoned by their owners and then squatted in by undocumented workers, who hid out there until they were to be torn down.

It may have been a coincidence, but the dog led him over to the building known as the Arab League, which the court had awarded to al-Labban's four sons, ordering the eviction of seven families, including their sister, Umm al-Sa'd, and her husband, al-Ashi. The sons had bribed judges and psychiatrists to get their late father ruled as not having been of sound mind when he'd drawn up the deeds, thereby invalidating them. As for the basement, they'd pretended not to notice that the Turkish seamstress was still there. He could see the broken collection box still hanging on one collapsed door. Nasser stopped to watch if anything was going on. Although there was hardly any movement around the basement at all, one or two women did go in then came out again after about an hour. Nasser was waiting for a sign.

It was probably around ten at night when Nasser saw the begloved eunuch making a quick exit from the lobby on his way out of the neighborhood. He was carrying a black leather briefcase, which looked like something a lawyer would carry. The dog followed him, but Nasser just let him be. He summoned up his courage and went into the lobby himself. He didn't hesitate to make for the door that led to the studio; it was ajar. He knocked and waited. He knocked again, more loudly this time. He entered, fearlessly, and hadn't taken two steps forward before he was greeted by that hoarse laugh. He didn't even have to guess who it was who'd just peeked her head out from behind the curtain that surrounded the gallery, which looked like a floating room up near the ceiling; she didn't come down to greet him, or beckon to him to come toward her, but nevertheless he did. She was looking at him with an amused smile, trying to guess how far he'd go. And Nasser had nothing to lose. He felt like a dog lured by a bone. Her smile widened as he climbed the stairs to the balcony. She looked more like a lioness, now, than a wild bitch, waiting for a signal from him to pounce. Like an expert, she turned around, letting her curvy ass invite him further. By the time he got up to the balcony, she was leaning vulgarly on the bed, and Nasser's cheeks flushed. All that time he'd spent pacing the alley, he'd never noticed this invitation, open to any and all passersby. He ignored the call to dissipation. His voice broke through the cloud of her heavy breathing like a plank of wood.

"I want you to answer one question."

She raised her heavily penciled right eyebrow quizzically. "Is this an official inquiry?" she asked.

"Do you know where Aisha is?"

Her laughter shook him.

"You'll really give me the honor of letting me be your informant?" she whispered. "You want me to be the one to tell you?" He looked stupefied. When he said nothing, she added, with feigned sympathy: "Are you afraid of love?"

"Can you answer my question?"

"I've got an answer for anyone who asks, anyone in charge, anyone in need."

He was lost. The hound inside of him responded to this animalistic woman. He just had to close his eyes for events to call each other forth and for him to be transported somewhere else. Somewhere off this path he'd followed his entire life. He knew that if he shut his eyes, he'd cross light-years, toward places he'd never dreamed of before. But not before he had an answer to the question that had brought him here.

"Answer me."

"I'll say it again: you know the answer." Despair tore through his insides when he heard that.

"Azza's dead," he sighed. "Her father buried her yesterday."

"Tell me something I don't know," she mocked.

"Give me an address where I can find Aisha," Nasser insisted.

"Only hyenas dig up graves, but . . . If that's what you want, we can dig it up for you. You're the king and I'm your humble servant."

NASSER WAS WALKING BACK THROUGH THE LANE OF MANY HEADS, BUT HE DIDN'T feel like he'd left the vaulted studio. It was beside him, inside him, as he walked along. He could smell it in his sweat. The end of his conversation with the Turkish woman was ringing in his head:

"The Turkish seamstress has no limits. Let her indulge you, and you'll relax and feel rested. If you please her, you'll be pleased."

"I won't rest until I find Aisha."

"I've got prettier ones, younger ones, freer and more fun . . ." She drew out her words, watching to see how he reacted. "My book of tricks has everything. Audio and visual. Fixed and moving. Live and pre-recorded. Automatic and manual. Home-grown and imported. Innocent and experienced. Soft and coarse. Silent and vibrating. Front and back . . . Oh, you poor thing. You're no angel. You're just flesh and blood, aren't you?"

From the gallery room where they were, he didn't notice the sun come up.

When he came to, the vaulted basement was full of people—and cameras. He tried to look away from the rows of women learning how to use the five sewing machines in front of the frosted window that was open out onto the street. In his confusion, he stumbled over the partition where finished orders on hangers were waiting to be picked up. Behind the partition he saw the basement's true dimensions. Three hundred square meters soaked in blasting music, eastern and western, full of women, their faces covered with men's headdresses, dancing wildly for the cameras in each of the room's four corners.

"Look, my girl used her tiny limp to invent a new style of hip-hop dancing. The fans went crazy, we got thousands of messages from fans aged eight to whatever God wills!"

When he went back out into the neighborhood, Nasser filled his lungs with the dry air. The blur of glaucoma pooled in his corneas. When he got back to his apartment that afternoon, he sensed that its tempo had changed. He was desperate for the dose of security he got from the emails and the diary entries, but when he looked under his bed, he found nothing, not even a scrap. When he ran over to his wardrobe, there was no sign of Aisha's sleeve, which he'd hidden there. The inside of the wardrobe hadn't been tampered with but a void was spreading. The ground was receding beneath his feet. Someone was erasing his memory, leaving only white noise . . .

Case Closed.
The End.

PART TWO

Madrid 2007

"NORA!" A TREMOR RAN THROUGH HER WHENEVER SOMEONE CALLED HER BY name. Her split-second hesitation made him doubt it was her real name. The potential of a concealed identity lent her an aura reminiscent of Andalusian women cloaked in mystery and passion. Whenever he finished his shift guarding her, something of her face would stay with him—that haughty look, the sense you had that her face was turned inward, like she was looking inward from a balcony folded around herself. She was totally unlike anyone else he'd ever had to guard: people who went about under pseudonyms or hid the skeletons of past professions or crimes. At the company he worked for, fellow bodyguards would come back with unbelievable stories—about complete nobodies who feigned importance by hiring bodyguards, or people who were never more than a hair's breadth from death on account of their long involvement in resistance movements or the criminal underworld. The recruitment agency that hired him took immense care in choosing among applicants: they only ever hired men with enormous physiques like his, they conducted thorough background checks—looking extra carefully for involvement in war crimes (hard to detect)—and on top of that they required a clean criminal record, proof of proficiency in martial arts and weapon handling, convoy and motorcade experience, and so on. He was an Arab migrant with a Master's in philosophy that hadn't helped him put food on the table in Beirut and wasn't any good here either—his name was Rafi, but he went by "Rafa" here—just one of millions of Arabs who had to shed skin, blood, and name to meet the needs of the other.

Around him, morning overflowed with warm sunshine and faces gathered in the garden and on the terrace of the Ritz Hotel. The white cane furniture in the garden made the sunshine brighter and the atmosphere more cheerful. Rafa sat at the table closest to the twin curved staircases which led up to the hotel lobby. From there he could see the whole area around his client, Nora, who was sitting opposite her female assistant, tasting the breakfast tapas, sipping a morning coffee and quietly watching the laughing customers mingle with the lush greenery. He examined her like he examined his own face in the mirror every morning: it too was masked, by a U.S. Marines–style crew cut and a gleam that hid the truth of forty years of life and disappointment. The name Nora was more than a veil, though: it almost gave away a past that hovered like a shadow at her temple and neck and covered her entire chest. Rafa felt like he was watching two people, one trying to peel the skin off the other. Nora's perfection lay in her unawareness of that duality, the unconscious rebellion beneath an acquiescent surface. Nora, he felt, was outside of time, sitting there anachronistically in Madrid's grandest hotel as if waiting for a sign that would allow her to slip back into the past.

Rafa observed with wry amusement the interest that Nora aroused among the hotel guests. The beauty of Arab women is legendary, he thought to himself. The myth has crystalized over thousands of years of civilization, and yet still they seem exotic and ancient to most men. Out of reach. The kings and princes they deserve now only exist in fairy tales. There are no men like that for them today. And so they're a doomed race. Most Arabs around the world have lost the special halo that once surrounded them; they're like any other race now, ordinary or worse.

Rafa looked away, attempting to resist the control she exerted over the whole scene. Sometimes for a brief moment, he'd stop being her bodyguard and she the object of threat. She'd become—in her absolute frailty—the threat itself. Like that morning two days before when she couldn't wake up. She'd slipped straight from sleep into a coma and had to be rushed to the hospital where she lay unconscious for a whole twenty-four hours before waking up, as if nothing at all had happened, showing no signs of functional impairment or any other damage. She came back from the dead, the doctors said matter-of-factly. And now here she was sitting indomitably before his eyes, fresh out of the whirlpool bath, bearing no resemblance to the apparition he'd escorted to the hospital two days before.

Without any warning, Nora got up to leave and Rafa jumped up to follow her. He performed his duty, like a shadow at her side, moving ahead and falling back to seek out any potential dangers that may have snuck into the lobby. She was a mere human being but she had an air of importance about her. He escorted her back to the royal suite where he cast an eye over the heaps of flowers. She was allergic to them all, but that didn't stop them arriving, without cards, from her absent lover, who was nevertheless present in every glance she cast around her, in the pretty fullness of her lips and in the avidity of her gaze, whose fatal potential she was wholly ignorant of. This was a woman always on the brink of disappearing with the next look. He looked across at her; her eyes were closed. He'd almost memorized this strategy of hers: she would close her eyes sweetly, then after a moment's lapse or retreat to somewhere inside herself where no one could reach her, she would surface with that look of loss in her eyes as she gazed around her, exposing how alienated she felt. Rafa thought the coma must have been an attempt to escape from that loss, a break from the piles of flowers that arrived in a steady stream and the servants and bodyguards who formed a cordon around her—around this girl in her twenties who was staying in a 5,000-euro-a-night suite in the fanciest hotel in the heart of old Madrid, a few steps from its most important museums—the Prado, the Reina Sofia and the Thyssen-Bornemisza—and the Teatro Español and Teatro Real.

Rafa waited patiently in the corridor outside his room, which was adjacent to Nora's suite, and then sprang to life again when she reappeared for her long morning walk around Madrid.

He'd been working for her for two months. He came programmed to please and he was used to working for Gulf millionaires who drove around in convoys just to attract attention. He hardly had to look at the very young woman to know that he was there to play his part in another of those displays of status. He would sit in the front seat watching everything that moved, and then he'd jump out before the car had even stopped so he could open the back door for her, and accompany her as she headed off into Madrid's streets, cafes, and squares, vigilant protector of her image. Until one morning, when a wry smile hovering at the corner of her lips unmasked him. She'd been perching on the banister at the side entrance to the Museo del Prado, which was already closed by the time they arrived. Sitting there, she was taller than him, and he'd taken a few steps backward into the plaza, so that the moving traffic of the Paseo del Prado was to his right and the calm greenery and Nora were to his left. He stole a few seconds to look at her. What was it he was supposed to be guarding? Jewelry? Another kind of valuable? She didn't seem to be obsessed with jewelry like the other women he guarded for the sheikh, whom people called the Emperor of International Investment. He couldn't make sense of the loneliness that enveloped her; she was a tiny gazelle trapped inside a glass paperweight.

That day, she'd been in a flighty mood—every day was different, as if she were a droplet of quicksilver that could never be pinned down to a particular psychological state. As she sat on the bare flight of stairs leaning back against the wall of the museum that towered over her like the wall of a temple, Rafa tried to read what was beneath her faint smile. He could've sat down but he preferred to stand; some sixth sense had him in a state of alert. He was observing her delicate teenage face and the sharp contours of her eyebrows, when she broke her constant silence to ask him a question: "Rafa, you escaped the war to come and do what? Guard people like us?"

"My name's Rafi, not Rafa." It wasn't just his name that had changed over more than ten years in that job; when Rafi looked at Rafa these days he almost didn't recognize him. "I didn't escape the war," he explained. "I left Lebanon when the last thing tying me to the country died." He looked away; he'd said too much. It would have been a big professional no-no to expose himself like that, to confess that the death of his mother, whose cancer they'd fought side by side, was what caused those ties to be severed. Nora didn't press him.

After that brief exchange, they'd dropped the bodyguard ritual, tacitly agreeing that she didn't really need a guard by her side the entire time. From then on he'd always left a few paces between himself and her, following and watching, giving her the space to wander around and mingle, so long as she remained in sight. Whenever she sat at a cafe, like she'd just been doing, he'd pick a table a little way away, at the back, where he could still see her.

"You think you're guarding me sitting back there?" He wasn't expecting her to pounce again. He hadn't even gotten over the shock of her first question when she hit him with the second. "What are you protecting me from, anyway?"

"That depends. What are you scared of?"

The look she gave him slammed against his face and slowly slid off, like a bird against a windshield. He could feel his pulse throbbing in his neck as he hurried to apologize, "I'm sorry, ma'am." She looked away and his words trailed off on his lips.

"What is it you usually guard in jobs like this?"

"Mostly politicians, rich people, valuable objects."

"No gangsters?"

"Sometimes."

That was the first time a client had mocked him. (Why aren't you guarding me? And what from?) He was intrigued.

"And what do you protect them from?"

"Their own pasts usually."

How could he have let that answer slip out? Her wry smile became a sigh and he didn't know what to make of it. Her mood had flipped and she stared blankly into space; it had dawned on her that a person couldn't simply bump into their past, stop to say hello, and then part ways amicably; your past either sprays you in a hail of bullets or it blows you up with an explosive vest. Either that, or it looks the other way and hurries past before you even realize it was there.

He felt like he might spend his whole morning apologizing for having allowed himself to speak. "I'm sorry—"

She cut him off. "Do you have to be prepared to die for your clients in this job?"

"The job doesn't usually require you to do more than mount a respectable defense." He continued after a brief silence: "You might say the only requirement is keeping yourself and the client alive."

"Against anything that could happen?"

When his job was put under the microscope of that question he didn't really know how to put what he actually did into words. "To be honest I think we're just here to send a message—this person is surrounded by people who can respond to any kind of attack. That's usually enough to stop any attempts being made in the first place."

"So you're just there to prove that someone's important?"

He shrugged, thought for a moment, and then added, "Maybe also to prove that someone belongs to someone prestigious."

The look that accompanied his choice of words put her relationship with the sheikh under the spotlight, but she didn't respond. "So do you actually keep people from getting killed?"

He smiled. "President Reagan was shot in the four meters between the entrance of a carefully guarded building and his armored car, while surrounded by elite bodyguards. Kennedy was assassinated in the middle of a high-security motorcade. Sadat was killed at a military parade by his own troops, Hariri bit the dust inside his own armored car, and Bhutto was flanked by bodyguards as she stood up in the American-made sunroof of her car. Keeping people from getting killed, like you put it, is a very romantic idea. Assassinations almost always happen in the most fiercely guarded places and you can never predict when one's going to happen. In the end, it's probably impossible to protect someone from that much anger and hatred." As soon as he finished speaking, he began to worry that he'd said too much, so once again he apologized quickly. "Excuse me, ma'am, there are boundaries that shouldn't be crossed in this line of the work, and one of those is irritating a client with silly conversations."

"You got a Master's in philosophy so you could do a job that requires you to keep your mouth shut?" She stood up and walked off; he followed.

Over the next few days, Rafa became more aware of the circle of silence that surrounded her, and he would listen in carefully whenever she talked to her assistant or to the sheikh on one of his fleeting visits, attempting to glean some information about who she was, something to explain the currents beneath the words on the surface. Her every expression was a puzzle. He observed her for long stretches to try to figure out why it was she needed his protection, what it was that threatened her.

"YOU WANT TO GO THERE?!" RAFA WAS SURPRISED AT THE BROCHURE IN NORA'S hand. "The British Cemetery?!"

The resentment in his voice made her want to go even more. "Why not?"

The brochure had caught her eye two days earlier. Sensing her interest, the sheikh pushed it under a pile of papers. The arrival of his barber gave her the chance to snatch the brochure and stuff it into her purse.

They went on a morning that reminded him of his American girlfriend's words: "rain's tiny kisses playing music on our faces." Live, stinging kisses stirred their longing as they drove through the Carabanchel district in the suburbs. The grass in the cemetery was padded with water and squelched under Nora's light footsteps. The wildness of the place answered a deep need for adventure inside her: a deserted oasis, shaded by cedar, cypress, and plane trees. Rafa was reluctant but had to follow the bewitched Nora, who flitted among the graves. Rafa was familiar with the cemetery, since he'd lived nearby for three years before he'd got a job, but it was so isolated he'd never been tempted to go in until the sheikh had visited it, and now Nora too.

He and the assistant had to hurry to catch up with Nora. They found her leaning against a cedar tree, looking alarmingly pale for a moment. The frailty was instantly masked by that grayish look, her soul absorbed in images of death. In the translucent drizzle, tombstones came to life, names and epitaphs emerged from the granite to share their silence. That morning, the usual void look was missing from Nora's face; standing there she was a woman torn between two worlds and aware of the yawning gap that separated them. When she was ready to leave an hour later, a morbid silence had descended over the three of them.

To Rafa's surprise, Nora woke up early the next morning to return to the cemetery. They were met there by bouquets of yellow flowers at the foot of each row of graves. It felt like they were floating on sunny death.

"There are nicer cemeteries to visit than this one," said Rafa.

She had the feeling that he was trying to get her to leave and when he saw that she was suspicious, he hurried to add, "This is just a cemetery for outcasts."

"Meaning?"

"It's kind of sentimental. A morbid repository for people whose mortal remains couldn't be sent home, but which didn't belong in the local graveyard either, for reasons having to do with religion and culture. Like other countries in Europe after the Reformation, Spain didn't allow people who weren't members of the established Church to be buried in consecrated ground. Long before the Spanish War of Independence, the British and Spanish governments signed a treaty to provide cemeteries for non-Roman Catholics. One government sold the land to the other and the cemetery was inaugurated in 1854. Over the years, it welcomed the city's dead: Christians—Anglicans, Protestants, and Orthodox—as well Jews and Muslims."

"Look! There's a line of Arabic poetry on that gravestone: 'Tread softly over this earth for it is made of bodies.'" Like a child, she wanted to venture ever further, and he had no choice but to follow.

"It's by the famous blind poet Abu l-Ala al-Ma'arri."

Rafa's attempts to put a stop to those visits just made them more alluring. Over the next few mornings, the death of those outcasts became a compulsive puzzle for Nora. Despite himself, Rafa joined her in discovering gravestones witness to nearly a thousand burials over 150-odd years, engraved with unique messages of love and bereavement in all sorts of languages: English, Latin, Spanish, French, German, Hebrew, Serbo-Croat. The cemetery became like a book, with each gravestone a granite page, and Nora the engrossed reader moving about, asking Rafa to translate for her, empathizing with the stories of adventurers who'd died far from home. She thought she too could die and probably feel at home there, where the boundaries separating the deceased had all been washed away. She might find a missionary lying beside a music-hall artiste, or an accountant or waiter or diplomat, nannies side by side with doctors, journalists, lawyers, teachers, and butlers. The cause of death might have been old age, war, sudden illness, traffic accident, or a plane crash, but they all ended up ruminating on the same serene death.

Nora made a ritual of visiting the cemetery. Every day she would choose a different grave to sit on, as if trying on dresses. Sometimes she would sit as she was sitting now, staring into space, but flinching back whenever something caught her attention. She'd blink and find herself in the distant past, then blink again and be back. Her mood changed most when she tried to communicate with the tombstones, tried to decipher their messages.

"Don't you feel the urge to break through death with a message for all these spirits? I wonder how expressive they could really be. How well they could convey what they're experiencing right now, in death. Doesn't it blow your mind how we have this need to go on communicating and writing, long after death? Despite death?" Her question was more rhetorical than it was aimed at him, but Rafa responded by translating the lines written by Sophocles and spoken by Antigone:

> *"Come, Fate, a friend at need / Come with all speed! / Come, my best friend, / And speed my end! / Away, away! / Let me not look upon another day!"*

Nora felt the spirit breathe those words down her spine. She chased Sophocles' scattered words through the cemetery, searching for a hidden gravestone.

"When I have suffered my doom, I shall come to know my sin; but if the sin is with my judges, I could wish them no fuller measure of evil than they, on their part, mete wrongfully to me." *—Antigone.*

She flinched, as though those words were a message directed at her. It made Rafa hesitate before translating the words of Oedipus on another gravestone:

"When he discovers the truth of his actions, he is wrought with horror and self-loathing. He now devotes himself to his own punishment. He plans to walk the earth as an outcast until the end of his days."
—Oedipus.

Rafa shivered at the echo of those words, augmented by her deep silence. He sensed she longed to hear more of the tormenting messages. She turned to face Zoroaster's words on the gravestone behind her:

"What am I? and how and whence am I? and whither do I go?"
—Zoroaster.

That summed up her mood. Trying to avoid Rafa's inquisitive look, Nora noticed some Hebrew lines:

"A loving son and father, I am to be remembered as number 10, creating and animating matter, expressed by 0, which, alone, is of no value."

She found refuge in that zero, surrounded by invisible voices and emotions unfolding within her. She was connected to the longing in those messages, finding some vindication in Neruda's lines:

"Dies slowly he who avoids a passion, / who prefers the dots on the i to a whirlpool of emotions."

Near the gate she met another Arabic inscription:

"Here lies an Iraqi poet who faced many winters, stuffing his clothes with Arabic newspapers, ruminating on their defeats, and still dreaming here, amid the kindled ashes of outcasts, of a land that seeks respite so it may catch its breath and gather the ashes of its scattered sons."

Nora usually ended up resting under the poplar tree. There, she discovered an unmarked grave hidden deep in the grass, a sheet of gray stone blending into the earth as though it wasn't a grave but the torso of a man who'd laid down for a short rest, leaning his head against the poplar trunk, and then turned into stone. There was an old key affixed to the stone with two hooks, beside which an Arabic inscription read "The Keyholder." The deceased's name was buried beneath a thick protrusion of poplar roots and Nora didn't bother to try to uncover it.

"Very few burials take place here now because the site's full, but they do allow people to bury ashes still," Rafa said.

"The idea of a land saturated with dead, the soil closing over their faces— it's horrifying. Where I come from graves are filled and emptied continuously, like buckets, so that every newcomer has a place to rest."

"Here, people own their burial plots." The idea did seem odd at that moment even to him.

Over the course of their visits to the cemetery, Rafa could see the change in Nora. It was as if a door had opened between her and those people, as if she had been smuggled through the usually sealed door in the back of her head. Rafa was sure that some kind of barrier separated her from her past.

"So you grew up without a dad. What's it like to be fatherless?" The question came out as naturally as a line on one of those stones, and his answer was equally spontaneous:

"Cancer was there with me and my mother from the second I opened my eyes. We made such a compact little triangle. Between my mother's needs and school, I didn't have a spare second to pity myself. All I wanted was for the chemotherapy to stop the disease advancing in Mom's liver, but they eventually had to remove it."

Nora saw her own face in the mirror of his; death was the morning coffee they shared under that poplar tree. "Was it easy to find a donor?"

"They used a piece of mine. It's amazing. You can grow a whole new liver from a tiny piece of someone else's!"

"Like the will to live. Even when you chop off its head, it grows leaves again." The gravestones around them listened, sucking on their peeled hearts. "Was she sick for long?"

"We were very close for a long time. We didn't think of those years as years of sickness but as years when we were close to each other. I considered her an extension of my own liver! You might say I got to know her better than I'd ever been able to get to know myself. Taking care of a sick body is totally different from taking my obliviously healthy body for granted. I knew her needs better than my own. Anyway, the piece of liver lasted ten years before it finally failed us both."

The surrounding graves felt restless, and pigeons flapped in the air. The dead were eavesdropping, releasing their stories to provoke the memories and nostalgia of the living.

"Do the graves make you think of the torment going on inside of them?" she asked. "I grew up thinking of death as a date with torment."

Looking around, all Rafa could see was the abstract map of his life: the dreams he'd left behind, the children he hadn't brought into the world.

"Graves remind me of the torment that happens on the outside, to tell you the truth." His answer revealed in front of her eyes a map whose contours spiraled out from inside the grave, to show that those who'd died weren't cut off from the world they'd once inhabited. They carried their ordeals with them and smuggled them into their graves, into their dry bones and sodden soil, constantly pushing and spreading their death into the outside world. Death was a re-reading of the map.

"Sometimes I think death's a decision we make with our eyes all the time." The fine drizzle faded away and the sun poured through the clouds, freshly washed and shimmering. Nora continued, "When the eye fails to see, the heart follows, dragging the whole body down. Death is blindness, a total eclipse of insight." She was absentmindedly rolling a lock of her hair around her forefinger, bringing it up to her nose and sniffing. Lately, her hair had begun to smell like grass warmed in the sun.

A way off, a homeless man was kneeling at a grave with a bouquet of yellow roses. Nora watched him taking the bouquets from grave to grave, kneeling, mumbling verses and moving on, joining each grave together in his prayer of yellow flowers. The row of graves he visited looked like they'd been freshly dug that morning, but she knew that no burials took place there any more.

Like the birds chattering helplessly, Nora went on. "It might have been a blessing if my father had got cancer. But he was above cancer—in the sense of the rapid proliferation of cells. For him, any excessive growth at all was considered a sin."

Rafa breathed slowly; by breathing he allowed her to dip farther into the past. A poplar leaf blew at Nora and she squeezed its juice between thumb and index finger. "I remember the lemon leaves that the woman who raised me used to crush and rub under my armpits before sending me to say good morning to my father at dawn on feast days. I'd sit there itching all over in my gold brocade dress while my father lay in the corner, dozing, oblivious to my existence. I would wait breathlessly for it to be morning, tugging at him to take me to the special holiday prayer at the Holy Mosque. I remember one particular morning, with the silence heaped in mountains separating me from him. In the darkness I knew what was wrong: father never looked me in the eye, never really saw me. He saw nothing but the male heir I'd deprived him of. That dawn, I wanted him to see me. I came so close with the gas lantern, peering into his closed eyes, that suddenly his beard caught fire, waking him up and startling us both. I put it out with my bare hands." She opened her palms wide for Rafa to see the traces of burn. The lines on her palms, for life, heart, and head, were gone. "I don't think Father ever forgave me for it. He haunted me with that pale, charcoal-blackened face, a permanent nightmare."

Rafa had no idea how many spirits passed back and forth in between them, scooping up the echo of their words, as he looked into Nora's cloudy, faraway eyes, gone somewhere he couldn't even reach to pull her back. He sat silently waiting for her to re-emerge, and when she did, her voice was a sarcastic whimper. "For the first seven years of my life, we—me and the woman who raised me—used to look down on him from above. Sometimes he'd send me a bar of candy, noting down its price in his list of goods that had gone past their expiration date, but apart from that all I shared with him was that yearly feast-day breakfast of cheeses, olives, and date paste. When I took off the plastic tablecloth, the annual encounter would end, and I'd run back upstairs to the woman I regarded as my second mother." Nora avoided using names so that she could see her past self from a stranger's perspective. "People don't die of old age, they die from cutting all the threads that link them to the living. That's exactly what my father did."

"If there are threads that tie us to those we love, then my mother is a spider web that guards me. I can still feel her all around me, even now."

"A bodyguard guarded by the dead!"

He looked up, stung, expecting derision, but he was received by her enveloping seriousness instead. He was moved.

Insomnia

"I CAN'T SLEEP." THE WORDS ESCAPED HER INVOLUNTARILY, AND HER ASSISTANT stopped what she was doing. It was the middle of the night, and they'd just gotten back from the hotel swimming pool where Nora, in her knee-length swimsuit, had struggled bravely in the water for hours. When she was defeated in her attempts to swim, she floated on her back and let time settle and clear around her. Only rarely during her stay at the hotel had she had to share the pool with anyone else at that late hour.

The deep wound on her left knee floated inside its bandage and the waterproof layer around it. Three days earlier, Nora had given them all a fright by disappearing from her hotel suite while her bodyguard wasn't paying attention. She'd woken up very early and slipped out without telling anybody, heading to the British Cemetery; the short time it'd taken Rafa to guess where she'd gone and catch up with her was enough for something to happen. When Nora reached the poplar tree where the gravestone with the key was, she'd found the homeless man—the one who usually wandered around placing yellow flowers on the graves—chiseling at the gravestone, bent on destroying the inscription. Her sudden appearance startled him, and for a moment he remained crouched where he was, staring into her eyes. The empty look sent chills down her spine, giving him the chance to lunge at her. He shoved her and she fell back, her knee crashing against the broken gravestone.

When Rafi arrived, he saw blood on the gravestone and the grass, and in the gaping wound across her knee. Nora sat watching in shock as Rafi knelt down in front of her and lightly but deftly smoothed the torn flesh back over her knee, then tore his white shirt into strips to wrap around the wound and stem the bleeding. Shock had numbed the pain and all Nora could do was watch like an onlooker. The words she did manage to string together didn't mean much to Rafi: "The hobo with the yellow flowers. . ."

When they took a look at the tombstone, they discovered that the old key was missing, leaving only a depression in the gray stone, and that the name had been chipped away entirely, except for a few letters: "Sh . . . i." Luckily Nora's wound—her knee needed ten stitches—wasn't as bad as it could have been.

"Don't worry," Nora's assistant hurried to comfort her sleepless, frightened boss, picking up the clothes Nora had just taken off and watching her nestle into the hand-embroidered bed sheets. She left the light above her and the light in the corridor leading to the bathroom on. The assistant had never seen anyone who slept bathed in so much light. "I could make you some chamomile tea and run you a hot bath if you want."

"I just want you to check on me every half hour while I'm sleeping. I'm worried that if I sleep too deeply, I'll go into a coma and die . . ."

A sympathetic fear welled up in the assistant's heart and she quickly reassured her. "I sleep as lightly as a bird; I fall asleep in a second and wake up just as easily. I'll sleep on the sofa in the sitting room and leave the door open so I can watch you all night."

The assistant's self-sacrificing promise coaxed Nora to confide further. "I've been scared of sleeping alone since I was little. I used to sleep glued to my second mother's ribs, and I'd make her hold me tight. Whenever I felt sleep pulling me toward death, I would hear her murmuring God's names over me and I'd resurface." She paused to push away an apparition, "I was sleepy all the time."

The assistant relaxed at this easing in her mistress's mood—though she couldn't claim to have gotten used to those fickle changes of temperament, which were getting even more pronounced lately. "How about I make a doctor's appointment for you?"

Nora didn't say anything. The assistant unobtrusively finished what she was doing, then left.

The night passed like an interrupted dream, in flashes of light in which her assistant hovered over her breathing to make sure she was still alive and then went out again.

It was eleven in the morning when the honking of saxophones outside woke Nora. A stream of protestors stretched from El Retiro and the Prado down to the Palacio de Congresos, stopping traffic, and they'd dyed the Fuente de Neptuno fountain bright green on their way. They were demanding raises for municipal workers. When Nora stepped out of her hot bath, she looked radiant and fresh; she walked barefoot across the thick carpet, delighting in the feel of handwoven silk. Her breakfast was waiting on a tray on the table in front of her beside a few embroidered cloth bags her assistant had lain there.

"I went out for a walk this morning and came across an old Turkish woman who was selling these handmade purses." A sharp look pecked at her momentarily, then relaxed. Nora picked up her coffee and calmly took a sip, looking out the window at the demonstration below. She picked up one of the bags; in her mind's eye she could see a similar purse tied around her waist and hanging down to the right. Her words flowed out like she was picking up an old story.

"The woman who brought me up invented a little bag like this for me to tie around my waist. She made it out of the fabric of my feast-day dress. She believed that every girl should start with a little bag that the world could pour good luck into!" Down below on the street, one of the striking workers delivered a speech to the entire city over a PA system in enthusiastic Spanish.

"She was so noisy and cheerful, dancing, praying the Ramadan night prayers and singing all in the same breath." Nora picked up another little purse, this one adorned with blue eye beads and tiny palms to ward off envy. "What would a girl like me put in a purse like that?" she snorted.

"I could put your hair pins in it . . ." ventured the assistant.

"Someone once gave my father a tin of agarwood and he kept it hidden away, never once using the incense. I stole the biggest piece, which nature had sculpted into the shape of a man. It was the first thing I hid in my purse. When I wasn't looking, the man used to leave me messages written with hair pins on my skin; he'd climb out of the bag when my eyes were closed. He said my hair couldn't stand being restrained by hair pins, so he took to braiding my untamable hair and winding it around my head like a crown. In the world I lived in, it was always men who held the keys to the world. That little agarwood man was my secret key . . . I always blushed when he'd dip his finger into his mouth before smoothing down my thick eyebrows . . ." Her voice was scarcely audible any more, a little girl murmuring in her sleep.

Super Emperor

RAFI JUMPED OUT OF HIS CHAIR TO GREET THE SHEIKH WHEN HE APPEARED, unannounced, in the hallway, but he headed straight for Nora's suite and entered without knocking. Rafi couldn't help but feel embarrassed, like he'd been caught red-handed. He'd gotten used to the sheikh's sporadic appearances and disappearances over the ten years he'd spent working as part of the man's security detail whenever he came to Madrid on business or pleasure.

The women he'd gotten used to seeing on the sheikh's arm never lasted more than a few days, though. There was always a new face, attracted to the forty-something sheikh's good looks and the financial empire he'd managed to build at a relatively young age. This time around, it was different though. Somehow Nora had succeeded in luring him back every time he went away. Through some unspoken arrangement, he'd made her understand what her role was in that equation of theirs: when he was around, she hardly ever left the suite, but as soon as he left, she'd be out of there in an instant as if fleeing his shadow. Whenever her mood darkened and the ties binding them began to break—because she was the one breaking them—he'd rush back to trap her.

RAFI LINGERED IN THE HALLWAY OUTSIDE, TRYING TO LISTEN IN ON WHAT WAS HAPPENING on the other side of the door. The sheikh's aftershave hung tenaciously in the air.

Inside the suite, Nora lay on her chaise longue and watched him come in. Something in her eyes drew him toward her like a magnet, like a shark sensing a drop of blood at the bottom of the ocean. He leaned over her, careful not to touch any part of her except for her lips, grazing them cruelly with his own.

His kiss penetrated her skull, burrowing down to her spine. She clenched the chaise to stop herself from wrapping her arms around his neck. When he pulled back, he could taste her blood on his lips. He licked them as he stared at her. "What do you do when I'm not around? Do you find a way to entertain yourself?"

The question groped at a deeper question: her intentions. It was absolutely vital for him that she remain exactly where he wanted her, when he wanted her, how he wanted her. Fulfilling his every condition. The taste of her saliva, her silence, they awoke the hunter inside of him. She knew that tone of his, it preceded a storm. "Your bills betray a lack of enthusiasm. What do you do to amuse yourself in my absence?"

"Nothing."

He'd failed to draw her into conversation, but it only provoked him further.

"Nothing? Don't you miss me?" Their arguments usually started with something stupid like that.

"Do you want me to lie? No, I don't."

"Maybe you miss hi—"

"Hold it right there."

"Who are you to tell me where I should hold it?"

"They're your rules. You came up with them and now you want to break them. If you get to break the rules, then I'll break them, too."

"Really? I'd love to see that."

"Fine. You will," she said with implicit defiance. He grabbed her by the throat.

"Are you threatening me, you bitch?" He squeezed her neck; he seemed to enjoy watching her face turn carnelian red. "You want to make a laughing-stock out of me? Is that your plan? You stup—". She hit him with her arms and fists, catching him unawares, and broke free.

"Say one more word, and I swear you'll never see me again."

She got up from the chaise longue and ran toward the bedroom. He caught her by the bedroom door and threw her against the cold, clean wall, grabbing convulsively at her body.

"Oh really?! I've obviously spoiled you then. . ." That was the last thing he said. His thirst for destruction was beyond words. Rafi tried to ignore the fight raging on the other side of the door even though he could hear bodies crashing together.

She ascended from pain to pain, from climax to further climax, staring into eyes that delighted in her suffering. No matter how much she gave in, he would never trust her. Her eyes cut into him like a tightening noose, penetrating through him and around him. He left no room in her for a rival. Time passed them by. She dived down, drawing him in, toward the hunger that always followed. She was always two steps ahead and he was always panting to catch up. If he'd managed to beat her to it, he'd have left her there without a backward glance. She bit, it hurt, he groaned. He was searching for hatred in her, she was searching for destruction in him. When he was plunged inside her like this, her body betrayed her with desires that weren't her own: it mimicked him so that he could take her over. She was finding it harder to overcome this thing that brought them together, that enslaved them, that always lured him back. No matter where else he went or who else he lusted after, he was as stuck as she was in the trap he'd laid for her.

Caviar

That night, the sheikh hovered around Nora, tracking her every move like a vulture, ready to swoop the moment she flagged. He forced her to eat caviar on bread topped with slices of lemon, but he himself didn't touch the stuff. He liked to order things his ulcer prevented him from eating and watch her eat them instead, as though she were a dog or a cat, relishing the sight of each bite as it went down. He liked forcing every bite down her throat, which always tightened up after he plundered her body. He put her on and took her off as if she were a glove, but when her body rejected him, he would break through her defenses by force-feeding her.

When he was done, she'd curl up on the end of the sofa and he'd ignore her and carry on drinking alone, looking weary and grim. The further he drifted from consciousness, the closer the two of them grew. She remembered the texture of the caviar, reddish, jelly spheres exploding against her tongue and the roof of her mouth, washing away the taste of him in sea-saltiness. At one point, she laid his head down in her lap so that he could stretch out on the sofa. She was calm in those moments of truce when everything was laid bare. In sleep, he was just an innocent boy from a working-class neighborhood. His forehead was sweaty at the hairline and the volcano inside him lay dormant. Maternal instinct filled her and for a moment she was woman pure, with no need for ornament, or danger. When his breathing got heavy, it was easy enough to lay his head on a pillow. Then she stood up.

She shut the door to her bedroom, and then several others: one that led to the sitting room, another that led to cramped maid's quarters, as well as the door leading to the Jacuzzi and the door to the bathroom. She felt like she had to shut every door within a hundred-meter radius.

Through the windows in the corner of her bedroom she stared out onto the two tree-shaped sculptures in the park below, which peeked back up at her. She didn't want to sleep. She didn't want to sit down. She wasn't afraid, but her mind was aglow, split open like a gorge. Fiery explosions surged upward, blazing wildly in the corners of her mind before melting away. Nothing could be translated into a coherent image. She made a decision: leaving her fur coat behind, she wrapped a gray scarf around her head and slipped through the service room into her assistant's bedroom where she put on the woman's coat. She slipped out through a door that opened out onto the end of the hallway and took a quick look back at Rafi's room; he left the door ajar even when he was sleeping. She was relieved not to have him hovering around her either. She wanted to be alone for a night. Alone. Face to face with the world.

In the road, whipped by the cold night, her disquiet grew. She understood the risk she was taking going out by herself this late, but she didn't care. She only cared about the earthquake inside of her. She didn't know when it was going to erupt onto the surface. It was the first time she'd ever dared break his rules. She walked uphill, the Palacio de las Cortes on her right, and veered left down narrow streets. Bars and restaurants were woven into the web along with laughter and flirtatious cries that trailed her as she passed. A young man circled around her singing gypsy songs and kneeling down theatrically until his girlfriend pulled him away. Nora carried on walking, staring ahead, her steps falling in time with the cackling of the woman behind her. The woman just kept on laughing and laughing. Nora floated on, mesmerized by everything she saw, totally unaware of the figure who'd been stalking her since the moment she'd left the hotel. She carried on further down narrow lanes toward the surprises they held. From deep within the darkness of one alleyway, a tall matador rushed toward her with a massive dog on a leash. When they shot past her, a soggy tongue licked the index finger of her right hand and the sensation of wet animal contact caused her to gasp. When she turned around to look, no trace remained in the darkness. The wetness puzzled her. *Do you wash it seven times with water and a final time in sand?* She hurried forward in the direction of guitar music and stamping feet. The melancholy Andalusian singing drew her forward until she found herself in the Plaza Mayor, a massive square designed by Juan de Villanueva in 1790 after the great fire. She was surrounded on three sides by two hundred and thirty-seven balconies and nine gates.

In the center of the great square, Nora was swept up in the flamenco music and the exuberance of a pair of dancing spectators. It was both overwhelming and upsetting. She looked around in amazement. In the colonnade surrounding the square, the cafes and restaurants were packed with night revelers and on a wooden stage erected in the middle of the square, a flamenco dancer strutted in circles around a gypsy dancer, while circles in the audience imitated his moves. In this city, resounding with amplified music, people could laugh and cry and dance and quarrel in Spanish and English and German. All those languages were awakened inside of Nora, a river of language that flowed between the banks of her past on either side.

To her right, a female dancer sprang out of one of the arcades and Nora shrieked, her heart frenetic, her body giving itself over to the dance. Her finger was still wet with that animal's slobber. When she snapped out of her dancing reverie, she noticed the smiling, encouraging eyes around her. A young American came dancing up to her. He was imitating the male dancer, but mixing in matador movements, circling her as if she were a bull, in thrall to the agonized cries of the singer behind him. Nora felt that she'd been cut off from the world, from every bond, that her purpose in life was to be right there, to experience those feelings that summed up everything she'd lost. In that fleeting moment, Nora was one with the bulls' blood that stained the walls of the wide arena around her where bullfights had been held in years past. "This void is you." A voice inside of her commanded her cells and they responded. "Spread your limbs into every corner, occupy all space, spread out toward the never-ending. Your limbs will reach; they won't tire. Your body is a droplet as vast as the night and all its lights."

Suddenly, she realized the dancer was dragging her toward an alley, and when she tried to pull away, he wrapped his arms around her. In that moment, a hand reached out of the darkness, grabbing the man by the neck and throwing him to the ground, where he lay motionless under the arcade. The hand took hold of her, pulling her forcefully, and when she looked to see whose hand it was, she gasped.

"Rafi?" Her voice squeaked. A migraine struck her.

"Spend my money on whatever you want, big or small, but don't you dare use it to buy yourself a lover." That was the note the sheikh had scribbled on her mirror before he left. She could tell his hand must have been shaking.

Reptile

HE REACHED OUT FROM HIS DEEP SLUMBER AND OPENED HIS EYES IN THE oppressive darkness. Khalil was lying an arm's length away from the basement ceiling but for a moment he had no idea where he was. The ceiling looked damp. He struggled to remember how he'd died, when he'd ended up in this grave. Is this what death is really like? The power suddenly goes out and then when it comes back on, you find yourself underground? He couldn't remember hearing any receding footsteps. His head didn't feel concussed. He'd always been told that the first thing a dead person hears is the footsteps of those who've carried him to his grave receding in the distance. When he tried to sit up, he banged his head on the ceiling. His own groan confirmed: "Yeah, you're dead." That eternal sentence uttered at one point or another by all living beings. That sentence was like a door that opened up onto death itself. A little ways beyond it, the two angels Munkar and Nakir would no doubt appear and begin to judge his deeds.

The snake he'd been expecting to find beside him, ready to crush him, wasn't there, though; instead there were sticky mounds of fat. The smell of dough and frying meat jerked him out of his burial. The Turkish seamstress, who was lying beside him, sensed his movements and began to coil her limbs around him. For a moment, he struggled to breathe, but the dinosaur inside him broke through the curtain of the grave and the fat, ascending to the heavens and beyond. The current of those heavens floated him higher and higher, and when he fell back to earth like a rag the walls and the low ceiling began to watch him. They'd gotten used to tracking his movements. He would walk down the Lane of Many Heads—he preferred to come on foot, having parked his taxi far away—careful not to be noticed by anyone as he snuck into the basement studio. He didn't want Ramziya or anyone else's prying eyes to catch him in his tracks. No matter how well he blended into the darkness or how softly he stepped, he could feel the emptying houses of the lane watching him. The goddamned Lane of Many Heads didn't use the eyes of its inhabitants to watch him, it used its walls, ramshackle doors, cats, and trashcans, the dry air and the smell of desertion and sewage, the remnants of arguments that had taken place on every street corner, the slaps a wife laid on her husband. The Lane of Many Heads watched him with its every breath, and rebuked him.

Nasser's fist had left a searing pain which ran from his jaw to the back of his neck and reminded him of his car door, which Nasser had crashed his own car into during the pursuit. That was right before he arrested him. The Turkish woman took pleasure in the bloody bite-marks she left on his shoulders.

"Are you angry, precious?"

His stomach twisted in disgust at her hissing, but he didn't recoil from her bites. He thought back to the comic car chase, the sadistic pleasure he'd felt in his spine when his car crumpled as it crashed into the rubble on Qarara Hill. Nasser had forced him out of the car like a common criminal. Khalil couldn't help but laugh when Nasser clamped the Hollywood handcuffs on his wrists, but the scenario became a nightmare when Nasser took his police thriller fantasy to the extreme. He threw Khalil into a filthy cell with hardened criminals and put him through intense interrogations day after day. Like all corrupt cops, Nasser enjoyed torturing suspects and Khalil wasn't cut out for the challenge. He collapsed like the Twin Towers and confessed in the most exacting detail to having taken his passengers hostage, frightening them and dropping them off miles away from where they'd wanted to go.

Under torture, Khalil would have confessed to anything had the cursed Turkish woman not intervened. He had no idea what strings she'd pulled to get him released, back into this fetid bed. He turned over and deposited those days of torture in her fleshy punching bag of a body. She, in turn, received his brutality with a satanic hiss, "Give me your rage, all of it." She egged him on while he simply buried his face in the pillow, hoping to suffocate, to rid himself of this revolting thing. That pillow was the only thing he had left in the world. He took it everywhere with him like a turtle takes its shell, from Mecca to the U.S. and back. When he'd brought it with him to the basement that night, the Turkish woman had spotted it straight away, her teeth chattering like a rat-trap. Her entire body chattered when she danced.

Beneath the gallery, music blasted and then stopped. It started playing again and then stopped. Somebody was going through their entire vulgar collection. Khalil didn't bother to look to see what was happening. He was stuck like a bug in the wooden nest that the Turkish woman had installed beneath the basement's vaulted ceiling so she could spread out her large bed.

"Don't be afraid! So long as your Turkette is alive and kicking no one will dare lay a finger on her pleasure-saurus."

She bit his earlobe hard and what sounded like a pack of hyenas roared within her. Jail had broken something in him—not his body, but his sense of superiority, the idea that he was *untouchable, a heavenly creature*.

The night he got out of jail it was Mu'az who found him. From the bus, the imam's son had spotted Khalil's car on the side of the road some distance from the Lane of Many Heads. It looked like the sand at the edge of the Umrah Road had reeled the electric-yellow car in and swallowed its front tires. It was past midnight. Mu'az jumped out of the bus before it had even stopped, muttering the Throne Verse as he approached the car. It looked broken down and like it was surrounded by demons. Up close, in the light of passing cars, Mu'az spotted Khalil's face, ashen, smashed against the steering wheel. The sweat on Khalil's unconscious face poured hot out of Mu'az's temples and forehead, blinding him. For Khalil, time had come to a standstill. He had a vague sensation of being manhandled and stuffed into the first passing car, and then ending up at Zahir Hospital where they succeeded in reviving him. That was when he came face to face with the dinosaur inside of him, the creature that he no longer controlled.

"This time the cancer is spreading out from your right kidney." The doctor began that way so as to soften the blow of what was coming next: "This form of cancer is the most aggressive." A week passed in the blink of an eye, like it does sometimes in movies. The surgery to remove the tumor behind his kidney went smoothly and Khalil came out of it cracking jokes, almost pleased that the dinosaur had taken a bite out of his body.

The relapse hit hard, though. In the days that followed, it seemed as though the cavity that the surgery had left in his back and abdomen had given the dinosaur a foothold and it began to spread through his body. The blank look on the doctor's face as he examined the X-ray terrified Khalil. He was trying to hide the fear from Khalil's body, to communicate what was happening without getting Khalil worked up. "Your condition is disconcerting. Such rapid and aggressive cell division is extremely rare. It's like a fire through dry straw. It won't take more than a few days, a month at most, before, uh . . ." The doctor struggled to collect his thoughts. Khalil seemed to have gone deaf, lost in a Hollywood daydream-thriller in which he'd have to play the part of crowd-pleaser and insist on leaving the hospital to confront his dinosaur nemesis on the streets of Mecca.

"But where would they discharge you to?!" The walls were deaf to Mu'az's pleading questions. He was the only person in the audience, the only person there to object to the suicidal plot. Khalil was running away from the prospect of further amputation. "You can't convalesce in a taxi!"

For the first time, Mu'az understood what kind of person Khalil really was: he was hostage to a fatal solitude. He belonged to no one and the sadness that enveloped him was unbearable. It tore at him.

The first course of chemotherapy was the worst. It laid waste to Khalil's bones, all the way through to the marrow, but despite how frail he was, he was up on his feet an hour later, paying no mind to the nurse standing by with a wheelchair as he staggered out of the hospital.

Beneath the fiery Meccan sun, he was blinded by the sweat pouring from his forehead and the rest of his body. He turned to Mu'az suddenly, clutching at the arm that propped him up, and stopped in the middle of the boiling asphalt. He held Mu'az's head between his feverish palms, ignoring the prickle of his coarse hair and squeezed as if to wipe the events of the past week from his memory. "This movie isn't to be replayed for the gawkers in the Lane of Many Heads, got it? Just forget you ever saw me like this." Mu'az nodded, assenting to a command that came across as part plea and part threat. He hid his pity for the former legend of the Lane of Many Heads, the Hero of the Streets, who stood shrunken on the black asphalt, as pallid as quicklime.

Privacy seemed to matter more to Khalil than anything else. The first time cancer attacked him was back when he was in flight school in Florida and he'd kept it a secret—from his own father even. Ever since then, whenever he spoke about his illness it was as if he was talking about a film he'd once seen. Privacy and a creative imagination were the only weapons Khalil had against his self-destructive impulses. In one way or another, cancer was something he felt he could be proud of. To him it was like an excess, or an eruption, of cellular production in which he played the role of nuclear reactor, setting off a chain reaction, producing boundless energy.

Khalil took his time outside the crumbling Zahir Hospital building where he'd received a dose of radiation that spread through his body, poisoning his cells. He stood up straight. He wanted Mu'az to see him as the six-million-dollar man, a hero who'd just received an injection of enriched uranium and was off to do battle with viruses from outer space.

"I swear on the Quran, I won't tell a soul. But you really should follow the doctors' advice and stay in the hospital for another week. The food here is good at least, and they'll keep tabs on your treatment."

Comforted by the promise, Khalil drove off in his cab, escaping from the look of cancerous fear in Mu'az's sad eyes.

He was careful not to show any hint of illness in front of the Turkish woman. All she could talk about was how Nasser had rammed Khalil's cab with his car.

"Don't let them beat you down with a couple of dents. When you get better, just hobble over to the nearest car dealership and pick out whatever toy you want. Just so long as you promise never to take my favorite toy away," she said, wrapping her iron grip around him. "If you treat your Turkette right, she'll get you all the latest toys." The look of disgust he gave her was like a slap across the face. He would never let that succubus buy him. Not because he wasn't for sale—no, there was definitely a price-tag hanging around his neck—but because the interested buyer was such trash. Whenever she bragged about being Turkish, he felt like spitting on her and calling her *trash*. A word like a cleaver to decapitate her with.

She pressed her lips like blotting paper against his face, murmuring, "You're this Turkish woman's soul." An atomic meltdown of hatred was unleashed inside of him, stronger than the cancer that had exploded out from behind his recently operated-on kidney. He trembled with the pleasure of oppressive hate, and right away—as though her body were a finely tuned vibration-sensor—her desire was awoken. She reapplied herself, but for the first time in his campaign, the dinosaur inside him let him down. No matter how many times he swung at the Turkish woman, the dinosaur wasn't moved by the violence, the spilled blood. It played dead, lying there like a limp worm. The Turkish woman, on the other hand, had been taken over by a nymphomaniac lioness. She was bashing his dinosaur around in her claws, desperately trying to excite him, only vaguely aware of his sudden impotence, while his mind raced, thinking of all manner of possible cures and remembering how he'd once snickered at the warnings about the increased risk of heart attack from those blue pills he used to take. He wished he could have had a heart attack right then; it would at least spare him the embarrassment of impotence. On a third level of consciousness, he was aware that he was smashing those bulges of fat with his fists and feet in order to compensate for his impotence until her bubbles floated climactically to the surface.

Finally, miraculously, he managed to drag his worn-out body away from that fatty mass, and with superhuman strength pulled his clothes on. He stumbled over to the wooden staircase that led down from her bedroom to the dance floor below. He didn't even glance at the bodies gyrating around him, and they just watched him indifferently as he struggled to find his way out, any way out.

As soon as his lungs filled with the air of the lane, he began to cough and he hawked up something yellow. The last of the smell of her. As he staggered on, he stepped on an alley cat's tail; it hissed, baring its teeth. He stepped on the filth that had turned the white cat's coat gray, the signs of its last dust-up with some stray dogs.

"You and I are a lot alike, kitty. We've got eight souls, but have you heard of cancer? It's not just a stray dog that wants a bite. It's a dinosaur with gigantic feet that chases me and stomps on my souls, one after the other. The first time it attacked, it destroyed all my sperm, robbing me of the chance to have children. Now it's crushing the rest of me, Khalil the devil, my manhood."

He drove off in his cab. Alone in the car, the last thing the Turkish woman had said to him, the last he'd smelled of her, came back to haunt him. He scratched at his face because it still bore the marks of her lips. Her constant generosity always aggravated his dreams.

"Without your dinosaur, you'll never be anything but a sewer worm, Khalil."

Defeat. He slammed on the brakes, stopping his cab in the middle of an overpass, and considered everything he'd lost.

Every attempt at arousal had failed to revive him, but his lower half, which seemed paraplegic to him now, shot back, "How long is the Turkish vampiress going to let you get away with it?" He drove on recklessly, arriving at Mina, where he turned off the engine and sat in the blackness of the darkest night. He summoned the genies of Mina to revive his dinosaur. He wasn't in the mood to acknowledge that he was a man devouring the very last crumbs of life. If all he had left was a single day, he'd spend it as drunk as an animal. The thought of being drunk made him laugh. How could he hope to get drunk in the midst of all the garbage that seemed to be his lot in life? He was so deep in the mound of garbage the only way to get rid of it was to burn it all. It wasn't just the cancer, it was also his addiction to that piece of Turkish trash.

"That Turkish woman is the only one who can tear the dead flesh off your heart to see through to your true, unadulterated, desires," a voice inside chastised him. "She's the only one who can go toe to toe with your dinosaur, may he rest in peace. You deposit all the hatred you feel toward those people who are waiting patiently for the Mahdi inside of her. You belong to a race of people who are trying to engineer Judgment Day. You nurture wars so that they'll wash the earth away with pure blood. You dream up all these plots that will wipe the slate clean, but they're about as realistic as a Bollywood film. And yet it still pisses you off that they won't even give you a supporting role."

It killed him that they insisted on giving the lead role to the Antichrist in the war to come. They were even going to give a speaking part to a rock by the side of the road that will say "There is an infidel behind me" to believers, but they continued to ignore his talent. Come on! Khalil was a walking database of every action scene in every American movie ever made. He could act. He could tell you which corner every bullet and missile came from and the exact type of cruelty they would visit on human tissue, both living and dead. He used to drive to the edge of Mecca and park amidst the brutal volcanic mountains, just to think about the different types of homemade explosives that existed and how to pack them. All his passengers could attest to his encyclopedic knowledge of hydrogen bombs, their mass, and how deep through the ground their blast radii would reach.

"Out of all of us, I'm the one who's best prepared to kill but still you guys go out and attack the Antichrist without me!"

All throughout their peculiar relationship, the Turkish woman had listened carefully to all his complaints. His every drop of rancor produced more evil in the lane. In the darkness at Mina, surrounded by demons and the ghosts of slaughtered animals, Khalil felt like he himself was the cancer that gave rise to the saga of the malignant cells that were ravaging the neighborhood: the appearance of the body was just the opening scene. It was followed by the destruction of Mushabbab's priceless orchard and the story really reached its climax when Yusuf was hounded into exile. He suddenly had the feeling that he was writing the script, in invisible ink. Khalil remembered sitting with the Turkish woman, watching her copy down his story in magical ink as he dictated it. He pretended that he'd been enlisted to help her, that he was under hypnosis, that there was a whole troupe of Hollywood actors waiting in the lane, preparing to film scenes for a film about the role of Arab minorities in global terrorism. They were the ones who put up the YouTube video that broke open the scandal of the Lane of Many Heads.

"Khalil the pilot, always escaping from reality into your cinematic delusions."

No matter how much Khalil gave into his love of Hollywood's plots and sacred jungles, he always guarded a few things fiercely: his life, his cab, his special pillow, his mother's ashes and his resolve never to let the Turkish woman record Azza's story in her magic ink. His heart was seized by a fear that writing these things down would produce a chemical whose capacity for disfigurement was beyond comprehension. As soon as that nightmare struck him, his fingers jerked and he shook the hypnotized agent inside him awake. "That Turkish woman is Ottoman trash!" He'd upturn the Turkish woman's table and break her inkpot, rip the role of spying and whoring out from beneath her, banish her from the most important plotline in her heart.

Sometimes, when his dinosaur overpowered him, he was desperate to sacrifice Azza, who was taming him like Jessica Lange tamed King Kong: he thought about dropping her from his gorilla palm and giving her as a burnt sacrifice to the Turkish woman. At moments like that, their demonic qualities brought him and the Turkish woman closer together, evil pulsed through their veins, their heads drew nearer, and being alone together was like being in an opium den filled with the smoke of devilish intentions. In bed together, perched near the ceiling of the basement, above the dance floor, they looked like they were sitting on a bench suspended in the air like demons who sit in the sky eavesdropping on humans below and dodging God's angry shooting stars. Together they listened in on the bloated or anorexia-stricken fates of the female dancers below as the lights from the different dance sequences played across their faces. Against the backdrop of that lighting, which wouldn't have been out of place in a nightclub, there was no limit to the photographic tricks his cinema-soaked mind could play. He imagined that he was the Turkish woman and that she was him, as if they were starring in the film *Face/Off*. She had his elongated face with his long, wide, even nose, his ears that pointed backward with clipped tips like a bird's wings, his mouth, and his drop-shaped eyes. It was easy to imagine his own stretched-out face atop the rolls of fat on her neck, and her own monstrous face above his Adam's apple and body, the muscles of which had slackened after all those immobile hours behind the wheel in the unbearable Meccan heat.

When had the Turkish woman changed her strategy so she could attack Khalil himself?

Khalil drove on blindly, aimlessly, nearly running into pedestrians and other cars at intersections that appeared out of thin air. He knew he needed to get out of the car before he caused a massacre.

He eventually made his way back to the Arab League Building, and discovered that it was ready to be knocked down. He snuck up to the rooftop, careful not to let the eunuch see him, and headed for the storage unit where the old film projector was stored. His body was a sponge heavy with his sweat. The moment he opened the door and stepped inside, he sensed some strange presence was in there. An evil laugh lay behind the box where he'd hidden his rare projector, the only thing he'd inherited from his father. He yanked the cover off to find a smashed mess sneering back at him. The only thing that had survived the destruction was a single reel: the black-and-white dinosaur. The vandal had left it untouched among scraps of other reels stuck to its tattered scenes.

Khalil fell to the floor sobbing, the roll of film lying in his lap like a dead child. He slouched, allowing the cancer to spread from his kidney to his liver, tearing through his gall bladder and spurting bile all through his insides. For a moment, he died there violently, and he only came back to life so he could experience the suffering of an even harsher death.

He sat there, glassy-eyed, replaying the shredded dinosaur film in his mind just like he'd done night after night on the rooftop when he lived in the building. He used to watch as the tears in the reel showed larger and larger on the dinosaur's body with every viewing, waiting for the one showing when the dinosaur's entire body would disappear and he would finally be stripped bare of his beastliness, forced to face the neighborhood as mere skin and bone. Khalil had never managed to beat his addiction to watching the dinosaur on the walls of the rooftop, its tail swooping in the air, falling down on the Lane of Many Heads.

Finally when his tears were dry and his heart exhausted, Khalil fell into a deep sleep and dreamed of doing a remake of the dinosaur movie. He'd turn the dinosaur into the huge reptile that would emerge from Ajyad Mountain on the heels of the Antichrist and slap its tail against the surface of the earth, flipping everything upside down and heralding the apocalypse.

The sun rising over the roof woke Khalil. He stuffed the reel back into his hiding spot. "No projector will ever play this reel again," he reassured himself. No more decay, no more patching it up. The dinosaur is finally somewhere where it can never be wiped out."

Garbage Red

"MOON-SHAPED AMULET . . . PARKING LOT, JAWHARA TOWER." A SINGLE EMAIL of seven words had brought Yusuf to a parking lot outside one of the towers that overlooked the Haram Mosque. Living in the Lababidi building all by himself had affected his ability to see the world around him for what it was. Reality was no longer a simple tissue to him: his dreams, his memories, pictures, and every word from every book he'd ever read combined to form a new reality. Yusuf himself had turned into an apparition on a thin strip of film, liable to disappear if exposed to any light source. In al-Lababidi's house, as he moved from room to room, he made sure to shut every door he passed through, keeping up the habit of al-Lababidi's wife, Marie, and her servants: "Don't let the outside touch the pictures."

He gradually lost the ability to make sense of the world around him and the only reason he'd answered the message was because he was desperate to break out of the cycle of delirium he found himself in.

In plain view of the parking attendant, Yusuf walked past the gate, convinced that he was a ghost, and climbed up the exit ramp to the first floor of the parking garage. The attendant made no attempt to move toward him, he didn't even look at him, which only added to Yusuf's worry that he'd become invisible. When he got to the first floor, he saw that it was packed full of cars and stiflingly hot, like the inside of a boiling pot. The smell of electrical fires and fresh paint mixed with the sweat on the back of his neck. Yusuf wasn't sure which of the four floors he was meant to wait on, he wasn't even sure what he was waiting for.

He walked forward under the bright neon lights, cursing himself for coming to a place like this without even asking Mushabbab for advice. He felt the forest of concrete columns watching him and the glare of all the yellow signs and zone numbers blinded him. Some outside brain showed him the outlines of the car that came barreling toward him like a crimson lightning bolt. It emerged as if from some bloody patch beneath his eyelids. Even the hubcaps were painted dark red. The dream car grew larger as it headed for him. The moment lasted an eternity. Yusuf felt sluggish, his whole body froze as if to stay rooted to the spot. His body surrendered. His mind surrendered. His every muscle relaxed to receive the blow, his body went numb and indulged in the pleasurable sensation of being smashed before they'd even made contact. He tasted delicious death in that red second and savored it without knowing.

The deafening blow that followed brought him out of his reverie. Yusuf jumped, a delayed reaction, into any random direction falling onto the front of a blue garbage truck. The narrow band of red was squeezed under the truck's front bumper but Yusuf didn't have a chance to look at the thin red rivulets spreading out beneath the blue truck. He felt a hand yanking him, stuffing him into the front seat. Deep down he was certain that the red car would've crushed him to bits if the blue truck that had appeared from out of nowhere hadn't wiped it out first.

He knew he was inside the blue truck because of the faint smell of rot that enveloped it. It made him feel woozy. He spread out, as if decomposing, peaceably and discreetly, within the grave. Nothing bad could happen to him any more.

He realized he was squeezed in between two men: a short man who was driving the truck and a tall man who'd rescued him. The tall guy, his face covered by a red-checked scarf, was as reedy as a scarecrow. As the garbage truck roared through the gate of the parking garage onto the road, Yusuf's hand felt for the door handle, but was soon seized by an iron fist. The scarecrow turned to look at him. They were both panting. Sweat pooled between their shoulder blades and beneath their arms. Yusuf caught a whiff of something from the intimate past and noticed that the eyes staring back at him were gray. The man pulled the scarf away, slowly. Yusuf gasped.

"The Eunuchs' Goat?" The harsh look on his face didn't soften in the slightest. "I thought they deported you. Or left you to rot in some prison somewhere."

"Yes, though are we not all destined to rot in this earthly hell?"

"What are you talking about? Are you j—" He wanted to say "joking" but something in the Eunuchs' Goat's gray eyes stopped him short.

"Go ahead, say it. I was always the clown."

"What are you doing riding around in a garbage truck? And what happened before? Was that all real?"

"Only as real as you." The Eunuchs' Goat gave him a withering look, sweeping his gray gaze from top to toe, but Yusuf ignored the affront and carried on talking.

"Did you go back to the Lane of Many Heads? It isn't safe there any more. Things aren't the way they were back before you got arrested. Did you hear? Azza was probably murdered."

"When was she ever alive? When were any of us? Women are insects. At least for us men, death is a victory. It liberates our souls . . . What is all this crap?" Yusuf sensed danger in the bizarre words.

"I'll get out here, please."

"No. You're coming with me."

"With you? Where?"

"You'll see. You have to see."

The hot wind whipped at their faces, yellowing them. Yusuf wanted to shut the window but he didn't dare move. For the first time in his life, he was frightened of one of his childhood friends.

"I have to at least know where you're taking me." His voice betrayed his terror.

"Don't forget I just saved your life." Every word that came out of his mouth sounded strange. There was no trace left of the simple Eunuchs' Goat he'd known since childhood.

"What happened to you?"

The Eunuchs' Goat looked back and forth between Yusuf and the driver, who hadn't said a word the entire time, as if expecting one of them to rescue him. Yusuf's eyes fell on the Eunuchs' Goat's hands, the dirt under his fingernails. Not even his hands resembled the old Eunuchs' Goat's polished marble hands, whose elegance had defied the hardships of life in the Lane of Many Heads. Yusuf's searching look made the Eunuchs' Goat uncomfortable so he quickly tried to distract him.

"Get ready. We're about to go through a checkpoint." Yusuf didn't have time to respond or even comprehend. "Get down now." Without any warning, he shoved Yusuf's head into a black sack and Yusuf felt hands and feet like steel on his body, holding him down beneath the seat.

The truck seemed like it would keep going forever. Every time they stopped, Yusuf could feel the steel limbs crushing him down further beneath the seat. It was more to punish him than to keep him out of sight. Finally when they parked, they yanked him out of the truck roughly and pushed him forward. The ground felt soft and moist beneath his feet and the stench of rotting garbage blinded him. He knew he was walking on a trash heap. Just then, the black sack was pulled off his head to reveal the Eunuchs' Goat smirking at him:

"Welcome to my kingdom! Now, follow me." He led him through a network of tunnels and chambers so tortuous that Yusuf couldn't tell whether they were penetrating deeper down into the earth or up into the sky. He would've lost his way if it weren't for the deep earthy smell that guided them like a compass. Yusuf recognized the muggy smell that used to hang over the kitchen scraps dumped outside in the Lane of Many Heads. He realized that the tunnels below weren't deep like a cave, but ran beneath the thinnest layer of dirt, as shallow as the city's pride.

The Eunuchs' Goat finally pushed through a reed mat and cleared their way to the surface. They passed layers of rags, rotting vegetables, food, plastic tubs, soda cans, electronics, massive piles of broken mobile phones. There were mounds and mounds of garbage as far as the eye could see and the dump was surrounded by developments of what looked like doll's houses. It didn't matter if they were in Mecca any more or somewhere else. The garbage dump might as well have been the whole world, Yusuf felt.

All around them faces appeared from behind stacks of boxes, curtains strung up haphazardly between piles of trash, and sheet-metal doors stuck into the ground, guarding the void behind. With a single glance, the Eunuchs' Goat informed him that he'd found refuge; his breath gave off the stench of decay.

Yusuf's lungs seized up when the Eunuchs' Goat led him to the massive trenches that were used as ovens. The African dump kings lit fires there to burn plastic and aluminum, sending massive plumes of smoke into the air. Yusuf's eyes began to make out the flocks of grimy children swooping like birds of ash through the smoke, laughing and coughing, feeding the flames. Women the same color as garbage heaps were scattered around the edge of the trenches, picking containers and food out of the piles and scurrying back to their hovels tucked away in the stinking mounds.

The Eunuchs' Goat led him straight toward the volcanic ditch, which was surrounded by a ring of trash piles. It looked like a conference room. They were met by a group of five men. Their decrepit smell was nothing compared to their skin: ashy, dry, cracked; he could see it peeling and flaking from where he stood. When they got nearer the odor was unbearable. "Finally. There he is." Two of the men grabbed him, pulling his arms back behind him, pushing his head forward, constraining his movements. No matter how hard he tried, he couldn't break free.

"What's going on?" Yusuf shouted at the Eunuchs' Goat. A short man with a thick beard came forward and blocked Yusuf's vision.

"No questions allowed. This is a trial." Yusuf cast his eyes stupidly over the dirt-smeared faces. "So where's the key?" It took him some time to decipher those words in broken Arabic. It became apparent that the Ethiopian man with the unkempt beard was the one in charge. A surprise kick broke one of Yusuf's ribs. When he cried out in pain, the Eunuchs' Goat jumped up to intervene.

"You promised me you would leave that task to me. I'm the one who succeeded in bringing him here and I'm the one who'll rip the answer out of his disgusting body," he said as he pushed the Ethiopian man away from Yusuf.

"Yusuf, give me the key." A caravan of garbage trucks arrived at the dump and deposited their fresh cargo. They attracted flocks of children dressed in tatters who appeared from out of nowhere, from behind every mound and pile, running and diving into the new harvest, collecting the treasures and treats, fighting with starving women and women who looked like they'd just arrived. To Yusuf, the scene appeared a nightmare.

"What key?" he murmured.

"We know it was you who fought the thief in the Haram Mosque. You don't deserve to keep the key or even to live in the vicinity of the Haram."

"What do you mean 'I don't deserve to'?"

"You're unclean," the Ethiopian answered. "You're an idol-worshipping journalist. You want to revive pagan Mecca, not the Mecca of Islam. You direct your prayers toward stone walls." The Eunuchs' Goat got between them.

"Are you going to let me take care of this or should I just go? This man is mine. I'm the one who brought him here."

"You can have him, just shut him up and spare us this little girl's whining," he said turning to Yusuf with a spiteful look. "You know full well who you are. You know who your father was. You infidels are forbidden from living within the vicinity of our Sanctuary."

Yusuf seemed completely taken aback by it all, but the Eunuchs' Goat didn't spare a moment:

"Just give us the key to the Kaaba already. It's the Lord's House, our Holy Mosque."

"Your mosque?" Yusuf's head was pounding.

"We are his servants, earth-renouncing," said the third man who'd been silent the entire time. "You're dirty, boy, and you're defiling the Lord's House. Your hand defiles the key."

"Yusuf, the key . . ." The Eunuchs' Goat repeated himself like a broken record. "If you don't cooperate, my brothers will kill you. If you continue being stubborn, it will be out of my hands."

"You've got brothers now?" Yusuf's question embarrassed the Eunuchs' Goat.

"Give me the key, and I'll drop you off at the nearest highway."

"Believe me, there's no way I could I even get my hands on it. I don't have it."

"You lying infidel!" the Ethiopian shouted. "We read all your articles. How dare you say that God is in our hearts and in every morsel we eat, when everyone knows He is in heaven exalted?" The man seemed totally convinced of the idiotic things he was saying and he strode past the Eunuchs' Goat to deliver a kick to Yusuf's torso. The Eunuchs' Goat answered this by shoving the man back and then the two men squared up, ready to fight. Just then, a cacophony of pots and pans broke out and people began to disappear; they melted back into the piles of garbage and the sky swallowed up the hordes of children. The Eunuchs' Goat grabbed Yusuf and ran off into the volcanic mountains surrounding the garbage dump. He dragged Yusuf's limp body over the trash mounds with superhuman strength. Yusuf was scratched and bruised, numbed by the putrid smell; his body was unreal. The time he'd spent in isolation in al-Lababidi's house had made it more transparent, and the odor that permeated everything was enough to tear his limbs apart. All he wanted was to be left there to die. He pulled at the Eunuchs' Goat's hand to stop him, to ask what was going on, but he was so worn out all he could do was gasp, "Leave me here. I'll find my way." The Eunuchs' Goat just dragged him on further, not breaking his stride.

"You don't even know where you are. You're not in Mecca any more and you're not allowed to go back. This is Jeddah."

"What?"

The Eunuchs' Goat had no choice but to stop. "Yusuf, you know who your ancestors were. Mecca has no choice but to exile people like you."

"Like me?"

"Come on, we both know it. I was with you when you went up to Bull Cave to prove the Yemeni man was your father."

"But I don't understand. Why would who my father was mean that I was evil?"

"I'm not the naive Turkish boy made of marble any more. I'm a soldier in the Mahdi's army and he's commanded that you be killed."

Yusuf began laughing hysterically, but a slap from the Eunuchs' Goat shut him up.

"I just can't believe you've become so violent." Yusuf pleaded, ladylike, with the Eunuchs' Goat's hardened marble exterior.

"You'll never believe how far I'm willing to go to win the coming battle."

"What battle?"

The Eunuchs' Goat dragged him forward and began running again. "The police are raiding the dump. If they catch you here, you'll end up rotting in jail. This isn't a joke, it's a warning. Now move as fast as you can!"

Yusuf ran on, fueled by every last drop of fear inside him. He ran on and on, he didn't know how long for or where to, but by the time the Eunuchs' Goat finally stopped him they were at the top of one of the volcanoes and the police cars that had raided the dump looked about as big as matchboxes below. They were roving all over the place, rounding up the undocumented workers who used the dump as a hideout.

At the top, all around Yusuf, the residents of the dump were celebrating their escape from the raid down below and feasting on half-squashed fruit they'd rolled up in the folds of their clothes. Biting down, nearer and nearer to the rotten bits and then even those. Yusuf thought back on the rotten charity his own body had been raised on. As an orphan, he had attracted all manner of unwanted "gifts" of food and clothes. Only then, did the Eunuchs' Goat turn to answer him.

"So you asked me why I'm here? As you can see, our world is sinking under all your garbage. If we don't put a stop to this, you're going to swallow up the entire world." Yusuf found the emptiness in his eyes chilling.

"Our garbage? Are you serious? Do you even hear yourself? You've got the same name as my childhood friend the Eunuchs' Goat but other than that, everything about you has changed. Who are you?" The Eunuchs' Goat couldn't bear to look at him. They were standing face to face among a hellish-looking crowd. No one there paid any attention to Yusuf; the other leaders had each escaped to the nearest mountaintop.

"I have orders to get rid of you. Your life isn't worth so much as a trash bag if you can't lead us to the key."

"But I don't have it."

"There are some people, some very powerful people coming after you. They hacked into your email to lay this trap for you. You saw the red car. They want you gone. You're fair game, either to me or to them. The only difference is they won't give you a second to breathe."

"And you? Are you going to give me a second?" The Eunuchs' Goat looked unsure. "Are these your brothers now?" Yusuf asked, gesturing at the haggard faces surrounding them.

"This is the army of the Mahdi, which will soon conquer the world."

Yusuf didn't dare argue with his boilerplate answer. From where they were standing, the policemen and police cars down below were nothing more than toys amidst a cloud of shrieking crows.

A loud boom rang through Yusuf's head, a tremor that reminded him of the bulldozers in the Lane of Many Heads. He was vaguely aware of a streak of blood trickling down the Eunuchs' Goat's left cheek and in the moments before he lost consciousness, he understood that they'd been attacked.

Nasser began his morning with the news, which filled him with panic:

> . . . while Jeddah Police spokesman Col. al-Mi'ayd said the force had launched a number of raids on a garbage dump in east Jeddah, arresting dozens of illegal aliens. He noted that routes leading to the site were notoriously treacherous, enabling a small number of criminals, who reacted quickly, to escape, but he offered his assurances that they would soon be apprehended. Meanwhile, the mayor of Jeddah has announced that the municipality is nearing completion of a new garbage dump of four and half million square meters, at a cost of thirty million riyals. The mayor added that the new dump, which was constructed in accordance with the strictest international guidelines for environmental preservation, would be open to receive the city's garbage soon.

A Key for a Drink

YUSUF WOKE UP BESIDE IBRAHIM GATE. HE CAST HIS EYES OVER THE ROWS OF worshippers; his memory was a blank. He had no idea how he'd gotten back to the gates of the Haram Mosque. Had those hours in the garbage dump been a nightmare? His eyes fixed on the tops of the minarets whence flocks of pigeons soared into the sky with every prayer and prostration. He couldn't understand why the most critical moments in his life were always getting mixed up with his dreams and nightmares.

He felt a surge of pain when he tried to stand. His broken rib was testimony to his miraculous survival. "They want you dead." The words echoed inside of him, urging his feet along. Limping, he hurried back to al-Lababidi's house. Every time he passed a trashcan, he had visions of the barricades, hidden trenches, and escape tunnels at the dump. He was certain that every trashcan was a lookout post for the army of the Mahdi who were advancing from the Eunuchs' Goat's camp to launch their apocalyptic war against the one-eyed Antichrist who was being formed in the bowels of the city and its kitchens and was about to be resurrected.

THE EVENTS AT THE GARBAGE DUMP BEGAN TO INFILTRATE YUSUF'S DISTURBED sleep. Night after night he woke up, alone, screaming for help. He carried the Eunuchs' Goat's jaw in his hands and blood poured out of the knife wound that stretched from his temple down beneath his eye to his ear and the veins in his neck. The sticky dark red blood it spurted covered Yusuf's chest. Even when he was wide awake, Yusuf could still feel the stickiness of that blood on his neck and fingers. The blood was thick and it took ages to congeal in the dark chill that enveloped him. He knew for certain that the Eunuchs' Goat had been stabbed at the dump. His many attempts to convince himself that the stabbing was just part of the nightmare failed in the face of the intense terror he'd felt at seeing a face split apart like that. It was like some vein of clarity had burst open, exposing a perfection buried deep inside Yusuf; a perfection that overcame the horror of the Eunuchs' Goat's disappearance.

The nightmare that plagued him only added to Yusuf's discomfort with the outside world and his frailty in the face of it. He gradually lost the face that had guided him in the Sanctuary and he could sense a strange, pearly cloud passing over the rooftops, trying to find a way into the house. The light outside, he was convinced, was enough to strip his face of all its features. Yusuf stopped going up on the roof, for that reason, and instead he spent whole days in one of the reception rooms, barricading himself inside, blocking every vent, hibernating among the photographs on the walls.

His entire being was reshaped during his long seclusion in the upstairs parlor where the distinguished old men of Mecca were gathered. He stayed awake for days, searching desperately through those faces for one that would give definition to his own. The electrical charge in his brain rose steadily and the countdown to an explosion tick-tocked all around him. He was terrified of touching anything in the vicinity lest he burn to a cinder. He appeared more and more inhuman, he was a shadow, or an unexposed film strip, ready to burn up and disappear in the faintest glimmer of sunlight from outside.

On day seven of his dematerialization, Yusuf saw a man come out of photograph number sixty-four on the wall of one of the parlors. A live man taking form in the film strip that was Yusuf's body. Swarthy, with a beard that covered a third of his face, a broad nose, and piercing eyes that were trained on Yusuf, studying his features closely. For a second, Yusuf thought he was staring into a mirror; the man had the exact same features as he did. Perhaps the only difference was that he wore glasses and looked like a religious scholar from a hundred years ago, his white turban wrapped in slightly lopsided spirals that mirrored the downward swirling embroidery on his robe. The broad gold ribbons on the robe, which stretched down to the man's left big toe, glinted in the darkened room, suggesting hidden movement beneath the black robe. In the center of that scene, all attention was drawn to the man's right thumb from which the key ring hung miraculously. Yusuf desperately tried to memorize the outline of the key in his mind, but its gleam blinded him.

He remembered the forgotten caption on the wall beneath the photograph, which was empty now that the man had stepped out: "Abd al-Wahid of the Shayba clan. Custodian of the Kaaba during whose tenure the Great Key was stolen."

Yusuf looked to where the finger was pointing: the next page of this history book of photos, a picture of two Shaybi children, one of whom was dressed in a gold embroidered robe. Yusuf looked back and forth at the faces of the two children and they looked back at him. He shut his eyes and when he opened them again, he saw the boy on the right was winking at him. No matter how many times he blinked, the boy was still winking, nodding toward the door. Yusuf couldn't help himself: he turned around and walked toward the door. In the mirrors on either side of the door, Yusuf could see his reflection lit by the gold embroidery glimmering behind him. He realized that the boy in the embroidered robe had snuck up behind him and was trying to take over his body, so he threw him off and ran out of the room.

At the moment of manifestation, Yusuf forgot to take a look at the other child, the one on the left, but then he saw that it was a girl dressed in a gold embroidered robe, and that she'd pushed the boy forward to take over his body. He didn't stop to hear what she had to say.

He threw the door open, trying to erase what that instant had brought him, and neglected to shut it behind him. He went into the parlor next door and sat there clutching his Quran until he could collect himself. By the time he had gotten used to the dark again, the venerable old men on the walls had stepped out of their frames. They began moving between photographs, going in, coming out, trading places, waving to Yusuf. He could hear people moving around on the other floors and in the rooms next door, slamming doors. He could hear them rustling behind the photos, drawing water at the first sign of dawn to wash themselves in preparation for prayers.

Yusuf fasted for a long time. He subsisted on nothing but a few dates and some handfuls of water from the Well of Zamzam, which Mu'az left on the doorstep for him each day, until he too grew paper-thin and was able to join the old men in their frames and converse with them. For the first time in his life, he wasn't worried that he might go insane. He was finally free of the lifelong nightmare that his mind would one day lose its grip on reality. His eyes narrowed till they were thin slits connecting wakefulness and dreaming. They forgot how to sleep, but they no longer cared about sleeping. No longer did he struggle to win his body some fragmentary rest; all his other physical needs receded as well. He became a bundle of energy unlike any other. He felt the terrifying energy of the house all around him, pulling all the doors wide open, climbing up the stairs to the sitting room on the top floor, which is where he saw the old woman who blew him away the moment he laid eyes on her.

As soon as he opened the door, he felt a pearly cloud preceding him into the room. He recognized the scent but he didn't know from where. The air was oppressive as Yusuf passed through the cloud; he stood in the middle of the parlor, feeling stripped bare, looking around as the cloud passed over the old black-and-white photos. As the cloud passed over the photos, the black fell right off, leaving all the photos to the right of the door a bare white strip.

When the cloud reached photograph number five, the old woman whom Yusuf had come looking for fell out of the frame, materializing directly in front of him. The moment she stepped out, the wall behind him turned the color of green silk. The woman pointed to an inscription written in red above the door. Yusuf read it; it was a verse from the Quran: "God's first House was established for the people at Becca." She turned to the man whom the cloud had pulled out of his frame after her and introduced him to Yusuf. "This is my father, Hulayl al-Khuza'i." Al-Khuza'i came forward, carrying the key to the Kaaba in his hand.

He held it out toward his daughter. "Take this key and keep it safe. Hobba, you are my only heir."

"Father, how I can assume responsibility for the Kaaba when I am already responsible for Qusayy's heart?"

"You would allow Ibn Ghabshan to take custody of it then?"

Yusuf realized he was living through the moment in history that had been driven out of the photo frame.

"No. He's a drunk."

"But he'll sell the key for a jar of wine; your husband Qusayy, who's worthy of it, will buy it. That way the key will pass from master to master."

Hobba turned to Yusuf, wrapping her arms around his neck, running her palm lightly over his jugular, and down to his chest where the key hung. Yusuf could feel the woman clinging to him, begging him to rescue her.

"The heart is the key to everything," she whispered. An electric shock ran from Yusuf's brain down to his heart when she drowned his key in hers, but her father interrupted gruffly:

"And you? What are you waiting for?" Yusuf stammered a reply, but the man didn't pause to listen. "Go, now. Get yourself to the Kurd's bookstore at the head of Ali's Pass at the foot of Abu Qubays. Dig through the mounds of sand and dirt that cover the remains of the old square house underneath. Uncover everything that's inside: the ten windows, the column topped by two arches over the prayer niche, and the hole beneath the prayer niche in which the green marble slab lies, marking the place where our beloved, the Prophet was born. Take out the silver ring. The silver ring marks the birthplace that is the center of all birthplaces. This is your inheritance. Do you understand?"

Just then the cloud completed its revolution around the room, leaving all the photographs behind it a blank white. When it reached Hobba and her father, their color gradually drained, before they vanished into the air. Yusuf heard a crow caw, and when it flew up out of his mind into the room in front of him, he saw that it was no longer coal-black; it was white.

"What are you waiting for?" It chastised him.

"A sign. A message."

"The messages are in everything around you. In your blood, even, and in that key around your neck."

"But my eyesight is getting worse. I'm seeing double. How can I trust my vision when this concentration has clouded it?"

"Just shut your eyes and let the world come to you. Let it translate you. Let it define you. Choose a book and find your sign." Yusuf picked a book at random off the bookshelf: al-Jahiz's *The Book of Living Creatures*. "Now just pick a word."

Yusuf opened the book at random to a long chapter and read the first word he saw: "Crow."

"What connects the crow to Abd al-Mutallib?"

Yusuf flipped through the chapter to read the story of the Prophet's grandfather and the crow. The crow showed him where to dig up the buried Well of Zamzam and bring Mecca to life again."

"And what connects the crow to Cain?"

Yusuf didn't need to read the *Book of Living Creatures* to answer the question, he already knew it: "The crow showed him how to bury Abel."

"And what's the connection with the Kaaba?"

"Dhu l-Suwayqatayn, the bow-legged, blue-eyed, broad-nosed, fat-bellied one who will appear at the end of time and dismantle the Kaaba brick by brick with his comrades and throw its remains into the sea."

Yusuf wondered what could connect all those things: al-Jahiz, the crow, the universe, Mecca, the Kaaba . . .

"Now you understand the secret orbits of a single word and the power of resurrection that lies within it. The key that can unlock the entire universe lies within the most basic word. Don't let locks and borders stop you. Gather your will and go forth."

Yusuf obeyed the command that rose within him and stood up. He followed dutifully as it shone, like the crow before it had shone, from door to door, room to room, to the green marble and the silver ring. He dived down to the bottom of its shine. He washed like all those around him who were preparing to dress in pilgrim's robes. Then he performed his ritual ablutions and unleashed the bright light of purity. In his pilgrim's robes, he looked just like the perfectly white photos on the wall, just like the eternal pilgrims in them. As he stepped out of the Lababidi building, he joined the flood of pilgrims.

It was the seventh day of the month of Dhu l-Hijja, two days before the pilgrims would gather to stand on the Mount of Mercy at Arafat, where Adam and Eve met after they were banished from heaven. As he walked through the Haram Mosque, Yusuf saw that a storm was brewing. Soldiers were driving the masses of pilgrims away from the mosque and panic had turned the faces of everyone in the crowd monstrous.

"We've been cursed! God's house cannot be opened. The Kaaba has shut us out." They'd made this discovery when the Emir of Mecca, and other visiting grandees, had come to wash the inside of the Kaaba and wrap it in white cloth as was always done on the seventh day of the month of Dhu l-Hijja. Soldiers searched for Abd Allah al-Shaybi in the mosque's colonnades so that he could come unlock the Kaaba, but they found neither the forty-something-year-old man nor the key, not in the mosque and not at his house.

It was then that a rumor spread about how a fire had raged through the houses of the Shayba family the year before, wiping them all out. All attempts to open the Kaaba with freshly cast keys failed. Outside the Farewell Gate, the sheikhs who specialized in Quranic recitation were searching for a verse that would drive away the curse, when a blind sheikh spoke up.

"The Kaaba will only open for a Shaybi. All of Mecca knows the story of when cholera struck the Shaybi family and nearly wiped out every last one of them. The only Shaybi left was an infant in diapers and when the Emir of Mecca failed to unlock the Kaaba, he had no choice but to call for the infant, place the key in his little hand, and turn the key in the lock. Only then did the Kaaba open."

"What about now? Aren't there even any infants left?"

Yusuf joined the flow of pilgrims, dissolving into the masses headed for Arafat. All the pilgrims could do was carry on with the rituals they'd come to perform. The sky was dark that day, not because of the clouds upon which the angels perched to hear the pilgrims' prayers, but because of the terror caused by the curse that hung over their heads, threatening to wipe out the very earth from under their feet.

Yusuf flowed with the pilgrims flooding toward Mina, where the devil was trapped in three stone pillars. Each pillar of Satan was surrounded by circular galleries over eight levels, supporting the masses of pilgrims, who were delivered there by futuristic escalators and moving walkways. Three million pilgrims that year throwing seven pebbles before sunset at each of the three devils for three days equaled one hundred and eighty-nine million pebbles thrown at Satan from eight levels of modern engineering. They weren't pebbles raining down on Satan, however, they were little pieces of living flesh, which the pilgrims tore off their bodies and sins to hurl onto Satan's body, which grew larger. Yusuf stood in the middle of all the throwing hands so his flesh would be torn off and hurled down. He felt he'd been washed in that downpour, relieved of his every infirmity. For a moment, Yusuf was one with the devils being bombarded and the sins of the pilgrims and their dreams, one with the holy ground he stood on, with its geography and its history.

By sundown after the third day, Yusuf felt as light as could be, and he was carried by the masses of pilgrims back toward Mecca, arriving at the Holy Mosque by nightfall. He was guided by the minaret at Bab al-Salam, the Gate of Peace, the fourth oldest of the mosque's minarets.

Purity opened Yusuf's body up to a memory that began in the past and ended in the present. His senses were liberated. They could travel unimpeded, summoning that past into the present and moving within both simultaneously. He didn't go through the modern marble entrance, but through the old gate, which had been implanted in his memory by everything he'd read, by al-Lababidi's photos and by the detailed maps and drawings that Mushabbab had put together from the recollections of Mecca's oldest inhabitants. The Gate of Peace consisted of three large arched doors, each five meters tall, divided by two two-meter-wide columns, topped by calligraphic decorations in naskh script, names written inside circular cells: God, Muhammad, Abu Bakr, Umar, Uthman, Ali, Sa'd, Said, Abd al-Rahman ibn Awf, Abu Ubayda, Talha, al-Zubayr, Hasan, and Husayn, may God bless them all. Yusuf decided to go through the small opening inside the doorway that was cut out of the larger door, following in the footsteps of those who came to the mosque back when the doors used to be shut at night. He saw his grandfather, as he saw his father, as he saw himself there and then. He used to sit, every dawn, on the pebbled sections between the pathways of stone and marble, among the study circles of master reciters from Indonesia, Egypt, Syria, and Morocco. He would open the pages of al-Azraqi's history of Mecca and begin to memorize its passages and copy them out.

That morning at dawn, there was someone searching for Yusuf amidst a sea of pilgrims, so he had to hurry through Mecca's history in order to penetrate deeply enough that those pursuing him would be unable to strip him from its pages. The overpowering yearning for a page of al-Azraqi, where he could lie down never to wake up, drove him toward the steps of the Bab al-Salam minaret. There in the throng of pilgrims, the book fell from his hands and was lost. More than once, the book had nearly disappeared among those bodies, which had succumbed to a vague impulse to tear it away from him. The page, which the book had been open to, was torn by the crowd's jostling. He'd read it before—like every page of the three-volume work—a thousand times and it was imprinted on his memory, and yet this most recent re-reading, as it was torn out of his hands, was like the very first. He learned that the historians and jurists used to call The Gate of Peace "the Shayba Clan's Gate," because it faced a door by that name inside the mosque, which had marked its eastern boundary in the Prophet's time.

Yusuf stood there at a loss, searching for the missing piece of the puzzle that would connect the Shayba clan to the key and to the river of the booksellers. He himself was the link between the key and the river; at that moment, in his yearning for things to intersect, Yusuf realized that owing to all that he'd read, all the historical depths he'd plumbed out of love for Mecca, it was his destiny to stand there before the Gate of Peace, which cast the features of the last of the Shaybi key-holders over his seeking face. His passion and the strange resemblance he bore to the custodian was what drove his adversary to hunt him down, to tear him out of the puzzle of the city and create a new puzzle. Despite this realization, Yusuf was overcome with an old sadness; all the holy city's discontent washed over his body. His shoulders hunched and he understood the true meaning of absence.

A woman's soft laughter shook Yusuf from his thoughts of loss. He recognized that delicateness. When he turned to look, he was shocked to find the ancient idols moving around the Gate of Peace. Hubal raised his head from beneath the doorway of the bookstore where he'd lain buried for centuries, and peered into Yusuf's eyes. He knocked the dust of ages and old books off his hideous body as he slowly got to his feet and began chasing after Yusuf. Yusuf was terrified; lightning tore through his brain. He took off running but almost instantly he crashed into two intertwined bodies, a man and woman embracing. Yusuf recognized the tender body of a woman making love, and from the photos in al-Lababidi's house he knew this was Asaf and Nayla, the couple who'd been turned to stone for making love inside the Kaaba. When Yusuf appeared, the woman's pliancy retreated from the man's rigidity. Yusuf knew those light, hurried footsteps from somewhere deep in his memory. He tried desperately to see the present, but the past and the present were mixed into a single stream and that was all he could see at that moment. It no longer made any difference whether women in love had been turned to stone or stone had been turned to women in love. He ran after the woman Nayla. With every stride, he grew more certain that he was chasing after one of the Eunuchs' Goat's stolen mannequins, but a profound longing told him that she was in fact Azza. He moved, as softly as night, toward the courtyard of the mosque, past circles of worshippers keeping vigil, as the imam led prayers for the redemption of the believers and for the key to rain down from the sky and grant them entry to God's house, lifting the curse hanging in the air. The soldiers had erected a cordon around the Kaaba, preventing worshippers from approaching; the mobile staircase stood forlornly by the impassable door in the same place it had been since the Emir of Mecca came to wash the Kaaba and failed. Yusuf imagined the staircase darkening and being transformed into the body of Hubal, with his one severed arm, shoving against the Kaaba with his dreadful body. Behind the rows of worshippers, one of the soldiers was telling his buddy about the first time he'd seen the Kaaba being cleaned.

"They told us we'd be accompanying the Emir of Mecca when he went to wash the Kaaba before the pilgrimage. I was new to the special security detail. I didn't sleep at all the night before because I was so excited that I was going to get to see the holy object being cleaned up close. I soon realized that stones are just like us, though. They take off their clothes and wash in water to get clean and then they put on perfume. Me and the other guys quickly performed our ablutions so we could get down to the cleaning. I'll never forget how the staircase looked, footsteps on incense. By the time the sun rose, the courtyard of the mosque was soaked in the most amazing scented oils: agarwood, sandalwood, and amber, brought by the mosque servants in buckets. I slipped under waterfalls of luxurious perfume and halfway up, I began to stagger out of dizziness. The crowd began its circumambulation, and I was carried around by the perfumes and then into the Kaaba itself. The inside of the Kaaba is as dark as a pupil. It looks straight at the Lord of the House. All I could hear was: 'You are in His house. You've come to wash the threshold.' If someone hadn't pushed me deeper inside to the right of the entrance, I'd have been smashed in my fall to the courtyard below. My body floated on perfumes unlike any other inside that entrance, until the horns of the golden gazelle seized me and pierced my chest, lifting me out of the well without any movement. When the emir ascended, smiling sweetly, the doors opened wide, and we poured out our buckets full of perfumed water. As soon as the emir left, our commanding officer said, 'Now pray!' The order came as a surprise, like when a falconer takes off a falcon's blinders and nudges it toward the sky. I rolled up the sleeves on my uniform and raised my hands up beside my ears to begin my prayers. My hands hung in the air as I turned my head; I didn't know which direction to pray in. For the first time in my life, I didn't know which direction to pray in, now that I was in the heart of the Kaaba itself. My commanding officer saw me hesitate. 'Pray in any direction,' he said. I said 'God is Great' and prayed in the direction I was standing, two cycles of standing, bowing, prostrating, and sitting, and then I turned around and prayed another two cycles in the opposite direction, then two cycles to my right, and another two cycles to my left. I gathered all the directions of prayer into my heart and prayed toward it."

Without disturbing prayers or attracting the guards' attention, the female form snuck up the staircase as quickly and silently as night, luring Yusuf after her. Again he had the horrible feeling that the staircase was actually Hubal's back, but he held his fear at bay and moved forward as the courtyard filled with incense smoke. Yusuf found himself on the staircase as the shocked guards looked on; some power that overpowered his will was leading him upward. It was as though he'd climbed those steps hundreds of times before, as though that ascent was in his genes. When he got to the top, all eyes were on him, from the birds in the sky to the people down below. To the desperate pilgrims below, he looked like the winged horse with a human face that carried the Prophet to heaven, like a black dot moving nearer the door decorated with Quranic verses in gold. The woman disappeared, and Yusuf found himself face to face with the door, profoundly black and profoundly enchanting. As the door drew him forward, the worshippers below noticed black moving against black and lurched forward. For a moment, Yusuf had no idea what he was doing up there. He could've pressed himself against the door and begged God to heal him of his ills. But then the black dot stirred and the key around Yusuf's neck found its way into the keyhole. Instinctively it plunged forward and turned. Yusuf felt the door give, drawing him forward. It wasn't the key that opened that figure of miracles, it was the touch of unmitigated impotence, unmitigated desire. He was completely soaked for a second, completely blinded, while below the evil presence was gathering its strength to transform the staircase into the body of

Hubal, which began to recede from the doorway, tearing the key out of the lock and dragging his body from the Kaaba. Yusuf felt he was being ripped from the Kaaba; he suddenly understood the meaning of death: his entire being was sucked away while specters of universal life bled on the walls of his brain, flashing in the distance and disappearing like lightning bolts. He couldn't get hold of anything, couldn't lean forward to reinsert his stiff body into the sacred keyhole. His body was becoming one long wound and the key was weakening and slackening from the injury.

The crowd below surged and the minarets of the Gate of Peace suddenly sprang to life. Night prayers for mercy rang out from the minaret windows: "Praise be to God, the Most Compassionate. Bless and preserve our Prophet Muhammad, O Most Forgiving and Most Merciful Lord." The voices of aged muezzins filled the sky over Mecca with prayers for mercy and forgiveness.

At the sound of tearing and the key turning in the lock as the Kaaba was about to open, the soldiers ran forward. They didn't care about catching the trespasser, they just wanted to get up close to the door, so they found themselves chasing after the moving staircase as if it were a missile with Yusuf at the top. It moved so gently that Yusuf wasn't aware of any danger or indeed of who was abducting him by pushing the staircase past the rows of worshippers across the courtyard of the mosque toward the colonnades. Yusuf felt he was floating on the sweet tones of the nighttime supplications. Some of the soldiers chased after the staircase while others looked back at the Kaaba to see if it had indeed been opened so that they might steal a glimpse of the inside.

When he moved past the steps of the Gate of Peace, Yusuf felt the nighttime chill against his skin. All around him voices screamed at him to wake up and flee his captors. He became aware of some ancient presence in the air and all of a sudden the famous witnesses of the Gate of Peace from his history books came to life. They used to follow the Chief Judge of the Shafi'i Law School up Mount Abu Qubays to verify the appearance of the crescent moon that marked the beginning of the fast and the two Eid festivals. These men delivered all of Mecca's feasts and they were now stretching their arms out to Yusuf, who grasped them tightly and leaped into the crowd. He had the feeling that the key, the gate, the Shayba family, the river of books, the prayers, and he were nothing but a plot dreamed up in those men's heads—those men who'd dreamed of a being greater than themselves, an all-encompassing being; or rather perhaps it was Mecca that had conjured itself inside their minds.

Yusuf moved within that dream. He knew where to find Mushabbab now. Mushabbab had warned him not to come looking for him until he was ready for the final move. He snuck onto the back of a truck hauling the pilgrims' tents down from Arafat and Mina and squeezed himself in between the rolls of tents. He remained there until they arrived at the al-Labani Tent Company's warehouse on the Jeddah Road. Mushabbab had once told him that some people he knew had given him a temporary job there as a guard. As he stood there in front of the building, he recognized a familiar scent. He didn't even look at the waiting figure who'd peeked out of a small side entrance. He jumped down from the truck and slipped into the warehouse. The guard didn't seem to have noticed him. All around him in the warehouse, heaps of tents lay like weary travelers who'd just arrived after a long journey. Yusuf walked through an ocean of tents as the workers began unloading the still warm, still smelling of pilgrim tents off the trucks.

As night wore on, activity in the warehouse dwindled; that was when Yusuf spotted Mushabbab, sitting in a corner on top of a pile of 125-year-old tent thread, one of the al-Labani family's heirlooms. The family had grown famous in Mecca for their craft. Their ancient grandfather used to sign his name on the tents in black and white: Ahmad Abd Allah al-Labani, and his descendants later added the man's lifetime—"1307–1382 AH"—beneath his signature.

When Yusuf surrendered to the pile, flopping down beside Mushabbab, he forgot all about their rivalry and disagreements. They breathed in the same breath from those flowing beneath them: three quarters of a century of a man's life, and those of countless pilgrims, were stored in those seams. The stacked-up lives of sons and grandsons stretched out before them, starting with Abd al-Rahim (1350–1411 AH), who modified the tradition by sewing the tents with blue and white thread and signing his own name.

He was followed by the Nigerian tentmakers whom Abd al-Rahim had brought over to sew the tents. The journey taken by the tents and thread surrounding them was like the journey taken by the people of Mecca: forced out from the Shamiya district in the heart of Mecca to areas like al-Shisha and Hawd al-Baqr on the outskirts and eventually to the road out of Mecca. Just like Mushabbab and Yusuf as they caught a ride on a truck, this time sitting beside the driver in the cab, headed toward Medina. Mu'az would follow after them with the amulet.

As they drove away, the warehouse grew smaller and smaller until it eventually disappeared from view. The blue and the black and the white all vanished, as did those threads and that history. There was a bulletin in the newspaper the following day: "The heirs of the al-Labani Company announce that they have decided to sell their family's warehouse and have ceased renting tents to pilgrimage agencies. For further inquiries please contact————. Sale filed with Records Office, year 1428 AH."

Not a Patch of Shade Left

THE NEWS, WHICH HAD PASSED YUSUF BY ON THE MORNING HE LEFT MECCA, came below a bold headline on the back page of *Umm al-Qura*, January 1, 2008:

> *Following extensive planning with world-renowned consultants, Elaf International Holdings Real Estate Division has announced plans for the creation of a mixed-use site at Darb al-Nour (formerly known as the Lane of Many Heads) on the Umrah Road, as part of its development strategy for the area. The company has released plans for two towers, one boasting 123,000 sq m of commercial office space and a 30,000 sq m five-star hotel, and the other offering 77sq m luxury apartments. The area between the towers will house a 36,000sq m luxury mall and parking for approximately four thousand vehicles. Developers say the project's proximity to the central commercial and historical district will give strategic value to the project in the form of distinctive design features. The multi-billion riyal project is expected to be completed in 2011. Among the companies contracted to work on the scheme by Elaf International Holdings Real Estate Division are MZ Global Consultancy Ltd., who will be responsible for designing the site, and international consultants GP Ma.*

The detective followed the story on comment forums on the Internet, where supporters and detractors were coming to blows over the dramatic rise in land prices to the north and northwest of the Holy Mosque—from thirty thousand to a hundred thousand riyals per square meter—since the announcement of the decision to expand the mosque complex northward. The expansion would push settlement and amenities northward toward Mount Shahid and al-Tan'im—and who would benefit from this but Elaf Holdings, who owned most of the land in those areas, and who based on this had just released their plans for the five coming years?

Having been so preoccupied with the Lane of Many Heads, Nasser hadn't been aware of the deluge that had swept the Holy Mosque, or the apocalyptic rumor that accompanied it: the Shayba clan were on the brink of extinction. He carried on reading the comments appended to the article:

—The direction of the Holy Mosque's expansion is like a magic finger: wherever it points, a square meter of soil suddenly becomes more valuable than a cubic meter of solid diamond. And it's a lucky fellow who can predict the direction it'll point before the official announcement comes out!

—More than 300 of Mecca's historical sites and monuments have been destroyed so far. It isn't the authorities who are destroying them, but some shady third party. It started right after the end of King Abd al-Aziz's reign, God rest his soul.

—The Arabs used to demolish any building taller than the Kaaba, like Qusayy, for example. They also used to demolish any which imitated the Kaaba with a cuboid shape. But we're like Las Vegas now, huge towers and imitation cubes all over the place.

Suddenly, sitting on his chair in front of the screen that morning, Nasser stopped reading, sucked in by a huge void. He sensed a change in the rhythm of the city; a seventh sense was telling him Yusuf wasn't in Mecca any more, as if Yusuf's departure from the environs of the Haram Mosque right then had sucked the vitality out of the air around him. He felt drawn, as if to a black hole in the universe that centered around Yusuf's movements, drawn to follow. He didn't finish reading the rest of the comments. He got up to leave, not wanting to waste any more time.

The moment he left, another comment popped up about a news item on the planned demolition of houses on Mount Hindi, in preparation for the removal of the entire mountain by early 2011 at the latest.

Tread Softly

Mu'az set off up Mount Hindi carrying the burden he'd been entrusted with. After he'd gotten hold of the amulet, he'd had to wait a while before Mushabbab's instructions reached him. At first he simply attributed the silence to the weight of three million pilgrims slowing Mecca down, and waited for the city to shed its human scurf so Mushabbab would be free to devote time to the task; the doubts in his mind grew, though, when he started hearing the rumors about the extinction of the Shaybas and the story people were repeating about the attempted break-in at the Kaaba.

When Mu'az had woken up that morning, it had been to a silence which called to mind the silence before Israfel blew his trumpet to announce the Day of Resurrection. He'd lain frozen on his mattress on the floor in a corner of the studio, waiting for the trumpet to sound and for those in their graves to be resurrected. When nothing happened after a while, he got up, denied the sense of resurrection that was in the air. He headed for the Holy Mosque, to see for himself what had happened to the Kaaba, dawdling beneath the lofty door while he circumambulated as if he expected it to creak open at any moment, refusing to stay closed and revealing the interior to the circumambulating worshippers. According to the story doing the rounds, there had definitely been an audible click, the sound of a key turning in the lock; the door had submitted to that strange young man who'd slipped past the soldiers and climbed up the stairs. Mu'az wanted to get closer to see if the door was still slightly ajar, but the soldiers had formed a tight cordon around the Kaaba so nobody could get anywhere near it. The vague threat of a curse still hung in the air.

As he made his way up the mountain, Mu'az imagined it was the last shot taken of a Mecca whose Kaaba then closed in its face—a shot burnt up with bleak white. The shots he'd taken during his time as a professional photographer, he thought to himself, could all be summed up in this image of Mount Hindi rising above the city for the last time. He clutched the bag in his hand tighter and continued on up, his mind's eye seeing front doors marked with red *X*s, which meant "unfit for habitation," and houses that didn't even have front doors. A lean dog regarded him wanly from one house, and on another crumbling house a dovecote still stood, doves cooing in every corner. When would the doves leave too? Mu'az felt like he'd been away from that mountain for an age, from that Barbie wrapped in a mangy red rag lying on a doorstep, from that broken water cooler with the leaky pipe sticking out and the seven kittens lapping at the water that pooled underneath it while their mother eyed Mu'az from a distance. The house above it, whose windows were all closed, bore a cornice of immaculately illuminated blue calligraphy, of which Mu'az could make out only two words of a verse by Abu l-Ala al-Ma'arri: "Tread softly." Damp had caused the rest of the words to crumble.

His hand reached out to knock at the door of al-Lababidi's house before his mind caught up with him, but when only silence yawned back at him despite repeated rapping, his heart was clutched in a cold grip. Only then did he notice the words FOR DEMOLITION daubed in red paint across the wall in front of him. The phrase was repeated the length of the facade, stretched out in places: DE—MOLI—TI—ON. The last letter was half cut off by the window of the downstairs sitting room. Mu'az stood staring at the repeated words. The meaning simply couldn't penetrate his skull. He was there but not there—until he felt a hand clamp down on his shoulder.

"At last." The words plopped down with finality, accompanied by a victorious look on Nasser's face, their full weight slumping onto Mu'az's head. When Nasser reached for the bag in Mu'az's hand, Mu'az didn't attempt to resist. Nasser fingered the hard object inside the bag and his mouth went dry. They'd told him there was no case, but right away he'd solved it. They'd accused him of not reaching a satisfactory closure, but he'd found one. He didn't give Mu'az any chance to object, but opened the bag to reveal the amulet right away. Their eyes were instantly drawn to its bright gleam. It was the shape of a half moon, pure silver, and decorated with the breathtaking engravings of the Jewish craftsmen of Yemen. Nasser could sense Mu'az's stiffness and glanced around him, aware of the eye watching him.

"You were bringing it to Yusuf?"

It wasn't a question, so Mu'az didn't bother to confirm or deny. He felt drained of any will to move or speak, but finally managed to mumble, "This is a personal affair."

"Don't play games, Mu'az," warned Nasser. "I know Muflih al-Ghatafani, and he told me. So just tell me where Yusuf is now." It was a plea as much as it was an order. "I know he's somewhere waiting for this amulet."

Mu'az seemed caught off balance. After thinking for a moment, he replied, "We're not doing anything illegal or anything that should concern the police."

"And I'm not speaking as a police officer. I'm a private investigator, and I happen to know what you guys are up to."

Mu'az made a sudden grab for the amulet and said, "If you'll excuse me—"

Nasser was alert and ready for the movement. He kept a firm grip on what was in his hands and looked sharply at Mu'az, who just smiled. "You know I'll find you," said Nasser.

A loud crash interrupted them, and looking up in fright they saw that the wind had slammed open a line of windows above. Mu'az's heart gaped with an arid abjection which turned his black skin an ashy gray. It was the first time a window in that house had opened; his earthly paradise was lost. His keys had gone, leaving him discarded in Mecca like a strip of film burning up under the glare of a torch. His shoulders slumped and he gave in to Nasser's insistent pressing.

"Now that Yusuf's not here it's meant to go to Mushabbab."

There was a silence, and the two men listened to the distant sound of bulldozers chewing up the mountain's insides. Mu'az's eyes were glued to the amulet in Nasser's hands. Speaking over the strangled roar, Mu'az added reluctantly, "At the Mosque of the Prophet in Medina. That's where the circle that holds the secret of the amulet is." At that, Mu'az turned and walked away, light as a mountain goat. Nasser watched him go, winding down the hillside between outcrops and houses.

Nasser was left standing there alone with the amulet, with the mass of mystery that had fallen into his hands. He suddenly got gooseflesh at the thought of opening it, and for the first time in his career—throughout which he'd never known any fear—his heart felt the touch of death's grasping fingers when he imagined what might attack him from out of that amulet. His sense of security was all gone; he sensed an enemy was watching him. Everything around him threatened.

He stuffed the amulet into his breast pocket, folding his arms over it, and walked back to his Infiniti. In front of the car, he stopped for a few moments, not sure where he could go to stop this dreamlike series of events from turning into a nightmare. His eyes were closed; he longed to open them and find himself somewhere else. The city around him was as full as a balloon and wherever he drove, his car was soon surrounded by giant coaches and trucks and monster four-wheel drives and zipping motorcycles that shot in front of him, past him, and back and forth through all three mirrors. When he finally headed for the Jeddah road, he knew he wasn't coming back. He drove as far as the first cafe on the highway, the Mahawi.

The same Pakistani waiter watched him sit down. Time dissolved around him into a dark gray and he couldn't tell whether it was daytime or night, whether he was moving in his own internal time or the external time of the cafe and the city. There no longer existed a boundary within him that could prevent the things around him from melting into that indeterminate clump of gray time and being sucked into the ticking of the clock inside him: the cheap cafe chair was part of his body and the ground was threatening to be sucked in and subsumed into the mixture too.

He pulled up at the side of the highway and fingered the silver amulet in the dark. It came to life under his fingers: a semicircular box, hollow, the lid beautifully worked, smooth. The upper surface responded to his touch and slid back to reveal a dampish interior lined with red velvet and containing some yellowing, sooty-edged paper that had been tightly folded and stuffed inside. Nasser turned on the car's interior light to see the delicate, discolored parchment properly. He took it out, taking care not to tear it, and eased apart the folded, moth-eaten edges as delicately as he could, not wanting to lose a single letter of what was written on them. In the dim light, he recognized the script. His feelings were conflicted.

A bus suddenly honked loudly and gave a squeal of brakes on the other side of the divider that separated the roads going into and out of Mecca. Nasser cursed. It had almost flattened a dented blue GMC, which pulled up suddenly half a kilometer further on. Just ready for someone to leap out and come after him, thought Nasser. He felt like he was being targeted, like he should get going. He suddenly heard the siren of a police car that had appeared out of nowhere on the road behind him, and hurriedly turned the engine on, but a voice over the police car's loudspeaker instructed him, "Infiniti! Stop and park."

His toes twitched over the gas pedal, but the sand around him was hostile wherever he looked. He pushed the parchment back inside the amulet, closed it then stuffed it into the folds of his clothes and pulled himself together.

"Driving license and vehicle registration please, sir."

Nasser could see no option but to comply.

"Detective al-Qahtani? I'm so sorry." His nervous laugh was louder than it needed to be. "I'm from the traffic police department. Can I help you at all?"

Nasser joined in his laugh. "That's okay, thanks. I just stopped to look at some papers."

Her Footsteps

IT WAS AROUND FOUR IN THE MORNING WHEN SHE AWOKE TO FIND THAT EYE PEERing into her face. Like a marionette, she was tied by cords from her fingers and toes to the four corners of the room. A hand was moving back and forth over her body, clothing her in silk and draping her in jewels like a mannequin or an ancient idol. Hands washed her and oiled her limbs with aromatic substances; then she became aware of a dribbling sensation on her feet—grains of wheat? Milk? Every droplet on her nude body stormed through her every cell. She was swinging in the air and there was nothing she could hold onto to cut the strings or escape that unbearable touch. For a moment she left her body to the ransacking; recently her sleep had essentially become that swinging movement where nothing could pin her down, not even death. For the first time, she lost her fear of sleeping alone where death might manage to catch her unawares. Somehow, she'd become invincible.

In one swift move, Nora leapt out of bed, breaking all the strings. In the same movement, she pulled on her jeans and a tight sweater, and then, seeing the spots on the window, a raincoat too. The moment she went out into the sitting room, her assistant jumped up out of her sleep—"Good morning, Ma'am,"—and hurried to call Rafi, who appeared from out of nowhere like a phantom to open the elevator door for her. *Are you watching out for me or just watching me?* She pushed the provocative question to the far corner of her mind so it would fall off the edge.

When she emerged into the reception hall, the receptionist's gaze followed her from one end to the other. They always put the most inexperienced ones on the night shift, either trainees or foreigners, to fill the void of the dark hours. Nora left the hotel followed by her suited-and-booted shadow. She'd decided to take photos of the places she liked going, to grasp hold of the life she'd gotten to know in this city, that had pulled her out of her old loneliness.

In the park to the left of the hotel she stopped and waited. She wanted to sit, unnoticed, on a bench looking out on the street as it slowly woke—just sitting at a bench on the sidewalk was enough to awaken in her the momentum of freedom—but the only two benches were occupied by homeless people in dusty sleeping bags patched up with all kinds of scraps and leftovers, and they were both fast asleep. All you could see were their faces, exposed to the gently drizzling sky. Nora walked along one of the paths into a flock of ring-necked doves, which took to the air and scattered, then descended and settled somewhere else. They danced on the ground, pecking at seeds and pointing their tails into the air like arrows; when the arrows poked into the frame of the picture Nora was just getting ready to take, something she'd read long ago floated back in flashes so she couldn't distinguish between the photo she was taking now and the one in her head:

Ring-necked doves are in the courtyard of the Holy Mosque, too,

They wrap a dark towel around their neck before going off to wash.

Until evening comes

When they put on a smart scarf, to attend a wedding.

We grew up with those dark gray collared doves who fly in circles over the Holy Mosque: they're holy.

We watch their courtship dances as they tussle over females, and their droppings on our heads and on rooftops bring good fortune.

Because when we were little, we were told: these are the doves of the house of God. They live nowhere and serve nobody but the Holy Mosque of Mecca.

So don't hurt them.

But yesterday I saw the same ring-necked doves everywhere in Holly-

wood films. Are the doves migrating and spreading, or is there now a house of God everywhere? In Jonah and Moses' whale, Moses' pleasing yellow cow, Ishmael's ram, David and Jacob's sheep, Joseph's brothers' wolf, Solomon's horses, the monkey and the pigs: they're all animals of the holy books, so what harm would it do if I squeezed us all into these words, and then squeezed all the words into a book, and then brought that book to life?

The streets of Madrid seized on Nora's loneliness, enticing her to respond to those endless alleyways and their unceasing clamor. Like every other morning, she'd rushed straight out into the street before eating anything at all or even washing her face, letting the morning cold peel the sleep from her face. Nora walked faster than she breathed, her footsteps racing the air in her chest, as if the ground was about to be stolen from beneath her feet before her next step.

It was five in the morning when Nora stumbled across the Chocolatería San Ginés in the very heart of Madrid. It was famous for its churros with Spanish hot chocolate.

The young waiter swiftly and gracefully led them to a table in the far corner, all the while eyeing Nora approvingly. With an imperious look, Nora indicated that Rafi should join her at the table, and he had no choice but to comply, seeing that she needed him as a shield. He observed how she was aware of her reflection repeated in the surrounding mirrors as she sat down. The waiter returned with a tray of small appetizers and chocolates wrapped in brightly colored paper, leaving it on the table with a flirtatious wink at Nora.

Nora waited, avoiding looking at her reflection mingled with the reflected crowds. When the waiter reappeared, he spread his palms on the marble table with obvious pleasure and leaned shamelessly toward Nora. "We don't have a menu," he purred, taking a thick card out of his back pocket. "Just this." It showed a photo of their specialty churros con chocolate. "Hot chocolate and fried dough fingers are an inseparable pair. You dip one in the other for a taste of Spanish pleasure unlike anything you'll ever try again. So, heh, want to try? Spanish stallions like me feed this to their lovers for breakfast . . . Heh, so? Don't miss the chance, it's a once-in-a-lifetime experience!" He went on flirting until he managed to get Nora's smile to become a grin.

The chocolate finally came, in a ceramic bowl almost as big as a soup bowl with a row of droplets, like melted chocolate, drawn around the rim. The thick, not-too-sweet liquid sent a delightful charge through Nora's body and burnt her tongue—she insisted on drinking it straight from the bowl, leaving a chocolate smear across her upper lip. Only at the end did she dip the fried fingers into the liquid and crunch on them with enjoyment, as Rafi sipped his coffee in silence.

When she stood up, ready to leave, Rafi stopped to pay the bill. He always paid for everything she needed, small or large. "This is a woman whose bills are paid for her," he thought. "She picks what she wants, and they settle the bill and carry the stuff. Her purchases are lined up in her hotel suite or stacked in her bags, which are always packed ready to leave." She seemed bored of shopping; she rarely stopped to buy anything but ice cream—usually passion fruit flavor. Whenever she had one she was reminded of those words from somewhere in the recesses of her mind:

> *For you, this herbal shampoo, with chamomile, aloe vera and flower of pain*

That was how the import company chose to translate passionflower: flower of pain!

RAFA FOLLOWED NORA'S ATTEMPTS TO PENETRATE THE LIFE AROUND HER, SLIDING through scenes and occurrences, mingling with people and groups who seemed happy and engrossed in their own stories: kids on school daytrips running around, spinning and shrieking all at once, while one skinny child sat alone on a bench at the entrance to the Prado, scribbling trees on a piece of paper. The sight awoke a longing in her fingers for the blankness of paper or walls. Then there was a group of six people—three men and three plump women wrapped in headscarves, popping kisses on the face of a groom in his flowing morning suit while the bride's short improvised veil flapped in the wind like a fountain on top of her head. Inside her own head, two veils and two brides chased Nora and her heart began to pound. She stood alone in the street, watching, while Rafi watched her; cars and motorbikes sped by aimlessly without stopping or glancing back. Nora couldn't stand looking back. She fought off a headache. She wanted to plunge into life and the depth of its currents, but could only manage to float on the surface of the endless waves of that city. She'd lost no time in getting to know the place but she remained bobbing like a cork, trying to catch up, because when she returned to her own city—which had plenty of time, or rather froze its time—she'd find herself on hold, like those houses left as charitable endowments whose name, *awqaf*, suggested they'd been paused—*waqafa*, to halt—until who knows when. Nora chased away the word *desperation* and walked on.

Her story featured lots of departures. Her sheikh had moved her from a zone of heat to a zone of frozen waiting. After each temporary departure of his she would always return to her hotel, to the emptiness, then go out to face the world once more, buy a stack of paper, and sit for hours in the cemetery trying to write (what a strange relationship she had with pen and paper!) and extract something comprehensible from what was happening to her and around her. Rafi felt the stuttering of the words, which suddenly became long lines stretching the length of the page. He thought, if he was meant to be guarding her from her past, then at moments like these he was failing abysmally, moments when she disappeared off his radar with the same calm as that faint smile of hers, which floated over the world, never engaging.

One morning he found out she was left-handed. He allowed himself to go a little closer to her, and from three meters away, he watched her sketch.

"You're really good at that," he marveled. "You draw like you're digging up treasure, or like you're writing in braille. I could close my eyes and follow your lines with my fingers."

She looked back at him impassively.

"You know, there are lots of cultural events in Madrid. If you want, you could start by going to see the big modern art collection in the Reina Sofia."

Nora didn't reply. Her hand moved rapidly back and forth over the paper, inking words that became bodies, speaking into the paper. Her left hand didn't stop chasing the words.

Only when she's agitated does her left hand sweat. She's left-handed: her lines take the shortest route from the heart.

She started creating a girl with open arms and a fluttering braid but short legs planted in the ground.

When the hand turned and twisted, and she wanted a hug, I realized with embarrassment that my darling had started to menstruate.

My darling's foot freed itself from the earth's gravity and entered the gravity of the facing body.

She started coursing with a desire for a body we cannot see.

Somebody left those words in her head, and when they fell silent, Nora realized she was totally alone. She'd spent most of her life pretending to be mute. She hadn't uttered a word for months; was that pretense or really muteness of the heart? In that cemetery of outcasts she was able to stand outside herself and look back in on the forgotten head she carted around with her, on the words stacked carefully and infinitely on the walls of her skull. If she pulled one little word out, the whole stack would collapse. At the base of those shelves she found anger, like shards of glass inserted into the archive of her words. In her relationship with her father, anger had been the only spark that could ignite his attention and make him see her. One day, she'd awoken to find that her little face had lost its ability to make him angry, so she hurried to shove her body out of childhood, and freed her female hormones early one morning, alone, allowing her features to mature, her lips to fill out, and her eyes to shoot sparks. It happened in one night, with a single leap from childhood to the peak of femininity. She hoped he'd wake up to feel the threat of that femininity, resume his anger, and see her.

Without planning to, Nora stepped into a chic hair salon whose smart window featured pictures of androgynous, ultra-modern cuts. She pointed at a close-cropped head in the window and freed her long tresses from their braid. The stylist gave a sharp intake of breath. "No no, Señora—" he protested, and steered her to a mirror, explaining in a flow of Spanish how beautiful that thick cascade of hair was and what a shame it would be to sacrifice it. He stroked the ends of her hair lightly as he spoke, and hovered around her examining her like a precious artifact. She faced him in the mirror with a determined look and pulled her long locks from him.

The negotiations finally came to an end with a long sigh and the stylist took out his scissors. Decisively, like a sculptor bringing to life the image in his head, he cut a line upward from the back of Nora's neck to the top of her head. Nora's hair fell to the floor like a curtain. The cleaning lady hurried to gather it up and laid it on the table like a dead body. Nora had one sentence in her head: "Blocking the way back." She scored it onto the forehead of the woman facing her in the mirror. A stylish French bob that fell over her left cheek to just below her chin and was almost shaved at the back. Dawdling outside the salon, Rafi was struck by her lightness when she emerged.

Rushing happily, almost hysterically, ahead of him, flying on her new bangs, she asked him to take her to the Reina Sofia; Rafi hid his pleasure at her response to the suggestion he'd made. Now and then he stole glances at the radical departure in her silhouette.

The first artwork to greet her when she entered was an installation: two lines of half-columns forming a colonnade like a tunnel, down which a figure in a black habit halfway between a monk's and a clown's was making his way. The artist had captured him in a hurry.

"Look at the eyes," said a young man in English, embracing his girlfriend theatrically. Nora looked. At first glance they reminded her of a pair of eyes she knew well but whose name escaped her. Rafi followed her like a shadow. She submitted to the eyes of the monk, which were looking into another world, at beings other than the beings they knew, and for a moment she lost all sense of who she was and found herself in the place where he was looking.

"This is quite a well-known artist." The voice speaking Arabic pulled her back. When she turned around discreetly, she saw a photographer, holding a camera, with his girlfriend. "He disappears in the Far East for months at a time, staying in forgotten, impoverished villages and up in the mountains, then reappears with eyes that say nothing, but tell hidden truths about us, ordinary people. With just one look into those eyes you see hidden truths inside yourself and in the outside world."

In a desperate attempt to recover what she'd seen, Nora slipped between the columns and began walking down the colonnade toward the monk-clown, to look into his eyes, when one of the museum guards noticed her and intervened politely, "Excuse me, ma'am, no walking inside the installation, please."

She couldn't go on. She rushed through the upper floors like a wind sweeping across those artistic visions, storing them. Her head was empty; she had to build new cultural reference points out of the mountains of knowledge around her, snatching handfuls of context. But the edifice she was building was so frail, and it didn't bear the names of its creators, nor their biographies or dates, like the artwork she was looking at now. She didn't know how to read the name of an artist and place them mentally, or glance at the production date and identify the movement they belonged to. She just looked and absorbed the spirit of the work, decontextualized. After all, she herself was fleeing from her context, and a fragile culture. Before leaving, Nora stopped in the museum bookshop to look; she bought a book called *Vitamin P: New Perspectives in Painting*, which Rafi had hesitated over for quite a while before suggesting it to her. When she flicked through it quickly, she felt even less burdened, faced with that quantity of names and artistic movements. That map of knowledge, and the destruction of that knowledge in comparison with the one torn page that was the sum of her knowledge and which twisted and turned and ruminated like an isolated, veiled alley, busy with its veils, like women whose patience had deserted them. Defensively, Nora conjured in her heart her own vast spiritual map, which bore dates steeped in nobility and antiquity, but she couldn't express it or turn it into a currency valid for any human exchange.

That night, alone in bed, Nora heard a faint sound, the sound of a shutter quickly opening and closing, coming from the edge of the pillow. When she looked round in her dream, she couldn't see anyone, but there were light footsteps heading for her, the light footsteps of a threatening wind, so she began to run. The footsteps were chasing her. The world looked like theater curtains and paper backdrops showing scenes she knew, but she didn't slow down to look at them or examine their details. Her body was pushing onward at high speed, bursting through the backdrops and leaving them torn behind her. Whenever she wanted to clutch at something in the furnishings or images, the footsteps chasing her sped up, her panic flared, and her lungs threatened to explode. She stopped to take a breath and glanced behind her, glimpsing the owner of the footsteps—a thin young man whose dark complexion contrasted with the bright white of his sneakers and his radiant smile. He didn't say anything to her; she only had time to glimpse him before the scene froze and the backdrops suddenly lost their relevance, Nora falling in among them like an apparition. The young man came closer and squatted at her feet, pointing his camera and smile right at her. He snapped a shot then ran away again. He seemed to her to be crossing the earth by foot to return to his own remote country.

She awoke in the morning with an emptiness in her chest where the photographer boy had taken his shot.

Between Two Mosques

NASSER COULDN'T REMEMBER WHEN IT WAS HE'D LAST SLEPT. HE HALLUCINATED, eyes wide open, as he drove. He could hear a voice mocking him: "You're addicted to medals, aren't you?" He was driving through Bahra when toilet paper overwhelmed him suddenly. He was remembering the most important advancement in his career, which had been thanks to Bahra, this village on the old Mecca–Jeddah road. His investigation had grown out a rumor that was going around about an illegal recycling plant run by a gang of infidels, who were turning old school books and newspapers into toilet paper that was carcinogenic.

"You're lying on my blood," Aisha's voice breathed directly into his chest. He woke, terrified, and found himself driving through the martyrs of the Battle of Badr. "I lay here waiting for an ambulance. I felt no pain. I looked at the bones protruding from my broken pelvis through torn flesh; it appeared and sat beside me for hours while I waited. There's a delicate body that emerges from our bodies to save us if we experience a trauma: it gathers our broken limbs and sits with them, far from all pain—it chooses a spot as far as possible from the pain for us to sit together. It sat with me all through the night, and together we looked upon the spot where pain lay waiting, until we heard the ambulance sirens approaching and it handed me over to a paramedic, who plunged a needle into my artery. It was then the pain shot through me, but only for a moment, and then I lost consciousness. In that moment, I heard my pelvic bone smash. I could no longer differentiate between our two injuries."

"Was it you who died?" His feet stamped on the gas, thrusting body and dream forward to catch up with her answer, but he'd woken himself up, and all that remained was the trace of an answer: "Death isn't difficult. It's life that's so unwieldy."

The road stretched black before him. He fingered the amulet resting against his chest, and resisted the urge to take it out. He'd have to postpone reading the papers inside till he reached somewhere safe. He clutched at Yusuf's Window:

> *When Mecca's dreams thicken in the world, they flee to Medina. The historian al-Azraqi, who catalogued the marvelous qualities of Medina, noted the strange fact that wolves in pursuit of gazelles would stop in their tracks if the gazelles crossed into the city limits!*

After Bahra, the road stretching ahead to Medina was empty but for a smattering of cars, all going way over the speed limit despite the camels roaming freely in the dunes on either side of the road; Azrael urged drivers to hurtle through the thin wire fence on the median, smash into the cars going the other way, and wrench out the souls of their passengers.

He had no idea how he made it to Medina or where he parked his car. He found himself in front of the Mosque of the Prophet, loitering near the main entrance, where he had a good view of everyone going in and out, and he scanned their faces for either Yusuf or Mushabbab. He remembered that he didn't know either of them, but so long as he had the amulet they would find him. He was certain of that. Or perhaps they'd been in touch with Mu'az. His knees trembled as he made his way forward. The night prayer was underway, and worshippers were kneeling for the closing tashahhud. He waited until the moment of absolute silence that followed their final greeting before entering the mosque compound through the Gate of Gabriel, walking past the bench where the eunuchs who'd devoted themselves to serving the mosque sat. He leaned against the Column of Repentance and fell asleep; he was exhausted. As he dozed, he could hear one of the eunuchs explaining something to an Egyptian pilgrim:

"—the Column of Repentance. When Abu Lubaba tied himself to this column to atone for giving away the Prophet's plan to attack the tribe of Qurayza, he nearly lost both his sight and hearing. His daughter would only untie him when he needed to pray or relieve himself, and when he was done she'd tie him back up again. He swore his bonds should remain fast until they were untied by the Apostle of God himself. And that's what happened, after forgiveness was granted by a verse of the Holy Quran. The Prophet used to receive at the same spot the weak and the wretched and those who had no home but the mosque, and he would speak with them and comfort them."

Nasser wasn't sure if it was the eunuch's voice he was hearing, or a message directed solely at him. He opened his eyes and looked at the white lines that divided the women from the men, they were like the calcareous lines that ran from his heart to the hearts of those seeking the Rawdah, the section of Paradise that lay between the Prophet's pulpit and his grave. He didn't dare go over to the grave, but from where he sat he offered up a small prayer: *God, even though I've resorted to evil so that I might reach You, by standing here in Your Rawdah I return to You all power to choose, and from this moment I am guided by nothing but You.*

Emptied of choice, he slumped back against the Column of Repentance, feeling light and translucent, as if he were fusing to the gossamer ground beneath him that held the bodies of the Prophet's companions. He began to see the foot of Omar, may God be pleased with him, taking shape in the dust before him—just as it had once come out of the ground long ago, and had had to be reburied—and he realized that the dead were buried not in the ground but in the hereafter, which was all around him, and that he could look at them and marvel at how their bodies resisted decay even in torment. He felt that he was a part of the luminous existence that stretched into future centuries and emanated from distant eras, from the original hijra to the end of all things, its path to resurrection. He eased the parchment from its amulet with a feverish hand and began to read:

> LAST WILL AND TESTAMENT OF SARAH to her son Marid, sheikh of the tribes of Sabkha, written in the year six hundred and twenty-six AD.
>
> It had been two days since we left Khaybar, and we had spent them in silence, smelling like desert wolves. I was wrapped in an abaya of coarse camel-hair that hid my femininity and protected my body with a moist layer of sweat. The burning sun was tyrannical as we headed north up Wadi Himd to avoid the routes the caravans took, but our hearts remained among the cool waters and palms that gave Khaybar the nickname "Garden of the Hijaz." The taste of your father is still in my mouth. When he let me leave, he said, "The whole Land of Canaan awaits the child in your womb, while Khaybar is destined to fall and we, Abraham's chosen descendants, are fated to be destitute, because of the rebellion in Moses's tale,

to change and blend different nations and religions endlessly before we finally reach our eternal home." That man, who so longed to be your father, placed on my shoulders a very momentous responsibility: the fate of the Jews and their return to Canaan, as promised them in the Arabian Peninsula.

I was thus entrusted with taking you to a mighty tribe where no one could uproot you so that you could continue the miracle of transformation. And so I had to continue onward, never looking back, shedding with every step my identity, my religion, my father Ka'b, my husband al-Nidr, and my family, and exchanging the sweet waters of Yathrib for the bitterness of the wells we stopped at along the way, crossing the eternal sands, toward the oases of Najd and Wadi Bani Hanifa and the tribe known as the Suns, in the hope that they would accept me into their invincible protection and their fate, which had been divined by our seers: it had been ordained that at the end of time, they would inherit the Peninsula and ride the steeds of history and take up the reins of many nations, for wherever their hooves touched the ground, gold sprang forth, kindling fires in lands that the sun could not reach. At a certain point in the journey, I looked ahead of me and saw a blur of darkness: black horses covered the horizon of those wastelands your mother crossed so that she could place you at the mane of the lead horse.

Nasser realized the significance of that ancient parchment he was holding. He wasn't meant to open it and read it, but he refused to be a donkey, carrying a load of books he couldn't read. From now on, he'd have to watch where he stepped, and with whom. These exaggeratedly crumbling and moth-eaten, tangled and untangled letters: it was no longer clear whether he was reading what he read from the parchment or from breaths imprisoned in his chest or from white birds concealed in the sky above the mosque, which had flown out of a fire raging in the past to intercept a bolt of lightning before it struck the Prophet's resting place. The flavor of the words and the old parchment forced him to keep reading; he was curious to know where the will would break off. The anonymous author had given all the faces around him the aspect of the divineress Turayfa, who had predicted the collapse of the Ma'rib dam and led the nations of Arabs to spread outward in waves: one wave to birth and spilt blood in Mesopotamia, another to papyrus and writing in the valley of the Nile, another to stone and building with the angels in Mecca, another to prosperity and palm trees in Yathrib, and another to passion and poetry in the Fertile Crescent.

Ishmael

IT WAS PAST MIDNIGHT. SCREAMS OF TERROR AND DESTRUCTION ISSUED FROM THE roof of the Arab League, where bloody scenes filled the TV screen and poured out over the neighboring rooftops. The dawn prayer would soon burst through the endless fog of violence that *Jaws*, which was nearing the end, had brought. Mu'az shuddered at the thought of the dawn angels descending for prayer and seeing all that violence, but as soon as the shark had been exterminated and the TV faded to black, he got up to put on another video all the same.

Khalil sat facing his silhouette reflected in the black screen. His hair—thin, receding, and increasingly wispy—was pitiable, but it had valiantly resisted every dose of chemotherapy. He raised his hand in a salute of bulging green veins and perspiration to the band of brave soldiers who appeared as the opening scene of *Mission Impossible 2* wiped his face from the screen.

Once again the sound of gunfire filled the air and dead bodies were strewn everywhere for the dawn angels to wade through. This was the tenth movie Mu'az and Khalil had watched in the last fifteen hours. Mu'az was sitting at the top of the stairs, resting against the bare mud wall, which had been warmed by the sandstorm wind. He looked at Khalil's profile: it was growing longer and thinner, like the nose of an airplane waiting until air resistance was at its lowest to take off. Khalil was sitting in his permanent spot on a sponge mattress on the bare floor of the roof, facing the TV. It had been two weeks since his last chemo session; the doctors had halted his treatment and sent him home to die.

"We can't ignore this low white blood cell count any more. His body can't take the treatment; it's doing him more harm than good . . ." That was their way of saying nothing was working. "The shortness of breath you're experiencing isn't just a side effect of the chemotherapy," they explained. "The cancer has spread to your lungs and is now moving toward your heart, which, as you know, is already in critical condition." Theirs was less a diagnosis than the description of a battle in which the massed ranks of cancer advanced on his heart and no counterattack was in the offing.

"How can you send someone away to die alone?" The thought weighed on Mu'az. What recitation could keep him company in his loneliness? He wanted Khalil to recite the Surah of Sovereignty but he didn't dare suggest it, so he got into the habit of sitting a short distance away and reciting under his breath and blowing the words toward Khalil while he was engrossed in cinematic bloodshed. The flames of the Surah of Sovereignty battled with the explosions and amplified Hollywood sound effects; Mu'az stumbled sometimes but he continued reciting. Khalil looked over at him and noticed his twitching lips.

"It's no big deal," he tried to reassure him. "It's just like bringing a child into the world . . . Its very first breath is the beginning of a countdown that always ends in death."

The cancer had filled the void left by the loss of al-Lababidi's house, which had removed him from the scene. Mu'az and Khalil had formed a front so tight that the cancer could have probably continued its spread from Khalil's liver straight over to Mu'az's. With the determination of the early mujahideen, Mu'az neglected his photography so he could devote all his time to fighting the war. When Khalil decided he was too tired to visit the hospital three times a week—once for chemotherapy and twice for serum—Mu'az learned how to administer the subcutaneous injections so he could do them himself.

When the pain got too much for Khalil, he would lie stiffly on the mattress staring at unending scenes of compulsive violence on TV. The Surah of Sovereignty would sink, with heavy sadness, into Mu'az's heart, as he muttered it, sneaking looks at Khalil who was growing thinner by the second. He couldn't keep a morsel of food down, and the poison of the chemotherapy, which had sapped the strength from his muscles and joints, left his movements sluggish and clumsy. He'd begun to appreciate science fiction more, though, and he watched the action movie that was playing out on the screen of his body with pleasure, wearing a smile of happiness and nausea.

"Imagine if Ramziya were here now." He always came back to Ramziya and her faith. During their one short week of marriage, she hadn't given up. She'd spread herself all over him as though she were a miracle fertilizer that could revive his dead sperm to create a child. Maybe that was what scared him: she had challenged his love of self-destruction, which he'd begun cultivating with his first death, when at the age of twenty he encountered those science fiction liquids—5FU, MVAC, CMV—for the first time. They were like strange weapons out of Star Wars that the doctors dripped, infused, and pumped into his blood, where they remained for hours, days, months, transmuting him and exterminating his sperm . . . He was nearly fifty now and the invading creatures had lost interest and flown away in their spaceships; there was nothing left in him worth destroying.

"What does a person do when modern science gives up on them?!" The question he posed to Mu'az tugged at his own heart as well. This "modern science" they talked about was like a present-day god who'd turned his back on Khalil and denied him his miracles. The storyline chattered away incessantly inside his head: "They said go and die. But Ramziya's faith said, 'Be patient and you shall see those same doctors drop dead before the cancer ever reaches your heart.' You're a cancer old-timer now, I might add . . . Death can't stand to live inside you!"

Mu'az stuck to Khalil's conviction that he'd make it through, picking out the Quran's miracle verses to strengthen his hope that a miracle would land on the roof of the Arab League to rescue Khalil. The imam's son clung for dear life to Khalil, the last of the heroes of his lost paradise: he snuck up to the roof of the Arab League every day to sit there with one eye following the movie and the other watching Khalil's breaths for fear they might suddenly stop while he wasn't paying attention. The cancer might penetrate Khalil's ribs and leave him rotting up there in the heat . . . Khalil put up with Mu'az because he brought with him his flashlight smile, his cunning way of looking at life, his faith that images were a worthy substitute for reality. The two shared that sinful faith in the image as a path to resurrection.

Sometimes Khalil was silent for hours, each second an age during which he directed all his senses to the pain, following the cancer's rapid progress and the decisive moment when it penetrated an organ. It passed from kidney to liver and liver to stomach, and then it broke through his diaphragm decisively. He felt his fragile lungs quaking as it advanced, felt the suppurations at the base of his trachea anticipating the final surrender of his heart at any moment. It was times like that that Khalil would go blind and deaf and lose his ability to concentrate; a feverish pallor would come over his skin, as if all of the supply train of life had been cut off. At times like that, nothing could get through to him except jokes about Ramziya and violent action movies. Mu'az realized that the violence answered some deep need in Khalil, so he began feeding him those movies to keep him going. He came by in the morning to pick up two hundred riyals and returned in the evening with a dozen videotapes at fifteen riyals each, old and brand-new releases alike: *X-Men: The Last Stand*, *The Bourne Ultimatum*, *300*, *Spider-Man 3*, *Pirates of the Caribbean: At World's End* and *Dead Man's Chest*, *Transformers*, *Miami Vice*, *Poseidon*, *BloodRayne*, *Underworld: Evolution*, *Second in Command*, *The Guardian*, *Road House 2*, *Living & Dying*, *Cut Off*, *Snakes on a Plane*, *The Detonator*, *The Fast and the Furious: Tokyo Drift*, *Hellboy: Sword of Storms*, *Fearless*, *Bon Cop, Bad Cop*, *Undisputed 2*, *Connors' War*, *Machine*, *Lord of the Rings*, *Ocean's 11*, *12*, and *13*, *The Matrix 1* and *2* . . . After a while the titles and actors became irrelevant, sunset and darkness followed sunrise and still Khalil's eyes were glued to the 45-inch plasma screen. He scarcely noticed when one movie ended and another began: the main thing was to keep the scenes of war coming, to stab the enemy inside him with every heroic move or brave martyrdom performed by a character in his stead. The movies grew into one endless reel, starring Khalil's own cells.

And so the son of Qarara Hill sat with the son of the Ethiopian imam devouring movies like potato chips salted with the verses Mu'az never stopped reciting. Together they kept Khalil's life going from one fight scene to the next, as the realities of life and death became a mere game on a TV screen. Mu'az was watching Khalil die and he was certain that his solitary fight against the disease was more heroic than anything Hollywood could ever produce. He was filled with a deep respect for the loneliness of that fighter. It did occasionally occur to him that he was spending his evenings with a dead man and he would be haunted by his father's terrifying words: "We will be resurrected doing what we died doing . . . In the grave, we'll relive the last moments of our lives, over and over until Judgment Day." Would Khalil lie in his grave and be resurrected like this, watching American cinema? Was that fate worse than being resurrected driving his taxi through traffic in a sandstorm?

He was surprised, then, when on his way to deliver the call to prayer early one morning, he heard no sound at all coming from Khalil's roof. He raced to the Arab League building and took the stairs three at a time, blinded by a single thought: Khalil had died behind his back. He reached the roof, panting, and was met, to his amazement, by an emaciated apparition kneeling naked against the sky, shoulder bones poking out as he pressed his shining forehead against the ground. Tears welled up in Mu'az's eyes: was this Khalil praying for the first time? He didn't stay to find out, but turned and hurried back downstairs, hoping with all his heart that Azrael would descend at that very moment to snatch Khalil's soul as he was prostrate and record that he was praying, regardless of what for. With that fervent supplication, Mu'az intoned, "Come to prayer . . ."

In the early stages of his disease, Khalil continued to drive his taxi, except on Wednesdays when he went in for chemotherapy. He'd leave the taxi miles from the Lane of Many Heads and make his own way back to the Arab League, where he lay sweating and vomiting, turning a metallic blue. The next day, he'd wake up with a supernatural determination to get back in his taxi again, sometimes even driving past customers without stopping just to piss them off.

Khalil had taken up driving his taxi again during the past two weeks following a break after the doctors issued his death sentence. A chiseled-out skeleton swimming in a huge robe, maybe there was nothing left of him for the cancer to eat. What was certain was that Khalil had decided to go out to face the cancer. With sallow skin pulled taut over his bones, and reeking of garlic, he looked at the city with new eyes: the eyes of a dead man.

Every morning, Khalil hesitated at the junction between al-Hujoun—left—and al-Zahir—right—but his hands would instinctively turn the steering wheel and he'd show up on time to his appointment with the stranger who had been appearing every day for the last ten days in front of the Martyrs' Cemetery, always in the same white robes and gray waistcoat.

The night before, the same smell of coffee had risen from the wounds that the Turkish woman had left on his impotent body. He'd hidden his illness from her—though she herself was more monstrous than cancer—but of course his frailty gave him away. Nothing satisfied her any more but a bite of his liver. He gasped in the silence of the taxi when his passenger's eyes alighted on the bite-mark on his right forearm.

"She satisfied her hunger on you but now she's sick of you, like everyone around you." This man had been tyrannizing Khalil for days, asking again and again to be taken to addresses that they would then find had vanished from the map of Mecca. That day he'd gotten into the taxi without giving an address, leaving Khalil to drive in confusion; instead, he kept repeating, "This is a nightmare, Khalil. You're dreaming. You'll wake up soon. At the next bend in the road, or the next red light. You'll wake up and this hallucination will go away, so will the dead body with the yellow beard in the seat behind you . . ."

Khalil tried to relax at the wheel and force his thoughts to submit to what was happening in his car, knowing intuitively that he'd soon wake up to a screech of brakes. That nightmarish situation called to mind the bad dreams that had plagued him since the body had appeared in the Lane of Many Heads along with Detective Nasser. Nasser often came to Khalil in his dreams and subjected him to the usual mockery and the same repeated question: "Did you ever eat a chicken breast, Khalil? Because people who eat chicken breast can't keep secrets. Anything they're told is soon blowing in the wind. So what is it you've been spreading about the Lane of Many Heads and Mecca, huh?" He'd interrogate him with a torture instrument that resembled the hands of a watch, letting it loose on his heart and leaving it to tick round, tearing the edges. Every time, he'd wake up choking on his own sweat in the Turkish seamstress's bed, to the sight of her eyebrows arched in such annoyance that the previous night they'd jumped right off her forehead. *One floating eyebrow told him that she'd lost her animality and that her magic had been discovered, and her features began to crumble; she turned into a gray-haired heap decaying in a grave of fat before his very eyes, and he knew that he'd have to pay the price for having stripped her naked.*

"And the seal-dies, who did you give them to?" The word *seal-dies* punctured his front wheels like a nail and the car swerved violently, while a voice in his head warned him, "Whatever happens, don't brake. The car will skid off the bridge." As coolly as the most sophisticated airplane autopilot, Khalil stiffened his grip on the wheel and forced the metal structure around him back onto a straight path. All that remained was for his passenger to choose where he wanted to go.

"Stop anywhere and sniff. You know most of the ground in Mecca is graves, right? The ground where the pilgrims walk around the Kaaba—between the Hijr of Ibrahim, Abraham's footprints, and the Well of Zamzam, ninety-nine prophets who came to Mecca on pilgrimage were buried there, and Ishmael's virgin daughters—and the peaks of Mount Khunduma, where another seventy prophets were buried. Don't ever think you can get rid of a grave. The ground is stuffed full of death—take a handful of earth from al-Shubbayka or The Martyrs and sniff it. That's the smell of your ancestors. Death is a destination in Mecca; the ground and the sky never forget a dead body. Sniff your own corpse and you'll smell your ancestor Uqayl ibn Ateeq al-Hadrami. He stole the seal-dies, and you took them as your inheritance to do whatever you felt like with them."

He tried to claim innocence in vain. This time, the wheel didn't wobble at the sound of the name; the ancestor, Uqayl ibn Ateeq al-Hadrami, was sitting in the car with them, naked and buried under the pile of rocks that had been thrown at his corpse, one hand still holding the dagger that had pierced his heart. In the speeding taxi, Khalil was stripped of the nickname "the Pilot" that the Lane of Many Heads had given him, and regained his family name, al-Hadrami.

"Both of you committed suicide—he with the dagger he was given as a present, and you with the gift of the seal-dies." Khalil was frozen like stone, passively taking in this ransacking of the grave of his ancestor Ibn Ateeq al-Hadrami, the minister who'd ruled Mecca tyrannically in the final years of the first hijri millennium.

"They were inside that pillow you always keep in the trunk of this car of yours. They were the only thing you took from your inheritance and your sister. You didn't rush into the fire to save your mother—you just grabbed the pillow that held the bundle of dies and got out of there." Khalil saw he'd fallen into the trap his uncle Ismail had laid for him from beyond the grave. He'd been looking for Ismail's musical instruments and songbooks when he stumbled across the seal-dies, which were hidden inside a large brass incense burner: six dies bearing a line drawing of a gold-plated key. The moment he set eyes on them, waiting silently in the enormous incense burner ready to be lit, some sixth sense warned him that they were dangerous, that they were a piece of Mecca's very heart, and that he was the reason they'd lain there all those centuries since the end of the first hijri millennium, waiting. He was so impatient to possess them he didn't want to check their date or owner, but picked them up in humble silence and stuffed them into the pillow he took with him everywhere—to Qarara Hill and Florida and back to the Lane of Many Heads, where they were saved from the fire that took his mother—until they finally disappeared inside the stuffing of the Turkish woman.

"Your ancestor al-Hadrami, who served as the minister of the Sharif Hasan ibn Abi Nama, was highly adept at forging identities. He could impersonate a dead judge by using the man's personal seal, and get him to sign any deed he wanted from beyond the grave, or proofs of debt owed by deceased people, so as to rob people of their inheritance. In your ancestor's hands, dates became mere masks that he placed on papers to lend them historicity and respectability, or to deny events that had happened or loans that had been taken out; he had the power to fast-forward and rewind dates at will. Those six dies, or whoever possessed them, owned Mecca's heart."

Just the previous day, when the Turkish woman's disguise had fallen in front of his eyes, taking his good fortune with it, and he realized that his downfall had already happened, and at her hands, he took refuge in that pillow, burying his face into its soft stuffing looking for the reassuring weight of the dies whose ink never dried up. The pillow's unfamiliar lightness woke him from his nightmare; in a frenzy he tore through the pillow's insides, ferreting through the damp cotton but finding only a terrifying nothing. He began to punch the fat form lying around him and on top of him; the seals' disappearance had unmasked her and revealed the animal within. The battle that raged between him and the Turkish seamstress wasn't a fair fight by any means; still, he left her with a broken arm hanging limply, though she didn't even whimper, and she left him with bite-marks showing the imprint of every one of her teeth all over his body, stripping him like a tortoise ripped out of its shell.

"When Abu Talib came to power, Ibn Ateeq al-Hadrami was thrown in prison and there he began to scratch his memoirs onto the walls, confessing details of all the inheritances he'd misappropriated, all the witnesses he'd forced to sign his forgeries, and all the dates that he'd faked, explaining at length the secrets behind his power to manipulate time. He also recounted the stories of the old deeds he possessed, how he'd given them the authentic flavor of age and made denying them as impossible as denying the existence of Ibn Khaldun's *Introduction to History* or al-Tabari's *History of Prophets and Kings*. Your ancestor al-Hadrami didn't close his eyes once during the weeks he spent chiseling his biography on those walls, as though purging his insides of sin onto the walls of Mecca. He told the story of his involvement with Khidr Effendi in full, scratching the details with such fervor that Khidr rose up out of the grave where he was buried in exile outside Mecca to join al-Hadrami on the walls of his prison cell. Together they remembered the certificate Khidr had refused to forge and the vitriol that al-Hadrami had poured on him, the houses that al-Hadrami had expropriated and the furniture he'd auctioned off before the last of Khidr Effendi's footsteps, disappearing into exile, had even faded from Mecca. Khidr Effendi mocked al-Hadrami's attempts at suicide, pronouncing that 'suicide means you never wore the right mask to fool the Sharif into doing what you want. The right mask is more effective than all the judges' seals; a seal imprinted on the eye of a prince is like the lost seal of Solomon himself!' On one line on the wall, Khidr Effendi wrote, 'Do not hurry, for it will come to you: the demand of a wronged person cannot be resisted.'

"Together, they watched his end. The Sharif, Abu Talib, sent a dagger to al-Hadrami as a gift, together with a letter that read, 'If you want to kill yourself, here is my dagger: take it and send your soul to hell!' Khidr Effendi helped al-Hadrami engrave a copy of the letter onto the wall, and when al-Hadrami picked up the dagger, Khidr promised him he would record his death in all its detail, as befitted a legend; when al-Hadrami stabbed himself, Khidr made a note of the spot where the dagger had entered—just below the fourth rib and straight into the heart—and described how it remained there, stopping the blood from spilling out, and when they carried him away, Khidr Effendi walked with them like a devoted servant and composed a description of the mangy donkey and the cart that bore his corpse, the water nobody bothered to wash the body with, the prayer that wasn't said over his soul, the patch of earth in Umm al-Doud, the neighborhood of worms, where they tossed his body, the crowds of commoners who gathered to bid him farewell with a hail of stones, the angle of the sun over the heap of rubble they piled on top of him, the halitosis of the curses that steamed around him like a cortege for his soul.

"When the cursing crowds had finally dissipated, Khidr Effendi remained there devotedly, unperturbed by the frenzied crows that circled over the burial mound. He sat patiently among the cawing and the smells of decay to record the sessions of the angels of torment who, over long ages, counted every seal he'd faked and every one of the hundreds of orphans he'd cast into destitution. All the land he'd expropriated was weighed as sins on their scales of justice, not discounting a single handful of the dust he'd arrogated to himself. The scales groaned under the weight—not of earth and masonry, but of the tears and suffering of those whom he'd wronged. It seemed as if it would all be too much for Khidr Effendi's handwritten historical record to bear. Khidr Effendi remained there, faithfully documenting the fate of his persecutor al-Hadrami, until his hair, even his eyelashes, had turned white. With his final trembles, he recorded the cries of anguish that issued incessantly from the heap of rubble: they always got louder and more intense toward the last portion of night, when God descended to the sky of this world. He never cast a single glance of mercy toward that mound and al-Hadrami, the buried wretch, could never find the words with which to beseech Him. The knot in al-Hadrami's tongue was the last thing Khidr recorded in his history, before the burial mound was swallowed up by Mecca's dust. The angels dug channels so his story could seep into the city's groundwater and never be forgotten."

The silence and air of mystery that Khalil had come to expect from that passenger had been exploded with that story. All the darkness in Khalil's features appeared to him for the first time that morning, and he saw himself in the rear mirror: when he glanced at the passenger in the reflection, he saw in the man's eyes his own face. He was an identical copy of al-Hadrami, his ancestor. The passenger wasn't relating a history, he was teaching Khalil to read the engravings on the wall of his own head and discover that he, Khalil, was the ancestor just risen from the grave beneath his ignominious burial mound, and that he was coursing with the will of that corpse.

In the rear mirror, the entire page of Khalil's life was out clearly for him to read:

Night after night, Khalil had hemorrhaged everything into that cursed woman's ears: everything he knew about the Lane of Many Heads, his mother and father, Mecca, its weak points, neighborhoods where the people were so worn down by poverty they could easily be cleared and the land taken from them, endowed properties whose heirs had died . . . He'd poured all that information into the ears of the Turkish woman and who knows who she'd sold it to? He'd left the seals there in her possession all that time, allowing most of Mecca's old houses and endowed properties to be stolen from their unsuspecting heirs.

Khalil had lost his magic touch and his ability to keep time with the pain at around three one morning, when the Turkish woman had finally thrown him out into the alley.

"Don't try to come back." With those words her eunuch pushed him out the door, brandishing a pair of blunt dressmaking scissors and leaving a swerving line of cold metal on Khalil's temple. He then tossed all his belongings out after him: heap after heap of smashed video tapes . . .

When Khalil regained consciousness, he didn't move but stayed where he was, prostrate in the dust of the Lane of Many Heads, watching everything from the superman-like perch his cancer had elevated him to. He was always a degree above the alley, looking down on its simple people from above, the only hero on the scene, with deeds to all those endowed properties that the passenger had taken him to. He—with his naïveté and the seal-dies stuffed into his pillow, was the tool that had given all those documents credence, and now the cancer had eaten Mecca.

Khalil needed time to regain his balance; by some miracle, he was able to drive his car. After the first bend in the road, he wanted to stop and get out to check the contents of the trunk: a bunch of Hollywood movies (among them the mangled reel of the dinosaur film), three yellowed robes, and a pillow in shreds, but not a single pair of shoes amidst those tattered disguises (though his own face was a better disguise sadly) . . .

Was he really leaving with all his belongings and taking this path? And under the gaze of this ghost-like being . . . "This is a nightmare, isn't it?" he wanted to ask the passenger, but his voice was coming out a weak croak. "Of course it is," he muttered to himself. "What do you expect? Best be careful. Make a wrong turn or doze off at the wheel and you and this creature you're driving will be sent to oblivion . . ."

The car suddenly sped up, and even though he was stamping on the brakes with the full weight of his foot, it refused to slow down, screeching through a stream of cars and buses headed to al-Rusayfa. Khalil hoped he could make it to the ring road, where he could drive at full speed without any danger; a voice was urging him to get to Mount Mercy, in Arafat, where Eve had met Adam after their descent from Paradise, in the hope that the game this ghost was playing would lose its danger in Arafat's empty, never-ending roads. But the car took the old Mecca–Jeddah road, making for the site of the denouement of al-Hadrami's history, and nothing could stand in its way.

"You were planted in the Lane of Many Heads to torture me. You're the cancer that was brought to life to toy with me . . . But you know I'll defeat you. You can't kill me—I'll simply race you and beat you to my own death."

When he reached Umm al-Joud, a neighborhood of munificence, which had once been Umm al-Doud, a neighborhood of worms, Khalil began to miss his father's voice, his words uttered with care and affection. Love opened up in all directions and pulled him in, and at the spot where the rocks were piled over the corpse of his ancestor, at that very millisecond, a huge tanker appeared, a dinosaur, making a turn across the road; it was met by a splatter of blood on Khalil's lips as he coughed. The cancer had finally penetrated his heart at that exact same millisecond, clutching both ventricles in its claws; Khalil the pilot's body flew—with four engines, autopilot, and manual—into the body of the petrol tanker, which stretched out like a screen showing a dinosaur made of fire, while Ismail's singing face filled the rearview mirror: "Meccan folks are doves, Medinans turtledoves, and the people of Jeddah are all gazelles . . ." An obelisk of white flame leapt up, penetrating the impassive, watchful sky.

Death of a Prophet

The eunuch watched him from behind the Column of Repentance. The more he stared, the more he felt the lines of age creeping over his own smooth face, which hadn't aged a day since he was castrated. Emptied of all desire, he was removed from the cycle of time; his body grew larger but his face remained that of a child, and his mind was filled with the memories of childhood. Nothing that entered his head ever faded; it was a patch of childhood innocence. But his face was being reflected in the face of the man leaning against the Column of Repentance, turning it into a frown, so the eunuch turned away, and moved toward the old man who was reciting from the Quran, tossing his head from side to side as he read, and allowed the old man's gentle movements to smooth the frown from his face.

Nasser stumbled over obstacles in the worn parchment, especially those places where the ink had faded completely. Whether he was a waking reader or a dreaming one, he could feel the changes in tempo caused by the interrupted sentences, and he had to skip over lines with the agility of a gazelle so as not to let the thread of meaning disappear before his eyes, like sand dunes shifting constantly across the page:

> The peaks of Mount Batha appeared in front of us, looking like ghouls' heads in the darkness of the dawn twilight. It was there that our guide, Ayif al-Ghatafani, left us and went to track the troops of Ghatafan, who we were expecting would march to our aid; the Jews of Khaybar were their allies. We used to give the sheikh of the Ghatafan tribe, Uyinah ibn Hisn, half of our date harvest in exchange for his protection.
>
> In the shade of a rock I sank into a pile of sand to rest, hoping to calm the ache that gnawed at my bones after the long ride, but I was so eager to

see our guide return with news of victory, news that would mean we could return to Khaybar, that I couldn't close my eyes.

Instead when he did return, the guide confirmed our worst fears. Ayif al-Ghatafani told us he'd seen no sign of any Ghatafani troops coming to our assistance, and that Khaybar would have to defend itself against the onslaught. No one he'd met along the way expected Khaybar to hold out long against two hundred Muslim warriors who were eager to be martyred and who'd already proven their strength with the victories they had won at Badr and the Trench and the truce they'd concluded with the Quraysh in Hudaybiya.

From Mount Batha we made our way eastward. That turn to the east was the end of our entire existence, like a death to be followed only by a rebirth. We had to move in secrecy, and we also had to forget: we had to hide everything that could tie us to Khaybar and its Jews. We dressed like Bedouin of Ghatafan, in attire our guide had given us; I could sense a warning in his gaze—until then, I had only known men's looks of lust, and I attributed it to the miserable shape I was in from the journey. We were forced to walk through the night, only resting for a short while at the hottest hours of the day. Behind us, the defeat of besieged Khaybar became fact, and it didn't take long for a flood of Jewish survivors, who'd been expelled from Khaybar and Medina, to cover these deserts, seeping into other tribes. I had to keep my distance from the survivors, to carry you into a new existence and a religion that would reign over Canaan and spread far beyond it.

I spent the first nights of my flight defending images of my rapidly receding childhood, of the girl who was carried in a solid gold howdah in the procession of her marriage to the knight chosen to impregnate the most beautiful girl in all Khaybar and ennoble its Jewish blood. I was the girl who succeeded in claiming that honor; it happened one day when he saw me racing grown men up the trunks of palm trees. He spotted that mixture of animal, ghoul, and bird in the mound of my breasts and in my nose, which pointed to the darkest springs lying underground. The gurgling streams of basil-scented forest in my laughter delighted him.

To the rhythm of the camel's footfalls, I recalled every face and beard that came out to greet the wedding procession and shower us with Medinan roses. Every last fortress we passed on our journey came out to congratulate and bless us. And with every step we took, the caravan—with the camel of my father Ka'b ibn al-Ashraf at the head, and the howdah of my Ghatafani servant bringing up the rear—grew bigger. We crossed the plains, passing the citadels of the tribes of Qurayza, Qayniqa, and Waqif, who all blessed my marriage to Khaybar's spiritual leader. Throughout the journey, I was haunted with doubts about the sudden change in my life and my dreams: I'd been plucked from the plains that were my home and sent to live in my husband's fort, the all-powerful nucleus of the rural Hijaz where, my nanny assured me, I would not be treated merely as mistress of the fort, but as a prophetess. As a fifteen-year-old, the thought terrified me and my terror came to a head when a horseman with a short robe and long beard appeared, cutting through the ranks of the caravan, and headed straight for my howdah as our men did nothing to stop him. He snatched me from my howdah in his strong arms and put me in front of him on his saddle; we made it to Khaybar in the blink of an eye, my heart thumping wildly. There, he lay me back on the white cotton sheets of his bed and crushed roses on my neck, drinking me through their petals. His breath smelled of grease and firewood, and he roused whirlpools in my body to receive him; I opened and contracted with unflagging violence, until it was night and the cotton sheets around us began to unravel. It wasn't until the following morning that I became sure of his identity—he was my husband, the man who would plant the seed of you inside me—up until the moment you were born, I wasn't sure whether you came from his loins or from the sandstorms that would later receive me in my flight.

It was he who sent me on this path; I had no choice but to obey and depart with this Ghatafani, who'd served in the temples of the Persians and Byzantines and learned the secrets of Petra and the Valley of the Kings in his search for immortality, and ended up an ascetic among the sand dunes.

"The mosque closes at ten," the eunuch said, interrupting Nasser as he was reading.

Nasser looked up at the large green-belted body and effeminate face; he could hear the thin voice but he couldn't understand. "On your way, please, the doors of the mosque will now be closing."

Nasser folded the parchment into the amulet and got up stiffly. Seeing the distress in Nasser's face, the eunuch added sympathetically, "Starting tomorrow, they're going to break the tradition of closing the mosque, even though it's been this way for fourteen centuries. They plan to keep the doors open all night." He searched Nasser's eyes for a reaction, then went on, "At the end of the day, this mosque is the Prophet's house, and we eunuchs have sacrificed our bodies to guard the tranquility of this honored site so that the dead, peace be upon them, may sleep in peace until the dawn prayers are called and the doors are opened to worshippers who may stay until the night prayers are over."

The eunuch contemplated the iron fence and the many barriers between them and the Prophet's grave. He thought about his Ottoman-era predecessor, who would hurry, with due reverence, to open the door leading to the grave when the dawn prayer was called. He would place a pitcher full of water and a bowl polished with perfume and the Surah of Prostration on the edge of the stone so the Prophet and his companions could perform their ablutions. The young eunuch sighed, and Nasser echoed him, saluting and praying for the Prophet and his companions, and sensing the Prophet's soul, which was resurrected to return his greeting, just as when any worshipper, be they at the very end of the earth, greeted the Prophet and said a prayer for him; a million thousand thousand thousand thousand resurrections took place inside that grave every second, not allowing the buried Prophet's eyes to close for a moment's death, even though he lay in his grave. The eunuch hid a shiver deep in the folds of his jubbah, beneath his wide belt, so that the reason for it wouldn't offend the beloved Prophet to whom he'd devoted his life, and whose Rawdah, the area between his grave in Aisha's house to his pulpit, he served. The eunuch gazed tenderly down at his palms, and then spread them out to show Nasser. They were yellowed with perfume.

"They exude a never-ending perfume. The more I wipe the grave, the more they perspire. I've grown lighter, too. I was a child in 1971, when I snuck in behind my father one morning before dawn, my teeth chattering from the cold, and hid behind the curtains to watch the workers replace the cloth hangings in the sacred burial room. As long as I live, dawn for me will always be associated with those layers of pure green silk lined with heavy cotton and crowned with a band of dark red embroidered with bright cotton threads and gold and silver wire, Quranic verses covering a quarter of the surface. Just from looking at it, you could hear the Surah of the Conquest being recited in the dim light of the noble chamber, where yellow decorated weavings showed the locations of the three graves. It was the first time I'd snuck into the burial room, among the scent of ancient prayers. I did it again on several consecutive nights to watch the workers who'd been chosen to carry out the renovations in secret."

"They change the cloth on the sixth of Dhu l-Hijja every year, don't they?" Nasser asked, but the young eunuch was too lost in his memories to reply. It was as though he could only hear and see what was before his mind's eye.

"The cloth they took down was seventy-five years old, according to the date woven into the fabric—unchanged for three quarters of a century. I trembled in the dawn twilight when I looked toward the fourth, empty, grave. My father told me afterward that the prophet Jesus, peace be upon him, was to be buried in it when he descended to earth in his second coming. My father, the head eunuch, stood reverently under the shimmering star that appeared on the wall of the room that faced the Kaaba, above the head of the noble Prophet. He replaced the silver nail with a diamond the size of a pigeon egg, and beneath it another gem larger still; both were set in gold and silver. I seem to remember—whether I was awake or dreaming—a skinny young architect approaching the cloth that lined the room. He went round folding up the heavy, embroidered, perfumed fabric, then threw the bundle onto his shoulder and left the venerable chamber, placing it on the ground of the Rawdah outside, just a few steps from where I'm standing now. As I watched, the workers gathered around it to carry it to the truck; it was so heavy they couldn't even lift it!" The eunuch sighed, looking Nasser in the face, then went on.

"The chamber stands over one of the rivulets that water the gardens of Paradise. The inside of the chamber belongs to a different time, bodies exist with a different energy, and whoever enters that chamber over the rivulet and pool is relieved of all infirmity and stripped of everything but their true nature, becoming a new species formed of all the prayers and salutations ever said over the noble grave of the beloved Prophet. As children, my predecessors slept on pillows that their parents had covered with a piece of that cloth, breathing in the scent of all those prayers, so our souls are connected with that immortal inner soul."

The eunuch turned to leave, and Nasser followed him silently. He was thinking about Sarah, the Jewish woman, and her wedding, and how she had lain with her husband on those cotton sheets but had never eaten with him or approached him, how she'd been hidden away from strangers, fasting from everything but the food of her people. In his mind, he could see a long reel of images of extremists from the histories of the many religions: those who call anything that they don't believe in "heresy," those who declare themselves God's chosen people, those who worship gold and accumulate vast wealth, who corner the market and determine people's livelihoods, all so that they can take over the world some day and make everyone else their slave.

Nasser contemplated the fourteen centuries that separated him from that time. The grand plaza outside the Mosque of the Prophet opened out before him, and he lingered there in the hope that Yusuf or Mushabbab might seek him out. He had no idea how long he spent in that wide square in front of the mosque, but he began to feel hungry. A black woman was selling drinking yogurt from a mat spread on the ground at the edge of the plaza, ladling it from a large bowl into small clay ones. She was watching him, and when he approached her she immediately filled a clay bowl and held it out to him.

"Good health! That's the last of today's prosperity, with the Prophet's blessings. Drink up, say grace, and send him your salutations."

"God's prayers, salutations and blessings be on our Prophet Muhammad."

"And his family and companions," she concluded.

Nasser thanked her, thrusting a hundred-riyal bill into her hand. Her hand trembled as she grasped the bill. He drank the bowlful in one go, and was deliriously filled with the faint but rich flavor of sweet woodruff. When he raised his eyes from the bowl, they fell upon a muscled back, and he felt as light as the short robe that covered it, the white waistcoat, the yellowish scarf thrown over the shoulder and the wide belt. Nasser felt like he was watching a character from a novel wandering, carefree, in his sleep; the man was headed to the market, and without hesitating Nasser followed him. He vanished into the covered market, with Nasser just behind him. Around them, the stores were saying goodbye to their last customers of the day and closing up, and the stalls were lowering their awnings over rows of prayer beads, prayer rugs, and cheap imported clothes. The man was in no hurry, and neither was Nasser, since any movement might have roused the man from his torpor; from a distance, it looked as if they were walking with a fine thread stretched between them, in their own sphere parallel to that of the people around them. They passed a Pakistani man with a straggly beard sitting at a stall selling prayer beads, miswak toothbrushes, and folded keffiyehs in bundles of three in boxes of cardboard, then an African woman standing propped against the damp, peeling wall. In front of her was a huge wooden cart laden with rows of small plastic bags containing red chili powder and deep scarlet hibiscus, and stacks of soft, but bitter, baobab fruit hiding inside white quartz-like exteriors. The woman didn't look up as Nasser passed; she was dozing on her feet, hardly expecting customers. She was simply waiting the last short while until night came and she could say she'd made it through another day. The man Nasser was following seemed to be on an endless journey into the depths of sleep, until he took a sharp right into an alleyway next to a man selling sugarcane. Nasser had scarcely entered the alley when a body hit him with the weight of a rock. He hit the floor, crushed under his attacker's weight; there was no use resisting. When he opened his eyes, he was in a hallway, and in front of him was a slim, dark face, watching him. Nasser didn't need to ask to be certain it was Yusuf, and Yusuf's words confirmed it.

"You've taken an amulet that belongs to me, Detective."

Nasser resolved then and there that he wasn't going to let anyone rob him of his dream of getting a medal for solving this case. But in the darkness of the cold corridor he felt an eye watching him and reading his thoughts, and without turning to look he realized who the man who'd led him to that spot must be. The faint smell of mastic strengthened his suspicion that it was Mushabbab. Just hearing the name in his head pulled him out of the cloud he'd been floating in. In a panic, he patted his clothes, but he couldn't find the amulet anywhere, and his heart sank at the thought he'd lost it. Suddenly, Yusuf tossed the amulet onto the ground in front of him. "No need to look very far," he taunted, then snatched it up again.

"So how far did you get with your reading?" he went on mockingly, holding up the parchment as if to read aloud. "It's pretty easy following you, by the way. I was right next to you in the mosque. The state you were in and the way you were so engrossed in reading had everyone staring at you."

Connections

Rafi followed Nora and her assistant as they approached the tiny restaurant, Casa Gades. None of its three floors was more than a single room, and all were filled with small tables, cigarette smoke, and conversation. Diners greeted Rafi left and right as he led Nora straight to the cellar room. Before they'd got out the car, he'd explained to her, "This brilliant restaurant was Señora Mirano's idea. She runs it for a group of art patrons; she's very respected in Madrid's young art circles. She puts on exhibitions here of unusual experimental work by up-and-coming artists." Over the past several days, Rafi had ventured to suggest several places Nora could go to get to know the real Madrid, and this restaurant was one of them.

The cellar was a small room with niches in the walls for paintings, and it led to a small office where an eclectic collection of contemporary artwork was exhibited, abstract paintings and stone and bronze sculptures. Nora felt totally out of place, though she in fact did fit in with the clashing incongruity of the collection, and felt a kind of tacit mutual comprehension with its dissonance. It was like walking through an artist's brain amidst the crackling static of their visions.

Señora Mirano, the ninety-something restaurant owner, was thin with short platinum hair, and she overflowed with energy. She led them up to the third floor, which was the quietest, drawing Nora's attention as they climbed the wooden stairs to the strange works of art that hung on the walls. "Young artists regard this as a place many different trends and movements can meet and interact," she explained. "It's vital for a developing artist to spend time in a place where debate is encouraged." She pointed out the photos of the celebrities who'd dined in her art den. "That's Joan Miró . . . And Picasso, and a Russian ballerino . . ."

The top room looked over the room below it. Nora chose the furthest table for herself and her assistant, while Rafi made for a seat in the corner. On one side of them was a window looking onto the street below and on the other a wooden screen separated them from the other diners. When the owner reappeared, stopping at Rafi's table, he murmured to her, "Señora Mirano, this is the woman whose sketches I showed you . . ." From where she stood, Señora Mirano gestured at a drawing on the wall, which looked like a Picasso nude. "Your sketches bear some of Picasso's influence," she said, directing her words at Nora.

Nora almost laughed out loud. What would this art lover say if she found out that in the twenty-first century there were people who'd never heard of Picasso? "The lines convey a charged energy," the woman went on, oblivious to Nora's self-deprecating expression. "You speak to the world through these lines."

Nora felt uncomfortable under the woman's gaze. "You've only seen one or two sketches."

"That may be so, but they are interesting," Señora Mirano replied. "And I say this with some authority, since I was born into the art world and I've spent nearly a century around artists by this point. It isn't just my personal opinion—" she came closer to Nora, and leaned over the table. "I showed the sketches Rafa gave me to my critic friend at the Fundació Joan Miró. She was very taken with them. You're what, twenty-four? Twenty-six? You could go on to achieve a lot from where you are now. Did you study art?"

Nora was caught off balance, tongue-tied. Rafi took the spotlight off her by drawing Señora Mirano into a conversation in Spanish. By the time the waiter arrived with the Italian salad she'd ordered, Nora had regained her composure. The four looked like any other group of friends out to dinner. "Bon appetit!" Señora Mirano said.

Nora reveled in the rhythm of the artworks on the wall, the conversations of the regulars around them, each with their distinct, individual features, and in the fragrance of herbs, the taste of thyme, virgin olive oil, bread freshly baked in a wood-fired oven, and seafood. When the plates were cleared, and cups of coffee and Nora's chamomile tea appeared, Nora took her folder of papers out of her bag. Señora Mirano found her glasses and began to look through the papers with interest; Rafi translated for Nora.

"Your lines are very mature, it's like you've spent a lifetime struggling with these greedy pen strokes, almost tearing the paper. Look at this violence, Rafa, how the lines dig and scratch... The force of the retreat, the spontaneity of the movement. This is lust, appetite, desire, veils being torn off all over the place! The human torso is spread out here like a thunder-filled sky, exploding as if in lovemaking . . ." Rafi was too embarrassed to translate the last part for Nora. The woman eventually stopped exulting, but a look of surprise remained on her face.

A gypsy appeared on the narrow street, playing the violin in a red dress that was partly covered by her black shawl, its tassels trembling every time her bow slid over the strings.

"Ah! Madrid's night moves in time with the ebb and flow of the second movement of Bach's violin concerto . . . Music is like Arabic: poetic but highly disciplined. The structure of harmony is like the system of patterns in Arabic, like the verbs composed of three letters which form the roots of the whole language. Chords are made up of either three or four notes, you know, and they can be arranged to create infinite variations, just like Arabic letters. The mysterious secret behind Bach's compositions is just like *alif-lam-ha*, the letters that make up the word 'God'; Bach thought his compositions proved God's very existence . . ." Sinatra, Picasso, Bach: these were names that struggled desperately to steady themselves, but could find no foothold on the slippery walls of the empty water tank that was her mind.

"Bach wrote forty-eight preludes and fugues, using all twenty-four major and minor keys, just to prove that it could be done. He wrote so much, and for so much, like a real Sufi, convinced that numbers mattered. The *Goldberg Variations* were written for an insomniac prince who wanted Bach to compose a piece that he'd never get bored of listening to on nights when he couldn't sleep . . ." Nora realized at that moment that her own insomnia was not the product of an overburdened memory but an empty one. It stemmed from the aridity of the place she came from, a place that was becoming amnesiac even though it knew that the rest of the world was testing and examining and rebuilding itself through debate and criticism, that there were places like Madrid where arts and sciences and architecture and music collided with people going about their everyday business in a civilization that had managed to retain its noble exterior. All those names and their achievements, of which she knew nothing, caused Nora to feel a sense of loss.

Her train of thought was interrupted by Señora Mirano's laughter. "It's no wonder, is it, that they included his *Brandenburg Concerto No. 2* on the 'golden record' that they sent into outer space on one of the Voyager probes along with other examples of sounds, languages, and music from Earth." If they'd sent that record to the city where she was born, would the people there recognize it as the sound of their Earth, Nora wondered.

"This is Beethoven's *Violin Sonata No. 5* in F major, the Spring Sonata. The difference between him and Bach is that Beethoven broke the rules, though that doesn't mean that Bach wasn't one of the most important rule-abiding composers."

Nora knew that it would be a huge undertaking for her to absorb this encyclopedia of human achievements, and that she was embarking upon it at a relatively late age. The gypsy violinist outside had dropped a coin and was groping for it on the ground. It was only then that Nora had realized she was blind. Nora was blinded by her own pity.

"How do you feel about preparing for an exhibition? Not necessarily here—maybe in your own country?" Nervously, Nora fingered the edge of her scarf, looking at the gypsy woman's tasseled shawl as the ninety-something Señora Mirano went on, "I came from a nomadic gypsy background too, and I learned that art in all its varieties can make the world a safer place for us. Art's like a planet that grants us citizenship and gives us papers of its own, different from those of real nations." Nora felt naked; the more this woman looked at her drawings, the more her internal life, which she herself didn't dare confront, would be uncovered.

"But I don't have the knowledge to produce anything that could match that kind of art," murmured Nora, surprising even herself. "I didn't learn to create art by studying it. I drew this"—she fingered her sketches—"because I needed to push the walls away and create some space. To create balance."

"That might be the best description of what art is that I've ever heard: opening a place up into infinite spaces in the total creative consciousness! Maybe this need is what compels primitive peoples and children to create the art that has always been such an important part of human creativity. After he became famous, Picasso said he wished he could go back to drawing like a child. You must break through and exhibit something. Open up your innermost self to audiences and let them walk around in it, examining your deepest secrets . . ."

"I appreciate the suggestion. I'll think about it," she whispered into the corner of her scarf, and without thinking she tied the corner for the promise she'd made, twisting the fabric into a knot the size of a pigeon's eye.

"Where did you learn this gypsy magic?" asked Rafi affectionately. Nora's face shone. The features of the three people around her looked like part of the clay and ceramic tableau behind them, illuminated by the magic of the dim lights floating over the violin strings mixed with the longing of lute strings, which night drew toward the depths of the soul; there was her second mother's hoarse voice and her headscarf with knots in each corner like a rabbit's teats.

"The woman who raised me taught me to tie a knot in my scarf for each wish I made. We were supposed to make big wishes, and tie a knot for each one, and only undo the knot when the wish came true, as our joyous ululations rang out across the rooftops. The bigger the wish, the wider the votive knot and the more people who'd benefit from your offering. Never leave your headscarf without a knot, she said."

There were so many knots in her second mother's scarf, every one representing a different joy awaiting her down the road: Nora's graduation from primary school, her first period, finally managing to memorize the Surah of Sovereignty, which warded off the approach of hell as one slept, learning to sew properly.

"Like this gypsy's shawl, with hundreds of knots," she observed. "Do you think each one of them is for a wish or a dream?"

"Sometimes one dream is enough," ventured Rafi.

"One dream?!" she exclaimed. She thought for a moment, and then she added, "Yes, maybe—maybe even one would be too much."

Señora Mirano stood up, excusing herself, "The question is how much space we create for the audience within the dream that consumes our life."

A burst of music sent a flock of pigeons flapping down the alley and away into another alley in the distant basin of her memory; they returned like a wave of night directing the rhythm of her body.

"I came from an alley like this. Two walls . . ." Rafi listened as Nora's mind wandered to the night when she'd been woken by an almighty gasping, banging, and scraping beneath her window. For a moment she'd thought someone was trying to break through the barred window, but then her consciousness began to distinguish the sounds, and a deep instinct impelled her to peep out of the window. She saw a man's head below her window; he was unconscious, his eyes were closed, his head was rolling back and forth against the wall. She leaned further forward, thrusting her nose between the bars of the window, and was able to make out the black mass between his legs: it was a head in an abaya, glued mercilessly to the spot, gorging itself. When the epileptic spasms ebbed, the head detached from the body and out of the black appeared the face of a woman with dribbling lips. The epileptic man bent forward to kiss them quickly. "You cursed woman . . ." he murmured hoarsely.

The woman's eyes widened, anticipating an equally epileptic response, but the man began to move away, cautiously tidying himself up before he left the secluded alley. The man's face disappeared and Nora saw Rafi's face again. "At night, our alley was a theater where the actors never got tired, a strange shadow play. I used to lie in my bed and listen, hearing but never seeing the actors—footsteps bursting out of nowhere and running, voices walking the length of the alley acting out angry or debauched amateur dramatics, spurred on by the sense of privacy that the narrow alley lent their performance. They all played their roles safe in the sense of secrecy that surrounded their climaxes and exhibitions. The voices of men arguing or talking with drunken slurring tongues or sharp angry tones; mumbles and pants, women clapping in upper-story windows to catch the attention of those lower down; in the background, laughter or crying, or the hurried footsteps of that woman coming home at dawn from her shift in the hospital. The only thing I knew about her was the smell of a day's sweat, Dettol, and strong disinfectants as she dragged her exhausted body onward to the sweat-drenched future. I never saw her but I could picture her with her white gloves raised in the face of our alley's indifference. The alley always picked itself up and kept going, never stopping save for the cries of women, or the call to prayer, or fathers, indoors mixing with outdoors in that unique mixture that was our daily bread, interrupted now and again by the applause of the audience outside . . ." Nora's gaze shifted from the gypsy across the street to her assistant and from there to Rafi's heavily lined face. Everything that was yet to come was also part of that obscure map of life.

Señora Mirano suddenly interrupted them. "Would you like to join our discussion of *The English Patient*?"

Rafi declined politely, echoing Nora. "Have you actually seen *The English Patient*?" she asked him as they made their way back to the hotel.

He nodded. "I thought it was wonderful, but there's no way I could sit through it again. I've seen enough violence in real life, in the civil war, had enough shocks, experienced enough adrenaline rushes, that I've found I get pretty upset when I watch a sad film or read a sad poem. I think I'm getting worn out."

"Maybe not—maybe you're just learning to appreciate the value of a peaceful life."

"Also, I can't stomach this Western thing of watching real life through movies any more. Señora Mirano once told me that we've invented a duality, a second reality and I think I agree with her. Our mental world is a reflection of what we see around us, civilization is the shell that represents our inner spiritual selves. Without it, we're just animals in search of food and sex. We want to exist on a higher plane, but we can't get there or we can't stay up there. Most of us never will. In the end, it's just a dream . . ."

Reading Triangle

In the endless void of the corridor, an epoch of sand stretched between the three men. The whole time they were in the corridor, Mushabbab had remained calm, and when at one point Nasser's throat went dry, Mushabbab was poised and ready. Whenever Nasser's doubts became too much for him and he looked like he was about to tumble from the nightmarish plane of reality they were exploring, Mushabbab quickly handed the will over to Yusuf so he could pick up where Nasser had stumbled:

> Everything changed when we entered the heart of Najd. We left the soft sands saturated with the Hijazi breeze. Even the air tasted dry and harsh and began to dig into our skin. My body must have become stiffer somehow, as well. I have no idea how long we climbed, teetering on our camels, as we followed our Ghatafani guide across the ribs of great sand dunes on the edge of the Nafud Desert. It took us a while before we realized that we'd been surrounded by a group of men riding bareback on massive camels. In the burning sunlight, it wasn't entirely clear whether they were men or mirages or demons. The men, and the camels they were riding, were the color of sand, even their eyelashes. There was no way we could've gotten away from them; it was hard enough to figure out what direction they were headed in. They were kicking up a sandstorm that either lashed at your back, or blinded you, or suffocated you. They tied us to our saddles by the feet and forced us to follow them. At one desperate moment, I thought the horizon was a sheet of molten copper rising up to the sky, propelling us forward with flames until we finally reached the top of the copper wall, where the wind rose up and began pelting us with what felt like sandstones. "Locusts!" Ayif al-Ghatafani shouted.
>
> We had to protect our eyes and faces from the locust attack. It was well known among the Bedouin that locusts were so vicious that they ate humans alive. I raised my abaya over my head like a tent, while the giants faced the onslaught head-on and didn't seem at all bothered. They didn't even cover their faces and they laughed at al-Ghatafani as he tried desperately to keep the locusts off the terrified camels. I don't know what caused it but my camel bolted and I could do nothing to control it. It was

all I could do to hold on to the reins as locusts buzzed all around me and inside my abaya. The camel didn't stop until we'd made it out of the locust swarm. When I opened my eyes, I saw the other camels were outrunning the last of the locusts and the giants appeared around me, riding alongside. It was as though I hadn't crossed the locusts and the desert, rather that the desert had receded. I could see gouges on my camel's neck and around her eyes; the locusts had left what looked like a tattoo across the belly of al-Ghatafani's camel.

"We're lucky we made it out of there."

An oasis in the Rimmah Valley lay before us, looking like a ruin. The palm trees were stripped bare, the locusts having decimated their crowns and clusters, and as we neared the village, we could see the uncovered graves of the children and the elderly done in by smallpox, which the locusts carried.

The camels instinctively gave that hell a wide berth, looping around toward the southeast. It was as if the giants were leading us from one disaster to another more horrific as our detour continued. Smallpox ran alongside us, borne by the locust swarm, leaving oases of death in its wake until it disappeared inside the bones of the desert.

We ran past the tribes of Tayyi and Asad, and our captors drove us like a storm between the tribes of Hanifa and Tamim on the way to their oasis.

Delicacies

Night fell over Madrid and the activity around the Prado Museum across the street began to die down. Nora listened closely as she'd grown used to doing in her distant alley:

She heard Nazik the Turkish woman emerging from the cluster of alleys and poverty. She was dressed in her navy blue coat, with embroidered sleeves, and she'd wrapped a white scarf around her head—she didn't cover her face like the other women in the neighborhood. Her fiery locks fell over her forehead, attracting everyone's gaze and quivering with every word she spoke to her companion the eunuch. He walked two steps behind her, following her every command like a loyal dog. Every Friday morning when Nazik appeared, the women of the lane would duck into entryways and teenage girls would bury their fingers inside their abayas.

"Nazik can capture a girl with just one finger!" The rumor came about because of how her eyes bulged and hovered above the girls' hands like a hawk, examining them, picking out the finest, longest fingers. She was always negotiating with parents to get them to allow their daughters to work for her doing embroidery.

That Friday, the girl didn't run away. She stood there among the pots of herbs, like a dove at rest, and watched the Turkish woman. When Nazik got closer, she walked out to the outer gate to get a whiff of her perfume, Paris Nights; it made the whole neighborhood sigh. Nazik had mummified that perfume bottle, which she'd inherited from her ancient grandfather, allowing herself only a single drop every Friday. Nazik didn't waste a second. She grabbed the girl's right hand and started checking out her fingers.

"These are good fingers. Real Turkish delight! If you send her to me, I'll teach her how to sew, and trim, and fit, and drape, and pin . . . These fingers will feed you honey and ambergris." The words wafted on ambergris into her father's mind and the very next morning he lifted the siege under which she'd lived and sent her to Nazik's workshop.

At the doorway, she was met by the scents of women. It was mostly sweat but there was a perfume which she couldn't quite identify. It made the blood rush to her temples. There was nothing of Paris Nights about this place. For the first time in her life, she understood that she was an adult woman.

"Girl!"

Nazik greeted her like someone clinging to a lifesaver. It was a surprise to see the Turkish woman without her wig, her hair as white as a corpse-washer's sponge. "Welcome to my kingdom, where the girls shake their asses but never break their backs!"

She led her to a row of sewing machines that faced the wall like schoolchildren being punished. A chubby girl sat there, engrossed in her sewing. Her arms were each the size of an infant. She was spinning the machine, a Singer, violently; it looked as if she might tear the wheel off at any moment.

Nazik handed Nora a heart-shaped embroidery hoop holding a piece of white cotton taut. "Should I teach you the fluffy satin stitch?" she asked. "We use it to embroider flowers on women's dresses. A woman wearing a dress with that flower always turns heads . . ." When she said "flower," it sounded like "flavor."

Nazik began stabbing blindly, lewdly, at the fabric, creating the bright red heart of a flower out of her stitches; it was so suggestive that sweat broke out on Nora's upper lip. Nazik watched her closely. When the girl tried to take the hoop and have a turn, Nazik tossed it aside. "Don't waste your time with sweaty slaves' work!" she cackled.

She walked Nora over to a clothes rack with dresses of every color and shape. She grabbed a red and white head-covering like men wore and wrapped it around Nora's head until only her eyes showed. She pushed Nora forward in her black dress to a section of the studio that was curtained off. Nora was shocked to see drumming and dancing. "Let yourself dance!" urged Nazik.

Swaying gracelessly ahead, she led the girl forward like water down a sluice. When sweat began to run down Nora's neck to her chest, the head-covering gave off a scent that gripped her by the throat. Her body heaved with passion and desire. Something inside her took over. She tore herself away from Nazik and fled the dance floor. Nazik didn't follow after her. The girl understood that they sewed together more than clothes, and that the snips went as deep as each of the chosen bodies dared allow. Some stopped at being stripped, while others were content to be consumed and recycled.

"I'm never going back there, no matter what," Nora vowed to herself.

"NOTHING PROVIDES SECURITY LIKE LEARNING A TRADE. WITHOUT ME, YOUR daughter will starve!"

Her father fell for Nazik's threats and pleas and allowed her to go up to his daughter's bedroom alone, where she menaced her.

"Do as I say," she said, pulling on the girl's arm as if to make her understand. "You're luckier than all my best girls, believe me. During that split-second appearance you made, the scepter fell into your hand. Do you understand me, girl? The scepter!" With every word Nazik spoke, the girl could smell the scent in the head-covering that had stirred an indomitable desire inside of her.

"JUST LIKE MY HAIR SMELLS NOW," NORA SAID, SHRUGGING HER SHOULDERS AS SHE sat in the large bedroom she occupied in the Ritz Madrid. It was only now that she could get her head around the storm that she'd stirred up during her brief presence in that basement studio. "The scepter," she repeated to herself. "The scepter you refused to take from Nazik all those years ago."

In a city without any call to prayer, she woke every morning at dawn to the sound of a dove flapping its wings. She knew when it was time for prayer from the gust that rose up out of the silence, a dawn presence, which pulled her out of her deepest sleep. She knew he was coming. The man who loved her started his motorcycle in a faraway courtyard, startling the pigeons that took to the air to circle the length of her narrow alley, like a wave that pierced her and settled in the back of her neck, causing her entire body to quake in anticipation.

Getting There

Al-Ghatafani warned us that we would be passing through hell and then suddenly we were being led into the southern simoom wind. The wind dug the sand out from beneath our feet and erected graves above our heads that reached the sky.

The look in al-Ghatafani's eyes told me that he'd survived all those nightmares only to fall into my trap. It frightened me.

"Wherever they take us, let's pretend that we're brother and sister." He closed his eyes in assent. The oases of the Hanifa tribe lay before us.

We made camp there, and for the first time since we'd set off, the hush of night combined with the exhaustion of hunger, thirst, and desperation knocked us out. We slept as if we were dead. I lay there until I was pulled back by a brutish growling and gurgling, and found the giants sitting in a circle, chewing on camel meat, tearing the limbs and the sandy insides to pieces. It was like they lived off sand. All around us the sand smelled of the previous night's light rains, and the camels grazed on Eve plants, which had sprouted overnight like green spikes on the dunes. I realized that we had finally left hunger behind us and were now making our way through the heart of the Najd oases.

I lay awake, imagining the abyss we'd left behind. The only thing holding me was al-Ghatafani's night-sculpted, wind-chiseled body lying beside me. I could hear wolves howling inside me, or out in the desert around us, demanding a drink of his blood. When I got up at dawn, he was standing, facing away from me, stroking his camel's neck. I felt that persistent movement between my ribs. As I drew nearer to him, passionate dawn and the waking universe rose up inside of me. I interfered with his finely honed senses and ability to read the weather or the scent of a place. He was defenseless. He trembled like a slaughtered sand grouse when my body touched his, but he knew to surrender. Our careful calculations, the cause of our people, our mission were all betrayed because of a wolf's howl. I heard my father Ka'b's warning: "Choose the best lineage for us so that we may be resurrected!" and was suddenly terrified at what I'd got myself into. I pulled away. He could tell I meant it, so he kept his distance.

Drawing

THAT NIGHT WHEN SHE GOT INTO BED, SHE TUMBLED INTO A BOTTOMLESS WELL, hands that reeked of beer and garlic groping her body as she fell. She was woken by a metallic clatter against the marble floor, and a man's voice. When Nora opened her eyes, she saw it was past midnight. She slipped across the marble floor in bare feet—a rude awakening—and peeked through a crack in the bedroom door. She saw a paunchy man who looked a little like a cartoon character: greasy, oozing evil, about to burst. He bent down to pick up a shiny object from the floor and when she focused, she immediately recognized the key that had been taken from the gravestone in the cemetery of outcasts. A sudden terror came over her and she could no longer breathe. She didn't want him to see her. She knew he could hurt her and the thought made her hair stand on end. The man compared the key to a sketch on a piece of old parchment he was holding.

"A perfect copy," he said. "The same wide teeth and a bow in the shape of three mihrabs. But you're right. It's obviously a fake."

The man bit down on the thin layer of gold with his yellowed teeth to reveal the cheap metal underneath.

"Of course, it is, you idiot." The icy look on the sheikh's face sent a shiver through Nora's bones. She could feel his rage on the other side of the door. "You're a bunch of fuck-ups and you're wasting my time. You brought me all the way out here to watch you screw everything up?" He snatched the parchment and the forged key and stuffed them into a white envelope before bundling the man out of the suite and walking out himself.

The next morning, Nora's bags had already been taken to the private plane, which awaited her at the airport. The hotel corridors and basement were a beehive of activity in anticipation of their departure, which she'd been informed of the day before. When he opened the door to her bedroom to collect her, the emptiness hit him like a punch in the face and he fell back against the wall. Her silver earrings, the agarwood perfume he drank from her skin, her inhaler, small possessions were scattered here and there on the table beside her messy, empty bed.

A storm roared through the hotel, turning the entire place upside down in search of Nora, who'd disappeared without a trace.

It was her deep fear of the sheikh that had caused her to sneak out of the hotel before dawn, but by the time she'd reached the Fountain of Neptune, Rafi had already caught up with her.

"Let me take you wherever it is you're going," he said, getting out of the car. He was tidying up his papers on the backseat so she'd have somewhere to sit, but she simply opened the passenger-side door and got in the front seat. He hesitated for a second before he got in next to her; it felt awkward to be that close to her.

"Where to?"

"Somewhere that isn't Madrid. I don't care where."

"Are you sure about this?"

"Either take me or let me out so I can get in a cab."

He drove off, in no particular direction, until they found themselves at the highway that led south out of Madrid.

"Please, let me help you. What is it you're running away from?"

She stared at him for a while and then she told him what she'd seen the night before. "You're his bodyguard, I'm sure you know all about it. What's he doing with that key and the man who nearly killed me?"

He was silent for a moment. "I'm glad that you trust me, but the only thing I know is that the sheikh was interested in that grave for some reason. Based on what you just said, I can only assume that he was looking for that key." She seemed dissatisfied so he elaborated: "A month before you two got here, he came here on his own and went to the cemetery, but he didn't find what he was looking for. He also went to Toledo for the same reason, I think."

"Let's go to Toledo then."

He hadn't been expecting that. "Listen, if you think you're in any danger, then the safest thing to do would be to go in the opposite direction." He saw the stubborn look in her eye so he started the car.

They drove in total silence along the highway to Toledo, which lay seventy kilometers south of Madrid. They passed the line of fortresses erected by the Muslim rulers of al-Andalus as a barrier between themselves and the Kingdom of Castile.

"Come on, tell me something: something about art, or Andalusia, history, highways, anything." She seemed amused. "At least we're following Señora Mirano's advice. Did you hear her telling me that I had to go to Toledo to see the painting by El Greco in the Church of Santo Tomé? It's called *The Burial of the Count of Orgaz*, she said." He felt for his pistol. "Don't worry," she said, laughing, "I'm not planning to do anything bad!" He didn't say anything. "In any case, I don't have anything to lose any more even if I do do something bad."

He relaxed and allowed himself to speak. "If we're not worried about losing something, that means we don't deserve to have it in the first place. You're young and full of life. That in itself is a miracle, and you should be afraid of losing it."

"The only thing I can lose is the search itself, if I stop trying to find myself. You should have never gotten involved."

"I'm here to protect you." The stubborn furrow in his brow met her radiant, if enigmatic, smile; she needed to push things as far they could go: if not to break the monotony, then to test how determined he was to protect her.

"All right, then. We can at least look forward to seeing *The Burial of the Count*." She opened the window to enjoy the first breath of release. The soft music, the wind in her air, the endless countryside; it soothed her and she allowed herself to consider the path her life had taken. She'd stumbled from one holding pattern to another, passing by two true loves as she chose a third, leaping blindly into the unknown. Ever since she was a child she'd harbored that suicidal instinct. The only lover she wanted now was herself—it made her laugh how dramatic she was being, but honestly what was wrong with learning to love herself? Had she done all this to punish—who? Her father? Herself? She was young when she'd learned that one wrong turn could take you past the point of no return. She'd called it life's minefield: one careless step and—boom! Was that what she'd stumbled over during her one and only trip to Nazik the Turkish woman's basement studio? From now on, she was going to walk the walk and talk the talk—whatever that meant. If the only thing she had left was a last shred of determination, she was going to put it to work to keep herself from going back to where she'd started. At the same time, she knew that the idea of going back to where she'd started was a fantasy. There was no such thing as going back to what had been. If she ever did try to return to her birthplace, she'd find that the city and everyone in it had moved on, in thought and in deed. Nothing was waiting for her exactly as she'd left it; she wasn't even the same person who'd left. She was in the place best suited to her new and shockingly modern configuration, an island that had shot up to the surface from the bottom of the sea, propelled by a volcanic eruption. She could do nothing except continue to live in places that resembled her, and it was by no means a given that the place that resembled her would be the city in which she'd been born.

She realized that Rafi was watching her. The only thing he could see through the windshield was a single nagging thought: this is a race. His mission wasn't to take Nora away from her past like she'd asked him to, but the opposite. He had to try to stitch together a moment from her past with a moment from the past of a city that she'd never known, like Toledo. He knew where the connection would come: through art. Or through the suffering or death contained within the art. The constant movement, which resembled her, whose revolutions she fit perfectly like a gear, where she was made whole. He was certain that the only way she could have peace of mind was if she could see herself as a cog in a machine she knew well, the machine that created her dreams and made them come to life. The point wasn't to go back into the past but to catch up with it at some point in the future. The eternal *journey* alongside and away from an event that was headed in the same direction as her dreams, as part of that eternal process of change and transformation. She had to have some trust. She knew she couldn't run away, couldn't get her hands on people or things. All she could do was hop on at a station and ride through countless moments past.

As they approached Toledo, they saw the red mountain looming on the horizon surrounded by the blue of the Tagus River, which had repelled invaders from time immemorial. The city was like an island atop the great mountain. Rafi could see that Nora was struggling to take it all in.

"Toledo was one of the most important cities in all of Spain during the so-called Golden Age. It was once part of the Umayyad Caliphate of Cordoba, but King Alfonso the Sixth of Léon and Castile captured the city in 1085. Toledo later became known as a holy city in the seventeenth century, and gained a reputation for being open, tolerant, Eastern . . .

"It's full of treasures from when it was the capital of the Spanish Empire. Lots of important historical figures were born here or lived here: El Greco, King Alfonso the Tenth—they call him Alfonso the Wise because he was learned, and started the translation movement in the thirteenth century. They translated Islamic learning into Latin and helped spark the European Renaissance. Toledo was a center of culture and home to three monotheistic religions: Christianity, Judaism, and Islam. At one point, they lived together in harmony, but then came ghettoization and finally in 1492 the Jews and Muslims were expelled. Any who remained were forced to convert to Christianity in 1500. They used to call these people Moriscos, 'little Muslims'—another way of saying heretics. Of course, the Christians discriminated against the converts and that's when they started coming up with ideas like pure bloodlines and heresy trials. From the second half of the fifteenth century onward, they suppressed Islamic-looking architecture and the Gothic style began to dominate the city."

"'Little Muslims,'" Nora repeated. Everything he'd said rang a bell; it was as though he'd been recounting a history that Nora knew intimately. He pointed toward the gate up ahead.

"Existential conflicts are embedded in the soil of this red mountain like fossils. They go all the way back before the Muslim conquest to the Goths and the Romans and the Christians, actually all the way back to Heracles of Libya and to Tubal, Noah's grandson who became the first king of Spain."

Rafi parked his car at the foot of the mountain. Side by side, they made their way up the stone steps, which took wild and sudden turns, watching the city come to life, smelling the coffee brewing behind stone walls. "There's something magical about entering this city on foot; there's nothing like it. I always feel like one of the invaders who scaled its defenses and destroyed them. Here, this way."

Nora flew ahead, her ankle-length white cotton dress billowing around her as she surrendered herself to the rhythm of the mountain, allowing the cramped stone passageways to slip through to her heart, ascending from the foundation of one house to the roof and then the foundation of another. Suddenly she found herself before several narrow paths paved with red stone, which led up to the summit. She teetered at the edge.

"Be careful," he said. "This city takes artists prisoner." The sun rose just in time to receive her laugh. He looked at her for a moment. She might have flown away on the wings of that smile.

"El Greco himself became one with the city. He was born in Crete, but he felt at home here. He did everything here: he was a sculptor, painter, architect. He was the first person to see art as a process of discovery. We can go to the El Greco Museum and see his house while we're here." He looked at her in profile: thick eyebrows, long, dark eyelashes pointed downward as if she were being pulled sleepily to the point of no return. Rafi wanted nothing more than to pull her up out of the abyss. He wanted her to explore the city as though it were one of its many painted avatars.

"El Greco was actually just passing through, but the city took hold of him. The rebel inside him found the freedom he'd been searching for in these peaks. He had a lust for life and he was constantly chasing after beauty so he found it depressing to be as lonely and independent as he was. He put it all into his paintings. Even his death seemed to carry a message: he died a poor man in large empty rooms, surrounded by his meager possessions. All he had was his books and paintings and artists' fancies, nothing substantial. That was what he valued and needed; that was how he lived. He never had the money to fulfill his grand ambitions so he fulfilled them in art."

She felt life tingle in her fingertips as she ran her hands over the red stones warming in the sunlight. He was telling her all this to try to distract her from what she'd come to look for.

"It's as if money has the last word, even in art and dreams."

They lingered in the square between the rooftops and his words reached deep inside her. In the dark corners of her mind, she sensed an accusation. She let out a hot breath she'd been fighting back.

"Is that so?" She said as if sticking her tongue out at him before hurrying daintily forward, climbing up, as he followed. He'd never seen her happy before.

By arriving in the city so early, they had the magic of sunrise all to themselves, and it lingered in the glow of Nora's astonished face for hours.

"So, you're going to take me where the sheikh went, right?" He hadn't expected the tone of implicit command.

As they approached one of the silent stone houses, a woman popped out from behind a wooden door. She was mesmerizing, dressed all in white. She gave them an exaggeratedly warm greeting. "Don't tell me. You're on way your way to the El Greco Museum?" She didn't wait for an answer. "I think I know you," she said to Rafi. "Have we met?" He was afraid she'd remember that he'd visited her school with the sheikh some months back. He gave Nora a look of warning, and tried to divert the woman's attention.

"Do you know when it opens?" He asked her in Spanish.

"Follow me. It's in the Jewish Quarter. I know a fantastic route we can take." She walked them over as if they'd had a longstanding appointment. She would walk two meters ahead and then turn around and walk back to say something about the sights, like a tour guide they hadn't employed. "This is when I usually have my coffee, and I hate it when people interrupt me and spoil my tranquil mornings." They had no choice but to follow her. Her thin body was stuffed into white cotton trousers and a top tight enough to suffocate, with a gold design on the front. They could barely keep up with her as she teetered up and down slippery paved paths in stiletto heels—a terrifying sight. She was so light that the constant stream of chatter that poured out from between her dark-red painted lips threatened to blow her away. It was as though she were dying to talk and she mixed her own personal history in with that of the city.

As he translated what the woman was saying for Nora, Rafi slipped in a word of warning. "The sheikh met this woman, but he didn't get the answer he was looking for. So we need to gain her trust." She took them across slopes and up hundreds of steps to show them the conflict between modern and ancient architecture. She made them stop in front of the Arts Center and the City Hall, hulks of concrete isolated in the midst of all those stone buildings, to lament the victory of modern brick. She showed them secret passageways that led to the heart of that bloody mountain, taking them all the way up to the summit. She didn't let them stop, not even at the Church of Santo Tomé where El Greco's *The Burial of the Count of Orgaz* hung.

"El Greco is life itself," she opined. "He was a Jew who disguised himself as a Christian and some people say he was the real author of *Don Quixote*, rather than Cervantes. He was a literary character as well, like in the story of *Sidi Hamid Benengeli*, the Arab historian who was the inspiration for Cervantes' character Hidalgo or the melancholic knight, who's identical to El Greco. El Greco's paintings are all about how art can transform human beings into something holy and he was always trying to commemorate the beauty of Toledana women."

There was a sudden tragic note in her voice. "We are very sad. I don't mean us women, I mean those of us who are life's missionaries. People who have a message don't really live in this world so much as in a world of ideas and disguises. They're cut off from life and desire and all petty things." She'd make some comment on art and then politics and her own personal tragedies, before turning to religion and architecture. Her conversation dizzied them.

"Here's an example of religious architecture in the Islamic style from the Almoravid period. This is Puerta Bab al-Mardum and that's the Church of Cristo de la Luz. This piece of artistic genius was brought here by the Almoravid ruler Yusuf ibn Tashfin in 1086 when he came to the aid of the party kings at the Battle of Sagrajas and took Toledo back from Alfonso the Sixth of Castile. Look at the imposing gates and the decoration on the roofs. It reminds you of the exquisite architecture of Marrakesh, Fez, and Tlemcen."

Without even pausing to take a breath, the woman led them over to the Synagogue of El Transito. "This synagogue was built in 1356 as a family synagogue for the king's treasurer. It's the oldest synagogue in Toledo, but it was turned into a church in 1492 after the Jews were expelled from Spain." She led them to the center of the synagogue, where through two arching windows a mosaic of sunlight fell over their faces. She paused in front of three gypsum arches. "Here we see where my forefathers and yours, Jews and Muslims, came together to create a most outstanding example of Sephardic artwork." She drew their attention to the intersecting web of plaster with Hebrew and Arabic calligraphy, Islamic motifs, and the name of God repeated many times. She sighed. "If only all this hadn't been suppressed, mostly in the sixteenth century, you would've been able to see the variety of religious architecture for yourselves. Art used to fight over this city. Whoever set foot in Toledo would fall in love with the city immediately, and it didn't matter how protective the city's other lovers were, how they plotted to keep the city for themselves and eliminate their rivals." Nora giggled suddenly, her laughter as slight and airy as the woman herself.

"It's time for my morning coffee."

They insisted that she let them take her for a coffee. She sat across from them in a cafe on the Plaza de Zocodover and told them her story. "You know the building where we met? It's sort of a home-cum-school for orphan girls, run by the Church. They provide them with all their basic needs until they're old enough to get married and then they move on to a different life. I was one of those girls, except for one small difference. I spent my entire life in that dark, bare school and although I could've left its austerity behind by getting married, I was too scared to go out into the world when I finally grew up, so I became a teacher at the school. A prophet of austerity, in a way, but I at least hope I'm able to teach the girls to be braver than I was so that they can go out and have their own lives. In the midst of that asceticism, I preach the gospel of escape; I feel like an infiltrator. I've taken my vows to be a spiritual hypocrite." Rafi looked deep into Nora's eyes as he translated what the woman had said. She was prepared to spend the whole day with them, talking and listening, as if she loved nothing more than filling the time with her own stories as they climbed through the city like she didn't even have to breathe; and, of course, it was intoxicating to hear herself being translated into another language. She insisted on writing her address at the school for each of them in her severe handwriting, paying most of her attention to Nora.

"Will you send me a postcard? You will? I don't believe you. I want to have a collection of postcards from the world outside. Places I don't dare to go myself. I hope you come from somewhere very far away so I can hear a voice from the other side of the world."

"I'm from Mecca. The city that Noah visited to retrieve the bodies of Adam and Eve from the floodwaters just as his grandson would later visit Toledo." It was the first time Rafi had ever heard Nora mention her hometown.

"O merciful God!" the woman said before standing up and walking off—without acknowledging them at all—ducking into the first lane she came to. Rafi knew they'd missed their chance to ask what the sheikh had come looking for. He settled the bill while Nora went into the cafe to look for a bathroom.

As she was washing her hands, the woman in white appeared beside her all of a sudden. "Did you really say you were from Mecca? Meeting you and you promising to write to me on this beautiful, sunny morning is the highlight of my life." She pressed yet another piece of paper with her address on it into Nora's palm.

"Please write to me a lot. Write with the dust and the sweat and the dreams of your city. Maybe I'll give your postcards to my students. It's good for them to imagine different cities, different religions." She turned to leave, but then she turned back again. "Are you another one of those religious types that come here pretending to be tourists? Deep down, we all suffer the burden of our religions. A city like this attracts people in disguise from all over the world. Here, being this high up, we're closer to God, so we don't need all the different names religion goes by. God himself is near to us and nameless. We can free ourselves from our masks and ambitions; it's enough that we're meek. Here we can forget about the world down below and stop caring about life." She walked away again, no explanation given, no response expected. Nora hadn't understood a word of what she'd said, of course. Rafi was astonished to see them walk out together. The woman leaned down over the table.

"The El Greco Museum is closed on Mondays, but you can still go see *The Burial of the Count of Orgaz* in the church." As soon as she stepped away from the cafe, her expression became humorless once again. She was preparing to reenter a world that knew everything there was to know about her and about which she, too, knew everything.

"Should we follow her?" There was enough skepticism in Nora's voice that Rafi felt able to acknowledge that it wasn't worth it.

"I think she must be insane, that woman. That's the conclusion the sheikh came to." At that altitude, the sheikh had begun to matter less. Nora was swept up in the moment; she wanted to pursue an adventure that would take her far away from everything she'd left behind.

They walked along, winding their way back through the Roman and Islamic-era buildings along stone alleyways, which seemed always to ascend. Nora stopped in front of a house, which looked to them like a spearhead at the tip of the other houses, like a river between sloping banks. It was a small stone house with an old arabesque door, inlaid with brass. The door knocker was in the shape of a circular constellation.

"For Sale—Please call," Rafi read the sign that had been posted on the wooden shutter.

"If he forgets me and I end up—maybe we should write down the number, just in case . . ." Her request took him by surprise, but her enthusiasm was electric. He jotted down the number: 37 63 29.

As they crossed back through the Plaza del Ayuntamiento, Nora stopped in a small bookshop. When she found a book about El Greco that she wanted to buy, she realized that she hadn't brought any money with her. She put it back. Nothing could spoil her mood on that sunny morning.

All around them, as if out of nowhere, a flood of tourists and flashbulbs appeared and they were pulled along in their wake. They ate paella with snails, topped with black beans, at a table with four chairs and a loud orange umbrella. The umbrella didn't really shelter them so when the sky began to sprinkle, raindrops stuck to her hair and gave off a scent of passion in her heart. It was raining hard suddenly, a downpour, and then equally suddenly, it stopped. The sky folded the rain clouds and tucked them under its arm as it watched them from the edge of the precipice where the orange umbrellas ended.

Rafi took the book about El Greco out of a paper bag and handed it to Nora. "Oh, you shouldn't have!" she said, and it sounded like she was saying, *I needed to own this!* She flipped the pages, possessively, giddily, and there, between the pages, she found a slip of paper with the phone number for the house that was for sale. She smiled and pressed it deeper toward the spine of the book.

"Don't mention it. I'll just put it on your bill." The words floated through the air that separated them, meaninglessly; they weren't intended to burst her happy bubble. Rafi was watching her, as if with a sixth sense, trying to decipher the small reactions behind her natural smile and between her exuberant chatter and heavy silence.

They finally traced their steps back to the Church of Santo Tomé, which held the painting depicting the burial of the man who was Count of Toledo and Lord of Orgaz in the fourteenth century. Rafi could tell that she was uncomfortable letting him pay for the tickets. "Don't worry," he said. "This is on me."

They walked into the hall, which looked to them like a vestibule, and stood, awestruck, behind a rope that separated them from the painting, which stretched from floor to ceiling. They looked down on the gently lit burial scene and the Count of Orgaz's body.

"Humans wearing heavenly faces. This painting shows two saints known for being lavish and vibrant, Saint Augustine and Saint Stephen, descending from heaven to attend the burial of the departed nobleman. One stands at the man's head and the other at his feet as they lay him in the earth. It's as though this is the miracle that the worthy can expect to receive when they die. It was a way of getting the people of Orgaz to donate liberally to the church," explained the guide, who was himself under the painting's spell.

She stared at the gold embroidery on the robes of the saints laying him to rest while the messengers of death themselves became obscured. Then Picasso's painting *Evocation, The Burial of Casagemas,* which she'd seen in the Museo del Prado one morning, materialized before her eyes. *The Burial of the Count of Orgaz* was overlaid with Picasso's painting, the blue of *Evocation* cast over the heavenly gloom of the angels descending to carry out the funeral rites.

There was another body where the count's body had been, but it wasn't the body of Picasso's friend Casagemas. It was someone else, someone Nora felt she knew. Naked women took the place of the angels, and there were two who stood out in particular. They were wearing sheer thigh-high stockings: one in red, the other in black. They both looked like they'd just walked out of a cabaret. They stood, watching the macabre scene below. Then, the two women turned to look at Nora. The woman in black stockings looked just like her; it was like looking at a mirror. When she turned to examine the woman in red, her heart stopped.

The Devil's Horns

> "THIS TRIBE IS LEGENDARY—people call them the Devil's Horns," al-Ghatafani cried out to us, "but they may be nothing more than a mirage created by our own fear . . ." We slowed down to interpret the terrifying sight: mountaintops pricked the sky like devils' horns, blocking the horizon. The giants took the lead, urging our camels to hurry forward and penetrate the rocky slopes by way of narrow hidden passages carved out by goodness knows what. The camels rushed along in a frenzy, scratching themselves against the rock, so excitable that they threatened to throw us off. They were bloody by the time they reached the open space that materialized behind a wall of rock. There was an entire universe hidden behind that abominable rock face: palm trees, grazing animals, people—all the same sandy color—surrounding an enormous idol of blazing black. A shiver ran through the devil's horns around it, adding to the stench of burnt flesh that it gave off. Our worst fear had risen up out of the sand.

Pages and pages of the parchment were missing, and Yusuf had to skip lines obscured by patches of blood or henna.

> THEY PULLED ME FROM THE SAND and threw me at the feet of their leader, who watched me struggle. He caught hold of my right hand and examined my birthmark, a vein that ran across my palm from my index finger to my wrist, where it disappeared into the bundle of veins there.
>
> Their leader's body was a fierce sandstorm; it ravaged me for nights and days during which my eyes never closed once. I fulfilled that sheikh's every desire, as the blood boiled in my eyes. My screams were

even louder than those of al-Ghatafani coming from whatever hell they were subjecting him to.

"The woman who bears this birthmark will carry the demon who will inherit the earth. Through him, our spawn will penetrate all tribes and become ageless demons that roam the earth, breeding with the survivors of storm-struck caravans and ships on the shores of the Gulf of Suez and the Persian Gulf . . ."

Burial

"Sometimes I get woken up by a deep feeling of remorse. About what, I don't know . . . There's always the same idea jammed in my head: 'You're a fighter,' it says, but it sounds more like criticism than praise." She fell silent, trying to hear the reproachful voice replay itself. The two paintings, the Picasso and El Greco, had fused in her mind, and it disturbed her. "I've never fought for anything. Not for principles, or a better life, or love of country. None of that matters to me. Now I'm fighting for the sake of my silly little whims. I embarked on a total of one battle—for love—and it vanquished me." She waved the dream away with a flick of her hand.

"The only thing I ever fought for was the love of a man who was aging with frightening speed. His body grew weaker by the minute, everything except his heart, which was cast iron and sealed shut. It ticked assiduously but never to the bigger beats that cause hearts of flesh and blood to tremble. My father was proud to be a descendant of those striving men of rock-hard conviction who'd fought both for and against the unification of the Arabian Peninsula. I had to learn to live with that iron heart, to make important decisions on my own, without letting my emotions get in the way. The first emotion I ditched was fear, because nothing mattered." Her voice quavered at the bruising words.

A tourist bent down, smiling politely, to pick up the book that had slipped from her hand and fallen in front of the grave, setting it beside her. She placed it gravely on her lap, open at *The Adoration of the Shepherds*, who were arrayed reverently around the child and his mother Mary. It was El Greco's last painting; he'd intended for it to hang over his grave in the Church of Santo Domingo el Antiguo. Her words flowed, barely above a whisper, bringing the past to life, and Rafi strained to listen, not wanting to miss a word, as the infant in the painting cast a glow onto Nora's face as well as those of the shepherds around him.

"Some mornings you wake up and you know it's not like other mornings. You're on top of the world, everything you dreamed of the night before is waiting for you just outside the door, you just need to push it open with your toes and everything will rush in, climb into bed with you, right into your lap. That morning, it was her lap that was overflowing. I froze; the moans she was suppressing were coming from my body. 'Help me . . .' she begged. Pleas, sweat, bloody-tasting tears: I had no idea what to do, and the contractions were coming thick and fast, there was no time to think.

"'How did you hide this the whole time?!' A spasm of pain and my reproach was batted away; her water broke at my feet. The stink of bloody water covered my limbs, blinding me. I could feel the heat of the fetus against my thighs as it swam in that water. I was pressed up against her thighs, face to face, as a storm tore through my body. I had no time to look for help; it was just me and that laboring belly and the world closing in on us.

"'No one can know . . .' The breaths she wasted on that plea closed the womb around the baby's thighs. I don't know how long the child had to wait on the threshold of the world like that until I slipped my fingers inside her. Even today, my hands tremble when I reach for something . . ." She raised her trembling fingers in the air.

"I can still feel her vagina and the baby drenched in water. I tried to free a tiny leg trapped by a tear in the vaginal wall, and I pushed the left leg, which was in a hurry to step over the threshold, back against the right so they could slip out together; I was afraid the frantic leg would tear the pelvises of both mother and child. In those hours, which felt to me like a single viscous second, I sank inside the woman who'd been my only friend; the only person who could read me like a silly poem memorized in school. I'd never been more than a flimsy imitation of the passion and tenderness that she imposed on the world around her through books and words . . . There, on the knife-edge between life and death, I lost the ability to communicate with her slow rhythm. She was in no hurry to push that child out, despite the fear of scandal; if anything, maybe she was hoping to keep the baby hidden inside her. But then a violent spasm in her womb decided the matter: the baby was out. He didn't cry. With two bloody masses on either side of me, I waited: for her placenta and for the first breath to blow open his lungs. For a moment, I allowed her to die, worried that the walls of the womb had collapsed around the placenta, but then out of the corner of a terrified eye, I saw her belly contract as she squatted, and the placenta slithered slowly out on to the ground. I was conscious of nothing but the tiny, slippery, utterly mute body in my hands. I had nothing to cut the umbilical cord with, so I sealed it off near the belly with a bobby pin, and instinctively turned him upside down and rubbed his body between my palms so the lungs would open and drink air. For a few moments, time stopped: the tiny body in my hands watched me silently with closed eyes that peered through me, and then, in an instant, my lips were on his blue lips, my forefinger parted them, and I sucked deeply. The taste can't be described in words—it wasn't salty, it wasn't bloody—it was the taste of life. The liquid filled my throat, and it still does; I often wake up coughing in the middle of the night, trying to spit it out. A last desperate suck at what was behind those lips and a shudder convulsed the little chest. He cried! Joy gripped me, but fear, too, fear that someone might hear, and he sensed it too and fell definitively, finally, silent. Living and dying in the space of a moment.

"How long did we sit there, those two heaps, once living, now dead, lying between us? I felt guilty for the vitality that had come over me. I couldn't bury him; he was still lying against my chest, his blood clotting on my nipples. When she got up, limping her usual slight limp, she pulled the placenta to her chest; I followed her, and we walked almost pressed side-by-side. Under the stairs, I dug with one hand and with the other held the baby firmly against my chest. All my longing to give birth was embodied in that pliant bundle of life, and when the hole was long enough I let her snatch him from me. I ignored his male organ, preferring to bury him gender-less, and turned and went upstairs before the soil could touch him."

On those naked steps high in Toledo, Nora and Rafi sat in silence, the radiant energy of the painting of the child and shepherds animating the dance-like figures of the tourists around them. The striking contrast between the degrees of dark and light in the painting and the city heightened the drama of the scene. The long shadows of tourists, the laughter of a girl sitting on the shoulders of a young man with long hair, the babbling of an old woman who'd begun dancing, alone, to the melody of the violin played by a homeless man in colorful gypsy clothes. Nora's voice blew toward them like wind from a distant time and place. She absentmindedly stroked the naked infant among the shepherds on the page.

Nora got up, as if fleeing from that birth, and Rafi followed her. They walked through the brilliance of the clashing darkness and light in the painting, and their feet led them to the fourteenth-century bridge of San Martín. The Gothic surroundings were the most beautiful setting for a sunset in all of Spain.

"I snuck under the stairs with my paper and charcoal, that night, and drew that baby in dozens of sketches, but none of them pulsed with the warmth of the tiny body that had died on my chest. None of them tasted like that water. I couldn't bring myself to breathe a single word for months after that, it might have been seven months, or maybe more—I was afraid I'd lose the taste in my mouth, the taste of the inside of a woman from a child's mouth. It was my secret taste, and without it the world would drop dead and abandon me. That child should have been born from my womb so he could shatter this worry of infertility. I never dared to ask what had made a married woman deny that she was pregnant."

Around them the violin's song blended with the crimson sunset and the bodies around them began dance, everything swayed as though drunk in the sunset, and Nora fell silent. It only added to the feeling that they were still walking through *The Burial of the Count of Orgaz*, the distorted proportions of human bodies that dominated the painting mingling ecstatically with the tourists on the bridge, whose faces had become exaggeratedly tragic or comic, their laughter shriller and their silences more profound, as longing floated in the air above like a blood smear that dissolved the city in the red peaks of the mountains.

The disc of the sun looked like an oil painting pinned to the horizon. Stone Toledo loomed above them, its head in the sky and its feet in the waters of the Tagus. Time froze. Nora was like a creature from a different era, stamped—no matter how she tried to shake it off—with features of primitiveness and imminent extinction. A voice inside her explained to her what she was seeing around her.

"There's an eternal process of displacement, a constant concealment, in which people are forced to hide their religion, their loyalties, their pregnancy, their reality, their battles, even their gender. People disguise themselves as something other than what they are: man as woman, genius as idiot, Muslim as Jew as Christian, debaucher as prig, fundamentalist as liberator, so they can guarantee that they'll be accepted, or so they can worm their way into people's hearts or places or positions of power, or just so they'll be left alone to live in peace." The people around her, and Nora, herself, were part of that human flock, in a state of denial, hiding, masking. All those living creatures, minerals, humans were nothing but masks of the Divine Power, who became visible in extremes of infidelity and faith, piety and sin, moving away from Himself to practice His wholeness. The alley of her childhood was all about unmasking; that truth had come to her early, when she was still a child, though she may not have been able to translate it into words at the time. How many masks had been pulled off in that faraway alley? There, when a passerby felt certain that they were alone, silent and unseen, they would play out their reality, revealing their face for God alone to see without judgment or punishment. The difference between seeing and seen would dissolve. Tragic and comic storylines were acted out in that alley, and only the doves replayed the same act over and over when they answered the sound of her lover's motorbike with a flutter of their wings and flew in a complete arc over the alley like passion flowing. Her heartbeats quickened, warning of exposure, and she stuffed the masks inside her breast though she longed to release them. The departure of the motorbike, more than that of the man, was what had caused her to feel a tyrannical urge—like exhaust fumes—to flee and spread.

The flow of her past was suddenly interrupted by the appearance of the woman from the morning. "O merciful Father, you're here! I was worried you'd left!" she cried, still panting. Rafi couldn't hide the shock from his face; some deep presentiment told him the woman's appearance would bring evil.

"I've been all over Toledo looking for you. I knew this place was my last chance to find you." When she took Nora's hand, Nora didn't start; the woman pressed it to her own, upturned so as to read the palm. With her left hand she dabbed the sweat from her temples and wiped it on her pants, passing its dampness on to Nora's palm.

"Your face has been in my mind since I left the two of you. I knew I'd seen it somewhere before." The movement around them stopped, and the red of the setting sun darkened, throwing sinister shadows across the walls and gargoyles. Neither Nora nor her companion uttered a breath; Rafi felt like he could do nothing to stop the fates that were being entwined around Nora.

"Come with me, I have something to show you." She gave them no chance to object and set off, leading them back toward the Mosque of Cristo de la Luz. When they got there, they gazed up at the decorated brick facade and the series of arches that called to mind the mosque in Cordoba.

"This mosque dates back to the year 999, but it was converted into a church in the twelfth century. A statue of Christ that had been bricked into the wall to avoid profanation was re-discovered in the time of Alfonso the Sixth and El Cid." She grasped them by the arm and stopped them in the threshold, where they could see both the watching silence inside and the redness of the setting sun, which was unable to penetrate into the mosque. "That was when this transept was added, and with it a Mudejar semicircular apse."

The woman kept them there under the three arches of the door for what felt like a long while. The mosque felt totally deserted, like it was holding its breath. There wasn't even a janitor or imam there. To Nora, it seemed like a toy mosque with its cuboid shape and fine decorations. Rafi retreated a few steps to read the Arabic inscription in the brick facade: "In the name of God, Ahmad ibn al-Hadidi built this mosque at his personal expense, desiring God's reward. With God's assistance, and that of the architects Musa ibn Ali and

Sa'da, it was completed in the month of Muharram in the year three hundred and ninety-nine."

The woman took advantage of Rafi's preoccupation with the inscription to whisk Nora inside the mosque and slam the door behind them, leaving Rafi outside. With devilish suddenness Nora found herself alone with that woman in the empty apse. The silence drowned out Rafi's angry knocking.

Nora hesitated, wondering whether to escape. Was it the unhinged gleam in the woman's eyes, or the newfound recklessness that had taken hold of her that had Nora so excited? Nora wanted to be swept to the very limit of danger. She followed the woman through the calm emptiness of the mosque silently.

The dark red sunset pooled in bloodlike darkness between the successive keyhole arches. Nora avoided looking up at them; they looked like open doorways leading to death. The woman's besieging eyes could read her reaction to the call of the place and its spirits.

The nine square vaults on the ceiling followed their steps like the eyes of giants. The woman made Nora stop and listen beneath each vault; Nora stole furtive glances at the beautiful square structures, not daring to look closer for fear she'd be sucked into their darkness. Stopping Nora under a vault that featured a seven-pointed star, the woman forced her to look twice, and said, "Before we go any further, remember that what I'm about to reveal to you concerns the rivalry between our two great ancestors: mine, Samuel ibn Nagrela, and yours, Ali ibn Hazm. The Jew and the Muslim, who both believed that man's fall did not take place when Adam and Eve fell from Paradise but when Cordoba fell and the centuries of harmony that had existed between the different religions was lost." It dawned on Nora that the woman was speaking to her in fluent Arabic.

"You're not imagining it. My Jewish ancestors used languages as the key to their fortunes, and one of those languages was your own. My ancestor Samuel displayed a remarkable talent for the Arabic language and calligraphy. That was what brought about the great change in his fortunes." Nora sealed off her thoughts against this woman who seemed to be able to read them so easily.

"After the fall of the Berber kingdom and the wars between the party kings, the two men's fates took different paths as they each searched for a door that would take them to the Paradise they'd lost here on earth. Ibn Hazm sought refuge near Seville, mourning Cordoba and its green revolution, and the destruction of its massive library, for which caravan-loads of books on astronomy, astrology, the sciences, and nature had been brought all the way from Baghdad. Ibn Hazm chased the dream of a resurrected Caliphate and the universal civilization it had nurtured. He believed that it was key to the door of Paradise and that was what made him side with the underdog in every conflict. He spent his life between exile and prison, an itinerant; after he was released, he isolated himself to write—on theology, matters of doctrine, and philosophy, trying to record the contents of that great lost library. He was way ahead of his time. He wrote a series of books comparing the three religions—the key to the faiths—which culminated in his book *The Necklace of the Dove*. Love was the only thing that could bridge the gaps between people, he discovered.

"Ibn Nagrela, on the other hand, was a physician from Cordoba, who was welcomed by the royal court in Granada, an Andalusian city that was home to the largest mixed community of Jews and Muslims. He lived two lives: one, in Arabic, as the ruler's secretary and general of the Granadan army, leading campaigns against the neighboring kingdoms; and another in Hebrew, the language of his community in which he wrote poetry. Both men mourned the loss of their earthly Paradise in al-Andalus, the end of coexistence. They both spread the wisdom of eleventh-century Cordoba, whose scholars had been killed and whose library had been destroyed."

The woman brought her face right up to Nora's, engulfing her in heavy chamomile breaths.

"Both our ancestors left us their version of the key to Paradise: Ibn Hazm gave us *The Necklace of the Dove* and Ibn Nagrela his son Joseph, who inherited his father's poetry and carried on his ideals and his obsession with Eden. He believed that translation was the solution to the puzzle of the absolute mind, or absolute Paradise. Translation would preserve the dialogue that had taken place between civilizations when Islamic rule flourished in al-Andalus. That gave us the Jewish Golden Age in the kingdoms of Northern Andalusia and the transfer of scientific knowledge to Europe. My ancestor Joseph's translations opened the door to the world. I was obsessed with him when I was younger—this man who, it is said, was slaughtered along with thousands of other Jews in the streets of Cordoba when contact between religions became a crime known as heresy." Half-hidden in the darkness, the woman led Nora forward, gradually but firmly, toward the apse, her chamomile-laden breaths intensifying Nora's concealed longing for the place.

"Joseph provoked his enemies—he wasn't as humble as his father—and people say that he was killed for it, crucified along with the members of a hundred and fifty Jewish families. The truth is, though, that Joseph managed to escape Granada. According to the story, he went in search of a door that had been revealed to him in a vision, in Aden, at the tip of the Arabian Peninsula." The lights suddenly went out, and the woman pushed Nora into the apse, closing the door behind them. The darkness swallowed them.

"Sit on the ground. Lean back and look at the sky above and below . . ." Nora found herself being pushed down into the darkness, where she sat with her back against what felt like stairs carved into the wall. Meanwhile, the woman had vanished, and Nora began to think she'd been left there to die. Her body felt so drugged by the darkness she couldn't even bring herself to get up to look for a way out.

The temple receded into deeper and deeper darkness, to the quickening thump of her heartbeats. The cold floor gnawed at her body through her light dress. Suddenly a shaft of light from the setting sun poured through a central window, illuminating the double rows of golden windows that went all the way around the wall of the temple. The round body of the temple came to life, flooding the space around Nora with rose-colored gold. Nora thought, for a moment, that the sunset was cascading into the temple like a waterfall, and she couldn't be sure whether the temple was shooting upward into the sky or plummeting down into the earth to burst through to the sky on the other side of the planet. The inside of the temple was engulfed in a pink halo that revealed narrow steps carved in a spiral around the wall; they couldn't have been there for climbing because they were too narrow and there was no banister. It took a while for Nora to make out the sunlit patches on the walls: from the ground to the sky, the wall was covered not with windows but with brightly colored doors that looked tiny from below and were covered in engravings that deceived the eye in the evening light, which was rosy in some places, bloody in others, and elsewhere absent, leaving an ominous pitch-blackness. Nora blinked, unsure of what she was seeing, and in that split second, the rectangular patches dissolved and whirled into the form of a single, huge door open to the sky above.

"This is what Joseph, who bore the dream of Samuel ibn Nagrela, saw when he finished his nighttime vigil outside Solomon's Seal near Aden."

The sun dipped behind the mountains and the temple was plunged into darkness, complete and thick, like a living thing; the darkness embraced Nora, who had no choice but to slump back, feeling the chamomile breaths flow from the fading church murals outside. A distinctive smell—from her childhood—filled Nora's senses, bringing tears to her eyes. It was just like the smell of the qat the Yemenis chewed at sunset to get high—the woman was trying to drug her, she was certain of it. Her limbs felt heavy and sagged into the ground, and her vision was blurry. She could see through things, and through her own body, which was disintegrating and diffusing into the layers of darkness. It gradually become one with the darkness, and she began to hear distant voices speaking in Arabic; was it the woman resuming her story on the other side of the closed door, or was the story itself flowing through her, as if she were walking through an absolute mind that stretched into the past. Maybe it was the mind of Joseph ibn Nagrela as he stepped out onto the deck of the ship that plowed the Red Sea on its way to the tip of the Arabian Peninsula. Yemeni singing rose around him as the crew moored the ship. The waves lapped at Joseph ibn Nagrela's feet as he stood alone on the seashore at the port of Aden, carrying nothing but the robe on his back, lost in thought and fingering in his pocket the damp, salt-encrusted scrap of paper that bore a drawing of the door.

A stranger woke him up after he'd spent two days sleeping, hungry and forgotten on the beach, licked by the tide. "Brother, go find some shade from this sun!" He gradually became aware of the Arabic words and realized that someone was trying to coax him to consciousness. As soon as he had woken, Joseph pulled the drawing out of his pocket and thrust it at the stranger, gesturing toward the golden door. "This is what I'm looking for."

Salt-soaked Arabic words flooded from his mouth, reminding him that it had been months since he'd spoken to another human being. Traveling in the infernal hold of one of the ships of the invading Portuguese fleet was like being incubated in a womb from hell.

"It came to me in a dream, a door between heaven and earth. I searched and searched and found that this city, Aden at the base of the Arabian Peninsula, is the gateway to the village of Solomon's Seal, which contains every door on earth. That's why your city is called 'Aden'—because it leads to those doors . . ."

For days, Joseph ibn Nagrela traveled across the land of Yemen, repeating the story in an Arabic too heavy for the simple people he met to understand; still, the moment they set eyes on that drawing of the door, they realized that he was a man possessed by thoughts of a world other than theirs.

He kept repeating the story until one day he crossed paths with a beggar. "Happy Solomon at your service," the man greeted him merrily. When Happy Solomon clapped eyes on the door, he fell silent, listening to his genies and subjecting Joseph to careful scrutiny, then said, "My tongue speaks the tongues of all those who believe, every language on earth spoken by men who breathe, even the speech of beasts, so accept my wisdom. I'm a miniature version of the prophet Solomon himself!" He examined the drawing with the help of his genies and explained, "What you are seeking is beyond the destiny of Eve's sons. My genies speak of a mountain of doors, but there none of those doors will open for a living human."

"Will they open for a dead person?"

"My genies know about life, nothing else. Don't tire them out with your riddles about death."

In the face of Joseph ibn Nagrela's determination, Solomon the Happy assented to be his guide to the Hadramawt Valley. On foot, they crossed the happy mountains of Yemen, avoiding Seiyun and its famous market where craftsmen sold their products, including doors. Joseph nevertheless saw many Seiyuni women in their wide straw hats and brocade-embellished dresses, stopping travelers with songs and dances and inviting them to come to the market; they tried to tempt Joseph himself to buy one of their doors.

Happy Solomon also avoided al-Hajarayn, the town in the mountains famous for its beekeepers and their curative honey, warning Joseph, "You can say goodbye to your door if you drown in the honey of al-Hajarayn. The mountain's like our mother Eve, who opened her legs to tempt Adam from Paradise."

They avoided Shibam, climbing the mountains facing it so as to look across the Hadramawt Valley from their peaks. The city was filled with towering mud buildings of five, six, seven stories, which stood like a crowd of giants gathered in a space of no more than five hundred meters across, destruction masochists, so fragile was their position on the plain, which was constantly at the mercy of mountain floods.

"You must pass by the reservoir of underground water before you reach the temples," advised Happy Solomon. He led Joseph ibn Nagrela to the outskirts of Ma'rib, a city that stood on the remains of the Great Dam and was known as the "city astride the two gardens of paradise."

"I will leave you here to continue your journey," said Happy Solomon. "If you're fortunate, the lord of the genies and birds will permit you to enter the village of Solomon's Seal." He vanished then and there, as if he'd never existed.

Joseph ibn Nagrela found himself alone, standing between the two temples—Baran, temple of the sun, which was also known as the throne of Bilqis, Queen of Sheba, and Awam, temple of the moon, which was known as Bilqis' Sanctuary. He looked out on the vast sand sea that was the Empty Quarter.

The first night fell pitch black, erasing Joseph's features, forming deep pools of shadow in the valley and hovering over the temple of the moon, revealing to Joseph the place where lovers from all over the Arabian Peninsula came to die. As night proceeded, the nine-meter-high crescent-shaped temple wall, carved from a single block of stone, came to life. It emerged out of the great sand guarded by eight eastward-facing pillars inlaid with seashells or moonshells, which invited him to enter, luring him into the Holy of Holies whose translucent marble walls were woven out of silver and gold and precious stones.

Joseph spent his nights in a trance between the four columns of the Holy of Holies, listening to the two tableaux that stood seven meters above the ground on either side of the entrance, whispering prayers for love and prosperity, begging the Queen of Sheba to materialize out of the milky sand, naked and as lithe as the moonlight, which gleamed on the temple floor as she walked on tiptoe to take up her ceremonial gown of shimmering silver that left her shoulders and arms bare, two slits running from the top of her thighs to her bare feet. Wearing her crown, she then approached her seat among the stone seats that surrounded the stone table at the entrance of the Holy of Holies. The seats of mother sun and father moon and Venus were taken up as well as they all met to discuss how to lure back her lover Almaqa from Awam. The pale, translucent marble would light up with his presence, reflecting the faces of the resurrected lovers who had risen up from the graves that lay in row after row to the south and west of the temple.

Joseph spent his nights in a fever for Bilqis, listening and emptying his soul of everything but his longing for that door.

Finally, when the moon waned and withdrew, Joseph ibn Nagrela followed it, with the flood of lovers illuminated by Bilqis' breaths, walking three kilometers to the west and crossing the plain of henna and coffee trees of the left garden of paradise, led by five pillars and a sixth broken pillar to the temple of the sun where he waded through the wide water channel to the south and then entered the gate to the main temple, crossing the vast courtyard, which was still alive with the echoes of feasts held in Almaqa's honor. Inscriptions threatened curses on any thieves who dared to enter the sanctuary. He climbed the stairs in the courtyard to the huge dais to the Holy of Holies, where the bull planted its four-meter-high legs to fertilize the soil and the lovers.

Joseph spent his days deciphering pledges of love inscribed in cuneiform on the eastern columns of the dais and the offerings that lovers brought from the ends of the earth: jars of herbs, perfumes, incenses, silver that the lover-pilgrims laid along the length of the wall of the external courtyard and on both sides of the main gate. To Joseph the temple seemed a polished expanse of translucent alabaster, breathing in the sunlight and exuding a faint cinnamon-scented incense, a pool of goodness that healed his senses and filtered the light around him so that it magnified the image of the door inside him.

News of Joseph ibn Nagrela spread: they said he was a hermit who had brought to life the pilgrimages Bilqis and her lover Almaqa made to visit each other, traveling constantly between Baran and Awam, and had taken up residence in Almaqa's Holy of Holies, where he received the lover-pilgrims who came to Almaqa seeking the moon's spells and the farmers and shepherds who came seeking the sun's. With the lust of a miser, Joseph ibn Nagrela devoted himself to receiving the pilgrims and collecting from their mouths and hearts their harvest songs and love poems, learning from their dances the primitive, animal, chest-splitting cries that begged a lover to be swayed, a plant to grow, a harvest to be enriched.

Joyful pilgrims traveled to see him from all over the Arab lands, to meet him between his two gardens of paradise, among the sweet clouds of song gathered around him, raining torrents over the Hadramawt Valley for three consecutive moons and showing Joseph the secret that gave that land its nickname, "the Happy Land of Yemen."

On Joseph's seventh sunrise between the two temples, he was awoken by the soft scent of incense, and when he opened his eyes, glittering strips of light on the horizon dazzled him. The mountain opposite looked like it was covered in solid gold bricks; when he looked more carefully, he could make out hundreds of doors covering the entire surface of the mountain. He rushed toward them blindly, desperate to get inside, but when he reached the mountain the doors had melted into one huge gate that was firmly closed against him. No matter how hard he knocked, no answer came. At sunset, the doors faded away and he wondered if it had all been a mirage; nevertheless he didn't dare leave.

Dawn after dawn, those shining doors reappeared, but each time he approached they would be transformed into that single, closed gate. He got thinner and thinner, surviving only on the water and goat's milk brought to him by the girls of Solomon's Seal, near Ma'rib, girls who were the descendants of Solomon and Bilqis.

"These are doors between the parts of Creation," they told him. "Between animal, vegetable, and mineral, between tongues, between life and death and God knows what else . . . Some of them opened for the prophet King Solomon, and that's how he earned the name "King of the Genies," but those doors have never opened for another living being. It all comes down to keys. You'll have to find the original key before you start dreaming about one of those doors opening for you!"

The sun peeled Joseph's skin and grilled his flesh a dark, aromatic teak while the moon polished him to a silver gleam; his coal-black braids grew longer. He was getting thinner still, as thin as a key, but whenever he approached a door, the closed gate would stand in his way. At the age of seventy, having never lost hope, he woke up to find that his seed had caused the bellies of the Solomon's Seal girls to swell. When the pains of labor took them, and the ground of the two gardens shook, all he remembered was the first girl to be born. She had a moon-shaped birthmark on her palm. Joseph's memory kept the sandstorm that had covered the mountain: when it finally abated, the mountain had vanished behind a veil that made it difficult to see; countless doors were scattered all over the valley bed and figures that looked like a band of beggars flocked from everywhere on earth and began to collect the doors, piling them up on a huge bonfire that they'd lit to help them see.

"It is not the destiny of Eve's sons to possess these doors, and it is a curse to try to break the locks preserved in the tablets," he was warned, but Joseph ibn Nagrela slipped away from them and plunged his bare hands into the fire to save the doors, forgetting all about his newborn daughter who had disappeared with the rest of the village of Solomon's Seal and forgotten the earthquake she'd been born into.

Joseph ibn Nagrela returned with a cargo of doors to Andalusia. In Toledo, he went to visit all the most famous blacksmiths whose skill in forging knives and swords and casting keys was incomparable, and wasted the last quarter-century of his life in its hills, casting key after key with the locksmiths, casting and re-casting in search of the one key that would open all those doors. The locksmiths said that he used all the songs, poems, dances, prayers, and charms he'd learned at the temple of Almaqa to help him, but none of the hundreds of keys that they cast was the ultimate key that could open those locks.

When Joseph ibn Nagrela was one hundred, they forged a key that opened door after door, until there was only one door left, but the excitement split Joseph's heart in two and he dropped dead in this mosque. In the commotion surrounding the death of such a legend, the key was lost. When this apse was built, the doors were affixed around the walls, where they appeared only to those endowed with vision, inspiring creators like El Greco to search, in their own works, for the ultimate key that would open the door between humans and the divine.

A back window smashed and Rafi burst in. He was irate, but he stopped to see if Nora was alright. "Are you okay? You can't imagine how scared I was," he gasped. In the same breath he turned to the woman, yelling, "Are you insane? What the hell were you thinking?" The delicate touch of Nora's fingers on his arm calmed him, and the strange gleam in her eyes struck his heart like a feverish glow, but with a queer luminosity; he felt her gaze restrain him.

"What a great bodyguard I am," he muttered to himself. "Letting an old woman trick me!" He pushed forward into the dark mosque, shining all his suspicion at the corners to uncover the woman's schemes, but she paid no attention to him and carried on telling Nora her story. Nora flopped back against the wall, suddenly tired, and ran her tongue over her lips to moisten their sudden cracks.

"Now. Close your eyes and imagine your Arab ancestor: once, a man came here burdened with the same longing as is in your face now. He made the opposite journey to Joseph ibn Nagrela's voyage to Aden in search of the door: your ancestor from the Shayba Tribe crossed the seas from Aden to here looking for a key that would open a single door, that of the house of God, but instead all he found was these doors and locks." Nora was lost amidst those mirror-image journeys; one man went after a door and another came after a key.

"Here." She pointed to a patch on the floor of the temple and pushed Nora toward it so she could receive the vision. "Al-Shaybi spent a quarter of a century in this spot looking after the mosque, tracing the steps of Joseph ibn Nagrela, and the key to the absolute." Rafi lingered in the apse, looking fervently for the doors that had been revealed to Nora, but the woman dragged him out. It was then that they noticed the parchment in a wooden frame, studded with shimmering gold and tiny red and green flowers, which hung on a ravaged fresco as if guarding the entrance to the apse. The woman stopped to explain: "In this sheet, al-Shaybi recorded his faith; it always pointed toward his qibla, your city, Mecca." The writing on the parchment captured Nora's attention; it was an old form of writing that bore no dots, so each word could be any one of numerous words and its meaning any one of many meanings.

"It's the first page of the Surah of the Night Journey," Rafi explained in an attempt to break the magic the woman was spinning around Nora.

"I'll tell you more about this al-Shaybi," she went on. "Many people have come looking for him, but I've kept his story a secret, waiting for a sign." She looked at Nora. "Follow me." She set off out of the mosque, striding through the cold high Toledo night. Around them and at every corner as they climbed the hills they could hear unseen footsteps kindled by their thudding heartbeats. Nora shivered and clasped Rafi's arm, and he pulled her to his ribs, placing his hand over her icy fingers.

They ended up at the boarding school where they'd first met the woman that morning. In the night, the building showed its bitterness; it looked ready to jump off into the abyss behind it.

"Come in. Shhhhhh—any movement might wake the building . . ."

Rafi hesitated, but Nora stepped through the short wooden door, clutching his arm. The woman led them into a narrow corridor and down the staircase at the end of it to a vaulted cellar that stank of damp paper and desertion. She turned to look at them. "I'll take you to the refuge where I hide from every fear and weakness." Her voice stumbled thickly as if fumbling its way through the darkened alleyways of the purplish night. Nora felt dizzy in the dim light and a shiver ran from her body to Rafi's; they were now more certain than ever that this woman was deranged. She waved at the walls, which were covered in overflowing bookshelves. "We all have our own Mecca, where we take refuge from our fear and loneliness; this is my Mecca. I find solace here among the manuscripts of your Arab ancestors and my ancestors—who were Jews before they converted to Christianity out of fear of oppression and dispossession. Look . . ."

She began reading out the titles of the works and Rafi realized she was speaking Arabic. "*The Incoherence of the Incoherence* and *The Long Commentary on the Metaphysics of Aristotle*. Both by Averroes, the twelfth-century Cordoban philosopher, physician, and theologian who wrote about the immortality of the human mind through its connection to the effective mind, and the effect of that mind upon it. We still hold to his belief that we will all be resurrected in a more perfect body. I like to sum it up by saying that our open minds and hearts are the gateway to absolute knowledge and absolute existence!" She took a breath then moved to the next shelf, reciting title after title.

"But I promised to tell you about al-Shaybi . . . He was kidnapped by a Portuguese pirate ship on the shores of the Red Sea and brought to Iberia, where he finally escaped and made his way to Toledo. Poor al-Shaybi spent his life here as a busking storyteller, recounting stories of Aden and the women of Solomon's Seal, who were all born with an outline of the moon on their palms, to children. He acted the stories out again and again without ever getting tired, and if you listen carefully, you can still hear the echo of his stories in the city's walls and hills . . ."

Rafi and Nora strained their ears; they could no longer tell whether it was the woman speaking or the echoes of al-Shaybi's tales echoing off the walls: "My mother was descended from the line of King Solomon and Queen Bilqis, like everyone else in the village of Solomon's Seal. The daughters of the Seal are born with a moon on their palm, which they never close in a stranger's face, because they believe that if the moon ever falls or is crushed, a fire will spread northward from Aden to clutch the whole of the Arabian Peninsula in its fiery grip, heralding the Day of Judgment." With his thin teenager's voice, al-Shaybi continued his story as the woman flitted from book to book.

"My father was the great-great-grandson of the man who bore the key to God's House on Earth, the Kaaba in Mecca, and he went to Solomon's Seal to search for the stolen key to the Kaaba. He settled there after falling in love with the moon-shaped birthmark on my mother's hand. I was born there, on the mountaintops of Happy Yemen."

The woman interrupted the echoes of the past to continue in a hoarse voice. "Al-Shaybi spent his nights in the mosque, withdrawn into the apse drawing the doors that I showed you. He was about my age, and he used to visit me to ask me about my ancestor Joseph ibn Nagrela's journey to Aden, and they'd both sing with the same magical voice, lamenting the love they had found in the hands that bore the moon, which meant they'd both come from the same Aden. Sometimes when I looked at al-Shaybi's head bent over those doors, it felt like he and my ancestor were one and the same. Joseph ibn Nagrela was reincarnated in al-Shaybi . . ." She held her breath, listening to the echo of her voice.

"Al-Shaybi never stopped coming here. I used to think he was in love with me, but he was actually coming to sift through every single poem that Joseph ibn Nagrela had left behind, believing that the key had been smelted and cast in poetry, and that he would find it hidden in a single verse . . . He and I went through every poem Joseph ibn Nagrela brought back from the temple of Almaqa, hoping we might find an image of the key. Here, look."

She opened a yellowed manuscript in front of them. "This is a collection of the poems of Joseph ibn Nagrela, who was moved to write poetry by love."

The room got darker as the woman continued talking. The two tried to focus on what she was saying, hoping that she might finally get to the point of all this. Nora felt lost amidst the cascade of words; she imagined figures in nuns habits slipping into the cellar and watching them surreptitiously from behind the shelves.

"I buried half my life in these poems, and ruined my sight. I remember one night, the night of my fifteenth birthday, when al-Shaybi and I were leaning over our work with our foreheads touching, we were so tired after hours of reading and re-reading a single line of a long poem in search of the key that we fell asleep right there. The line was: *Exile is the ink in the book of God with which every straying soul is written and in which every soul searches for a mouthful of bread*. That poem and the promise it carries returned to me when I saw your face this morning, Nora." The deranged gleam in her eyes shone on Nora's face.

"I dreamed of your face. When they introduced you, they said 'This is the one who fled from the ink of doves and pigeons, the one who was delivered from the greed that surrounds the House of God.'" She brought the lamp closer to Nora's face. "In my dream, a war waged around you and over you. That's what brought you here. As if you were kidnapped."

Frozen as if made of marble, each squeezing themself against the other's ribs, Nora and Rafi stared aghast at the face that wouldn't stop talking.

"I spent half a decade dreaming of you. Your face harassed me every single night, and then you suddenly disappeared. You were absent from my dreams for another half-decade. How naive was I to think that I could ever forget your face. I did forget it, but this morning, your features looked familiar to me. It just goes to show that even the lucky ones in our midst scarcely notice when they meet their dreams walking down the street."

Her gaze bored through Nora as she repeated her words, slower this time and with a crazed edge. "I dreamed you in war." Nora's face was drenched in the purplish glow from the old building's night-soaked stone walls. "In fact, the whole world awaits war . . ." She shifted her warning gaze back and forth between them, impressing her fear on them.

"In our books we call him the Savior, the one who will appear to lead us into the war that will open the door between the four rivers of Heaven and allow them to flow on earth, running together as one, purifying the earth before the descent of the Messiah, peace and glory be upon him, who will unite humanity in peace and the word of God, the word that will resurrect the dead and transform your deserts into a Cordoban paradise." She took Nora's hand, spreading it against her own left hand, and closed her right hand over the poems.

"We're all hiding our faces behind other faces, but not all faces are burdened with as many contradictions as yours. I see fortune and death in yours. I've dreamed about you so often—too often. So often that your features became tattered and worn." She said it like an accusation.

Rafi and Nora looked like wax figurines in the dim light of the cellar, like the miniature models of sheep clustered around the infant Christ on the shelf. The air moved thickly when the woman reached out for a book on the table and opened it. It was about the gardens of the Alhambra.

"I knew you by your smell. The measure of a garden in al-Andalus was always its sound and its scent. That's why our ancestors always made sure to plant great beds of scented flowers where nightingales, peacocks and doves would roam. Soon, your deserts will flow with perfumes and songs, as one body from one word."

She stared piercingly at them, urging them to say something. Rafi shook his head. "The fall of Cordoba was the fall of the whole world's dream."

The woman looked toward the door in surprise; this time, Nora was sure there was a figure in a nun's habit moving about, watching them through the shelves. The woman raised a trembling hand and picked up a small book, which she handed to them.

"Take a little of me with you in this book, even though you'll never be able to read it because it's in Hebrew. It's a copy from a manuscript of Ibn Hazm's book *The Necklace of the Dove*, a book about love: love as a door that opens at first sight onto the heart of the other, love as a place of being, as a race, as blood that flows through us, bringing all bloodlines together, giving us an eternal, heavenly body . . . A look of love is magic capable of transcending masks and veils. It is the key or the door to a supernatural creature hiding forgotten inside of us." She fell silent for a moment, listening to the darkness as if straining to follow the sound of footsteps.

"Don't forget that love, like life, begins as a game but ends gravely. It's contagious, it can be passed on by voices and scents, so there's no point in us fighting it. We must open our senses and hone them to receive its assault. We must surrender when it remolds and transforms us . . ."

A minute that felt like an age passed slowly before the woman led them up the stairs and out. She took a good look around in the doorway to check there was no one spying on them and then leafed through *The Necklace of the Dove* and took out a sheet of canvas showing a small charcoal drawing of the El Greco painting *The Burial of the Count of Orgaz.*

"This is a copy of a real sketch."

Darkness ran in a shiver from the woman's touch to Nora, and they sensed even more strongly the stir of watching figures around them.

"As I told you, al-Shaybi spent a quarter-century in the Mosque of Cristo de la Luz, communing with our ancestors in his dreams and his waking hours, hoping they would show him the key. They accused him of disturbing the dead. He used to dream about El Greco. He fell entirely under the artist's spell and claimed that he was a Don Quixote fighting windmills so as to open doorways to eternity in these peaks. Al-Shaybi spent entire days making copies of *The Burial of the Count of Orgaz*, looking for the door. He made countless sketches, including this one. He added many details to the scene, but what comes up most often is this." She looked around, checking again that no one was listening, and then raised her lamp beside the sketch. She traced the strokes of charcoal. "He inserted this key into many of his drawings, perfecting it over time. He would place it on a shoulder, or tuck it into the folds of a gown or the curls of a cloud. But—look—here the key's in a very prominent position, and it's almost the size of a man, it dominates the whole scene. See, in the outstretched right hand of the celestial figure reaching up to Mary's lap. They said the Meccan was possessed by what he called the 'master of all keys,' whose bow was shaped like three interlocking mihrabs. It pursued him in his dreams, but he never managed to find it when he was awake; and yet, al-Shaybi never stopped predicting that soon there would come a time when God would close His house and His mercy in the face of erring believers, and no treaty or war could open them back up. Only that key, in the hand of the right man, could re-open the doors of heaven, and the doors between life and death . . . They say that al-

Shaybi was on his way back to Mecca when he was found dead outside the gate of the outcasts' cemetery in Madrid, completely naked, clutching a forged key to his chest. It had been cast for him by the most famous blacksmith in Toledo to fit the description revealed to him in a dream by Joseph. Al-Shaybi was forty-three or fifty-three when they buried his body in that same cemetery without epitaph or name—without anything at all but a forged key that was fixed to the tombstone right above his heart. That was seventeen years ago now.

Nora knew she was talking about the key that had been stolen from the tombstone in the British Cemetery. But how had the sheikh got his hands on it? Was he connected to the Shayba Clan of keyholders in some way? She remembered the drawing on a piece of paper, which the two men had compared with the key from al-Shaybi's grave.

"I found this drawing right here inside this book, *The Necklace of the Dove*, the last thing al-Shaybi was reading before he left."

Suddenly the woman seemed tired, and she snapped *The Necklace of the Dove* firmly closed on the drawing and handed it to Nora. With the same firmness she propelled them out the door and closed it silently behind them, but not before pointing a warning finger at Nora: "It's been waiting for you all these years."

The moment the door closed and they heard the finality of the key turning in the lock, they woke up with a start. They stood, amazed, in front of the desolate-looking door; the copy of *The Necklace of the Dove* in Nora's hand was the only evidence that what had just happened to them hadn't been a product of their imagination.

They were driving aimlessly when they glimpsed a column of smoke rising from Toledo. Nora felt a tug at her heart. Up in Toledo, crowds were watching the fire consuming the old school and its large library.

She placed a hand on the steering wheel and turned to Rafi. "Listen," she said urgently, "I'm not interested in war of any kind, not even for the sake of a key that will unlock the four rivers of Paradise. Let's forget about that story. It doesn't concern me. Just take me back to Madrid, please."

"Anywhere but Madrid, I'm begging you."

"Madrid." She was desperate.

"I'm sure I can—"

She interrupted him softly. "The sheikh is the only way I'll get back."

Amulet

YUSUF PUT DOWN THE SHEETS OF PARCHMENT HE'D BEEN READING AND HANDED them to Nasser. He walked away, limping slightly as he always did, while Nasser eagerly picked up where he'd left off:

THE VOICE OF THEIR AGED PRIESTESS rose up from the very bottom of my fever to confirm that I was pregnant with you. Once they heard that, they took me to the hidden springs where my body was washed and soaked for days before they placed me in the shadow of their tar idol. My skin was humanly supple once more.

When al-Ghatafani appeared, leading my still-saddled camel, I didn't bat an eyelid; I supposed he was just another one of the hallucinations rising up from my delirium. No one stopped us when we rode past the wall in the mountains by the Devil's Horns.

"They're sending you away to give birth in the bed of a chief from an influential tribe." Neither one of us knew whether I was carrying his seed or that of the Devil's Horns.

We were received by ecstatic dogs wagging their tails, girls dressed in red, and the gurgle of running water as we approached the Sabkha tribe.

"Sheikh Sa'd is the chief of the most powerful tribe in the desert. They're descended from Wa'il and Rabi'a ibn Nizar," al-Ghatafani said to reassure me. The palm trees stirred a longing for Khaybar in my heart. It had been an age since I'd been bathed in the sight of green. Sheikh Sa'd ibn Ibrahim ibn Ka'b's men came out to meet us and make sure that we were safe and in good health. Najd was in uproar. There were reports that Muhammad ibn Abd Allah's followers were planning to seize the Najd trade route. Ayif al-Ghatafani and I were taken to the sheikh's house, which was surrounded by his loyal servants, and we stood by the mud-brick door, which was always open. Sheikh Sa'd was on his way out when our eyes met; a falcon fell from his eyes straight into the trap in my eyes. For nights on end, I'd been gathering my magical powers to carve a cradle for you in the arms of that peerless knight of the desert. I didn't fail you. The tribe lit torches and married me to their sheikh. I lay in his bed and gave him my body, though he had no idea that you were already inside of me. In seven months, I would give birth to you in that bed and you would carry his pedigree.

Don Quixote

OUTSIDE THE HOTEL, AS THEY WERE SAYING GOODBYE, RAFI HANDED HER TWO CDs. "This is de Falla's *Don Quixote*, and this is the one I promised you, Bach's St. Matthew Passion." She took the CDs from him and put them in her large pocket. She smiled.

"We need to listen to things we can't comprehend so we can learn to comprehend the things we can't hear." She reminded him of Señora Mirano, and he suddenly heard her voice in his mind:

"I once read that people consider *St. Matthew Passion* to be the most beautiful piece in the history of Western music. They say that Bach was as strict about music as a rabbi is about the Halacha. That's the law that Jewish philosophers like Spinoza rebelled against because they felt it was too concerned with outward behavior, instead of the faith in one's heart. They said it made a robot of man and a façade of religion. Bach's music exists within harsh tradition; an act of obedience, a deep study of pleasure. Through his pure orthodoxy, he builds something greater than orthodoxy, which allows us to plumb aesthetic depths that we can discover within forms themselves. It allows us to find the source within the solid construction. He recreates exhausted possibilities."

Without thinking, he brushed her hair out of her eyes with his shaky hand and tucked it behind her ear. Her forehead tingled.

"Don't listen to things you can't comprehend, just listen to the joy in the music. Don't try to examine every drop of water, the important thing is for our bodies to be exposed to the pleasure of the rain." She wanted to laugh. Whenever a man was sweet to her, she giggled like a child. She listened to him, patronizing, protective. She knew he could tell how inexperienced she was the entire time. The shame in her blushing temples receded when he looked as if he were about to say goodbye.

"Don't force yourself to think about what could never happen. I can't remember who it was who said: in the limitlessness surrounded by walls on four sides, and within the thick fortification of nuclear reactors, there is a being about to come to life and rise up. The great transformation happens through the greatest of explosions." The sound of his own words annoyed him as they listened to what sounded like last words, like goodbye.

A little girl got loose of the hand of her mother, a beggar, and ran ahead. She stopped a few steps away from Nora and stared with big eyes. The girl was encouraged by Nora's smile and came closer. Shyly and in her sweet Spanish, the girl asked Nora, "What's your name?"

Rafi could sense her hesitation, but he had no intention of translating it for her. He was certain that Nora had understood the question. He watched as a tear rose up out of Nora's hesitation and slid down her cheek. The name Nora was like a dam keeping the story of her past and present at bay. Rafi didn't know what to do. He said, "Her name is Bella," to the girl in Spanish to smooth things over. Nora took off her black leather bracelet and wrapped it around the wrist of the little girl, who surprised her with a quick kiss on her wrist and a "gracias" before running off to show it to her mother. Rafi noticed there was a strip of metal on the bracelet, but he wasn't sure what was engraved on it. It looked like the peaks of some towers or maybe it was just a brand: A&A.

He caught up to Nora and handed her the two books: the one about El Greco, and Ibn Hazm's *The Necklace of the Dove*, between the pages of which she'd slipped the drawing of El Greco's painting, a gift from the Toledan woman.

"These are yours. Don't forget them." His finger stretched out to trace the course of the tear that had run down her cheek; she looked away.

"I'm not sure there's room for these here."

His outstretched hand trembled in the air between them. "Maybe for the girl who looks like you?" From the distraught expression she wore as they walked into the lobby of the hotel, he could tell that there was no room there for that girl, nor for him either.

"You know that woman was crazy, don't you?" His throat felt tight as they rode in the elevator together, feeling like strangers. He knew this was the last time they'd ride in an elevator together and that the doors would soon open and that she would disappear as if she'd been nothing but a mirage all along.

"Nora," he whispered, stirring the air in the elevator. "Would it shock you to hear that I can't stop thinking about making love to you? About connecting with you physically? It's a riddle that occupies the space between imagination and geography. Maybe our imaginations are actually a part of our real physical existence. Something more like a necessity. Without our dreams, we're left with nothing but our existence to keep us company. And that's something we can't get our heads around. We don't even understand the reasons behind it. Life has no meaning unless we can hone it with our dreams." Her eyes were fixed on the elevator doors and she was holding her breath.

"You're a woman now. You don't have to go back to the sheikh. You can just turn your back on everything that's happened and come with me. It doesn't even have to be with me. But . . . Just get yourself away from all this. Embrace your freedom."

Not again, said the look she gave him. They parted outside the door of her suite and she disappeared behind it, going to face what awaited her.

Wallpaper Tree

NASSER HURRIEDLY EXAMINED THE WORN SECTIONS OF THE PARCHMENT. Mushabbab could no longer fill the gaps with what he'd heard the elders say. He could do nothing. He handed the worn parchment to Yusuf, who skipped to the end:

> I COULDN'T COAX SLEEP TO COME to me there in the soft mud. Whenever I managed to doze off, I was swept up in a storm. A storm with you at the head, riding on a horse of fire, black. It shot up out of the sand and into the sky, carrying you and your men back from Khaybar. My dreams felt like I was skipping lines and pages in the book of destiny, looking ahead to what awaits you.
>
> Labor came to me. Hand in hand with death. I was in agony for days and eventually I realized that I only had enough life left in me to save one of us. That's why I sent for al-Ghatafani. I used up the very last sparks of my life writing this testament for you—in the blood of my labor—so that you would know everything there was to know about the truth of your lineage and origin. I slipped it inside my amulet, a silver half-moon that my father gave me when I married. It was made by our best silversmith to symbolize how the moon secretly penetrates our minds and even the rocks around us.
>
> In the morning, al-Ghatafani visited me in my birthbed and deathbed beneath the palm trees. He looked like a ghost. Like one of the sand ghosts we defeated on our journey.
>
> "I'm going to give you this testament, but you must first swear to me that you will protect it, you and your descendants. They must memorize my family tree and all its branches in the different tribes until my people return to Khaybar. Until they regain the Hijazi countryside, which is rightfully theirs."
>
> Glancing possessively at my round belly, where I was carrying you, he took the silver amulet and promised to store the family tree inside it.

> He also swore to engrave my lineage on the walls of the fort of my father Ka'b ibn al-Ashraf at Khaybar so that my descendants would be able to recover it even if the amulet were lost or destroyed.

The parchment ended there. The three of them had no way of knowing how al-Ghatafani and his descendants had served Sarah's son and his descendants over the next fourteen centuries as the amulet was passed from one generation to the next.

Nighttime Arrival

The clock read ten p.m. as Nora opened the door to her suite and stepped into the gaze that examined her from her damp hair all the way down to her sports shoes. It was as if she'd walked into a cloud; an electrical storm, emanating from where he was reclining on the sofa, battered her face. He was dressed in a suit and he was still wearing his tie, his overcoat even. He'd been in the exact same position since the morning he discovered she was gone and no one had dared to disturb him.

She had no idea how long she'd been standing there, besieged, when he eventually stood up and walked toward her in silence. She froze as he reached out to her and tore off her white cotton dress, buttons flying in every direction. She didn't so much as blink, not even when the window that overlooked the gardens came into his line of vision and he pushed her toward it, cold and menacing like the sky in one of El Greco's paintings. He showed her body to the people passing below, her entire torso exposed to the road. Neither of them said a word. There was nothing to hear but his heavy breathing and screaming rage. When it became clear that she wasn't going to resist, the game stopped being fun. He shoved her toward the door of the suite and then dragged her into the corridor, which stretched before them, holding its breath. She followed passively all the way to the elevator doors. He pressed the button. As they waited for the elevator to ascend, she gritted her teeth and racked her brain. She was trying to think up some way she could defend herself when he threw her out onto the street, naked. She found some steely determination within: she decided she'd pretend to be dead and allow her naked body to be discovered by anyone who chose to. The elevator opened and the brutal air cloaked her naked body. He pushed her into the chilly elevator and she ceased to see. He pressed the button for the ground floor. He seemed to have lost the ability to think—like an animal frozen in headlights. Only one instinct controlled him now: revenge, the need to humiliate her.

"In case you're finally tired of acting solo, I'll choose the audience from now on." When the elevator reached the ground floor, the air inside was thick, tense, then the doors parted with a cinematic flourish to reveal the reception desk and every eye in the lobby. Piano music drifted toward them from the end of the corridor. As the door opened—it felt like it was taking ages—he stripped off his overcoat roughly. She didn't make a move; her arms were pressed firmly against her sides so he wrapped it around her tightly and growled, "Keep defying me and you won't even find a rag to cover yourself with."

His voice was colder than the wind that pummeled them when they walked out of the hotel. She saw a darkness in his face that reminded her of Death in the background of *The Burial of the Count of Orgaz*. She looked away, provoking the resentment that held him in its thrall. He grabbed the back of her head and kissed her hard and when she opened her eyes again she found herself in the back of his large Mercedes. As soon as the door was shut, they were off. Rafa could taste the blood in her throat all the way from where he was standing, out of sight, in a pool of yellow beneath a streetlight.

Paper Tree

NASSER WAS EXAMINING THE LAST SHEET OF PARCHMENT FOR A TRACE OF THE family tree when Yusuf grabbed it out of his hands. "Don't waste your time looking for the family tree. It isn't here. You should be helping me look for the remains of the fort."

"What kind of fort do you think could survive centuries of erosion?"

Mushabbab made them go back over the testament from the beginning, but no matter how much they searched they couldn't identify where the ruins of Ka'b ibn al-Ashraf's fort should be. Mushabbab pulled out a bunch of maps for Yusuf. "My friends went to great pains to produce these maps and they were reviewed for accuracy by the Center for Hajj Studies and Muflih al-Ghatafani, may he rest in peace. They give us a rough idea of the fort's location. It was the fourth side of a square formed on three sides by the Mudhaynib Valley, Ranuna Valley, and the Qaba Mosque." There were some rough schematic drawings, which showed the fort at the intersection of the line running south from Baqi Cemetery and the line running northeast from the Qaba Mosque at a proportion of two to one. That is, the distance between the cemetery and the fort was twice the distance between the fort and the mosque. The two of them combed the entire area, though the city had begun to encroach, spreading out in every direction. It was like searching for a needle in a haystack of fourteen hundred years.

Bundug

THE AIRPLANE MADE A HALF-CIRCLE OVER THE MOUNTAINS THAT BLOCKED OUT the horizon as it prepared to land. Nora looked out over the peaks, which pointed menacingly into the sky like devil horns. Her heartbeat quickened and she began to tremble, as though she was expecting something horrible to happen.

The plane touched down lightly on the primitive airstrip in the middle of the empty desert. From the ground, the mountains blocked any view of the horizon and Nora felt like she was being held captive behind the devil's cloak. She looked around as she descended the steps to the runway; there was no sign of life anywhere. The only thing she could see was a pair of signs in the road: one pointed to Khamis Mushayt and the other to Najran. On the six-hour journey, Nora had listened as the sheikh talked to his assistant about maps and plans and budgets for a deal they were about to sign. He was ignoring her on purpose. He was still angry, and he wore his anger was like a layer of fire immediately beneath the skin. It singed her even though he was focused elsewhere. As soon as she stepped onto the plane, everything about Madrid disappeared. Nora was used to it. Every time she hit the ground she was born anew, her memory wiped clean.

What she gleaned from their conversation was that they were about to meet someone very important. Someone they called the Building Crow. She was half-asleep when she heard the sheikh mocking the man, though he obviously envied him. "Our competitor's a beast. You know he has several different citizenships. He's a multinational citizen and he's out of any one nation's reach. He could get his hands on Satan's property if he wanted to."

"Well they don't call him the Building Crow for nothing."

"We need to think like devils to get him on board so we can complete this stage of the project. We can use his greed to get our hands on the whole world. Whatever property he wants, he gets. He could shake the ground beneath us. He's this century's King Shahriyar. He always gets the most beautiful women: he marries them and then when he divorces them, he gives them a house to be heartbroken in. If we want him to get on board, we have to go to him, all the way out to the Devil's Horns where he's hunting and camping."

"Don't worry, sir. We've made sure to bring him a mouthwatering bit of prey," the assistant said, winking at the two female flight attendants waiting on them. "He has a soft spot for Egyptian sweets."

Human falcon eyes tracked the motorcade of Mercedes as they entered the small, nameless village, disappearing between the run-down two-story buildings at the side of a pothole-ridden asphalt road. Nora shut her eyes in the face of all that decay, which had the power to revive buried fantasies. As far as she could see, the fruit orchards and beautiful mud-brick houses had given way entirely to soulless cement cubes, but the few orchards that remained at least gave the town a familiar feel.

By ten p.m., the town was dead and the only sounds they could hear were the rush of the river and the creeping thick night. She wouldn't see the sheikh for three days; her assistant told her that he had to stay with the Crow at his camp. This was confirmed by a train of Land Rovers that drove into town, kicking up a dust storm against the evening sky and carrying her sheikh along with the Crow's son to a nighttime hunt. A cacophonous show of walkie-talkies, blindfolded falcons and their trainers whistling, clanking rifles, and reckless driving. The women ate the party up with wheat bread and butter and the procession of Land Rovers invaded the dreams of the children sleeping inside the town's dark houses.

It was clear to Nora that she would be spending the evening alone in the midst of that silence. After a long shower, she went back to her room, barefoot, a red bath towel wrapped around her. She'd been getting ready for bed when she heard a few soft knocks at the door. So soft she felt the knocking must've risen up from her distant memories. She turned away from the door and faced the bed: a five-star hotel in a village, it was clean but without an ounce of taste. Everything smelled like abandonment. The knocking got louder and she forgot she'd ever been sleepy. "Who's there?"

Out of all the people it could've been, Nora never would have expected to open the door and find the head flight attendant standing there in an embroidered red silk dress with a plunging neckline. "Get dressed. You've been invited to dinner at the Building Crow's camp."

"Oh, but I'd rather sleep."

"He sent for you specifically. No one turns down an invitation from the Building Crow. You'd never be forgiven."

"But I'm not ready for a party. The only clothes I have with me are pajamas and a pair of jeans. My bags are still on the plane."

"That's not a problem. Just put on some makeup. You need some bright red lipstick. I'll be right back." The woman was gone before she had a chance to object, and a few moments later there was a fancy set of underwear and a hand-embroidered, brilliant gold caftan laid out on the bed waiting for her. Nora couldn't get her head around anything. She knew that the sheikh would never forgive her if she turned down the invitation. A few moments later, she was sitting beside the two flight attendants in the back of a black Mercedes, dressed in an outfit conjured up by goodness knows what magic wand, as the desert night ushered them to the campsite.

An assemblage of lights pierced the darkness on the horizon, and when they got closer, they couldn't believe how grand the campsite was. Large brocaded canopies had been erected against the desert sky. When the car stopped, they were greeted by a guard in white robes and a checked red headscarf who led them to the canopies. In the middle of each canopy, there was a fire that gave off warmth against the austere sand. They walked through a fantasy realm. The walls of the canopies were embroidered with Arabic writing in red, blue, and golden thread. Here and there, the large tents were studded with pieces of art, which reflected the gleam of night and fire. Their footsteps were muffled by exquisite Persian carpets that stretched as far as they could see. Confronted with that splendor hidden within the infinitude of desert and the scents of Arabic coffee and cardamom and ginger, Nora relaxed. What was she thinking when she said she didn't want to come out to an oasis like this? Every canopy was air-conditioned and brightly lit with the power supplied by generators, whose roar could be heard far off into the dark night.

The three women were led toward a large tent raised over a triangular platform of white canopies. The Building Crow was presiding over the tent, dressed down in his white robes, bare-headed, without even his striped black cloak. Just the simple man himself, his dyed black hair, the farthest thing imaginable from his formidable reputation. Nora and the other two women sat on his left, in a line against the red damask, which had been laid out to hide the tent poles. To the Building Crow's right, there sat a black man who stood like a plume of smoke reaching up to the top of the tent. His eyes pierced her like spikes of fire and paralyzed her down to her toes, crushed her. She was looking into the face of Satan himself. She turned to look at the Building Crow himself, who for all that he was large and intimidating was less terrifying than his right-hand man, Bundug. Out of all possible names, Bundug—Bullet—summed up the character of a devil who was ready to shoot fire at the people around him at any moment, who acted with an uncanny sense of his master's confidence, who used his satanic strength, even, to control his own master. The odor of his body filled the entire tent, a mix of devil's sweat and pungent eastern musk. His body was a coil of steel cables without a single lump of fat; a network of disgusting nerves, which could easily be tracked and deciphered, darting and pulsing vividly. Nora was certain that she'd receive a physical shock if she were ever to touch those nerves, that she'd be turned to ash. She was careful not to look that devil in the face again while he commanded the party and the Building Crow himself. Bundug, Bundug. No name has ever been repeated so doggedly, so madly, like his name was that night. Everyone savored the tune of it, accentuating its dissolution, they repeated it, begging for its consent and good favor, flattering the absolute ruler who held them in his thrall.

Servants appeared, spread around the room, and in the blink of an eye gracefully removed the palm mats and the large platters of rice topped with whole lambs freshly slaughtered that evening that had been laid before them. Dinner was over, but Nora hadn't been able to bring herself to force down a single bite. A cloud of the devil's sweat hung over the assembled guests. It turned her stomach and spoke of his desires and intentions. The trays of lambs staring back at the diners was just the first sacrificial offering of many. Bundug began moving among the diners like a storm of contradictory passions. He ate voraciously, swallowing unfathomable amounts of red meat, but he didn't touch the milk- and butter-steeped rice or the vegetables or fruit. Only meat, as blood-red as the tongue he wiped across his lips after every bite, and the inside of his mouth, which was revealed with every lunatic laugh. The meat was burned up to produce energy in the furnace of that bundle of nerves, without even a single globule of fat.

"Where does it all go? It's like the devil himself is eating alongside you." The Building Crow chuckled as he teased Bundug, his creation. His fondness was apparent. Every time he looked at him, he was even more astonished, but Bundug just fed on that satanic riddle, which confused everyone and was him at the core.

Bundug's furnaces blazed and the party kicked off. The music grew to a roar and the guests could suddenly hear the throbbing drumming of his coiled nerves in their own. Moving, writhing to the beat, Bundug came nearer and motioned to the girls shamelessly, pointing at their shoulders, and their breasts, and their thighs, which clamped together in defense. That was when the Building Crow made his move and all hell broke loose. He came out wearing nothing but a sarong around his waist, his flabby, hideous, burn-scarred torso completely bare. He pulled the three women to their feet to dance, and Nora found herself buffeted by the dancing bodies, blinded by the mass of burn-striped flesh. It was as if Satan's teeth were still stuck in his body. The rhythm of the drums became more insistent and frenetic and Nora was terrified that he might lay his hands on her body. But Bundug was flitting around like a blood-sucking fly, buzzing and swooping. The fleshy mass came nearer and nearer, grazing her, the burn-scars enveloping her, giving off a thick sulfurous fug, and the women dancing realized that underneath his thin sarong he was completely naked. Bundug made that plain when he danced over and pulled his boss' sarong right off. The Building Crow was naked before them. Nora shut her eyes, but she could still feel the idol's eyes enveloping her. Flesh began crashing against flesh. Nausea ripped through her insides. Her eyes looked away, to Bundug's coil of nerves, sculpted as if from steel.

Her refusal only attracted the demon. He channeled his perversity toward her and approached, pointing with his index finger at her throat. She choked on her saliva and stumbled, twisting her ankle. Nora felt dirty and stupid for dancing so she tried to make her way back to her seat, but the demon's blazing eyes followed her. He could see her refusal plainly and it only made him circle more lecherously around the two remaining dancers, his lust goading them.

That scene went on forever. The thunder of a coil of nerves whipping clouds of flab. And the flab spread out to engulf all three women and that was when Nora wrenched herself away. Lightning tore through the demon's black body. He pounced on her, his eyes shooting fiery daggers.

"Where do you think you're going?"

She tried to stifle her hysterical wailing. His pupils were coal black and his eyes were like clotted blood, there was no sign of white. An eye of sand, creeping, pitch-black, bottomless, was dripping blood onto her face. Bundug pulled away from the dancing party and wrapped his burning fingers around her wrist. He dragged her outside the tent and shoved her into another tent nearby. He shoved her with all his strength and she fell to the floor.

"You slut! You want to play the virgin? Your fee's in the envelope already, in dollars. A hundred grand for this cheap sack of flesh. And an extra thirty for your two whore friends. Are you trying to bargain for more by pretending to be chaste?" Nora looked like she'd lost her mind. She was shaking and she'd stopped breathing; her skin was turning blue. The cry of a wounded animal came bawling out of her chest. Even the demon seemed to be moved by it.

"Take me home. God help me. Please, I'm begging you, take me home."

The demon took offense at that. "You think you're worth a cent to me? Cheap flesh like yours? The world's a market and it's packed full of the best kinds of fresh meat, fresher than you even. Every day hotter, fitter bodies are brought to market. It makes me sick just to think about all the flesh that gets thrown at my feet. Who do you think you are? This is a hypermarket with shelves and shelves of tits and ass, so much for so cheap it turns your stomach. I could import bodies like yours and stock them in my freezer. You're nothing.

Nothing." His eyes flogged her as he waited for her to say a single word so that he could snap her neck. Nora's voice had disappeared deep down within her chest and she herself was sinking into the darkness.

"You're nothing. Shut up. I swear to God if I so much as hear you breathe, I'll smash your head in and leave your filthy body for the hyenas." He turned and walked out. She wasn't breathing. Her eyes had dried and were fixed, bulging, on the tent wall in front of her. There was writing, in golden thread, on the wall of the tent and it began to spread and cover the four walls of her horizon. She couldn't move or hear, she couldn't see anything but those verses of the Quran, the word of God in the heart's heart. She realized that she was entering into, looking inside, the heart of the Quran itself, the Throne Verse, which was said to protect and dispel fear. She didn't read the verse, she crawled over it and slipped inside, seeking shelter. She sank deeper and deeper as the verse grew lighter and lighter, until Nora became aware of the white idol that was the platform with three faces. The idol bent down—the entire campsite listing as it bent—and picked her up, setting her down on its crest. She could see a woman's face joined with that of a man and a child, and with her own. She and they became a single mass of life shooting up toward the sky, while in the tent next door, the tender flesh had been laid out and was topped by burned flesh, and both were topped by a network of cables sending its shocks through them, and giving off an acrid smell of sulfur.

On the last night, before they reached her sheikh's camp, Nora was sleeping deeply when she was woken by a horrific burning smell. Her eyes sprang open in the dark and she could see Bundug towering over her in the tent like a plume of smoke. His fiery eyes paralyzed her as she lay there and without even breathing he raised his arm into the air and brought it crashing down onto her body. She could make out the feel of his headdress band tearing at her flesh. Only his execrable breath disturbed the total emptiness of her tent. He whipped her silently. The headdress-band dug deeper into her flesh and Nora received the blows in silence. Any notion of pain or self-defense had left her. The pain was too deep to scream for or move away from. As if her soul was being torn away, her body surrendered to the flogging, as her two companions watched, goggle-eyed, from their beds, paralyzed in their own nightmares. The blows sought out her face especially, as if to break her pride, blindly striking at her neck and chest. Nora raised her arms to cover her face and her body turned to stone to absorb the pain. Part of her embraced it, using it to wash away an old sin she'd been hiding somewhere deep inside her.

Bundug's demonic laughter interrupted the rhythm. "Ah, so it was a flogging you were lusting for all this time? I knew just the kind of whore you were from the moment you started playing the virgin and praying every chance you could." He waited in vain for her to respond. "If you breathe a word of what I did to you, I'll crawl into your sleep and break your neck. And I'll crush your bones under my camel's hooves and throw them in the desert far from any trails." He spat at her and disappeared.

Her sheikh pretended not to see the signs of whipping on her body. He knew, but he chose to obey the rules of a vital partnership that enabled him to enact the final stage of his plan.

Media

NOTHING BUT THAT DEEP SENSE OF ISOLATION. ALL THE FACES THAT HAD GIVEN Mu'az's shots their meaning had vanished: al-Lababidi's house, then Yusuf, then Mushabbab, then Khalil. The feeling of a curse frosted the air. "Mecca paused on the verge of Doomsday": this was the shot that summed up for Mu'az the crushing emptiness around him. To coexist with it and within it, Mu'az surrendered to the seasonal rhythm of life in Studio Modern, where he worked, this time looking for some purpose to his life.

The studio was no bigger than three meters by three meters, with a wooden screen that was bare on the outside, and on the inside bore a poster of a waterfall whose water droplets remained perfectly static, night and day, never refreshing Mu'az with a cool mist. He felt like the studio was too small to accommodate his dangerous thoughts these days—especially when the owner turned up late and Mu'az was left alone with a female face. Then, it would no longer be the camera taking the photo, but Mu'az's whole body that took the shot and developed it underneath the skin. Sometimes a young woman would take a risk and smuggle a few locks of her bangs into a photo, and Mu'az would know that the bangs would be sent straight back to him the moment they arrived at the passport authority, for him to take a new photo without; then, he'd watch as the girl tried to slip some other signature of herself into the picture, this time pulling her headscarf back a little to reveal just the roots of her thick black hair, outlining her forehead with a dark border, and this time she'd succeed in getting it past the hands of the passport office employee. In the unofficial shots, the girls would relax, smuggling a glimpse of cleavage into the frame, or the edge of a leg. What got him most were the women's slender ankles, totally unlike his mother's thick camel-hoof ankles covered by a layer of dust. These were softly rounded, like flower buds.

"I'll devote myself to photographing nothing but women's ankles one day, thousands of ankles spread out like wallpaper, and I'll stand at the very center of the wall amidst them all." That was his most recent dream, which he was sure was a sin-free zone, since he couldn't recall any religious texts that prescribed a punishment for ogling women's ankles.

Mu'az firmly believed that he'd been taking photos before he even owned a camera. Today, as he climbed the minaret's spiral staircase and stood hidden at the tiny window, looking out onto the alley from above, he could see the old men he'd grown up knowing—they looked isolated, each a portrait of loneliness or weakness or worry—and the little drawings sketched by young boys who were dusty and confined to tiny areas around their houses, just like he had once been, but his generation, he could see, had found ways out and were now smoking water-pipes at the cafe or chasing the shadows of the girls, who'd gotten bolder. Mu'az could see that the younger girls of the Lane of Many Heads tried harder now to peek out from behind their abayas, attempting to look the world in the eye and seeing more than his sisters had seen.

IN THE NEWSPAPER *THE STAFF*, WHICH A CUSTOMER WAS HOLDING, A LARGE PICTURE taking up a whole quarter-page caught Mu'az's eye; the customer was busy tidying himself in front of the mirror and smoothing his eyebrows with spit, so Mu'az took a longer look. It was a painting of a human torso in black on a white background. A quaking longing shook Mu'az's heart all of a sudden; he knew that form. He skimmed the first lines of the article:

"Under the auspices of his Excellency the Minister for Culture Faysal al-Mu'ayiti, an exhibition by contemporary artist Nora will open at 8 p.m. tonight, Wednesday 20th February, at Earth Gallery, Jeddah. Nora has been hailed as one of the most promising female artists of Saudi Arabia's contemporary art movement . . ."

The customer's eyes pierced him from where he sat before the camera's lens with a stretched-out smile like a baguette dotted with sesame seeds and notched by the baker's knife, waiting to be photographed. Attempting to control the tremble in his hand and his heart, Mu'az automatically reached out and switched on the glaring lamp, illuminating the baguette; his lens hovered for a while as he looked for an angle that would soften the dark, knotted eyebrows. Suddenly a cascade of shots hit Mu'az, static ones, moving ones, all Azza's drawings he'd spent his nights with, those severed human trunks that inhabited the Lane of Many Heads and which he'd spent his childhood peeping at to the point that he started dreaming about them, even when he was awake, and now they were here, poured into that quarter-page of newspaper right in front of him. His hand froze over the captive face inside his viewfinder, as if receiving a long-awaited divine visitation that contained everything he had devoted himself to, contained his whole life; impatiently, he pressed the button, crushing face and baguette, and let the man leave. Mu'az himself was out the door in a flash, running down Gate Lane. It wasn't long till the opening, but seeing the notice about it had left him no time to think: he had to be in Jeddah that evening and find the address: Earth Gallery, The Seafront, opposite Jamjoum Mall, Jeddah.

As usual Mu'az paid no attention as he slipped easily between the public bus stops and found the blue and orange bus with broken air conditioning that dropped him at the stop behind the Mahmal Shopping Center in downtown Jeddah. Mu'az surrendered his eyes to the salty air of the artificial seawater lake created where the neighborhood known as Clay Sea used to be. It had formed the city boundary and was full of quarries out of whose Manqabi stone Jeddah's most beautiful old buildings were built; the stone breathed humidity, salting the bones of its inhabitants. But the greedy, ever-expanding city known as the Mermaid was swallowing it up now, trapping it between cement and giants like the National Bank, the Queen building, and the Seafront and Mahmal shopping centers.

From the bus stop Mu'az took a taxi to the exhibition venue. He flung himself into the car seat and let go, allowing his body to become a numb reflection of the nights he'd spent alone once Khalil was gone, and his feverish search for some battle of his own. With a hazy, wandering gaze, Mu'az absentmindedly sliced Jeddah, the Mermaid City, into mental images, ignoring the driver's ploy to stimulate the meter by taking a diversion over Crown Prince Bridge to the new tunnels over Road 60, instead of the Andalusia Road shortcut to the Palestine junction then the short distance west toward the sea, thereby crossing the entire Mermaid from east to west, along the full length of Palestine Road. In one panoramic shot, Mu'az captured the whole road stretched out like a tightrope for circus clowns to walk across through the air: it began pulled tight with poverty and tumbledown buildings, then, as it approached Jeddah's central nerve, known as al-Medina Road, the oil boom buildings and glass towers began to appear, leaning toward the sea, and it ended with the fountain of King Fahd's palace, which sat right in the Red Sea, so famous for its rare coral. Between Road 60 and al-Medina Road, on both sides, was cellphone kingdom, where cars crawled slowly, horns honking, amidst the armies of workers buying and selling the latest cellphones, new and stolen. As they passed the almost-deserted U.S. consulate building with its cement security barrier, he couldn't resist taking a mental wide-lens shot of the machine guns mounted on armored cars at the gates.

"Can all that protection hide images of peace and safety inside?" he wondered. Before him, the disc of the sun was a vivid orange, setting at the very end of Palestine Road. On both sides, clouds of crows gathered to roost in the trees of the villas' gardens, and every time the wind blew or a car horn shrieked, a black torrent rained from the treetops, blotting the edges of the orange sun. Mu'az recalled one of Yusuf's Windows, entitled "The Crow in History," which had caused a storm—also sending al-Ashi into a bout of depression and doubt—and led to Yusuf's column being banned for several months:

> *We once imported crows as a way to eliminate the rats that were multiplying with the increased garbage that our cities produced. Now, whenever the crows gather and rain down from the treetops, debate flares up in Mushabbab's orchard, and many of his companions repeat the old saying that Arabs used to call crows "the one-eyed ones," because they close one of their eyes and make do with looking out of the other since they're so keen-sighted—so keen-sighted, in fact, that they can see a beak's depth under the ground! But Mushabbab also moves the discussion on to portray crows as the one-eyed false Messiah who represents one-eyed Western civilization: with one eye on the material, it is blind to the spiritual!*

The taxi passed Palestine Commercial Center, and women's bodies captured Mu'az's lens: one hurrying through the mall's horseshoe-shaped parking lot, her face uncovered, and behind her another covered entirely in black, even her hands covered in black gloves, and behind them both a group of girls with their headscarves falling around their shoulders, the sea breezes sending locks of their brightly-dyed hair streaming behind them. Mu'az would have been gripped by the sense he'd touched down on some planet other than Earth had it not been for the wooden cart parked at the mall entrance, right in the shade of the ATM, and the African woman leaning against the blue logo of the Saudi American Bank, with an orange tiger-print scarf lazily covering her hair, three braids escaping to the right and the curve of her neck revealing her prominent collarbones. He took a quick snap of the girls sweeping by in fancy abayas decorated with frills, silver designs, and colored edging at the sleeves that matched their headscarves, and rings and bracelets made of all kinds of leather, beads, metal, and crystal. "Wallah, al-banat fallah!" thought Mu'az, remembering the ditty from his childhood: "Goodness, the girls are loose and free!" His finger was poised over the button inside his head as he sighed. "How could you forget your camera?!"

The Pakistani driver was watching Mu'az's face the whole time, and his laugh brought Mu'az back from his surprised reverie.

"You are new in country?" asked the driver.

Mu'az shook his head. "Imagine!" he chuckled.

When they approached the King Fahd fountain in the sea, Mu'az's lens widened in anticipation. The driver pointed to the left, announcing their arrival at the address. Mu'az could see a fancy-looking gallery with a throng of cars outside it; it was a quarter of an hour until the opening. He indicated to the taxi to stop outside the Jamjoum Mall and crossed Palestine Road on foot to get to the gallery.

He quietly slipped into the crowd and was enveloped in a cloud of perfume: heady Oriental spices for the men and cloying sweet essences for the women. At the entrance he could isolate the smell of his own sweat and the developing agents still clinging to him; the powerful developers that could reveal features out of nothingness in his darkroom were dwarfed by the presence of those bulldozing perfumes.

Mu'az found himself facing the final painting. In its emptiness he could make out a faint blue halo encircling two female figures whose backs were turned to the world. One, though, was looking back at him, with a mixture of pain and mockery in her face. Mu'az shuddered and closed his eyes, denying Azza and Aisha's appearance on that blank canvas and ridiculing himself for his fanciful ideas. "You're the son of an imam—you know nothing about the female sex except for Azza and Aisha, so you imagine every woman looks just like them!"

Someone was talking to the artist. "Picasso once said that art is the memory of sadness and pain. He saw pain as the backbone of life. He said, 'I started painting in blue when I learned of Casagemas' death.' So what it is that makes you paint in this ashy gray, Nora?"

"Laziness!" she replied instantly, with a laugh, but her real answer was hidden from Mu'az by the Pakistani waiter holding a tray of appetizers who had moved in between Mu'az and the crowd. Mu'az snatched a glass of water and gulped it in one go to quench the sudden dryness in his throat.

"No, no—the truth of your art must be exhibited in Riyadh too. Just call me."

Mu'az's skin closed like a sheet of Polaroid film over the horse-like neck that arched back in response to the compliment. He craned to get a better look at the image of her face, framed in black silk. As he looked, the developing agents inside his head turned the artist into a picture of a filly, the finest of all of Solomon's horses. The journalists' cameras and eyes crowded out Mu'az's lens, already misted with old images of another woman—but this one veiled—that overlapped with the gleaming face of the artist. Mu'az struggled to peel away the past's layers of veils, so as to compare what was silenced underneath with today's clarity. The fullness of the lips always gave away what was behind the veil, yesterday and today; so what was that contradiction he sensed inside his private archive?

Mu'az's line of vision was blocked by the personality opening the exhibition, and the lengthy, simpering speech with which he attempted to capture the artist's attention. "The art movement is booming at the moment, with the reform movement reaching all of our cultural institutions. The Association for Culture and Arts in Riyadh would be delighted to host an exhibition of your work at the Center . . ."

Mu'az was dazzled by the stark contrast between the men's white robes and the blackness of the women's silk abayas. In the margins between black and white Mu'az used his developing and editing skills to recreate the past of the artist's face: peeling away the veneer of foundation and powder, enlarging the pixels, returning the eyebrows to their original untamed thickness, filling the cheeks out a bit, sharpening the eyes with a glint of expectation and desperation. The bodies in the canvases poured out of those pixels, all without legs, yet running. In one corner, in the penultimate painting, the artist had just managed to capture the back of a knee, but the body was still managing to flee. Mu'az's entire memory was captured in the void of that delicate painting, his lens clouded by the movements of some invisible internal ghost who blurred into the shining figure of this artist.

It was impossible for Mu'az to confirm his suspicions or identify the ghost; the disappearance of the veil and the figure polished by beautifying procedures and novelties had spoiled the delicate traces preserved in his archive as a reference point. The full parted lips were the same, that was certain. But the ears, each dotted with a diamond, were ready to flee. They didn't match the ears in the archive. The biggest distortion was in the ankles: printed in his memory, they were crossing the Lane of Many Heads in the middle of the night, and he knew them well, but here they sat in high-heeled shoes, perfumed, oiled and manicured and stretched upward like a dancer's. There was something vital missing: the dashing flight in pursuit of life, the will to escape. This ankle was fixed like a stake. It didn't flee and it didn't pursue life.

The throngs of men and women chatting, laughing raucously and flashily competing for the attention of the media were getting unbearable, and Mu'az bolted outside, gulping for air. He crossed Palestine Road and immediately sat down on the bare sidewalk in the parking lot of the Jamjoum Mall.

Abstract Past

MUSHABBAB DECIDED TO LOOK FOR THE FORT IN THE HUMAN STRUCTURE OF the area. He dawdled in front of every building and store to chat to people, combing their words for a slip of the tongue that might lead him to it, while Nasser and Yusuf went back and forth over the square of land they'd identified. It looked like a tattered scrap of parchment. No matter where they looked, they found nothing but houses and palm orchards, to the point that they began to give up hope of ever finding any remains of the fort underneath the rubble of fourteen centuries of abandonment. There was nothing at all in that neighborhood of erratically built mud buildings to indicate that it might also house the ruins of an ancient stone fort. Again and again all they found were cement walls and trucks parked outside decrepit, box-like houses. Yusuf's limp was getting worse.

NASSER SEEMED PRETTY CHEERFUL, AND SURE ENOUGH THEIR STUMBLING SEARCH finally led them to an old stone column. The remains of the fort were right there; they'd missed the spot more than once, because it was hidden behind a dense curtain of dry creepers and guarded by a line of palms, looking as if people and long abandonment had conspired to hide everything that remained of it.

As they pushed onward, they were amazed by the ancient stone building buried under wild plants in the backyard of an empty mud brick house. Through an opening in the wall that they assumed must have been the main gate, they managed to get inside the circle of the tower, where the dim light rooted them to the spot. Everywhere around them were dried droppings and the echoes of thoughts, military strategies, conspiracies, and noble-sounding words of peace that still slumbered in that stone temple, interweaving with the wild plants to veil the truth.

Yusuf and Nasser wandered in the small rooms that adjoined the main hall, some of which were buried in earth or had been incorporated into the mud house, or were blocked up by stacks of boxes covered with cobwebs and plants. They kept coming back to the main hall, and to the wall that looked like a mihrab covered up with plaster. The plaster was coming off in places near the base, revealing engraved letters here and there.

When Mushabbab caught up with them they'd already begun chipping it off. Together they entered a single, hazy dream, with no light save that of the flashlight whose batteries were rapidly running down. It was difficult to say which of them was awake and which dreaming, or which was guiding the dream that was carrying them all toward discovery.

Beginning from the base up, they worked in total secrecy, continuing for as long as the daylight lasted. Until the wall finally disappeared into absolute darkness, they carefully probed for where to scrape off the plaster, afraid to switch on a flashlight in case its light advertised their presence. They kept at it for days, and when night became day again they still hadn't slept a wink. Yusuf limped energetically about on his steel knee, and they survived on dates and dry wheat bread, taking turns to go to the market to fetch bottled water and to empty their bowels behind the fort wall. Often, Mushabbab would lean silently like a dot on the wall opposite, summoning the will of the ancestors to help them continue in their excavation.

Sometimes, Nasser would lie down, taking up a position at the furthest end of the hall and feigning sleep, allowing the silence to spread over him until he might as well not have been there, so that nothing remained before the wall but Mushabbab and Yusuf's breaths. The two were virtually joined together; it was essential to contract all the individual goals and wills in that hall into a single will, a single chisel to dig into that tree and pry the covering from its hidden roots. At the distant edge of Yusuf's being, Mushabbab was breathing into him all the history and wisdom of the centenarians he had known, drowning in images he assembled from what they'd read in the writings on the wall, while Yusuf patiently continued scraping away at the layer of plaster.

As the will of that historical being pressed forward, the roots emerged bit by bit, and then its trunk: climbing it was the name Ka'b ibn al-Ashraf. The three went on for days, scraping rhythmically, until the wall finally surrendered the full spread of branches, bearing the names of well-known tribes, which it had been concealing all those centuries. At times, Yusuf became detached from the memory of the tree, and Mushabbab from Yusuf's memory, and they both became detached from Nasser's dream; then, the three would lose their direction, their sight growing weak in the darkness, their eye sockets contracting and their fingers trembling. They were like addicts isolated from the outside world. Nasser's eyes widened as he imagined the hand that had engraved the tree, and evoked its strength of will; in that faint light it looked to him like a giant's hand reaching to the sky.

Desires

Mu'az sat on the curb in the Jamjoum Mall parking lot for a long while. The massive shopping center windows behind him were obscured by the sea air and the blue steel. He was aware of a fountain in the ocean spraying salty water into the damp air. This fountain, he thought to himself, was a challenge to the historical process of the eventual collapse of all nations and heroes. It hadn't been switched off since the death of King Fahd, during whose reign it was installed. It still raised its plume dozens of meters skyward. He took several photos in succession of the spray spanning across the sky over the sea. He knew when the photos were developed that the spray of the fountain would look like men in white robes patchy against the sky like stains. He could have his own solo exhibition of his imaginings of these dissolved men. Mu'az realized that he'd been deceived by the artist's face. He'd been so preoccupied he forgot to look at her body language, her walk, her voice, failed to compare her to the audiovisuals of his memory. From his hiding place on the minaret stairs, he used to watch Azza's nightly escapes, cocooned in a black as black as the asphalt, which was what now separated him from the truth of her identity. All he had to do was cross over and take another look at her from far away. He'd ignore the face—cast a veil over it—then he'd know the truth of her. His feet failed him, though. No matter how hard he tried to stand, he couldn't. The idea that this woman might be Azza frightened him. If she were Azza, it would destroy the Azza he'd built his photographic world around. The Azza of the Lane of Many Heads was an impossible creature, a being that reality couldn't capture. As he sat there paralyzed he thanked God that she hadn't seen him and that he hadn't gone up to her. No matter who this artist was, she wasn't Azza. Or, then, what if all women were Azza? The one he'd tried so hard to keep under wraps, like the first outlines of the human form on the walls of a cave. As soon as it is exposed to light and breath, its color fades and the flame, which has lasted for tens of thousands of years, is extinguished. Mu'az stubbornly closed his eyes in the face of that Azza, whom he'd preferred not to recognize at the moment, fearing he might go blind.

He still hadn't recovered from his first shock when a specter appeared against the fog. When he looked up, he didn't need to pause a second to think or to check his mental database of faces to know who it was who was speaking to him. The resigned look in his eyes was an invitation for the Eunuchs' Goat to take a seat beside him, but he didn't. Mu'az could barely hear what he was saying over the din of the cars:

"When the girls of the Lane of Many Heads died, our world died alongside them. What else are rats like us supposed to dream of? I heard they put up barriers around the Kaaba now since the key's been lost." He wasn't speaking to Mu'az; he was preoccupied with his shopping cart, which carried a mannequin dressed in muslin and lace. It turned Mu'az's stomach, and he was certain that he'd be struck with the disease if he so much as looked at the crazed, trembling fingers—like talons—running over the strips of velvet that covered the mannequin's plastic waist, and at that dead marble face stuck onto a woman's body, unsmiling, unable to look out on the world. For the first time, Mu'az noticed the feminine features of the Eunuchs' Goat's face, and his shiny shaved head, the red scar on his left cheek that cut through his onion beard down to his neck.

"I went inside." Mu'az's voice was almost sad. "I was careful not to let her see me, but I accomplished what I came to do. We—you and me and maybe the whole of the Lane of Many Heads—have no business being inside there. There are professional photographers in there. There are probably also newspaper editors in there and an army of reporters from international news outlets. Who could ever die with all those lights on them?" The Eunuchs' Goat tried to ignore the signs of age in Mu'az's face. He'd been a mere teenager, mimicking the adults, when he'd last seen him back in the Lane of Many Heads. Now he was more like a mannequin who'd suddenly come to life, the signs of the past twenty years becoming instantly etched into his face in the process. A mannequin that was being subjected to an acid peel of time gone by and specific doses of light therapy.

"I don't think so," he said and drained the last of his soft drink. A piece of acting fit to be caught on tape.

"If you're here because you're curious, go inside. Do you want her to recognize you, is that it?" Mu'az's words were like a snapshot that couldn't be retouched, but it was received soberly.

"I don't think so." Mu'az took a mental portrait of the Eunuchs' Goat's head at precisely that moment: empty, echoing with words. If he looked for his own reflection in the Eunuchs' Goat's eyes, all he saw was the stolen mannequin in the shopping cart.

"It's idiotic of you to keep saying 'I don't think so' when you're feeling hindered by this inferiority complex you inherited from Yusuf. So tell me: what grave did you crawl out of? Last I heard you were a fugitive from the immigration authorities."

"It would shock you to know what desperate people like me can accomplish. They don't have anything to lose. You should see our little kingdom: castles on the mountainside, hiding places beneath rotting garbage heaps that even dogs wouldn't venture into. Police and Immigration can't reach us there. We're an army of people waiting to be discovered for what we are. We're not the subject of legend any more. Down in the ground we extract the gold from your garbage. Each day we come face to face with the monster that threatens to devour our planet, and we burn it day after day to replenish our forces. If we stop recycling, garbage will overwhelm you and us and swallow the entire world. Everything you throw away is added to the monster; that's why we can't just shut our eyes, relax, fall in love, and settle down somewhere outside the dump where our kids won't get asthma and cancer." Mu'az noticed that the Eunuchs' Goat's skin wasn't marble-white like it used to be; there was a layer of ash on his skin, as if he'd just left a crematorium.

"In the garbage dump?" He couldn't hide the disgust in his voice.

"Your garbage is more valuable than anything you buy in your super-hyper-mega-stores."

"Like the cursed nations in the Quran? You were cursed because of what you did. I figure the immigration police never did arrest you that night, never booked you for deportation, and you didn't actually escape. No. You stole the money out of the Eunuchs' Goat fund and abandoned your poor father and your deranged mother. You destroyed your parents who rescued you from garbage and embraced you, so you could return to garbage. We thought you ran off with a woman but you ran after this . . ." He said, pointing to the mannequin, disgustedly.

The Eunuchs' Goat broke out laughing. "All the women you know are just the same woman. You can't fool them. They know that love can't sprout from fear and that mannequins and human beings can't fall in love. Imagine this cork body in love! This is like a disease that's eating away at me: I need them to feel my touch. I need them to love me back. But who can bring them to life? I collect all the mannequins I can get my hands on and recycle their parts so I can create one real living woman out of them." He waited for a response from Mu'az. "Look. You have no idea what I've been through. You spent your entire adolescence memorizing the Quran and trying to get away from your father's stubborn agenda. How could you know? I'm the only one who knows what it's like to miss the feeling of flesh and blood in your arms. That's what the girls of the Lane of Many Heads were," he said pointing to the mannequin in the shopping cart. "Your sister Sa'diya . . ." Mu'az blinked rapidly, but he was too drained to tell him to keep Sa'diya out of it. "Fine, let's say Azza, or whatever girl, lived in constant fear that we would touch them." He scratched the mannequin's body without thinking. "They didn't want us to discover this: a cylinder where their pelvises should be and metal rods instead of thighs and calves."

Mu'az's expression didn't soften; he looked on the verge of anger. "You think I wasn't like you guys, the other boys in the lane? That I don't know what it means not to feel the touch of another body? You say I was too busy being trained to call prayers to notice any of that. No, I felt what you were all going through and I loved all of you. I'm going to level with you: you're all cowards. You were the Veil Monster, who used to sneak into our rooms at night, but that too was a cowardly thing to do. You and my sister Sa'diya didn't do a single thing to win each other's hearts. That's why you ran away like a kitchen rat and why she didn't shed a tear after you left."

The Eunuchs' Goat started removing the clothing from around the blank space between the mannequin's legs. "There's a nymphomaniac in Ta'if who's demanding that we circumcise women, so that they'll be like this. So that they won't want to touch us. And pretty soon, he's going to call for the castration of all men—after milking us for our semen, of course, so they can create embryos in test tubes and reproduce the human species without a man and a woman ever making contact, not even husbands and wives." He was silent, then added, "Yes, I live among a super-human race. I take advantage of their superiority and anger, but the whole time all I can ever think about is burning the world down and recycling it."

The audacity in the Eunuchs' Goat's tone, which sounded to Mu'az almost like a threat, annoyed him.

"Why am I talking about women with a boy like you? I bet it shocks you!" He listened to the echo of his own words, then carried on, "The girls of the Lane of Many Heads lived in terror of becoming real flesh and blood themselves. They were so frightened of scandal, they sought refuge in death, and men like Yusuf, or Khalil, or the Eunuchs' Goat, or even you, the son of the imam who has the entire Quran memorized, are accused of the crime. They expect us to bear the guilt of killing the prey without getting to taste its blood. Tell me something: why would a girl in love want to kill herself?"

Mu'az was now certain that the Eunuchs' Goat had lost his mind. "As soon as a girl is born, they lock her up in a mannequin's body. All girls are possessed by a mannequin that wants to control them, but then you and me and him are trapped by it. Look at us! Yusuf should never have stopped writing to her, that way she wouldn't have disappeared into death. And I should never stop hoarding and burning mannequins or else the neighborhood girls will all drown! The head of the Lane of Many Heads and everything inside it needs to be recycled, and we need to go on smuggling. Smuggling in love and words and candid photos, magnifying lenses, women's hands and faces. To show that we are made of flesh, and blood, and desire."

Mu'az was staring at the mannequin in the Eunuchs' Goat's shopping cart. It turned his stomach. "Can you honestly tell me, Mu'az," the Eunuchs' Goat went on, "which one of us is real: me or the mannequin? We have to figure out whether this is all just the paranoid fantasies of a lunatic. Am I a real human being or just one of these?" He asked, pointing at the mannequin in the cart. "What if somebody is hoarding me in this city? Who can promise me that I'm not just a puppet? That I won't just be unplugged one day and that another newer model won't take my place? That I won't be tossed onto a trash heap while the souls of real humans are transported to some other existence that will forever remain a mystery to us . . . To some paradise somewhere."

Mu'az gave up any hope he'd had of following the thread of the conversation so he just tried to tie together the strains that interested him. "Do you think Azza was taken away? Or was she the one who died?"

"While Yusuf was still writing to her? We're the philosophy of garbage, that's what we are." His entire body was transformed into an exclamation mark for a moment, but he regained his previous apathy almost instantly. Without so much as a backward glance he set off, pushing his cart toward the shopping center exit. As soon as he'd disappeared into the darkness, Mu'az noticed a black driver, dressed in white robes and a red-checked headscarf, jump out of a black Mercedes to open the rear door for the artist, who slipped gracefully inside. Her ankle flashed in his memory. The driver shut the door and took his place behind the steering wheel, and they set off.

"That's the same driver. The one who was driving the woman from social insurance. The Cadillac at dawn. Azza's driver." He leapt to his feet. "When you get this close to her, you're bound to lose your mind. Just like all the other men who've gotten to know her. Life's too big to revolve around a woman." He didn't know who it was that kept repeating that phrase inside his head. The gallery was suddenly still and it was as though the lights had never been on. There was no chance of taking any more pictures. Mu'az looked around him. He wasn't sure anything would come out in the dim light, but he took one final shot of the great emptiness all the same. The only thing that interrupted the perfect emptiness was a single car-washer, sitting on the motionless escalator counting his takings. He was chatting to a man selling wreaths of jasmine flowers, who was standing at the very edge of the frame, waiting for one last customer. He'd spent the entire evening walking up and down the seafront, selling his wreaths to day-trippers, the wreaths hanging from his wrist slowly withering in the hot, salty air. He caught up with the last of the mall's shoppers, a family laden with bags, none of whom so much as noticed him except for the young daughter, whose black braids looked like a curled snake. She clung to her father's arm and asked him to buy her a wreath as he was loading their purchases into the trunk. Almost all his customers that day had been girls like this one, younger than ten; they were life-savers, these girls with their slanting eyes—far from the Barbie model—who were captivated by his wreaths of jasmine flowers.

In that instant, Mu'az realized that as his imagination was taking in a stream of photos, it also was taking in a virus of diaries and mannequins, and was manipulating them. The gallery was the perfect place to meet Azza. He looked around at the crows that, startled by sporadic honking, took refuge in the trees and on the walls of surrounding villas. He paid no attention to them and instead tried to get a shot of the small birds. "Birds move in such a strange way when they're flying. It's as though they're swimming and diving and then catching themselves and diving again."

He was talking out loud, to the night. "Birds are nature's desire to be free. It takes the form of little winged bundles, which we know as birds, but which are actually freedom itself. It departs from our bodies, like these little bundles, when we take a photo of a dream that has grown within us, one that we chase after no matter where it leads. When we grab hold of it, even in a picture, these handfuls stream down from our bodies. I saw all this in the dozens of photos I took of the boys and girls of the Lane of Many Heads chasing after their dreams. But did I see those kinds of birds flying out of the artist's body at the opening?" He didn't know who it was who'd planted these words in his head, nor from which stolen scrap they'd reached him; he was desperate for his body to speak in those tiny wings, to be freed of all limits, but a blackness settled over his heart.

"Crows are nature's predatory desires, and that's how they get their form: smudges of pure blackness." He felt like he was trapped between the two: bird or crow? That was the choice the Turkish woman had laid before him, and she was waiting to hear his answer. For the first time, he was honest with himself about what she wanted from him: to put his faith in her hands. He was the one who claimed that there was an invisible line, which if crossed would tear one's body apart. Therefore there must also be a line that assembles the disassembled to create a body. Every photograph he took and edited, every verse of the Quran he'd memorized was part of his search for that line. He tried with his every bundle of freedom, every bird, the desire for freedom in his eye, to break through to the point where everything was gathered together: Azza, life, the city, in a single body that would speak to him. The Turkish woman may not have translated her wish into words, but she would inevitably drive him to collect those disparate strings for her.

Mu'az made up his mind as he was standing there. He approached the glass exterior of the gallery and pressed his face up against the glass. He focused with his every layer of seeing—perception, interpretation, dissection, composition—on the very final painting, the last in the exhibition. He focused on the absent figure in it, on the pool of light, which was the absent figure's remains, a fog of breath, gradually allowing the handfuls of absence to cloud his eyes. His eyes wide and tearful, his sight was extinguished; the last thing he saw was the dripping lines of longing left behind by the figure who had disappeared in front of him, flowing into the city, and submerging the image of her in his mind, flooding his systems, which came together in the completion of the picture. The pupils of his wide eyes turned completely white. Surely that was the color of Adam's eyes, from whom he'd inherited the pain of leaving Eden, and the color of Jacob's eyes, from whom he'd inherited the pain of losing Yusuf.

When he turned to look back at the city and all he could see was a spot of light dancing over the blood fountains in his eyelids, he knew he'd gone blind. Within the blackness that had taken root inside Mu'az, shadows, memories, and reality were all rolled into one. He recognized two faces in there somehow: the face of the Turkish woman's eunuch, who was sexy even to men when dressed up as a woman, and Azza's face as she'd appeared to Yusuf, the summation of everything gathered together in the Lane of Many Heads, a mirror, a face that stood for Mecca itself. Mu'az shut his blind eyes against the mirror, squeezed them; he could hear the glass shatter. All he could think about was telling someone what he'd seen. He took out his cell phone and dialed the number he'd been warned never to call unless it was an emergency.

"Listen. This is Mu'az. I have something important to tell you."

"I don't understand."

"Azza's Aisha."

"......"

Silence. Mu'az repeated himself. "Azza's still Aisha." Hearing his own words, he understood the problem. He was saying the word *Aisha*, which meant alive, but it was the same word as the name. So he rephrased: "Azza's still living, Yusuf. She's not dead. She's alive. She's with Long Belt, Khalid al-Sibaykhan."

He licked the salt spray off his lips thirstily and got ready to head back, but there was no Lane of Many Heads left and the Kaaba was surrounded by barricades. He thought of going back to his father, wherever he was. For the first time in months, he found himself missing the sardine rows his father used to pack them into to sleep after night prayers. When he considered the blackness behind him, and in front of him, and on either side, and above, and below, the thought of how far he'd traveled away from that sardine can frightened him. He desperately needed those blind recitations, which his father forbade. Going to bed after performing the night prayers together and being up for dawn prayers in the mosque. None of the Imam's children dared miss either of those two appointments. Dusk was when the demons spread through the world and dawn was when the angels appeared. His journey stretched before him between those two appointments.

Blue

THE WHOLE TIME SHE WAS IN JEDDAH, NORA HAD THE TOP FLOOR OF THE SEA-front tower he owned all to herself. All she wanted was to forget about what she'd been through in the desert. She'd been alone with the sheikh on the flight back, but the sullen look on his face told her never to mention what had happened with Bundug.

She had no idea what had gotten into her that day to make her want to cross his clear red lines, but in the end she decided to shove open the glass door that led to his office, which had always been off-limits to her. Once she was inside, she had no idea what to do, though. She plopped herself down onto a chair in front of the desk and sat there, bewildered, like a pathetic little auditor who was out of her depth. As she aimlessly admired the expensive antiques dotted around the place, a box suddenly caught her eye. Perhaps it was the contrast of the rough box to the luster of everything else that drew her attention.

Her curiosity was piqued. She pulled the box toward her and tipped it upward, peeking inside. In the midst of a stack of papers, damp and charcoal-smeared, she spied a blue folder bearing the label AISHA'S EMAILS, standing up against the side of the box. Blood rushed to her head and without thinking she grabbed some of the contents of the folder and ran back to her room. She stuffed them under her mattress and sat down on the bed in the dim light, trying to steady her heartbeat.

That night her sleep was interrupted by the stolen words, shifting and pulsing beneath her bed, enveloping her in their nightmares.

"What's this gloom? Is this a funeral?" The phrase broke through her shallow sleep. He barged in like a storm, and she leapt up in bed. He pulled the curtains back, allowing the sun to reach her bed, as she spread her arms over the bed as if to protect it. She could tell he was drained from the dark circles around his eyes, and when he examined her, the signs of sleeplessness in the disturbed bedding around her didn't escape him either. "Get the hot tub ready," was his order to her assistant and to his own on the phone he said, "Make sure to burn everything. Don't miss a scrap. I want it over and done with." When he hung up the phone, he turned to Nora. "We both need to wake up." Nora was frozen in place, terrified. Had he discovered the missing papers? He stared at her. "Or do you prefer trying to wake up while you're still in bed?" he asked her sarcastically. She let out a deep sigh and smiled devilishly. His cell phone rang, interrupting them. "Lord let this be mercy not torture!" He jumped onto the bed as soon as his phone call was over. "I hate missing out on these sweet, lazy moments with you, but there's nothing I can do about it. An empire of demands awaits. Though I do prefer you when you're this starved lioness."

It was ten in the evening by the time he put on his embroidered cloak, careful not to disturb the wave in his brilliant headscarf. He left her, swimming in the scent of his agarwood perfume. She knew from the extreme care he'd taken with his appearance that she had several hours, perhaps days, to herself before he'd be back. She locked her bedroom door and took out the few papers she'd managed to nab from the folder. She inhaled the damp smell, with the faintest hint of pine, and ran her eyes over the page.

From: Aisha
Subject: Message 48

Dear ^,
You read all my charts: the CT scans, MRIs, ultrasounds, my medication schedule.

So tell me: is there any part of me that's still alive? Worthy of surprise, of another step toward life?

I think maybe I'll gather that all up into an amulet and put it around Azza's neck if she comes to bid me farewell.

I'll let you in on a secret:

~~Azza~~ is on the verge . . . of taking a leap.

Am I her reflection?

Should I let you in on one last, final secret?

Me Aisha, I'm the one who's always been ready to walk away from this world and everything in its packaging. Everything the world gives us comes in packages, which we then open so we can absorb life from them. If it weren't for you, I'd have taken those unopened packages to the grave with me. I discovered that I barely touch my perfume bottles, never turn on a new device, never dare cut up an entire cake; that I squeeze every last drop out of my toothpaste, carefully skim the surface of my lotions and lipsticks, never scrape out my eye shadow or sharpen my eyeliner, my new clothes yellow where they lay folded in a suitcase at the top of my wardrobe. I pass over things as if not passing over them at all. Only lightly touching the surface of things, never reaching their core or even denting them (just like my hymen). I haven't had a haircut since I was born. It just creeps down my back. I was planning to hand it all back over to the angels on Judgment Day, to be bare once again like I was on the day I received it, the day I was born. If it hadn't been for you, my can opener. You were the one who bothered to cut my hair one Sunday as we sat beneath a breathtaking willow tree. The tree made a palace just for us, shielding us with its branches. You surprised me by undoing my braid and wetting my hair with a splash of Evian. You layered my hair like cascades on either side, which shimmered with every nod or laugh. I was so graceful with that hairstyle.

~~Azza~~, on the other hand, has to open everything and rummage through it. She has to burrow down to the bottom of every box she sees, and the angels have made a note of that habit.

Being able to jump is a miracle.

I know you'll laugh at me, but:

I used to be too worried to sleep on my front in case I damaged my perfectly shaped breasts. I never let anyone touch them, not even myself. God knows what Azza did with that perfection. She used to tease me: "What's the point of having those perfect, perky breasts? What have you ever done with them?" They're like the breasts of a mannequin, but it's not as if I had them molded and formed and brought to life.

I failed to discover either body: human or bionic.

If Azza ever had to deal with a computer, she'd wear it out by running programs, and hooking up peripherals, and adding more memory. Me, on the other hand, I'd run away from the buttons at the first warning beep. That's why I'm going to die before ever discovering the basic boot-up functions of my own body-device.

Can we diagnose my condition as a life's blessings inferiority complex? ~~Azza~~ might have called it a mental inferiority complex, but I would call it a self-awareness inferiority complex.

My emotions and fears and desires, my frivolity—is there anything frivolous about me?—in boxes, with their documentation, sealed up to keep you out.

Azza and I would've stood like that before the angels of death: me and my boxes all sealed tight, she and hers licked clean. Am I just passing through? Is she the permanent one, the permeating? I wonder.

Impossible P. S. I wish I could sit with you one last time with all my boxes laid out before us. We'd open each one together and drink it down to the dregs.

P. S. Boxes of chalk, left over from my days as a schoolteacher, collecting dust. What was I supposed to do with a box of chalk? But then as soon as I gave them to ~~Azza~~, look: she moved them and the world followed.

If only you could see ~~Azza~~'s room. Spaces packed full of black and white figures, which have surpassed the limited range of their colors and who move constantly, going in and out of the Lane of Many Heads as they please.

P. P. S. Even my breathing is short. It's rapid, it doesn't last a whole second, so that none of my cells split open. That was until you taught me how to breathe. Deeply. Count to ten as I breathe in. Hold it for ten seconds as every cell explodes and its stores burn up. Then for ten seconds as I breathe out, right up to the very last molecule of CO_2. And for another ten seconds, I leave my body empty. Forty seconds of life in a single breath. God, pleasure is so slow. Pleasure hides between the oxygen of life and the two in carbon dioxide.

I can live for forty seconds in a single breath.

The pleasure hidden within a single breath is so intoxicating. Forty tick-tocks of joy spent between oxygen and carbon.

In the ten seconds of emptiness, I make sense of the thirty seconds of burning.

P. P. P. S. This is the music of de Falla. Once again, I wonder: me and ~~Azza~~, which one of us is Sancho Panza and which one is Don Quixote?

From how many to how,

~~Azza~~ is the one who deserves to be transferred into life.

Because she is able (without having the means to be able) to exist beyond the circumstances of existence. She wasn't given the opportunity to be educated, like I was, let alone the access to books that I had.

Her skeleton is made of gold (pliant and hard). It jumps into the fire and comes out in never-ending life-shapes.

Final P. S. Love is all there is to life.

That is to say, to live is to yearn. Or, to love. Or to love by yearning for what you can never have back.

My name is Aisha, not Hayah. It means living, not life. That sums me up, don't you think?

Aisha

Nora wailed and wailed until her tears ran dry, as de Falla's music reverberated in her bedroom. Her breathing slowed as if she were under a strong anesthetic. The words jostled her and tore at her clothes. Everywhere she looked there was blood. Her heart fell out onto the paper before her, buzzing, followed by her lungs, and the words penetrated through her cranium, sinking all the way to the bottom of her spine. That crossed-out name stopped her short. Who? And who crossed it out? A deep sadness was troubled.

As Nora went through the small stack of emails, her fever rose higher. Through her veins flowed mutual betrayal, between her and the author of these emails: was this Aisha? The one who presumed a personality that wasn't her own? Wearing her face? Her features? Her reactions to life? The Aisha who stole the girl who resembled her, who stole her name and hid her in the ruins, while she lived off the death of the girl who resembled her? Angry knocking at her door ripped her from that other world. She discovered that she'd spent the entire night reading and crying; she hid the documents and opened the door.

"Why'd you lock the door?" Her hazy look raised his suspicions. He scanned the room as though looking for evidence of a crime and repeated the question. "What's the matter?"

He embraced her roughly, pushing her head down against his chest, staring deep within her. "Your eyes look blindfolded like a falcon's. What are you hiding from me inside that head of yours?"

She shut her eyes. She collected the saliva in her mouth and swallowed, worried that her breath would give away the smell of emails. "It's because of the sleeping pills. I haven't slept ten hours straight in months," she said, trying to sound blithe.

"I can't detect any Valium on your tongue though. Give me a taste of the truth." He clamped his lips onto hers, jealously, possessively. She covered him quickly, in fear. Might he taste the bitterness that overpowers the bitterness of waking up from a strong anesthetic? The bitterness that discovering the emails poured into her throat: the awakening of her clouded mind, which was proceeding toward her end, with trepidation, as though it were trying to delay it.

Abraham's Palm

FOR DAYS AFTER MU'AZ'S PHONE CALL, YUSUF MOVED ABOUT FEVERISHLY AND agitatedly, torn between the tree that was revealing itself to them on the wall and the woman he'd dreamed of, for all those months, being dead and risen, in her death, to a place where she could no longer be sullied. News of the phone call had disturbed Mushabbab. They shared the task of going out to gather information that might lead them to the one they called Long Belt. Where was he? And what possible link could there be between him and Azza?

IT WAS DIFFICULT TO SAY HOW LONG IT TOOK THEM TO UNCOVER THE TREE CREATED by the guide Ayif al-Ghatafani, who had traced, over the course of his own lifetime, nearly three quarters of a century of Sarah's branching lineage in the Sabkha Tribe, and her son's marriages outside the tribe. Finally they arrived, with surprise, at the abrupt end of the tree's branches, presumably marking the point when the guide himself died. No matter where else they scraped at the wall, they found no other word or branch.

Then Nasser came across a device in the form of Ursa Major at the bottom of the tree. The three stood looking at it for ages, some intuition alerting them that it contained a sign, until their flashlight died and the darkness became dense around them. Suddenly, a silver beam penetrated the pitch black, and they became aware of the full moon outside shining in through a hole in the roof and falling upon the furthest corner of the hall, the spot where they had been bedding down at night. The silver beam revealed the disturbed surface of the soil, and when they scraped it away they found a stone marked with seven depressions representing the stars of Ursa Major. It felt as if the remains of the fort were conspiring to shed their every last mask before them in one go, or as if, because of all the time they'd spent there, they'd been accepted into the fort's mind. They applied themselves immediately to digging up the stone, and it lifted as soon as Yusuf slid the shovel beneath it. Underneath was a copper-lined wooden box, and inside it lay a piece of parchment spread carefully between two sheets of blotting paper. Mushabbab held it up to the faint light, displaying a tree illuminated with colored inks: they were certain that it could only be the missing final page of the parchment inside the amulet, containing the rest of the tree that began on the wall, and whose later branches Ayif al-Ghatafani's descendants must have diligently added over the centuries.

In the dim light, the three heads fused into one and the three hearts throbbed with a single beat, as their sleep-deprived eyes took in the complete tree, spread between wall and parchment. They traced the tree's two oldest branches—the first beginning with Moses and Aaron and leading to Ka'b ibn al-Ashraf in the year 629 A.D., and the other descending from Wa'il, Rabi'a, and Nizar—to where they met in Marid, Sarah's son born in the bed of Sa'd, sheikh of the Sabkha tribe.

On the paper was the more recent half of the tree, which showed the descendants of Marid Sabkha born of Arab women exclusively from the heart of the peninsula. The ink was faded, blotched, and smeared in places, varying with the skill of Ayif al-Ghatafani's many descendants at handling the fine old parchment, and revealing the difficulty they faced in documenting the lineage over fourteen centuries to the present day. Impatiently, the three pairs of eyes scanned the branches passing through Iyad, Qays, Saleem, Ma'ad, Bakr, Mu'awiya, and Awf to the present, where Nasser's eyes settled on the final entry in the document, which Muflih al-Ghatafani had added to that long branch of Marid's descendants. The name was clear and unmistakable: Khalid al-Sibaykhan.

Nasser laughed hysterically, while a shudder ran through Mushabbab. "This is Long Belt! Al-Sibaykhan a descendant of Sarah and her son Marid, and right in Mecca!" He sputtered.

A single sentence uttered about that parchment pierced their dream, destroying it and expelling them. A glaring light flooded the hall and figures in khaki uniforms appeared.

"Give yourselves up!" they barked, quickly closing around the tree on the wall. Nasser stepped forward calmly with his hands in the air, but Mushabbab hurled himself blindly and without warning at the source of the light. Hands attacked him and everything became a confused tumult; Nasser hit out in the darkness and was hit back at, and it was impossible to tell who were the attackers and who the prey. In the chaos a shadow slipped out and limped away, vanishing into the darkness.

Cyber Attack

From: Aisha
Subject: Message 90

It scares me sometimes the way you read my thoughts. The last article you sent me was about the legendary game designer Miyamoto, who's banned by Nintendo, the company he works for, from talking about his hobbies and dreams because they're worth a fortune. This is the man who has transformed the most banal aspects of his daily life into obsessions that have gripped the entire world. He invented Nintendogs after his family got a dog and he invented Pikmin because he loves gardening.

I've been watching break-dancers who walk on their hands and move their bodies as though they're made of rubber. And I've been watching Usain Bolt, the Jamaican sprinter who broke the world record for the hundred-meter race at the 2008 Olympics, reaching the finish line so far ahead of six of the world's best sprinters no one could believe it. All these physical accomplishments make me feel like there's a new species of humans being created that we're not part of. My species, physically and emotionally stagnant, ought to just die out.

No dreams worth mentioning, or movement.

Nora set the message down so she could take a look around the military plane that was taking her to Medina. The art exhibition had come and gone and now she was back to the series of sporadic moves that determined her life on the sheikh's chessboard. She resumed her silence thousands of meters in the air. A few luxurious chairs and a circular meeting table were all there was to the troop-carrier they were flying in. That and the roaring engines, which shook her heart and relieved her from having to speak or listen. She shut her eyes and pictured her paintings hanging on the gallery walls. Beings not male or female, limbs severed, in the paintings and the gallery, visitors were all on a single plane. They held animated conversations. Saying things they'd never dared to say before, or hadn't been able to fit in, as the sea air salted their exchanges. They missed their missing limbs, or criticized them, or justified their absence. The female university students who'd come to the exhibition on an organized visit were a challenge. They provoked the darkest lines, they dug up the empty canvas and poured their rebellion or apathy onto it. They stood in front of her paintings, laughing and winking to one another, giving the figures a taste of life's sting, if only for a few seconds. Nora was standing there, facing life's onslaught, when they dragged her into conversation.

"Are you scared?" one of them asked.

Nora nodded, indifferently. "Maybe. It's fear that makes us fight," she said sarcastically.

"Your paintings make me feel beaten down," another one of them said. "Why are you so cruel to bodies? You should leave them alone."

Another girl laughed, not bothering to hide her malice or lower her voice as she sniggered. "This is the work of a butcher's daughter."

Nora's skin was tanned for the first time in her life, by the sea air, and it came to life. For a few days, her figures were more than a monologue delivered by her fingers to the canvas. They'd become human in those gazes, but the exhibition was over and at that altitude, she allowed her figures to be wrapped up, like a cinema reel, back to their hiding place, back to the faint El Greco sky on the grave. The airplane banked sharply and when Nora looked out she could see the lava fields spread around Medina, as if a volcano had dipped its giant fingers into the earth's core and sprinkled its coal around. Another look was enough to transform all that coal into diamonds, like the source of all her paintings. At that moment, she wished she could come back as a line of coal over that land, which had given shelter to the Prophet in his flight, and could be safe. She drove the black lava fields from her mind as, in the midst of a cloud of palm trees, the minaret of the Prophet's Mosque came into view. Nora had missed those minarets, "which will never cease calling people to prayer until they hear Israfil blow his horn for the resurrection, and they shall be the first, and their dead shall be the first to come up out of the earth to answer the call."

The thought made her shiver. She was like someone facing resurrection, weighed down with choices.

Nora was alone in her suite at the Intercontinental Hotel, though she was used to her sheikh being away at private meetings by now. Then, just like any other time she was left on her own, she found company in the handful of emails, which she secreted away like illicit drugs. If only she'd stolen the entire file. What might've been revealed to her—matters of life and death. Something like this short message:

From: Aisha
Subject: Message 66

Something inside me has broken. My satellite receiver maybe.

But. Here. There's a signal.

You present it to me with a single orchid. You say, "Orchids remind me of you."

My body believes you. My body mimics and learns how to be haughty.

My head spins from dancing on the inside.

A

Nora took pleasure in examining the orchid just like she took pleasure in the millions of tiny spiral loops that Aisha laid down in her messages to express herself, carrying herself from the peaks of life down to death. Her reflection had disappeared from the mirror: every time Nora looked she saw Aisha. She flipped through the guestbook from her exhibition for the hundredth time, asking herself who these comments were written for: Nora or Aisha? As de Falla played in the background, she scanned the book word by word to see which of them was the dead Sancho Panza and which of them was the living Don Quixote. How long would it take for one of them to come back to life and for the other to recede into death? She kept reading until the entire universe had shrunk to the size of a man's head, and then to the size of a thought in a man's head, and finally to the size of a ray of light in a man's eye. Was it an Arab's eye or a Westerner's? Perhaps the eye belonged to the person who was stoking all these events and turning them into a time bomb. She was the one who'd dropped her name and identity: anything that would cause her to be born out of pre-existing memory, the memory of the woman who'd written these emails, which inhaled and exhaled her in their naked lines.

From: Aisha
Subject: Message 77

I gave the baby to ~~Azza~~.

It's for her to bury, or bring back to life.

I'm tearing up the sheets of my mind one by one to see where he might have gone. Where he might end up. Can one jump with a baby in one's heart?

Some nights, I hear him crawling up the staircase to my cubbyhole.

Some nights, I slither down to meet him.

I curl up in a ditch in the bare earth. Not a drop of rain. Oh, how the dead miss the rain!

I used up my entire stash of perfume bottles to get rid of his scent.

But he smells of my insides.

The scent stays hot, my every breath stokes it.

A

P. S. They found the apeman, whom they believe to be the missing link, frozen in a block of ice on the side of a mountain in North Carolina. When they melted the ice, they discovered he was nothing more than a rubber gorilla suit.

What will they find after we've melted? I would hate to die in a freezer. Don't let them put my body on ice.

Aisha

Nora pushed those words to the back of her mind. Toward the hole into which she'd thrown all her memories. And took refuge in the only thing around her: in the autograph book that certified that she was the one who was still alive. Suddenly her eyes fell on a sentence in the book that she hadn't seen before. The handwriting sent a shiver down her spine.

One day you'll wake up and bury us all.

The phone rang. She picked up the receiver without thinking.

"It's for you, ma'am." The receptionist's upbeat voice dispelled the gloom of that sentence, but then there was a second voice:

"Azza." The word hung in the air, as if forever. "Azza." Azza. The name echoed in her ears as though Yusuf were shouting to her from the roof. The name echoed around her bedroom, against the shut window. It fell on naked Aisha and Jameela at her father's sink.

"Azza. Azza." Nora was the name Khalid al-Sibaykhan had bestowed on her—the phone was still buzzing—after he stripped her of the name Azza so that he could own her by his mother's name. He wanted her to understand the kindness he was doing her, wanted her to understand the name's significance: "A powerful woman who was worn down by my father's other wives."

She couldn't tell when the buzzing stopped and the knocking started. Was it the knocking of the distant past or the here and now? Not until she opened the door and saw him looking back at her.

"Azza." His voice had always been warm, but now it trembled: frightened, desperate, cold. She reached for the phantom edge of her veil, to cover her head, to hide from his eyes. From that all-seeing familiarity she knew so well. His voice and his face matched the image she called up from the very depths of her lost memory. She came face to face with her own name: Azza. With that name's burdened legacy. A burden he'd set on her shoulders. She fell. Yusuf fell down with her and they touched the ground at the exact same moment. She could hear nothing but the name she'd so longed to hear: Azza. A gaping void inside of her hungered for it. For the precise way Yusuf said it. He said it with gravity, like he said Mecca. It gave the name a formidable depth. He said it as though he were bashing against the Meccan ground to unearth the Well of Zamzam or Judgment Day. No one but Yusuf could do so much with just a name.

"Azza. Let's go. Now."

Pink

"DO YOU KNOW WHO KHALID AL-SIBAYKHAN IS? HE'S THE BULLDOZERS ON all our mountains. He's the buyer, he's the deeds that strip people of their properties, the one eliminating and demolishing. He's your father, who contracted, annulled, and sold . . . Sold you, and your house. Al-Sibaykhan is the sin that has possessed us all. The Lane of Many Heads, you, and I are nothing but dots being erased on a map of genocide. We're dots floating in the dust after a city has been ravaged. Dozing eyes, the moment before a city, many cities, are razed to the ground. Do you understand, Azza? You're hanging in the air with a rope around your neck. You shouldn't be on that side. It's too dangerous. Jump to me, Azza."

"Don't talk to me about jumping!" she replied. "The only time I ever dared to open the window my father nailed shut, I saw my death, because her death was our collective death. What I saw made me jump right out of the alley, forever. Don't you know me best, Yusuf? I can never jump, except to the wrong side."

"We can change things, Azza. Help me expose all this!"

"You want exposure? More than this?"

"Help us get you out of this first, Azza of the Lane of Many Heads. Then we'll expose what's going on. Al-Sibaykhan is the reptile that will swipe its tail and cause the ground to swallow us all up."

"Yusuf, please, make contact with the real world around you. Come out of your bubble of history and Doomsday. Who's going to listen to all this?"

She steeled her heart and led Yusuf next door, into Khalid's office. Adrenaline was pumping in her veins, and she tried to separate her mind from her shaking body. His maid or his coffee boy or his assistant could come in at any moment and see what she was doing, but she couldn't back out now. They hurried to the desk, where they saw a safe underneath the drawers; when they knelt to open it, they found it unlocked.

Inside, the first thing they saw was the amulet, lying in the lower compartment. Yusuf's hand shook as he picked it up and checked that the parchment was still folded carefully inside.

"I didn't want to scare you," he began. "But I've just escaped an ambush. There's no doubt it was Khalid's men. That's when they took the amulet. I spent the night wandering around, hiding, looking for a way to get to you." He spread the family tree in front of her, and quickly took her through it, skipping most of the lines, but the blood was pumping in her ears and a sudden thought occurred to her. She looked again in the safe, and there was the copy of the El Greco painting. She froze; how had it gotten there? And what had happened to Rafi? Was he one of them—or another of their victims? Had they used her as bait to get this drawing? She pushed the thoughts aside and opened the sketch for Yusuf, drawing his attention to the key held in the hand of the celestial creature reaching toward Mary's lap. They stood motionless as he looked at the key; holding his breath, he took out the key hanging around his neck.

"It's the same key," breathed Nora, then told him about the man who had spent a quarter-century of his life in the peaks of Toledo, obsessively looking for that key, and left a copy of it fixed to his gravestone.

"Maybe you're related to that guy—maybe he's your lost father! Your mom Halima always talked about how Andalusia had kidnapped her husband . . ."

Nora went back to the safe and took out the drawing Khalid al-Sibaykhan had showed her one morning in Madrid, to compare it with the copied key stolen from the grave.

"All these are copies of that," she said, pointing to the key around his neck. "It must be the key." She emphasized the words *the key*. She looked around them, struck by the deafening, blinding discovery. Her ears were ringing and her saliva tasted like blood. Her mind was racing against time to create a bomb as big as this explosion Yusuf had caused in her blood.

"What do you think this is all about?"

An obscure instinct was honing in on that threat hung around Yusuf's neck.

"You're a Shaybi, Yusuf."

They stood either side of the key, looking at the two interlinked mihrabs on the bow, and the third, bearing the verses of the Surah of Fidelity, in engraved gold, which watched over their embrace from above.

They returned to the safe to look for more clues, but there was nothing except for a DVD on the top shelf. Yusuf quickly played it on the computer: it was a promotional film, which opened with the logo of Elaf International Holdings. They couldn't fathom the images of the Mecca of the future that rolled across the screen: everything around the Kaaba had been erased and replaced by a vast marble space that extended northwest from the Haram Mosque, rising in three tiers, like a sundial, to another five tiers that led to a flat, paved plain stretching to the very edge of the city, sweeping away the Lane of Many Heads. Skyscrapers enclosed the horizon on three sides, a line of seventeen giants on the right and the same on the left, meeting in the center in a vast idol that looked like the Empire State Building and was flanked on each side by a miniature version of itself. Next came another ring of skyscrapers, seven to the right and seven to the left, and in the center two enormous creatures guarding the great idol. They all looked like spaceships that had landed on Earth to besiege the Kaaba in a postmodern metallic standoff. The whole lot was surrounded by an outer ring of inferior towers that stood like wretched guards protecting the backs of the giants against the assault of the sand and the poor who were massed like ants outside the massive conurbation. It looked like life itself had been chased outside the circle of the Holy Mosque.

"Look, these zones around the Kaaba are what gave Khalid al-Sibaykhan his nickname, Long Belt. He's tying the whole city around his waist . . ."

When the promotional film ended, it took them some time to make sense of the idea that this what the Kaaba would look like in the future. The stone structure covered in black silk had been taken away, and in its place was a metal box of the same dimensions as the old one but elongated like an obelisk pointing to the sky, and around it were countless levels of walkways that would hold huge numbers of circumambulating pilgrims. The new Kaaba was like the shaft inside the grinding cogs of a huge mill.

Their hearts scarcely beat any longer. Their mouths felt dry. Yusuf was frozen in the desk chair and Azza stood motionless behind him, the scent of Medinan mud rising to her from his dirty hair, their eyes still fixed on that vision of the postmodern Kaaba. Azza could feel the emptiness behind her, the abyss brushing the back of her neck. At any moment, al-Sibaykhan could walk in and the hair-fine line would be broken, pushing them to some zone as extreme as the designs that had just left them speechless.

"Now I understand. It might sound like some crazy film plot, but I think the disappearance of the key, and all the rumors about their failure to cast a new one, were planned to make way for this . . . To redesign the Kaaba . . ."

"Would you really mind if it looked like this? Stone or metal, what difference does it make? The important thing is it's a symbol."

"Azza, this isn't the Kaaba we know. This is Hubal. The idol, the same idol that's worshipped by the Devil's Horns tribes, is taking over the House of God, rising to the sky on the Kaaba's foundations. Those foundations were built by Adam and the angels out of stones from heaven. It's a human treasure . . ."

"But didn't you say those emeralds from Heaven were dug up and thrown into the sea so nobody would worship them?"

"Not the foundations . . . I really hope they haven't done anything with the foundations. Any attempt to dig up those foundations would destroy Mecca. The least we can do is expose these documents so the authorities can see what these people are planning to do!"

She stared at him in silence. He looked skinny and pale, but unshakably determined. "Expose them to who?"

"The organizations that protect cultural heritage in London and New York, the royal court, the Consultative Assembly, the Committee for the Promotion of Virtue and the Prevention of Vice . . ." He sounded naive, even to himself. "But first, you have to come with me, we have to get you out of here." He gathered the papers, ready to leave.

"I'll repeat what a crazy woman once told me: this key, in the hand of the right man, can open all the doors to God's houses, doors you've never even imagined . . ."

"But look at the metal Kaaba of the future . . . What key could open that contraption?"

"Even that," she replied, touching the key around his neck. "This key is everything. You need to get it out of here, now."

"No, Azza, you are everything," he said desperately, hoping it would penetrate her head this time. "You and Mecca. I'm not leaving unless you come with me."

Her head was spinning, so her body moved automatically. She put on her abaya and followed him out of the suite.

As the elevator door opened onto the lobby, they spotted al-Sibaykhan coming in through the main door with his assistant, his bodyguards spread around the entrance and the lobby. Yusuf yanked her back into the elevator and pressed a button, but the minutes it took to respond seemed like forever. Azza moved forward, lifting her abaya in an attempt to hide Yusuf from sight, but a man suddenly appeared in front of the elevator, his eyes meeting Yusuf's. He was one of the ones who'd surprised them at the fort. The man's hand shot out to stop the door closing, and like a flash across Azza's line of vision, Yusuf's hand struck the arm, pushing the man backward. With a grimace of pain, the man hit the floor just as the elevator doors slid closed.

They didn't know what floor they were going to for a moment, but the elevator took them to the second floor, and the moment the doors opened they raced to the nearest emergency exit. Yusuf smashed the glass on the fire alarm, sending the hotel into an uproar. They bounded down the emergency stairs, pushing through endless doors until they finally burst out into the parking lot. In front of them, Nasser was just getting out of his Land Rover. He stood paralyzed at the sight of the two figures that had suddenly appeared in front of him, his eyes a waxy white as he stared agog at the woman. Azza retreated, while Yusuf rushed forward eagerly with a sigh of relief.

"Detective, thank God you managed to get away!"

The distance gaped between him and Azza. He glanced behind him, only to find her staring accusingly at him.

"You're working with him?" she hissed.

"This is Detective Nasser! He knows everything . . ."

She retreated further. "I saw your father's grave in Madrid. He traveled to all those countries looking for that key. He was probably the one who led me there so I could help you discover who you are—and now I find out you're working with this guy?" Her voice had the fury of a person betrayed.

"Azza, listen—" Nasser stepped forward, into the space between them. "Wait, that's not Azza!" he exclaimed in disbelief.

Azza was already moving back toward the hotel entrance.

"Hold it, where are you going?"

"There's something I have to sort out," she muttered to herself; they could barely make out what she said.

"There's no one called Azza," said Nasser desperately. "She was invented by Aisha the cripple! Aisha's dreamt us all up . . ." Yusuf wanted to follow Azza, but Nasser stood in his way. He watched her retreat out of the corner of his eye. Was that a faint limp? Could it be the Aisha he'd always hated?"

The second the abaya vanished inside the hotel, Yusuf felt the same tearing of flesh from flesh he felt when they pulled him away from the Kaaba and ripped the key out of the lock. The same violent separation. He was in a trance, and when he felt the blow to his stomach he was unprepared, struggling uselessly to break free of his attacker and reach the door that had swallowed Azza, any door . . .

Click

THE ELEVATOR TOOK AGES TO REACH ITS DESTINATION. ONE CORNER OF HER HEAD was shouting, "Get to the door. Get out. Out!" But the other three were pushing her toward the other door, past the single purple orchid that reminded her of her mother's dress stuffed into the window that had been nailed shut and of Aisha's murmur in her ear:

> *The first time we were alone together you asked me, "Who is the man who's touching you now? Who's the one who makes you feel? Who brings you to life?"*
>
> *I am black,*
> *My eyes are black,*
> *My hair is black,*
> *My heart is black,*
> *My blood is black. Does blackness come from too much touching?*
> *Or from never being touched?*

She opened the door to the suite slowly and walked in, coming face to face with him immediately. The only thing separating them was the wild purple of the orchid, and the brilliant green of those words:

> *Azza isn't even a tree. She's like a kind of indestructible grass: drown her, scorch her, stamp on her, freeze her with frost. She'll grow again the next day like new.*

A click: she felt it deep in her spine, like the sudden flowing feeling after a tooth's been pulled out. Had the door clicked shut or had she snapped?

Lighter

Amidst the expectant silence that lay over the Intercontinental Hotel, Khalid al-Sibaykhan's assistant stood in a room at the end of a corridor, feeling utterly lost. He tossed the envelope he'd received from al-Sibaykhan onto the bed, the bank transfer receipt still inside it. So many zeros his eyes got lost and his heart skipped a beat as he skimmed to the end of the figure, while al-Sibaykhan watched him mockingly, expecting him to cry. Yes, it was all tragic and overblown, but he was much too dry on the inside to wring tears from the veins beneath his skin.

Those zeros were beyond his wildest dreams. Not just that; there were also the promotions that would see him reach the highest ranks possible in the field of criminal investigation. With al-Sibaykhan, life was all elevators, and steel and glass structures soaring into the skies. Life was nothing but endless zeros—everyone recognized al-Sibaykhan's zero-shaped logo—to the extent that you couldn't even keep up with your account balances. Al-Sibaykhan's word was an axis for the whole world to collapse and revolve around; he himself had spent his life revolving . . .

He opened his wardrobe and took out the huge Samsonite case. He opened it and felt about inside to be certain all the papers, which he'd virtually memorized, were still hidden inside, then closed it and left the hotel, his shoulders slumped. Even the exhaustion that had overcome him after the events of the past week was nothing in comparison to the rotten taste rising in his throat. A rat had chosen to burrow a hole into his body and die there. He took a deep breath, afraid of contaminating the air and disturbing the people around, or infecting them too with his rat.

The gleaming white Land Rover's brakes squealed as it exited the hotel parking lot under watchful eyes. He drove aimlessly, leaving the city and its mosque behind him. He pulled over at the edge of the road north of the city, got out, and stood by the passenger door, at a loss. Then he got the case out, and, with trembling lover's fingers, took out the blue file, and squatted down by the back wheel of the car. His body shrank as he reached into the file: there, inside, was the essence of his beating heart, the snakelike rollercoaster that lifted him up and twisted him round and whirled him three hundred and sixty degrees only to return him to the point where he'd begun and to the first woman whom he'd wrapped, whose words he'd wrapped, around his neck like a collar before jumping into the void. Siren Man shook at the first touch after a long separation.

"My God, woman . . ." he moaned, crushing his head against the hot metal of the car. Why didn't I burn you before, like I was told to? Why did I dare disobey al-Sibaykhan for you when he ordered me to destroy all your emails? Why are we too weak to change our nature? I'm a coward and a traitor to my very last drop of blood, and I'll die that way. In the end, you led me to confront myself, to confront two choices: run away with you, or pursue Yusuf . . . And I chose the bank account! Why was I too weak to put up a decent fight against my own emptiness? Why was I too weak to be a better man, Aisha?" Her name rent his chest like the howl of a lost wolf.

"Aisha, only your hands can make me come." With the flame of his lighter, he set the first email alight, as tears dripped to the scorching sand. Detective Nasser al-Qahtani let himself cry freely, and Siren Man sobbed as the papers, one by one, were consumed by flames.